Emma Blair Omnibus

GOODNIGHT, SWEET PRINCE

WILD STRAWBERRIES

Also by Emma Blair:

WHERE NO MAN CRIES
NELLIE WILDCHILD
HESTER DARK
THIS SIDE OF HEAVEN
JESSIE GRAY
THE PRINCESS OF POOR STREET
STREET SONG
WHEN DREAMS COME TRUE
A MOST DETERMINED WOMAN
THE BLACKBIRD'S TALE
MAGGIE JORDAN
SCARLET RIBBONS
THE WATER MEADOWS
THE SWEETEST THING
THE DAFFODIL SEA
PASSIONATE TIMES
HALF HIDDEN
FLOWER OF SCOTLAND
AN APPLE FROM EDEN
GOODNIGHT, SWEET PRINCE
WILD STRAWBERRIES
FORGET-ME-NOT
MOONLIT EYES
FINDING HAPPINESS

Emma Blair Omnibus

GOODNIGHT, SWEET PRINCE

WILD STRAWBERRIES

EMMA BLAIR

timewarner
paperbacks

A *Time Warner* Paperback

This omnibus edition first published in Great Britain by
Time Warner Paperbacks in 2003
Emma Blair Omnibus Copyright © Emma Blair 2003

Previously published separately:
Goodnight, Sweet Prince first published in Great Britain in 1999 by
Little, Brown and Company
Published by Warner Books in 2000
Copyright © Emma Blair 1999

Wild Strawberries first published in Great Britain in 2000 by
Little, Brown and Company
Published by Warner Books in 2000
Reprinted 2001
Copyright © Emma Blair 2000

The moral right of the author has been asserted.

*All characters in this publication are fictitious and any
resemblance to real persons, living or dead, is purely coincidental.*

All rights reserved.
No part of this publication may be reproduced, stored in a retrieval system,
or transmitted, in any form or by any means, without the prior permission in
writing of the publisher, nor be otherwise circulated in any form of binding or
cover other than that in which it is published and without a similar condition
including this condition being imposed on the subsequent purchaser.

A CIP catalogue record for this book is
available from the British Library.

ISBN 0 7515 3511 7

Typeset in Adobe Garamond by
Palimpsest Book Production Limited,
Polmont, Stirlingshire
Printed and bound in Great Britain by
Mackays of Chatham plc, Chatham, Kent

Time Warner Paperbacks
An imprint of
Time Warner Books UK
Brettenham House
Lancaster Place
London WC2E 7EN

www.TimeWarnerBooks.co.uk

GOODNIGHT,
SWEET PRINCE

To Jane, with love

Now cracks a noble heart. Good night, sweet prince;
And flights of angels sing thee to thy rest!

HAMLET Act V, Scene 2

Chapter 1

'What!'

Tommy Riach dropped his gaze to stare at the floor, writhing inside. 'I'm sorry, Dad,' he mumbled.

'That's not bloody good enough. Expelled from school! What on earth possessed you, boy?'

How could he explain? He couldn't, simply not having the words. The streak of rebelliousness that ran through him was deep as any canyon and, to him anyway, defied description.

Jack Riach sighed, removed the dark glasses he wore and ran a hand over the sockets where once his eyes had been. He loved his son with all his heart and yet there were times when he could have knocked the bugger senseless. 'Smoking and drinking, you say.'

'That's right,' came the whispered reply.

'Wait till your mother finds out. She'll be beside herself. Cry herself silly no doubt. What do you make of that?'

Tommy was lost for an answer, hating the thought of

1

hurting his mother in any way. Or his father come to that.

'Do you have cigarettes on you now?'

'Yes, Dad.'

'Then you'd better light up. Why the hell not. If that's what you want to do.'

'Thanks, Dad.'

Tommy quickly fumbled for the packet of ten he had in his jacket pocket and moments later smoke was curling towards the ceiling.

'And, according to you, it's happened before. This was the second occasion you were caught.'

'Yes.' That again was said in a whisper.

Jack came to his feet and crossed to the window where the cold November light played across his face. For some reason he found himself remembering the war and what it had been like before he'd lost his sight. There had been so many young men only a few years older than Tommy, most of them now dead. Buried over there in France and Belgium. Somehow that put things into perspective. Smoking and drinking weren't so bad after all. Insignificant really. Nor was being expelled from school.

Jack recalled . . . and shuddered inwardly. 'So what are we to do with you now?' he queried softly.

'I've no idea, Dad.'

'Another school?'

'That's up to you.'

Jack smiled wryly. 'Is it indeed. I would have thought it was up to you. What's the point of sending you off to another school if you're only going to be expelled again. Don't forget this isn't the first time we've had trouble. You seem to have a real talent when it comes to that.'

Tommy looked round for an ashtray already knowing

there wasn't one. He flicked ash into the fireplace instead. 'Are you asking or telling?'

'Don't be impertinent, boy,' Jack growled threateningly.

'I didn't mean to be.'

'Then I'm asking.'

Tommy considered school which he loathed. It seemed so . . . senseless. All right, it was necessary to learn the fundamentals, reading, writing etc. But beyond those a total waste of time as far as he was concerned.

Jack suddenly laughed.

'Dad?'

'Wee Linda Millar.'

Tommy flushed, knowing exactly what Jack was referring to. 'She's moved away.'

'So what in the hell has that got to do with it? Can you imagine what it was like for me to have to face her father.'

'She agreed, Dad. It wasn't as if I forced myself on her. She was as keen for me to look at her drawers as I was to see them.'

'At that age!'

Tommy shrugged. 'Curiosity, part of growing up I suppose. I don't know.'

'You were only ten at the time, Linda eight. And you weren't peering at her drawers but what was underneath. What I could never understand was why you didn't lock the toilet door.'

It hadn't only been the toilet with Linda, Tommy reflected with amusement. No indeed.

It struck him then that was another thing he hated about school, all chaps together. Not a female in sight, discounting matron that was. It simply didn't seem right to him. Unnatural.

'How's the book coming along?' he inquired casually.

'Fine, as far as I know. Your mum says it's going well.'

'She's always a good judge.'

'So far anyway.' Jack paused, then said, 'Are you trying to change the subject?'

Which was precisely what Tommy had been hoping to do. 'I just wondered, that's all.'

Liar, Jack thought. Though full marks for trying. He turned and returned to his chair which he eased himself into. He might be blind but there wasn't an inch of the house he didn't know like the back of his hand or could find his way round. He'd be meeting his great friend Andrew that evening, this was something to discuss with him.

Tommy flicked the remains of his cigarette into the fireplace. 'Can I go now?'

'If you wish.'

Tommy hesitated in the doorway. 'Dad, I'm really sorry. Truly I am.'

'I know that, son,' Jack replied softly. 'Now go and make your peace with your mum. If you can that is.'

Tommy left Jack to his thoughts.

'Well,' Andrew Drummond mused. 'That must have been a bit of a shock for you and Hettie.'

Jack groped for his pint and lifted it to his lips. It was a Friday night when he and Andrew always met up, when possible that is, in the local pub. They'd been doing so for years.

'You can say that again.'

'How's Hettie taking it?'

'As you'd expect. Feeling ashamed, which is hardly surprising considering her background.'

Andrew recalled the Hettie of old, a farm worker and Jack's paid mistress before the war. Now his wife, and the best wife Jack could have had. He'd always thought highly of Hettie. More than that.

Jack slowly shook his head. 'What's to become of that boy? I wish I knew. There's a wild streak in the lad which most certainly doesn't come from me.'

Andrew couldn't help but laugh. 'That's rich, Jack Riach! Who are you trying to kid? Talk about self-delusion. You were as wild as they come when young, as many a lassie could have testified to.'

Jack had the grace to look shamefaced. 'You're exaggerating.'

'In a pig's ear. As you well know, if you're honest that is.'

'I'm always honest,' Jack protested halfheartedly.

Both men laughed.

'Besides which, you were hardly an innocent yourself. Particularly where the lassies were concerned.'

'True,' Andrew mused. And wonderful days they'd been too. He had many fond memories of his youth.

'Do you remember . . .'

The pair of them fell to reminiscing.

'I suppose I could always buy another farm,' Jack declared later at the kitchen table where he, Hettie and Tommy were having a late-night supper. He'd originally been a large landowner but had sold up on returning from the war because of his disability.

Hettie frowned. 'Whatever for?'

'Not for me of course, but Tommy. We could hire a manager to teach him the ropes. And I'd naturally be on hand to advise.'

A thoroughly appalled Tommy stared aghast at his father. 'Are you serious, Dad?'

'Quite. We've got to do something with you and since you've decided you've finished with school then that would seem the obvious thing.'

Tommy's knife clattered on to his plate, all thought of food forgotten. 'It's a terrible idea. Completely ridiculous.'

Hettie gazed coldly at him, still furious over what had happened. The shame of having a boy expelled! She was quite mortified and hated to think what the good people of Dalneil would say when the news got round. 'And why is it ridiculous?' she snapped.

'It just is, that's all.'

'I should have thought it would have appealed,' Jack said mildly.

'Appealed! Grubbing around in the dirt for a living. No thank you.'

'Don't speak to your father in that tone of voice,' Hettie admonished, fighting back the urge to slap Tommy. Damn it, but she was close to tears again.

'You'll have to get a job of some sort, you certainly can't sit around here for the rest of your life,' Jack went on.

'We had hoped you'd go to university one day. Which is hardly likely now,' Hettie glared.

'I'd never have got into university, Mum. My marks must have told you that. I'm just not clever enough.'

'You're clever enough all right,' Jack stated. 'What you mean is that your marks, and I admit they have always been poor, merely reflected the fact you wouldn't apply yourself. That's a different matter entirely.'

Tommy's lips thinned. He could hardly deny the accusation because it was true. Lack of application and a certain amount of laziness on his part. 'I'm still not going to be a farmer,' he muttered stubbornly.

'What then?'

'I don't know yet. I'll think of something.'

'Hmmh,' Jack mused. 'The old McPherson place is up for sale, and at a reasonable price too, I understand. It doesn't have a lot of acreage but would do to get you started.'

Tommy came abruptly to his feet. 'Farming's out, Dad. It may have suited you once upon a time but it would never suit me. I mean that.'

'Sit down and finish your supper,' Hettie gestured. She was beginning to realise for the first time just how spoilt Tommy had become, and wilful with it.

'No thank you, I've had enough. Now if you'll excuse me.'

Jack sighed, thinking along the same lines as his wife. His expression had become strained when the kitchen door clicked shut.

'There were a few moments there when I could easily have clouted him. Little sod,' Hettie hissed.

Jack silently agreed with her.

Tommy, not yet bothering with the candle, threw himself on to his bed and stared up into the darkness. There was an awfully big adventure out there somewhere waiting for him, he'd known that for years. But what? That was the question to which he didn't have an answer.

An African explorer maybe. That would be jolly interesting. But how did you become one of those? He could just imagine himself cutting a swathe through the jungle, fighting man-eating lions and the like.

A grin crept over his face. A big-game hunter, that

was another possibility. Or big-game hunter *and* explorer. There was no reason why you couldn't combine the two.

These fantasies were something he'd never confided to a single soul, certainly not the chaps at school who'd have ragged him rotten.

School, he wasn't going to miss it one little bit. Thank God his father had agreed those days were over. For the most part they'd been boring in the extreme. Tedious beyond belief.

Just as being a farmer would be. That was the very last thing he wanted, the very notion made him squirm.

When younger he'd dreamt about being a pirate, hoisting the jolly roger and all that. But in the end he'd had to concede that was too fanciful, not to mention impractical. As far as he knew there just weren't any pirates nowadays. All sadly gone.

'Ho ho ho and a bottle of rum,' he murmured, and laughed quietly.

Tom Riach, the feared and dreaded pirate. Chests of gold, silver and jewels captured on the Spanish Main. And women, oh yes there would be lots of those. Lots and lots. All sorts and types. All swooning at his feet. Fabulous women and oodles of booty, what a life, he reflected. How glorious that would have been.

The awfully big adventure was definitely out there waiting for him. No doubt about it.

And one day it would happen.

The next morning Andrew was in the process of getting dressed when a sudden pain lanced through his stomach causing him to gasp and bend over.

'What's wrong, Andrew?' a concerned Rose, his wife, demanded.

The pain lanced again, though this time not so severely as before.

Rose hurried to his side, her brow furrowed. 'Darling?'

He managed a weak smile. 'Indigestion I think. It just caught me unawares, that's all.'

She laid a hand on his arm. 'Come over here and sit down for a bit.' It was unusual for Andrew to suffer from indigestion, almost unheard of actually. Normally he could eat the richest of foods without suffering any ill effects. The legacy of years of army cooking, he sometimes joked. A regular officer until resigning his commission to take over the family distillery, he'd been stationed in Ireland for the duration of the war.

Andrew straightened. 'There's no need for that. I'm fine now.'

'Are you sure?'

He took a deep breath. 'Whatever, it's gone.'

'Can I get you anything. A tablet perhaps?'

'No, Rose. But thank you anyway.'

He stared into her eyes, thinking how beautiful she was, and how much he loved her. It had always worried him that the twenty-year age gap would one day affect their marriage, but it never had. Although . . . well childbearing had proved a different matter. Rose had never been the same after Drew had been born. Where previously she'd revelled in their lovemaking that had all changed with the arrival of their son.

'I suppose I'd better get on,' Andrew smiled. 'Mustn't be late for work. What would the staff say.'

'Indeed,' Rose agreed, also smiling. Andrew was a stickler for timekeeping and made it a point of honour to always be at his desk on the dot. Mr Kelly, his book-keeper, was forever declaring you could set your watch by Andrew.

9

'I'd only have a light breakfast if I was you,' Rose suggested. 'You don't want to bring on that indigestion again.'

He nodded. 'A slice of toast and cup of tea will do me.'

Rose started to turn away to continue with her dressing which she was only halfway through.

'Rose.'

He drew her to him and once in his embrace tenderly smoothed her long, as yet uncombed, hair. 'Do you ever have any regrets? About us I mean.'

She frowned. 'What a silly question. No, of course I haven't. Now why suddenly ask that, for goodness sake?'

He continued smoothing her hair. Then, on impulse, he brushed his lips over hers. 'I'd hate to take you for granted.'

'You hardly do that. At least, I don't think you do.'

'Nor do I, Rose. You're probably the best thing that's ever happened to me and I'll never forget that.'

How sweet he could be at times, she thought. Sweet and romantic. She'd been extremely lucky to meet Andrew Drummond. 'I've never regretted a single day of our marriage, so there. And that's the God's honest truth.'

'Me neither,' he confessed.

'Good, that's that out of the way. Now you'd better hurry up or you will be late.'

'Heaven forbid,' he laughed.

He was troubled, she thought, not knowing why. There had only ever been one bone of contention between them and that hadn't been mentioned in years. Was that it? Was that what had prompted his question?

She was acutely aware of his eyes riveted on her back as she walked away from him.

*　　*　　*

Nancy Thompson ran a hand over her weatherbeaten face, wishing there could be just one day in her life when she didn't feel totally and utterly exhausted. No wonder so many of her kind died relatively young, worn out by the unremitting toil and harshness of their situation.

Nancy was a bondager and had been for two years since the age of twelve when her mother had taken her along to the Hiring Fair to find her a labourer, or hind as they were called, who'd take her on.

That day she'd caught Bill McCabe's eye and the deal had been struck. Shortly afterwards she'd gone to live with him in the cottage he'd been allocated by the master.

There were many outside the Border valleys who knew nothing of the bondagers' life and would have been scandalised to think such a thing still existed. But exist it did, although it was not quite as prevalent as it had once been. Slavery some called it, serfdom by others.

Bill, a short squat man of twenty-three who could never have been called good-looking by any stretch of the imagination, pushed his plate away. 'Any more tea in the pot?'

'There should be some left.'

Bill grunted, Nancy's cue to fetch the pot and refill his cup. When that was done she went to the sink where she emptied the remains into a draining dish.

Bill scraped back his chair, picked up his cup and crossed to the fire which he sat in front of. There he lapsed into a brooding silence which was common for him at that time of night.

'Annie McGillvary's baby's due any day now,' Nancy declared. Annie was another bondager who lived in the next cottage along with her hind.

Bill didn't reply.

'She's scared about it as it's her first one. Some of the older women tell terrible stories, you understand. Enough to put the fear of God into anyone. You'd think they'd know better.'

Nancy got on with the clearing up, then started on the dishes. As she washed she thought of her ma whom she'd never seen from the day she'd joined up with Bill, nor was ever likely to again. She'd been the oldest of three children whom her mother, another bondager, had been only too pleased to be rid of.

Bill glanced at the battered clock on top of the mantel-piece. Almost time to go to bed. The best part of the day as far as he was concerned. He enjoyed his bed, with Nancy in it.

Prior to Nancy his bondager had been a lassie called Pat. Pleasant enough, to begin with anyway. But then she'd started to show a tendency to nag which hadn't pleased him one little bit. He couldn't bide a nagger. And so she'd had to go to be replaced by Nancy. If he missed Pat at all it was because she'd been an excellent cook, far better than Nancy whose meals were nothing out of the ordinary. Still, he reflected philosophically, you couldn't have everything.

'Right,' he announced a little later, noting that Nancy had finished at the sink. 'We'll go through.'

Nancy didn't dislike what was coming next, nor did she particularly like it either. It was simply one of the many things expected of her.

How long before she fell pregnant? she wondered. And what then? Would Bill renew her yearly contract or find someone else to take her place?

Bill wasn't a great one for children. He'd said so on a number of occasions.

Nor would he ever do what she'd asked many a time which would have greatly lessened the chances of her getting in the family way. He was far too selfish about his own needs and gratification for that.

Thankfully that night, which wasn't always the case, he was quick and soon snoring his head off.

The next thing Nancy knew he was shaking her and telling her it was time to get up.

Another hard slog stretched wearingly ahead.

'That's enough for today,' Jack Riach declared, and yawned.

Hettie glanced up at him in surprise, having been taking his dictation which she'd later type out and place with the rest of his manuscript. A manuscript which was growing steadily towards completion.

'What's up? You've given me a lot less than usual. Isn't it coming for you?'

Jack shook his head. 'It's Tommy, I'm worried about him and it keeps intruding on my mind.'

Hettie closed the large notebook in which she'd been writing and laid it aside. 'Would you like some coffee?'

He considered that. 'No, what I'd really like is a dram.'

'At this time of day! It's far too early.'

He grinned sheepishly at her. 'Rules are made to be broken, Hettie. I've always said that.'

'Even though.'

'And we could really break them by you joining me for a couple.'

'A couple now, it was only one a moment ago.'

He shrugged. 'Will you fetch the bottle or will I have to do it myself?'

'I'll get it.'

'Still happy with how the book's coming along?' he asked as she poured the drinks.

'If I wasn't I'd say. You know that.'

'Then it's fine?'

'Believe me, Jack, it's fine. I'm just dying to know how it's going to end, that's all.'

He laughed softly and tapped his nose. 'That's for me to know and you to wonder about. Besides, I'd spoil it for you if I told you the ending in advance.'

'I don't believe you know what it is,' she teased.

'Oh, but I do.'

'Maybe you're fibbing.'

'Now why should I do that?'

'You just would, being you.'

'I never tell you the ending, so why change now?'

'Rules are made to be broken, Jack, you just said so.'

He laughed. 'Point taken. But I'm still not giving you the ending. That remains my little secret.'

Truth was he didn't have an ending yet which was unusual for him. Normally he knew it early on, if not before he actually started to dictate.

'Where's Tommy?' he queried.

'Gone out for a walk, I believe. He mentioned something to that effect after breakfast.'

'Well that certainly won't do him any harm.'

'No,' Hettie agreed.

Jack sighed.

'You are worried about him, aren't you?'

'Very.'

'So am I. It's only natural.' Hettie paused, then said tentatively, 'Jack?'

'What?'

'There's always the army. It would be a good career for him. Or one of the other services.'

Jack's expression clouded over and then darkened even further. 'No,' he replied harshly. He finished what was left in his glass and immediately held it out for a refill.

'It was only a suggestion.'

'You weren't there, Hettie,' he said so softly she almost couldn't hear. 'Oh I know you've heard people, including myself, occasionally speak of it. And you've read about it. But the reality . . .' He trailed off, mind filled with awful, terrible memories.

'That was in the war, Jack. It's peacetime now.'

A grim smile slashed his face. 'Peacetime yes, but for how long with that fellow Herr Hitler in power. He's already gone into Czechoslovakia and once he's conquered that, what next?'

Jack shook his head. 'There could well be another war, Heaven forbid, and before too long either. It doesn't bear thinking about. Certainly not for us who were in the last one.'

'Do you think . . . it really could happen, Jack?' Fear was clutching her insides as she asked that.

'You wouldn't believe people could be so stupid, and yet they can. It's possible, Hettie, very very possible.'

He took a deep breath, then said bitterly, 'I loathe and hate the Germans, you've no idea how much. Because of them millions died, not to mention the untold misery they caused. If they drag us into another carnage then I hope their entire race roasts in perdition for all eternity.'

Hettie didn't know what to answer to that so said nothing. She could well understand Jack's feelings though she didn't entirely agree with them. It seemed to her there had to be many decent Germans, that stood to reason after all. You could hardly condemn an entire nation, no matter what that nation had done.

'So the army and other services are definitely out,' Jack stated. 'Understand?'

'Yes,' she whispered.

'Not another word on the subject.'

Hettie was sorry she'd brought it up in the first place. She should have known better.

'Push,' Nancy urged.

Annie McGillvary's lips were drawn back in a wolfish snarl. 'I'm trying,' she gasped. 'I'm bloody trying.'

The onset of pains had been sudden and violent. Nancy had tried to get her friend home to have the baby there but that hadn't been possible. Which was why Annie was now lying on her back in a field, legs drawn up and splayed, while Nancy was doing the best she could. It wouldn't be the first time a bondager had birthed in a field, it was quite a common event.

Annie screamed, eyes bulging. Her whole body convulsed.

If only it hadn't been such a raw day, Nancy thought, but what did you expect at this time of year. The wind was whistling all around them causing a nearby hedge to rustle and sway.

It was going to be quick, even the inexperienced Nancy knew that, which was something of a relief. 'The head's coming,' she exclaimed excitedly. 'I can see it now.'

Annie couldn't believe such agony was possible. It was as if she was being ripped in two. Literally torn apart.

'Push,' Nancy urged again.

'I fucking well am!'

Nancy wished one of the older women had been with

them but Annie had insisted she go with her. One in accompaniment was all that was allowed.

Now the head was born and the shoulders were straining to be free. Blood and goo were dribbling down the inside of Annie's icy-cold thighs.

This time the scream was the most horrendous yet, a scream whipped off by the wind to be lost in the distance.

A mercifully short while later it was all over, Annie having collapsed in on herself after the final titanic push. 'A boy or girl?' she croaked.

Nancy held the child to her breast, partially covering its blue-tinged body with her smock. 'A boy.'

Nancy glanced at her friend through eyes filled with tears.

'And the wee mite's dead.'

Chapter 2

'It's Andrew and Rose,' Hettie exclaimed, ushering them into the room where Jack and Tommy were.

'This is a pleasant surprise,' Jack smiled.

'We were on our way to my sister Charlotte's and thought we'd drop by,' Andrew explained. Charlotte was married to the Dalneil minister, John McLean, and lived in the village manse.

'Take a seat,' Jack declared, coming to his feet. 'I don't suppose you'll refuse a dram.'

'Only if it isn't Drummond,' Andrew joked, knowing full well Jack kept nothing else.

'And you, Rose?'

'A small one with water would be nice.'

Tommy felt the foursome should be alone and decided to take himself upstairs. 'I'll leave you lot to it,' he stated affably.

'No, you stay, Tommy. Our visit here concerns you,' Andrew replied.

'You've grown since I saw you last,' Rose observed. 'Quite the young man now.' Then, teasingly, 'Is that the hint of a moustache I can make out?'

Tommy blushed. He'd always fancied Rose Drummond rotten, though of course she was far too old for him, not to mention married.

Hettie laughed. 'Shame on you, Rose, you'll embarrass the lad. That's cruel.'

Andrew's statement had intrigued Tommy. Concerned him? In what way? he wondered.

'Would you like a hand there?' Andrew queried, moving to Jack's side.

'If you'd pass them out.'

'Aye, no trouble at all.'

'Any excuse for a dram,' Hettie said, though not entirely unapprovingly. Whisky and Scots went together. Some men just needed a wee bit of restraint, that's all.

Jack shook the bottle he was holding. 'The damn thing's empty, Hettie. Is there another in the larder?'

'Isn't there always. I'll go and fetch it.'

Rose eyed Tommy kindly, having known for years that he had a soft spot for her. 'You've left school I understand.'

'Expelled,' Jack qualified. 'Let's not be mealy-mouthed about it. The bugger was expelled, kicked out for smoking and drinking.' He paused, then added, 'Who knows what else he was up to either.'

'You mean lassies?' Rose further teased.

This time Tommy went scarlet.

'The thought had crossed my mind.'

'Well, Tommy?' Rose queried, still with a teasing tone.

He was tongue-tied, being asked such a thing by Rose. 'Well?'

'Fat chance of that at an all boys school,' he finally managed to stammer in reply.

'I contrived to meet a few when I was at school,' Andrew commented drily. 'No doubt it was the same with you.'

Hettie breezed back in with the new bottle. 'It's lovely having some company. We were listening to the wireless earlier but there wasn't much on.'

Jack listened a lot to the wireless for obvious reasons. It was a great solace to his blindness.

'We're not intruding then?' Rose queried.

'Och no, you and Andrew could never do that. The pair of you are always welcome in this house as you well know.'

'What's the occasion at Charlotte's?' Jack inquired of Andrew.

'Nothing special. A natter and some supper, that's all.'

Andrew noted that Tommy was looking uncomfortable, and apprehensive. He smiled inwardly.

'Smoking and drinking,' he said to Tommy. 'A touch of the cratur I hope. Do you like whisky?'

Tommy nodded.

'And yet I see your dad hasn't given you a glass.'

Jack hesitated for the briefest of moments. 'I suppose it's all right. You are sixteen after all. Straight or with water?'

'Straight please, Dad.'

Andrew grunted his approval. 'I'm delighted to hear you like whisky, lad, for that's what I've come to talk to you about.'

Tommy couldn't imagine why. He was quite bewildered.

'*Slainthe!*' Jack toasted, raising his own glass.

'How's the book coming along, Jack?' Rose asked after

she'd had a sip. 'Andrew never mentions anything about what's said at those get togethers of yours on a Friday night.' Which wasn't true, though Andrew was selective. He had told her about Tommy and discussed the matter with her.

'He won't let on the ending and I'm dying to know,' Hettie chipped in, eyes twinkling.

'Nor will I.'

'You horrible thing,' Rose said, now teasing Jack.

'What I have taken down so far is extremely good,' Hettie declared, immensely proud of Jack and his writing. 'Nor would I say that if it wasn't so, as you all know.'

'I look forward to reading it then.'

'And as always you'll have one of my free copies,' Jack retorted.

'Thank you.'

'Getting back to whisky,' Andrew said, sitting beside Rose on the settee. 'Would you be interested in making a career in it, Tommy?'

That startled the youngster. 'I beg your pardon?'

'You heard me. Would you be interested in making a career in it? With Drummond Whisky to be more precise. As a traveller for the firm.'

Jack was dumbfounded. 'Are you serious, Andrew?'

'Never more so.'

'Well,' murmured Jack. Tommy working for Andrew, that would be perfect.

'Tommy?' Hettie prompted, also delighted by this suggestion which would solve all their problems.

'I, eh . . .' Tommy swallowed. 'I honestly don't know.'

'You wouldn't start off as a traveller of course,' Andrew went on. 'You'd have to learn the ropes first. From the bottom up so to speak. But given time and progress you would eventually go on the road for me.'

Tommy's mind was whirling. His first reaction was to reject the offer, but that would be ill mannered and his parents would be furious. A traveller for whisky hardly matched being an African explorer and big-game hunter.

'Speak up, son,' Jack enthused. 'You can't just say you don't know. This is an ideal opportunity and one you're lucky to have, considering the circumstances.'

Andrew laughed and waved a hand dismissively. 'His being expelled makes no difference to me. It shows spirit, that's all. A quality I much admire. The trick is to harness that spirit . . .' He treated them all to a beaming smile. 'In this instance with spirit of another kind. If you'll pardon my little joke.'

He rounded again on Tommy. 'The remuneration wouldn't be much to begin with, but fair, I promise you that. And there would be a yearly review.'

'This is very kind of you, Andrew,' Hettie declared.

'Not really, it depends how you look at these things. Anyway, in life it's often who you know, eh?'

Tommy finished his whisky which he didn't even notice going down.

'Well?' That was Jack again.

Tommy was horribly aware of four pairs of eyes staring intently at him. 'It's . . . an awfully big decision to make just like that,' he prevaricated.

'Quite right too,' Rose declared, taking his side. 'It is an awfully big decision. One that should be thought through. He's showing sense.'

Tommy shot her a smile of appreciation.

'I understand.' Andrew nodded.

Jack's lips thinned. As far as he was concerned Tommy

should have jumped at the chance. What was there to think about? Damn all, in his opinion.

'Can I speak to you, give you my decision in a couple of days' time?' Tommy asked Andrew.

Hettie was aware of how displeased Jack was and was none too happy herself. But Rose was right, there was absolutely no point in forcing the boy.

'Of course,' Andrew replied.

'That way a mistake won't be made,' Rose said, again coming to Tommy's aid.

'Then we'll leave it at that for now,' Andrew agreed.

Tommy knew there was going to be all hell to pay when the Drummonds had gone.

Nancy paused in her darning and shook her head. These socks had almost had it, she thought. They'd been darned so many times there was nearly more darning than original wool. She idly wondered if other men were as hard on socks as Bill.

She glanced up and frowned when there was a knock on the door. Now who could that be at this time of night? Had to be Annie over for a blether she presumed.

She was wrong. She gasped in surprise when she opened the door and the master was revealed. 'It's you, sir.'

'Aye, me.'

Nancy wasn't sure what to do, being all alone. 'If it's Bill you want I'm afraid he isn't here,' she said.

The master already knew that which was why he was there, it being the one night a week the labourers went to the pub. 'Damn,' he muttered, pretending disappointment.

'Can I help you, sir?'

The master banged his hands together. 'Fiendishly cold night. Is there any tea going?'

'I can put the kettle on if you wish.'

He immediately stepped past her. 'Then do that. Nancy, isn't it?'

'Yes, sir.'

Once inside the master glanced around. At least she kept a reasonably neat and tidy house he reflected, though it wouldn't have mattered if she hadn't.

He brought his attention to bear on Nancy now busy at the sink pump. An attractive figure, as far as he could make out that was. And the face wasn't bad either. He was going to enjoy this.

Nancy was nervous, so much so her hands were trembling. She wished Bill had been there.

The master removed his coat and tossed it aside where it fell across a chair. His jacket followed the coat. The pub was open for a good hour yet, plenty of time for what he had in mind.

Damn the wife and her monthlies, it was so inconvenient. There again, it gave him the opportunity to branch out when he wished. Not that he always needed an excuse when the mood took him.

'It won't be long, sir.' Nancy smiled, busying herself, wondering why he'd taken off his jacket as well.

Nice smile, he thought. He walked towards her, stopping a few feet away. His eyes fixed on the bulge of her breasts.

Nancy knew then with a certainty why he'd come. A hand flew to her mouth. She'd heard it went on, of course, the other women whispered about it from time to time but never really discussed it openly.

She swallowed hard, hoping against hope she was wrong

24

and it really was Bill he'd come to see. Please God that was the case.

'Lovely little creature, aren't you,' the master said in a husky voice, suddenly filled with desire.

Nancy edged sideways. 'Please, sir.'

He smiled, a smile that quickly transformed itself into a leer. The blood was pounding in his veins. 'There's nothing to be afraid of, Nancy. I'm not going to do anything you ain't done before. How old are you, lass?'

She told him.

Young and no doubt juicy. Just the way he liked them. Slowly he began undoing the front of his trousers.

Nancy whimpered. She could try and dodge round him and flee the cottage. But if she did escape, what then? She and Bill would be out on their ears, no doubt. She felt like an animal caught in a trap.

'You'll enjoy it, girl, I promise.' Not that he gave a damn whether she did or not. All that mattered was *he* did.

Nancy's vision blurred. This was a nightmare. She'd been sitting at home, totally at peace with herself and surroundings. Then that knock on the door and . . .

She gave a muffled scream as he grabbed her.

The master got up from the floor where Nancy lay spread-eagled. Like shagging a bloody corpse, he thought in disgust. Worse than useless. At the very least she might have struggled but hadn't even done that. He wouldn't be coming back again, he decided. Wasn't worth it. He liked his women to have some oomph in them, a bit of appreciation. But her . . .

Nancy didn't open her eyes till she heard the door click shut.

* * *

'Christ Almighty, what's happened to you?' Annie McGillvary exclaimed. She too was alone, Hector having also gone to the pub.

A dishevelled Nancy fell into Annie's arms. 'Oh Annie, Annie,' she sobbed.

Annie guided her friend over to a chair and sat her down. 'Now what's this all about?'

'The master . . . the master . . .' Nancy broke off and shook.

Annie sighed. Bastard. It was obvious now what had happened. 'He called on you, I take it?'

Nancy nodded.

'Did he hurt you?'

'Not really,' Nancy choked.

'Then count yourself lucky. He's been known to do that before. Belle Gibbons was black and blue after one such visit. The swine punched her all over.'

Nancy was thankful she'd been spared that. 'It was so unexpected, Annie. So very unexpected. Suddenly he was there and then minutes later . . .'

Annie wished she had some drink in the house, but unfortunately didn't.

'I've only ever had Bill until now you see,' Nancy babbled. 'And I had time to think about that, get used to the idea before he bedded me. But with the master . . .' She shuddered. 'I thought I was going to puke.'

'There there,' Annie crooned, stroking her friend's cheek. 'It's all over now. Finished and done with.'

'I feel so . . . dirty inside. Dirty as sin.'

'But you shouldn't. It wasn't your doing after all. What happened is common enough hereabouts. If a master takes a notion to a bondager then that's that, she has no say in the matter. None at all. The only thing to do is grit your teeth and let him get on with it. That's the way it is, Nancy love.'

'It's so unfair though,' Nancy sobbed.

Annie smiled bitterly. 'You've never said a truer word. Unfair it is, but that's the way of the world I'm afraid.'

A traveller for Drummond Whisky, Tommy reflected, staring up at his bedroom ceiling where light from his candle cast flickering shadows. That meant a car, which would be terrific, something he'd always wanted. He had an aptitude for mechanical things and was sure he'd make an excellent driver.

He closed his eyes and imagined himself as a racing driver whooshing round bends, then opening up on the straight, going at a fantastic speed.

The car would be in British racing green livery of course, and he would be the premier driver in the whole country. He saw himself receiving the winner's cup and all the admiring glances, mainly from women, coming in his direction.

The champagne would pop and froth, then he'd be pouring it into the cup and drinking deeply. A god, that's what you must be at a moment like that, a veritable god.

Tommy sighed and brought himself out of his reverie. He had a decision to make and it wasn't easy. Even with the inducement of a car.

The thing was, what was his alternative? Run away from home, take his chances like that? It was a possibility of course, one he'd been mulling over. Trouble was he didn't have any money to back himself up. If he did run away it would be with only a few measly pounds in his pocket. He was practical enough to know that wouldn't get him very far.

27

Working for Andrew Drummond wouldn't be too bad, he thought. Andrew was a decent man and, by all accounts, a good employer. He could do a lot worse. Oh aye, he could do that.

It would be a start, he rationalised. And you had to start somewhere, even if the jungles of Africa were your ultimate aim.

Tommy sighed again, already knowing what his answer was going to be when he next saw Andrew.

'What have you been up to?' Bill McCabe slurred as Nancy came into the cottage. He was clearly drunk, though not belligerently so. His eyes were rheumy and squinting slightly.

Nancy had already tidied herself before leaving Annie's, which she did when Hector had arrived in. She explained where she'd been.

Bill grunted.

'How was your night out?'

'Och fine. The usual.'

She'd discussed with Annie whether or not she should tell Bill what had happened, and decided she wouldn't. There was nothing Bill could do about it anyway except be upset. Which he may or may not be, she wasn't sure.

'Would you like some tea?' she asked.

He shook his head, then belched. 'Not on top of that I wouldn't. It would be spoiling good beer.' Bill yawned and stretched. 'It's bed for me. I'm fair done in and that's a fact.'

Nancy found herself staring at that part of the floor where the master had taken her, remembering anew the ghastliness of it all.

'You all right?'

She nodded.

'You look a bit funny like.'

'Do I?'

He lurched towards her. 'What were you and Annie talking about?'

'Nothing much. The things we normally talk about.'

Bill didn't believe that. Even in his befuddled state he could sense something was amiss. 'Come on, what was it?'

She hadn't been going to but should she now change her mind? 'Mainly the baby Annie lost,' she lied.

'Oh!' That explained it. 'She'll soon have another if Hector has anything to do with it. You take my word. He enjoys his oats does Hector.'

Just like you, she thought. Just like you.

'See to the fire and come on through. I'll be waiting.'

Not tonight, she wailed inside. Not after the master. That would be too much to bear.

But go through with it she'd have to. She knew that, even though she would feel total revulsion and hatred against men and their rutting ways throughout it all, and afterwards.

The master sat astride his horse watching three of the bondagers, one of whom was Nancy, hard at work. His expression was dyspeptic.

What a disappointment that had been, he reflected. And, now he thought about it, an insult to himself. Why, halfway through he'd almost felt like giving up there and then.

An insult right enough. And he wasn't a man to take insults. By God, he wasn't. A corpse, he thought yet

29

again. That's precisely what it had been like. Shagging a bloody corpse.

Small flakes of snow started to fall, causing him to glance up at a heavy, grey leaden sky. There had been the smell of snow in the air for days and now it had arrived.

His horse whinnied and then snorted, making him smile. He remembered that she didn't like snow. It made her nervous, especially falling snow.

Nancy paused in what she was doing to catch her breath, well aware that the master had been staring at her. Now what was going through his mind? she wondered. Was he thinking about the other night or something else? Beside her Annie, who'd gone back to work the day after she'd given birth, toiled relentlessly on.

The master, noting that Nancy had stopped, glared at her which sent her instantly back to the task in hand. He smiled inwardly. You'll have to go, bitch, he decided. Nobody insults me and gets away with it.

He wheeled his horse about, intending to return home for a hot meal and drink.

McCabe would go at the end of his contracted year, and with McCabe would go that Nancy.

His mind was made up and once that happened he never changed it.

Tommy halted to gaze at the Drummond Distillery, a building he'd known all his life though he'd only ever been inside on very few occasions. Now he was seeing it in a quite different light.

He had an appointment with Andrew in ten minutes and mustn't be late. That would never do, Hettie had impressed on him when he'd been sluggish in getting ready. So here he was, in best bib and tucker, about to take the plunge that would alter his life for ever.

It wouldn't be too bad, he told himself yet again. A start anyway, if nothing else. And the awfully big adventure was always out there waiting for him. He knew it was. That was something he must cling on to, never forget.

He suddenly smiled to himself, remembering the car that would one day be at his disposal. A car to take him all over the country and even down into England.

Sucking in a deep breath he continued towards Drummond's and his immediate destiny.

'Is it true?' Bill demanded, voice loaded with anger.

Nancy, who herself had only arrived home a few minutes previously, glanced round at him. His expression was frightening.

'Is what true?' she gulped.

'That the master came here and you displeased him.'

Oh Christ, she thought. 'Who told you that?'

He balled his hands into fists and advanced on her as she swiftly retreated. She'd never seen Bill like this before.

'Never you mind, is it true?'

'How do you mean, displease?'

'Exactly that, you stupid bitch.'

Her breath was coming in short pants while her skin had gone cold all over. A different sort of cold to that caused by the weather. 'Who told you?' she repeated.

'I said it doesn't fucking well matter. All that does is you displeased him.'

Nancy hung her head in shame. 'He turned up one night when you were at the pub and forced himself on me. I had no choice, Bill, believe me. If I hadn't given in you and I might have been turfed out.'

'And we still might,' he hissed. 'If you were going to open your legs for him the least you could have done is make a good job of it.'

'I'm sorry,' she whispered.

'Sorry! That's no bloody use. None whatsoever.'

She felt the tears begin to well, her thoughts muddled at that moment. 'He's such a horrible man, Bill. You've no idea what it was like.'

Bill made an exclamation of disgust and moved away. He wanted to smack Nancy, knock her from one end of the room to the other. What had been a secure little billet was now in jeopardy.

'You must have known he'd tup you at some point, young and pretty as you are. It's to be expected. It's his right after all. He's master, ruler of all on his land.'

She couldn't help herself. 'Have you no thoughts for me? No consideration for my feelings?'

'Sod your feelings, I care nothing for those. Not in these circumstances. A complete let-down I heard. Worse than useless.'

Nancy doubted that had come from Annie, or even Hector via her. The origin must be the master himself.

'What's a little shag, eh? Nothing, nothing at all. Happens every night of the week. The trouble with you, lady, is you're high and mighty. 'Tis a fault in you I've noticed many times. And now you've displeased the master. God damn you!'

'I didn't mean to displease him,' she replied, now almost hysterical. 'I didn't mean to do anything.'

The anger suddenly evaporated in Bill and he sagged where he stood. He was fond of Nancy, in a funny sort of way. In fact, if he was truthful, he felt . . . quite affectionate towards her. As much as he'd felt towards

32

any woman that is, which wasn't saying a great deal. Now this . . .

He ran a hand over his face. Crossing to a chair, he slumped into it.

'Bill?'

'Aye?'

'I am sorry. Please believe that.'

'Aye, sure,' he muttered.

Nancy was trying to bring herself back under control, the momentary hysteria having almost got the better of her. She'd wondered how Bill would react, now she knew. No concern about her wellbeing, only that she'd displeased the master.

'Well, what's done is done I suppose,' Bill mumbled. 'Can't help that now. No use crying over spilt milk as they say. Except . . .' He swung on Nancy. 'If he calls again you put things right, you hear?'

'Right?'

He grimaced. 'I don't know what was wrong but whatever it was don't do it again. Make sure he goes out that door with a smile on his face and a spring in his step. Now promise me?'

She nodded.

'Let me hear you say it.'

'I promise, Bill.'

'You want to stay here, don't you?'

She nodded again.

'Then that's what you've got to do. And just pray to God he does come back. Or at least forgets the whole matter. The master isn't one to cross or upset, Nancy. Believe me. He's got a black heart that man. Black as coal.'

Bill lapsed into one of his brooding silences and after a

while Nancy turned away and got on with their evening meal.

'I've got a surprise for you,' Rose announced to Andrew.

He glanced up from his Sunday paper. 'A surprise?'

'A nice one too.'

'So what is it?'

Rose was enjoying this, and had been looking forward to the moment. 'Any ideas?'

He considered that, then shook his head. 'None at all.' A surprise? He couldn't imagine what.

'I'm going to have a baby.'

Chapter 3

'A baby!' Andrew exclaimed, stunned.

Rose smiled at his reaction. It had been eleven years after all since Drew had been born. She'd quite convinced herself she'd never have another child. That Drew was all there was.

Andrew leapt from his chair, the paper falling to the floor. He swept Rose into his arms and whirled her round. 'Darling, that's absolutely wonderful! I can't tell you how pleased I am.'

'I think you are,' she laughed in reply.

He stopped and stared at her, eyes blazing with pleasure. 'How far gone are you. I mean, is it certain?'

'It's certain, all right. And I'm three months gone. I wanted to be absolutely sure before telling you.'

Like Rose, Andrew had come to believe they'd never have another child. And now this. Right out of the blue.

'It'll be a little girl of course,' Rose declared. 'I've always

35

wanted a girl and that's what we're going to have. I'm convinced of it.'

'Now hold on, Rose,' Andrew cautioned. 'Let's not get carried away. It might not be a girl . . .'

'It will,' she interjected firmly.

'But it might not be, I don't want you being disappointed. As far as I'm concerned as long as the bairn is born healthy with all its bits and pieces in the right places then that's all that matters.' He'd been about to add, with no after-effects to its mother, then changed his mind.

Now he came to think of it, there had been an added glow to Rose of late, and some sort of difference about her. 'How do you feel, my love? Any morning sickness?'

'If there had been you'd have known about it, silly. And I feel wonderful. Absolutely on top of the world.'

'Have you been to see the doctor yet?'

'Several times. He says there's nothing to worry about. Everything is exactly as it should be.'

Andrew breathed a sigh of relief. A baby! He was still grappling to take it on board.

'If you don't mind I thought we'd call her Mary after my mother.' Mary Seaton had died from influenza when Rose was young, leaving her father Willie to bring both her and her brother Ian up on his own. Until Willie had married Georgina, who'd then become their stepmother.

Andrew frowned. 'I've nothing against that, but isn't it unlucky to name a baby before it's born?'

'Nonsense!' Rose retorted. 'There's nothing unlucky about it. Old wives' tales. So you agree?'

'If it's what you wish.'

'I do. Very much so.'

'And a boy?'

She waved a hand. 'It's a girl, a boy's name won't come

into it. Trust me, I know. We women have intuitions about such things.'

That might be, Andrew thought, but he didn't like her building up her hopes about the baby's gender. He didn't want her being disappointed. He had heard of cases where it had been difficult afterwards when the wrong, or unexpected, sex had turned up.

'Now I want you taking good care of yourself,' he stated brusquely. 'No more horse riding for a start. Far too dangerous. Especially at your age.'

'My age!' she exploded mildly. 'I'm only thirty-two.'

'Even so, it's old enough to be pregnant. We mustn't take any chances. I insist on that.'

'Do you indeed,' she teased.

'I do. Most emphatically.'

She'd already decided to stop riding, but wasn't going to let Andrew know that. Let him think she was obeying his wishes. 'All right, no more riding,' she pretended to concede. 'Anything else?'

'A sleep every afternoon.'

'Whether or not I'm tired?' That again was said in a teasing manner.

'Precisely. And alcohol is completely out.'

She had to smile, not being a great drinker at the best of times. She was far too mindful of her figure for that. As a teenager she'd been inclined to plumpness and had got into the habit of watching her food and alcohol intake as a result.

'Agreed, Rose?'

'Agreed.'

He relaxed a little. 'Now, how about Drew?'

'What's he got to do with it?'

'Are we going to tell him?'

A smile twisted Rose's lips. 'I think we'd better. I'll probably begin to show before long anyway.'

'Then you can tell him.'

Rose laughed. 'Me! Why me? Why not you?'

'Because ... because ...' He couldn't think of an answer.

'Might it be because you'd be embarrassed?'

'Not at all,' Andrew blustered.

'I think so.'

'Then you think wrongly.'

Rose knew she didn't. 'I know what, we'll compromise,' she suggested. 'We'll tell Drew together.'

Andrew could see he wasn't going to wriggle out of this one. Well, if it had to be done so be it. Though he'd have much preferred Rose to have had a word on her own. 'When?'

'How about after lunch?'

He nodded. 'We'll do it then.'

Mary Drummond, Rose mused to herself, not for the first time. That had a fine ring to it. And Mary it would be.

Drew, home from school two days previously for the Christmas holidays, stared aghast at his parents. 'You're expecting!'

A smiling Rose nodded while Andrew glanced away.

Which meant ... At their age that was disgusting! No, it was more than that. It was obscene. Why, his pa was positively ancient while ma was ... He just couldn't credit his mother and father were still doing *that*.

'Are you pleased?' Rose prompted.

'We certainly are,' Andrew added in a mumble, supporting his wife.

'I suppose so,' Drew replied hesitantly. He was nothing of the sort. He was far from pleased. Apart from anything else it meant he was going to have to share the limelight. Or worse still, be completely shoved aside while all attention would be focused on this new addition to the family.

'It's going to be a little sister for you,' Rose declared, still smiling.

Andrew sighed. 'You don't know that for definite, Rose.'

She rounded on him, continuing to smile. 'I told you earlier, Andrew, it *will* be a girl. I'm positive.'

Drew couldn't get over the fact his parents still did it. He wasn't supposed to know the facts of life, they certainly hadn't been explained to him by Andrew and Rose, but he had picked up the rudimentaries at school. And incredulous he'd been too when he'd heard them. He found it amazing that people actually did that to one another. The very idea made him sick.

He stared at his mother, seeing her through new eyes. And disapproving eyes they were too. 'When?' he stuttered.

'In the spring, darling.'

He hoped he was at school when it happened. 'That's nice,' he managed.

Rose positively beamed. 'I'm glad you approve.'

Huh! Drew thought bitterly. It was as if his childhood had somehow, suddenly, begun to slip away. Right now he wanted to be on his own, think this through. It had never entered his mind; why the whole idea was preposterous, that his parents still went in for that sort of thing. He'd considered them well past it.

'Is there anything else you want to ask?' Andrew queried gruffly.

Drew shook his head.

'Fine.'

Drew wanted out of there, away from that room, the very house itself. And his parents. He'd run to the distillery and back. Further probably. Run as fast as he could, like the wind.

A few minutes later that's exactly what he was doing.

'So how did you get on?' Hettie asked Tommy who had just returned from his first day's work.

He pulled a face. 'Uncle Andrew wasn't joking when he said I'd be starting at the bottom. I've been humping sacks of grain all day.'

Jack chuckled.

'It's not funny, Dad! My back feels as though it's broken.'

'My wee lamb,' Hettie sympathised.

'You'll soon get used to it,' Jack stated. 'It won't take long.'

Hettie was recalling her time on the farm when a few sacks of grain had been nothing to her. But she'd been brought up differently from Tommy whose life to date had been one of ease.

Tommy flopped on to a chair and sighed, 'I won't have any trouble sleeping tonight.'

'Why don't you go and have a nice bath and then we'll eat directly afterwards.'

'I doubt I've enough energy left to go up those stairs, Mum. I'm whacked.'

Tommy gazed down at his hands, grimacing to see the beginnings of blisters. He couldn't help but glance at the clock and figure out how many hours there were till he had to return to purgatory.

'Of course you've enough energy,' Hettie declared in a no-nonsense tone. 'Now on you go. You'll feel the better for a bath, I promise you.'

Tommy groaned, 'I suppose so.'

'I know so,' Hettie stated.

Tommy pulled himself out of the chair, finding he was already starting to stiffen up. He'd be like a board before long, he reflected ruefully.

Tommy was so tired he fell asleep in the bath and Jack had to wake him up for supper.

'Why are you wriggling like that?' Nancy demanded. 'You've been fidgeting all evening.'

Bill glared at her, and mumbled a reply.

'Eh? I didn't hear what you said.'

'A boil!' he exclaimed. 'On my arse. It hurts something chronic.'

Nancy grinned. 'I was wondering why you were squirming in bed last night. It's not like you to be so restless.'

Bill shifted his position yet again. 'Damn thing.'

'How do you know it's a boil if it's on your backside? You can't see there.'

'I had a good feel earlier. It's a boil all right. And a big juicy bugger at that.'

Nancy had a think. 'My ma used to say that bread poultices were the very dab for those. Shall I make you one up?'

Bill gritted his teeth. He didn't like the idea of Nancy fiddling around with his backside, but he'd do anything for some relief. He grunted in reply.

'Is that a yes or no?'

'Yes damnit!' he swore.

'Right then, I'll get on with it. You'd better strip off.'

Bill was shy about that. He and Nancy might sleep together but nudity was something else.

She guessed what was bothering him. 'It's the only way, Bill. Unless you want to go on suffering.'

Which was the last thing he wanted. 'Aye, all right,' he answered ungraciously.

Nancy put the kettle on to boil while Bill got out of his trousers, deciding to stay in his long johns, until the poultice was ready.

Nancy crumbled bread into a bowl, ready for the water, then rooted around for some bandages she knew she had somewhere. She was going to enjoy this, she thought gleefully.

'I've never had a bread poultice before,' Bill said. 'Will it hurt?'

'Och, not to a big man like you. Nothing you can't cope with.'

Bill grunted again.

Nancy laid out her scissors in preparation for what was coming next, humming to herself in the process.

'Will you stop caterwauling,' Bill complained, nerves on edge. 'You sound as if you're being strangled.'

'Thank you very much,' she replied sarcastically, thinking that was it, the poultice was going to be as hot as she could make it.

'Well, you do.'

Bill ran a hand through his hair. He hated being unwell, positively loathed it. Not that having a boil was being unwell, far from it. But it was the same sort of thing in a way. It meant he wasn't a hundred per cent and that made the grafting more difficult.

Nancy waited till the kettle was fully boiling before removing it and pouring some of its contents into the bowl, clouds of steam issuing from both bowl and kettle.

In the interim she'd made up a pad of muslin on to which she now scooped the bread, mashing it down with the back of a tablespoon.

'Drop those long johns and lean across a chair,' she instructed. 'And hurry up if you want the benefit of this.'

Bill did as he was bid, feeling a proper fool with his naked backside sticking in the air.

Nancy approached him with the steaming pad in one hand, bandages and scissors in the other. She was doing her best to keep a smile off her face.

What a ridiculous sight, she thought. If Bill could only see himself. Better still, if others could. Especially those he worked alongside.

'Now then,' she declared, and slapped the poultice across the large boil that had erupted on his left cheek.

Bill howled and jerked.

'Keep still!' she snapped.

'It fucking burns.'

'Och, don't be a big jessie. Hold still.'

Bill's teeth were clamped shut, his eyes firmly closed. It was as if he was being branded.

'Next we'll get this bandage on to keep it in place,' Nancy said quietly.

Bill wished he'd never mentioned the bloody boil. This was terrible. 'Hurry up,' he gasped.

Nancy sadistically pushed down on the pad which made him writhe in agony. Oh, but this was grand. It wasn't often she had the upper hand where a man was concerned.

Her bandaging was far from expert, and she wasn't at

all sure the pad would remain in place, but she'd done her best. When the poultice cooled it would begin to draw, hopefully sucking all the poison out.

Nancy had to stop herself from slapping Bill resoundingly on the rear. That wouldn't have amused him one iota, though it certainly would her. 'Now how about a cup of tea? That'll cheer you up?' she suggested.

Bill began tugging at his long johns, keeping his face turned away from Nancy so she didn't see the tears in his eyes. He gave her another grunt.

Nancy resumed humming, much to Bill's annoyance. Only this time he didn't complain or pass comment.

One of the lassies in the bottling department glanced up as Tommy appeared. Here was a bit of sport, she thought, nudging her pal Irene in the ribs and nodding in Tommy's direction.

'Well, if it isn't Little Lord Fauntleroy himself,' the lassie, whose name was Bell Mathieson, called out.

Irene giggled, as did several of the others present.

Tommy reddened slightly and hurried on his way. He knew all these women, who lived in Dalneil and the surrounding area, but by sight only. Their being 'common', he hadn't had any truck with them in the past.

'Hello, Lord Fauntleroy, come on over here and give us a big smacker,' Irene declared brazenly.

Tommy's face reddened even further. This was awful, not to mention humiliating.

'Och, you're no interested in a wee runt like that, are you, Irene?' Isa Weir said, tongue firmly in cheek.

'He might not be wee all over,' Irene instantly retorted, which raised a filthy laugh.

'Is that right, Mr Riach?' Bell queried, heavily accenting the Mister. 'Are you no wee all over?'

'But big,' Hannah McIlroy added.

All the girls kept working during this teasing, their hands deftly moving as they corked, labelled and finally boxed the ever moving line of bottles that clattered between them.

Tommy desperately wanted to make a withering reply, but couldn't think of one. Then he stepped on something on the floor that sent him skidding, nearly losing his balance and falling over.

Bell and her companions screeched with laughter.

'It's a bit early for him to have been at the whisky already,' Sandy McAlpine commented loudly.

'He's too young for whisky. Aren't you, Mr Riach?' Isa Weir jibed.

Mr Balfour, the gaffer, came back into the department having been to the toilet. 'What's going on here?' he demanded.

The women immediately fell silent.

Mr Balfour harumphed and swept them all with a disapproving glance. 'Ah, Tommy,' he smiled. 'What can I do for you, lad?'

'Nothing, sir. I'm just passing through.'

Mr Balfour nodded. 'On you go then.'

Hannah McIlroy sniggered as Tommy passed her. '*Are* you big?' she whispered.

Rose had already run her bath and was waiting for it to cool before getting in. Meanwhile she was sitting in front of her vanity table brushing her hair. It was mid-afternoon.

She stopped brushing to stare at her abdomen reflected in the mirror, smiling to herself at the thought of what was inside. Their baby, little Mary.

45

She couldn't remember when she'd last been so ecstatically happy. It was as though all the colours in the world had somehow been made brighter. Shining as never before.

Rose sighed with pleasure. This pregnancy was proving quite different to the one she'd had with Drew. Then she'd been depressed and irritable, while this time round she was just bursting with energy and enthusiasm. That difference was yet another reason she was convinced she was carrying a female child.

Oh what fun it would be having a daughter. The fun of dressing her and all the other little joys that made having a daughter so different to a son.

A doll's house, she thought, they must get one of those. Then she remembered the doll's house she'd had when young and how much she'd enjoyed that. She'd spent hours at a time playing with it, all on her own, no need for other company.

She wondered if her father Willie had held on to the doll's house or if it had been thrown out or given away. It was quite possible it had been kept, in which case she would have it brought here for Mary. And the dolls that went with it.

The idea excited her. Her old doll's house and dollies, Mary would adore those.

She made up her mind to telephone Willie that very evening and inquire about them.

'How does it look?' Bill queried anxiously.

Nancy stared at the cavity where the boil had been, thinking it a right mess.

'Well?' Bill demanded.

'The poultice has done the trick.'

46

Bill uttered a sigh of relief, thinking that was that then.

Nancy wished she knew more about boils. The cavity and flesh directly round it were purple and red, shot through with whitish feathery lines, and the whole thing was still very angry in appearance. She wondered if Annie had any ointment she could put on that might help.

'I'm going to wash the area down and put on another bandage,' Nancy declared. 'That'll have to do for now.'

'It's still sore.'

'Aye, bound to be. But you're on the mend.'

'Thank God for that,' Bill mumbled. It was going to be lovely to sit down properly again, and lie on his back of a night.

'Just stay where you are till I get things ready,' Nancy instructed, and moved away leaving Bill bent over a chair with his long johns wrinkled round his ankles.

What she hadn't told him was that another boil had started to appear close by the original.

Andrew pulled Rose closer to him. 'That was wonderful. Thank you,' he crooned.

'It was wonderful for me too,' she replied coyly.

Andrew could only wonder at their recent lovemaking, a complete turnaround to what it had previously been. It reminded him of the times before Drew had been born.

She was actually eager now when he approached her, compliant to his wishes. What a change from the mental distance he'd endured for years when he'd felt, or at least that was the impression he'd got, she was only allowing him out of wifely duty.

If this was what a second pregnancy did to her then he praised the day it had happened.

'Oh, I forgot to say, I rang Pa when you were out at the pub with Jack,' Rose informed him, her voice warm and cosy, just like the body pressed against his.

'Oh?'

'He and Georgina would like us there for Hogmanay.'

'Indeed.'

Rose stroked a naked thigh. 'We haven't been to see them for ages, Andrew. I think we should go.'

'You want to then?'

'Very much so.' She smiled up at him. 'Besides, I have an ulterior motive for visiting The Haven.' That was the name of the estate Willie owned.

'Ulterior motive? Sounds intriguing.'

She told him about the doll's house and wanting to bring it back with them.

Andrew frowned. This business of Rose insisting the baby was going to be a girl really worried him. The idea had quite taken her over.

'So what do you say?' she prompted.

Andrew was always slightly uneasy about going to The Haven and visiting Georgina, though since his marriage to Rose nothing had ever been mentioned between them about the affair they'd once had. Or the fact that the son Willie thought was his, was actually Andrew's own. Not for the first time he thanked the Lord that young James, a year older than Drew, took after his mother in looks.

'I don't see why not,' he conceded. It had been a while since they'd been to The Haven; if anything a visit was overdue.

Willie was a long-standing friend of his from army days when they'd served in Ireland together. It was after the war, while passing through the area, that he'd met up again with Willie and through him Georgina and Rose.

Rose knew about the affair with her stepmother and had long since forgiven him, or at least come to terms with it. She had no inkling about the true parentage of James – and pray God she never found out.

'Drew will enjoy it,' Rose persisted. 'He and James get on so well together.'

'True enough.'

'Shall I accept their invitation then?'

'Of course. I'll look forward to it.'

Rose snuggled up even closer and moments later her hand was on his groin, instantly arousing Andrew again.

He marvelled at the change in her.

'Kiss me,' she whispered.

He did a lot more than that.

Andrew was day-dreaming, which was quite unlike him at work, when there was a tap on his office door. He roused himself. 'Come in!'

It was Mr Kelly, the book-keeper. 'Am I disturbing you, sir?'

'No, not at all, Mr Kelly. What can I do for you?' He noted that Kelly wasn't carrying any files, papers or the like.

Mr Kelly was only a few years older than Andrew but, with his white hair and thick bushy eyebrows, might have belonged to the next generation up. He was a small wiry man who always moved quickly and with apparent determination.

Andrew, feeling he couldn't do it all by himself any more, had advertised a few years previously for a book-keeper and Kelly had been one of the applicants.

Kelly was a local who'd moved to Edinburgh in his late teens where he'd taken up employment with an insurance company. A confirmed bachelor, he'd sent in the application because he wanted to return home to live with his ailing widowed mother. Within a short time of taking up his new post Kelly had proved himself indispensable and had certainly lightened Andrew's workload. Andrew thought the world of him.

Kelly cleared his throat. 'I've just heard the news, sir, about Mrs Drummond, and I wanted to offer my congratulations.'

'Why, thank you, Mr Kelly.'

'No doubt you're delighted, sir.'

'Indeed I am. As is my wife.'

For a brief moment Kelly thought of the children he'd never had and never would. If there was a regret in his life, that was it. It would be a fine thing to have children of your own, especially a son and heir like Andrew. But that was not to be. Truth was, he'd never felt comfortable in female company. Not in that respect anyway. He'd never have admitted it to a soul but they scared him somewhat. The idea of having to be physical with one would have sent him running a mile.

Andrew glanced at his watch. 'I'll tell you what, Mr Kelly. Shall we have a dram on it?'

Kelly was shocked, though he did his best to try and hide it. 'Aye, if you wish, sir,' he replied reluctantly, heartily disapproving of drinking while working. And certainly before noon as it now was. But Andrew was the boss.

A few minutes later both men were holding fully charged glasses, Kelly wondering if he should take it upon himself to propose the toast or leave that to Andrew.

Andrew did the honours. 'To the new baby, eh?'

'The new baby, sir.'

Kelly grimaced as he swallowed his dram, not being

much of a drinker at the best of times. The spirit made his eyes water.

'And will you convey my best wishes to Mrs Drummond, sir. I'd be obliged if you did.'

'I shall indeed, Mr Kelly. You can rest assured.'

Kelly placed his empty glass on Andrew's desk. There had been some matters he'd wished to discuss with Andrew but now decided to leave them till later.

'Is that all, Mr Kelly?'

'Yes, sir. Thank you, sir.'

'Then how about another . . .'

'No, no, sir. I must be getting on.' And with that Kelly hastily left the office.

Andrew chuckled quietly when Kelly was gone. A funny old stick, but his heart was in the right place and he certainly knew his job.

Chapter 4

N ancy shook her head. 'It's getting worse, Bill. You've three whoppers now and signs of another on its way.' The cavity belonging to the original boil also remained unhealed. This despite the ointment, borrowed from Annie, that she'd rigorously applied.

Bill swore.

'I honestly don't know what to do. I think you're going to have to go to the doctor.'

Bill straightened up with a jerk. 'That'll be the day. I'm not going to any doctor. I don't trust them. Quacks one and all.'

'There's nothing else for it that I can see.'

He turned and glared at her. 'No doctor, understand!'

'All right, it's your funeral.'

He gingerly felt the boils and groaned. They were like red hot pokers stuck into his bum. He was tired, even more than usual, not having slept properly for nights.

'Shall I put on some more ointment?' she queried.

'Aye, go ahead.'

'Though it doesn't seem to be doing any good.'

'Put it on anyway.'

'Then bend over again.'

This was getting past a joke, she thought as he presented his backside to her for a second time. At which point one of the boils burst sending a dribble of thick, yellow pus running downwards.

Nancy winced at the sight, thinking how horrible it looked. Very nasty indeed. 'Perhaps you should take some time off work?' she suggested.

'Don't be soft, woman. I can't do that. No work no pay, and that means you as well, for if I don't get paid then neither do you.'

She'd been well aware of that. 'It was only an idea.'

'And a stupid one at that.'

'There's no need to be abusive, Bill. I'm only trying to help.'

He stared into the roaring fire, biting his lip as she began mopping up the pus. He was damned if he'd go to any doctor. Not only did he not trust them, they were expensive to boot.

The barman at The Sheugh glanced at Bill in surprise. 'What are you doing here, Bill? It's not your night.'

'There aren't any rules that I always have to come in on the same night I take it?' he snapped in reply.

'Of course there aren't.'

'Then give us a dram and a half pint.'

Bill stared moodily about him as the barman got on with his order. It wasn't his night but he'd desperately wanted a drink to take his mind off these effing boils that were driving him mad.

He wasn't pulling his weight at work, he knew that only too well. Not that he'd said anything to any of the others, none of their bloody business that he had boils on his arse.

And where was it going to end? One had led to two and that to three with another on its way. Was he going to have a whole backside full before he was finished? The thought of that brought a cold sweat to his brow.

'There you are, Bill,' the barman declared, placing his drinks before him.

Bill grunted, fished out the correct money and paid for them. There was enough in his pocket for a few drams, thank God. Anything to ease the pain and discomfort.

As the pub was nearly empty the barman considered lingering to chat, then decided against it and moved away, guessing Bill wanted to be left alone.

Bill picked up his dram and threw it down his throat, giving a small cough afterwards. He'd just had to get out of the cottage. He didn't know what it was about Nancy lately but she sure as hell was getting on his wick. Everything she did seemed to irritate him.

Why hadn't she been able to cure these boils! She was a woman, after all. Women could do these things. Patsy certainly would have been able to. Patsy would have had them cleared up quick as a wink.

Go to the doctor indeed, he sneered to himself. No bloody fear. He'd much rather swallow his money than give it to those charlatans.

He thought of John Bald whom he'd grafted alongside a few years back. A grand bloke had been John till he'd fallen ill and gone to the doctor with pains in his chest. Well, that had been the end of John. Six months later he was dead and planted. So much for going to the doctor.

The bastard had been quick enough to take John's cash all right. Oh aye, he had that. And a fat lot of good it had done John. No good at all.

Bill crooked a finger at the barman and indicated he wanted another dram.

He again thought of Nancy, certain she was laughing at him behind his back. Bitch. How dare she laugh at him, he couldn't help having boils. They were the last thing he wanted. And she found them funny.

He placed more money on the bar when the dram arrived, not speaking to the barman or the barman to him.

Irritating, that's what she'd become. Annoying in the extreme. The second dram swiftly disappeared followed by a gulp of beer.

A slight numbness was taking hold of him which eased his pain. A few more drams and he wouldn't be feeling much at all. Perhaps he might get a decent night's sleep later on.

And then the bandage that Nancy had secured round him somehow slipped, to fall off his buttocks altogether.

Fuck, he swore inwardly. She couldn't even put a bandage on properly. Now he'd have to go to the bog and do something about it.

He was raging inside as he headed for the toilet.

Nancy sat in the dark, wrapped in a warm shawl. She'd let the fire almost die out. She was waiting for Bill to come home; he was a lot later than she'd anticipated.

She enjoyed sitting in the dark letting her mind roam free. Sometimes she thought about things, other times nothing at all. She found great solace in this, particularly the latter.

She'd seen the master watching her again that day, his expression inscrutable, those hard eyes of his fastened on to her. She'd found it scary.

She wondered if he'd call again, dreading that he might, shuddering at the memory of him pawing at her, driving himself into her flesh. It had been sheer humiliation and a frightening violation.

She started when there was a rattle at the door which then swung open.

'Bill?'

He swore, and lurched towards her, knocking over a chair in the process. 'Where are you?' he slurred.

'Here.' She rose and went to meet him.

Bill reached out and grabbed the front of her smock. 'Why are we in darkness?'

'I like it that way sometimes. You know that.' Christ, he was pissed, she thought, the reek of alcohol wafting over her as he swayed on the spot.

'The bandage fell off in the pub. A proper tangle I was in,' he snarled.

'I'm sorry.'

'And so you should be. Can't you do anything right? Can't you even put on a fucking bandage so that it stays up properly?'

'I did my best.'

'Well, that's not good enough. You hear. Not good enough.'

He threw her from him. 'You stay here the night. I don't want you in my bed. It'll be more comfortable without you.'

He staggered from the room, stumbling several times as he went.

Nancy stared after him for a few seconds, then returned

to her chair and sank into it. Couldn't do anything right? Was that really true or just the drink talking?

She'd often felt alone in her short life but never more so than at that moment. Alone, and worthless.

Nancy dropped her head into her hands and sobbed in despair, hot salty tears coursing down her cheeks.

'Despite his moans and groans I think he's settling into the job,' Hettie said to Jack. 'Do you agree?'

'It would seem so.'

Hettie was happy to have that confirmation, glancing up at the ceiling beyond which Tommy's bedroom lay. As was usual with him since starting at the distillery he'd gone to bed relatively early.

Was it her imagination or was there a change in him? He seemed more grown up somehow, more mature. She was certain there was an air of gravitas about him that hadn't been there before.

Hettie sighed with contentment. Children, they were just one long worry from the day they were born. Nor did it end when they left home and got married, she'd been told. Even then you kept on worrying yourself sick about them.

Not that she'd have changed anything. It must be appalling to be childless, she reflected. Particularly for a woman whose whole being craved to reproduce.

Men had that urge as well, she thought, but not in the same way as women. Their urge was for sex, to plant their seed, whilst a woman's was to give birth. The completion of the cycle which she'd seen so many times on the farm, from the earth and ever-changing seasons, to the animals in the field.

Jack suddenly smiled, a beam that lit up his face. He began to chuckle.

'Jack?'

'Huh?'

'What's wrong with you?'

He was still smiling broadly. 'Nothing. Nothing at all.' He'd just come up with the perfect ending for his new book but wasn't about to tell Hettie that.

'Are you sure?'

'Absolutely positive.'

He chuckled again. It was a cracker all right. An absolute cracker.

Tommy, shoulders hunched against the cold and hands deep in his coat pockets, trudged on his way home for lunch. He hoped Hettie had something warm and filling to serve up, he was starving.

He halted when he heard a drone in the distance and, shading his eyes, glanced up at the sky.

What a beautiful sight, he thought, the plane's sleek lines gripping his imagination.

And then the plane went zooming overhead affording him a full view of its underside. One of those new fighter planes he'd read about, he decided. Had to be.

His heart was in his throat as he watched it recede into the distance, thinking what it would be like to fly one of those. Even more exciting than a racing car for you were operating in three dimensions as opposed to only two.

For the space of a few moments the Spitfire was silhouetted against the weak, watery winter sun. A shining bullet of pure power. Then it was lost in cloud.

Tommy sighed. What he wouldn't have given to be the chap in its cockpit, a lord of the air as all fighter pilots were.

For the rest of the way home he envisaged himself at

the plane's controls, putting it through its paces. Banking left, right, diving, pulling out of the dive at the last possible moment. A dashing daredevil to be regarded with awe wherever he went.

For the rest of that day the fantasy kept popping back into his mind.

'Glasgow!' Rose repeated in delight.

'I have to go down on business and thought you might like to come with me. You could do some Christmas shopping while I'm tied up, then we could have the evening together and stay overnight.'

Rose's mind was already racing, the shops she'd go to, what she might buy. 'It sounds wonderful.'

'I thought you'd be pleased.' He suddenly frowned. 'I need the Rolls looked at anyway. I can't quite put my finger on the problem but there's been something wrong with it of late. Probably only a bit of fine tuning but while in Glasgow I'll take the opportunity of putting it into the dealer's for a check over.'

The Rolls had originally belonged to Andrew's father Murdo, in fact had been his pride and joy, and had come to him on Murdo's death. The old lady was getting on in years now and several times he'd thought about replacing her with a newer, more updated model. Thoughts he'd always eventually dismissed, coming to the conclusion on each occasion that there was no reason why the car shouldn't last him out. A Rolls was special after all, built not only for the luxury and perfection it provided, but to last.

'The day after tomorrow, you say?' Rose queried.

'That's right.'

'You might have given me more notice.'

He laughed. 'I might have done if the idea had not only come to me this morning.' He paused, then added, 'Besides, the break will do you good. You've been cooped up here for ages.'

'I shall shop for baby clothes,' Rose announced enthusiastically. 'Apart from Drew's christening gown we haven't anything left of his. Anyway, this time round I'll want pinks not blues.'

Andrew sighed. There she went again, determined it was going to be a little girl. 'Perhaps neutral colours to start with?' he suggested. 'Until we know what's what.'

Rose fixed him with a withering stare. 'Oh ye of little faith, Andrew. I've told you to trust my instincts on this.'

'Even so . . .'

'Not another word,' she interrupted. 'You'll only spoil my fun if you go on and on.'

'I'm just thinking of you, Rose,' he said lamely.

'I appreciate that. You don't want me to be disappointed, and I won't be. You could put money on it.'

Andrew recalled a period in his life when he'd been addicted to gambling. An embarrassing affair that had ended up with Murdo having to pay off his debts. He cringed inside at the memory.

'It'll be an early start,' he declared. 'You'll have to be up and ready. I shan't be hanging around as I have appointments to keep.'

'I'll be ready,' she assured him.

Crossing to Andrew, eyes sparkling, she pecked him on the cheek. 'You're a darling man, Andrew Drummond, and I love you very much.'

'As I love you.'

The smile she gave him contained the promise that she'd be showing her gratitude, and love, later on that night.

Drew stood in the window watching the Rolls drive off to Glasgow, angry and jealous that his parents had not taken him with them. Despite his pleadings the answer had been an emphatic no.

He thought of the forthcoming child his mother kept burbling on about non-stop. It was 'Mary this', and 'Mary that', and 'when Mary comes I'm going to' . . .

He loathed this Mary before she was even born. Loathed and detested her.

'Are you all right, Master Drew?'

He turned from the window to find Christine, one of the maids, staring at him in concern.

'Why shouldn't I be?'

His tone was rude, she thought. There were times when Master Drew needed his arse skelped, which he certainly would have had if he'd been hers.

'You just looked a bit upset, that's all.'

'Haven't you got something to do?' he answered coldly.

Skelped and skelped again, Christine told herself. The little bugger was spoilt rotten. 'Plenty,' she replied equally coldly and swept away, leaving him to it.

Drew was instantly contrite, knowing he shouldn't have spoken to Christine that way. But he hadn't been able to help it. Besides, she was only staff after all, no one of real importance.

At least he'd be going to The Haven for Hogmanay, there was that to look forward to. He and James would have lots of fun together. As he would with Grandpa Willie.

That helped dissipate his anger somewhat. Hogmanay at The Haven would be great.

'How about this, sir?'

The necklace was eighteen strands of eighteen-carat gold roped together by a length of fine gold wire. Andrew liked it immediately, but would Rose?

'It's very nice,' he murmured.

'And tasteful, sir. Definitely that.'

Andrew glanced at the assistant, then back again at the necklace, trying to imagine it round Rose's neck. During their stay in Glasgow he too was searching for a Christmas present, making himself find the time to do so.

'How much?' All items in the shop, Glasgow's most exclusive and prestigious jeweller's, were unpriced.

The assistant told him.

Expensive, Andrew thought. But he'd wanted the best and you had to pay for that. Besides, it was to be more than just a Christmas present. It was also a celebration of Rose's pregnancy. In other words, a very special gift to mark both occasions.

The assistant moved away to return with another necklace. 'There's this one, sir.'

Andrew shook his head. That one didn't appeal at all.

'We have others.'

'No, no,' Andrew interrupted, making up his mind. He tapped the double-stranded piece. 'This will do admirably.'

'A wise choice if I may say so, sir. Very wise indeed.'

Andrew reached for his cheque book. There was something else he intended buying Rose before returning to the hotel.

The thought of it made him smile.

* * *

'For me?'

'For you, my angel.'

Rose stared quizzically at the fancifully wrapped box, wondering what it contained. The box was about a foot long and several inches wide.

'Well, aren't you going to open it?'

She laughed. 'Don't hurry me, Andrew. Let me enjoy speculating about what's inside.'

He watched her closely as she attacked bows and ribbons.

'Oh, Andrew,' she breathed when the lid was off and the tissue paper unfolded. 'It's beautiful.'

Rose laid the box on the bed and pulled out a pale pink négligé edged with matching hand-made lace. A nightdress of the same colour, also edged in lace, was revealed underneath.

She held the négligé up against herself, then ran a hand over the smoothness of the fabric.

'It becomes you.' Andrew smiled.

Pure silk, Rose thought. Trust Andrew.

'Pleased?'

'Of course.'

He indicated the nightdress. 'And there's that to go with it. I was rather hoping you'd wear them both tonight.'

She smiled wickedly. 'I can imagine what you have in mind, you old seducer.'

'Anything wrong with that?'

'Not in the least.'

Rose placed the négligé beside the box and whisked out the nightdress, which shimmered in the overhead light. 'Why don't you try them on?' he teased.

'Not yet, thank you very much. We'll never get any dinner if I do.'

'I can always have it sent up. That and champagne.'

The wicked smile returned. 'You are impatient.'

He went to her and caught her into his arms, drinking in the sweet smell of her. 'You're right. We should wait. Tonight will come round soon enough. And in the meantime I want to wine and dine you. My favourite girl.'

She cocked an eyebrow. 'Does that imply there are others?'

'Don't be silly. I've never looked at another woman since marrying you, and you know it.'

'Do I?' Now it was her turn to tease.

'It's the truth. You're all I want and ever will. Where women are concerned that is.'

'Is that a fact?'

'It's a fact.'

It could be so good between them at times, she thought. So very good. 'There's only one drawback about the nightdress,' she said softly.

He frowned. 'Which is?'

'I don't have to put it on to know it'll be tight fitting. Give me another month or two and I won't be able to get into it.'

He hadn't considered that, nor had thought to mention to the saleswoman that his wife was pregnant. 'I can always change it. Though not tonight, the shop will be closed by now.'

'I don't want you to change it. I was only telling you, that's all.'

'There are still those couple of months,' he murmured, and blew gently in her ear.

'Indeed there are. And *after* Mary arrives.'

He wanted her there and then, to strip her naked and . . . He broke their embrace and cleared his throat.

'What's wrong?'

'I'm having evil thoughts.'

She laughed, gathered up her négligé and nightdress and draped them over her pillows.

'Rogano's,' he breathed huskily, his imagination running riot.

'Can we still have champagne with our fish?'

'You can have whatever you want, Rose. A bucket of the stuff if you wish. Tubsful of the stuff if it'll make you happy.'

He'd temporarily forgotten she wasn't supposed to be drinking, she thought gleefully, testament to his 'evil thoughts', as he'd put it. 'I don't need champagne for that. Simply being with you is enough.'

A lump came into his throat as he gazed deep into her eyes.

'The table's booked for eight thirty. We'd better get a move on,' he said eventually.

Ever since seeing the Spitfire Tommy had been reading up on the air aces of the Great War. What splendid chaps they'd been, heroic in the extreme. Flying their Spads, Sopwith Camels and SE15s.

He closed his eyes, picturing himself high aloft in one of those fabled machines, a white streamer attached to the back of his helmet crackling behind him as he shot down yet another Hun.

'Stop idling, boy! You're being paid to work not daydream,' Mr Kelly snapped, having stopped in front of Tommy's desk.

Tommy's eyes flicked open. 'Sorry, sir,' he stammered.

'And so you should be.'

Kelly stared sternly at Tommy who'd come to help him in accounts. The lad was a liability in his opinion, couldn't add for toffee, forever making mistakes, having to go over columns of figures again and again and still getting them wrong more likely than not.

'Then get on with it. And remember I'll be keeping an eye on you at all times.'

'Yes, sir.'

Tommy busied himself once more with the ledger book open before him. How boring this was, how excruciatingly boring. One long yawn.

Tommy stared at the ledger's pages, but it was the skies over France and Germany he was seeing.

'Is there something in the dictation you can't make out?'

Hettie glanced across at Jack, having stopped typing for the past few minutes while transcribing her notes. 'No, I was just thinking.'

'Now there's a dangerous occupation,' he joked. 'About my book?'

Hettie sighed. 'No, Rose. Envying her really.'

Jack could hear a wistfulness in her voice. 'In what way?'

Hettie decided to take a break and got up from her chair. 'Would you like a cup of coffee?'

'Not for me.'

'I would. I won't be long.'

Jack waited patiently till she returned and sat opposite. 'It's unlike you to be envious, Hettie,' he said softly.

'I suppose it is. But in this case I am.'

'Is it the baby?'

That startled her. 'How did you guess?'

'A couple of things you've said recently.'

Silence fell between them while Hettie sipped her coffee, then nibbled the biscuit she'd brought in to go with it. 'The book is coming along well,' she declared.

'And I'm still not telling you the ending.'

'I've given up all hope of that.'

'Good, let it surprise you.' He paused, then said, 'Shall we go for a stroll after you've finished?'

'If you wish.'

'I could use some fresh air blowing round my cheeks.'

Me too, she thought. She and Jack often went for a walk which she always enjoyed. She'd describe anything that might be different and there were always people to stop and pass the time of day with.

'The baby,' Jack said, bringing the subject back to that.

Hettie gazed into her cup. 'It would be nice to have another child. I think Tommy missed out on not having a brother or sister.'

'I agree,' Jack stated. 'But as they say, man proposes, God disposes. It apparently wasn't his will for us to have another.'

'Or Rose, until she suddenly fell pregnant again. So, in our case who's to say. It might happen yet.'

'It might.'

'And wouldn't that be wonderful, Jack! I'd be so thrilled.'

'Who knows,' he teased. 'Maybe these things are catching.'

'Maybe,' she grinned.

That cheered Hettie up and her gloominess and self-introspection vanished.

'Why don't we go out for that walk now and you can finish your typing when we get back?' he suggested.

'Would you mind?'

'Not in the least.'

Jack decided he was going to buy Hettie a puppy for Christmas. It would need lots of attention and could give her something to fuss over. It would hopefully stop her being so broody.

Chapter 5

'Where's Mum?'

Andrew laid his whisky aside to gaze at his son. He'd been lost in thought, remembering the days when he'd been young. Those and times in Ireland as a Second Lieutenant. Other memories too, some of which he wasn't proud of.

'Gone to Aunt Charlotte's,' Andrew replied. 'She shouldn't be too long I wouldn't think. What do you want her for?'

Drew shrugged. 'Nothing much.'

'Can I be of any help?'

Drew shook his head.

How well did he know his son? Andrew wondered. Probably as little as Murdo had known him at that age. And older come to that. Murdo had seemed forever tied up at the distillery just as he supposed he was.

He gestured to the chair Rose usually sat on. 'Come and join me.'

Drew viewed Andrew with suspicion, this being rather out of the ordinary. 'Why?'

'Just for a natter, that's all. No other reason.'

He had nothing better to do anyway, Drew decided, heading for the chair. Truth was he was bored rigid and impatient for their departure to The Haven. With James about there was always plenty to do there.

'A penny for them?' Andrew probed.

Drew didn't really enjoy being alone with his father whom he found stern and forbidding at times.

Drew shrugged.

Andrew reached for his drink and had a sip. 'We don't get enough time together, you and I.'

And even less when the rotten baby arrived, Drew thought bitterly. He was getting heartily sick of his mother forever going on about it.

'Then what shall we talk about?'

Drew was beginning to wish he hadn't accepted the invitation to sit down. 'Anything you like,' he mumbled.

'What about when you grow up and one day take over the distillery?'

Drew blinked. 'You mean when you're dead?'

That made Andrew smile. 'Before then I hope.'

'Maybe I don't want to run the distillery. Maybe I'll want to do something else.'

Andrew stared at his son in astonishment. That possibility had never crossed his mind. 'But it's yours, your inheritance,' he stated slowly.

'So?'

'So it's your duty to take over where I leave off. If nothing else, think of the people who rely on you for employment. What about them?'

'Whoever bought the distillery would keep them on, I suppose.'

Andrew's expression became grim. 'Don't you understand? It's Drummond single malt whisky, it should be owned and run by a Drummond, not someone else. An outsider.'

'Maybe I'll have a baby brother and he can run it,' Drew said slyly. 'Just as you took over when my uncle Peter was killed.'

'Don't ever mention a baby boy in front of your mother,' Andrew swiftly rebuked him. 'You know she has her heart set on having a girl.'

'But she might not.'

Heaven forbid, Andrew thought. Heaven forbid. He saw off what remained in his glass and, rising, crossed to the decanter. That possibility was something he'd been trying desperately hard not to think about.

Drew was enjoying his father's discomfiture, watching Andrew keenly through slightly slitted eyes 'Mum doesn't know it's going to be a girl after all. She's only guessing.'

Andrew had a quick gulp from his glass, then topped it up again. 'We'll simply have to wait and see what happens,' he said gruffly.

Drew secretly hoped it would be a boy. It would be a sort of revenge. Then he had an alarming thought. 'There won't be any others after this one?'

Andrew returned to his chair. 'It's feasible I suppose. Why not.'

'But . . . but . . .' Drew stopped spluttering and gazed at his father in horror. 'You're so old. So ancient. Why, you're almost as old as Grandpa Willie.'

That hurt, Andrew reflected. It truly did. He was sensitive enough about the twenty-year age difference between himself and Rose without that kind of statement being made.

'Ancient, am I?' he repeated, forcing himself to chuckle.

'You've even got white hair.'

Andrew self-consciously touched a patch above his left ear which had lost its natural auburn colour and was now a distinct white. 'Only in parts,' he attempted to joke.

'It's still white.'

There was a long silence between them, then Andrew said slowly, 'You resent this child, don't you, Drew?'

Drew didn't reply.

'Don't you?' That was said softly, but with an edge to it.

'Yes,' Drew eventually whispered.

'But why? Won't it be nice having a brother or sister?'

And then the dam burst, the pent-up resentment Andrew had so correctly recognised. Drew blinked back tears. 'I just can't believe you and Mum . . . at your age. It's . . . unbelievable . . . horrid . . .' He broke off, trembling all over.

An embarrassed Andrew did his best not to show his emotions. 'It's perfectly natural, Drew, when people love one another as we do. That's what happens between them.'

Drew didn't want to hear any more of this or discuss the matter further. 'I think you're both disgusting!' he shouted and, leaping from his chair, ran out of the room.

'Drew! Come back here!'

When his son didn't Andrew contemplated going after him, then decided it was probably best not to.

'Oh dear,' he sighed. They were going to have problems with Drew. He might come to terms with the inevitable, but Andrew had his doubts.

Should he tell Rose about this conversation? She'd be

dreadfully upset and that was the last thing he wanted in her present condition.

He'd leave it a while and talk to the lad again. Yes, that was what he'd do. A month maybe, perhaps more. After all, it was early days yet. It was only a short time since Drew had been told of Rose's pregnancy.

'Children,' he breathed. What a handful they could be.

He knew it must be his imagination, but he was certain he could hear Murdo laughing in his grave.

'Enjoying yourself, Mr Kelly?' It was the distillery's Christmas 'do' and every single member of staff was there. A great deal of food had been laid on plus crates of Drummond whisky. And should the latter run out there was always plenty more where that came from.

'Oh aye, very much so,' Kelly lied in reply. He didn't enjoy this sort of occasion one little bit.

Andrew gazed about him, thinking it was going well. But then it always did. He spotted Rose chatting to Bob Mowbray, one of the maltsters. Bob was shortly due for retiral and would be sorely missed.

Over in a corner Tommy was starting on his fourth dram. He didn't realise it but there was a rather silly grin on his face, the effect of the other three.

This was a bit of all right, he was thinking. Free booze and all you could eat. It certainly beat that ledger book he'd been struggling with earlier.

'This is rare, isn't it,' Bell Mathieson, from bottling, said to her pal Irene.

Irene patted her stomach. 'I'm full as a pig, so I am. I can't remember the last time I guzzled so much.'

'And it's good stuff too. Not plain like we get at home.'

'Aye, it is that,' Irene agreed.

Bell nudged Irene with her elbow. 'There's Tommy Riach. Fancy going over?'

'What for?'

'To talk to him, you eejit.'

Irene considered that. 'I don't think so. He's posh, Bell, management and all that. No' one of the workers like us.'

'That doesn't make any difference on a night like this. Even Mr Drummond and his wife speak to everyone. Real friendly like.'

Irene studied her friend curiously. 'Have you got a notion, Bell Mathieson?'

'What do you mean a notion?' She knew exactly what Irene was getting at.

'For Tommy Riach.'

'Och, away and bile yer heid. He's far too young. I don't go in for cradle snatching.' Bell was the grand old age of eighteen.

'You seem keen though.'

'I'm nothing of the sort,' Bell retorted. 'I only suggested chaffing with him. Look, he's all alone, standing by his ownsome.'

Irene studied Tommy. 'He is quite handsome, I give you that. But no' for us, Bell. When he gets a girl it'll be some high falutin lassie. Don't forget who his da is. A famous writer and all. Not to mention stinking rich from all accounts.'

'He is attractive though,' Bell mused.

'And they say he's got a big one.'

Bell laughed. 'Don't be daft. That was only a joke yon day in the department to embarrass him.'

'Maybe so. But there are those who swear it's true.'

'Never!'

'I'm telling you.'

'And how would they know?'

Irene shrugged. 'Search me. Perhaps one of them found out for herself and passed on the word.'

Both females were virgins and would have hotly denied being anything else. Yet, as was common amongst their kind, they would pretend otherwise when it suited them A wink here, a glance there, a knowing look when certain types of remarks were passed. They saw it as good fun and all part of being grown up.

'Here, my glass is empty,' Bell observed.

'Have you finished that already!'

Bell giggled. 'It doesn't half go down quickly when they're giving it away.'

Irene nodded her agreement. 'May as well make the most of the situation then, eh?'

'You're dead right there.'

They looked over at a long trestle table festooned with bottles. It was strictly help yourself.

'Shall we?' Bell proposed.

'I'm with you.'

In unison, they moved towards the table.

'Are you getting tired?' Andrew queried anxiously as Rose joined him having left Bob Mowbray.

'Not in the least.'

'I don't want you overdoing things. Perhaps you should have a sit down for a while.'

Rose laughed. 'Stop fussing like an old mother hen, Andrew. I'll sit down if I need to.'

'Just make sure you do,' he cautioned.

She touched him lightly on the hand. 'You really are sweet.'

'I do my best,' he smiled.

'I think I should mingle again. What do you say?'

'We'll do so together.'

It was getting terribly hot in there, Rose reflected, and she was beginning to perspire a little. Another ten or fifteen minutes and she'd retire to cool off and check her make-up.

'Why so cheery?'

A startled Tommy turned to find he was being addressed by Bell Mathieson with Irene beside her.

'You were scowling as if you had a bad smell under your nose,' Irene explained.

Tommy laughed softly. 'Was it as obvious as that?'

Bell nodded.

'I was thinking . . .' He hesitated. 'Perhaps I shouldn't say.'

'Go on,' Irene urged.

Still he swithered, then the alcohol got the better of him. 'I was thinking about Mr Kelly. He's been getting at me all afternoon. The man makes my life a misery.'

'Oh?' That was Bell.

'He hates me for some reason. I'm sure of it.'

'I find that hard to believe,' Irene commented.

'It's non-stop niggle as far as he's concerned. I just can't seem to do anything right.'

'Surely you're exaggerating.' Bell frowned.

'Not in the least. I got one lousy column of figures wrong this afternoon and that was that. He wouldn't get off my back until it was time to go.'

Tommy glared across the room at Kelly who was deep in conversation with Davey Grant, an elderly engineer. 'Bloody swine,' he muttered.

'It's that bad, eh?' Irene smiled, trying to lift Tommy's spirits.

'Worse. You've no idea. I can't wait to get out of his

clutches and into another department. Thank God I'm not here as a trainee book-keeper. Life under him would be ongoing hell.'

Bell nodded her sympathy. They were lucky with Balfour their gaffer. He might be a hard taskmaster but he was very fair. 'I've heard you're eventually going to be a traveller for us. Is that right?'

'That's right.'

Bell's eyes lit up. 'That's a smashing job so it is. And well paid too I should think.'

'Very.' Tommy preened. 'And I'll have a car. Well, I'll have to being on the road.'

'Jammy you.' Irene beamed.

Kelly was now forgotten as Tommy set out to impress the girls. 'It's a very responsible position you know. And terribly important.'

'Oh aye,' Bell agreed, thinking there was something rather angelic about Tommy's appearance which she hadn't noticed before. It appealed.

'You must be awfully clever,' Irene declared, her eyes shining also.

'Not where columns of figures are concerned,' Tommy joked, and they all laughed.

'You're really nice,' Bell grinned.

Tommy went slightly red. 'Why thank you very much.' Then, not to be outdone where compliments were concerned, and thinking it only polite anyway, 'And so are the pair of you.'

'Och, we're just wee working girls,' muttered Irene. 'That's all.'

'You're still nice. And easy to talk to.'

'Do you normally have trouble talking to lassies then?' Tommy stared at Bell. 'Depends on the lassie.'

Bell nodded her understanding.

'Well I'm going to get myself another dram,' he declared. 'How about you two?'

Bell and Irene instantly swallowed the remainder of their drinks. 'That's very kind.'

He took their glasses from them. 'I'll only be a couple of minutes.'

'We'll be here,' Bell retorted.

'We're not going anywhere,' Irene added.

Bell thoughtfully watched Tommy's retreating back. Like an angel, she thought again.

'Pity there isn't any dancing,' Irene commented.

'Aye, true enough.' Bell wouldn't have minded getting up with Tommy Riach.

'I could really go a bit of the jigging.'

'Me too.'

Pity about his age, Bell reflected. And the difference in class between them.

'I think we'd better be getting you home,' Bell declared to Tommy some while later.

'But why? I'm enjoying myself. Aren't you?' he slurred in reply.

'You've had enough, Tommy. Any more and you might make a fool of yourself.'

Despite the fuzziness in his head Tommy could see the sense of that. He had had quite a lot. He tried to tot up how many, but couldn't. He quietly burped and the taste of whisky flooded his mouth.

'Have you got a coat?' Bell queried.

Tommy nodded.

'Then you get that while we get ours. We'll walk you back.'

'Will you?' He was delighted.

'You might fall down or get lost otherwise. We can't take the chance. It would be awful for someone going to be a traveller to disgrace himself.'

'Oh, the humiliation,' Tommy replied in a mock tone.

'It would be too. Especially if Mr Drummond got to hear of it, which he probably would.'

'It might even get you the sack,' Irene chipped in.

Tommy shook his head, and held up crossed fingers. 'My dad and he are like that. He'd never sack me. Not in a million years.'

'I wouldn't count on that,' Bell replied sternly. 'Now come on, let's be out of here. It's almost finished anyway.' She gazed about her. Many of the staff had already taken their leave, though Mr and Mrs Drummond were still present.

'Aye, all right,' Tommy consented. 'But just a last dram before we go.'

'No,' Bell stated firmly.

'Another won't hurt.'

Bell stared into glassy eyes. 'In your case it would. Now do as you're told and that's an end of it.'

'Bossy women,' Tommy sighed.

With Bell and Irene flanking him on either side they headed from the room.

'Christ!' Tommy exclaimed, and went tumbling on to the road.

'He is well and truly pissed. Even more than I thought,' Bell said to Irene.

Irene smiled. 'It won't do him any harm. At least he didn't make an exhibition of himself inside and that's the main thing.'

'Aye, you're right there.'

Neither girl was particularly perturbed by drunkenness, it being a common enough state of affairs. Neither was exactly sober herself.

'Upsadaisy,' Bell declared, grabbing Tommy by the arm and hauling him to his feet.

'I slipped on the frost,' he mumbled sheepishly.

Bell and Irene didn't bother arguing. 'Not far to go now,' Bell informed him, as they started off again. To stop Tommy weaving she hooked an arm through his.

Just before Tommy's house Irene hesitated. 'I'll let you take him up to the door,' she said to Bell, giving Bell a fly wink. She then hung back as Bell and Tommy completed the last few yards.

'Must be quiet. Don't want to wake the parents,' Tommy whispered.

'Now you go straight to bed, you hear?'

'I hear,' Tommy answered, the same silly grin that had been on his face earlier now back again.

There was a few seconds hiatus between them, then Bell kissed him full on the mouth.

Tommy was momentarily taken by surprise, more so when a probing tongue found his. Taking hold of Bell he pressed her hard against him.

Bell squirmed away when a hand started moving towards her breast. 'Goodnight, Tommy.'

'Goodnight, Bell.'

'Don't fall up the stairs now.'

'I won't promise.'

She pecked him swiftly on the cheek, after which she rejoined the waiting Irene.

Tommy crept inside.

*   *   *

Hettie, lying awake with Jack fast asleep alongside her, heard Tommy come in. She could tell from his erratic footsteps that he'd had a few.

Tommy's bedroom door clicked shut and silence again descended on the house.

He was growing up, Hettie thought, pleased yet worried at the same time. He was still her baby after all. Her wee son.

She rolled over and cuddled up against Jack. Now Tommy was back safe she too could go to sleep.

'Well?' Irene demanded as they continued on their way.

'Well what?'

'Is it a big one?'

Bell knew she was being teased. 'A real whopper. Absolutely enormous. I nearly fainted when I held it.'

Irene's jaw dropped open, such was the sincerity in Bell's voice. 'Did you really?'

'Oh aye, I took it out and gave it a waggle. Huge as a donkey's it was.'

'You're having me on.'

'Who me!' Bell replied, pretending innocence and not succeeding.

Irene laughed, knowing she'd been had. 'I actually believed you there for a moment.'

'We did kiss though.'

'I saw that. What was it like?'

'Just a kiss, that's all.'

'Nothing special?'

'Maybe. Maybe not,' Bell prevaricated.

'Anyway, you just remember he's no' for the likes of us so don't go setting your cap at him.'

Which was a great pity, Bell reflected. Despite the fact

he was younger than her that's exactly what she'd like to have done. She'd taken quite a shine to Tommy Riach.

It was Christmas Eve and Bill was sitting staring grimly into the fire. Every so often he grimaced slightly and shifted his position.

'Would you like a cup of tea?' Nancy queried.

Bill glared at her, then shook his head.

She decided not to bother either. 'Is it bad the night?'

'Of course it's fucking bad, you stupid bitch.'

Nancy winced. 'I only asked.'

'Then don't.'

The silence between them stretched on and on. Eventually Nancy rose and put some more coal on the fire. That would be it for the evening, from there on the fire could just die down.

It was the last thing Nancy wanted to say, but she felt she had to, mentally preparing herself for the abuse that was bound to follow. 'You're going to have to give in, Bill, and go to the doctor. You can't go on the way you are.'

The look he shot her was one of sheer malevolence. 'Don't mention doctor to me. You know how I feel about those bloodsuckers.'

'There's no alternative, Bill. I've done everything I can. What's worrying me is you could get a worse infection. What then?'

He didn't reply.

'Then it would become even more serious.'

Bill's lips set into a thin, determined line. 'I will not spend my hard-earned money on a doctor.'

Temper suddenly flared in her. 'Then go on suffering. And hell mend you!'

'Quiet, woman!' he snapped viciously.

Nancy came to her feet. 'I'm off to see Annie and Hector. I won't be too long.'

'What are you going there for?'

'Because I can't stand this atmosphere any longer, that's why. Now is there anything you want before I go?'

'No.'

'Right then.'

He listened to her take her shawl from the peg behind the door and whirl it round her shoulders. There was the snick of her hand on the latch.

'Nancy.'

She paused, and turned. 'Aye?'

'I'm sorry.' He almost choked on the apology but got it out nonetheless.

Nancy immediately softened. 'I'm on your side, Bill. I think you sometimes forget that.'

He swallowed hard. 'I know.'

'Then will you do something for me. Please?'

'What's that?'

'Reconsider the doctor. For your own sake.'

There was no answer.

'Bill?'

'The money . . .'

'To hell with the money,' she interrupted fiercely. 'You're in agony with those boils. If money's what it takes to get rid of them then spend the damn stuff. And just be thankful you've got it to spend.'

Bill took a deep breath. Nancy was right, he knew that. But what she was proposing went against the grain. Completely so.

'I'll think about it,' he mumbled.

Nancy knew then she'd won. 'You do that.'

There was a gust of icy cold air and she was gone.

* * *

'All aboard!' Andrew called out.

Drew opened the rear door of the Rolls and dived inside. At long last they were on their way to The Haven.

'Here, where are your manners? What about your mother?' Andrew admonished. 'Ladies first, don't forget.'

'He's anxious to be off, that's all,' Rose smiled.

'Even so.'

'Sorry, Mum,' Drew said from the interior of the car.

'And so you should be,' Andrew replied, though smiling now. Turning to Rose he said, 'I'll drive slowly and carefully, I don't want you to be bumped in any way.'

His concern really was touching, Rose thought. If she'd told him once she'd told him a dozen times she wasn't made of porcelain. 'Not too slowly or it'll take us all day to get there.'

She kissed him tenderly on the cheek, glanced round at Drummond House which they'd only be gone from for a few days, then was helped to her seat by Andrew.

A few minutes later the Rolls was purring on its way.

Chapter 6

'Andrew!'

Willie Seaton came bustling down the steps of The Haven to shake his son-in-law and old friend warmly by the hand. 'How wonderful to see you again.'

'And you, Willie.'

James Seaton, face alight with excitement, came running after his father. Drew, who'd shot out the opposite side of the Rolls, joined him.

'Rose, my darling,' Willie beamed, and hugged his daughter tight.

'Be careful, Dad. Don't forget my condition.'

Willie immediately released her. 'I do apologise, for the moment there I'd quite forgotten.' He eyed her from head to foot. 'And don't you look radiant with it.'

'I can't tell you how happy I am.'

'You don't have to, it's obvious.'

Andrew glanced sideways at James, eternally thankful that the boy didn't take after him. The secret of

James's true parentage remained safe between himself and Georgina.

'Let's get out of this cold,' Willie enthused, grasping Rose by the arm. 'I'll send someone out to get your luggage.'

'Be back later!' James shouted, as he and Drew dashed off.

'Children nowadays,' Willie said, shaking his head. 'Always so impatient.'

'I doubt they've changed all that much since we were that age,' Andrew commented drily as they mounted the steps towards the front door.

Georgina, who was waiting in the drawing room to greet them, wore a navy blue fancy print frock enhanced by a softly draped streamer tie collar of lustrous plain tone satin. Soft shirrings accented the moulded hip-line while the circular flare-cut skirt showed off the smart uneven hemline.

She hadn't changed much since the last time they'd met, Andrew noted. Still the attractive woman she'd always been. For some reason he found himself self-conscious of the greying at his temples.

Georgina took Rose by the hands and gazed at her in delight. 'We were so pleased to hear your news,' she declared. 'We'll discuss it all later when we're alone and can talk freely away from these men.'

Rose laughed. There had been a time when she'd disliked Georgina, resented her for taking her mother's place. But those feelings and emotions were now long gone. It was hardly Georgina's fault her mother had died.

'So, who's for a snifter? You two will be needing one after your journey,' Willie proposed.

'Not for me thank you,' Rose smiled. 'I'm keeping a

strict limit on my alcohol intake on account of Mary.'
The sojourn in Glasgow had proved a minor exception
to that rule.

'Mary?' Willie frowned.

'That's what I'm going to call the baby when she arrives.
After you know who of course.'

Georgina was also frowning. 'You seem awfully certain
it's going to be a girl.'

'I am,' Rose replied confidently. 'There's no doubt
about it being a lass. Isn't that so, Andrew?'

He shrugged. 'So you say.'

'I've never been more convinced of anything in my life,'
Rose added.

'I naturally approve of the name,' Willie mused. 'But I
think you shouldn't have your heart so set on the gender.'

'That's what I've been telling her,' Andrew commented.
'It's going to be a terribly big disappointment if it's a boy.'

'It won't be. Wait and see. And by the by, Father, do
you still have my old doll's house?'

'Doll's house?' Willie repeated. 'I really have no idea.
Georgina?'

'I've none either. If it is still around it's probably up in
one of the attics.'

'Then I shall look for it there,' Rose stated. 'I want it
for Mary.'

'You're not going wandering round any attics,' Willie
rebuked her. 'I'll send up one of the staff. If it's there it'll
be found.'

'And my dolls. I want those as well.'

'Dolls as well,' he agreed, and turned his attention to
Georgina. 'Now what can I get you, my love?'

'Something soft would be lovely. Tonic water if we
have it.'

Willie nodded his understanding. Georgina was most abstemious where alcohol and rich food were concerned which was why she'd retained the youthful figure he so adored.

'And you, Andrew?'

'Drummond please.'

'What do you have planned for this evening?' Rose inquired of Georgina, for they'd arrived on Hogmanay itself.

'A quiet night with just the family. We'll undoubtedly have a number of first-footers after the bells are rung, but until then it'll be only us. Willie thought lots of people and noise wouldn't be appropriate in the circumstances.'

That was a relief to Rose. The last thing she wanted was to be involved in a big get-together which would have been too tiring by far. As it was she'd retire fairly soon after the new year had been seen in.

'Sounds splendid to me,' Andrew declared.

'Good,' Willie nodded.

Rose couldn't help but glance at the spot where her brother Ian had been murdered by an intruder. What a ghastly memory that was. She still carried a sense of guilt about the way she'd mercilessly teased Ian when he'd been alive. Ian whose life, so full of promise, had been ended at such an early age.

She'd visit the grave before returning home, and that of her mother. She always did when at The Haven. And while with her mother she'd tell her of little Mary.

Willie gave Andrew his glass, the last to be handed round. 'A toast?' he queried.

Andrew's expression became troubled. 'Can I propose one?'

'Of course, old boy.'

Rose was expecting a toast to the new baby, wrongly so as it transpired. Andrew was thinking about current events in Europe.

'To the continuance of peace,' he said softly.

'Aye,' Willie murmured, his good humour abruptly vanishing. 'I'll certainly drink to that.

'Peace,' Willie echoed.

'I'm glad that's over,' Willie sighed, ushering Andrew into his study. It was nearly six a.m., the last of the first-footers having just departed.

He went straight to the decanter, poured two hefty measures, gave one to Andrew and slumped into a comfortable leather chair, indicating that Andrew do likewise.

'I always find Hogmanay a funny old time,' Willie mused, lighting a cigarette. 'Somehow neither one thing nor the other.'

'I know what you mean.'

'One moment you're happy as Larry, the next sad as all get out. At least that's how it affects me.'

'Same here. More or less.'

Willie regarded Andrew keenly. 'And what do you think 1939 holds?'

Andrew shrugged. 'All sorts I should imagine. Some good, some bad.'

'Will it be war?'

Andrew briefly closed his eyes, then slowly opened them again. Were those dreadful horrors to return? It made him go cold all over just thinking about it. 'It certainly seems to be heading that way. I wish I could say otherwise but I can't.'

'Please God you're wrong.'

'Oh aye, I couldn't agree more. Please God I am.'

Both men fell silent, remembering the previous conflict. They had been lucky to have spent it in Ireland which, though still dangerous, had been nothing compared to the Western Front and other theatres.

'At least . . .' He trailed off.

'What, Willie?'

He gave Andrew a weak, sickly smile. 'Our boys are too young to get caught up in any new hostilities. There's that to be thankful for.'

'Indeed.' The relief in Andrew's voice was evident.

'They're too young and we're too old. Past it, Andrew, you and I, well and truly.'

'Bloody Germans,' Andrew hissed through clenched teeth. 'Don't they ever learn? Weren't the millions who died on all sides enough for those butchers?'

'It was Versailles and the French. The conditions of the peace treaty were too harsh thanks to the Frogs. The Jerries have never forgiven either them or us for that. Particularly Herr Hitler, and he's the one who counts.'

'This country isn't ready for war, we all know that.'

'If it did happen all over again do you think . . .' Willie broke off and swallowed hard. 'We could lose this time round?'

The prospect of German domination was an appalling one. Those arrogant, heel-clicking, cold-hearted bastards strutting up and down every street in the land. Andrew's hand tightened on his glass till the knuckles shone white.

'We have to face the possibility.'

'Surely the Americans would come in again?'

'We could only hope and pray so. Without them, and even with the might of the Empire behind us, I would fear the worst.'

'Christ,' Willie swore.

Andrew saw off what remained of his drink. 'Can I?'

'Help yourself.'

'You?'

'Aye, I will.'

Andrew was dog tired, bed would be more than welcome when he got into it. He thought of Rose already well tucked up and fast asleep. Waiting for him to join her.

'It's been a long day,' Willie yawned.

They talked about the threat of war for a short while longer, then both men headed off to their respective rooms.

'Please, Dad?'

Andrew glanced at his wife. 'Well, Rose?'

'It won't hurt for him to stay on a few days longer. He's enjoying being with James so much and there's no company for him at home.'

'I'll personally put him on the train,' Willie assured Andrew. 'He won't come to any harm.'

'Please, Uncle Andrew?'

Andrew thought back to the conversation he and Willie had had late on Hogmanay, thankful again these boys were not older. 'All right,' he consented.

Drew whooped with glee and did a little jig on the spot while James laughed and clapped his hands.

'Well, that was a popular decision it seems,' Andrew commented to a smiling Georgina.

For a moment, no more than that, she was looking at him the way she once had when they were lovers. And then it was gone. 'Yes,' she agreed.

That had jolted Andrew, made him feel uncomfortable. He wasn't proud of the fact he'd cuckolded Willie, though to be fair he wasn't the one who'd made the running.

On the other hand if he'd been more strong-willed he wouldn't have got involved no matter how hard Georgina had tried to seduce him. But in those days women had been a weakness of his, a weakness he'd overcome since marriage.

'I mustn't forget the doll's house when we leave in the morning,' Rose said. That had indeed been discovered in an attic. One of the maids had spent several hours cleaning it up so that it was again fit to be played with.

'We won't forget it,' Andrew assured her. 'You have my word on that.'

On impulse, Rose crossed to him and kissed his cheek. 'Thank you.'

'Or the dolls,' he added.

'I have to go out on the estate for an hour or two. Do you want to come with me, Andrew?' Willie asked.

Andrew considered that. 'Yes, I would. I'll enjoy the exercise.'

'While they're away we can have tea and another natter,' Georgina smiled to Rose.

Rose ran a hand over her forehead. She was feeling tired and would really have preferred an afternoon nap. She also felt strangely drained which was quite unlike her. Perhaps she could do both, natter and nap, before the men returned.

Rose came groggily awake. 'Andrew?'

He sat on the edge of the bed beside her. 'You should start getting ready for dinner.'

'Is it that late?'

He stroked her hand. 'This is the third time I've been up to see how you were.'

'I must have been more tired than I realised,' she apologised.

'It's entirely natural, considering. You are expecting after all.'

'Little Mary,' she grinned.

'Little Mary,' he agreed, knowing that would please her.

'Georgina and I had a lovely chat,' she said. 'We've had quite a few since you and I arrived.'

'Anything in particular?'

'Oh, my pregnancy, after the baby arrives, local gossip. That sort of thing. Women's talk.'

Rose sat upright and sucked in a deep breath. 'I feel a lot better for that sleep.'

'Shall I run your bath?'

'Please.'

He stared her straight in the eyes. 'I do love you, Rose.'

She smiled. 'I know. And I love you. Very much.'

She grasped the hand that had been stroking hers and laid it on her bosom.

Andrew knew this wasn't an invitation to lovemaking but rather a gesture of affection, that she simply wanted to be touched by him.

They sat in blissful silence for a short spell, then he roused himself. 'I'd better attend to that bath, otherwise I'll be wanting to get in there with you.'

Rose gave a low laugh and swung her legs out of bed. A laugh that became a gasp when a slight wave of nausea swept over her.

'Rose?'

'It's nothing. I think I'm just hungry, that's all.'

'You're eating for two we mustn't forget.'

'That's something I'm trying not to do,' she chided in reply. 'Now on you go and see to the bath so that I can get on.'

Rose watched him fondly till he'd left the room, then reached for her dressing gown, the nausea having disappeared.

She started to hum, a jaunty traditional tune that she remembered from her youth.

'I think it's going to snow,' Andrew said, peering up at a leaden sky. 'It has that look about it.'

Rose snuggled even deeper into the fox fur coat she was wearing. 'Wouldn't it be wonderful to be marooned somewhere. Just the pair of us.'

He chuckled. 'Hardly.'

'I think it would.'

'Do you now?'

'Oh yes,' she replied brightly. 'Just you and I, snowbound in a little croft somewhere. With nothing to do but . . . entertain ourselves.' The latter was said meaningfully.

'You brazen hussy, Rose Drummond.'

'With a roaring fire to keep us warm.'

'I see,' he murmured, delighted by her mood.

'It would be so romantic, don't you think?'

'Oh, undoubtedly.'

'And I like it when you're romantic.'

'Aren't I always?' he teased.

'Most of the time. Especially when you buy me things.'

He laughed. 'Is that what this is all about. You want something?'

'Could be,' she demurred.

'Such as?'

'Oh, I don't know.'

He was thoroughly enjoying this. 'Yes you do. Now come on, out with it.'

Her eyes sparkled but she didn't reply.

'Rose?'

'Why don't you try and guess.'

'I've no idea what you're after, honestly.'

'But try and guess.'

He pretended to be serious. 'A gold watch. Diamond bracelet?'

Rose giggled. 'Wrong.'

'A new wardrobe then.'

'Nope.'

He tried to think. Now what could it possibly be. 'Can you give me a hint?'

'Hint schmint. No schmints.'

She was getting outrageous now, he thought. 'If I didn't know better I'd say you'd been at the bottle.'

'Who me!' That was expressed with a combination of mock outrage and innocence.

'Yes, you, my sweetest darling.'

'As if I would. And it not even noon yet.'

He glanced at his watch. 'It's not far off.'

Rose sighed with contentment. She was enjoying this journey which, for some reason she couldn't quite fathom, had a rather surreal air about it. The Rolls might have been a gilded coach, she a fairytale princess and Andrew a . . .

'Kiss me,' she commanded.

He gazed at her in astonishment. 'I beg your pardon?'

'Kiss me.'

He leant across and pecked her on the mouth. 'How's that?'

'Not good enough. I want a proper kiss.'

'But I'm driving.'

95

'So pull over and stop. We're hardly in the middle of dense traffic.'

Which was true enough. They were the only car on the road and hadn't passed another vehicle for the past twenty minutes or so. 'If you insist.'

'I most certainly do.'

'Right then.'

He turned into a natural layby and killed the engine. 'You asked for it,' he declared, reaching for her.

The kiss was long and passionate, yet tender at the same time. A kiss between man and wife still very much in love with one another.

'There,' he murmured when the kiss was over.

'You still haven't guessed what I want you to buy me.'

'I'm stumped, Rose. Haven't the foggiest. Is it going to cost me much?'

'An absolute fortune.'

'Then so be it. Now what is it?'

'Lunch.'

He blinked. 'Lunch?'

'That's all.'

'Are you hungry?'

'Not yet, but I'm getting that way. I will be soon.'

What had got into her, he wondered. Not that he was complaining, far from it. 'Then lunch you shall have. The most expensive and lavish to be had in these parts.'

The smile on her face suddenly froze into a hideous grimace.

'Rose?'

She grunted and clasped her middle.

'Rose, is this another game? Because if it is it isn't funny.'

'Sore,' she complained. 'Pain.'

Alarm flared in him. 'What sort of pain?'

Rose swallowed. 'I think . . . I think . . .' She swallowed again. 'Oh Andrew, I'm bleeding.'

He swore viciously. 'Are you sure?'

The look in her eyes told him she was. 'Must get you to a doctor,' he said, fumbling with the ignition key.

Rose whimpered.

He turned the key and nothing happened, not a flicker of anything from the engine. He desperately tried a second and then a third time with the same result.

Rose leant forward, still clutching her middle. This wasn't happening, she kept telling herself. It wasn't happening!

Andrew banged the steering wheel in frustration. Mustn't panic, he thought. That was the last thing to do. He forced himself to take a deep breath and then try the key again. The engine remained lifeless.

'I had the damn thing seen to while we were in Glasgow,' he said through gritted teeth. 'They assured me everything was fine, that the old lady was running smooth as a nut.'

Rose jerked. 'It's coming, Andrew!'

He stared at her, appalled. 'The baby?'

She managed to nod.

'Jesus Christ.'

There were now tears flowing from her eyes that had nothing to do with the pain she was experiencing. 'Mary,' she choked. 'My wee Mary.'

Andrew knew it to be useless but nonetheless tried the key again, praying the engine would miraculously start. It didn't.

He was frantic. What in the hell to do?

Then he saw her, a girl in the field opposite. She was

walking parallel to the road, heading in their direction. He immediately threw open his door and slid out.

'I won't be a moment,' he yelled to Rose, already sprinting towards the girl.

'Don't leave me, Andrew!'

'I'm not!' he yelled back over his shoulder.

Nancy Thompson stared in amazement at the stranger bearing down on her. She frowned, wondering what was going on. The man was clearly in distress.

'We need your help. We need your help!' Andrew cried.

He vaulted a low stone dyke to stand beside her. 'It's my wife, she's miscarrying,' he blurted out.

Nancy glanced at the Rolls, then back again at the distraught stranger. 'In the car?'

He nodded vigorously. 'Please do what you can.'

'Let's go,' she declared. They clambered over the dyke and hared across the road.

Nancy's mind was in turmoil at this rapid turn of events. She wrenched Rose's door open and peered inside.

Rose had slumped over both seats, her face contorted in agony, tears still flowing.

'Oh my angel,' Andrew groaned.

Nancy thought of her friend Annie McGillvary and the baby born dead in a field. At least she was now experienced in these matters.

'The master's house is about half a mile away,' she informed Andrew. 'It would be best if you drove there while I try and comfort the lady.'

'Engine won't start,' Andrew explained. 'I've tried it again and again.'

A spasm racked Rose's body.

Nancy knelt just inside the door and hurriedly undid

Rose's coat to reveal a blood-stained gaberdine suit. There was no doubt about what was happening.

'We'll get this skirt off,' Nancy said.

Andrew reached in and took Rose's hand while Nancy busied herself. 'I'm so sorry, Andrew. I'm so sorry,' Rose choked.

'It's not your fault.'

'Wee Mary. My wee bonny Mary.'

Andrew was horribly aware of the doll's house sitting on the rear seat with Rose's memorabilia alongside it. The sight of that ensemble sickened him.

Nancy pulled the skirt free, having slid it out from underneath Rose's bottom, and tossed it on to the road. It was ruined anyway.

'Where is this house? Which direction?' Andrew demanded of Nancy. 'Has the owner a telephone?'

'Straight ahead,' Nancy replied. 'You can't miss it. And no, there isn't a telephone.'

Andrew swore.

'I'll run there anyway. There must be a car . . .'

'Don't leave me, Andrew,' Rose pleaded, her hand tightening in Andrew's. 'I want you here if I should die.'

'You're not going to die,' Andrew swiftly replied, not knowing if that was true or not.

'I feel I am.'

'Well, you're not,' he delivered sternly.

Nancy had rucked up the half-slip Rose had on and was now removing the fashionable frilly knickers underneath.

'It hurts so much, Andrew,' Rose whispered.

'I know.'

Nancy used the already sodden knickers to wipe away some of the blood awash on Rose's thighs. The birth hadn't yet happened but was obviously imminent.

Andrew felt so helpless standing there. He should really go to try to fetch a doctor but his leaving would only cause Rose more anguish. He fully understood her wanting him there with her.

'Is it a constant pain or are they coming and going?' Nancy asked Rose.

'All the time.'

'I have whisky in the glove compartment. Is that any use?'

Nancy shook her head. 'Not unless you want some.'

'No.' He did really.

Nancy had noted the well-packed luggage rack. 'Do you have any towels in your cases?' she queried.

'I'm afraid not.'

'I'm so sorry, Andrew,' Rose repeated in a whisper.

'I said it's not your fault. These things happen and there's nothing we can do about them.'

Nancy mopped up fresh blood that had oozed out, this darker in colour than the rest.

'It's going to make a mess of your nice leather seats,' Nancy commented.

'Bugger the sodding seats, they're unimportant,' Andrew snapped back.

'I was only saying.'

Andrew bit his lip, then apologised. He was beside himself.

'I understand, sir. Don't worry. No offence taken.'

'It isn't fair,' Rose mumbled. 'It just isn't fair. What have I done to deserve this?'

'You've done nothing, darling. I promise you.'

Andrew realised that Rose had stopped crying while her eyes had taken on a slightly glazed look.

'Andrew . . . Andrew . . .' Rose threw back her head

and shrieked, causing the veins in her neck to stand right out.

'Dear God,' Andrew muttered, fighting back tears of his own.

Rose shrieked repeatedly, each cry a knife in Andrew's heart, until finally, and thankfully, it was all over.

To his dying day Andrew never told her that the foetus had been male. When asked he'd lied and said they couldn't make out what sex the baby was.

Chapter 7

'She's asleep now,' Sister Eason whispered.

Andrew stared dully at Rose who'd been given a strong sedative. What a nightmare this had all been. What an awful, terrible nightmare. He gently unclutched the hand holding his and laid it on the bed.

'How do you feel?'

He glanced at Sister Eason. 'Pardon?'

'I said, how do you feel?'

Andrew shook his head. 'As you'd expect I suppose.'

'Well you come away with me now and I'll give you a cup of tea.'

'I don't want to leave her.'

'She won't wake for hours, Mr Drummond. I assure you your wife won't know you've left her bedside.'

'But . . .' He trailed off. The sense of inadequacy he was feeling was now even more profound than it had been earlier.

'Come along, tea and a biscuit. That's an order now.'

He'd have the tea, but not the biscuit. He wouldn't have been able to hold that down.

'You're in a state of shock, Mr Drummond,' Sister said once they were outside the screens surrounding the bed.

'I suppose I am.'

There were three other beds in the small ward which was part of Leithan Cottage Hospital. Leithan itself was a middling-sized market town approximately twelve miles from where Rose had lost the baby.

There had been a car which had stopped, the couple in it bringing him and Rose to the hospital. He couldn't remember if he'd thanked the girl who'd helped them. Nor did he know her name, she'd never said what it was.

'Would you prefer coffee?' Sister asked once they were in her office.

'Tea's fine.'

'I could give you something stronger if you wish.'

'No, tea please.' He wouldn't have been able to keep that down either.

Dr Laidlaw, a middle-aged man with a jolly, cherubic face, came into the office. 'Ah, Mr Drummond. I was just on my way to see you.'

Andrew, who'd sat down, stood up again.

'Sister?'

'The patient is asleep.'

Laidlaw nodded. 'Good. Sleep's what she needs. The more the better.'

It was the question Andrew hadn't been able to ask up until then. 'Is she going to be all right, doctor?'

'Oh aye, she's a healthy young woman. Physically there shouldn't be any after-effects and there's no reason why you can't have another child in time. So put your mind to rest, Mr Drummond.'

Andrew sagged with relief. 'Thank you.' He sucked in a deep breath. 'Have you any idea what caused the miscarriage?'

'None at all I'm afraid. Nature does that sometimes for no apparent rhyme or reason. It just happens.'

'And she'll be all right?' he repeated.

'As rain, given time to recover. Now that could take a while, she's been through quite an ordeal as you know. Rest, rest and more rest is my recommendation. Her body has taken a battering but it'll mend itself. I don't envisage any problems there. As I said, she's a healthy young woman.'

'Would you like to wash up before your tea?' Sister Eason queried of Andrew.

'Yes . . . I would, thank you.' There was a smear of blood on the back of his hand that needed to be got rid of.

'Can I make a suggestion?' Laidlaw said.

Andrew nodded.

'Wash up, have your tea and then book into an hotel. Your wife will be here with us for the rest of the week at least. And you might want to change your clothes.'

Andrew glanced down at his rumpled suit which also had blood on it. 'Yes, of course. But I don't want to leave Rose.'

'She'll be asleep for ages yet. That draught I gave her was a strong one. There's plenty of time for you to get yourself sorted out.'

Andrew saw the sense in that. He would need some place to stay after all. He closed his eyes and frowned. 'My luggage is with the car which broke down. The police said they'd send someone from a local garage to fetch it.'

'Sister, why don't you get on the phone and find out what's what. You might also ring the Strathspey.'

To Andrew he explained, 'That's a comfortable hotel only several streets away. Nice and handy for the hospital.'

'I'll arrange everything,' Sister Eason declared.

'Is there anything I can give *you*, Mr Drummond?'

'You mean a prescription?'

'That's right.'

'No, I'm fine.' Andrew laughed bitterly. 'Well hardly that, but you know what I mean. I can cope.'

'You're certain of that? It's no bother to give you something.'

'I'll cope, I assure you. Now I'd better go and get washed.'

'Turn left as you leave the ward,' Sister Eason smiled. 'And your tea will be waiting for you when you get back.'

Andrew stopped outside the office to stare at Rose's screened bed.

There was a lump in his throat big enough to choke on as he tore his gaze away and made for the toilet.

A thoroughly shaken Georgina hung up the phone. The call had been from Andrew to tell them what had happened. He'd asked if Drew could stay on even longer than they'd arranged. He'd also requested that Willie explain the situation to Drew.

Poor Rose, Georgina thought. And how ghastly to miscarry in a car in the middle of nowhere. What a dreadful plight for the pair of them to have been in.

At least Rose was in safe hands and being well looked after. Andrew had said the attention she was getting at the hospital was first-class.

She crossed to the bell tug and pulled it, then went to

the window to watch Drew and James playing on the lawn. She could see they were having a whale of a time.

'You rang, madam?'

Georgina turned to face Sadie, the maid who'd answered her summons. 'Find one of the men and ask him to get Mr Seaton. He's needed here at the house as soon as possible.'

'Yes, madam.'

'Drew!'

An ashen-faced Drew had jumped up from where he'd been sitting and fled the room when Willie had finally concluded what he'd had to say.

'Drew!' Willie called again, to no avail.

'Let him go,' Georgina counselled. 'He'll return when he's ready.'

'I need a drink,' Willie declared. 'That wasn't the easiest of tasks.'

'No it wasn't.'

A few moments later James appeared. 'Have you finished?' He glanced around. 'Where's Drew?'

'I think he wants to be alone for a while. Your father had some bad news to give him,' Georgina replied.

Drew forced his way into the middle of some bushes and, not bothering that the ground was freezing cold, sat down. In the distance he could see The Haven, from which he'd run non-stop.

His breathing was laboured, his chest heaving. His thoughts were in turmoil.

It was as though . . . as if . . . he'd actually *willed* the child to die. He shuddered and tightly clasped his hands together to stop them shaking.

He'd loathed that child, detested it. Resented its coming. Why, hadn't he actually admitted the latter to his father?

And why? Jealousy, that's why. Because the baby would take away, had already taken away, the spotlight being solely on him.

And now the child, wee Mary as his mother had insisted on calling it, was dead, gone for ever.

Guilt racked him. If he hadn't had such evil thoughts Mary might still be alive. Alive in Mummy's tummy waiting to come into the world, instead of . . .

If he'd loathed Mary he now loathed himself even more. What sort of boy was he to hate an unborn child? Despicable, that's what. Totally despicable.

If only he could do something, if only there was some way to make amends. Take back those thoughts, have things as they were. But there wasn't, and never would be.

Drew sobbed, filled with self-pity and disgust.

Then there was his mother. She too could have died, what then? He simply couldn't imagine life without Rose. The comfort of her touch, the warmth of her embrace. Basking in her love.

'Oh, Mum,' he croaked. 'Please forgive me. Please. I didn't mean any of it, honestly I didn't.'

But that was a lie. He had. He'd wanted the baby gone, disappeared. Which was precisely what had occurred.

A great fear took hold of him. Fear of God. For wasn't he a murderer, killer of his own sister?

He might not have stuck a knife in the child, but what he had done was as good as killing her.

He unclasped his hands and rammed a finger across his mouth, biting hard on its flesh and bone.

This was a day he'd remember and regret for always. Of that he had no doubt.

No doubt at all.

'Is there anything we can do, Andrew?' a heavy-hearted Hettie asked, glancing yet again at Jack sitting listening to her. 'Well let us know if there is. You only have to say.'

'What's happened?' Jack demanded when she'd come off the phone.

'Rose lost her baby.' She went on to give the details.

Tommy, also in the room, stared from Hettie to Jack and then back again. He remained silent.

'And there's nothing we can do?'

'Not according to Andrew.'

'Damn,' Jack muttered. Then, 'Damn,' again. Andrew must be in a frightful state, Rose a great deal worse. 'Did he mention when they're coming home?'

'That hasn't been decided yet. The weekend perhaps, or the beginning of next week.'

Tommy laid aside the newspaper which he'd been pretending to read, in reality day-dreaming. 'Shall I put the kettle on?'

Hettie smiled her gratitude. 'That's a good idea, son.'

'He's finally nodded off,' Georgina announced to Willie on rejoining him after a lengthy absence. The clock informed her it was just past midnight.

'He took it very badly I'm afraid,' Willie commented morosely.

'He did that. Even worse than I would have expected. He was sodden when he got back and will come down with a cold I shouldn't wonder.'

'Did he say anything further?'

Georgina shook her head. 'Nothing more than those

few words when he arrived in. Even James couldn't get him to speak.'

Willie recalled the conversation he'd had with Andrew about what 1939 might hold. Neither of them had even considered this possibility. Their speculations had been entirely national and international, not domestic.

'It's a blooming shame,' he said rather weakly.

'Aye, it is.'

Georgina produced a wisp of hanky and blew her nose into it, her eyes suddenly wet with tears.

'Come here, lass,' Willie said huskily.

She crossed to him and sat on his lap, curling her body against his.

'It's times like this we should be thankful for what we've got,' he murmured.

'Yes.'

He gently stroked her hair, then the arch of her neck, thinking what a lucky man he was.

Andrew was hollow-eyed and haggard-looking as he sank on to the wooden chair beside Rose's bed. He'd had a word with Sister who'd informed him that Rose had been given another draught of sedative in the middle of the night.

Some while later Rose's eyes blinked open and she gazed uncomprehendingly at the ceiling above her.

'Rose?'

She slowly turned her head to look at him. For a few seconds there was no expression at all, then the hint of a smile twisted her lips. 'Hello.'

'How are you?'

Her hand fluttered, and he reached over and took hold of it. He noted how cold it was.

'Tired.'

He nodded.

'And . . . empty.'

They stared at one another, understanding and love flowing between them. In a way, they'd never been closer.

'I thought I might have imagined it, but I didn't, did I?' she said in a faint, tortured voice.

'No.'

'In the Rolls . . . and there was a girl.'

'A farmlass who helped. I never caught her name.'

Rose nodded imperceptibly.

'Are you hungry?'

Rose considered that. 'I'm not sure. I don't think so.'

'You're going to be fine, Rose. Tiptop. The doctor has assured me there's no reason why we can't have another child.'

He immediately wished he hadn't said the latter when her face contorted.

'Wee Mary,' she breathed.

Andrew bit his lip.

'I didn't see . . . I never saw . . .'

'Ssshh, Rose,' he crooned, squeezing her hand.

'So empty,' Rose repeated. 'So very, very empty.'

All the goodbyes had been said, the thank yous made, and now Andrew, at long last he felt, was taking Rose home. She halted outside the main door and drew in a deep breath. 'Freedom,' she joked.

Andrew laughed. 'I can well understand you saying that. Even with the best of care and attention hospitals can't be fun.'

'They certainly aren't.'

He took her by the elbow, carrying her case in his other

hand. 'Now watch these steps. I don't want you taking a tumble and ending up inside again.'

'Heaven forbid.'

She was putting a brave face on it, he thought, his heart going out to her. He couldn't wait to get her ensconced again at Drummond House.

At the bottom of the steps Rose paused and glanced around. 'I thought you said the Rolls was here waiting for us.'

His expression became grim. 'No, I said the *car* was. That's ours, the red Austin Twenty over there.'

'And the Rolls?'

'I sold it and bought the Austin as a replacement.'

She didn't have to ask why he'd got rid of the Rolls, she knew why. And was extremely grateful for it. Many men might not have been so thoughtful, or sensitive. 'Is it a good runner?'

The moment of tension had passed. 'So I was assured by the garage. It's jolly comfortable too.'

She was hobbling slightly he noticed as they walked over to the Austin, but that was only to be expected. It shouldn't take her long to be properly back on her feet again.

'Jack, Hettie, it's good to see you!' Andrew exclaimed, coming to his feet as they were ushered into the drawing room.

Hettie immediately flew at Andrew and threw her arms around him, squeezing him hard.

'Here, hold on there, Hettie. You'll crack my ribs,' he protested. Years of hard graft on the farm had left Hettie unusually strong for a woman. At least, the sort of woman Andrew was used to.

Hettie pushed him away, but kept hold of him, staring deep into his eyes. She nodded at what she saw there. 'Where's Rose?'

'Upstairs resting. She's tired from the journey.'

'I'm not surprised after what she's been through. Are we your first visitors?'

'No, Charlotte's already been and gone.' Charlotte was Andrew's sister, the minister's wife.

'Can I see Rose, or is that not a good idea?'

'Go on up and have a natter. Jack and I will remain here and do the same.'

'If that's all right then. I'll only stay a few minutes.'

During this exchange Jack had made his way to a chair. 'So how is Rose really?' he asked when his wife had left them.

'Drink?'

'No thanks.'

Andrew went to the mantelpiece and leant against it. 'To be honest, Jack, I'm not quite sure. Up one minute, down the next. An enigma at other times.'

Jack could hear the strain in Andrew's voice although Andrew was doing his best to disguise it. 'We felt for the pair of you when we heard the news,' he said with meaning. 'It must have been awful.'

'It was, Jack, believe me.'

'Right there in the car?'

'I stopped the bloody thing and then it wouldn't start again. Lucky for us a local girl was on hand to help out. Otherwise I don't know what I'd have done.'

Jack grunted his sympathy.

'Are you sure you won't have a drink? I could certainly use one.'

'Aye, well on you go then.'

Jack listened to the chink of glass on glass. 'When are you going back to work?'

'I haven't really thought about it. That's been the last thing on my mind,' Andrew replied over his shoulder.

'Can I give you a piece of advice?'

'Of course. Fire away.'

'Get back as soon as you can. What's done is done, there's no point dwelling on it more than you have to.'

'But Rose . . .'

'It was your loss too, old boy. Don't forget that. You too are grieving. Just don't wallow in it, that's all. Remember the saying, life goes on.'

'You're a hard man, Jack Riach,' Andrew mocked.

Jack recalled being told he'd lost his eyes, and then learning how badly scarred his face was, 'I've had to be,' he replied drily 'There are certain things you simply have to come to terms with. If you don't you go under.'

Andrew realised to what Jack was referring, and was instantly contrite. 'I'm sorry,' he stated quietly.

'Don't be. Just take my point on board. That's all I ask.'

'I'll return in a couple of days. I need some time to be with Rose.'

'That's understandable. In the meanwhile why don't you drop by the distillery. I would imagine many of them are worried about you.'

'I hadn't thought of that,' Andrew mused, giving Jack his whisky.

'There's a lot of goodwill towards you and the Drummond family in that place. You've always been good and fair employers, after all. And they like and respect you as a man, same as they did your father. They care about you and yours.'

'Stop it, Jack, you're embarrassing me,' Andrew mumbled, pleased Jack couldn't see he'd gone rather pink.

'Well, it's true.'

Andrew resumed his spot by the mantelpiece. 'Sometimes you wonder what it's all about, don't you, Jack?'

Jack laughed. 'Oh aye, you do that.'

Rose had stayed in their bedroom all day, taking her meals there. Andrew was therefore surprised when later that evening Rose suddenly appeared, to smile wanly at him.

'Darling!' he cried in delight.

'I want to talk to you,' she explained, pulling her dressing gown more tightly about her.

He immediately set about stoking up the fire, throwing fresh coals on it. 'Rather chilly in here,' he commented.

'That doesn't matter. I'm only down for a moment.' She hesitated, then went on, 'I hope you don't mind but I've asked the staff to make up a bed for you in one of the guest rooms. I need to . . . well, be on my own.' She stared beseechingly at him. 'I hope that doesn't offend you?'

'Not in the least.'

'It's just . . . That's how I want it for now.'

'If that's what you want then so be it. I'm not offended at all. I certainly don't want to disturb you during the night by tossing and turning or something silly like that.'

She smiled her relief. 'I knew you'd understand.'

'Of course I do. Perfectly.'

'Then I'll go back on up again.'

He watched her head for the door, a wraith of a figure that made his insides ache. 'Rose?'

She turned to him, a strange look on her face. 'Yes, Andrew?'

'Am I allowed to kiss you goodnight when I come up too?'

Rose nodded.

'Then I shall.'

She smiled wanly again.

It might have been a trick of the light, or purely his imagination, but she seemed to float from the room.

'Mr Drummond sir!'

Andrew stopped, *en route* out of the distillery. As Jack had suggested he'd come in and spoken to a few of the staff, chiefly Mr Kelly. He'd let it be known he'd be at his desk the following Monday morning. Punctual as usual, he'd informed Kelly, whose response had been a wry smile.

'Miss Mathieson, isn't it?' he said when the girl came hurrying up.

Bell blushed with pleasure that he knew her name. 'From bottling, sir.'

'So how can I help you?'

'I've been elected, sir, by the rest of bottling, including Mr Balfour the gaffer, to give you this.' She thrust an envelope at Andrew.

He stared at it in astonishment. 'I see.'

'It's nothing much, sir. We wanted to get flowers but there's none to be had for love or money this time of year. So we've made do with that.'

The envelope was addressed to himself and Rose.

'It's a card, sir, signed by all of us. I hope you don't think we're being forward, sir.'

'Not at all Miss Mathieson.' He remembered Jack's words of the night before. This was no token, but something heartfelt. 'Tell everyone that Mrs Drummond and I thank them. Tell them . . .' He had to break off and clear his throat which was suddenly clogged with emotion. 'We're deeply touched.'

'I'll get back then, sir.'

'Yes, you'd better.'

Bell saw enormous sadness etched into Andrew's face, and he somehow appeared older than she recalled. Not that she was used to being in his actual presence, but had often observed him in passing. He regularly went through the department, often having a chaff with Mr Balfour when there.

Andrew cleared his throat a second time as Bell hurried off, her long black skirt swishing over the floor.

Touched, he'd told Miss Mathieson. Truth was, it went even deeper than that.

Much.

The Scots have a word *dwam* which means a daze, or state of mental abstraction. Rose, lying in bed, was in exactly that when her door burst open and Drew came charging in.

Next moment, tears streaming down his face, he was wrapped in her arms, his own hugging her as tightly as she was him.

'I'm sorry, Mum, I'm sorry, I'm sorry. . .' he sobbed over and over again.

'There there, Drew,' she crooned, starting to rock slightly. She thought he was upset because she'd lost the baby and had no idea of what this was really all about – his guilt in believing he'd caused her to lose it, and put her life in jeopardy as a result.

Drew gazed up at her, his adored mother. The sweet, comforting, familiar smell of her filled his nostrils.

'Rose?'

She glanced at the open doorway where Andrew stood framed.

'Just leave us alone for a few minutes, please.'

'Fine. Willie and Georgina are here.'

She knew that, otherwise Drew wouldn't have been. 'I'll get up shortly.'

'Right then. I'll tell them.'

'Dreams,' Drew whispered. 'Bad dreams, Mummy.'

'About me?'

'Yes.'

She stroked his hair. 'There's no need for that. I'm fine, as you can see.'

'It was all my fault.'

'Don't be silly, poppet,' she laughed. 'Of course it wasn't. You had absolutely nothing to do with it.'

He wanted to tell her about his thoughts, had intended doing so, but now faced with her found he couldn't. The words simply wouldn't come. He laid a wet cheek on the swell of her breasts.

'I've missed you so much,' he mumbled instead.

'And I've missed you. Dad and I both have.' That wasn't quite true, she not having given much thought to Drew, being used to him being off at school anyway. But it was clear the boy needed reassurance.

'I'm going to be good from now on,' he declared. 'Extra specially good.'

'That's nice.'

'I promise you, Mummy. I promise you.'

Chapter 8

Nancy was scrubbing the floor, and hard graft it was too after a long day in the fields. But it had to be done along with all the other seemingly endless household chores. Sometimes she felt she'd already died and was living in hell.

She sat back on her haunches for a breather, laid down the brush and massaged her red, chapped hands. How long before arthritis set in? The bugbear of most people, male and female, who did the same sort of job as she and Bill.

He was sitting by the fire staring into it, his features hidden from her by the angle between them. She wondered what he was thinking, if anything at all. He was as still as a stone statue.

At least his boils were now a thing of the past, thank the Lord. The doctor had soon sorted them out. You'd have thought he'd have shown a little gratitude, however grudging, at her having talked him into going. But not one bit of it. The only reference he ever made of his several visits to the doctor was to complain how much money it had cost him.

Jesus, he was a mean bastard. Tight as a midge's arse. You'd have imagined at Christmas he might have given her a wee something, a minding, albeit that wasn't really the custom amongst adults, at least working-class adults like themselves. Not him, not Bill McCabe. Not even a sweetie or plain handkerchief.

Still, she reminded herself, there were worse than Bill about. Oh aye, far worse from what she'd heard. She should count herself lucky.

'Bill, can we speak?'

There was no reply.

'Bill?'

He stirred himself. 'Wheesht, woman.'

She got up, wincing at the pins and needles which suddenly stabbed her legs, and went to him. 'We should speak, Bill, and now's as good a time as any I suppose.'

He glared balefully at her. He was in a filthy temper, though there was no reason why he should be. He just was, that was all. 'Have you finished the floor?'

'Not yet.'

'Then I'd get to it if I were you.'

'It'll be done soon enough. Even I have to take a break. I'm not a bloody horse, you know. Or come to that, you'd give a horse more breaks than you would me.'

'You can be right yappy at times,' he snarled.

'Can I indeed.'

Nancy dried her wet hands on the pinny she was wearing, noting that the pinny would have to go in the wash. 'It's not long now till our contract comes up,' she stated. 'Have you any idea what's going to happen?' She was referring to the yearly contract between Bill and the master.

Bill hawked into the fire which caused her lips to thin in disapproval. She'd repeatedly asked him not to do that, considering it a foul habit, but he always ignored her. She sometimes thought he did it just to spite her.

'None at all,' he replied sourly.

Nancy sighed. If the contract wasn't renewed then it meant the Hiring Fair and a new master to find. It also meant leaving this cottage which she'd grown fond of. Like hinds, there were a lot worse about.

'You and he get on well enough, don't you?'

They had, he thought bitterly. Though not recently. Not since the master's calling on Nancy and going away displeased. Stupid bitch, why couldn't she have put herself out a bit. Done some play acting if that was what was required. He didn't know a great deal about women but had realised the majority of them weren't past that when it suited them.

'Well?' she prompted.

'Leave me alone. I want some peace.'

'You're not answering my question.'

He glared at her again, fighting back the temptation to slap her one. He would have enjoyed that. Christ but she could be irritating. Like an itch that never stopped no matter how much you scratched it.

'He wasn't too happy with me a while back, those bastarding boils. But that's over and done with. In the past so to speak.'

'So he will be renewing the contract?'

'How the fuck am I supposed to know!' Bill suddenly shouted. 'The master hardly takes me into his confidence.'

'There's no need to get shirty about it, Bill McCabe. I've every right to ask after all.'

'Have you now,' he sneered.

'Yes I do. If you're out then so am I, and all the upheaval and uncertainty that goes with it.'

He'd already made up his mind that if he was out he was getting rid of Nancy. It just hadn't worked between them. Oh, she was fair enough in bed, though not a tremendous cook. Certainly nothing like Patsy when it came to the pots and pans. He'd been thinking more and more of Patsy recently, regretting his split with her.

'I'm off through,' he declared, standing up and yawning. He rubbed the bristles on his chin, making a rasping sound.

'It's early yet.'

'So what? There aren't any rules about when I have to go through, are there? I mean, I am a tree man where that's concerned.'

This time it was she who glared.

'I'll be waiting,' he smiled ominously, and left her fuming.

'You're hurting, Bill,' Nancy complained later on. She was bone dry as was sometimes the case just before her monthlies. Usually Bill was understanding, but not on this occasion.

'Tough shite,' he hissed, and thrust even harder.

Nancy gritted her teeth.

Bill grinned to himself. He was getting a little of his own back for her being so bloody irritating.

'Hello, Tommy, how are you getting on?'

He came up short as Bell Mathieson joined him. They and others from the distillery were on the way home for the evening.

'Oh it's you, Bell.'

'In the flesh.' She shivered. 'I can't wait for spring to get here. I hate this cold and snow.'

He resumed walking as she fell in beside him. 'Where's your pal Irene? You're usually with her.'

'She's off the day. Down with the flu.'

'Aye, there's a lot of it going round.'

'Have you had it yourself?'

He shook his head. 'Not so far, touch wood. How about you?'

'Me neither I'm happy to say.'

'That's good then.'

'It was a shame about Mrs Drummond's baby,' Bell commented a little further along the road. 'How is she doing?'

'Fine, as far as I know. Well as could be expected.'

'It must be awful to lose a baby,' Bell reflected wistfully. 'And imagine, in a car as well. That's what I heard.'

'It's true,' he nodded.

'Poor woman. It must have been real humiliating for her. I mean, can you imagine. Your skirt pulled up and . . .'

'That's enough, Bell,' Tommy interrupted quickly. 'I don't think we need to go into the sordid details.'

She smiled. 'Have I embarrassed you?'

'Not in the least,' he lied. 'I just don't think it's something we, or anyone else come to that, should be talking about.'

'Aye, maybe you're right.'

'Certainly not like that anyway.'

She glanced sideways. What a catch he would be. Good-looking, not to mention charming. He'd make a fine husband, she thought not for the first time.

Bell giggled.

'What's up with you?'

She tried to keep a straight face, and couldn't. Did he have a big one or not? She'd never find out. 'I was just thinking of something that was said when we were working,' she replied, which was true enough. Her face creased even more.

'So arc you going to tell me what it was?'

That made her giggle again. 'It wasn't important. Forget it.'

Tommy dug his hands deeper into his coat pockets. It was a raw night and going to get worse. He hoped his mum had some soup waiting, just the dab in weather like this.

'Did you enjoy kissing me?'

That startled him and caused him to flame scarlet. 'What sort of question is that?' he protested.

'An honest one I should have thought. So, did you?'

He looked away and muttered something inaudible.

'I didn't hear that.'

'Of course I did.'

'And I enjoyed kissing you. Even if you were drunk.'

'I wasn't that bad!'

She laughed mockingly. 'Pull the other one, Tommy Riach. You were stotting. I doubt you'd have made it back if we hadn't been there to help you.'

'Nonsense.'

'Kid yourself if you like, but it's true. Stotting drunk enough to piss your pants.'

'I did nothing of the sort!' he retorted, scandalised.

She had him on the hop, she thought gleefully, considering it great sport. 'I never said you did, only that you were so bad you might easily have done.'

'You're exaggerating.'

'I don't think so.'

'Yes you are.'

'Am not.'

'Are so.'

'Not.'

'So.'

They both burst out laughing at the absurdity of this exchange.

'You're fun, Bell.'

'And so are you, Tommy. We get on well together you and I.'

He couldn't deny it. They did.

'There's a dance a week on Saturday. Are you going?'

'A dance? I haven't heard of it.'

'Aye, in the hall. There's to be a proper band and everything.'

'You mean Scottish dancing?'

'No, dance-hall dancing. The real stuff. Irene and I will be there. We wouldn't miss it. Should be a good night.'

Tommy had not been to one of the local dances, never having had the inclination to do so. He now wondered about this one.

'So are you going?' she queried.

'I shouldn't think so, Bell.'

'Why not?' She was trying to mask her disappointment.

He shrugged.

'That's no answer.'

'I just don't think so, that's all.'

'You could always come with Irene and me if you're shy,' she teased.

He was tempted, he had to admit. And it would be nice

to dance with Bell and maybe kiss her afterwards. Yes, he would certainly like that. 'Who else will be there?'

'Village folk and others from round and about. They won't all be young either. Quite a few of the older people will turn up. These dances are always popular.'

'Tell you what, I'll think about it. How's that?'

Again she was disappointed, certain that meant no. He was turning her down. Served her right for inviting him in the first place; she should have known better.

'We always go to the pub first and have a bevy or two,' Bell persisted. 'That puts a rosy glow on things.'

'They wouldn't serve me. They know I'm underage.'

'Ach, I wouldn't worry about that. They turn a blind eye on occasion. As long as you behave yourself that is. Which I'm sure you would, being a gentleman and all.'

A gentleman! He almost preened.

She laid a hand on his arm. 'It would be lovely if you came, Tommy.'

He looked into her eyes, then glanced away. 'Would it?'

'Oh aye.'

'I'm back!' Tommy called out. He was starving.

Hettie appeared and stared steadily at him. 'Was that Isobil Mathieson I saw you with, son?' She knew fine well it was, having watched the pair of them saying goodbye through the window.

'Yes, we walked down together. She's usually with her friend Irene but Irene's off ill with this flu that's going round.'

That placated Hettie a little. She followed Tommy on through to where Jack was. 'Good day?' Jack inquired cheerily.

'All right.'

'The dreaded Mr Kelly still got it in for you?'

Tommy grimaced. 'In spades, Dad. The man's a menace.'

'Well, it's just something you'll have to put up with for now.'

Tommy crossed to the roaring fire and vigorously rubbed his hands. 'When's tea, Mum?'

'Shortly.' She was still eyeing him suspiciously.

'Is there soup?'

'Vegetable broth.'

Tommy smiled in anticipation.

'That'll put hairs on your chest,' Jack chuckled.

'And yours,' Tommy retorted.

'Oh, I gave up hoping years ago. It never worked for me I'm afraid.'

'Tommy and Isobil Mathieson walked home together,' Hettie said casually.

'Oh?' That was Jack.

'Terrible family, you know. No better than tinks. That father of hers has a dreadful reputation in the district.'

Tommy stared at his mother in dismay. 'I was only talking to her, Mum, being friendly like. There's no harm in that, surely?'

'Not as long as it's only talking and nothing else.'

'They are a pretty rum family,' Jack agreed. 'And as your mother says, no better than tinks. Though I have to admit old man Mathieson has always been pleasant enough to me.'

Tommy now knew what his mother was driving at, which both amused and annoyed him. What she was really saying was that it was an unsuitable relationship which mustn't develop any further.

Hettie saw that Tommy had got her meaning and nodded slightly. There might be nothing between him and Isobil Mathieson, but if there was she would nip it right in the bud. The likes of Isobil, or Bell as they so commonly called her, weren't for her Tommy.

Andrew hesitated outside their bedroom door, or Rose's bedroom as it had become since her return from hospital. It was another night when she'd gone to bed directly after the meal, leaving him to spend the rest of the evening alone.

A glance at his wristwatch told him it was just past eleven. Silently he partially opened the door and poked his head round, the light from the corridor spilling into the dark interior.

Rose's eyes were shut, her breathing steady. She was fast asleep.

He stared at her for a few seconds, wishing he was there beside her. Wishing . . .

Taking a deep breath he closed the door again, the only sound being a small click as the lock engaged.

Rose smiled to herself as she listened to his retreating footsteps.

McFarlane, the groom, touched his forelock. 'Morning, Mrs Drummond,' he said.

'Good morning, McFarlane. How are you today?'

'Never better, Mrs Drummond. Thank you for asking.'

She went to a stall where a brown horse with white facial markings stared mournfully at her. The mare snickered in recognition.

'And what about you, Strumpet? How are you?'

She scratched the mare's ears. Strumpet rubbed and tried to lick her arm in appreciation.

'I'm just about to take her out for her morning exercise, Mrs Drummond,' McFarlane informed Rose.

Rose had been in two minds up until then, but now being with Strumpet decided her. 'Don't bother, McFarlane. I'm going to change. I'll take Strumpet out myself.'

McFarlane raised an eyebrow in surprise, but said nothing. It wasn't his place to comment.

'It's been a while, hasn't it, my pretty,' Rose crooned, Strumpet whinnying in reply. Somehow the delighted animal knew that it was to be ridden by its mistress for the first time in many months. The mournful look had vanished.

'So have her saddled up and ready for me, McFarlane. I shan't be long.'

'Yes, Mrs Drummond.'

Rose kissed the horse on its nose, suddenly feeling light as air inside. She was going to enjoy this.

Nancy picked up yet another stone and threw it into the canvas bag she was dragging alongside her. When the bag was full she'd take it to the edge of the field and empty it.

Stones were forever being unearthed by ploughing in this particular piece of land which was why, once a year, they had to be collected and removed. On this occasion the back-breaking work had fallen to her.

She paused to wipe away sweat and catch her breath. There were hours to go before the dinner break, and then the long afternoon stretched beyond that. It was going to take her two days at least to do what was required.

For some reason she found herself thinking of the lady in the fancy car. A sorry episode if ever there was.

Nancy sighed, remembering the fine clothes the woman had been wearing. What a pity they'd been ruined, though that probably wasn't much of a loss to someone so obviously wealthy.

Why, no doubt the woman had wardrobes full of clothes, all as fine and expensive. The loss of a single suit would be nothing to her. Despite herself, jealousy stabbed through Nancy.

They must live in a big house, she reflected, with servants, lots of them to attend every need and whim. She smiled, trying to imagine herself in such a position.

The husband had been a good-looking chap too, beautifully tailored and manicured. She laughed aloud comparing him to Bill McCabe. What a joke!

Oh, to be well off, she thought wistfully. Wouldn't it be wonderful. Rich instead of grubbing around in a field picking up stones for a living. That and all the other hardships she had to endure.

How old would the lady have been? Difficult to say really. Though certainly much younger than the husband.

Nancy gingerly touched her face. How rough and weatherbeaten it was, brown from continual exposure to the elements. Totally unlike the lady's skin which had been smooth as velvet.

Oh well, she mentally shrugged. There was no use worrying about it. Her lot was as a bondager and all that entailed. A daily grind from early morning to late at night, out grafting rain or shine.

She glanced down at her hands, calloused and dirty, her fingernails chipped and broken. Now the lady's hands had been . . .

'Stop it, Nancy Thompson!' she declared aloud. This

was daft, utterly pointless. She'd been born to what she had and nothing on this God's earth was going to alter that.

Still ... and she smiled softly. A lassie could dream, couldn't she? Even if she had nothing else but dreams.

She bent again to pick up what seemed to be the millionth stone of the morning.

Hettie glanced at Tommy in exasperation. 'Will you stop prowling and sit down!' she exclaimed. 'You're giving me a headache with all that constant movement.'

Tommy halted in his tracks. 'Sorry, Mum.'

'What's wrong with you, lad?' Jack queried.

'Nothing. I'm just ... restless, that's all.'

It was Saturday night and he knew precisely why he was restless. He couldn't stop thinking about the dance being held later on and wishing he was going.

And he still could, if he really wanted to. Except he wouldn't. For to go would mean meeting Bell and his mother was right about her; Bell was most unsuitable for someone of his background and prospects.

'If you're that restless why don't you go for a walk?' Jack suggested.

'Good idea,' Hettie nodded. 'It might get rid of some of that energy bottled up inside you.'

'Aye, on you go,' Jack prompted. 'Give us a little peace.'

Tommy grinned. 'Am I upsetting you that much?'

'Yes,' Hettie stated emphatically. 'You are.'

'All right then, I will.'

'Round the village twice at least,' Hettie said. 'And don't come back till you've calmed down a bit.'

'I won't.'

And with that Tommy was gone.

*   *   *

'He isn't going to show,' Bell whispered to Irene, adding lamely, 'not that I really expected him to.'

'There's plenty of time yet,' Irene replied, glancing at the clock behind the bar. The pub was full, all the tables already taken when they'd arrived, which was why they were having to stand.

'There's Isa Weir and Hannah McIlroy,' Bell said, spying their two pals from bottling who'd just come in. Isa's boyfriend Ronnie was already there waiting for her to join him. He immediately waved to the pair who went over. Ronnie also worked in the distillery.

Irene stared down into her now empty glass. 'Are you for another?' She laughed. 'As if I have to ask.'

'Of course I am.'

'Right then,' Irene declared as Bell finished her drink.

'They say gin makes you sin,' Irene giggled, and headed off for refills.

Chance would be a fine thing, Bell thought glumly.

Tommy was standing across the road listening to the hum emanating from inside the pub. He could see several people he recognised through the window opposite, but not Bell.

He could go in for a drink, nothing more, he told himself. Bell had assured him he'd be served as long as he behaved himself.

Only if he did that he'd get into conversation with Bell and then it really would be difficult not to be persuaded to go on to the dance.

Did he fancy Bell? Actually fancy her that is? It was a question he'd been trying to avoid answering.

He'd certainly enjoyed kissing her. That warm mouth

and tongue, her eager body pressed up against his. An experience he'd love to repeat. And could. All he had to do was cross the road and go through that door. Nothing could be easier.

God, but he was tempted.

'I'm gasping for a fag,' Irene said quietly to Bell. Being in a public place she could hardly light up.

'Nip to the toilet then.'

'Do you mind?'

'Not in the least.'

'Will you wait?'

Bell eyed her friend dyspeptically. 'Well, I'm hardly about to piss off and leave you. Talk about a silly question.'

'You might get chatted up in the meantime. Find a click.'

Bell gazed about her. 'I shouldn't think so. But I promise you, if Don Juan appears and I get swept off my feet, I'll still be here when you get back.'

'Well, there's no need to be sarcastic,' Irene retorted.

Bell laughed. 'Away and have your cigarette.'

As Irene left her Bell's gaze fastened on to the doorway. There was still no sign of Tommy. He'd never said he'd come, she reminded herself. No promise had been made so none had been broken.

But it would have been lovely if he'd turned up.

'The trouble with Tommy is that, apart from Eric Taylor, and Eric's away at school, he doesn't have any friends in the village,' Jack commented to Hettie. The Taylors were a local naval family, the father, a high-ranking officer, usually absent at sea.

'That's true,' Hettie nodded.

'Eric has always been around in the past when Tommy was on holiday. Different now of course.'

'Eric will be home again at Easter. They'll get together then no doubt.'

'No doubt,' Jack echoed. 'The pair of them have always been thick as thieves. Ever since they were wee they've run together.'

Jack drew in a deep breath. 'Too much time on his hands after work, that's his trouble. All he does is kick around the house. Never really goes anywhere.'

Tommy *was* rather at a loose end in the evenings, Hettie reflected. What he needed was a hobby. Certainly an interest of some kind.

As long as it wasn't Isobil Mathieson, she thought grimly. She might have come from humble stock herself, but Tommy was not only her son but Jack's as well. That made all the difference.

Tommy had a certain status in life. And would be a wealthy man when the time came to inherit, which should never be forgotten. Least of all by him.

'We should make a move soon,' Irene said to Bell.

'I'm not in a hurry. Are you?'

Irene shook her head.

'Well then. I don't want to arrive at the beginning of the dance. I much prefer getting there when it's in full swing.'

'Aye, you're right.'

'My turn this time,' Bell declared, taking Irene's glass, which had rapidly emptied again.

Tommy had slowly walked the length of Dalneil's main

street, and was now retracing his steps equally slowly. His eyes flicked sideways when he came abreast of the pub.

He hesitated for the briefest of moments, then continued walking, listening to the hum from the pub fading behind him.

Chapter 9

Andrew was annoyed as he strode home from the distillery, the fountain pen he'd used for years having leaked all over his shirt. He intended changing it and then returning to work, which was a damned nuisance as he had a great deal to get through that day.

He wondered what Rose was up to as he climbed the stairs. She hadn't mentioned earlier that she had anything special on so she should be around somewhere. Unless she'd gone out riding which she'd been doing a lot of lately.

He came up short outside her bedroom where the door was ajar, frowning at what he saw within.

'Rose?'

'Hello, Andrew. What are you doing back at this hour?'

He explained to her as he went inside. 'Are you actually playing with those things?' he asked incredulously.

Rose was sitting beside the doll's house she'd rescued from The Haven, her childhood dolls propped against it.

'Yes, it's fun.'

'I see,' he murmured.

'Now don't look so disapproving. I said, it's fun. There's no harm in that surely?'

'None at all.'

Rose began laying out a porcelain tea set, placing a cup, saucer and plate in front of each doll. 'This is what I used to do when I was young,' she smiled disarmingly. 'And I always served scones to go with the tea. They all adore scones.'

There was a peculiar quality to her voice, he thought. It was as though . . . she actually was somehow young again.

'We're having a guest today,' Rose declared. 'A very special guest. Aren't we, dollies?'

'Yes, Rose,' she said, pretending to be one of the dolls answering her.

'And who's that?'

'Mary. Mary's coming to visit.'

Andrew went cold all over. 'Mary?' he queried softly.

'Our Mary. Our little Mary. Isn't that right, dollies?

'Yes, Rose.' That was supposed to come from another of the dolls.

He swallowed hard. Had she gone mad or something? A feathery sensation of alarm raced up and down his spine.

'Do you wish to join us, Andrew?' Rose asked.

He shook his head.

'You'd be most welcome. Wouldn't he, dollies?

'Most welcome, Rose.

'Andrew likes scones too. He often eats them. Don't you, Andrew?'

He nodded.

'In fact they're a great favourite of his. Just as they are of yours.'

'Rose, eh . . ,' He cleared his throat. 'Are you feeling all right?'

'Of course, darling,' she replied, eyes wide and beguilingly innocent.

'You seem to be taking all this . . . very seriously.'

'But naturally.'

'And this talk of . . . Mary. It, eh . . .' He trailed off, lost for words.

'What about her, Andrew?'

'Mary doesn't exist, Rose. She's dead.'

Rose's smile seemed to stretch on and on for ever. 'I know that, Andrew. I miscarried her in the Rolls. Remember?'

'Then why are you speaking about her as if she was alive?'

Rose came to her feet and the bizarre magical spell that had surrounded her abruptly splintered. 'It was only a game, Andrew. Nothing more. There's no need to look so concerned.'

'But I *am* concerned, Rose. What you were doing is hardly healthy.'

Rose turned her back on him. 'We all handle grief in our own way, Andrew. This happens to be mine. My way of dealing with things.'

He went to her and grasped her shoulders. 'Oh, Rose,' he whispered.

She shook him off. 'I'll get you another shirt. That one's quite ruined.'

Rose swept from the room leaving him staring after her. This was worrying. He'd have to speak to the doctor about it.

'McCabe!' The master crooked a finger indicating that Bill come to him.

'Yes, sir?'

'You're not a bad worker, McCabe. When you haven't got boils on your arse that is.'

'Thank you, sir.'

This was amusing the master who'd never forgotten, or forgiven, his displeasure with Nancy. He'd intended letting Bill go, but had changed his mind about that. What he now planned was better.

'The contracts are nearly up,' he stated.

This was the moment Bill had been dreading. 'Yes, sir. Next month.'

The master nodded, and didn't instantly reply, intentionally keeping Bill on tenterhooks.

He was for the chop, Bill thought in despair. Oh well, he'd been expecting it anyway.

'Do you wish to remain on?'

Bill's heart leapt. 'Oh yes, sir. I do.'

'Hmmh.'

'Very much so, sir. Nancy and I are happy here.'

'Indeed,' the master mused. 'Are you indeed.'

Bill's mouth had gone dry as he waited to hear his fate. Why didn't the damn man just come out with it?

'Then remain you shall,' the master said after a suitable, tantalising, pause.

Bill touched his forehead. 'Thank you, sir. Thank you kindly. You won't regret it, sir.'

138

'You, but *not* your woman. I don't want her around any more.' The master smiled inwardly.

'Me but not Nancy, sir?'

'That's correct. The choice is up to you. If you wish to stay you'll have to find yourself another female. Is that clear?'

'Quite, sir.'

'So what's your answer?'

'You want it right away, sir?'

'I do. Here and now.'

Bill took a deep breath. He was fed up with Nancy anyway, her and her irritating ways. This merely sorted the matter, making it easier for him.

'I'll tell her tonight, sir. Spell it out like.'

'Good, McCabe. Good. You shouldn't have trouble finding a replacement, a chap such as you.'

'No, sir. I shouldn't think so, sir.'

'That's settled then. Go back about your business.'

'Yes, sir. Straight away, sir.'

So much for Nancy Thompson, the master thought with grim satisfaction. His displeasure had been revenged.

'And that's the long and short of it,' Bill declared, having waited till he'd finished the evening meal before announcing the news.

Nancy's face mirrored her shock. 'He wants you but not *me?*'

'That was the deal.'

'And you agreed, just like that?'

Bill was having trouble holding her gaze. 'He demanded a decision there and then.'

'Did he?'

'Yes,' Bill stated emphatically. He'd go out, he decided.

He had a few bob in his pocket which would buy him a couple of pints. A celebration in a way now he knew what was what. At least he wouldn't now have to suffer the humiliation of the Hiring Fair, standing there like so much meat in a butcher's shop window. And who knew what a new master would be like? This one was bad enough without his having the misfortune to land worse.

He would still have to go to the Hiring Fair of course in order to find another female, but that was something to look forward to, the boot being on the other foot so to speak. He felt quite cheered at the prospect.

'You're a bastard, Bill McCabe,' Nancy said levelly. 'A black-hearted bastard. And after all I've done for you too.'

He pushed his plate away and belched. 'You ain't done no more than you should. Would be expected.'

Her eyes flashed anger. She was still trying to come to terms with the bombshell he'd dropped. Not that she had any tender feelings for Bill, that didn't come into it. It was simply they were a team and rubbed along together well enough. Now uncertainty loomed before her.

And what if she didn't find another hind? What then? That would be a catastrophe. Farm work and bondaging were all she knew.

Bill rose. 'I'm off out for a wee while. I'll see you when I get back.'

'Bastard,' she repeated.

Bill waited till he was outside and away from the cottage before bursting out laughing.

Nancy tensed as Bill's hand crept under her nightie. The smell of beer and stale breath hung heavily over them.

'Don't even think about it,' she hissed.

'There's no need to be like that, Nancy. It's only a shag after all. You like it as much as me.'

She pulled away from the groping hand. 'If you don't stop right this minute I swear I'll go through to the kitchen, get the carving knife and stick you with it.'

The hand was immediately withdrawn. She would too, he thought. Nancy didn't make idle threats.

'Aye, all right then,' he muttered, well put out. And a little scared too if he was honest.

Nancy knew that sleep would be a long time in coming. How dare he! To expect that after what he'd done to her. Talk about bare-faced cheek!

A month was all she had left in this cottage, no time at all. And then what?

Of one thing she was certain. There would be no more shagging with Bill McCabe. He'd had his lot where that was concerned. And if he tried to force her it would be the carving knife.

Her mind was still spinning when Bill began to snore.

'So what do you think, doctor?' Andrew asked, having just recounted the story of the doll's house and the imaginary Mary coming to tea.

Dr Lesley was in his mid-thirties and popular with the folk of Dalneil. He wasn't only a good doctor but had an easy bedside manner which went down well.

'It could be a breakdown of some sort,' Lesley mused. 'Have there been any other symptoms?'

Andrew glanced away, finding this next bit embarrassing. 'She won't have anything to do with me sexually since the miscarriage. We're sleeping in separate beds.'

'I see. Though I can't say I'm surprised. What Mrs

Drummond has been through is bound to have taken its toll. Mentally that is. She'll need a period of adjustment. It's quite normal.'

'I can understand that.'

'Was eh . . . everything all right in that department beforehand?'

'Not really,' Andrew replied quietly.

Lesley waited for him to elaborate.

'She hasn't been very keen since our son was born. It was as though it had become a chore to her. That she was only doing her duty.'

'And previously?'

'A very loving and passionate woman, doctor. I certainly didn't have any complaints.'

'Which has all changed since the birth of Drew.'

Andrew nodded. 'She did perk up after falling pregnant the second time. For a while it was as it had once been between us. I took her to Glasgow and that was like a second honeymoon. Then the miscarriage and now separate bedrooms.'

'Hmmh.'

Lesley leant back in his chair and studied Andrew thoughtfully. 'My initial reaction is to say leave things as they are. I'm a great believer in doing nothing rather than something for something's sake.'

Which made sense to Andrew. 'Only what if she is, has gone . . .' he could hardly bring himself to say the word . . . 'mad.'

Lesley sighed. 'That is a possibility of course. I have to admit. It wouldn't be the first time the trauma of miscarriage has had that effect on a woman. Put her over the edge.'

'If you'd seen and heard her with the doll's house,'

Andrew said, and shook his head. 'It frightened me I can tell you.'

'I'm due to drop by and see her sometime soon anyway, so while there why don't I do a wee bit of subtle probing. Sound her out in certain matters, more so than I would normally. That way I can make an evaluation.'

'Fine, doctor.'

'I'll telephone and make an arrangement with her.'

'You don't think . . . I'm being an alarmist, do you?'

'Not at all. You love your wife and are naturally concerned for her well-being. You were quite right to come and speak to me about that concern.'

Lesley rocked forward in his chair. 'Is she home tomorrow?'

'All day as far as I know.'

'Good. I'll ring then.'

'Thank you, doctor.'

Lesley took Andrew by the arm as he was escorting him from the surgery. 'I'm sure there's nothing really to worry about, Mr Drummond. Not in the long term anyway. But in the meantime we may as well just see what's what.'

Andrew felt a lot better as he drove away. Simply articulating his worry had been a great relief.

Andrew woke with a start and sat bolt upright in bed. Sweat was streaming down his face and shoulders.

He'd been back in Ireland, watching Alice, the woman he'd been going to marry, burning to death. Hearing the shrieks and screams from within the human torch she'd become.

'Christ,' he muttered, and ran a hand over his forehead, a hand he noted was trembling. He was thoroughly shaken.

Alice whom he'd adored and whom the Fenians had burnt alive when they'd set fire to the family home. She'd died with her mother and father.

The nightmare had been so vividly real he would have sworn he was actually there witnessing what had occurred. The tormented shrieks and screams were still reverberating round inside his head.

Alice whom he'd loved with all his heart before meeting Rose, and whose death he'd revenged by killing the bastard McGinty responsible for the atrocity.

He'd set ablaze the McGinty home in retaliation then shot and killed the family before throwing McGinty himself back into the conflagration to perish in flames as Alice had done.

Andrew fumbled with the bedside lamp and switched it on, flooding the room with soft yellow light. It had all happened so long ago, so many years before, and still it haunted him.

He'd often wondered what his life would have been if Alice had lived to become mistress of Drummond House. There would have been no Rose then, no Drew. And of course no miscarriage in the Rolls.

McGinty . . . seeing the man's face and still hating him for what he'd done. He hoped again, as he'd hoped many times in the past, that the Fenian bastard was roasting in everlasting hell.

He and Rose must try for another child as soon as possible, he decided. Surely that was the answer to the problem that had arisen from the miscarriage. And if she did fall pregnant, not forgetting how long it had taken for her to become so the second time, pray God it was with a lassie, the daughter Rose so desperately wanted.

The first thing was for them to resume normal relations.

A period of adjustment Dr Lesley had said. Well, that was fine, but a period was exactly that, a space of time which, by its own definition, must eventually come to an end. His immediate aim must be to bring that end about sooner than later.

A holiday perhaps? That might help. The pair of them thrown together without any work to intervene. Definitely a possibility to which to give some serious thought.

The trouble was the distillery, which he always loathed leaving for anything more than a few days. How bound he was to that building and what it produced! But he must put things in perspective, he told himself. Rose was his wife and her well-being, not to mention their marriage, must take priority.

Not just a week's break but a month at least. And somewhere far away, distance being essential in his opinion. A balm to help heal the deep wound afflicting Rose.

Andrew held his hands in front of him to see that they'd stopped trembling. His breathing was also back to normal.

He lay back and closed his eyes, recalling scenes from his childhood. His father Murdo and brother Peter. Peter whom he'd never really got on with and who, being the elder, should have inherited if it hadn't been for France and the war.

How he wished he was in bed with Rose. To feel her close, touch and cuddle her. Not for sex, that was the last thing he wanted at the moment, but for her presence and the reassurance that went with it. The sheer solace that man and wife should find in one another.

He could go to her now, explain how disturbed he was, that he'd had a nightmare. But he wouldn't, knowing that to be wrong. It would be putting pressure on her which she didn't need.

A picture of Rose with the doll's house flashed into his mind causing him to shudder. That had been scary, truly frightening. What if she had gone over the edge never to return? How dreadful that would be.

The shrieks and screams inside his head were gone now. The image of Alice faded to a pale shadow of that which had woken him.

Loneliness could be a terrible thing, he reflected, as could memories. Especially in the middle of the night when all sorts of ghosts and horrors, some real, others imagined, walked.

Jack Riach listened in sympathetic silence as Andrew recounted the story of the doll's house. The two of them were in the pub where they did their best to meet up every Friday night.

'Dear me,' Jack whispered when Andrew was finished.

'I thought a holiday might be a good idea. A long one to try to take her mind off matters.'

'It certainly wouldn't do any harm.'

Andrew gazed morosely into his dram. 'Lesley called in to see her then came over and spoke to me at the distillery afterwards.'

'Oh?'

'He was very hopeful and did his damnedest to put my mind at rest. He said he couldn't detect anything abnormal in Rose, that she was simply a woman trying hard to cope with an extremely difficult situation.'

'There you are then,' Jack smiled.

'Except he wasn't there that day in the bedroom. He never heard her voice or saw the look in her eyes.'

'That bad, eh?'

'Worse than you can imagine. It made me feel sick. I honestly thought I might vomit afterwards.'

Jack didn't reply to that. If only there was something he personally could do, but what? Be a friend, there when necessary. A shoulder to lean on, an ear to bend.

Andrew threw the whisky down his throat and then had a long pull from his pint. 'Anyway, I don't want to bore you with my problems any further.'

'You're not boring me, Andrew, honestly.'

Andrew could hear the ring of truth in his friend's statement. 'Thanks, Jack.'

'A problem shared after all.'

'Indeed.' Andrew smiled. He glanced around, his gaze fastening on a young couple sitting in a corner. They were both locals, recently married.

He couldn't help but thinking how attractive she was. A full-bosomed lassie with chestnut-coloured hair and, somehow, provocative features. He felt an old familiar stirring. It had been a while after all.

'Another drink?' he said gruffly to Jack, rising from his chair.

'Aye, sure.'

When he returned he repositioned himself so that the girl was completely out of his line of vision.

'There's a page here addressed to you,' Rose declared across the breakfast table.

'Me!' Andrew exclaimed in astonishment. This was something new, Drew never wrote specifically to him.

'It says "Dear Dad".' Rose smiled, handing the page across to Andrew.

'Wonders will never cease.' He took the page.

He began to frown as he read first one side then the other.

'Well?' Rose prompted.

'Drew wants me to know that when he grows up he definitely intends taking over the distillery. That he's looking forward to it and is sorry if he ever gave me the idea he might do otherwise.'

'I see,' Rose murmured. 'And did he give you such an idea?'

'There was some talk one day about the possibility of his not following in my footsteps as I followed in my father's and he in Grandpa's.'

'You never mentioned.'

Andrew shrugged. 'I was surprised but didn't really think him serious. I also got the impression it was a bit of a tease, that sort of a thing.'

'His recent letters have been strange,' Rose mused. 'Though don't ask me how. I'm not entirely sure.'

'It's probably just his age. All children go through peculiar phases. I know I certainly did.'

As had she, Rose reflected. Particularly during puberty. That had been a most difficult time for her. But it couldn't be puberty with Drew, he was still far too young for that.

There again, Andrew was thinking. The strangeness of his recent letters could well be the result of late events. Yes, that was it no doubt, he decided. The miscarriage.

Andrew was right about that, though he didn't appreciate how badly affected Drew was, not being aware of Drew's assumed guilt.

'Have you ever considered becoming a Sunday school teacher?'

Tommy gaped at his mother. 'I beg your pardon?'

'You heard me. Have you ever considered becoming a Sunday school teacher?'

'Why should I do that?' an aghast Tommy queried.

'You might enjoy it and it would give you an interest outside work. I'm sure you'd be welcomed with open arms.'

Tommy couldn't think of anything he'd like less. The very notion was preposterous. 'Lassies do that. There isn't a single male amongst them.'

Hettie smiled inwardly. The whole point, though she wasn't about to tell Tommy that. Not only were the teachers all lassies but, without exception, ones from good families. Who knew, it might be the start of something.

'I think you'd be rather good at it myself,' Hettie went on. 'It could be very interesting.'

Interesting, his foot. Boring beyond belief more likely.

'You were aye keen on Sunday school when younger,' Hettie declared. 'You used to love it.'

He had too, Tommy thought. 'That was then and now's now,' he stated firmly.

'I always thought you had a wee fancy for Miss McKeown, Mrs Ure as she is now, who taught you. You spoke about her often enough.'

'Did I?' Tommy replied, pretending innocence. He'd worshipped Miss McKeown who'd been the dishiest of all the teachers. The *only* dishy one, he now recalled.

'There are probably Miss McKeown types there now,' Hettie declared slyly.

Then, deciding she'd said enough for the moment, 'Anyway, it was only a thought.'

Miss McKeown types? Now that might not be as daft a suggestion as it had first seemed.

* * *

'Come on, girl, come on!' Rose urged Strumpet, flicking the mare repeatedly on the flanks with her crop.

Rose started to laugh from the sheer pleasure and exhilaration of the gallop. Her heart was thudding nineteen to the dozen.

A stone wall, or dyke, loomed into view which she decided to jump. Then she and Strumpet were soaring through the air to land with only the slightest of bumps.

'Faster, girl, faster.'

Strumpet did her best to respond. Her mane was streaming, her nostrils flared in the extreme. Somehow the mare found it within herself to quicken the pace.

Rosé knew she could be badly hurt if she came off at this speed, and didn't care a jot. Being hurt or even killed didn't matter, all that did were the sensations she was experiencing. Glorious sensations that were causing her blood to race and her spirits to soar. She felt as though she'd transcended this world and was inhabiting another.

'Give her a good rub down and feed, McFarlane. She's deserved it,' Rose instructed, patting the exhausted mare's nose. Strumpet was too exhausted to even whinny a response.

McFarlane took in the mare's sweat-stained and heavily lathered coat beneath which she was both heaving and trembling. He glanced at Rose, then back again at Strumpet.

'You have had a ride today, Mrs Drummond,' he said in a neutral tone. She'd completely knackered the bloody beast, was what he was actually thinking.

'I have indeed.'

McFarlane couldn't remember the last time he'd seen a

horse in such a state. As for Mrs Drummond, she looked done in as well.

'I'll be going out again tomorrow,' Rose informed him.

'Yes, Mrs Drummond.'

'Shortly after breakfast, same as today.'

'Strumpet will be ready and waiting.'

'Good.'

Rose kissed the mare, after which she wheeled about and strode from the stables, leaving a somewhat perplexed McFarlane behind. He'd found the look in her eyes quite unnerving.

Chapter 10

'God, this is tedious and never gets any better,' Bell commented to Irene, the pair of them halfway through the morning shift.

'Aye, well just be thankful we've got work. There's plenty in this country don't.'

'True enough. That wage packet at the end of the week is always welcome and no mistake.'

Irene sighed. 'I'm gasping for a fag.'

'When are you not?' Bell teased. 'I swear that when you die you'll come back as a chimney.'

'There are plenty worse than me,' Irene protested. 'Besides, who can afford to smoke all that much at the price of ciggies. It's scandalous so it is.'

'If you stopped think of the money you'd save.' Bell was teasing again knowing there was little likelihood of that.

'And the enjoyment I'd be giving up,' Irene countered, hands moving deftly over the line of bottles passing before her. 'You have to have some pleasures in life.'

'Well I know what mine is,' Hannah McIlroy called over. 'And it sure as hell isn't fags.'

That raised a laugh from the other girls with a few lewd comments and digs being made.

'That last dance was a bit of a disappointment,' Sandy McAlpine declared.

'In what way?' queried Isa Weir.

'The usual talent. No new faces. I didn't think the band were all that good either.'

'The dance seemed all right to me.'

'Of course it did,' Bell said. 'You had Ronnie in tow, love's young dream and all that. No wonder you had a good time.'

'Have you done it with him yet?' Sandy inquired with a twinkle in her eyes.

'I'm not saying. It's a secret between the pair of us.'

'Which means you haven't,' Irene snorted.

'It does nothing of the sort. It means exactly that. I'm not saying.'

'One thing about your Ronnie,' Sandy went on. 'He does have a lovely bum. I've always thought that.'

'Me too,' Hannah chipped in. 'Though of course I've never seen it in the raw. What's it like, Isa?'

'Is it all hairy?' Bell further teased.

Isa shot Bell a contemptuous glance. 'He's a man, no a bloody monkey for Christ's sake.'

'That doesn't answer the question.'

'It's the only answer you'll get out of me, Bell Mathieson.'

'It really must be love the way he was slobbering all over you,' Irene grinned.

'He doesn't slobber! Not over me or anything else.'

'Aye, all right, keep your shirt on. It's only an expression.

Though I could have sworn I saw him foam at the mouth at one point.'

'Really!' exclaimed Sandy McAlpine.

'Really. The sort mad dogs get.'

Sandy burst out laughing while Isa glared. Though, if she'd been honest, she was enjoying being the centre of attention.

'You lot are just jealous. That's your trouble,' Isa sniffed.

'As if.' Bell smiled.

'I didn't see you there with anyone.'

'I was with Irene,' she protested in a mock fashion.

'You know what I mean.'

'Maybe that's because I'm choosy.'

Isa was instantly outraged. 'That's an awful thing to say. You can't get more choosy than my Ronnie. He's a dreamboat.'

That produced a guffaw all round.

'What world do you inhabit?' Sandy jibed.

'Maybe she needs specs,' Bell leered.

'Ronnie a dreamboat,' Irene repeated, and cackled.

'I seem to remember you fancied him at one time,' Isa retorted. 'But he wasn't interested. That's because he's got taste.'

'Taste, my arse. He can't have that if he's going out with you.'

'Well, if you're talking of arses yours is certainly big enough.'

Now it was Irene's turn to be outraged, being very sensitive about her somewhat largish bottom. 'Bitch!'

'No more than you.'

Bell was grinning to herself, that barb had really hit home with Irene.

'Balfour!' Mrs Reid, one of the older married woman, suddenly warned. The chatter immediately ceased.

Bell glanced over to see that Mr Balfour had indeed reappeared in the department having been absent for the past half hour. He was accompanied by Tommy to whom he seemed to be explaining something.

Bell wasn't sure what her reaction was to seeing Tommy; her emotions were mixed. All she could think was how well he looked. She paused momentarily to wipe a stray wisp of hair from her forehead.

Balfour and Tommy, the gaffer talking non-stop, made their way slowly along the length of the department to pause only a few feet away from Bell.

She smiled at Tommy who couldn't have failed to notice. There was no response, none whatsoever. Not even a flicker of recognition in his eyes. Then he and Balfour were continuing on their way.

Bell dropped her gaze, stung to the quick. That had hurt, really really hurt.

It had been as though she didn't even exist.

'Well, I'm off to bed,' Rose announced, rising from the easy chair she was sitting in. They'd only retired from dinner fifteen minutes previously.

Early yet again, ridiculously so, Andrew thought in dismay. It was as though she didn't want to spend any time in his presence. Or at least, as little as possible.

'I was hoping you might stay up for a bit so we could chat,' he said.

Rose hesitated. 'About what?'

'Nothing in particular. Just chat, that's all. Spend a cosy evening together.'

'I'm tired, Andrew. Bed's the best place for me.'

'If you say so, Rose.' The disappointment was clear in his voice.

She went to him and pecked him lightly on the cheek. 'That'll save you looking in later.'

More disappointment. 'Goodnight then.'

'Goodnight.'

'Oh, Rose!' he said as she was moving away.

She stopped and turned, a quizzical expression on her face.

'I was wondering, how about the pair of us going for a ride this Saturday afternoon? I haven't ridden in ages and the exercise would do me good.'

The quizzical expression became one of slight irritation. The last thing she wanted was to go riding with Andrew, much preferring her own company.

'Still, if you don't wish to.' He smiled thinly when she didn't answer.

'No, it's not that,' she lied, desperately trying to come up with a reason for his not accompanying her.

'But?'

There was no way round this, she realised. She could hardly go out by herself and leave him behind. That would be too much like a slap in the face.

'No buts; it'll be fine,' she replied, trying to force enthusiasm into her voice.

'I shall look forward to it, Rose.'

'As shall I.'

Like two strangers, he reflected after she'd gone. That's what they'd become, like two strangers.

Rose stopped brushing her hair and stared at herself in the vanity mirror. Why was she being so horrid to Andrew? She did love him after all. And yet day after day, night after night, she found herself rejecting him. Pushing him away. Ignoring him.

Tears welled in her eyes to run down her cheeks. Large fat tears like escaping diamonds, each sparkling and dancing in the light.

She sobbed. Sorry for herself. Sorry for Andrew. Sorry for everything. Sorry for being born in the first place.

She really did try with Andrew, but somehow, something always came between them when she made the effort. She wanted him there, and didn't. Loved him, yet at other times hated him.

He was going away on business for a few days the following week which suited her down to the ground. Or did it? Why, oh why was she so confused, so muddled, so utterly wretched?

The baby of course. She knew that. It was the obvious answer. The doctor at the hospital had warned her there might be a period of emotional flux, but she'd never expected anything like this.

Would she ever be right again? Could she ever return to the Rose who'd married Andrew? The sweet uncomplicated young woman who'd been so full of hope for the future?

Things had changed with the advent of Drew, she was aware of that. Her feelings had altered, a coldness creeping in where there had only been warmth before.

She'd never denied Andrew, she reminded herself, even while knowing that wasn't entirely true. There had been nights where excuses had been made, a slight upset, or illness, exaggerated. But basically she hadn't denied him, though her heart wasn't in it.

And then the second pregnancy and what a difference that had made. She'd discovered joy again, and a taste for the pleasures of the flesh that had long lain dormant.

She thought fondly of Glasgow and the hotel room where they'd made such wonderful love. Then revulsion swept over her at the memory, causing her to shiver slightly.

A female Jekyll and Hyde was what she'd become. One moment this, the next that. A quite different animal entirely.

Perhaps she should call Andrew upstairs, invite him to stay the night with her. The poor man had his needs after all, and where Andrew was concerned they were considerable.

What if he tired of her excluding him and sought his pleasure elsewhere? How would she feel about that?

It would bother her, naturally so. And yet would it? She wasn't sure.

Part of her would be jealous, another part relieved. But which part would be the greater? For wouldn't he only be seeking what she was refusing him?

She could hardly blame Andrew if he did elect to cheat on her. He was no saint, not by a long chalk. What she knew of his past history, and she was sure there was a great deal she didn't, proved that.

What a useless creature she was, Rose thought, wiping away the still flowing tears. No good to anyone any more, least of all her husband who loved her as much as she loved him.

It was as though a great glass barrier had been built, a barrier she could see through but could neither get through nor over. A shimmering teasing tantalising barrier.

Reaching out she picked up one of the dolls she'd placed

earlier by the side of her mirror and clasped it tightly to her bosom.

Tears continued to flow as did her sobbing.

'Oh Mary,' she whispered.

'I'm going to miss you dreadfully,' Annie McGillvary said to Nancy. The pair of them were mucking out a cowshed, or byre as they called it.

'And I'll miss you and Hector. You've been smashing friends to me.'

'You'll find another man at the Fair. Handsome lass that you are. The buggers will be queuing up.'

Nancy laughed. 'I doubt that.'

'And you're young. Lots of work left in you which is one of the ways they'll see it.'

There were only days to go and . . . Nancy paused and drew in a deep breath. She was scared, frightened of what lay ahead. The uncertainty of it all.

'He's a swine your Bill,' Annie declared vehemently, her pitchfork thudding into the mound before them.

'Not *my* Bill any more,' Nancy corrected her, thinking with satisfaction that she'd kept her word to herself. Bill had gone without since the night he'd broken the news to her, and most unhappy he'd been about that too. It was the threat of the carving knife that had dissuaded him from forcing the issue. As time had gone by, much to her grim amusement, he'd become more and more bad tempered, the reason for that obvious. Nor had he hit her which she'd again put down to the threat of the carving knife.

'Aye, true enough,' Annie agreed.

Nancy suddenly became aware that she was being watched. It was as if she had a burning sensation between her shoulders and back of the neck. She swung round and there, standing in the shed's open doorway, was the master.

He was staring at her, an amused, triumphant, smile playing across his lips.

He was gloating, she thought. No other word for it, gloating. Well, as long as that was all he did she didn't care.

She returned to work and, when she looked again at the door several minutes later, he was gone.

At the conclusion of the hymn the congregation sat and the Reverend McLean, Andrew's brother-in-law, announced that they would now be joined by members of the Sunday school.

There was a slight rustling amongst those present when the children, herded by their teachers, filed in.

This was what Tommy had been waiting for, the arrival of the Sunday school teachers. Now what were they like?

He was pleasantly surprised, having been expecting the worst. Several of them weren't bad-looking at all. One of them he recognised, a lassie he hadn't seen in years. The others were unknown to him.

It was the last girl who really caught his eye. Hardly a ravishing beauty but she certainly had something that, as far as he was concerned, made her stand out.

Should she or shouldn't she? She hadn't been going to but now Nancy decided she would. She halted and turned round for a last glimpse of the cottage she'd just vacated.

There it was, the grey stone building that had been her home, and which she'd probably never see again. A place of memories, none of them happy ones.

Mist was swirling and eddying, rapidly becoming thicker

by the minute. She caught a glimpse of one of the bondagers but couldn't make out who.

Her goodbyes had been said the previous night, and sad they'd been. Annie had wept and wished her all the best. As had Hector, though he hadn't wept. Well, being a man he'd hardly do that!

Others had come to the cottage to mutter their farewells, the women mainly, with a number of dark looks being cast at Bill sitting silently by the fire.

He would also be going to the Hiring Fair that morning but hadn't suggested they travel together. He hadn't left yet and she had no idea if he was taking the same route as herself or another.

No words had been said between them earlier. She'd served him breakfast which he'd eaten, then, with a grunt, he'd gone out about some task or other. He still hadn't returned when she'd closed the door behind her and set off.

Well, it was finished. She and this place. She and Bill McCabe. It was a new day and a new beginning. A chapter in her life had finished, another was about to open.

There was one final look at the cottage, after which she hurried on her way. Plunging deeper and deeper into the ever-thickening mist, praying to God she didn't get lost.

The Fair would be over by early evening. To get lost and miss it could prove a catastrophe.

Andrew smoothly changed gears as he rounded a bend. He wouldn't have taken this road by choice but a new customer in the area had necessitated the different route.

'Leithan 2 Miles', the sign informed him. The small town where Rose had been in hospital after the miscarriage.

No, he wouldn't have come this way at all if he could have prevented it.

Andrew frowned as he entered the town; there seemed an awful number of people around. Far more than he would have expected. As he got closer to the centre the crowds became more dense.

Something was going on, had to be. And then he recalled that Leithan held a Hiring Fair once a year round about this time. That must be it, he thought. He'd arrived on Fair day.

He'd heard of Hiring Fairs but never actually been to one. He found the concept of what went on there rather intriguing and wondered if he should stop off and take a look around. He was rather hungry after all, and Leithan would be as good as any place to have a bite to eat.

Nancy shivered and tugged her navy blue shawl more tightly round her shoulders. This was awful, even worse than she remembered. The humiliation of it all made her cringe inside.

So far three hinds had stopped and talked to her, all moving on again. Several others had stood off and given her the once-over but not approached, one of these a horrible older man with black teeth and an inturned eye. The thought of going to bed with him had made her flesh creep.

She'd arrived later than planned, which hadn't helped matters, but the weather had held her up.

She stamped her feet to try and bring some feeling back into them.

Andrew had walked past the girl before it dawned on him that he'd seen her before. Though how he should know one of these wretched creatures he couldn't imagine.

Perhaps she bore a resemblance to someone, could that be it? No one sprang to mind.

'Toffee apples, sir. Would you like a toffee apple?'

The speaker was standing behind a barrow displaying them. His expression, as he studied Andrew, was hopeful.

Andrew shook his head. Toffee apples indeed!

'Have you got the kiddies with you, sir? I'm sure they'd like one. They don't come no better or tastier than my toffee apples.'

Disgusting-looking things, Andrew thought, perusing the items in question. 'No thank you,' he stated gruffly, and began retracing his steps.

In some ways the Fair was proving a bit of a disappointment. He'd expected there to be more novelty about it. Hoop-la stalls, coconut shies, those sort of things. Well, there were a few in evidence, but only a few.

There she was again, the girl he'd thought he'd recognised. The white scarf covering her head and tied underneath her chin, topped by a black straw hat, didn't do her any favours, he reflected. But then that was the same headgear worn by the other women standing about waiting to be hired for farm work.

The girl moved and now he could see her face quite clearly. He did know her, he was certain of it.

But from where?

'Excuse me?'

Nancy had noticed the well-dressed man heading in her direction but hadn't really paid any attention to him, not dreaming for one moment that he'd stop and talk to her. 'Yes, sir?'

'You don't recall me, I take it?'

Nancy shook her head.

'You helped my wife a while back when she was in difficulty. We were in a parked Rolls-Royce when she started to miscarry.'

Nancy's face lit up with amazement. 'Of course, sir!'

'So it is you. I wasn't absolutely sure.'

'A terrible thing to happen, sir. Right horrible so it was.'

'I don't know what we'd have done without you. And I never even thanked you afterwards or got your name.'

'Nancy, sir. Nancy Thompson. And you don't have to thank me, I only did what anyone would have done. How is the lady, sir?'

'Fine, well on the way to recovery.'

He owed this girl a debt of gratitude, Andrew thought. Five pounds perhaps, that should cover it. 'So you're here looking for a job, eh?' he said affably.

'A hind to be more precise, sir.'

'A hind?'

'Man, sir. Farm labourer. They take me on then contract themselves to a farmer. The farmer won't employ a hind without a woman, sir. He gets two for the price of one that way.'

Andrew shook his head. 'I must confess I know little about the system.'

'It's called bondaging, sir, and that's what I am, a bondager.'

Andrew was trying to digest this, understand it properly. 'You say you're waiting for a man to pitch up and offer you employment. Correct?'

'Yes, sir.'

'Any man?'

'Whoever'll have me, sir.'

There was clearly more to this than Andrew had thought. 'And what exactly would your duties be for whoever takes you on?'

'Keep his house, sir. That and work for the farmer.'

'Keep his house,' Andrew repeated slowly. 'You mean live with him?'

Nancy nodded.

Andrew was shocked. Why, this was no more than a form of prostitution. If he was understanding things correctly that was. 'Live with him as . . .' He cleared his throat. 'Man and wife?'

'Aye, sir. That's the way of it.'

'Dear God,' he whispered. He really had had no idea. This was barbarous. And it disturbed him hugely.

How old was Nancy? Difficult to say really. Her weatherbeaten face no doubt added years to her.

'Fourteen, sir,' she answered when he asked.

Andrew was appalled. Fourteen! And condemned to a life like this. At the mercy of whichever male should take a notion to her. Prostitution was precisely the word for it and of a most revolting type. His thoughts were whirling.

'What happened to the man you were with?' he queried.

Nancy briefly explained about Bill and the part the master had played in her ending up at the Hiring Fair that day.

By the time she'd finished Andrew had come to a decision. As he'd reminded himself, he owed this girl a debt of gratitude, and pay it he would. To hell with five pounds, he could do a lot better than that. And would.

'Are you hungry?'

She blinked at him in astonishment, thinking that a strange question. 'Yes, sir. I didn't bring anything with me and can't leave here in case I miss an opportunity.'

'A hind,' Andrew said grimly.

'That's right, sir.'

He glanced down at the small cloth-covered bundle by her feet. 'Are those your things?'

She nodded.

'Then pick them up and come with me, Nancy Thompson.'

'Sir?'

'I'm hungry as well so I'll explain what I have in mind over a hot meal.'

'In mind, sir?'

'You heard me.'

'I don't understand, sir. Are you a farmer?'

Andrew laughed. 'No, distiller. I make whisky.'

'Then what would you want with the likes of me, sir? I know nothing about whisky except that I enjoy a taste when I can get it.'

'You drink whisky?'

'I have, sir. Though not often. Don't get the chance you see.'

Andrew nodded his approval. 'My sisters were brought up to drink whisky, a family tradition. So you'll fit right in.'

'I still don't understand, sir.'

'You will. Now grab hold of that bundle and let's go.'

Confused and bewildered Nancy did as she was bid. She liked and instinctively trusted this man.

Andrew had ordered their food at the bar and now rejoined a nervous Nancy. 'It won't be too long,' he declared, placing a half pint of beer in front of her. His was a pint.

'I've never been in a pub before,' she stated quietly. 'It's . . .' She trailed off and glanced about her.

'Just relax, Nancy. There's nothing to be worried about. I assure you.'

'What do you intend, sir? You still haven't said.'

He regarded her thoughtfully. 'How would you like to work as a maid in a big house? You'll have your own bedroom and lashings of good food. The work is hard I grant you, but nothing like you've been used to I shouldn't think. And you get one whole day off a week.'

'I don't know nothing about being a maid, sir,' Nancy protested.

'That's all right, you'll soon pick it up. It's fairly simple really.'

A maid? Nancy was thinking. No more being outside in all weathers, no more Bill McCabe, or someone like him, to have to deal with. No more having to open her legs night after night whether she felt like it or not.

'Would I get paid, sir?'

'Of course.' Andrew mentioned a sum which, albeit modest, was enough to impress her. 'So what do you say?'

'Oh yes, sir. Thank you, sir. I'd be only too pleased to accept and you'll find me a grafter.'

Andrew smiled with satisfaction, pleased he'd been there to come to her aid. His debt had been paid.

'Can I ask your name, sir. Last name that is. I remember your wife calling you Andrew.'

'Drummond. Andrew Drummond. My wife and I live in Perthshire. A village called Dalneil. I don't suppose you've ever been to Perthshire?'

Nancy shook her head.

'A beautiful part of the country. More rugged than round here, more spectacular you might say.'

'Am I going there today, sir?'

'Indeed you are. With me in my car.' He laughed at the expression on her face. 'You've never been in a car either, I take it?'

'No, sir.'

'Then it'll be a new experience for you.'

'Yes, sir, Mr Drummond, sir.'

'Mr Drummond will do fine. Now . . .' He had a swallow of beer. 'I want to hear all about being a bondager and get to know something of your background.'

He listened in stony silence as she recounted her tale.

Chapter 11

Andrew halted the car when Drummond House came into view. It had been a long drive, but a cheery one. Nancy was an excellent companion with a dry, sometimes bawdy, wit. Andrew had warmed to her and felt quite relaxed in her presence, as he hoped she was in his.

'That's it,' he declared, pointing.

Nancy gaped with stupefaction. It wasn't just a big house, it looked the size of a castle to her. It was huge! The master's house was teensy by comparison.

'Well?'

'I'm going to actually live *there*?' she replied in a strangulated voice.

Andrew chuckled. 'That's right.'

Nancy swallowed hard and then shook her head. This was unbelievable. Who would have thought when she started out that morning this was where she'd end up.

'It's beautiful, Mr Drummond.'

Beautiful? Yes, he supposed it was. He gazed at the

house with fresh eyes trying to see it as someone would for the first time. 'Thank you, Nancy.'

Andrew strode into Rose's bedroom, formerly theirs, to find her lying on the bed staring vacantly at the ceiling. He frowned in irritation. She seemed to be forever lying down of late. When she wasn't out riding, that is.

She turned her head to gaze at him. 'Hello, Andrew. Good trip?'

'It went very well, as expected.'

He crossed and sat beside her. 'I had a bit of a surprise earlier. One I've brought back with me.'

'Oh?'

'Do you remember the girl who helped you in the car the day . . .' Choose your words carefully here, he warned himself. 'The day you were taken to hospital?'

'Of course I remember.'

'Well, on the way home I stopped off in Leithan and . . .'

Rose swept into the kitchen where Nancy was enjoying a bowl of cock-a-leekie soup. Up to that point she hadn't been able to recall the girl's face, but she did the moment she saw it.

Nancy immediately came to her feet and attempted a smile.

'I thought I'd better give the lass something after the journey she's had,' Mrs Moffat, the cook, explained, wiping her hands on the large white apron she always wore while on duty. 'Just to tide her over like. She'll eat properly with the rest of us later on.'

Rose nodded her approval. 'Quite right, Mrs Moffat.'

She brought her attention back to Nancy. 'How are you, Nancy?'

'Never better, Mrs Drummond, thank you very much.'

'You're to work for us, I understand.'

'That's right. Your husband came across me at the Fair and kindly offered me a position. So here I am, ready to begin right away if necessary.'

Rose laughed. 'I think tomorrow morning will be time enough for that. Meanwhile we'll have to get you settled in.'

'Thank you, ma'am.'

She studied the girl, her emotions mixed. The sight of Nancy brought back such painful memories. And yet, she was enormously grateful for the help the girl had given her. Things had been bad, but might have been a great deal worse if Nancy hadn't been there.

No, Andrew had done the right thing she decided. One good turn deserved another after all.

'We don't employ a housekeeper here,' Rose explained to Nancy. 'I take care of those duties myself.'

Nancy nodded.

'It keeps me busy you'll appreciate. Gives me something to do. Now then . . .' Rose took a deep breath. 'I'll return in fifteen minutes, which should give you time to finish that soup, and we'll take it from there.'

'Thank you, ma'am.'

'I hope you'll be happy here, Nancy.'

'I'm sure I will, Mrs Drummond.'

Rose left the girl to her cock-a-leekie, one of cook's specialities.

'It really is the most disgusting business,' Andrew declared angrily, pouring himself a dram. He and Rose had just retired from dinner giving him the first real opportunity to tell her about Nancy.

'I have heard of bondaging. Though I can't say I know all that much about it.'

'Slave labour, that's what it is. A combination of that and prostitution in my book. The whole rotten system should have been abolished years ago.'

Rose nodded her agreement. It sounded awful.

'She was at the Fair, out of a job, because she didn't please the farmer who raped her.'

'Raped her?' Rose repeated in a whisper. That was dreadful.

'Forced himself on her as his right of employer. Have you ever heard the like?'

Andrew slumped into a chair facing Rose and had a sip of whisky. 'She's had a hell of a life. I felt immensely sorry for her when she told me about it.'

He paused, then said, 'I presume it *was* all right me bringing her here. I mean, you don't object? It just seemed the least I could do.'

'Of course it's all right, Andrew. She'll be a welcome and useful addition to the staff.'

'She's only fourteen. Imagine having to live with a man as his wife at that age. Not only that but work like a trojan into the bargain. The sort of hard physical labour an Irish navvy might balk at.'

Rose settled deeper into her chair, intrigued by what Andrew was saying.

The pair of them talked and talked, mainly about Nancy, and for the first time in ages Rose didn't go early to bed.

Christine, who had the room next to Nancy's, stuck her head round the door. 'It's rise and shine,' she announced.

Nancy immediately slid from underneath the bedclothes.

It was early, but a later rise than she was used to. She couldn't wait to start her duties.

'Get washed and dressed and I'll be back for you,' Christine said and disappeared, closing the door behind her.

Nancy stretched and yawned. She'd slept well, the bed being warm, cosy and comfortable. Best of all there hadn't been Bill McCabe to contend with. That in itself was a sheer delight.

She wondered if Bill had found someone at the Fair. Bound to have done, she thought. Bill wouldn't have any problem there. She wished the newcomer to the cottage well. Especially if the master took a fancy to her.

After she'd washed at the bowl and jug of water provided she hastily donned the uniform Mrs Drummond had allocated her the previous night. The uniform was used but that didn't matter. It was only a little loose at the waist, otherwise it fitted perfectly.

She was ready and waiting when Christine returned.

There were five other girls who worked at Drummond House as maids, all of whom she'd met the night before. They were a friendly bunch and clearly all got on well together. Nancy had been made to feel completely at ease from the moment she'd arrived.

'Morning, Kelly!'

Kelly stared after Andrew who'd just strode past him. He had not seen Andrew in such a good humour for a long while.

Well, long may it continue.

'What was the war really like, Dad? You rarely mention it.'

Tommy and Jack were alone, Hettie having gone out visiting. She wouldn't be home again for a good hour yet.

Jack had been thinking about his book, mulling over the next section. 'The war?' he repeated softly, mind flashing back over the years.

'As I said, you rarely talk about it.'

'That's probably because I don't want to.'

Tommy could hear the wistfulness in his father's voice, that and more.

'The war is a period best forgotten about,' Jack said.

'Was it that awful?'

Jack could recall it so vividly it might have happened only yesterday. The sights, the sounds. Faces of comrades killed in the terrible carnage, Peter Drummond, Andrew's elder brother, among them. The mud that had claimed so many victims, men sucked screaming to their deaths. Others blown to smithereens. Arms, legs, body bits flying through the air . . .

'Dad?'

'Pray to God, son, that there is never another one. That's all I can say.'

'And yet the papers think there will be.'

'I know. I shudder when your mother reads them to me. The news fills me with dread.'

Another war, it seemed inconceivable that anyone, any sane person that is, would allow it to happen again. 'It's your birthday next week,' Jack said.

'Seventeen, quite grown up, eh?'

Seventeen, Jack thought, just the right age for war. Old enough to be brave, too young to know any better. It was the smell he remembered most vividly, he reflected. The rank stink of all-pervading fear.

'A land fit for heroes,' Jack smiled gruesomely. 'That's what they promised. A land fit for heroes. Only they never delivered. That wasn't what the poor bastards came home to at all. They were lying, the politicians that is, lying in their teeth. I've never believed or trusted a politician from that day to this.'

'Did you . . . kill anyone, Dad?'

Jack sucked in a breath. There was one in particular that had stayed with him. He'd been cowering at the bottom of a shell hole in no-man's-land when Fritz had jumped in beside him. There had been several seconds of stunned silence while they stared at one another, each surprised to find the other there, then he'd fired his revolver twice and that had been the end of Fritz. He'd spent sixteen hours in that shell hole with the corpse before being able to get away.

Fritz had been a middle-aged chap, quite portly too, wearing a thick gold wedding ring so there had been a family back in Germany. A woman suddenly widowed, children suddenly fatherless.

He'd escaped in heavy smoke. Diving, ducking, weaving, jinking to the safety of their own lines, tumbling into the trench like a frightened rabbit into its burrow.

'Dad?'

'Yes, son?'

'I asked: Did you ever kill anyone?'

'Not that I was aware,' he lied.

'Oh. I thought you might have done.'

'Perhaps I did. Often you simply never saw the result of what you were firing at.' Well, that was true enough.

'But never hand to hand?'

Jack was shaking inside though he didn't show it. Fritz in the shell hole, the bayonet slash that had disembowelled a young lad who'd shrieked and shrieked as his guts spilled out from between his fingers. And then there had been . . .

Jack shook his head, feeling he might drown in the memories as so many had drowned in the mud.

'Don't ever think war is glorious,' he said, voice tight as a drum. 'That's the last thing it is, believe me. And I should know.'

Pack up your troubles in your old kit bag and . . .

Jack was unable to cry having lost his tear ducts along with his eyes. If he had been able he'd have wept.

Rose was *en route* to having a lie down when she spotted Nancy, busy dusting, through an open doorway.

Fourteen, Andrew had said she was. A mere child, a baby really. And to have been through what she had. How she sympathised with the lass, especially the rape.

Rose couldn't imagine what that must have been like. To be taken against your will, forced. It was ghastly beyond belief.

Fourteen. She wondered what Mary would have been like at that age. Certainly not as mature as Nancy, Heaven forbid. She tried to conjure up a picture of Mary at fourteen and, strangely, it was Nancy's face she saw. Nancy, but different. A more youthful Nancy, an innocent Nancy. Nancy as a child should be at fourteen and as Mary would most certainly have been.

A laughing Mary, a giggling Mary, a wide-eyed Mary with her whole life before her.

As she would have been. *Should* have been.

Rose stifled a sob and hurried on her way.

'I'd be delighted for you to become a Sunday school

teacher,' John McLean, the minister, said to Tommy, who'd called on him at the manse.

Tommy had given this a great deal of thought and decided Hettie was right, it was a good idea. The lassie who'd particularly caught his eye that morning in church was called Barbara McTaggart. Her father was a local landowner in a smallish way. He'd found that out through discreet inquiry.

'Now when would you care to start?' John asked with a smile.

'This Sunday seems as good a time as any.'

'Even better. Then Sunday it is.'

'Fine then,' Tommy declared, rising from where he'd been sitting. 'I'll be there.'

The minister also came to his feet. 'Would you like a cup of tea before you go? My wife has just made a lovely chocolate cake which I'm sure you'd enjoy.'

'No thank you. I'd best be going.'

John shook Tommy warmly by the hand. 'I know you'll be a splendid success as one of my teachers. And, I daresay, the others will appreciate the male company.'

Yes please, Tommy thought, with Barbara McTaggart firmly in mind. 'I'll see myself out. I know the way.'

'Sunday then, Tommy.'

'Sunday.'

That was it, he'd done the deed, Tommy mused when he was outside. He just hoped he wasn't going to regret it.

Somehow he didn't think he would.

'The mistress has just never been the same since losing the baby,' Pattie Williams declared to Christine, as the two maids shared their mid-morning break.

'Things are all higgledy-piggledy right enough,' Christine agreed. 'You simply don't know where you are nowadays.'

Unknown to either, Mrs Moffat was in the larder listening to this conversation. The cook's mouth was a thin slash, for she too was worried about Rose. It was getting close to the point where she was going to have to speak to Mr Drummond. Only that very morning she'd asked Rose yet again for the coming week's menus and Rose had put her off saying she'd have them soon enough. Not at all like the Rose of old, and not good enough.

'In my opinion she should get a proper housekeeper. That would solve everything,' Pattie went on.

Christine nodded.

'Then things wouldn't be at sixes and sevens no more.'

'Maybe it's just a passing phase and she'll get over it,' Christine mused. 'I have an auntie who went a bit funny after she lost a baby. It didn't last long though, a couple of months at most I seem to remember.'

'I do feel for Mrs Drummond. I mean, you have to. For that to happen right there on the road.'

'Aye, poor woman.'

'No wonder she's been strange ever since. It's quite understandable.'

'Understandable all right, but that doesn't make it any easier for the rest of us. We're carrying the brunt.'

'Lucky for her Nancy was there.'

'Aye, real lucky so it was.'

The entire staff knew by this time how Nancy had come to be employed by the Drummonds, though weren't aware of the full situation. Nancy had merely said she'd worked on a farm and left it at that, glossing over the business of the Hiring Fair and bondaging. According to her she'd bumped into Andrew while looking for a new position and that had been that.

Christine finished her tea and sighed. 'I suppose we'd better get back to it.'

'No rest for the wicked, eh?'

'None at all.'

Mrs Moffat only emerged from the larder when both girls had departed from the kitchen.

Rose looked across the room when there was a tap on the door. She resisted the temptation to switch off the bedside lamp as Andrew would probably see the light go out. 'Come in, darling!'

Andrew had been downstairs swithering about whether or not it was too early to have this discussion. In the event he'd decided it wasn't.

'Reading I see.'

Rose laid the book aside. 'A novel I bought a while ago.'

He went to her and sat on the edge of the bed. 'Interesting?'

'So so. A romantic story that has its moments.'

A romantic story, was that a good sign or not? He had no idea. 'I've been meaning to talk to you, Rose.'

Somehow she knew what was coming and sighed inwardly. She'd been expecting this.

He reached out and took her hand. 'I think we should try and get back to normal. Have things as they were.'

She stared at him but didn't reply.

'It has been a while now and . . .' He cleared his throat. 'I miss you.'

Rose could well guess what it was he really missed. 'You have been patient, Andrew,' she conceded.

'I've done my best.'

'But it is early days yet.'

His heart sank to hear that.

'I don't know I'm up to . . . well . . . you know.' She glanced away and gently removed her hand from his.

'We could leave that for now. But I do believe we should be sleeping together again. Sharing the same bed. Don't you agree?'

Rose closed her eyes. This was difficult, and it wasn't as though she didn't sympathise with Andrew, she did. But the last thing she wanted was him back in the marital bed knowing full well that, despite what he might say or promise, it could only lead to the inevitable. That was Andrew.

'I need more time, darling,' she murmured.

Now it was his turn not to reply.

'Please?'

His determination melted. 'Of course. If that's what you wish.'

'I do.'

'Only . . .' Why did he feel he was about to propose something that was obscene. 'The sooner we get together again the sooner, God willing, we can have another child.'

'Another child,' she repeated slowly. 'A replacement for Mary you mean?'

'Not a replacement. You can't do that. But another child.' Hopefully a girl, he prayed.

For some inexplicable reason Rose found herself wanting to scratch Andrew's eyes out. Which didn't make any sense at all. Another child was the obvious answer. Then why was she so reluctant to try for one? That was a question to which she didn't have an answer.

'Rose?'

'I'm suddenly awfully tired, Andrew. I should sleep.'

Disappointment bit heavily into him. That and a certain amount of anger. She was being so unreasonable, but then that had been more or less the case since her miscarriage.

He thought of Glasgow and how good it had been between them, desire instantly taking hold of him. He would have given anything for it to have still been like that.

'I'll let you rest then,' he said, reluctantly getting up.

She gave him a smile of gratitude. 'Thank you.'

'But we must talk again about this.'

'We will, Andrew. I promise.'

He didn't believe her. At least, she wouldn't do so willingly.

Her bedside light snapped out as he closed the door behind him.

'Fascinating,' Jack murmured, Andrew having just recounted Nancy's story to him. And fascinating was precisely what he did find the story.

'Only fourteen too. A mere chit.'

'I've never heard of this bondaging. It's new to me.'

'Well, it still goes on, though it should be against the law in my opinion.'

Jack groped for his pint and had a swallow. This had certainly caught his interest and he was wondering if he could do anything with it. 'Can I meet the girl?'

Andrew stared at his friend in surprise. 'I suppose so. But why?'

'There's a book in this. I can smell it.'

'A book,' Andrew mused. He hadn't thought of that.

'But I'll need to chat to her first. Find out all the detail that I can. The ins and outs so to speak.'

Andrew considered the matter. 'I've no objection to you speaking to her, Jack, though it's up to her whether or not she'll agree.'

'Naturally. I didn't assume otherwise.'

'You sound quite keen?'

'I am, old bean. I am.'

'Then I'll tell you what, why don't we leave it for a couple of months. Let her find her feet up at the house. Then I'll broach it with her. How's that?'

'Capital. I'll be finished what I'm doing now and open to fresh ideas.'

Andrew was amused by this turn of events.

'Hello again.'

Barbara McTaggart smiled at Tommy who'd joined the ranks of Sunday school teachers that morning. 'Hello. How did you get on?'

He shrugged. 'Not too bad. I'm being allowed to take my own group next week.'

'That's good.'

She'd been smaller than he'd expected, and a little prettier. He liked the dark green of the eyes now studying him closely. 'Which way do you go?' he asked.

She told him.

'Why don't I walk with you for a bit. Unless you've another arrangement that is?'

'No,' she replied slowly. 'I haven't.'

'Right then, Barbara, walk together we shall. You don't mind me calling you Barbara I hope?'

She laughed. 'Well, you can hardly call me Miss McTaggart as the children do.'

He laughed as well.

'And my friends call me Babs.'

'Babs,' he repeated. It suited her.

'You're working at the distillery I hear.'

'That's right, training to be a traveller. In a few years' time when I've learnt the business I'll be on the road.' He didn't even bother to try and keep the pride out of his voice. 'Impressed?'

'Oh very,' she teased.

'It'll be well paid and I'll have a car. Though it isn't what I want to ultimately do.'

'Oh?'

He regarded her thoughtfully, wondering why he was even considering confiding in her. 'It'll have to be a secret though, just between the pair of us.'

She was intrigued. 'Cross my heart and hope to die if I breathe a word. That suit you?'

He nodded.

'Then come on, spill the beans.'

'An African explorer,' he announced triumphantly.

She stared at him in amazement. He was pulling her leg, surely. 'An African explorer,' she repeated, dazed. That was an ambition to say the least.

'And big-game hunter.'

Now he was having her on. 'I see,' she murmured.

He caught her by the arm having heard the disbelief in her voice. 'Honestly.'

'Well you . . .' She wasn't quite certain what to say. 'Certainly aim high.'

'Why not?'

'Why not indeed.'

'And one day I will be these things. I've sworn it to myself.'

He was serious, she realised. This wasn't a leg pull at all.

'Now you won't let on to anyone, you promised.'

'Our secret. Just between the pair of us.'

He beamed his approval at her.

There was more to Tommy Riach than met the eye she thought. Daft or not, she liked him for these absurd ideas. For absurd they were.

As for Tommy, he was thinking how much he liked Babs McTaggart. In fact he liked her a lot which was a most satisfactory state of affairs. Just what he'd been hoping would be the case.

Andrew came groggily awake as the naked figure slid in beside him. 'What . . . ?'

'Ssshh, darling,' Rose purred, placing a finger over his lips.

Rose! And naked. He was stunned.

Rose ran a hand over his chest, then slipped it inside his pyjama top. She wasn't quite sure why she was doing this, only that she had an overwhelming urge to make love. Her whole being craved it. To feel him inside her, for the release that would bring. Nor would the latter take long, in the first instance anyway.

Andrew was trying to collect his wits, this being completely and utterly unexpected. He groaned as her other hand found him and began teasing.

'My darling,' she crooned, shifting herself into the position she wanted. Her need was more urgent than she'd ever previously known.

Rose freed Andrew from the confines of his pyjama bottom, then sat astride him. A swift wriggle and he was in place.

'Rose?'

'Ssshh.' The finger again over his lips.

Andrew smiled wolfishly as she began to move. This was his dream of months come true.

As time passed he marvelled at how passionate, demanding and insatiable she was. It was as though she was trying to draw the very life force out of him.

When he awoke next morning it was to find her gone. All that remained was the sweet smell of her scent.

Chapter 12

Andrew frowned and glanced at his watch. 'Is Mrs Drummond coming down this morning?' he asked Pattie Williams who was serving breakfast.

'She's already had something and left, sir. Went riding I believe.'

His frown deepened. That surprised him. To go off without a word after what had happened the previous night. Odd to say the least.

His frown turned to a smile as he recalled their love-making. Rose had been simply . . . tempestuous. At one point her cries were so loud he'd feared she must wake the entire household. Luckily Drew, whose bedroom adjoined the one he was now using, was away at school otherwise he'd have been bound to hear.

Oh, but it had been wonderful, particularly after such a long spell of celibacy. He couldn't have asked for better. The sheer intensity on Rose's part had brought a whole new dimension to their lovemaking.

He hoped he was in for a repeat bout later that night.

'Come on, come on, you bitch!' Rose yelled into Strumpet's ear. The horse was running faster than it had ever run before, the countryside a blur flying by.

Rose's eyes were starting in her head, her expression one of ecstatic pleasure as the small whip she was carrying rose and fell.

McFarlane was appalled when Rose returned Strumpet to the stables. To bring the horse to such a state was downright cruelty.

'I'll take her out again tomorrow morning, McFarlane,' Rose announced.

'If you don't mind me saying so, the beast should have a few days' rest to recover. She's been going some.'

Rose eyed the groom coldly. 'I beg your pardon?' There was steel in her voice.

'The beast should have a few days' rest, Mrs Drummond. She might break down otherwise. That or do herself some real damage.'

'What are you implying, man?'

'Nothing, Mrs Drummond. Nothing at all,' he replied hastily. 'I'm only giving you my advice as a groom should. Whether you follows it or not is up to you.'

'Are you being impertinent, McFarlane?'

Christ, he thought. He was going to get the sack. And at his age where would he find another position? This one suited him down to the ground. 'No, Mrs Drummond. I'm sorry if it sounded that way. I certainly didn't mean it to.'

Rose relented. Perhaps Strumpet did need rest. But that wasn't a reason why she couldn't still have a ride. 'I'll take Moonbeam out then,' she said.

Moonbeam was Andrew's horse, a powerful gelding that McFarlane considered far too strong for Rose. But he had no intention of saying so, not after their last exchange. He touched his forelock. 'I'll have Moonbeam saddled and waiting, Mrs Drummond.'

'Good.'

She glanced over at Moonbeam's box, the animal staring back. A thrill of anticipation ran through her. 'You're not to mention this to Mr Drummond, understand?'

McFarlane nodded.

Now that should really be a ride, Rose thought gleefully.

Andrew was perplexed. Rose had been cold and distant all the way through dinner. You wouldn't have believed it was the same woman who'd come into his bed the night before. It was like comparing an iceberg to a fiery furnace.

'From what I'm told Nancy is doing rather well,' he said, swirling the contents of his after-dinner dram round in its glass.

Rose didn't reply. It was as though she hadn't heard.

'Rose?'

She blinked and seemed to come out of a reverie. 'Did you say something?'

'That Nancy is getting on rather well.'

'Yes. Yes she is. I'm pleased with her.'

'Is something wrong, darling?'

Rose cocked an eyebrow. 'Why do you ask that?'

'You don't seem to be . . . quite yourself this evening.'

'No?'

'No,' he stated emphatically.

'I wasn't aware of the fact.'

There it was again, that distant tone to her voice. As if

she was there and at the same time not. He had a distinct feeling of irrelevancy.

Should he or shouldn't he? He'd fully intended mentioning the previous night and how stupendous it had been, but now . . . in her present mood?

Well, of course he should. It had happened after all. It hadn't been a dream on his part. The smell of scent lingering round his bed earlier bore testimony to that. The smell of scent and his general feeling of well-being.

'Shall I now be moving back in?' he asked with a smile.

Rose stared blankly at him.

His smile began to slip. 'Shall I be moving back in, to our bedroom that is?'

She turned her face away from him, a face that had grown completely expressionless. 'Not yet, Andrew.'

'But I thought . . . hoped . . . after last night?'

'I need more time. I told you.'

'But that was before you came to me.'

'Well, it hasn't changed.'

He sighed with disappointment. 'Will you be coming again to see me?'

Rose didn't reply.

'Please say you will. For God's sake, Rose, don't make me beg. I am your husband after all.'

'Yes, you are,' she whispered.

Andrew was totally confused. What he'd thought was a break-through apparently wasn't.

'It was so good, Rose. So very good.'

She should never have gone, she thought. But she had been unable to stop herself. It was as if she'd been driven by demons.

Fear took hold of her. A fear she couldn't put a

name to. She abruptly stood. 'I'm going up now. Don't disturb me.'

'If you wish.'

She turned to look at him and for a brief moment there was a terrible torment in her eyes. Then it was gone.

'We'll work this out, Andrew, I promise.'

'I hope so.'

When he later passed her door light was showing underneath. As asked, he neither knocked nor attempted an entrance.

Heart heavy as lead he went to his own room.

'Tommy Riach walked Barbara McTaggart home from Sunday school yesterday. The second time he's done so,' Irene informed Bell who was working alongside.

That jolted Bell. 'Who's Barbara McTaggart when she's at home?' she replied nonchalantly.

'Some stuck-up cow with airs and graces. Part of the gentry. You wouldn't know her.'

'Do you?'

Irene laughed derisively, considering that a joke. 'Only what I've heard. She doesn't mix with the likes of us, the peasants.'

'And Tommy walked her home from Sunday school?'

'Twice apparently. She's a teacher there as is Tommy now.'

Bell paused momentarily to stare at her friend. 'He's what!'

'A Sunday school teacher. Joined the Holy Rollers.'

'Shit,' Bell muttered. That *was* a turn-up for the book.

'What are you two gabbing about?' Isa Weir called over.

'Don't be so bloody nosy!' Bell retorted hotly.

'Oh, pardon me for breathing,' Isa replied, voice dripping sarcasm.

They might be pals but that didn't stop Irene sticking the knife in. 'She's very pretty I hear.'

'Who?'

'Barbara McTaggart of course.' Then, teasingly, 'Do you think it's a romance?'

'How the hell should I know. I neither know nor care.'

Liar, Irene thought smugly.

There were lots of questions Bell wanted to ask, but wouldn't, not wishing to show any interest. But underneath she was upset, just as Irene had intended.

It might have been an Arctic wind blowing in as Rose entered the kitchen. A red spot on either cheek betrayed her inner fury. 'I want a word, Mrs Moffat,' she stated.

The cook, whose hands had been deep in a bowl of flour, wiped them on her pinny. 'Yes, Mrs Drummond?'

'I believe you've spoken to my husband to say you're unhappy with the way I'm managing things.'

Mrs Moffat glanced at Christine and Jamesina Laing, the latter another maid who was also present, as was Lena Johnstone the young scullery maid. Whatever was to be said should have been said to her alone and not in front of others. This was a breach of etiquette and undermined her authority.

Rose didn't give a damn about any of that, being hell-bent on having it out with the cook. 'Well?'

'Perhaps we could speak later.'

'We'll speak now!' Rose declared forcefully.

'Come on, Jamesina,' Christine whispered. It was best

they got out of there and fast. Lena, a slow but kindly girl, stood transfixed, not knowing what to do.

'Remain where you are,' Rose snapped to Christine and Jamesina who froze in their tracks.

'I have talked to Mr Drummond,' Cook acknowledged slowly. 'I considered it my duty to do so.'

'Why not me?'

'That didn't seem appropriate as it was regarding you.'

Rose took several steps forward, her gaze riveted on Mrs Moffat's eyes. 'Not up to the job any more is what I understand you said.'

Mrs Moffat blanched slightly. True enough, that was what she'd said, though not so bluntly. 'You have been ill, Mrs Drummond, and are taking some time to recover. I merely suggested it might be an idea to employ a housekeeper to take the strain off you.'

Rose's lips twisted into a sneer. 'Then *my* suggestion is that if you're unhappy here you hand in your notice.'

Mrs Moffat wasn't a woman to be bullied, not by anyone. 'I see,' she replied, anger in her voice.

'But if you do you won't be getting a letter of recommendation to take with you. Any letter I, or Mr Drummond, might write would be quite to the contrary.'

That was it as far as Mrs Moffat was concerned, her blood now up. She wasn't going to be spoken to like this, and certainly not in front of other members of staff. 'I'll pack right away,' she declared.

Christine sucked in a breath. They couldn't lose Mrs Moffat! It was unthinkable. Mrs Moffat was a brilliant cook who ran her kitchen like clockwork.

'You'll serve a month's notice. That was agreed when you were taken on,' Rose said, eyes flashing.

'Why should I bother with that when I won't be getting a letter of recommendation. Not that I need one, I have plenty others from previous employers. No, Mrs Drummond, in the circumstances I think it best I pack my bags and leave today.'

Rose hadn't been expecting this. To dismiss Mrs Moffat certainly, but not for the cook to leave virtually there and then. 'Do as you must,' she answered.

Mrs Moffat removed her apron, neatly folded it and placed it on the table. Then she swept past Rose and out of the kitchen without a backward glance.

Rose wondered why she felt defeated, as if she'd been got the better of.

Roast beef was scheduled for that evening, she remembered. That shouldn't be too difficult to cope with. She'd oversee, she decided.

'Put that apron on,' she instructed Christine. 'You're acting cook until we hire a replacement.'

'Bloody Norah,' Christine muttered when Rose too had gone.

'You did *what*!' Andrew exploded.

'You heard me. I had it out with Mrs Moffat and she resigned. She left this afternoon and good riddance I say.'

Andrew was furious. 'But she was . . .'

'I will not be criticised by any member of staff,' Rose interrupted. 'Especially behind my back. That was unforgivable.'

'It wasn't exactly a criticism, as I explained to you. She was simply showing concern and thought a housekeeper would take a weight off your shoulders.'

'Huh!' Rose sneered. 'You can be a fool at times,

Andrew. Quite naïve where women are concerned. It was criticism all right, and most unwarranted. I've been running the house perfectly.'

'Then why would she come to me?'

Rose shrugged. 'Jealousy maybe.'

That astounded Andrew. 'What on earth would she be jealous of?'

'I don't know. But I've always suspected her of being a bitch underneath, and this only proves it.'

'And you let her go without a reference?'

'She had plenty others she told me and wouldn't be needing one from us.'

'What about pay?'

'She didn't work a month's notice so forfeited anything already owed. She broke the contract, not me.'

Naïve with women – he resented that. He might have many faults but naïvety, with either gender, wasn't one of them. He thought Rose had behaved disgracefully and would never have told her of his chat with Mrs Moffat if he'd known this would be the outcome. His one consolation was that Mrs Moffat wouldn't be long out of employment, she was too good a cook for that. She had a sister in Stirling, he recalled. He would send a cheque there and ask for it to be forwarded. That and a note stating his regret at her departure.

'I've already drafted out an advertisement for a new cook,' Rose declared. 'We won't be without one for long.'

How Rose had changed since the miscarriage, Andrew thought. She'd become almost a different person, and not one he was sure he liked. He still loved Rose, there was no doubt in his mind about that. But did he like her?

That was something else again.

* * *

'I appreciate it's a silly complaint and I probably shouldn't be bothering you with it, but there we are.'

Dr Lesley regarded Andrew across his desk. 'There's nothing silly about indigestion, particularly persistent indigestion, it can be extremely painful.'

'I've tried everything I can think of but it just keeps coming back.'

Lesley nodded his sympathy. 'You've been under a great deal of pressure recently, Mr Drummond, perhaps that's the root cause. Pressure manifests itself in all manner of ways. Now what exactly have you taken?'

Andrew reeled off a list of pills and potions

'I have a mixture that's usually very helpful. We'll try that. In the meantime I suggest you eat only light meals for a while. Do you smoke?'

'No.'

'That's good. Smoking can often lead to various stomach upsets. As can alcohol. I presume you drink?'

Andrew treated the doctor to a wry smile. 'I'm a distiller, of course I drink. Whoever heard of one who doesn't.'

Lesley matched Andrew's smile. 'A rhetorical question I suppose. I'm certainly not adverse to a dram myself.'

'Drummond's I hope,' Andrew said quickly.

'Oh, always.'

'Then I'll see you get sent over a case.'

Lesley beamed. 'That's most generous of you.'

'Not at all.'

'But for now can you try and keep your consumption down to a minimum. That should also help.'

Andrew pulled a face. 'That's torture, doctor, not a cure.'

'Well, temporary torture, Mr Drummond. Just do your best.'

Lesley rose and crossed to a large, ancient, cabinet which he opened. He rummaged for several moments before finding what he was after, a bottle containing a white mixture.

'There we are,' he declared, placing it in front of Andrew. 'The instructions are on the label.'

'Thank you.'

Lesley sat again and made a pyramid with his hands. 'Now, how's Mrs Drummond?'

A look of anxiety creased Andrew's face. 'Physically she's fine. Goes out riding every day. But mentally . . .' He took a deep breath. 'She's becoming even more irrational.'

'I see,' Lesley murmured. 'And eh, relations between the pair of you. Have they resumed?'

Andrew found this line of questioning extremely difficult not to mention embarrassing. 'She did come to me one night. But one night only.'

'And was that a success?'

Andrew coloured slightly. 'Very much so. But with hindsight even that was irrational.'

'In what way?' Lesley saw Andrew's hesitation. 'I am your doctor don't forget, used to keeping confidences. The more information I have the better it is for me to diagnose correctly. Besides, I hear all sorts in this surgery. Things that would not only surprise but astound you.'

'She acted rather out of character,' Andrew stated in a low voice. 'Far more enthusiastic than I've ever known her. Quite bizarrely so when I came to think about it.'

Lesley leant back in his chair to consider that. 'The mind is a weird and wonderful device, Mr Drummond.

If only we understood it more. I think the best thing is if I pay her another call at the house.'

'You won't mention this conversation?' Andrew asked, alarmed.

'No, I'll pretend it's a routine call just like the previous one I made.'

'That's fine then,' a relieved Andrew sighed.

Mrs Drummond was beginning to worry him, Lesley reflected. Perhaps he should refer her to a specialist.

He'd decide that after he'd made his call.

'What's up with your face the night?' Agnes Mathieson, Bell's mother, demanded.

'Nothing.'

'Then why is it like fizz?'

Bell wasn't about to say why that was so. Agnes would have been mortified, not to say furious. As for her da, sitting snoring in a chair, if she'd told him what was running through her mind he'd probably have clouted her one.

She stared at Agnes's prematurely aged face, fag dangling from the corner of her mouth. Her hair was unkempt, greasy and straggly at the ends. Her dress was old and stained, fit only for the midden.

As for her da, he defied description. And he smelt abominably, but then he always had. It was a rare occurrence for him to have a bath.

Bell gazed about her. What a dump, hardly fit for pigs far less humans. Dirty too, clart everywhere. In the next room she could hear her two younger brothers going at it again. Why oh why were they forever fighting? Scruffs the pair of them.

She was the only one in the family who kept herself

decent, natural pride made her do that. The boys took
the piss from time to time but she always answered loftily
that it was because of her job. She had to be presentable
for that. It was necessary.

That usually shut them up as they knew how reliant the
family was on her regular money coming in. Without her
pay packet they'd be in a right old state and no mistake.

She thought of Tommy Riach and the lovely home he
no doubt came from. Everything there would be spick and
span, just like the home she intended keeping when she
got married.

'So why like fizz?' Agnes demanded again.

'Bad day at the distillery,' Bell lied, and shrugged.
Which satisfied Agnes who left Bell to it.

Bell closed her eyes and conjured up a picture of
Tommy. He'd be a wonderful husband. Kind, probably
generous, caring. And a good provider, unlike some she
thought, meaning her da. Oh aye, a traveller for the
distillery was bound to earn stacks.

It would be idyllic being married to Tommy. But there
was fat chance of that. The man in the moon would come
visiting first.

No, he'd probably marry this Barbara McTaggart or
someone like her. She had no chance, as Irene had told
her months back. She and Tommy Riach came from two
different worlds and nothing would ever change that.

Resentment filled her. Why couldn't she have been born
into a decent family. Why had she been landed with the
parents she had, and the background that went with them.
Life was cruel right enough.

Bell wrinkled her nose in disgust when her da broke
wind, following that up with a loud belch.

She'd go to see Irene, she decided. She had a couple

of bob in her purse and hopefully Irene might have the same. She'd suggest a visit to the pub.

Anywhere, to get away from this dump.

Rose hung up the telephone. That had been Georgina, her stepmother, wondering if she'd be interested in a shopping trip to Edinburgh. Of course she would, nothing would be nicer. And so they'd agreed to meet up the following week, booking into the same hotel where they'd spend the night.

It would be fun, she thought. And she did need some new clothes. Well, she always needed those.

Andrew was enthusiastic when she mentioned it later on that day, thinking a break from the house and Dalneil would do her the world of good.

Dr Lesley's report had been positive which had cheered him. Rose was depressed but, despite her bouts of irrationality, coping very well.

Time, Lesley had assured him. It would just take time.

'I don't know about you but I'm ready for lunch,' Georgina declared, having just bought a black gabardine suit that she considered did wonders for her figure. It had a slim little curved-in waist, big billowing push-up sleeves and a simply gorgeous jacket that flared at the sides with ripples in the back. On seeing her in it Rose had said she looked like a film star.

'There's just one other department I'd like to visit before then. You don't mind, do you?' Rose pleaded.

'My feet could do with a rest.'

'Mine too, but this won't take long. I promise you.'

Georgina heaved a sigh of resignation. 'Oh, all right. But not too long, mind.'

'You're a darling, Georgina.'

'Children's clothes?' Willie Seaton frowned.

'That's where we went. And believe me, Rose would have spent hours there if I'd let her.'

'But why on earth would she be wanting to look at children's clothes. She's not expecting again?'

'If she is she didn't mention and I didn't ask. It didn't seem right to after what she's so recently been through.'

Willie lit a cigarette. This was damned odd.

'But it didn't finish there. Later that afternoon she insisted we go into a toy shop. And again would have stayed for hours if I'd been willing.'

'You must have said something then, surely?'

'I did try to probe a little but without success. Rose wouldn't be drawn.'

'Did she buy anything?'

Georgina shook her head. 'Neither in the children's department nor the toy shop. She just seemed to want to browse.'

He regarded her steadily. 'So what did you make of it all?'

'I found it rather . . . I know she's your daughter, Willie, and this isn't exactly the nicest of words, but I found it rather creepy.'

'Creepy,' Willie mused.

'Definitely so. It quite spoilt the day for me.'

He laughed. 'It can't have spoilt it that much going by the amount of money you spent. Even by your standards you excelled yourself.'

'It's the prices, darling,' she lied smoothly. 'They've gone up dreadfully. I didn't buy more than I would normally.'

200

'Well, it's certainly your last shopping trip for a while. Another like that would bankrupt me.' The latter was nonsense of course but he felt he had to put some curb on her.

'About Rose,' she said, getting away from the subject of money. 'Do you think you should say something to Andrew?'

'I could do,' Willie replied reflectively. 'Telephone him at work and speak to him there. On the other hand, the fact she went to those places might not have any significance whatsoever.'

'It was still creepy,' Georgina insisted.

Willie wondered if his wife wasn't exaggerating matters Perhaps Rose had been searching for a present and hadn't found anything suitable.

Yes, he decided. That was far more likely to be the case.

'You sent for me, Mrs Drummond?'

'Yes I did, Nancy. I'm going to have a tea party with my dollies and thought you might like to be our guest.'

Nancy stared at Rose in amazement. 'That would be ever so nice,' she replied slowly, wondering what on earth was going on. Mrs Drummond playing with dolls!

Rose smiled beatifically. 'I brought the dolls and their house back from our visit to The Haven you know. They were mine when I was young. Did you have dolls, Nancy?'

'I'm afraid not.'

'What a pity. Such a shame. Anyway, let me introduce you to mine.'

Nancy struggled to keep a straight face. This was ridiculous. But play she would if that was what was required.

Chapter 13

'I really loathe that man,' Tommy declared vehemently, referring of course to Mr Kelly. 'He makes my life a misery.'

Babs McTaggart glanced sideways at him in amusement. He was walking her home from Sunday school as had become their weekly custom. 'Surely he can't be that bad.'

'He is, believe me. I don't know why but he has a go at me every opportunity he gets.'

'Are you sure you're not upsetting him in some way?'

'Well, if I am I'm not aware of it. I think he just doesn't like my face.'

Babs laughed. 'That's ridiculous.'

'No it's not. You must have met people you've taken an instant dislike to for no rhyme or reason. I know I have.'

Babs looked up at the sky. It was a beautiful June day, neither too hot nor cold. Just right in her opinion.

Somewhere in the distance crows were cawing, a peaceful sound she always thought.

Tommy was wondering if he dare take her hand. Up to now they had simply walked together. There hadn't been any physical contact. But what if he took her hand and she pulled it away again? How embarrassing that would be.

He thought briefly of Bell Mathieson, a different sort of girl entirely. He wouldn't have had any qualms about taking her hand. In fact, Bell would probably have taken his long before now.

'I'm enjoying this, but then I always do when I'm with you,' he heard himself saying, and blushed.

'And I enjoy being with you, Tommy,' she replied quietly.

'That's good then.'

An uneasy silence fell between them.

'I'm sorry about Mr Kelly. It must make life difficult for you,' she commented eventually.

'It does. Everything else at the distillery is fine with the exception of him. I wish he'd suddenly retire or drop down dead.'

She immediately halted and stared at him, her expression one of horror. 'You don't mean that.'

'I do.'

'No, you don't. You can't seriously wish anyone dead. That's an awful thing to say.'

He could see how deeply he'd offended her, and should have known better, Babs being a devout Christian.

'I suppose I was just letting my tongue run away with itself,' he conceded sheepishly.

'Don't forget, Tommy. "As ye give so shall ye receive", and that includes thoughts and ill wishes. They'll always come back on you.'

Her words were wounding, pointing up a charitable lack in himself. He felt ashamed.

'Still, it's only human,' she said, resuming walking. 'What we have to do is overcome those human frailties.'

'You're right, Babs. Of course you are.'

He frowned when her house came into view. It was such a short journey between the church and there and it always seemed to fly by. 'How about us walking a bit further?' he proposed.

'Oh, Tommy, I'd love to. But I have to get in. Lunch is always served promptly.'

He couldn't mask his disappointment. 'I understand.'

'It must be the same with you?'

'Well, not exactly promptly. Not on the dot so to speak. My mum is a little bit more easy going than that. But yes, there is a general time when it's dished up.'

'And your mum would hardly be pleased if you were late.'

'Hardly,' he agreed.

'There then.'

He kicked a stone which went skittering away. The rest of the day would seem interminable after this. Stretching on and on until it was time to go to bed. Sundays could be exceptionally dreary.

'Tell you what,' she said. 'We could meet up again after lunch. How about that?'

He instantly brightened. 'That would be wonderful, Babs.'

'Knock at three and I'll be ready.'

'On the dot, like your mum and her lunch.'

They both laughed.

'Where are you off to in such a hurry?' Hettie demanded.

'I'm going for a walk.'

It was quite unlike Tommy to be so eager to do that. She put two and two together and came up with four. 'Who with?'

He coloured slightly. 'Why does it have to be with someone?'

That confirmed it to her. It was a lassie all right. 'Oh, I just thought it would be, that's all.'

He briefly considered fibbing by naming Eric Taylor, on holiday from school, but decided against that. 'Anyway, I must go,' he declared, and rushed from the room.

'You thinking what I'm thinking?' Jack queried from his chair.

'A girl. No doubt about it.'

'Well, good luck to him.'

'Hopefully a lass from Sunday school. That would make sense.'

'Possibly. But don't you go interfering. Let things take their own course.'

'Interfering, me! The very idea.'

Jack chuckled. 'As if you would,' he said sarcastically.

At least she could find out who the girl was, Hettie thought. A wee word here and there would soon give her the answer.

They stopped under a large chestnut tree, one of the very few in the area. 'I used to come here for conkers when I was a lad,' Tommy said. 'Me and my pal Eric. We both climbed up it once and I fell out. I was lucky I didn't hurt myself.'

He gazed up into the branches in fond memory, remembering the sheer terror he'd felt when he'd slipped and gone plunging earthwards. He'd laughed about it afterwards but it hadn't been funny at the time.

'Did you steep your conkers in vinegar? I believe that's what you do to make them really hard.'

'Sometimes. Other times I baked them in the oven. It's considered cheating but I used to do it nonetheless.'

'I doubt there'll be any chestnut trees in Africa,' she said, tongue firmly in cheek.

'Africa?' For the moment he couldn't see the connection.

'When you go there as an explorer and big-game hunter.'

He realised he was being teased. 'But all sorts of other trees. The exotic kind. All shapes, sizes and colours of the rainbow. They'll be a wonderful sight.'

'What about snakes?' She shuddered. 'I've never seen a live one but the very thought . . .' She broke off and shuddered again.

'They've got snakes there that eat you alive,' he informed her. 'I read that in a book. Some poor chap went to sleep and when he woke up a huge snake had swallowed most of his leg.'

'You're having me on!'

'It's true,' he protested. 'They had to kill the snake and cut it in two lengthways to release his leg which was already part digested.'

Babs grimaced in disgust. 'And you seriously want to go to a place like that?'

'Oh yes, and I will. It'll be the most terrific adventure. The sort most people only dream about.'

Dream, she thought, not for the first time. That described Tommy perfectly, a dreamer. Well, it was no bad thing. Dreams of that nature were harmless, if kept in perspective. The reality of life invariably proved quite different.

Tommy found himself staring at her bosom, a gentle swell beneath her dress. He couldn't help but wonder what it would be like to . . .

'Tommy?'

He roused himself. 'Sorry.'

'What a strange expression you had on your face.'

'Did I?' he queried, pretending innocence.

'You looked transfixed.'

Transfixed in imagination, he thought. Most definitely so.

She moved closer. 'Are you all right?'

'Yes I . . .' He couldn't stop himself, didn't want to. His arm curled round her waist bringing her into an embrace. Her eyes opened wide but she didn't protest.

Then his lips were seeking hers, and finding them.

'Drew, I wish you'd stop following me around everywhere. It's very disconcerting.'

The boy shuffled his feet.

'Can't you find something to do?' Andrew asked mildly.

Drew glanced up at his mother, guilt heavy within him. If it hadn't been for him she'd never have lost the baby. The fault for that was all his.

'Well?' Andrew prompted.

'I've been thinking, Dad.'

'Yes?'

'As I'm going to be taking over the distillery one day I'd like to spend time there. Get to know how everything works.'

Andrew stared at his son in astonishment. 'But you're only eleven.'

'I know that. But you're never too young to learn, you've said so yourself.'

Andrew laughed. He had indeed. 'Rose?'

'Anything to stop him trailing around after me and continually getting under my feet.'

Andrew couldn't think what he could possibly find for Drew to do at the distillery, but no doubt he'd come up with something. And if he didn't, someone else would.

It pleased him, no, it delighted him, that the lad was showing an interest in his inheritance. No more talk about possibly doing something else when he was older. What a relief that was.

'Right then,' he stated. 'You can come with me in the morning. How's that?'

'Does that make you happy, Mummy?'

The question startled Rose. 'Yes, of course it does if it means I won't have you plaguing me for a while.'

Drew beamed, first at her then at his father.

'What are you up to?' It was early evening and Andrew had found Rose sitting in the garden.

'Just enjoying the sun,' she replied dreamily.

'Well, don't take too much of it. I don't want you spoiling that gorgeous complexion of yours.'

Her laugh was a bright tinkle. 'We hardly get enough sun in this part of the world for it to do that.'

'Even though. I don't want you even beginning to go brown. I prefer you the way you are.'

He could be so sweet, she thought. It was lovely.

'We're interviewing tomorrow,' she said. 'Or at least I am. There's no need for you to be involved unless you insist.'

'Aah, the new cook.'

'There are three applicants. On paper all of them are suitable. I suppose it's down to the one I consider will fit in best.'

Andrew sat on the bench beside her. 'I've been thinking about what Mrs Moffat said. Perhaps we should get a housekeeper.'

Rose's mood instantly changed. 'Are you also saying I'm not up to it any more?'

'No, I'm saying it might be too much for you right now. You have been through a lot recently, darling. You should be taking things easy. The housekeeping is a full-time job after all. I just don't want you tiring yourself out.'

That mollified Rose a little. 'I'm quite capable, Andrew. Honestly.'

'I've never doubted that for a moment, Rose. But I do think we should consider the matter. Even if it's only a temporary arrangement.'

Maybe she should agree, she reflected. Truth was, though she'd never admit it after what had happened with Mrs Moffat, she'd begun to find the housekeeping not tiring but boring, irksome. There were occasions, which didn't use to be the case, when she'd been going about those duties when she'd much rather have been doing something else. Riding, for example.

'I'll think about it,' she prevaricated.

'Good, Rose.'

'But only think, mind. I'm not agreeing to anything yet.'

'I'm sure your decision, whatever it is, will be the right one.' He paused, then said, 'There's something else I've been meaning to speak to you about.'

'Oh?'

'Why don't you and I go away for a holiday. Just the pair of us.'

Alarm flared in her. That would be awful. The two of them together morning, noon and – most importantly of all – night. Nights during which he'd undoubtedly want to share a bed.

She saw this for what it was. A ploy for them to resume regular lovemaking. The very thought made her wince inside.

'To where?' she asked.

'Anywhere you like. Abroad if you wish. It's entirely up to you.'

Rose took a deep breath. A holiday would be wonderful, but not under these conditions. Despair filled her. She did love Andrew, loved him dearly. But she didn't want him in her bed or to be with him all day long. The prospect was a nightmare.

'What about the distillery?' she queried, knowing how loath he was to leave it for any length of time.

'I'll sort matters out so that it'll run smoothly while we're gone. Kelly will manage just fine. It'll all be tickety-boo.'

Rose hung her head, horribly aware this had been proposed entirely for her benefit. 'I'd rather not if you don't mind, Andrew,' she said quietly.

'I see.'

'I . . .' She was frantically trying to come up with an acceptable excuse. 'I don't feel up to that yet. Perhaps next year.'

'Of course, darling.'

'I'm sorry.'

He reached over and took her hand in his. 'Don't worry about it. It was only a suggestion, that's all.'

'And a kind one too. I appreciate it.'

'But if you don't want to go then we won't. I fully understand.'

He was smiling, but she didn't miss the hurt in his eyes.

'I need some fags,' Irene announced, as she and Bell made their way home from work.

'And I want to buy a packet of kirbys. I keep losing the damn things.'

'I know what you mean. I'm just the same.'

Bell yawned. She was tired. Every day at the distillery was long but this one, for some reason, had seemed even longer. She'd wash her hair after tea and then have an early night. She smiled in anticipation.

When they reached the village shop they went inside, Bell collecting a packet of grips and joining the end of the waiting queue.

'That's her being served,' Irene whispered conspiratorially.

Bell was mystified. 'Who?'

'Barbara McTaggart, the lassie Tommy's been seeing.'

All Bell could make out was the back of a head and the top part of what looked like a rather expensive dress. 'Are you sure?'

'Oh, aye.'

'I thought you didn't know her?'

'Only by sight. That's her all right.'

Come on, Bell mentally urged. Turn round. She wanted a good look at the face.

'Thank you,' Babs said, picking up her change.

Mrs Wilson, who ran the shop with her husband, muttered something in reply.

Babs left the queue, halting to put the coins into her purse.

Well, she was no raving beauty, Bell thought with satisfaction. Not nearly as pretty as she'd been led to believe by Irene. But she was no gargoyle either. You could never say that about her.

Babs walked past them and straight out of the shop.

'What do you think?' Irene queried.

Bell shrugged.

'A wee bit jealous perhaps?'

Bell could have smacked her friend, for Irene was right. She was jealous. 'Of that? You must be joking.'

'It was a lovely dress she had on.'

'I never really noticed,' Bell lied.

'Classy. I bet that cost a bob or two.'

'It didn't suit her in my opinion. Wrong colour.'

'Ooh, I wouldn't say so.'

'Well I would,' Bell snapped.

Irene smiled. 'You *are* jealous.'

'I am nothing of the sort. Jealousy doesn't enter into it. If that's what Tommy fancies then good luck to him.'

'Well, I will say this for you, Master Drummond, you're not shy of work.'

Drew beamed at Ramsay Dodds whose job it was to fuel the peat furnaces. 'This isn't work, it's fun. I'm thoroughly enjoying myself.'

Ramsay laughed. It was hard graft as far as he was concerned, but then he had to do it day in day out.

Drew gazed into the flames dancing before him. What a strange mystical land this all was, he thought, one he found fascinating. It was a pity he'd have to go back to school at the end of the summer. He'd happily have continued on at the distillery.

How could he have considered doing anything else? he wondered. What a mistake that would have been. He knew with utter certainty that he'd been born to be a distiller, the latest in a long line of them.

It was as though . . . he'd somehow come home.

'Ah, Tommy, it's you. Come in.'

Andrew laid aside the pen he'd been using and smiled at Tommy now standing at his desk. 'How are you getting on then?'

'Fine, thank you very much.'

Andrew nodded his approval. 'The reason I've asked you here is that I want you to take a correspondence course.'

Tommy frowned. 'Correspondence course?'

'That's right. It's about distilling, of course, theory and practice, that sort of thing. I did the same course myself years ago and loved every minute of it. Found it most rewarding as I'm sure you will. I'll pay the fees naturally, so it won't cost you anything. Now, what do you say?'

'Yes please,' Tommy replied enthusiastically.

Andrew passed over a slip of paper. 'That's the name and address of the firm that runs the course. Write to them for an application form. When it's time to return the form come back and see me again and I'll give you a cheque to accompany it. All right?'

'I'll write this evening.'

'Good. The very dab.'

'I'll get on about my business then.'

Tommy was continuing to do well, Andrew reflected as the door snicked shut. He must mention it to Jack when they next met up.

* * *

'Why are you so restless?' Hettie queried of Jack, who was silently drumming his fingers on the arm of his chair.

'I look forward to my Friday night visits to the pub with Andrew. Only he's away for a few days and I don't like going on my own.' He didn't suggest Hettie accompany him; women of her age and standing in the village simply didn't enter pubs.

'I'll go with you, Dad, if you like,' Tommy volunteered.

'You!' Hettie exclaimed in surprise.

'Why not? If Dad wants company.'

'They wouldn't serve you.'

'Oh yes they will, as long as I behave myself and don't go daft.'

'And how do you know that?'

'I've heard, Mum.'

'Just heard?' she queried pointedly.

'Just heard. Now how about it, Dad?'

Jack came to his feet, thrilled at the idea of visiting the pub with his son. 'Let's get a move on then.'

Hettie sighed. Another sign of how grown up Tommy was becoming. She and Jack had been talking about that only the other night. He'd come on a great deal since starting at Drummond's, something of which they both heartily approved.

But the pub? She wasn't so sure about that.

'There you are, Dad,' Tommy said, placing a pint and chaser in front of Jack. He then returned to the bar for his own pint.

'It's crowded tonight,' Jack commented when Tommy rejoined him.

Tommy glanced around. The pub was rather full, though he couldn't have said whether that was normally the case or not. There were quite a few people he recognised.

There hadn't been any problem at the bar. He'd merely given his order then paid for it when it arrived. Nothing untoward had been said.

'*Slainthe!*' Jack muttered, tasting his whisky.

'*Slainthe,*' Tommy responded.

Jack cleared his throat. 'Well, this is a new experience for you, eh?'

'It is indeed, Dad.'

'So what do you think?'

Tommy grinned. 'I like it.'

'Aye well, just don't make a habit of coming, that's all. Apart from anything else pubs are expensive. You can't afford them.'

Not on a regular basis anyway, Tommy thought. But once in a while wouldn't do any harm. Especially as there wasn't any objection to his being served. It was just as Bell had said.

Tommy had no sooner thought of her than she appeared with her friend Irene, the pair of them all dolled up. Tommy hadn't realised it was dance night which was where Bell and Irene were ultimately headed.

'There's Isa and Ronnie,' Irene gestured. They made their way over.

'You've gone quiet all of a sudden,' Jack commented to Tommy.

'Sorry.'

'Seen someone you know?'

'There are a few people from the distillery here.'

'Oh aye?'

'No one in particular,' he lied. He certainly wasn't going to mention Bell who he thought was looking rather stunning.

'David, this is Bell and Irene,' Ronnie declared, introducing the chap with him and Isa.

'How do you do,' David smiled.

'David comes from Auchgloan. He's my cousin.' Auchgloan was a village about ten miles away.

'I can see the family resemblance,' Irene said.

'Aye, there is a likeness,' David acknowledged, thinking that Bell was a cracker. He'd fallen on his feet here.

Bell was staring over David's shoulder at Tommy. With his father, she saw. Barbara McTaggart nowhere in evidence. There again, you would hardly expect the likes of Barbara McTaggart to come into a common pub. A madam like her wouldn't be seen dead in one.

'So what are you ladies having?' David queried, eyes fixed firmly on Bell.

'Mine's a gin and orange,' Irene replied.

'And you, Bell?'

She brought her attention back to him. 'The same please. That's very kind of you.'

'Not at all. The pleasure's all mine.'

Isa winked at Bell when David went up to the bar, having noticed the interest he had in her. 'It should be a good dance tonight, eh?'

'He fancies you,' Irene whispered to Bell, disappointed, for she'd fancied him.

'I'll give David a hand,' Ronnie declared, and left the three of them together.

Bell was aware of Tommy watching her and wondered what he was thinking. Well, he wasn't the only one who could get a click. By God and he wasn't. She'd show him all right.

'What does David do?' Irene inquired of Isa.

'He's a postman.'

'A postman!' Irene exclaimed. 'He doesn't look like one.'

'And what exactly does a postman look like,' Bell said sarcastically. 'Is there a type?'

'He gets paid good money,' Isa informed them.

'Is that a fact,' nodded Bell.

'More than Ronnie gets at the distillery. Quite a bit more.'

'And he's free I take it?' That was Irene.

'He was going out with someone but that's finished. He's been down in the dumps which is why Ronnie invited him here tonight.'

David turned from the bar and smiled directly at Bell. There was no mistaking he was keen.

'Jammy sod,' Irene muttered, meaning Bell.

He was attractive, Bell thought. And seemed pleasant enough. A surreptitious sideways glance told her Tommy was still watching.

'Here we are then,' David said, appearing beside them holding two glasses. He handed the first to Bell.

Bell made up her mind. A click was on offer and a click it would be. To hell with Tommy Riach and his stuck-up fancy piece. He could go and take a running jump as far as she was concerned.

'Thank you very much,' Bell murmured coyly.

'As I said, the pleasure's all mine.'

Bell gave him a winsome smile. This was a fish that wouldn't take much landing. She'd have him firmly netted before they even left for the dance.

* * *

'Another?' Jack asked Tommy.

'If you're having one.'

Jack chuckled. 'Damned right I am.' He groped for his wallet. 'Will you go up or shall I?'

'I'll go again, Dad. It's a bit of a scrum over there.'

'There's a quid then. And don't forget my dram.'

When Tommy returned to the table it was to note that the chap Bell was talking to had his arm round her waist.

He forced himself to concentrate on what his father was saying.

Chapter 14

'I'm not interrupting, am I?'

'Not at all, Andrew,' Jack replied enthusiastically. 'Have a pew.'

Andrew handed Hettie the bottle of Drummond he'd brought with him. 'As you can see, I've come bearing gifts.'

Hettie laughed. 'There was no need for this, Andrew. We always have some in the house.'

'What's that?' Jack queried.

Hettie explained.

Jack rubbed his hands together. 'Just the thing. Get pouring, woman. And make them large ones.'

'Mine too,' Tommy chipped in, knowing there was little likelihood of that.

'You'll take what you're given and be thankful,' Hettie admonished him.

Andrew sighed. He was weary and troubled. He'd tried to talk to Rose but she'd been in one of her

219

unreceptive moods so in the end he'd given up and come to Jack's.

'Is there anything special on your mind?' Jack asked softly.

'It's going to be war, Jack. There's no doubt about it.'

Jack's expression became grim in the extreme. 'I agree, if the papers are anything to go by. Not to mention the news broadcasts. This nonsense in Danzig is going to be the spark that'll light the whole bag of fireworks.'

A wide-eyed Tommy sat listening to this. War!

'Hitler's a bloody maniac,' Andrew went on. 'Has he forgotten what it was like the last time? The damned man was in it, after all.'

Andrew accepted the glass Hettie gave him, noting that she had indeed poured large ones.

'Well, I won't be fighting this time,' Jack said gravely. Then, with a bitter laugh, 'I don't suppose they'll have any use for blind folk.'

'You've done your bit. And paid the price,' Hettie declared. 'And a high price it was too.'

'Aye, it was that,' Jack murmured.

'The crass stupidity of it all!' Andrew suddenly exploded. 'It makes my blood boil.'

Jack had a swallow of whisky, and shuddered. The shudder had nothing to do with alcohol. So many lives had already been lost, thrown away, and for what? So it could be done all over again it would seem.

Hettie placed a weak drink beside Tommy, trying not to think of his being caught up in all this. The thought made her feel sick inside, and scared. Not for herself of course, but for Tommy.

'What about you? What will you do?' Jack queried of Andrew.

'If they want me they can have me. Though I doubt they will. They'll wish me to stay put and run the distillery. I will lose men though, that's what happened in the last show. Some are bound to join up which will cause me problems. Still, we managed before and no doubt will do so again.'

'War,' Jack breathed. It seemed incredible.

'It still might not happen,' Hettie said tremulously. 'It's all supposition so far.'

'Anything's possible,' Jack demurred. 'Even miracles. And that's what it's going to take for war to be avoided.'

A thrill of excitement ran through Tommy. This could be the biggest adventure of all. 'How long will it last for, do you think?'

'Till it's finished, lad,' Jack replied heavily.

'Could we possibly lose?' Hettie queried.

Neither Jack nor Andrew replied. The possibility of that was horrendous. Life under the German jackboot would be intolerable.

'Well?' Hettie prompted.

'No,' Jack growled. 'By God and all his Angels we won't.'

Andrew wished he could be so certain about that.

'This is Miss Campbell, the new housekeeper,' Rose declared.

Andrew gave her a slight nod of recognition. 'Miss Campbell.'

'Pleased to meet you, sir.'

'And you, Miss Campbell.'

She wasn't at all what Andrew had expected. She was a lot younger for a start, and rather pretty in a bony-faced way. How old? He judged her to be in her early thirties.

She had raven-black hair cut just above shoulder length and was well breasted, her bosom amply filling the top of the black uniform she wore. Her hands were long and graceful, ivory coloured as opposed to pink. They rather fascinated Andrew.

'I hope you'll enjoy life here,' Andrew said.

'I'm sure I will, sir.'

'And where were you before?'

She told him, naming a place he'd never heard of, which she said was in Fyfe. Andrew wondered why she'd left there. He'd ask Rose later when they were alone.

'Well, what did you think?'

'She's fine. Though I have to say rather young in my opinion,' Andrew replied.

'She is young I admit, though I fail to see why that should stand against her. All I care about is her being up to the job, which I'm certain she will be.'

'Why did she leave her previous position?'

'She wanted a change, that was all. She fully understands the post is only temporary which she said suits her for the time being. We were fortunate to get her actually. The applications weren't exactly thick on the ground. Because the post is only temporary, I suppose.'

'I really am pleased you've hired someone, Rose. I'm sure it's the right thing to do.'

Rose had thought long and hard before making her mind up on the subject, but once decided had felt a lot better for it. For the present anyway she didn't have any housekeeping worries to contend with which was an enormous relief.

'I'm considering taking up painting,' she announced.

That surprised Andrew. Rose had never shown any artistic leanings in the past. 'Painting, eh?'

'Landscapes in watercolour. I think I'll rather like that.'

'Whatever, Rose, if it makes you happy then it does me. When do you intend starting?'

'I've already written to a shop in Edinburgh telling them my requirements which they will be forwarding on.'

'You *are* organised.' Andrew smiled, still bemused by this. But he certainly approved of her new project and wondered what standard of paintings she'd produce.

'I'll tell you what,' he enthused. 'If you're good we can perhaps arrange to have them shown in a gallery.'

Rose blushed. 'Don't get carried away, Andrew. Displayed indeed! I doubt it'll come to that.'

'You never know, Rose. You never know.'

Rose laughed, and for the space of a few moments it was like old times between them.

Moments that Andrew brought to a halt when he reached out to touch her and she flinched away.

It was nine o'clock on a Wednesday evening, bath night for Nancy. Something she always looked forward to.

She locked the door of the staff bathroom carefully behind her and then set down the towel and other things she'd brought along.

The bath itself was a huge, ornate affair which she now began filling. Clouds of steam billowed upwards as water cascaded from the silver-coloured taps.

There was an ancient wicker chair which Nancy threw her dressing gown over leaving her standing in her nightdress. As it was already warm in the room, thanks to heating pipes that ran along one of the walls, and getting warmer by the second, the nightdress swiftly followed the dressing gown.

Naked, she lifted her arms above her head and stretched. Smiling in anticipation of the long soak that lay ahead.

Crossing back to the bath she tested the water, judging the mix just right. She was standing upright again when she paused, thinking she'd heard a noise.

Nancy frowned. If she had heard something it certainly hadn't come from the bathroom as she was quite alone. Imagination, she mentally shrugged. Unless the noise had come from out in the corridor.

She started to hum, a folk tune she'd known for years and was a favourite of hers.

She laid her soap on the edge of the bath, and her flannel alongside. Then she scratched her bottom as the bath continued to fill.

There it was again! The same sound as before. Like . . . she wasn't sure.

Panic suddenly flared in her causing her to gasp. Surely there weren't mice in the bathroom. Or worse still, rats. Despite her country upbringing she'd always had a horror and fear of both, particularly the latter.

Quickly she looked under the bath but there was no sign there of either. She then scanned the rest of the room.

Nancy shivered, recalling a bondager friend of hers who'd once been bitten by a rat. A monstrous black brute who'd torn a chunk out of the lassie's leg before being dispatched by one of the men present at the time.

That had been horrible. It had taken them ages to calm the hysterical lassie down. Luckily the wound had healed without becoming infected. The bite from a rat could prove fatal.

There it was again! Coming from the nearer of the two old disused metal lockers standing against the rear wall. She grabbed her dressing gown and hastily put it on.

What to do? Call for help or investigate herself? She decided to investigate.

She glanced around for a weapon but there wasn't one. This was daft, she thought as she slowly approached the lockers. What if there *was* a bloody rat!

She stopped in front of the locker in question and listened. If she heard a scurrying from inside, or that of claws on metal, then she was off. Out of there like a flash.

What she did hear surprised her. Surely it couldn't be. But it damn well was. Heavy breathing.

'Right,' she muttered, angry now. Grabbing the locker handle she turned it and yanked the door open.

'Master Drewl'

He blinked at her, clearly terrified at having been found out.

'What are you doing in there?'

'I . . . I . . .' He swallowed hard.

It was blindingly obvious why he'd hidden in the locker which had a series of small holes three quarters of the way up the door. 'You were spying, you little swine,' she hissed.

'Please, Nancy, don't tell Dad. *Please.*' Tears welled in his eyes to fall tumbling down his cheeks.

'Get out of there while I decide what to do with you.'

He emerged from the locker and backed away from her. 'I'm sorry, Nancy. Really I am. Please don't tell Dad.'

She pulled the dressing gown more tightly about her. To think he'd been watching while she'd been standing there without a stitch on. Getting a right eyeful.

'I've . . . I've . . .' He gulped. 'I've never seen a naked woman before.'

Her face softened. It was quite funny really. Though unforgivable too.

225

'And I so wanted to see you, Nancy. You're so beautiful.'

'With or without my clothes on?' she replied tartly.

'Both, Nancy. I think you're wonderful.'

She wagged a finger at him. 'Spying like that. It's . . . disgusting.'

'I'm sorry.'

'No you're not. I can see it in your face. The only thing you're sorry about is being caught.'

He hung his head in shame.

Nancy took a deep breath. If she reported this God knew what his father would do to him. And it was innocent enough when you thought about it. A young boy's curiosity, that's all.

'And you are beautiful,' he insisted, head still hung.

'Am I indeed?'

'Oh yes. None of the other maids is nearly so pretty.'

She should be flattered, she thought, for him to have taken such a risk on her account. She was strangely moved.

'Do you forgive me, Nancy?'

'I don't know,' she replied hesitantly.

'Please do. And please don't tell Dad. I'd be so ashamed.'

'With a sore backside into the bargain no doubt.'

'Yours was gorgeous.'

She couldn't believe he'd said that. 'What!'

He looked up at her, mischief and lust in his eyes, the tears now gone. He was his father's son after all. 'Your bottom, Nancy. It was gorgeous.'

She opened her mouth to speak, but couldn't think of a thing to say.

'I'm going to marry you when I grow up.'

Nancy burst out laughing. This was getting ridiculous. 'Don't be soft, Drew. Your sort don't marry the likes of me.'

'But I will,' he stated stubbornly. 'I decided so weeks ago.'

The bath! She'd forgotten about that. Whirling, she hurried back to it and turned off the taps. Fortunately it hadn't overflowed.

'Nancy?'

She turned to find him behind her. 'What?'

'Can I have another look?'

His gall was amazing. Imagine him asking that? 'No you can't,' she snapped.

'You're not that much older than me you know. Only a few years.'

True enough, she reflected, somewhat in surprise. Well, it may only be a few years but there was a world of difference between them. She was a fully mature woman who'd lived with a man, while Drew was no more than a schoolboy.

She stared in astonishment when he reached out and covered her breast. He gently squeezed before she shrugged his hand away.

'You'd better go,' she said.

'You won't tell anyone, will you?'

She shook her head.

'Let me see you again, Nancy. I beg you.'

Beg! No one had ever begged her for anything in her life. Up until now that was. It was rather nice to be begged.

She didn't know why she did it, sheer madness she thought. Slowly she undid her dressing gown and held it open.

Drew sucked in a breath as he stared at her nakedness.

Then the vision was gone, Nancy's dressing gown firmly wrapped round her again.

'Now go,' she said.

At the door he turned to smile beguilingly at her. 'I will marry you, Nancy Thompson. I will.'

When he'd left she relocked the door and leant against it. She was trembling she noted. Excited too.

What to make of all this? she wondered. What indeed.

For Drew the episode with Nancy was a watershed. Childhood was gone, adulthood beckoned. Overnight he'd acquired a maturity that belied his years. He might still be only eleven, but he was a very different eleven to the one who'd climbed into the locker.

Nor had he lied to Nancy about wanting to marry her. He fully intended that he would one day.

It was only a matter of time and patience.

Tommy wiped sweaty palms on the back of his jacket, nervous as all get out at the prospect of having afternoon tea with the McTaggarts.

He cleared his throat, adjusted his tie, and then knocked. He could only pray he was going to pass muster and that they approved of him. This was a test, as he was well aware.

It was Babs herself who answered. 'Hello, Tommy,' she smiled.

'Hello, Babs. I hope I'm not late.'

'You're . . . right on the dot.'

They both laughed which made Tommy relax a little.

'Come on through then.'

He carefully wiped his shoes before stepping inside.

*   *   *

Barney McTaggart was younger than his own father, and rapidly balding. He was a tall, slim man with a fierce gaze and ruddy complexion. Tommy found him extremely daunting.

'A sandwich, Tommy?' The speaker was Anne McTaggart, slim like her husband and wearing spectacles. Despite the latter it was clear where Babs got her good looks from, and it wasn't Barney!

'Please, Mrs McTaggart.'

'Cucumber and cress or egg?'

'Cucumber and cress would be lovely.'

Tommy was horribly aware that Mr McTaggart had been studying him keenly ever since his arrival. He wished the damned man wouldn't be so blatant about it. It was most off-putting, making him feel like a specimen under a microscope.

'We grow the cucumber ourselves in our vegetable garden,' Mrs McTaggart informed Tommy, handing him a plate. Tea had already been poured, Tommy electing Indian rather than the China also on offer.

'Are you interested in gardening?' Mr McTaggart inquired.

'I'm afraid not, sir.'

'Hmmh, maybe later on in life. It's a wonderful hobby which Anne and I both thoroughly enjoy.'

'Delicious,' Tommy commented after tasting the sandwich.

Mrs McTaggart beamed.

'Tommy and I are going for a walk after tea,' Babs announced.

Mr McTaggart raised an eyebrow but didn't comment.

'That's nice, dear,' Mrs McTaggart said instead.

Tommy couldn't wait for the walk and to escape from the house. This was awful.

'And how do you like being at Drummond's?' Mr McTaggart inquired.

'Just fine, sir.'

'You're going eventually to be a traveller I understand.'

'That's right, sir.'

Mr McTaggart grunted, a neutral sound that was neither approval nor disapproval. Or if it was either that much wasn't apparent to Tommy.

'You're also a Sunday school teacher,' Mr McTaggart went on.

'Still learning to be one, sir.'

'Most commendable.'

'Thank you.'

Babs sipped her tea, eyes sparkling across the room at Tommy. They'd be going to their favourite spot for more kisses and cuddles. She was looking forward to that and had been since the previous week and their last visit there.

Like wading through mud, Tommy was thinking. He wasn't finding this easy at all.

The next moment a door banged shut. 'My brother Gerald,' Babs explained. 'He always does that. Bang the outside door I mean.'

'Terrible habit,' Mr McTaggart muttered. 'Never been able to break him of it.'

It was news to Tommy that Babs had a brother. She'd never mentioned him.

The chap who breezed into the room was in his early twenties and dressed in the uniform of the RAF. 'Ah, just in time for tiffin I see,' he declared, rubbing his hands vigorously together. 'I hope there are crumpets and strawberry jam, Mater. That would be just the ticket.'

'Of course there are, Gerald,' Mrs McTaggart replied. 'Let me introduce you to Tommy Riach, Barbara's friend.'

Tommy laid his plate aside, stood up and shook Gerald's hand. 'Are you a flying officer?' he asked, almost overcome with awe.

'That's right, Hurricanes. I'm on a spot of leave.'

Shaking hands and talking to a real live pilot. Tommy was stunned. He was remembering the Spitfire he'd once watched, what a beauty that had been.

'Wouldn't you prefer Spits?' he queried.

Gerald laughed. 'Damned fine machines, best in the world at what they do. But give me Hurrys any day.'

'Aren't they slower?'

'I hope we're not going to talk air force,' Mr McTaggart said. Then, to Tommy, 'That's all we have morning, noon and night when Gerald's home.'

'Sorry, Pater,' Gerald apologised.

Tommy's face had fallen. There was nothing he'd have liked better than to talk air force, as Mr McTaggart had put it.

'I'd love to be a flyer myself,' he stuttered.

'Really?'

'Oh yes. It must be marvellous.'

Babs thought of teasing him by saying she'd understood he wanted to be an African explorer and big-game hunter, but decided that might be too embarrassing for him. She certainly knew how her father would react. He'd think Tommy was off his chump and she didn't wish that.

Gerald glanced at his father, then turned his attention again to Tommy. 'I have some pictures up in my room. Would you care to see them?'

'Oh, yes please.'

'Spiffing. Just let me grab some tea and eats and then

up we'll jolly well go. I've not only pictures taken round the various 'dromes I've been at but also models that might interest you.'

'They would indeed,' Tommy answered enthusiastically.

As far as he was concerned what had been a rather dismal and uncomfortable occasion had suddenly become transformed.

'Your brother's a smashing bloke. I liked him enormously,' Tommy said to Babs as they were leaving the house.

'You were certainly up in his room long enough. I was beginning to think you'd forgotten all about our walk.'

Their walk had been the furthest thing from his mind when he'd been with Gerald, Tommy reflected. Though he wasn't about to admit that. He'd only remembered about it again when they'd eventually rejoined the others.

'Not me,' he lied. 'But your brother was jolly interesting.'

Babs glanced sideways at him. 'Up in the wild blue yonder were you?' she teased.

'Something like that,' Tommy admitted sheepishly.

She hooked an arm round his. 'You really are adorable, Tommy Riach. Quite scrummy.'

'You're fairly scrummy yourself, Babs.'

'Am I really?' she queried coyly.

'As scrummy as they come.'

'Go on, you're just saying that.'

'I am nothing of the sort! Cross my heart and hope to die.'

That filled her with the most wonderful warm glow. She pulled herself even closer to him. 'My parents took to you.'

That mildly surprised him, remembering Mr McTaggart's unrelenting fierce gaze. 'Did they?'

'Very much so. Believe me, I can read the signs. They took to you all right. Mind you, in all honesty, being the son of a rich and famous author helps.'

She laughed at the expression on his face. 'I only said it helps, Tommy. Not that it was the be all and end all. If they hadn't found you personable and acceptable I'd have picked it up. Especially from my dad, he'd probably just have upped and left us to it.'

Tommy closed his eyes for a brief moment, visualising the Spitfire he'd seen.

He decided he must read up more about Hurricanes. Fantastic planes, according to Gerald.

The flesh pressed against his was hot and burning, the hand caressing him promising delights to come.

Andrew smiled in his sleep. This was wonderful, so real it could have actually been happening.

Now a voice was crooning in his ear, whispering his name over and over. A tongue flickered in the same ear, darting sensuously in and out.

He shivered, feeling himself respond. 'Rose,' he heard himself whisper. 'Oh Rose.'

'Wake up, Andrew. Wake up.'

He didn't want to do that and lose this erotic angel. And yet still the voice was urging him to do so.

'Andrew.'

There was a little nip which made him jerk and his eyes flew open. The face peering into his was no fantasy, no figment of the imagination. He hadn't been dreaming at all.

'Rose?'

She was breathing heavily and even though it was dark in his bedroom he could make out that her eyes were dilated, nostrils flared.

'Oh, my darling Andrew.'

His hands were moving now, touching a breast, rubbing a nipple, the urgency in him growing with every passing second.

'Now,' she commanded in a rasping tone. 'Now!'

He twisted her on to her back, moved on top of her and thrust hard.

Rose screamed in ecstasy.

As had happened before, she was gone when he awoke in the morning. And, as before, all that remained was the sweet smell of her scent.

'Christ,' he muttered. Talk about wild abandon, she'd been positively demonic in her demands. How long had it gone on for? Must have been hours. Hours and hours.

He moved and winced, then remembered the fingernails slicing their way down his back. Not once, but over and over. His buttocks were also lacerated.

The previous visitation had been unbelievable, but last night surpassed even that. Vastly experienced as he was he'd never known anything like it.

Just what in hell was going on? he asked himself. Time after time it was the cold shoulder, not wanting to know. And then suddenly, out of nowhere, two visitations that were extraordinary to say the least.

How often had she told him she loved him? Again and again. And yet he'd be willing to bet if he met her over breakfast she'd be as distant as usual. Polite, pleasant, but distant.

The contrast between that Rose and the one who'd

shared his bed was incredible. It was as if they were two different women entirely. Jekyll and Hyde.

Yes, he thought. That was exactly it. A female Jekyll and Hyde.

He didn't know what to make of all this. He didn't at all. He was completely and utterly lost.

He'd speak to Lesley again. Well, he'd been going to visit the doctor anyway as his indigestion had returned even more severely than before.

But for now, for the moment, he was just going to lie there and savour the memories.

And what delicious memories they were.

Delicious, yet somewhat frightening too.

Chapter 15

'Here's the breakfast tray you asked for, Mrs Drummond.'

'Thank you, Nancy. Just put it on the bed and I'll have it shortly.'

Rose peered into the mirror of her vanity table and frowned. What was wrong with her today, she was all fingers and thumbs. She sighed in exasperation.

'Will there be anything else, Mrs Drummond?'

Rose swivelled round to stare at Nancy. 'Are you any good with hair?'

Nancy blinked. 'I beg your pardon?'

'I said, are you any good with hair?'

'I don't know. I mean . . . I just do my own, that's all.'

Rose decided she wanted company, and Nancy's was always pleasant. Nancy . . . somehow brought her comfort. Eased the terrible pain that gnawed at her day and night. Nancy whom she sometimes thought of as . . .

'Well come over here and see what you can do with mine.'

Nancy gulped. 'Oh I couldn't do that, Mrs Drummond. I'd be too scared to even try.'

That amused Rose. 'Brave heart, Nancy, brave heart. Have a go.'

Nancy was still hesitant. Rose had such beautiful hair which was usually immaculate. For her to put her mitts on it seemed a sacrilege.

'Come on, I won't bite.'

Nancy moved to a position directly behind Rose who handed her a large tortoiseshell comb.

'Pins, brushes, everything's here.' Rose smiled into the mirror. 'The rest is up to you.'

Twenty minutes later Nancy inserted the final pin. She didn't know the name of what she'd done to Rose but had tried to copy a style she'd admired in a magazine. It was a French pleat.

A little rough and ready, Rose was thinking, but excellent all the same. Certainly better than any of her morning's efforts.

'That's it, Mrs Drummond,' Nancy stated quietly.

Rose turned her head first to one side, then the other. There was talent here, definitely so. What had started out as a whim on her part had borne unexpected fruit.

'You're pulling my leg, Nancy, you *have* done hair before.'

'No, ma'am.'

'Are you certain about that?'

'Oh yes, ma'am. As I said, only my own.'

Rose patted down a few stray strands. 'Then you're to be commended. It's a fine effort. A very fine effort indeed. I'm impressed.'

Nancy blushed at this praise.

'Don't blush. I mean what I say otherwise I wouldn't say it.'

'Thank you, Mrs Drummond.'

Rose had another thought. 'Now you've done my hair why don't you help me get dressed?'

Nancy bit her lip. 'Miss Campbell will be wondering where I am.'

'Let her wonder. I want you here and that's an end of it.'

Rose got up from her stool feeling strangely buoyant and elated, though she didn't know why. She was enjoying this.

'Let's get started then, shall we?'

'In my opinion she's merely readjusting, Mr Drummond. As I mentioned previously, she needs time for matters to correct themselves.'

Andrew was deeply embarrassed, having related, though not in detail, what had happened when Rose had come to his bed a second time.

'It's early days yet, Mr Drummond,' Lesley went on. 'Believe me.'

What else could he do but take the doctor's word for it. He was the expert after all. 'I just thought I should bring it to your attention, put you in the picture.'

'Which was the right thing to do.'

'I was coming to see you anyway, doctor. It's my indigestion, it's back with a vengeance.'

Lesley frowned. 'Describe these pains precisely if you can,' he said slowly.

He listened intently as Andrew spoke. 'Hmmh,' he murmured when Andrew was finished.

Lesley rocked back in his chair and made a pyramid with his hands. 'I think maybe an examination is in order,' he declared eventually.

'An examination?'

'If you'll just slip behind the screen, Mr Drummond, and strip to the waist. Let me know when you're ready.'

That flustered Andrew who hadn't been expecting such a request. 'Certainly,' he replied.

A few minutes later Lesley joined Andrew behind the screen, instructing him to lie down on the black leather couch there.

Andrew emerged from behind the screen to find Lesley writing on a sheet of headed paper. 'So what's the verdict?' he asked.

Lesley finished what he was writing, capped his pen, a beautiful Mont Blanc Andrew noted, and regarded Andrew thoughtfully. 'I'm making an appointment for you at Perth Hospital. There's a good man there called Creighton whom I want to see you.'

Alarm flared in Andrew. 'Isn't it indigestion then?'

'It might well be. Certainly the symptoms would fit in with that. And yet . . . To put it bluntly my suspicions are that you have an ulcer.'

'An ulcer?'

'Worry, Mr Drummond, all manner of things bring them on. And nasty blighters stomach ulcers can be too if not treated properly.'

'Does that mean an operation?'

Lesley smiled disarmingly. 'I said I only suspect you might have one. Let's establish exactly what's what before we start worrying about operations, eh? In other words, let's not cross bridges before we come to them. I may be entirely wrong about this. But it's better to be safe than sorry. Don't you agree?'

Andrew nodded.

'I'll send this letter off today and will contact you when I hear from Creighton. I take it there won't be any problem in going to Perth?'

'None at all, doctor.'

'Fine then.'

Lesley rose and escorted Andrew to the door. 'I shall be in touch in probably about a week. I'll ring you either at home or the distillery to give you a time and date.'

An ulcer? Andrew reflected once outside the surgery. Lesley had said he might be wrong which must be the case.

He was quite convinced of that.

Andrew was restless, unable to concentrate, which was most unlike him while at work. Rose, the visit to Perth, what the latter might lead to should the ulcer theory prove correct, all kept churning round and round in his mind. He considered having a drink to try to settle himself, and decided against it. In his present agitated mood he'd probably drink the whole bloody bottle.

Maud, one of the typists, stuck her head round his office door. 'Tommy Riach is here asking if he can see you, sir.'

'Send him in.'

'Yes, sir.'

'And, Maud!'

'Yes, sir?'

'I'd like some coffee.'

'I'll make you some, sir.'

He'd settle for that, he thought ruefully. Though, in truth, he'd much have preferred whisky.

'Ah, Tommy!' he exclaimed when the lad entered.

'You said to come back when I'd filled out the application form for the correspondence course and here I am.'

'You'll be wanting a cheque then.'

'Yes please.'

Andrew opened a drawer in his desk, extracted a cheque book and placed it before him. 'How much are the fees?'

Tommy told him.

Andrew pulled a face. 'They've gone up since my day. But then, hasn't everything.'

When the cheque was completed he detached it and handed it over. 'There you are, send it off.'

'Thank you very much.'

'Start in September?'

'That's right.'

'It isn't so hard really. A chap of your intelligence will probably find it a doddle.'

Tommy flushed with pleasure. A chap of his intelligence! He liked that and would repeat it to Babs when they next met up.

'Any problems with the course, which I doubt you'll have, feel free to consult me. I'll be only too happy to give you any help I can.'

'Thank you again.'

Andrew suddenly wanted out of the office, to do something else that might take his mind off his worries. Being unable to concentrate was most unlike him, and another cause for concern itself.

'You don't drive, do you?'

Tommy shook his head.

'Ever been behind a wheel?'

'I'm afraid not. As you know Dad doesn't own a car.'

'How do you fancy a lesson then? Your first.'

Tommy gawped at Andrew. 'Do you mean that?'

'You'll have to learn to drive at some stage, it's going to be a huge part of your life when you go on the road. So why don't I get you started now?'

Andrew laughed at Tommy's stunned expression. 'Not scared are you?' he teased.

'Not in the least. There's nothing I'd like more.'

'Right then,' Andrew declared, coming to his feet. 'Let's go.'

En route he told Maud to cancel the coffee.

'That was kind of Andrew!' Hettie exclaimed after Tommy had told them about his lesson.

Tommy's eyes were burning with enthusiasm. 'It was wonderful. Absolutely wonderful.'

'How far did you go?' Jack asked quietly.

'Miles, Dad. Miles and miles. We did a big loop that eventually brought us back to the distillery.'

'And did Andrew comment afterwards?'

'He said I had natural ability as a driver. That I could pick it up properly in no time at all.'

'Well well,' Hettie smiled, proud as punch.

'He's going to take me out again fairly soon. He promised.'

'Well, if he promised he will. Andrew doesn't break his word,' Hettie declared.

'*Baroom baroom!*' Tommy growled, pretending to be turning a steering wheel. '*Baroom baroom baroom!*'

'And he took you out in his own car?' Hettie asked.

'The Austin. Pity it hadn't been that Rolls he used to own. I'd love to have had a go at that.'

'I doubt he'd have let you drive the Rolls,' Hettie

laughed. 'Far too expensive and precious a car for a beginner. It would cost a mint if you damaged it.'

'You're being awfully quiet, Dad. Aren't you pleased for me?' Tommy frowned.

'Of course I am.'

'You don't sound it.'

'Well, I am. Now when's tea being served, I'm starving.'

'Don't you want to hear more?'

Jack sighed. 'I suppose I'm going to have to.'

As Tommy launched into a blow-by-blow account of his lesson Jack was quietly reflecting how jealous he was of Andrew. In normal circumstances it should have been he, Tommy's father, who taught the boy to drive. But the circumstances, he being blind, were far from normal. Blind men didn't drive, far less teach others.

He'd long since come to terms with his disability but there were still occasions, this being one, when he cursed what had happened to him in the war.

He'd missed a great deal in Tommy's upbringing, things a sighted father would have done that he simply couldn't. And that hurt.

He'd never played football with Tommy, never taught him to ride, which had been a great passion of his before the war, never . . . oh the list went on and on.

And now this, driving.

Yes, he was jealous of Andrew, but in the nicest way. There was no animosity or rancour involved, Andrew was his dear friend after all.

If he'd been able to cry he just might have done so at that point.

'Oh Christ, you're lovely,' David gasped, having emerged

from a deep clinch with Bell. They'd been out to the pub and were now round the back of her house saying goodnight.

David had asked to see Bell again after the dance and kept on seeing her. They were now regarded as a courting couple.

A brief image of Tommy Riach flickered through Bell's mind, an image she swiftly banished. It was daft to dwell on what might have been and now never would. David was her beau, which was fine by her. More than fine for he was a helluva nice lad. She could certainly do a lot worse.

'Oh Bell,' he whispered, his hand rubbing her breast. He then began worming it inside her blouse.

They'd done this before, many times, so there was nothing new about it. She'd allow him to go so far, and no more. Up until then she'd steadfastly refused to go all the way.

She could feel his hardness pressing into her which excited her. She shivered, and broke out in goose bumps. Men never believed that women had the same intensity of urges they themselves had, but then most men didn't understand women one little bit.

His free hand fumbled with her skirt, rucking it upwards. Eager fingers tugged at the elastic of her knickers.

The breath caught in her throat when he found what he was after. She squirmed her hips, relishing the sensations coursing through her.

'I want to fuck you so much,' David moaned. 'You don't know how much.'

But she did, only too well. For she felt exactly the same about him. She'd often wondered, tried to imagine . . . Was it as good as they said? Did the earth

really move? She doubted the latter. But good it surely
must be.

'Baby, baby,' he further moaned.

Both hands were now up her skirt, one at the front, the
other kneading and stroking her rear.

'Bell, please. Please!' he pleaded.

'*No.*'

He groaned.

For the first time her resolve began to melt, the urgency
in her almost overwhelming. She touched him which made
him groan again.

Despite the writhing and squirming, part of her mind
was detached, clinical almost. It was that part which came
to a decision. 'Have you got a johnny?'

'In my wallet.'

'Came prepared did you?'

'Don't, Bell. Don't. That's not fair.'

She'd have preferred the comfort of a bed, but that
luxury was highly unlikely before marriage. And marriage
it would be.

'Why don't we get engaged?' she whispered.

He immediately stopped what he was doing. 'Are you
serious?'

'Never more so. Do you love me?'

'I . . .' He halted, aware of the commitment he was
being asked to make.

'You've never said.'

'That's jessie.'

'No it's not. I love *you.*'

His face broke into a beaming smile. 'Do you?'

'Yes, David, I do.'

He swallowed hard, and with that swallow he too made
a decision. Why the hell not? he thought. Why the hell

not! He certainly didn't want to lose her. That would have been awful. 'And I love you, Bell,' he declared in a rush of words.

'Are you sure about that?'

'Oh aye. Sure as sure. Just don't ask me to keep repeating it all the time, that's all.'

He may or he may not, but he would before she was through with him. He caught his breath as she began undoing his flies.

'The johnny,' she said. 'We have to use a johnny.'

Later she reflected that the earth hadn't moved. But it had been good. Oh yes, it had been that all right.

He'd sworn he'd bring a ring the following week.

'Engaged!' Irene squealed. 'Congratulations, Bell. When did this happen?'

'Saturday night. But you're not to say anything until I have a ring on my finger. Promise?'

Irene nodded vigorously. 'I promise.'

'Cross your heart and hope to die?'

'Cross my heart and hope to die.'

'Your word of honour?'

'My word of bloody honour. Now tell me all about it. I want to know every last detail.'

Bell glanced about her. It was Monday morning and they were on their way to work. After David had left her she'd gone inside and straight to a mirror to see if she looked any different. She hadn't. The Bell who'd stared back at her was the same Bell who'd stared back earlier when she was getting ready to go out. Yet she did feel different. A little piece of magic had been wrought and she'd never be the same again.

'I let him shag me.'

Irene stopped dead in her tracks and stared in astonishment. 'You what?'

'I let him shag me,' Bell repeated nonchalantly. 'But only after I decided we were going to get married.'

'You decided?'

'Damn right I did. There and then. There's no one better likely to come along so I'll settle for David, thank you very much.'

Irene was still trying to digest this as they resumed walking. 'What was it like?'

'What was what like?' Bell queried innocently. She was enjoying this.

'The shag, you eejit.'

Bell wanted to laugh at the way Irene's eyes were almost popping out of her head. 'Very nice.'

'Is that all you can say, *very nice!*'

Now she did laugh. 'It's difficult to describe. You know when you . . . eh . . . ?' She winked knowingly.

Irene coloured. 'Go on.'

'Well, it's something similar only a hundred times better.'

Irene was astounded. 'A hundred times?'

She nodded.

'Bloody hell.'

'You should have heard the noise I made. I'm surprised someone didn't come to find out what was going on.'

'Was it . . . his . . . big?'

'Huge.'

'Huge?'

'Ginormous.'

Irene gulped. 'Did he . . . have trouble getting it in?'

'He managed in the end. Though it was a tight fit. But that makes it all the better.'

'So I've heard,' Irene muttered.

'Well, it's true.'

Irene's mind was whirling. God, how she envied Bell. First a regular boyfriend, now a fiancé, and not only a fiancé but a shag into the bargain. She was green.

'I wouldn't have done it of course unless he'd agreed to us getting engaged.'

'Naturally.'

'I'll have the ring next week.'

'Oh Bell, I can't wait to see it.'

Me neither, Bell thought with enormous satisfaction.

'How long till the wedding?'

'We'll have to discuss that. But I would imagine next year. Well, I mean, once your mind is made up there's no use hanging around.'

'True enough. You'd just better make sure you don't get up the duff in the meantime.'

'There'll be no worry about that, Irene. I'll insist he always uses a johnny. I'm not walking up the aisle with a bun in the oven. No fears.'

'Can I be your bridesmaid, Bell?'

'I was going to ask you anyway.'

That delighted Irene. She'd never been a bridesmaid. It was something to look forward to.

They were fast approaching Drummond's. 'Not a word mind,' Bell cautioned. 'Not even a hint. I want the ring first before I let on.'

Irene giggled. 'I think it's tremendous so I do.' Then, soberly, 'Was it really ginormous?'

'I swear it.'

'Just like Tommy Riach's?'

Bell's good humour abruptly vanished. She wished Irene hadn't brought Tommy's name up. 'We don't know he's got a big one. That was only a joke, remember?'

'Oh aye, so it was. I'd forgotten.'

But what had gone up between her legs was no joke, Bell recalled with a smile. It had been nothing to laugh about. Shout about yes, but not laugh.

She mustn't make so much noise in future, she told herself. It would be awful if someone did get nosy and they were discovered 'at it'.

Particularly if it was either her mother or father. How humiliating, a real red-faced situation.

Oh, but she was pleased with herself. Pleased as could be. Things couldn't have worked out better. Especially as David earnt such a good wage.

'Christ, that was quick!' Sandy McAlpine declared enviously, staring at the engagement ring Bell was swanking to all and sundry, moving her hand so that the diamonds flashed and sparkled. 'You've only known each other five minutes.'

'It was love at first sight so it was,' Bell replied solemnly.

'The ring's a smasher,' Hannah McIlroy enthused. 'I couldn't be more pleased for you, Bell.'

They were all in the cloakroom prior to going on shift. It was the following Monday morning and that Saturday David had been as good as his word, presenting Bell with a little blue box containing the ring nestling in matching velvet.

To Bell's delight the ring had fitted perfectly so there was no need for her to go to the jeweller's in Pitlochry, where it had been bought, to have the band resized.

It was a smasher too, Bell thought proudly. Small

perhaps, a single stone surrounded by chips, but what else did she expect from a working man. The Koh-i-noor?

If her workmates were pleased for her it was more than her mother and father had been. They'd both hit the roof, her father most of all. His reaction was purely selfish, as was her mother's. Engagement meant marriage and marriage meant losing her weekly pay packet. No wonder they'd been put out. Tough shite, she'd thought at the time.

'What's his surname again?' Sandy demanded.

'Nelson.'

'So you'll be Mrs David Nelson.'

'That's right.'

'I'm to be a bridesmaid,' Irene informed the others.

'Are you indeed,' Isa commented caustically. She was jealous of Bell and thought she must cajole Ronnie into popping the question. The fact that his cousin David had done so might be an incentive.

'When are you seeing him again?' That was Hannah.

'Wednesday night.'

'Have your folks met him yet?' Sandy asked.

Bell's face clouded. That was something she was dreading and which she'd put off for as long as she could. 'Not yet,' she replied airily. 'But they will. All in good time.'

'Aye, well you know best.'

Bell glanced at Irene whom she'd confided in about her parents' reaction. Irene's response was to raise her eyebrows.

'I still think you're awfully quick off the mark,' Sandy went on. 'I hope you aren't going to regret this.'

'Never,' Bell stated emphatically. 'As I said, it was love at first sight. There's no doubt in either of our minds.'

'Come on you, lot.' Mrs Reid, one of the older members of staff, intervened. 'Engagement or not, we have to get to work or else Balfour will be hammering on the door.'

That had gone well, Bell thought with satisfaction as they all trooped from the cloakroom. As pointed out it had been a short courtship but there was nothing wrong with that.

Nothing whatsoever in her opinion.

Nancy was about to climb into the bath when there was a tap on the door. 'Who is it?' she called out.

'Drew,' came the whispered reply. 'Let me in.'

Of all the cheek! 'Go away.'

'Oh, Nancy, let me in.'

'Get lost!'

'I'm going back to school in a couple of days and want to see you before I go.'

See being the operative word, she thought. Well, she was having none of it. 'I said, get lost, and mean it.'

'Nancy, it'll be months before I'm home again.'

'That's your lookout.'

She slid into the steaming water, sighing with pleasure as it closed over her body. On several occasions since the last incident she'd caught Drew eyeing her, the look on his face clearly reflecting what he was thinking, or remembering to be more precise.

'Nancy?'

She didn't reply.

'Oh come on, Nancy. This is my last chance.'

She should take it as a compliment, she thought. Even if he was so young.

'Nancy?'

Marry her one day, he'd promised. She almost laughed. Aye, cows would fly first.

'Nancy, please?'

After a while the pleadings stopped.

Chapter 16

A wild eyed Kelly burst into Andrew's office without knocking. Albeit a Sunday, the entire distillery was working that weekend due to the pressure of orders. Andrew glanced up at him in astonishment.

'War's been declared,' Kelly stated abruptly.

The two men stared at one another. Neither was surprised as the news had been expected, but both felt sick to the pits of their stomachs that it had actually happened.

'The PM announced it on the wireless at eleven o'clock,' Kelly added.

Andrew let out a long drawn-out sigh and then ran a hand over his face. There it was, they were going to go through the whole damn thing again. The words Kelly had just uttered were a death knell for God knows how many millions.

Kelly slowly shook his head. 'I can't believe it. I really can't.'

Nor Andrew. But it was apparently fact. 'Get a bottle and glasses,' he instructed. If this didn't call for a drink nothing did.

Thank the Lord Drew was only eleven and well out of it. Surely the forthcoming conflict wouldn't last until he was eligible for the Forces. That was a ridiculous scenario.

But there were countless men who wouldn't be so fortunate. Tommy Riach for one. He thought of Jack and Hettie, how were they taking this? He dreaded to think.

Kelly placed the glasses on the desk and poured, Andrew noting that Kelly's hand was trembling. He could well understand that.

'I lost a brother in the last lot,' Kelly said quietly.

'Me too.'

'Yes, I know. I've heard.'

Andrew picked up his glass and stood. 'What shall we toast, Mr Kelly?'

'Victory I suppose. What else?'

'Yes,' Andrew replied bitterly. 'What else indeed. Do the workforce know?'

'The word's going round like wildfire.'

Andrew nodded, wondering if he should call a meeting and address them. He decided against that.

He crossed to the window and stared out. It seemed just an ordinary September day. Nothing special about it at all. But it *was* different. Oh yes, it was most certainly that.

When Andrew turned round again he found Kelly standing there, lost in thought, with tears in his eyes.

'I'm sorry, Mr Drummond,' Kelly mumbled, groping for a handkerchief.

'Don't be. There's no shame in it. As far as I'm concerned the whole bloody country should be weeping.'

'Aye,' Kelly agreed softly.

'All I can say is, no matter what happens, I hope that bastard Hitler and his cohorts roast in hell for ever more.'

'Amen,' Kelly nodded.

Andrew finished his drink. 'Another?'

Kelly considered that. 'You know, I think I will.'

Andrew and Rose were in the middle of dinner, neither having spoken much, the atmosphere funereal, when Pattie Williams appeared.

'Sorry to disturb you, sir, but Mr Riach is on the telephone.'

He'd been going to ring Jack after the meal, this saved him the trouble. He pushed his plate away, not having an appetite anyway. 'I'll take the call.'

'Yes, sir.'

'I'll only be a few minutes,' he said to Rose, and departed from the room.

'It's Tommy, isn't it?' Andrew said softly, he and Jack having met up in the pub at Jack's request.

'Yes,' Jack croaked in reply.

'He's seventeen, hopefully too young yet.'

Jack laughed mirthlessly. 'I served alongside many lads that age on the Western Front. Good lads all, most of them now . . .' He trailed off, and shook his head.

'How's Hettie?'

'Crying her eyes out. She'd recovered before I left but knowing her she probably started up again as soon as I was out of the house.'

'And Tommy?'

Jack's hand crunched into a tight fist. 'The idiot thinks it's wonderful. Imagine, wonderful! No doubt he sees himself winning a VC and becoming a hero.'

'*If* he's called up, Jack, it won't be for a while.'

'We hope.'

'Yes,' Andrew said quietly. 'We hope.'

'I can't bear the thought of him going through what I did, Andrew. The sheer horror, the total nightmare of that.'

He'd been lucky, Andrew reflected. Ireland had been a doddle compared to France and Belgium. There had been no comparison.

Another customer in the pub laughed loudly and shrilly causing Andrew to frown in irritation. Then he saw the chap's face and realised the laugh was no doubt a nervous reaction to the day's events.

'I prayed this wouldn't come about,' Jack went on. 'Night after night I prayed that someone, somewhere, would see sense. Fat lot of good that did.'

'I wonder what will happen next,' Andrew mused. 'I mean, in the immediate future.'

'The first thing they want to do is get rid of Chamberlain. He's worse than useless.'

Andrew nodded his agreement.

'Churchill should lead the country in my opinion. He's the man for the job.'

'But will he get it? That's the question.'

There was a pause, then Jack said softly, 'Do you know one of the worst things about being blind, Andrew?'

'What?'

Jack took a deep swallow of whisky and carefully replaced the now empty glass on the table between them. 'Having children and not knowing what they look like. Oh, I've had Tommy described to me often enough but it's hardly the same thing. I know what you look like, and Hettie, because I'd seen you both before I lost my eyes.

And it's easy to imagine the pair of you grown older. But Tommy? He's a complete mystery.'

Andrew didn't know what to reply to that, thinking of Drew, picturing his son in his mind. It was amazing the everyday things you took for granted, he reflected. Things denied to others.

'It might not last long,' Andrew said hopefully.

Jack laughed. 'All over by Christmas? That sort of guff. That's what they said the last time and it took four long hellish years for it to finish. Well, this won't be any shorter. Anyone who thinks differently is kidding themselves.'

Andrew was sure that was right. Four years, maybe more. And what if the Germans did win? He went icy cold all over at the thought.

'Do you fancy getting pissed tonight, Andrew? Really pissed. The falling-down kind.'

That appealed. 'It's not every day war is declared after all.'

'No, it isn't.'

The same customer as before laughed again, this time even more loudly and shrilly. He was in his early twenties, Andrew noted. Prime fighting material. The poor bugger was probably shitting bricks.

'Let's do that,' Andrew said.

'Pissed as farts.'

'Rat-arsed.'

'Deid mockit.'

'Boaking drunk.'

A few seconds' silence passed between them after that exchange. 'I'll get them in,' Andrew declared, and headed for the bar.

Jack sat still as a stone statue thinking about Tommy, fearing what might lie ahead for his son.

* * *

Andrew had slept a little then woken with the most fearful stomach ache. It was the whisky of course, he and Jack having consumed copious quantities, first at the pub then back at Jack's house. The strange thing was, although they'd set out to get drunk neither had actually become so.

Andrew groaned, and rubbed his belly. This was awful. If it kept up he wouldn't get another wink of sleep that night which meant going to work like a wrung-out old rag.

He tossed and turned for a while longer, but the pain remained. He'd go down to the kitchen and get some bicarb he finally decided. That should help.

He halted briefly at Rose's door, imagining her inside all tucked up. With a shrug he continued on his way.

He stopped again when he came in sight of the kitchen, wondering why the light was on. He found Miss Campbell sitting at the table hunched over a cup and saucer.

'Mr Drummond!' she exclaimed, blushing. 'What are you doing here at this hour?'

'I might ask the same thing, Miss Campbell.'

The housekeeper self-consciously pulled her dark-blue velour dressing gown more tightly about her. 'I have a confession to make. I'm something of an insomniac and often come down for cocoa about this time. I hope it's all right?'

'Of course, Miss Campbell. Feel free to do whatever you wish.'

He tried not to stare at the deep cleft between her breasts, one of which had a tiny mole on it. She really was well bosomed, he thought, not for the first time.

'I'm looking for the bicarb,' he explained.

'Stomach trouble?'

He nodded. 'Jack Riach and I rather overdid it earlier and now I'm paying the price.'

She rose. 'You sit down, Mr Drummond, and I'll fetch the bicarb for you.'

'Don't let me disturb you, Miss Campbell.'

'You're hardly doing that.'

Lovely backside too, he thought as she moved away from him, the material of her dressing gown accentuating its curves.

'What do you think of today's news?' he asked, sitting as instructed.

'It's dreadful.'

'Aye, it is that.'

'It's been coming for a while, mind. But it's still a shock now that it's actually arrived.'

'I agree.'

He watched her spoon bicarb into a glass of water and swirl the contents.

'That should do the trick,' she declared, placing the glass in front of him. 'Now drink it all down at once.'

'Bossy boots,' he smiled.

She blushed again. 'Sorry. I didn't mean it to sound like that.'

It tasted foul, but he managed to swallow it in one go. 'Horrible,' he grimaced.

'Quite disgusting, I agree. But if it helps that's all that matters.'

Definitely a handsome woman, he thought. There was a basic honesty and openness about her face which he liked. She seemed the sort of person you could easily confide in.

'We haven't really had a talk, you and I,' he said.

'No.'

He glanced around. 'It's a bit spooky here this time of night. I hadn't realised.'

'I can't say it bothers me. But I can see what you mean.'

They smiled at one another. 'How are you settling in, Miss . . .' He broke off. 'I can't keep calling you Miss Campbell. Not in a situation like this. What's your Christian name?'

'Elspeth.'

'Elspeth,' he repeated. 'It suits you. And I'm Andrew.'

She'd thought him rather austere up until then, but could see now that wasn't really the case. There was a warmth there she hadn't experienced before.

'The answer to your question is I'm settling in fine. I'm enjoying it here,' she replied.

'Good. It's a pity the position isn't a permanent one. Though, just between you and me, I suspect Mrs Drummond won't take over the housekeeping duties again.'

'No?'

'It's only a guess, but that's what I think will happen. So it may be you'll be here longer than you anticipated. If you wish to stay on that is.'

Elspeth frowned. 'I'll have to think about that.'

'Of course.'

She had a sip of cocoa.

'Have you always suffered from insomnia?'

'Ever since I was a child. I've no idea what causes it. Just the way I am I suppose.' She shrugged. 'One of these things.'

He should leave her now, he thought, and found himself reluctant to do so. He was enjoying their conversation, and her company. She was relaxing to be with. Such a change from Rose since the miscarriage.

'Would you mind if I smoke?'

'No, go ahead. I didn't know you did.'

She smiled conspiratorially. 'Only a few per day. And I really shouldn't in the kitchen of all places.'

'Well, I won't tell Cook on you. That's a promise.'

He watched her light up, thinking again how fascinating her hands were. Long, elegant and ivory coloured. He could just imagine . . .

He coughed, putting that straight out of his mind. 'My stomach seems to be settling a bit.'

She exhaled, sending a stream of white smoke spiralling towards the ceiling. 'Give it a little while longer and it should hopefully be gone altogether.'

'I've had a lot of trouble with my stomach recently,' he confessed.

'Oh?'

'I thought it was indigestion but Dr Lesley has other opinions. He believes it might be an ulcer.'

Her face immediately clouded with genuine concern. 'How awful if it is.'

'I'm seeing a specialist in Perth next week which I'm not looking forward to at all. If it is an ulcer that could lead to an operation and being away from the distillery for a time, recuperating and all that.'

'Does that worry you?'

He contemplated his reply. 'If you imagine a ship. Well I'm the captain who doesn't like being away from his bridge for too long.'

'I see,' she murmured, thinking how conscientious and responsible he was. They were admirable traits, ones she admired.

'Still, health comes first,' she said.

'I suppose so.'

'Work is only work after all, even if you do own your own business. Anyway, a distillery isn't a ship. A distillery won't founder if you're off for a few weeks.' Then, teasingly, 'I shouldn't think there are many unexpected icebergs in Dalneil.'

He laughed at the absurdity of that. 'Heaven forbid.'

'Drummond's hardly the *Titanic*.'

Andrew was lonely, she realised. She could read it in his eyes. Lonely and . . . sad. Somewhat lost even. That surprised her.

'Can I ask a personal question, Elspeth?'

'If it's too personal I don't guarantee I'll answer.'

He fiddled with his empty glass, thinking this was embarrassing. But he was curious. 'How come a good-looking lassie like yourself isn't married?'

She sucked in a breath, and turned her head away. Where she'd blushed before she now went a deep shade of red.

'Perhaps you haven't found the right man?'

'It isn't that,' she replied slowly. 'I did. Once.'

He didn't speak, waiting for her to go on.

All the old hurt and humiliation came welling back. Black memories, terrible ones. She flicked ash into her saucer.

'Sorry, I obviously shouldn't have asked. It was rude of me.'

'So why did you?'

'Curiosity,' he confessed.

Elspeth inhaled deeply, then ground out what remained of her cigarette. 'We were supposed to be married, except he jilted me.'

'At the . . .'

'Yes,' she interjected quickly. 'At the altar. He took fright, I was told afterwards, and ran for it. Last I heard he was somewhere in New Zealand.'

'I'm sorry.'

Elspeth hung her head 'It was a long time ago now. I try not to think of it. Remember. That's why I went into service, to get away from the wagging tongues and whispers behind my back. Everyone was very sympathetic and yet . . .' She trailed off.

'And yet what?' he prompted gently.

'I got the distinct impression they blamed me. Thought there was something wrong with me that had made Stuart take fright. Oh, you know what village people are like, Andrew. The gossip, the speculation, the downright lies that are circulated. It was just too hurtful for me to stay there and so I also left. Better that way.'

'I shouldn't have been so nosy,' Andrew apologised. 'I had no idea.' He felt for the woman, he really did. What an appalling thing to have happened.

'I was so ashamed,' she choked.

'But the fault wasn't yours. Was it?'

She shook her head.

'There then. As you say, the young chap simply took fright. It affects some people that way. Marriage is a huge step after all.'

Pull yourself together, Elspeth berated herself. She couldn't imagine why she'd confided in Andrew. It was a piece of her past she rarely divulged.

'You mustn't let it put you off men for life,' Andrew advised. 'They're not all like that. You mark my words, someone else will come along in time. You'll see.'

She managed to smile. 'Perhaps.'

'No doubt about it. So there.'

Elspeth stared him straight in the eyes. 'Please don't let on to anyone else in the house?'

'I won't. You have my oath on that.'

'Thank you.'

He wanted to go to her, put an arm round her shoulders and give her a comforting squeeze. But that would hardly be right. Up until a few minutes ago they'd been relative strangers after all.

'How's your stomach now?'

His eyebrows shot up. 'I do believe it's better, thank God.'

'The pain's gone?'

'Completely.'

There were a few seconds during which they gazed at one another, then he rose from his chair. 'I'd better get back to bed.'

'And I'll clear up here.'

'Thanks for talking to me, Elspeth.'

'I'm not usually so forthcoming. Maybe it's the lateness of the hour, my mood.'

'Whatever, your story's safe with me.'

She flashed him a smile of gratitude. 'And someday you must tell me yours.'

That jolted him. 'Mine?'

'Oh, I think there's one to tell. I can sense it.'

At the kitchen door he stopped and turned again. 'I'm glad you've joined the household, Elspeth Campbell. I approve of you.'

He was gone before she could reply, even if she could think how to respond.

* * *

'We had a letter from Gerald yesterday,' Babs stated quietly. 'He says he's going to be in the thick of it.'

Tommy's eyes gleamed. 'Lucky blighter.'

That angered Babs. 'Don't be so stupid! He could get killed. My brother could get killed.'

Tommy was instantly contrite. 'I didn't mean that the way it sounded.'

'Oh yes, you did. You're just like him. All gung ho and charge! What neither of you seems to appreciate is this is for real. It's not a story out of the *Wizard* or *Hotspur* you know. But *real*.'

Tommy glanced about him. They were in their favourite spot where they always came for kissing and cuddling. So far there had been none of that.

He picked a blade of grass and rubbed it between two fingers. Women, he thought. They always overdramatised everything. His mother was just the same. Ever since war had been declared she merely had to look at him and tears came into her eyes.

'At least you're safe for the time being,' Babs went on. 'Until you're eighteen anyway.' Compulsory military service had been announced for all men in Britain between the ages of eighteen and forty-one.

Tommy didn't reply to that.

'I couldn't bear it if you had to go off as well. Have two of you in the firing line, so to speak.'

Tommy was aching to 'go off', as she put it, but had more sense than to say so. He could well imagine the reaction if he did. From Babs and his mother.

Silence fell between them.

'What are you thinking about, Tommy?'

'Nothing,' he lied.

'I keep wondering . . .' She shuddered.

'What?'

'If I'll ever see Gerald again.'

'Of course you will,' Tommy replied scornfully.

'But I might not.'

'You will.'

'I wish I could believe that,' she muttered.

This was rapidly becoming a bore, Tommy thought. He wanted to talk about the war, but not like this. Didn't she understand how exciting the whole thing was? As for Gerald, he *was* a lucky blighter. He'd have given anything to be in Gerald's shoes. Shoes *and* Hurricane.

Tommy briefly closed his eyes, picturing himself at a plane's controls, zooming through the sky, a Hun squarely in his sights. *Rat a tat tat tat!*

Got you! The Hun blew up in a glorious ball of flame. Another miniature swastika to slap on to his fuselage.

'Why are you smiling?'

The smile abruptly vanished. 'Am I?'

'Like a Cheshire cat.'

'I wasn't aware.'

She regarded him suspiciously. 'You wouldn't suit a uniform anyway.'

That she'd more or less read his mind startled him. 'Why not?'

'Wrong shape. You'd look daft.'

He bristled. 'I wouldn't.'

'Oh yes you would.'

'Wrong shape?' he mumbled with a frown.

'As I said, you'd look daft.'

It simply wasn't true, he told himself. Babs was only trying to put him off any thoughts in that direction. Well she hadn't succeeded. Not by a long chalk.

'I think we'd better get back,' he declared.

She stared at him in surprise. 'If you wish.'

'It's getting late.'

'Not too late though,' she replied hesitantly. When she tried to catch his gaze he glanced away.

'Let's go then,' she said.

They usually held hands when they walked home, but didn't on this occasion. Their conversation was sparse and stilted.

At her door Tommy kissed her quickly on the lips. 'See you during the week.'

Her smile was stretched and strained. 'Yes.'

Babs bit her lip as she went inside. It was the first time things hadn't gone well between them.

McFarlane was rubbing down Moonbeam when a dishevelled Rose appeared before him. It was clear she'd taken a tumble.

'Mrs Drummond, are you all right?' he asked anxiously.

'Strumpet's dead,' she answered in a cracked voice.

'Dead?'

'We were galloping when she collapsed.'

McFarlane knew with certainty that Rose had pushed the mare too hard. It was something he'd been half expecting, dreading. 'Where is she now?'

Rose told him.

'Right, leave it to me. I'll attend to matters.'

'Thank you, McFarlane.'

He hesitated, unsure of Rose's reaction to the next question. 'Did she . . . suffer at all?'

Rose glanced down at the straw-covered floor, the memory of those terrifying few moments clear in her head. Luckily she'd cleared her stirrups otherwise she could have become entangled with the horse with who knows what result.

It had been madness, sheer madness. But at the time the thrill had been almost ecstatic. Urging Strumpet on, trying to go faster, faster. And then . . . suddenly . . .

Rose shook herself. 'I don't believe so, McFarlane. I'm sure she was already dead when she hit the ground.'

'Well, that's a mercy at least.'

'Yes,' Rose agreed.

'And you didn't hurt yourself?' He almost wished she had, the callous, cruel bitch. If she'd been his wife he'd literally have knocked her from pillar to post for what she'd done.

'I'm shaken, that's all.'

'You'd still better go to the doctor and have yourself checked over.'

'Yes,' she muttered, having absolutely no intention of doing so. She'd be fine after a long hot bath and rest.

McFarlane couldn't help himself. 'Strumpet was a bonny mare. A right willing beast.'

Rose didn't reply to that.

Without uttering a further word she left the stables.

This was it, Andrew thought, staring up at the grey hospital building. His appointment with Mr Creighton was in ten minutes' time.

He unconsciously touched his stomach which hadn't bothered him since the night he'd chatted with Elspeth Campbell, and that upset had been brought on by overindulgence, nothing else.

Rose knew nothing about this visit, just as she didn't know about his visits to Lesley. As far as she was concerned he was off on a business trip, nothing more.

He'd been nervous since waking that morning, which was perfectly natural after all. Ulcers could be nasty, as Lesley had warned him.

Not that he believed he had one. He didn't, convinced it was indigestion that had been plaguing him. Still, it was best to have that confirmed.

You're wasting time, he told himself. Dawdling, putting off the evil moment.

He took a deep breath, squared his shoulders and began mounting the steps that led to the main entrance.

Chapter 17

'I've been thinking,' Rose said to Andrew, who was sitting opposite. 'How would you feel about making Nancy my personal lady's maid?'

Andrew, engrossed in the newspaper full of the latest war news, glanced across at her in surprise. 'I beg your pardon?'

'How would you feel about making Nancy my personal lady's maid?'

He frowned. 'Do you need one? You haven't up until now.'

'It would be a tremendous help. I've discovered Nancy is terribly clever with hair and extremely useful when I'm getting dressed.'

'I see,' Andrew murmured, wondering what had brought this on.

'Besides, she's marvellous company. The pair of us chatter away for hours at times. She's ever such fun.'

'Isn't it . . . Well the idea of a lady's maid, isn't it just a wee bit pretentious nowadays?'

Rose scowled. 'Not at all.'

'It might be construed as such.'

'I don't give a fig how it's construed. Other people's opinions don't bother me one whit.'

Andrew sighed. 'I'll have to speak to Miss Campbell.'

'Don't speak to her, *tell* her,' Rose snapped. 'She's only another employee when all's said and done.'

'Still, it would only be polite to consult her.'

Rose snorted in irritation. 'Honestly, Andrew, you can be so damned weak on occasion. I despair.'

'Weak?' he repeated. He knew he had many faults but didn't consider weakness to be one of them. Quite the contrary.

'That's right, weak!'

This could very easily get out of hand, he thought. If he wasn't careful it could blow up into a major row.

'It would mean taking on another maid, a replacement for the duties Nancy does now.'

'Are you trying to say we can't afford another maid? Have you become mean as well as weak?'

Rose really had her heart set on this, that was obvious. But there was no need for her to be so disagreeable about it. As for name calling, that was most unlike her. Or at least, he reminded himself, *had* been unlike her. So many things about Rose had changed since the miscarriage.

'I am neither weak nor mean,' he stated levelly, becoming ever so slightly angry.

'Then prove it.'

He laughed. 'I don't have to prove anything, Rose. Not to you or anyone else.'

'See!'

See what? He wasn't sure. 'I'll consider the matter. How's that?'

Rose glared at him.

'Well?'

'I *want* her as a lady's maid, Andrew. Understand?'

Now he was angry. A request was one thing, being dictated to quite another. Even by Rose. 'We don't always get what we want you know.'

The glare had become venomous. 'And what if I insist?'

He shrugged. 'Won't alter things. I said I'd consider the matter and that's final.' He was damned if he was going to be bulldozed into anything. He would probably have readily consented if she'd gone about this differently.

'I'm going to bed,' Rose announced abruptly.

'Goodnight then.'

Rising, she flounced from the room.

Bitch, he thought. Which surprised him. He'd never thought of his wife that way before.

He doubted he'd be having a visitation that night.

On the other hand, and he smiled, it might just be that he would, Rose trying to persuade him where she considered him most vulnerable.

But it wouldn't make a blind bit of difference, no matter how great the temptation. If it was blackmail then she could go whistle Dixie.

Nancy was *en route* to the village shop to buy some kirby grips for Rose when she came across a group of lassies playing 'ropes'.

She halted to stare at them, observing how much they were enjoying themselves. Two of the girls each had an end of the rope, a length of washing line, which they were cawing, as the expression went. Whirling it round in an arc, the girl in the middle having to jump over it when it hit the ground. All the while they were singing a ditty that went with the game.

Nancy smiled wistfully to see the fun. How unlike her own childhood where fun was almost unknown, life simply too hard for levity. Even as a tiny child all she could remember was work of some description.

Sadness filled her at what she'd missed. Envy too watching these girls.

It suddenly struck her that several of the taller lassies were only a few years younger than herself. How old she felt by comparison, but then that was only natural after what she'd been through, not least living with, and being used by, Bill McCabe.

She moved closer, letting the happiness from the group wash over her. Beginning to feel as carefree as they, as innocent – if that was possible – as they.

She could almost imagine there had never been a Bill McCabe in her life, and that she'd never been a bondager and all that entailed. The sheer slavery of it.

A roar of laughter combined with jeers went up when the lassie in the middle mistimed her jump and fouled the rope. Now it was her turn to caw.

Nancy glanced about her. There was no one else in sight, just this group.

She moved even closer. 'Can I join in?'

The girl she'd addressed turned to look at her. 'Aye, if you wish.'

'You won't mind?'

'Can she have a play, Effie?'

One of the older girls nodded. 'She can start in the middle.'

Nancy eagerly hurried forward, thinking this wonderful. A real treat.

'One, two, three a leerie . . .' the group started to sing as the rope spun into action.

Nancy didn't last long, but no matter that. She was humming jauntily and beaming broadly when she continued on her way.

For a few minutes there she'd been a child again. A child experiencing a normal childhood.

'David!' Bell exclaimed, having answered a knock at the door.

'Do you fancy a trip to the pub? I have to talk to you.'

David's appearance had thrown Bell into a tizzy, it being completely unexpected. There hadn't been an arrangement.

'Who is it, Bell?' her father called out from the sitting room.

That alarmed Bell. The last thing she wanted to do was invite David in to meet her parents. Not there and then. That meeting was still in the future. God knows what he'd make of her father sitting unshaven and stinking, her mother rattling around like a female scarecrow.

'The pub?' she repeated.

David regarded her anxiously. 'Aye, that's right. We have to talk.'

Bell's hand went to her hair. She too was something of a mess; she certainly couldn't go out in public as she was. 'Can I meet you there in about fifteen minutes? Let me tidy myself and put on some fresh make-up.'

'I'll be waiting then,' David smiled.

Having closed the door again Bell flew up to her room. Now what was this all about?

*   *   *

'I got you a gin and orange,' David said as Bell joined him at the corner table he'd selected.

Bell hadn't liked coming into the pub on her own. It wasn't proper. But she was meeting someone and that made all the difference. She quickly sat. 'Is something wrong, David?'

He picked up his pint and had a long swallow, feeling totally and utterly wretched. 'Aye, it is.'

'To do with us?' My God, she suddenly thought, he was going to break off their engagement. How could she face the lassies at work if he did?

'I had a letter this morning,' he stated slowly.

'And?'

'Well, more of an official form actually. It came as quite a shock.'

He didn't seem to be breaking off the engagement, Bell thought with relief. But why was he looking so miserable?

'What sort of form?'

'You must have heard or read in the papers about the compulsory military service. Hundreds of thousands have been called up.'

She went cold all over.

He nodded. 'That's right. I'm one of them.'

The gin and orange vanished down her throat. 'Can I have another?' she croaked.

'Of course.'

Called up! It had never crossed her mind that might happen to David. Only to others, people she didn't know.

She stared at him standing at the bar. This would put the cat amongst the pigeons where their marriage was concerned. It had all seemed so cut and dried before. Now this bombshell.

'I made it a large one this time,' David said, sitting down again.

'When?'

'Do I have to go away?'

'Aye.'

'It doesn't say. It merely informs me that I'm to be drafted and to await further communication.'

Well that was something at least. A little respite.

'But it'll be soon, Bell. A couple of weeks probably.'

'You don't know that for certain.'

'No,' he admitted reluctantly. 'But it's my guess. Mobilisation is moving swiftly by all accounts. They're hardly likely to keep me and others hanging around. They'll want us in the army and square-bashing as fast as possible. It stands to reason.'

'Oh David,' Bell whispered, a hint of tears in her eyes. 'This certainly puts the kibosh on things.'

He nodded.

'So what are we going to do?'

'Well, I can't be exempted and it's highly unlikely I'll fail the medical.'

'And what about us getting married?'

He pulled a face. 'That'll just have to wait, I suppose. There's nothing else for it.'

Reaching out she took his hand and squeezed it. 'No wonder you were looking so miserable.'

'I so desperately want you to be my wife, Bell. For the pair of us to set up home together.'

'Me too.'

'For the pair of us to share a bed night after night and forget about going round the back of your place.'

She smiled. 'It would certainly have its advantages. There's no denying that.'

'Besides, I want to wake up in the morning with you lying beside me. There's a lot more to it than just the nookie side of things.'

'Yes,' she agreed softly, thinking him ever so romantic. What a lovely thing to have said.

'And children. Our children, Bell.' He took a deep breath. 'We can still have all that, it's simply that we're going to have to wait longer than expected.'

What if he didn't come back from the war. What if . . . ? Fear gripped her, that and a terrible sense of foreboding.

She was letting her imagination run away with her, she berated herself. Of course he'd come back. Safe in life and limb.

But what if he didn't? Oh God, what if he didn't?

Dr Lesley stared at Andrew across his desk. 'I have here your report from Mr Creighton in Perth, and I'm happy to tell you that the tests were negative. There's no sign whatsoever of an ulcer.'

Relief flooded through Andrew, followed almost instantly by a surge of triumph. He was in the clear, just as he'd known he'd be. If it hadn't been undignified he'd have let out a whoop.

'I'm delighted for you, Mr Drummond.'

'Not half as delighted as I am,' Andrew beamed. 'That's a real worry off my back. Though, I have to say, I never really believed I had an ulcer.'

Lesley didn't comment on that. 'Which leaves us with the ongoing problem of indigestion.'

'That hasn't been so bad recently,' Andrew replied jauntily. 'I haven't had an attack since I went to Perth.'

'Good. How do you feel generally?'

'Right as rain, doctor. Never better. Though I do find

I have a slight loss of energy now and again. But I put that down to advancing age.'

Lesley smiled. 'I'm afraid that's something no doctor can cure. Advancing age I mean.' Then, drily, 'We even suffer from it ourselves.'

Andrew laughed.

'So that's that then. A clean bill of health.'

Andrew rose from his chair feeling buoyed in the extreme. 'All that's left for me to do is thank you for your trouble.'

Lesley also rose, intending to see Andrew to the door. 'How's Mrs Drummond?'

Andrew frowned. 'The same.'

'Still sleeping apart?'

'Yes, sad to say. She continues to insist on it.'

'As I said before, Mr Drummond, time. Just give her time.'

Andrew had begun to wonder about that. Perhaps Rose had changed for ever. If that proved to be the case . . .

It was an appalling thought, one he mustn't dwell on.

'I wondered if I'd find you here,' Andrew smiled.

Elspeth Campbell, hunched over cocoa and smoking, smiled in return. 'You obviously can't sleep either.'

He came and sat facing her. 'Not a wink. I got fed up staring at the ceiling, so here I am.'

'The insomniacs' club,' she joked.

'Apparently. At least this time there's no stomach upset I'm pleased to report.'

'Can I get you something?'

'A cup of tea would be nice.'

Elspeth ground out the remains of her cigarette. 'That won't take long.'

He stared admiringly at her as she busied herself with the kettle. Beautiful backside, he noted again. He tried to visualise her naked, and the picture he conjured up made the breath catch in his throat.

Down, boy, he warned himself. Down. He mustn't get any ideas in that direction. It would be quite out of order.

Damn Rose, he thought bitterly. A man of his nature shouldn't be going without, it wasn't natural. To do so was sheer, and continued, torture.

For a wild moment he contemplated simply bursting into Rose's bedroom to have her there and then, whether or not she objected. It was his right after all. She was his bloody wife, for Christ's sake!

But that would be an awful mistake, no doubt about it. Rose would never forgive him for forcing himself on her. It could literally, in all but name, be the end of their marriage.

'Sugar, Andrew?'

'Please.'

A few minutes later she returned to the table and placed a cup of tea in front of him.

'I hope your cocoa hasn't gone cold,' he said.

'I doubt that, I'd only just made it.'

'I had my report from Perth yesterday,' he informed her.

'And?'

'I don't have an ulcer.'

'Wonderful!' she exclaimed.

'As you know it was taking time off work which was causing me the most anxiety. Now I can forget that. And any possible operation.'

'You must be thrilled.'

'Oh, I am, Elspeth. There's still the indigestion of course. But hopefully it'll simply disappear in time.' He cleared his throat. 'I've been meaning to talk to you.'

'Oh?'

'My wife wants Nancy as a personal lady's maid. How do you feel about the possibility?' He'd purposefully kept Rose waiting for a decision on this, a small punishment for her rudeness.

'I've no objections,' Elspeth replied slowly, thinking this rather grandiose of Rose. But then who knew what went on in that woman's mind? Certainly not her.

'I have to admit it took me somewhat by surprise,' Andrew confessed. 'She's never had a personal maid before. Anyway, as far as I'm aware, lady's maids went out of fashion years ago, except in the largest and wealthiest of households that is.'

'And she particularly wishes Nancy?'

'She was quite specific about that.'

'I see.'

Andrew had a sip of tea while Elspeth lit up another cigarette. 'They seem to get on very well together,' he explained. 'Rose is quite taken with her.'

'It'll mean employing someone else.'

'I realise that. Can I leave the arrangements to you?'

Elspeth nodded. 'I'll start inquiries straight away.'

Andrew had the sudden insight – it might have been something in Elspeth's tone, or her expression – that the housekeeper didn't like Rose. Well he could hardly blame her for that. Nowadays Rose was difficult, to say the least. As he well knew.

He stayed for over half an hour before excusing himself, the pair of them chatting away about all sorts of things. When he did finally leave it was with a sense of regret.

As she'd done on the previous occasion Elspeth remained behind to clear up.

Tommy's temper snapped. 'That's it, I've had enough. As far as I'm concerned, Mr Kelly, you can go jump off a cliff for all I care.'

Kelly stared at him in astonishment.

'You're never off my back, forever getting at me. Whatever I do is wrong and I'm sick to the back teeth with it!' a red-faced Tommy raged on.

'Don't talk to me like that,' Kelly barked.

'I'll talk to you any way I wish from now on. Because I'm leaving. I can't stand working here one moment longer. Not with you around I can't.'

Tommy was close to tears, amazed at his own audacity. But this had been building for months and the latest sarcastic criticism had been the last straw.

He didn't care that he was putting himself out of a job, or any of the consequences of this. He just couldn't take any more.

'You're a tin-pot despot, Mr Kelly, and a bully with it. You've had it in for me since the moment I arrived. Had it in for me in spades. I don't know why. I've tried to do my best and all I get from you are snide remarks. Well, up yours, Mr Kelly. Right up yours!!'

And with that Tommy crashed from the room, knocking a chair over in the process.

Kelly was left gazing grimly and angrily after him.

Tommy picked a blade of grass and rubbed it between two fingers. He'd come to his and Babs' favourite spot to cool off.

He was damned if he was going back to Drummond's.

He was finished there for good. No matter what, he was determined about that. He simply couldn't face another single day with Kelly.

What would Mum and Dad say? he wondered. Well, they wouldn't be best pleased, that was certain. And what about Andrew? He'd let him down.

No, he hadn't, he told himself. He hadn't at all. If anyone had let Andrew down it was Kelly. Kelly the tormentor. Kelly whom he'd come to hate with an unbridled passion. Kelly whom he could happily have seen boiled in oil.

The big question was, what next? Where did he go from here?

He brought the blade of grass to his mouth and blew on it to produce a whistling sound. He smiled. It was years since he'd done that. Somehow he found it strangely consoling.

Then there was Babs. What was her reaction going to be when he told her? She'd probably call him a fool. An idiot. But she hadn't had to put up with Kelly. She hadn't had to endure the daily agonies of being continually belittled and sneered at.

Tommy sighed. What a mess. What an awful mess. Thankfully he hadn't punched Kelly as he'd so wanted to. That would only have made matters a whole lot worse. But part of him wished he had for the pure satisfaction of it.

He tossed the blade of grass aside thinking he couldn't stay where he was for ever. He was going to have to go home and face his parents, explain what he'd done. And more importantly, why. He could only hope there would be some sympathy for him.

Kelly, how he loathed and detested the man. The beady-eyed, bushy-eyebrowed little runt. It was too much to hope that Andrew would sack Kelly over this. Knowing Kelly he'd give a distorted explanation of what had happened, with himself totally in the clear. What would his word count against that of the book-keeper? Not a lot. Kelly was a senior member of staff after all, he a trainee. No better than an apprentice.

And then he had it. The perfect answer to all this. The only one.

'Oh cheer up, it's not the end of the world,' Irene said to Bell. The pair of them were in Irene's bedroom where they'd gone to chat away from the rest of the family.

'Like hell it isn't.'

Irene crossed over and sat on the bed beside her friend. 'Look at it this way, it just means you're going to have a long engagement instead of a short one.'

'Long!' Bell snorted. 'It could be years.'

'Aye, well, it's not within your control. There's nothing you can do about it.'

'No,' Bell agreed morosely. There wasn't.

'Besides, I think it's all rather exciting.'

Bell stared at Irene in disbelief. 'What's exciting about it?'

'You know . . . war and all that. David being called up. Off fighting for King and Country.'

Bell gave a small hysterical laugh. 'He could get his fucking head blown off. What's exciting about that for God's sake?'

'He won't.'

'What are you, an oracle? Can you see into the future?'

'Don't be daft.'

'Then don't talk such nonsense.'

Irene hung her head. 'I'm sorry. I was only trying to help. Be a pal and that.'

Bell took a deep breath. All this meant she was going to have to continue living with her parents instead of having a house of her own which she'd been so looking forward to. It was as though she'd been released from prison only to be suddenly dragged back in again.

'Are you going to see him off?'

Bell nodded. 'I had a word with Balfour and he's agreed. He was very understanding about it.'

'Aye, he's no' a bad old stick Balfour. There are a lot worse.'

'A week this Saturday,' Bell mumbled. 'The ten o'clock train from Pitlochry.'

Ten days, Irene thought. They'd fly by. At least she didn't have to worry about a fiancé being called up. She didn't have one, not even a boyfriend. And now with the war there were bound to be fewer men around, less chance of finding a chap at all. It was a sickening prospect.

'What do you think of this Tommy Riach business?' Irene asked.

They fell to discussing that.

'Where have you been?' Hettie demanded indignantly as Tommy strode into the room.

Jack immediately came to his feet. 'Is that you, lad?'

'That's right, Dad.'

'We've been out of our minds with worry. Your mum was beginning to think you'd run away.'

'We've been up all night,' Hettie declared. 'So where were you?'

'Have you heard?'

'If you mean about Drummond's, yes. Andrew called in yesterday evening to speak to you. But of course you weren't here.'

'I went to Perth. I stayed in a boarding house.'

'Perth!' Hettie exclaimed. 'What on earth were you doing there?'

'I couldn't bear Kelly any longer. I just couldn't.'

'But why Perth?' Hettie persisted.

'I'm never going back to Drummond's. So I've joined the RAF.'

There was a stunned silence. 'You've what!' Jack choked.

'Joined the RAF. I'm going to be a pilot.'

'Oh my God,' Hettie breathed, thinking she might faint.

For Jack his worst nightmare had become reality.

'I'll have to go into the Forces eventually anyway. So why not sooner rather than later?'

Tommy gave them a broad smile that was entirely forced. This was turning out as bad as he'd feared.

'Your age . . .' Hettie started to say.

'There wasn't any problem about that,' Tommy interjected. In fact he'd lied about his age just in case there might be.

'You stupid bastard,' Jack hissed. 'You don't know what you've done.'

'Yes I do, Dad.'

'*No you don't!*' Jack shouted. Stumbling backwards he fell into his chair. Tommy in the RAF, right at the sharp end. In the Great War the average lifespan of a pilot had been three weeks. Three weeks! Many a time he'd watched a plane tumble from the sky, pitying the poor sod trapped inside. Some ablaze, others trailing smoke. It didn't matter. They all ended up dead.

'It'll be an awfully big adventure,' Tommy whispered, stricken by his parents' distress.

He reeled, crying out when Hettie slapped him hard across the face.

Then Hettie burst into floods of tears.

'So what's up then?' Babs asked as they came to a halt on a stone bridge below which a broad burn murmured gently on its way.

Tommy took a deep breath.

And told her.

'That was the best yet,' Bell sighed. She and David were round the back of her house for the last time before he went off.

'Yes. It was quite something.'

'You can say that again.'

'Oh Bell,' he whispered. 'I don't want to go. It's the last thing I want to do.'

'I know.'

'You will write?'

'Of course.'

'And so will I when I get the chance.'

She couldn't help herself. Throwing her arms round him she pulled him tightly against her and sobbed her heart out.

'Here's the train,' Andrew said. He'd brought them to the station and would be taking Jack and Hettie home again.

There were quite a few people waiting, a number of them young chaps who were obviously off into the Forces. Further down the platform were Bell and David whom Tommy had spotted earlier, correctly assuming

David to be the young man he'd heard Bell had got engaged to.

He thought of Babs who'd declined to join them which had disappointed him no end. But she'd been adamant. They'd said their goodbyes several days previously. And a cold parting it had been. He'd been left with the definite impression it was all over between them. Babs hadn't been amused by his joining up.

Bell suddenly glanced in his direction and their eyes met. He smiled and she smiled back. For a few brief seconds their gaze held, then she broke contact to say something to her young man.

'All the luck in the world, Tommy. We'll be thinking of you,' Andrew declared, holding out a hand.

Tommy shook with him. 'It was kind of you to drive us here today.'

'Not at all. The least I could do.'

'Well, son,' Jack said, also holding out a hand. 'This is it.'

Tommy suddenly realised with a shock how much his father had aged in the past few days. He'd become stooped and somehow a lot thinner. There were lines on the scarred face that hadn't been there before. Or if they had, Tommy couldn't remember them.

'Goodbye, Dad.'

'Goodbye, son.' Jack swallowed hard, not trusting himself to speak further without embarrassment.

'Now come on, Mum, you promised you wouldn't break down,' Tommy smiled as the train drew alongside.

'I won't.'

He gave her a hug and kiss on the cheek. He could feel her trembling in his arms.

A few minutes later he was ensconced in a first-class

carriage, leaning out of the window. He was bitter about the fact Babs hadn't come.

The last door slammed shut and the guard waved his flag. Jack half raised a hand in farewell, while Hettie desperately clung on to his other arm.

The train juddered, and then moved off in a great exhalation of steam.

'Good luck, Tommy,' he distinctly heard Bell call out as he passed her.

He watched the station and Pitlochry recede until they finally vanished round a bend.

Settling back in a seat he smiled. The big adventure had begun at long, long last.

Regrets? Yes, he had those. But above all he was feeling a sense of excited anticipation at what lay ahead.

Chapter 18

'Tommy Rinch got away safely,' Andrew announced on finding Rose sitting painting by the drawing-room window. He frowned when he saw Nancy there as well.

'That's good,' Rose muttered in reply, concentrating on her brush.

'Have you nothing else to do, Nancy?'

The brush paused in mid-stroke. 'I want her here with me, Andrew. All right?'

That irritated Andrew. The lass should have been busy, not idling her time away. 'If you wish.'

'I do.' That was stated emphatically.

Andrew crossed over and poured himself a whisky from the decanter. 'How's the painting coming along?'

'Fine.'

'Can I have a look?'

Now it was Rose's turn to be irritated. 'I've told you before, not until I'm finished.'

He shrugged. 'I'm just dying to see it, that's all.'

'When it's ready, Andrew, and not till then.'

This was Rose's first attempt at a picture which she'd been labouring over for several weeks now. She'd started it outside but had come in when the weather had turned colder. Her easel was surrounded by cloths to avoid getting paint on the carpet.

'How are Jack and Hettie?' Rose inquired.

'Not too bad, considering. I might drop by later to try and cheer them up. Want to come?'

Rose shook her head.

'I'm sure they'd appreciate you calling.'

'I've got far too much to do.'

That was a lie. She had precious little to do round the house now that Elspeth Campbell was in residence. She clearly just didn't want to go.

'Can I get you a drink, darling?'

'No thank you.'

Her tone was dismissive, he thought. It was obvious she didn't want him there.

'How long before you do finish?'

Rose paused in what she was doing and gave a long, drawn-out sigh. 'I really have no idea. But the more you keep interrupting me the longer it will be.'

'I'm sorry.'

She didn't reply to that.

Andrew could see that Nancy was embarrassed by this exchange which, under normal circumstances, would never have taken place in her presence. He wondered what the girl was making of her new role as lady's maid – and now companion it would seem. For more and more that's what Nancy was becoming. Rose's companion and shadow.

He found himself at a loss as to what to do with the rest of the afternoon stretching ahead of him. He could always go to the distillery of course, immerse himself in paperwork. But for once that didn't appeal.

'Will you stop fidgeting, you're distracting me,' Rose snapped angrily.

'I wasn't aware I was.'

'Well you are. It's hard enough to concentrate as it is without that.'

'I presume you prefer to be left alone,' he commented drily.

'It does help.'

Alone meant with only Nancy in attendance. 'You've done a lovely job with Mrs Drummond's hair today.' He smiled at the girl.

'Thank you, sir.'

'Is it a particular style?'

'No, just one I made up.'

'It certainly suits her.'

Nancy flushed.

'Andrew,' Rose murmured threateningly.

He drained his glass. 'I'm off then.'

Again Rose didn't reply.

He left the room, closing the door firmly behind him.

'Hello, McFarlane.'

The groom touched his forelock. 'Good day to you, sir. I haven't had you in here for a while.'

'No,' Andrew agreed. 'I haven't been in the mood for riding recently. How's Moonbeam?'

'In the pink, sir. In the pink.'

'I hope you've been exercising her regularly.'

McFarlane looked pained. 'Naturally, sir.' What he didn't say was that Rose had been riding the animal presuming, correctly, that Andrew knew nothing about that.

Andrew went to the horse who whinnied at his approach, trying to nuzzle into Andrew's hand when his nose was rubbed.

'It was a great shame about Strumpet,' Andrew said over his shoulder.

McFarlane's face clouded. 'Indeed, sir.'

'She was a good mare that.'

It was on the tip of McFarlane's tongue to tell Andrew what had really happened, but knew it would cost him his position if he did. Mrs Drummond would ensure that.

'Just dropped dead, eh?'

'That's correct, sir.'

'Terrible shame. Still, we should have a replacement soon. I know Mrs Drummond is trying to find one.'

Poor beast, McFarlane thought. He'd been asked by Rose to keep an ear to the ground and let her know if he heard of a suitable horse for sale. Well he hadn't, and even if he had, or did, he wouldn't be passing the information on. He loved animals too much to have that on his conscience.

Andrew was tempted to take Moonbeam out, but wasn't dressed to do so. Nor did he fancy returning to the house and getting changed.

'Do you have an apple, McFarlane?'

McFarlane smiled. 'Of course, sir. A right sweet and juicy one too. A proper treat.'

Moonbeam snickered as though he understood.

A proper gentleman, McFarlane thought as he went to fetch the apple. A joy to work for.

Unlike some he could name.

'I think I'll give the book a miss today,' Jack said as Hettie was clearing away the breakfast things.

She stopped and stared at him in astonishment. 'Are you feeling ill, Jack?'

He shook his head.

'Then what's wrong? Monday to Friday, you never take a day off once you start a project.'

'There's always the exception to the rule.' Jack replied softly.

'Are you stuck?'

'No.'

'What then?'

'I just don't want to write. I don't feel like it.'

Hettie replaced the dishes she was holding on the table. 'It's Tommy, isn't it?'

There was a long silence. 'Yes,' Jack finally admitted.

Hettie's shoulders sagged. 'I'm worried sick too, Jack. But we can't let it get on top of us. Life goes on regardless.'

Oh no it didn't, he thought. There were many in this war for whom it would cease abruptly. And Tommy, God help him, might be amongst them. But he knew that she meant life in general, not in particular.

Jack was in that state halfway between sleep and consciousness. Perhaps that was why it was all so vivid and real. Not just re-running memories, but as if he was actually back there.

It was a bright day somewhere on the Somme, and a dogfight was taking place high overhead.

He was drained, emotionally and physically. He'd slept after the previous night's foray into no-man's-land, but felt as though he hadn't. He'd have sold his soul for a shave, hot bath and, equally, a hot meal. As for a nice cosy bed with fresh linen, he'd have sold ten souls for that.

He stood with his back against the trench wall, watching the dogfight. The British planes were outnumbered, their German counterparts creating havoc.

A Nieuport exploded, he could clearly see bits of debris flying in all directions. Another boy lost. The German assailant sped off, seeking further victims.

Another British plane, a Sopwith this time, was hit, turning turtle and diving earthwards trailing a thick pall of black smoke in its wake.

A figure tumbled from the cockpit, the pilot. Enveloped in flames he frantically flapped his arms as he plummeted through the air. It was sickening to witness. Was the lad flapping to try to extinguish the flames or in a bid to fly himself? Who knew?

And then he heard it. Real or his imagination? He wasn't sure. A death scream of pure agony that made his flesh crawl and his breath catch in his throat.

How slowly the human ball of flame seemed to fall, and all the while the lad was still flapping.

It was an horrific, stomach-churning sight that made him want to vomit. Truly, a *danse macabre*.

Then the ball of flame vanished from sight, cut off by the top of the opposite trench wall. He slowly counted to three, by which time it must have been all over.

He stumbled into the dugout and sprawled on to his cot. Please God his own end wasn't like that, but clean and quick.

Please God.

'By the way, Nancy, I have a letter for you.' Elspeth had been waiting to catch Nancy alone, away from Rose for a change. This was because she'd recognised the handwriting. If Nancy elected to inform Mrs Drummond then that was her affair.

Nancy stared at the housekeeper. 'A letter for *me?*'

'That's right.' Elspeth fished in her pocket. 'Here you are.'

Nancy gazed at the letter in wonderment. Who on earth could be sending her a letter? She hadn't the foggiest. It was a mystery. 'Thank you.'

Elspeth went on her way while Nancy continued down the corridor to her room.

The trouble was, she couldn't really read. Bits and pieces, odd words, yes. But not read properly.

The signature was large, and bold, followed by crosses which she knew signified kisses.

D, she deciphered. Then R.

Nancy smiled. The letter was from Drew, her admirer. Had to be. Drew who'd sworn that one day he'd marry her. It was laughable really, he was only a boy. And yet, as he'd rightly pointed out, he was only a few years younger than herself.

She did her best, but couldn't make head nor tail of the letter's contents. The only way she was going to know what it said was to have it read for her. And she couldn't do that.

Still, and a warm glow filled her, it was nice to know he'd written. That he'd taken the trouble.

She recalled the night in the bathroom when he'd asked to see her naked and she, for some reason, had revealed herself. It made her shiver ever so slightly.

He'd be home again soon, she thought. The Christmas holidays weren't that far away.

He was going to be disappointed if he imagined he was going to get a reply. Even if she'd wanted to write, she couldn't.

She hid the letter amongst her belongings.

'What do you *do* all day long?' Pattie Williams asked Nancy, the pair of them sitting alongside one another at the evening meal.

Nancy glanced up the table at Mrs Owen, the new cook, a Welsh woman. Mrs Owen wasn't nearly as popular with the staff as Mrs Moffat had been. Nor was she as good a cook. In fact some of the dishes she produced were pretty unpalatable.

'This and that,' Nancy prevaricated. She didn't really want to talk about it, aware that some jealousy had grown up over her new status.

'But what exactly is this and that?' Pattie persisted.

Nancy wasn't enjoying the beef stew on her plate. The meat was tough, not nearly done long enough. But the vegetables were nice, if a trifle soggy. How she wished Mrs Moffat was back in the kitchen. You could never find fault with her.

'I do Mrs Drummond's hair,' Nancy said.

'And?'

'Help her dress.'

'And?'

'Oh, all manner of things, Pattie. I iron for her, of course, she's a stickler about that. I look after her wardrobe. Lay out clothes, put others away. Keep her company.'

Pattie shook her head. 'That's right jammy, so it is.'

It was too, Nancy reflected. Though she wasn't entirely happy with the situation. There was something very peculiar about Rose Drummond. A grown woman playing with dolls and a doll's house for example. Who'd ever heard the like? In many ways she wished she was back doing her old duties.

'I never asked to become a lady's maid,' Nancy reminded Pattie. 'It was offered. And don't tell me you'd have turned it down. I won't believe that.'

Pattie sighed. 'You're right. I'd have grabbed the chance.'

'So don't criticise.'

'I'm not criticising, Nancy.'

'Then stop being jealous.'

Pattie glared at Nancy. Then her expression softened. 'I suppose that's what I am.'

'It can be boring at times,' Nancy went on. 'Especially when she's painting. I have to sit there for hours on end, only replying when spoken to.' She smiled. 'It can give you a sore bum, sitting still for ages.'

Pattie laughed. 'I can imagine.'

'Tell me, can you read?'

Pattie blinked at this sudden change of subject. 'I'm not brilliant, but yes I can. Why?'

No, she daren't risk it, Nancy decided. If Pattie opened her yap it could get back to the mistress and who knew what the outcome of *that* would be. A son of the house simply didn't write to a maid, even a lady's maid. It just wasn't done. If Rose found out it would get them both in trouble, maybe for her even the sack.

'Oh, no reason,' Nancy shrugged. 'I just wondered.'

'Can't you?'

'I never really learnt. Didn't have the chance.'

'Well, perhaps some day.'

'Some day,' Nancy repeated wistfully. She doubted it.

* * *

'I've decided to spend a few days with Pa and Georgina,' Rose announced. 'Naturally I shall take Nancy with me.'

Andrew noted he hadn't been included. Not that he'd have gone, the present pressure at work was too great. But it would have been nice to be asked.

'Any particular reason?' he inquired casually.

'Should there be?'

Andrew sighed in exasperation. Why was she so often defensive. It wasn't as though he was trying to pry. Suddenly he wanted to be out of the room, away from Rose. It was becoming more and more difficult to be alone in her company. Truth was, he'd welcome a short respite from having her around and the strain it had become.

'I don't suppose so,' he muttered neutrally in reply.

Rose snorted. 'That's settled then.'

'When will you go?'

'Does it matter?'

He closed his eyes, took a deep breath, then slowly opened them again. 'Not in the least, darling.' He couldn't help the trace of sarcasm that tinged his voice when he spoke that last word.

'Shall we say Friday? Does that suit?'

'Perfectly.'

'And I shall probably return midway through the following week.'

He glanced at the mantelpiece clock. Too early yet to go to bed. He'd have another drink instead, he decided, his promise to Lesley about cutting down his intake long forgotten. He hadn't had a twinge of indigestion since going to Perth. He smiled ruefully to himself. Maybe the fright of possibly having an ulcer had scared it out of him.

'What are you grinning at? You look like a demented cat.'

'Was I grinning? I wasn't aware.'

'You were grinning, I assure you.'

He shrugged and continued reading his newspaper.

'Well?' That was said shrilly.

'Nothing, Rose, I told you, I didn't know I was grinning.'

She snorted again, this time in disbelief.

He glanced at her through half-lowered lids. There were occasions when Rose could appear quite ugly, and this was one of them. It was somehow the way she contrived to contort her features.

'I hope you'll give Willie and Georgina my regards,' he said.

'Of course.'

'And you might invite them for Christmas, should they care to come. Do you approve?'

Rose considered that. 'I'll decide towards the end of my stay there. It depends how that goes.'

'Well, it's entirely up to you.'

Rose knew she was being beastly, which upset her. One moment she could be happy as larry, the next . . . quite awful, wretched inside. And when like that she wanted to vent her spleen.

'It's a pity Drew isn't here,' Andrew went on. 'He could have gone along.'

'Yes, he and James are great friends.'

Andrew ran a hand over his forehead. He felt incredibly weary. Not tired, but weary. He was working too hard, he decided. He must do something about that.

Getting up from his chair he crossed to the decanter, pouring himself an extra large one. 'You, Rose?'

'No thank you.'

For a moment his head spun, then it was gone. How strange, he thought. He really was working too hard. 'I lost Duncan Sims today,' he stated.

'Duncan Sims?'

'One of the chaps at the distillery. He's been called up.'

'That's the second, isn't it?'

Andrew turned to face her and nodded. 'I'm going to be in a right pickle if there's any more. You can't just replace a skilled man as easily as that.'

'No,' Rose agreed.

'Still, I'll manage somehow. Dad did during the Great War and I will during this lot. Though it won't be easy.'

He downed his drink and poured himself another, instantly feeling better as the alcohol hit home. He contemplated going into the village and calling on Jack, then decided he wouldn't. He and Jack could have a few consecutive nights at the pub while Rose was away, if Hettie didn't object, that is. The prospect cheered him considerably.

Rose got up from where she was sitting. 'I'm off upstairs.'

He found that a relief. 'Have a good night's sleep.'

'I shall, thank you very much.' She hesitated, then added, 'And you.'

When she was gone Andrew slumped back into his chair. What a sorry state of affairs, he reflected. Not even a goodnight kiss, not that there had been for a while now. No sign of affection whatsoever. Strangers to each other they'd become, and strangers they remained.

It was enough to make an angel weep.

*　　*　　*

Some time later he paused outside her bedroom door. How often had he done that now? he wondered. Too often.

Should he make another effort or not? Try for a reconciliation between them. See if he could win his way back into her bed. *Their* bed.

God, how he ached with longing. It had been months now. His entire body was screaming for release.

She was being downright cruel in denying him, he thought in self-pity. Rose knew only too well what he was like. How much he needed the physical pleasures of life.

It would serve her right if he went elsewhere. She would only have herself to blame after all. Even if she didn't enjoy it, the least she could do, for his sake, was her wifely duty.

He turned away, stopped, and turned back again. The very thought of joining his body with hers had already roused him and caused him to break out in a cold sweat.

Taking a deep breath he tapped her door. 'Rose?'

There was no reply.

He tapped again, this time slightly louder. 'Rose, can I come in?'

Again there was no reply.

He bit his lip. As her light was off it could be she was fast asleep and just not hearing him. He tapped a third time, more a rap than a tap. 'Rose?'

Still no reply.

He sighed. What was he, man or mouse? Reaching out he grasped the door handle and twisted it.

The damn door was locked, he inwardly raged. Now where had she found the key for the lock, he hadn't seen it in years. He twisted again. No doubt about it, the door was firmly locked.

'Go away!'

Rose's voice was cold, commanding and had an authoritative ring about it that immediately took away all desire.

She wasn't sleeping after all, but wide awake. 'Bitch,' he muttered to himself. 'Bloody bitch.'

'The End,' Jack announced, and let out a long, heartfelt sigh.

Hettie glanced up at him, eyes glowing.

'That's it then,' he smiled. 'All finished. What do you think?'

'It's wonderful, Jack.'

'You wouldn't lie to me?'

She laughed. 'No, I wouldn't lie. It is wonderful. And if I may say, my heart's in my mouth.'

Now Jack laughed. 'Good. That's what I intended.'

Hettie shook her head. 'The twist in the final few pages caught me completely by surprise. I never saw it coming. And yet it's so right somehow.'

'I feel . . . liberated. Yes, that's it. Liberated. As though I've finally broken an extended bout of constipation.'

'Jack, that's awful!'

'But precisely how I feel. And a fabulous feeling it is.'

Hettie laid the dictation aside. 'I'll type this up later.'

'And in the meanwhile, why don't we celebrate?'

'In what way?'

'Upstairs.'

Hettie smiled. 'I can't think of anything I'd like better.'

'Me neither. Now come here, woman.'

She crossed to him, sitting on his lap when he patted it. He put an arm round her and drew her close. 'What would I ever have done without you, Hettie?' he said, a sudden husk in his throat.

'Or I you?'

'We were made for one another.'

'That's what I've always believed.'

'If only . . .' His expression darkened.

'If only what, Jack?'

'Tommy,' he whispered.

The happiness oozed out of her. The cloud that had descended over Jack now extended to her. 'Yes.'

'I worry so much about him, Hettie.'

'I know. As do I.'

He shuddered, his nightmares returning. Nightmares that were haunting him night after night. He wondered what Tommy was doing at that moment. Training, he presumed. Had to be. His letters said he was thoroughly enjoying himself. Revelling in it.

But it was early days yet. The real horrors of war were still to come. Lurking over the horizon.

'Let's go for a walk first,' Jack suggested.

'Good idea.'

'Get a breath of fresh air. Blow the cobwebs away.'

'Whatever you wish.'

Neither of them mentioned Tommy again that day.

Andrew had dined alone, Rose having departed for The Haven earlier, and was now off to meet Jack in the pub. With Rose away, and Jack having finished his book, no doubt it would be an extended session with the pair of them probably ending up back at Jack's. But first he wanted to stop in at his study to jot down a work reminder, something he often did in the evenings.

In a good mood, he was humming as he snapped on the overhead study light. He smiled in remembrance of how fond his father Murdo had been of this particular room. It

303

had been his sanctuary, the holy of holies, no one normally being allowed inside except Murdo himself.

Andrew started for his desk, then came up short when he saw what was propped up on it. A watercolour painting.

Rose's, he guessed correctly. She'd finally completed it and left it on his desk as a surprise. He thought that rather touching.

Swiftly he crossed over to study the painting up close. Not bad at all, he mused. He'd certainly seen a lot worse in his time.

He recognised the scene, there was no mistaking it, though Rose had added certain bushes, trees and shrubs that weren't actually there. Why she'd done that he had no idea. Artistic licence, he supposed.

The painting certainly merited being framed and he wondered where they might hang it. In the study perhaps? That was a possibility. But he'd leave the final choice of place to Rose.

She must be pleased with it, he thought. She'd hardly have left it on his desk otherwise. And she had every right to be.

And then he saw it. A tiny figure, almost obscured by bushes. It was that of a young child, a girl, staring out. A girl whose face was a combination of his own and Rose's.

'Mary,' he whispered. That must be who the child represented. Who else? The wee lassie Rose had lost.

Not only his face and Rose's, it suddenly dawned on him, but that of another person as well. Yes, quite definitely, that of another person. But who?

An icy coldness gripped him, his skin prickling with gooseflesh.

He felt sick inside.

Chapter 19

'So what do you think?' Willie Seaton queried.

The mare was similar to Strumpet in many ways, the same colour but with slightly different markings. A friendly beast, she nuzzled into Rose's hand.

'She's beautiful, Pa.'

'I thought you'd like her. She's yours. A present from me.'

'Oh Pa!' Rose exclaimed excitedly. 'What's her name?'

'Gypsy.'

'Gypsy,' Rose repeated in a murmur. 'You and I are going to be great pals.'

Gypsy snickered her pleasure.

'I'll arrange to have her taken to Drummond House so you've no worries on that account.'

'How old is she?'

'Three.'

Rose wanted to ride her there and then, and promised herself she'd do so at the earliest opportunity. 'I'm so thrilled, Pa. Thank you.'

'Do I get a kiss from my girl?'

'Of course.'

Willie beamed as he was pecked on the cheek.

'She's a perfect woman's horse,' Willie went on. 'Spirited, but not fiery. Easily managed. You shouldn't have any trouble with her.'

They stayed in the stables for a few more minutes, then emerged again into cold winter sunshine. Willie coughed. 'I haven't had a chance to speak to you alone yet. Are you fully recovered?'

She stared blankly at him.

'From what happened. The, eh . . . baby.'

'Oh, that! More or less.'

He frowned. 'What does more or less mean?'

'It's not something you ever fully get over, Pa. It'll always be with me.'

'Aye,' he sympathised. 'I can understand that.'

'It's like losing part of yourself. Which of course a baby is. It's terribly hard to explain.'

Willie thought of his first wife Mary who'd died from influenza and the pain that had caused him. He was no stranger to loss and grief.

'You'll be trying again, I take it?'

'For another child?'

He nodded.

'That's not entirely in our hands, Pa. We had to wait long enough the last time, who knows what'll happen in the future.' She smiled inwardly at her prevarication. She'd managed to answer the question without answering it.

Willie cleared his throat. 'Yes, quite so.'

They walked a little way in silence. 'Is Andrew well?'

'Couldn't be better. Working extremely hard mind you, thanks to the war. Demand has risen due to exports. In fact not only risen but is positively booming. There are times when Andrew says he doesn't know whether he's coming or going.'

'Booming, eh?' Willie chuckled. 'Well, that's no bad thing. More demand means more profits, a very satisfactory state of affairs. Pity it's due to war though.'

'Yes,' she agreed.

Rose slipped an arm round her father's. 'It's good to be back, Pa. To see you and The Haven again.'

'You should visit more often.'

'Perhaps I will,' she smiled. 'And thank you again for Gypsy. She's a lovely present.'

'There's absolutely nothing wrong with Rose,' Willie declared to Georgina later that day as they were dressing for dinner. 'I had a long chat with her earlier and there was no sign whatsoever of anything untowards. So I was right, we needn't have worried after all.'

'You must admit what happened in Edinburgh when she and I were there *was* strange, Willie. Rose looking at baby clothes and toys. Bizarre in the circumstances.'

Willie shrugged. 'If there was anything wrong, something playing on her mind, it's gone now. She's right as rain. I don't think I've ever seen her looking better.'

Georgina remained unconvinced. There was something about Rose that was eluding her, something she couldn't quite put her finger on. There again, as Willie had originally said, it might simply be her imagination.

'She was delighted with the horse,' Willie went on. 'Thrilled was the word she used.'

'It was very kind of you to give it to her.'

'Not in the least. She may be a married woman but

she's still my daughter. Anyway, I got as much pleasure out of giving it to her as she did receiving it.'

What a good man Willie was, Georgina reflected, not for the first time. One of the best. A real gem. She doubted there was a mean bone in his body.

It shamed her to remember how she'd once betrayed him with Andrew Drummond, and that James was Andrew's son. Still, all that was in the past, buried if not entirely forgotten. Willie would never find out. She'd never say anything, and neither would Andrew. Her secret was safe, thank the Lord.

'They've invited us there for Christmas and Hogmanay,' Willie announced.

'Oh?'

'I said we'd go.' He rounded on Georgina. 'That's all right I take it. Perhaps I should have spoken to you before accepting?'

'It's absolutely fine by me, Willie. I'll enjoy myself. And I'm sure James will.'

'That's what I thought. It'll be a nice break for the pair of us.'

He was fiddling with a gold cuff-link, one of a pair Georgina had given him. 'Damn thing,' he muttered.

She smiled. 'Here, let me.'

'She's all saddled up and ready to go,' the groom declared to Rose who'd arrived in the stables to take Gypsy out.

What a handsome creature, Rose thought. Dark swarthy looks, strong face, broad shoulders, narrow waist. He might have stepped straight from the pages of a romantic novel.

'What's your name?' she asked in a voice suddenly grown husky.

'Andy, ma'am. Andy Somerville.'

She was staring at him. He exuded raw masculinity and charisma. Rose was mesmerised by the oozing magnetism of the man.

Rose accepted Gypsy's reins when Andy handed them to her. 'And how long have you been at The Haven?' she inquired.

'Just over a year now. I was on the land before that but always fancied working with horses. When I heard this job was going I applied and was lucky enough to be taken on.'

'And which cottage are you in, Andy?' It was bound to be on the estate.

'Rose Cottage, ma'am.'

That made her smile. 'I know it. Tell me, are you married, Andy?'

'Oh no, ma'am. There's plenty of time for that. I intends remaining a bachelor for some while yet.'

Now that was interesting. 'I'll bet you have lots of lady friends?'

He regarded her curiously, wondering why she'd asked that. 'They come and they go, Mrs Drummond. Nothing serious, which is how I wants it.'

'I see.' She wanted to stay longer, but couldn't think of a reason for doing so.

'Is there anything else, Mrs Drummond? If not I'll get on.'

'That's all for now, Andy. Thank you.'

She led Gypsy outside and mounted, glancing back into the stables before she moved off. Her last glimpse of Andy Somerville was him bending over, backside pointing in her direction.

A wave of pure lust flamed inside her.

*   *   *

'Can I have a word, Mr Drummond?'

Andrew, sitting in front of the fire after his evening meal, instantly roused himself. He'd been lost in thought.

'Please do.'

Elspeth Campbell carefully closed the door behind her and came closer to Andrew.

He was smiling, pleased to see the housekeeper. 'Now what's bothering you?'

Elspeth folded her hands in front of her. 'It's a delicate matter.'

'Oh?'

'I believe Mrs Owen has been taking wine from the cellar.'

Andrew leant forward fractionally. This was serious. 'Are you sure?'

'Only she and I have keys and a number of bottles are missing. A dozen, maybe more.'

'It's a large cellar, Elspeth, even I couldn't say what's down there.'

Her face hardened. 'I know what I've removed on instruction and what I haven't. Bottles have disappeared that should still be there.'

'Well well,' Andrew mused. He was surprised to say the least. He'd never have guessed from Mrs Owen's prim and proper manner that she had a taste for alcohol. 'Have you found any empties?'

Elspeth shook her head. 'I took the liberty of looking in her room and there wasn't any trace. So wherever she's put them it isn't there.'

Andrew gestured to the chair opposite. 'Come and sit down, Elspeth. I could use some company.'

She blushed. 'I couldn't possibly do that. I'm on duty and . . . well it just wouldn't be right.'

Andrew rose from his chair. 'At least join me in a drink. In fact, I insist.'

That flustered Elspeth. 'I said, I'm on duty.'

'I heard you, and I still insist. One drink isn't going to do any harm.'

She relented, thinking she'd enjoy a drink with Andrew. 'What if someone comes in?'

He laughed. 'I'm the employer, Elspeth, don't forget that. If I wish to have a dram with my housekeeper then who's to criticise.' He added, ominously, 'They'd just better not, that's all.'

'In which case I'll have a sherry please.'

As Andrew was pouring he had a sudden thought, one that brought a smile to his face. He had the address somewhere and would write before going to bed that night. As for Mrs Owen, she was a rotten cook anyway.

Elspeth stayed for nearly half an hour before Andrew would let her go.

A half hour that gave them both great pleasure.

'I'm missing David so much,' Bell said to Irene, as they neared the end of the day's shift.

'Is he still writing?'

'Oh aye. Though not as often as I write to him.'

Their hands were moving deftly as they spoke. They'd been doing the job for so long it didn't need any concentration.

'Where is he again?'

Bell reminded Irene. 'He says it's a bleak place with none of the comforts of home.'

Irene pulled a sympathetic face. 'Any news of leave yet?'

'None. He was hoping to get back for new year's but that's not on apparently.'

'Pity.'

Bell thought of their sessions behind her house. She missed those as well, dreadfully. She wondered what she missed most, David or that? A combination of both, she decided.

'I heard on the wireless there's been some air raids on the south coast,' Irene stated.

'I heard that as well.'

'It'll be London next. You wait and see.'

'I've always wanted to go there.'

'London!'

'Just for a few days like. It must be wonderful.'

'Certainly diffcrent to Dalneil,' Irene replied drily.

They both laughed.

'Just a bit.'

'You could always go on your honeymoon there,' Irene suggested.

Bell had never thought of that. 'So we could. Mind you, it can't be that much fun at the moment, what with the blackout and all.'

'It must still be London. There might not be as much going on as before the war, but there again, possibly there is. Anyway, it couldn't fail to be a great experience for you.'

Bell decided she'd mention it to David in her next letter.

A honeymoon in London! That would be something to remember for the rest of her life.

Rose strode into the stables, her face bright with exhilaration. Steam was coming off Gypsy in clouds.

Andy paused in forking hay. 'You look as though you've enjoyed yourself.'

It was the third time Rose had taken Gypsy out, and she had thoroughly enjoyed herself. She hadn't pushed Gypsy too hard though. Partly because of what had happened to Strumpet, and partly because there were far more eyes on the estate than at home.

'I did, I can assure you.'

His shirt was sodden with sweat and consequently sticking to him, she noted. It threw his chest and shoulders into sharp relief.

What an Adonis, she thought yet again. The sort of man to make a maiden's heart melt. Well, she was no maiden, she reminded herself. Far from it. But she was affected nonetheless.

Andy crossed to her and held out his hands for the reins.

'No, I'll rub her down and feed her myself,' Rose smiled. That was simply an excuse to remain with Andy.

'If you like.'

'Is there any tea going?'

'I can brew up a cup if you wish.'

'Then let's have some. I'm parched.'

She could suddenly smell him which made her go weak at the knees. She fought back the mad, insane impulse to leap on him and rip the clothes from his body.

This was ridiculous, she thought. What on earth was making her think in such an outrageous way? It didn't make sense.

She stared hungrily at him as he moved off to where the kettle was kept.

'Jack!'

'Is that you, John?'

The Reverend John McLean, Andrew's brother-in-law,

hurried over to Jack standing just inside the church doorway. 'I've never seen you in here during the week before.'

A wry expression creased Jack's face. 'I felt the need to come. I hope that's all right?'

'Of course. It's God's house, open to all. You're more than welcome any time you wish.'

Jack took a deep breath. 'It's always so peaceful in here. That and . . . somehow reassuring.'

John nodded his understanding. 'A haven of tranquillity from the troubled world outside.'

'And troubled it surely is.'

'Aye,' John said softly. 'And it's going to get a lot more troubled before it gets better.'

'I wish I could disagree with you, but I can't.' Jack smiled. 'Are we alone?'

'Quite.'

'Am I disturbing you?'

'Not in the least. I wasn't doing anything I can't do later.' John hesitated. 'Is there something special brings you today?'

'Only to pray.'

'I understand. There are many have been coming to do that lately.' He hesitated again. 'It's Tommy, isn't it?'

'Yes,' Jack admitted quietly.

'A good lad.'

'He's joined the RAF you know.'

'Yes, I know.'

'They'll be at the sharp end. And not before too long I shouldn't imagine. I . . .' Jack trailed off as emotion welled within him. He couldn't bear the thought of losing Tommy. Or worse still, and there were many such scenarios. Some just too horrendous to contemplate.

'Would you like me to pray with you, Jack?'

'Would you?'

'Of course. Now where would you care to sit?'

'Not my usual pew, but right at the front.'

'Do you wish me to help or can you manage by yourself?'

'If you'll take my arm.'

When they reached the pew, instead of sitting Jack knelt on the floor and bowed his head. John did likewise.

'Let us pray,' John began.

Andrew hung up the telephone. That had been Rose to say she intended stopping off in Edinburgh *en route* to do some shopping. She'd stay overnight and then resume her journey on a mid-morning train.

She'd been distant during the call and that had been nothing to do with the line either. Cold, aloof almost. Not a trace of warmth or affection in her voice.

He'd made a joke about not going overboard and spending too much, which had gone down like the proverbial lead balloon. When he'd inquired how things were going she'd replied fine and not elaborated. Her goodbye had been almost curt.

Andrew sighed, ran a hand over his face, and thought how weary he was. Bone weary.

He'd have an early night, he decided.

'Where's Andy?' Rose demanded of Jenkins, the senior groom who was an old man teetering on retirement.

'Gone home, Mrs Drummond.'

'Home?' Andy had been there when she'd taken Gypsy out for a ride. 'Is something wrong?'

'No, Mrs Drummond. It's his half-day.'

'I see,' she murmured, bitterly disappointed. She'd been going to attend to Gypsy herself but now Jenkins could do that.

She left the stables in a right old temper.

'Are you all right, Rose?' Georgina inquired across the dinner table.

Rose started. 'Yes. Yes of course.'

'You've hardly touched your food,' Willie commented with a frown.

'I'm not really that hungry for some reason.'

The reason was Andy Sommerville; she just couldn't get him out of her mind. A mind running riot with lecherous thoughts which, on the one hand, were inflaming her, on the other, making her feel deeply ashamed.

She'd only ever been to bed with Andrew and couldn't help wondering what it would be like with another man. Andy Somerville in particular. A picture conjured up in her mind made her shiver.

'You're not ill, are you?' Willie asked anxiously.

'No, Pa. I've just lost my appetite tonight, that's all.'

Rose glanced at Georgina. She hadn't mentioned her intended stop-off in Edinburgh to either her or Willie in case Georgina suggested accompanying her. She didn't want her stepmother along this time.

Later she was aware of Georgina watching her keenly, which both annoyed and alarmed her.

It was as if Georgina knew what she was thinking.

The clock on the mantelpiece chimed midnight. Rose was sitting by her bedroom window staring out, a fire burning brightly in the small grate giving the room its only illumination. Ghostly shadows were dancing on the wall opposite the fire.

Rose was in her night-things including a heavy quilted dressing gown of a Far Eastern style. Despite the hour she didn't feel the least bit tired.

There was a fever in her that was keeping her awake. A red-hot fever of longing and desire.

She had to do something about this, she thought. She just *had* to. But what?

She couldn't just throw herself at Andy. Think of the humiliation if he rejected her.

But he wouldn't. She was almost certain of that. The previous afternoon she'd caught him staring at her out of the corner of his eye in a way that left no doubt he was attracted to her.

'Oh God,' she moaned, shifting in her chair. If she was on fire inside then it was a veritable furnace down there. A furnace clamouring to be attended to.

'Rose Cottage,' she said, and smiled. How apt. How very apt. An omen you could say. Of all the cottages on the estate Andy had to live in that one.

The mantelpiece clock ticked relentlessly on.

The house was deathly quiet, everyone, with the exception of her, abed when Rose slipped outside.

She shivered with cold, hastily pulling her coat more tightly about herself. It was pitch black, but that didn't hinder her. She knew exactly where she was going.

The cottage was in darkness as she'd expected it to be. There was a gentle wind causing the branches of some nearby trees to rustle spookily.

Rose stopped in front of the door and stared at it. What if Andy had someone with him? It was possible as he did have lady friends from time to time, though nothing serious he'd assured her.

She shook her head, aware of her heart thumping nineteen to the dozen. Turn back, she counselled herself. Turn back before it's too late!

But her body wouldn't allow her to do that. It was insistent, demanding gratification. Crying out for it.

She knocked and waited.

No reply.

Rose swore, and knocked a second time.

What if he wasn't in? What if he was elsewhere?

'Andy?' she heard herself call out. 'Andy!'

There were sounds from within, those of cautious movement. A light blossomed in the window only feet away.

'Who is it?'

'Rose Drummond.'

There was a pause, broken by the scrape of bolts being retracted. The door was thrown open to reveal Andy, clad only in a shirt that came almost to his knees, holding a paraffin lamp.

'Holy God,' he whispered. 'What are you doing here?'

She brushed past him. 'Shut that quickly,' she breathed.

The room she found herself in was relatively warm with the remains of a fire glowing cherry red in the grate. A glance round confirmed it to be a typical single man's domicile, messy with dishes piled in the sink. There were no feminine touches anywhere.

He came to stand beside her, his expression a combination of puzzlement and concern.

'Mrs Drummond?'

'You know why I've come.'

He studied her hard. 'Do I?'

'Don't play the innocent with me, Andy Somerville. You know precisely why.'

He visibly relaxed, his eyes twinkling. 'I reckon I does.'

She undid her coat, shrugged her shoulders and allowed the coat to drop to the floor. All she was wearing underneath was her nightdress.

'I reckon I does,' Andy repeated softly.

There was no reneging now; she was committed. 'Well?' She was amazed by her boldness.

Andy reached out and ran a calloused hand over her breast. Rose moaned in response.

Now using both hands he grasped hold of the front of her nightie and, in one violent movement, ripped it apart and from her, leaving Rose standing totally naked.

'Beautiful,' he whispered. 'You're a real beauty, Mrs Drummond. My oath and you are.'

And so was he, she thought. So was he. She trembled all over.

Taking her by the wrist he hurried her through to the bedroom.

Rose sat bolt upright. Had it been a dream? Had she imagined it? No, it had been real. She'd gone to Andy's cottage, returning to The Haven as dawn was breaking.

What had she done! screamed in her head. And yet she had done it. In the most wanton fashion.

She closed her eyes, remembering all that had occurred. How he'd . . .

Shame filled her, that and remorse. Guilt above all. How could she do such a thing when she loved Andrew?

For the first time it dawned on her they both had the

same Christian name. Andrew, Andy. Somehow that made it even worse.

And then a terrifying thought struck her. What if . . . what if . . . She swallowed hard. What if Andy had made her pregnant? How could she possibly explain a pregnancy to Andrew whom she hadn't slept with in months?

It was unlikely, true. But possible all the same. Who was to say the trouble she'd had conceiving in the past wasn't Andrew's fault? If that was so then it could be oh so different with Andy.

Fear gripped her, the fear of producing a bastard, the fear of losing Andrew, of divorce.

For she loved Andrew. When all was said and done she loved her husband. Incredible as that might seem after what had happened the previous night.

There was only one thing for it, she decided. As soon as she was home she and Andrew had to make love. That way there wouldn't be any discrepancy in dates, should she be pregnant, though God forbid!

Yes, that was it. Had to be.

Rose hung her head and began to cry. What had possessed her? What!

Chapter 20

'Is something wrong, Mr Drummond?'
'Just tired, that's all, Kelly.'
The book-keeper thought how pale and drawn Andrew
had looked recently. The man was clearly overdoing it.
'Would you like a dram, sir?'
Andrew considered that. 'You know, I believe I would.'
'I'll pour it for you, sir.'
'Will you join me, Kelly?'
'No thank you, if you don't mind.'
Andrew rubbed his eyes which were painful. That was
another thing, he was having trouble with his sight of late.
A visit to the optician would be in order he decided, smil-
ing at a vision of himself wearing glasses. Still, he couldn't
really complain. Many men wore spectacles at his age.
He recalled the dashing young blade he'd once been,
his sight had been perfect then. As had his figure which
had now expanded somewhat over the past few years. Not
too much, mind, but certainly a bit.

'There you are,' Kelly declared, placing a glass in front of Andrew.

Weary, God he was weary. Normally he would have considered a holiday, but he could hardly do that in wartime. It didn't seem right somehow.

Andrew glanced up at the attentive Kelly, another well past fighting age. 'Why were you so hard on Tommy Riach?' he asked softly.

Kelly blinked, having been caught off guard. 'I wasn't particularly aware I was.'

'Yet he said you were.'

Kelly's brow furrowed. 'If anything I was trying to teach him discipline, towards his work that is. He could be very lackadaisical.'

Andrew smiled. How often had his father Murdo accused him of that? He hated to think. But it had all come right in the end, time and maturity had seen to that.

'Your problem, Mr Kelly, is you don't have any children.'

Kelly frowned. 'Pardon?'

'You've never learnt to make allowances for youth. You have to when you're a parent.'

'There was never anything personal in it,' Kelly replied hurriedly.

'I believe that. But Tommy thought there was. He told Jack he disliked you as much as you disliked him.'

Kelly was appalled. 'I never disliked the lad, it simply isn't true. He irritated me, I can't deny that. And occasionally it went beyond irritation. But I certainly never disliked him. On the contrary, I thought he had the makings of a fine traveller. The potential was there.'

'Did you ever tell him that?'

'Of course not,' Kelly spluttered.

'Perhaps you should have done, eh?'

Kelly took a deep breath. 'Are you blaming me for his leaving, sir?'

'No, not really. I know he flounced off in the huff but I think he'd have come back again after I'd had a word with him and sorted things out. But he'd have eventually gone off to war anyway and been lost to us. At least for the duration.'

Andrew had a sip of whisky, closing his eyes in appreciation as it rolled smoothly down his throat. He'd put his single malt up against any distilled in Scotland. If it wasn't the best it certainly ranked high amongst them. A tribute to the skills of his forebears.

'I hope he returns safe and sound when it's all over,' Kelly said. 'I'd hate the idea of anything happening to him.'

'Amen,' Andrew murmured, thinking of Jack and Hettie.

'Amen,' he repeated.

The atmosphere during dinner had been frosty. In fact it had been more than that, it had been downright glacial. Now they were alone Andrew knew what was coming, and it amused him.

'So, why did you get rid of Mrs Owen?' Rose demanded in a steely voice. Her intention had been to be all sweetness and light towards Andrew but that had swiftly evaporated when she'd discovered what had occurred in her absence.

'She was stealing and I can't have that.'

'What did she steal?'

'Wine from the cellar. Miss Campbell noticed the missing bottles and as only she and Mrs Owen, plus me of course, had the keys then it had to be her.'

Rose harumphed. 'Is Miss Campbell certain about that?'

'Yes, she is.'

'There wasn't any mistake?'

'None.'

Rose was angry, seeing this as a direct challenge to her authority.

'Besides,' Andrew went on slowly, 'she wasn't much of a cook. Not a patch on Mrs Moffat.'

'Which is why you re-hired Mrs Moffat I suppose?'

'We were lucky there. I wrote to her sister in Stirling asking what had happened to her and surprisingly she was still available, not having found any other suitable employment in the meantime. I re-engaged her by telephone and, happily, back she came.'

Andrew smiled, not having told Rose that he'd had to be most persuasive for Mrs Moffat to agree. Nor that he'd upped Mrs Moffat's salary.

Rose's lips became a thin slash of disapproval. 'I find what you've done quite unacceptable, Andrew.'

'Oh?'

'Have you forgotten why she was dismissed in the first place?'

'Not at all. But she wasn't dismissed, she resigned. More or less forced to by you. Anyway, let bygones be bygones, Mrs Moffat belongs here. It's almost as much her home as it is ours.'

Rose stared balefully at Andrew, furious now. 'What you did was strictly against my wishes.'

He raised an eyebrow which infuriated her even further.

'I will not have her here,' Rose snapped.

'She stays, and that's that. What's more, you will stop

interfering in the kitchen now that you're not responsible for the housekeeping duties any more. Understand?'

Rose coloured. She wasn't used to being spoken to this way, by Andrew or anyone else.

'Understand?' Andrew repeated ominously.

'I want her sacked.'

'She stays.'

'I . . .'

'It's what *I* want in this case, Rose,' he interjected. 'She stays, and that's that.'

'I won't . . .'

'You'll do as you're bloody well told,' he cut in.

Rose scrambled to her feet and, looking straight ahead, without another word swept from the room.

Andrew waited till she'd gone before laughing softly. He'd enjoyed that. The trouble was he'd indulged Rose too much in the past. Well that was over.

And about time too.

How could she go to him tonight? It was now impossible. Out of the question after how he'd spoken to her downstairs. Damn that Mrs Owen for a thief. Stupid woman.

Rose was still seething inside. Positively livid. Well, a few nights either way wouldn't make any difference, she assured herself. Months yes, but hardly nights.

She'd go to Andrew when she was ready. But it had to be soon.

Just in case.

Dog tired as he was, Andrew had been unable to sleep. His mind had kept whizzing round and round. A jumble of memories from the past, matters concerning work, Rose.

In the end he'd decided to get up and seek out Elspeth

Campbell, hoping to find her in the kitchen. He only wanted to talk, have some company, perhaps get a little sympathy.

He stopped when he came in sight of the kitchen to see that the light wasn't on. 'Damn,' he swore, disappointed.

Go into the kitchen anyway and make a cup of tea, or return to bed? Elspeth might well turn up shortly after all. There was always that possibility.

Nearly an hour, and several cups of tea later, he gave it up as a bad job and went back to his room.

It was the following morning that Andrew ran into Nancy in the corridor. He came up short to stare at her in astonishment for she was wearing a tailored dress, an expensive one too from the look of it, instead of her usual uniform.

The dress had a neat, bloused top with pocket-like tabs. There was a swoopy skirt and set-in belt which gave it a smooth waistline, with half-sash ties at the front. The sleeves were long, the colour dark cadet blue.

These niceties were quite lost on Andrew who saw only a dress. 'Nancy?'

'Good morning, Mr Drummond.'

'Good morning to you.' He cleared his throat. 'That's a pretty outfit.'

She flushed. 'Thank you, sir.'

'But shouldn't you be wearing your uniform?'

'Mrs Drummond doesn't want me in a uniform any more, sir. She bought me this and other clothing in Edinburgh. Her instructions are that I'm to wear them now.'

Andrew recalled the painting Rose had left in his study as it suddenly struck him who the other face, apart from his and Rose's, had been reflected in that of the child. He could see now that it was Nancy's.

'I see,' he murmured. 'Most unusual I must say.'

'Those are her instructions, sir.'

'Then you must carry them out.'

'Yes, sir. Can I be excused, sir? Mrs Drummond is waiting for me.'

'Of course. On you go.'

He watched her hurry away with a chill of some nameless fear running through him.

'I haven't had a chance to say yet, but I liked your painting,' Andrew commented that evening.

Rose glanced across at him. 'I'm pleased.'

'It's very good. I thought I might hang it in my study, unless you have another preference?'

She shook her head. 'Your study will be fine.'

'When will you start the next one?'

'Not till the new year sometime. The holidays are almost upon us and Drew will shortly be home. And of course we have Pa and the family coming. So I think I'll leave it till the new year.'

'Yes, it was very interesting,' he said slowly.

He sensed her suddenly become wary, though it didn't show. Ask about the child, or not? He decided not.

A silence fell between them.

Andrew had never stopped halfway through making love before, far less with Rose, but he did now. Extricating himself he rolled over on to his back.

'Andrew?'

'What?'

'Is something wrong?'

'Only that I may as well be making love to a corpse. It's most offputting to say the least.'

Rose turned her head away. 'I'm sorry.'

'I can't think why you came if you're not really interested.'

She didn't reply to that.

He remembered the last time she'd been, and the time before. There was no comparison between that Rose and this. Then she'd been wild in the extreme, abandoned, passionate almost beyond belief. Now . . . nothing. No response whatsoever. As he'd said, it was most offputting. Eerie.

'I'm sorry,' Rose repeated.

'Is it ever again going to be as it once was between us?' he asked sadly.

Again Rose didn't reply.

Time, Lesley had told him. Time. But God, it was hard to bear. It was an ongoing torture. And now this which was even worse than her not coming to him at all.

Pity welled in Rose. For Andrew, for herself. How her entire world had changed in a relatively short while. She hardly recognised herself as the Rose who'd gone to Glasgow with Andrew.

'Was it a sense of duty? Or guilt perhaps?' Andrew queried, again sadly.

It had been neither of course, but the necessity to ensure she was covered where Andy Somerville was concerned. How she regretted that incident.

'Can we try again?'

There was no response from Andrew.

'Please?'

He twisted round to look at her. 'Is there any point?'

'Yes,' she murmured.

He'd completely lost the notion, which was extremely unusual for him. Unheard of even. He'd always had the notion where women were concerned.

'Please, Andrew?' Rose repeated, a sting of tears in her eyes.

Reaching out he drew her to him, she snuggling up against his chest. 'That's nice,' she whispered.

He stroked her hair, and she closed her eyes while he did.

After a while the hand moved from her hair to her shoulders, and then to her breasts which he gently caressed.

Rose thought of Andy Somerville. Up until then she hadn't realised how expert Andrew was in the art of lovemaking. Or that he was gifted with a stamina many men weren't.

With Andy it had been rough, he using her, plundering her body for his own satisfaction with no real thought to her needs. True, it had been exciting, but only up to a point.

It was so different with Andrew. He played her the way a master musician does an instrument, extracting sweet music of the very highest degree.

Rose sighed, feeling herself begin to respond to his touch. 'Oh, Andrew,' she whispered.

His own desire returned.

As had happened previously, when he awoke in the morning she was gone, leaving just a lingering hint of her scent.

Rose gathered Drew into her arms. 'Welcome home, son.'

He wanted to be with her, desperately so, and yet at the same time was uncomfortable. He'd never forget it was because of him that she'd lost the baby.

Rose held him at arms' length. 'Now what do you want to do?'

'Go over to the distillery and see Dad. I shall work there during the holidays.'

Rose raised an eyebrow. 'Really?'

He broke away from her. 'I enjoy it, Mum. There's so much to learn and do.'

'And what about when James comes?'

Drew shrugged. 'There will be the evenings and days off. We can be together then.'

'I'm not so sure I approve of this.' Rose frowned.

'Approve of what?'

'Your working at the distillery. During the summer's fine, it keeps you occupied. But Christmas and new year?'

His expression became stubborn. 'The distillery will be mine one day, Mum. I want to know everything about it there is. So why not start my education early?'

A Drummond through and through, she thought. There was a lot of Andrew in him. And Murdo, his grandfather. Perhaps even more of the latter from what she'd heard, never actually having met the man.

Drew wondered where Nancy was, at which point, as though on cue, she entered the room. He took in the fact she wasn't in uniform.

'Hello, Master Drew.' Nancy smiled. She'd been a little worried about his homecoming, but now realised she was pleased to see him. He'd changed a bit, she thought. He was somehow more mature.

Drew's eyes sparkled. 'Hello, Nancy.'

'When did you get in?'

'Just now. Only a few minutes ago.'

'Pleased to be back?'

He pulled a face. 'Anything's better than school.'

She laughed, thinking him lucky to be going to school in the first place. But she didn't say so.

'Nancy and I are off out shortly, a women's meeting,' Rose said to Drew. 'To do with the war effort.'

'Then I'll just get on up to the distillery.'

'Would you like something to eat before you go?'

He shook his head. 'Not till later, Mum, thank you.'

During his walk to the distillery all he could think of was how nice Nancy had looked. He'd somehow contrive to speak to her alone later.

Bell burst into the room where her two brothers, as usual, were squabbling. 'Will the pair of you shut the fuck up!' she screamed.

They stopped and stared at her in amazement.

'It's like bedlam in this bloody house. There's never any peace and most of that's down to you.'

Not waiting for a reply she went out again, slamming the door behind her.

Her father was in the living room sitting slumped in front of the fire still filled with ashes from the previous night. He was fast asleep and snoring, drunk, judging by the empty bottles strewn by the side of his chair.

'Jesus Christ,' she muttered, shaking her head. What a family. God alone knew where her mother had got to. And what a tip the place was!

She thought in despair of David, and the home they'd planned together, for the time being cruelly snatched from her because of this stupid war.

There was no tea, unless she made something herself, and she couldn't be bothered to do that. She'd eat later.

She'd go to Irene's, she decided. Have a natter with her. Anything was better than staying in this hellhole.

Her father, true to form, lifted a buttock just then and farted loudly.

Bell fled.

'She's a cracker right enough,' McFarlane declared to Rose, rubbing Gypsy's muzzle.

Willie and Georgina, who'd brought the horse with them, were also present.

'She's to have Strumpet's old stall,' Rose instructed McFarlane.

'Yes, Mrs Drummond,' he replied, touching a forelock.

'I'll be taking her out first thing in the morning. Make sure she's ready.'

McFarlane nodded that he understood.

'Let's have tea then,' Rose tinkled to Willie and Georgina. Talking together the three of them started back for the house.

McFarlane stared sympathetically at Gypsy, thinking what a fine beast she was. Well cared for too, that was obvious. Mr Seaton's groom clearly knew his business.

'Well, Gypsy,' he murmured, patting the horse's flank. 'I only hope that bitch doesn't ride you into the ground as she did Strumpet. But we'll have to wait and see about that.'

Shaking his head he led Gypsy towards her new stall.

Nancy yawned as she headed for her room. It was Christmas day, and a long one it had been. She couldn't wait to be tucked up.

There had been a drink in the kitchen earlier, Mrs Moffat and Miss Campbell dispensing sherry and cake.

They'd had their own Christmas dinner after the family had retired from theirs. And sumptuous it had been too. Mrs Moffat had done them all proud.

Good old Mrs Moffat, how pleased everyone had been to have her back. Not only to have her back but also to be rid of that sour-faced Mrs Owen whom nobody had liked.

Nancy had started to undress before she noticed the small tissue-wrapped parcel on her bed. Frowning, she crossed over and picked it up.

It was a slender gold chain that caused her to gasp with pleasure. There wasn't a card to go with it but she knew who it was from. Drew, of course. Who else?

She was deeply touched, and for the space of a few moments held it to her bosom.

She'd thank him when they were next alone together.

'Drew isn't fun any more,' James Seaton said to his mother Georgina.

'Oh?'

'He won't play like we used to. And he's always over at the distillery. I hardly ever see him.'

Georgina too had noticed the change in Drew. The lad was growing up fast. A little too fast possibly.

'Everything changes,' she smiled at James. 'That's the way life is. Nothing stands still. Or lasts for ever.'

She gave him a sympathetic cuddle.

'Nancy!'

She turned to find Drew hurrying after her. 'I hoped I might run into you,' he said.

'I'm off on an errand for your mother.'

'You're so hard to speak to nowadays. You're always by her side.'

'I'm afraid so.'

'What about during the party tonight?' he asked eagerly.

'I shan't be with her then. I'm not required, for once.'

He was drinking her in, thinking how lovely she was. 'So what are you going to do instead?'

'Nothing I suppose. I'll probably stay in my room.'

'Can I come and see you there?'

'Definitely not,' she laughed.

'Oh, Nancy. Please!'

'No,' she stated emphatically. Her hand went to the high collar of the dress she had on, underneath which she was wearing his chain. She still found it hard to believe it was real gold and that he'd bought it for her having saved up his weekly allowance. She remembered how the pair of them had laughed when he'd asked why she hadn't replied to his letters and she'd told him she could neither read nor write. He'd confessed he'd never thought of that.

'Can I have a hogmanay kiss then?'

'Drew, behave yourself,' she admonished.

'No one's about.'

'That's not the point.'

'Don't you want to kiss me, Nancy? I want to kiss you.'

Her good humour vanished, replaced by a more serious mood. She studied him, noting the changes in his features, particularly a new firmness that hadn't been there during the summer.

'Please, Nancy?' he repeated.

'You'll get me the sack.'

'No I won't. Mother adores you. Thinks the sun shines out that gorgeous bum of yours.'

'Drew!' she exclaimed, shocked. 'What a thing to say.'

'But it's true.'

She realised they were standing outside a large walk-in linen cupboard. Why shouldn't she indulge in a little flirtation and affection, even if it was with someone so young?

'Come here then,' she said, and crossed swiftly to the cupboard. Seconds later they were both inside, the only light being that coming through the crack at the bottom of the door.

'Oh, Nancy,' he whispered, taking her into his arms.

'Just one now.'

'Just one,' he promised.

A promise he broke. Nor did Nancy pull away or rebuke him, finding it a very pleasant experience, passionate too.

Afterwards she wondered how he'd learnt to kiss so expertly. If she'd asked him he'd have truthfully told her it just came naturally.

He was his father's son after all.

'Are you all right?'

Andrew started, not having heard Elspeth Campbell's approach. He smiled at her. 'I'm fine. I just came out for a breath of fresh air. It's rather fuggy in there with so many smokers present.'

'It is rather. I saw you leave and wondered if something was the matter.'

He shook his head. 'Just needed the fresh air, that's all.'

He'd drunk quite a bit that evening, but it was one of those occasions when it had little or no effect on him.

'I'll get back in then,' she said.

'Elspeth?'

She hesitated.

'Keep me company for a few minutes. Unless it's too cold for you that is.'

It was cold, but not unbearably so. She could manage a few minutes of it.

'I've got some news for you,' he declared.

'Oh?'

'Mrs Drummond has agreed for you to stay on full-time. If you wish that is.'

She'd been hoping for this, while at the same time wondering if it was such a good idea.

'Well, Elspeth?'

'I'd be delighted to accept.'

'That's settled then,' he beamed.

'You haven't been down to the kitchen at nights for a while,' she said slowly.

'No, I've been sleeping better of late.'

'That's good.'

He glanced round at the house. 'It's strange seeing all the windows blacked out. I find that quite disturbing.'

She didn't know what to reply to that, so remained silent.

'They'll all be up for hours yet. The usual hogmanay,' he smiled.

'I've never really liked hogmanay myself. The end of one year, the start of another. A sort of nothing time really. At least that's how I see it.'

'I understand what you mean.'

There was a silence between them during which neither felt ill at ease.

'I must get back,' she said eventually.

'Me too. You'd better go first.'

It wasn't lost on her he'd said that as though they'd conspired to meet up, a rendezvous.

'I was just concerned about you, that's all.'

'Thank you, Elspeth, and happy new year.'

'Happy new year to you, Andrew.'

She moved away, silent as a shadow, leaving a thoughtful Andrew behind.

Chapter 21

'Any news yet?'

It was September 1940, and the Battle of Britain was at its height. Tommy shook his head in reply. 'Not a sausage.'

Mavis Giddings, barmaid at the Lamb and Flag, gave him a sympathetic smile. 'Don't worry, you'll be made operational before long.'

'I hope you're right.'

Tommy and the rest of his training squadron were itching to get into the fight, hating kicking their heels while others got on with it. Normally their training would have extended well into the following year. But these were desperate times calling for desperate measures.

'The usual?'

'Please, Mavis.'

Tommy had struck up a friendship with Mavis, though, so far, that's all it was. He enjoyed her earthy humour. In many ways she reminded him of Bell Mathieson.

Dingo Roberts, an Australian also in the squadron, slid on to the stool beside Tommy. 'How are you going, mate?'

'Not too bad. You?'

Dingo shrugged. 'Anxious to get at the Jerries like everyone else. I've heard the Poles have been made operational now.'

'The Poles!'

'That's what I heard. If it's true then we can't be far behind.'

Mavis placed a half of bitter in front of Tommy. 'You, Dingo?' she asked.

'Make mine a pint. I'm dry as the Nullarbor Plain.'

'How are you getting on?' Dingo asked in a whisper after Mavis had gone back to the pumps.

'What do you mean?'

'With the fair Mavis there. Everyone's after her but she's only got goo goo eyes for you.'

Tommy blushed.

'Well, sport?'

'Mind your own business, Dingo.'

'Aha! Do I detect progress at last?'

'No, you do not. Now be a good aborigine and shut up.'

Dingo laughed. With his red hair and freckles he couldn't have looked less like an abo.

Others from the squadron sauntered in. All of them, including Dingo, were older than Tommy.

'Let's have a tune on the old ivories, Fitz,' Dingo called out to one of the newcomers.

Justin FitzHugh waved back. 'Let me wet my whistle first.'

More men from the squadron arrived, the small pub rapidly filling up.

'Come on, Fitz, get a move on, you lazy sod. We want entertaining,' Paul Wyborn shouted from the corner where he was ensconced with a girl from the village.

'I think it's going to be one of those nights, mate,' Dingo grinned at Tommy.

'Isn't it always,' Tommy replied drily.

'Can I have a word with you during the dinner break, Mr Balfour?' Irene asked him as he was walking by.

The gaffer stopped to stare at her. 'What about, Irene?'

'Private, sir.'

'Oh, all right,' he shrugged. 'Come to my cubbyhole.'

'Thank you, Mr Balfour.'

He moved off again.

'What was that all about?' a curious Bell queried.

'I'll explain after work.'

Bell didn't press as Irene clearly didn't want to discuss the matter further, guessing correctly it was because of others listening in.

'Well?' Bell demanded as they were leaving the distillery on completion of their shift.

'I've handed in my notice.'

Bell came up short to stare incredulously at her friend. 'You've what!'

'Handed in my notice. I go in a fortnight.'

Bell was stunned. 'But why?'

'Because I've joined up.'

Bell's mouth opened, then shut again. 'You've joined up?' she managed to say after a few seconds.

'The ATS. Auxiliary Territorial Service. They're going to train me as an ambulance driver. At least, that's what they promised.'

The pair of them continued on their way. 'You never said anything?' Bell complained.

'I didn't want to let on until I'd been accepted. The letter I've been waiting for came this morning.'

'But why, Irene?'

Her friend chuckled. 'Apart from the obvious reasons, helping with the war effort et cetera, it's a perfect opportunity to meet new men.'

Bell laughed. So that was it! 'You sly old thing.'

'There's no one round here seems interested in me. And I don't want to end up an old maid. By joining the ATS I might meet someone nice.'

Bell was jealous, but reminded herself she had David. Nonetheless, she too would have liked to join something like the ATS. It sounded tremendously exciting.

'Do you know where they're sending you?'

Irene shook her head. 'Haven't a clue. All I know is I've to report to a place in Glasgow. After that, who knows?'

Bell's eyes gleamed. 'Driving an ambulance sounds fun.'

'That's what I think. I should have a rare old time.'

Bell hooked an arm round Irene's. 'I'm dead pleased for you, so I am. But I'll miss you, mind. Oh aye, I will that.'

'And I'll miss you, Bell. But look on the bright side, think of all those gorgeous men I might meet. With a bit of luck there'll be a husband among them.'

They both laughed.

Their new CO strode into the operations room where Tommy and the rest of the squadron were waiting. They all rose to their feet.

'Please sit, chaps,' the CO said.

With a shock Tommy recognised him. He was older than he remembered, or at least looked older. He'd lost weight and there was an air of authority about him that hadn't been there before. That and something else Tommy couldn't put his finger on. Their new CO was Gerald McTaggart, Babs' brother.

Gerald introduced himself, then stared grimly at the assembly. 'You'll be pleased to know that as from midnight tonight the squadron becomes operational. Well done.'

A great cheer went up. It had happened at long last.

Gerald's smile was razor-thin, a smile that belied the look in his eyes.

It was a look Tommy was to encounter many times in the coming months.

'Top Hat, I have trade for you. Bandits at Angels 4000.'

Tommy glanced up through his canopy, quickly scanning the sky. There they were, Me109s. About a dozen of them.

'Here we go, chaps,' Gerald's voice came crisply over the R/T. 'Good luck.'

'Yoicks and tally ho!' someone added.

Tommy smiled, recognising Dingo's voice. His assumed English accent was diabolical.

The pub was muted when Tommy went into it later that evening. A sympathetic Mavis greeted him at the bar.

'I heard about Fitz,' she said.

Tommy's face was ashen, completely devoid of colour. 'I saw it happen,' he croaked. 'Fitz just . . . blew up.'

They both glanced over at the piano standing silent, both recalling uproarious nights when Fitz had played. Tommy knew it to be his imagination, but the piano seemed to have a dejected air about it. As though it was in mourning.

'The usual?'

Tommy took a deep breath, and nodded. 'Add a chaser as well, Mavis. I need one.'

'The CO wants to see you.'

'Thank you,' Tommy replied to Sergeant O'Dowd, a Liverpudlian of Irish descent.

Now what did Gerald want him for? he wondered as he headed for his office. So far they hadn't spoken together since Gerald had taken over.

'Hello, Tommy.' Gerald smiled as he closed the door behind him.

'Hello, sir.'

Gerald waved to a seat. 'I thought I recognised the face but couldn't place you to begin with. Then I looked up your file.' He paused, then said, 'A long way from Dalneil.'

'Yes, sir.'

'Call me Gerald when we're alone. But only then.'

'Right, Gerald.'

Gerald rocked back in his chair and studied Tommy. 'Well well, it was quite a surprise finding you here.'

'And I suppose for you to turn up.'

'A lot has happened since we met,' Gerald mused darkly.

'Indeed.'

Gerald's eyes took on a faraway look and became pained. He shook himself out of his reverie. 'Are you still in touch with my sister?'

'No, she didn't approve of me joining up.'

Gerald grunted, and a flash of disappointment and anger crossed his face. 'I see.'

343

'Maybe she did the right thing. I can't say.'

Gerald didn't answer that. Instead he got up and crossed to a window to stare out. He was about to speak when the klaxon sounded. Both men were galvanised into action.

'Heinkels, swarms of the bloody things,' Billy Moore commented over the R/T.

There were too, Tommy observed. And no fighter cover as far as he could make out. It would be like shooting ducks in a barrel.

'Help yourself, chaps,' Gerald instructed.

Moments later the first Heinkel tumbled from the sky.

Elspeth gazed at Andrew sitting across the table from her. It was just after three in the morning. 'How's the tea?'

'Lovely, thank you.'

She lit a cigarette while he stared morosely into his cup. 'A penny for them?'

He made a face. 'There's nothing in particular.'

'Worried about something?'

'No more than usual.'

A silence fell between them which Elspeth eventually broke by saying, 'You've never told me your story.'

He blinked. 'I beg your pardon?'

'Do you remember I told you my sorry tale some time back. I've never yet heard yours.'

'No,' Andrew said softly.

Elspeth waited patiently, but he didn't go on.

'I understand if you don't want to tell me. Some things are just too personal.'

How he enjoyed being alone with Elspeth Campbell. She was so relaxing to be with. He could have happily remained where he was, with her, for the rest of the night.

'It'll be strictly between you and me, Elspeth?'

'Of course.'

'No, I mean that. You mustn't breathe a word to anyone else. Members of staff in particular.'

'I won't. I swear.'

His expression became one of anguish as he spoke about himself and Rose.

It was more or less as she'd expected, Elspeth reflected as she got back into bed. She'd known there was something wrong between Andrew and his wife. Known it instinctively without having to hear the gossip that circulated from time to time amongst the staff.

There was the matter of separate bedrooms for a start. Understandable after the miscarriage, she supposed. And people of their class often slept apart, she knew that for a fact.

But not Andrew, not willingly, he simply wasn't the type. And so it had proved when he'd confessed his situation.

Her heart had gone out to him. How sad he'd sounded. Almost beaten somehow. It had taken a great deal of effort on her part not to weep on his behalf.

She'd already said her prayers earlier. But now she said them again, this time including Andrew.

'Get out, Dingo. Get out!' Tommy screamed into the R/T.

He'd seen Dingo's plane being raked with cannon fire, then, with smoke streaming from it, begin to spiral downwards.

The sky was filled with aircraft, a graceful ballet of death.

'Get out, Dingo!' he screamed again.

A figure detached itself from the doomed Hurricane, and seconds later a parachute billowed.

'Thank God,' Tommy breathed in relief. He could only hope no one shot Dingo before he hit the Channel.

He banked sharply to port as he glimpsed an Me110 zooming in on his tail.

Dingo was temporarily forgotten as the grisly dance went on.

Everyone looked round as Dingo strolled through the pub door. 'You bastards haven't got rid of me yet,' he grinned.

Tommy whooped and pounded the bar. 'Set 'em up for me old cobber!' he instructed a delighted Mavis.

There was a lot of back-slapping and hand-shaking before Dingo reached Tommy's side. 'It's sure as hell wet out there in that Channel,' he joked.

Tommy laughed, a trace of hysteria in his voice.

'And you know something?' Dingo queried.

'What?'

'I still can't bloody swim.'

'They've got the CO. Christ, they've got him!' Billy Moore's voice crackled over the R/T.

Tommy spotted Gerald's plane, identifiable by its distinctive markings, go belly up enveloped in smoke and flames.

He could see Gerald desperately trying to get out, but the canopy remained firmly in place.

'Dear God,' Tommy whispered. Gerald was being burnt alive.

It seemed an eternity before Gerald's plane eventually crashed into the sea.

* * *

'Time, gentlemen, please!' Mavis called out.

Tommy was sitting alone at the bar, Dingo having stayed in camp that night. The mood was funereal.

'You remain behind,' Mavis whispered to Tommy.

He only dimly heard her as he was lost in thought. What agonies Gerald must have suffered before he died, what excruciating torture. He kept thinking of his father's face, that being the result of burns. It was probably better Gerald hadn't survived.

The others present drank up and left, Mavis locking the door behind them. She poured herself a brandy and port before joining Tommy.

'I knew him from before,' Tommy said.

'The CO?'

'He came from the same village as me. I only met him once, mind, he was some years older. At his parents' house. I was seeing his sister Barbara at the time.'

Mavis had a sip of her drink, her eyes never leaving Tommy. Three of the squadron were now dead, two missing in action.

'Poor bastard,' Tommy choked, tears welling in his eyes.

Mavis put an arm round his shoulders and pulled him close. 'I can't say I knew him. He only came in here several times.'

'He was a decent bloke. I liked him a lot.' Tommy wiped away the tears. 'I suppose it was because of him I joined the RAF. Because of him and a Spitfire I once saw.'

'I'm sorry,' Mavis sympathised.

'My dad was in the Great War and never talks about it. Not unless you really push him that is. I'm beginning to understand why.'

She saw that his glass was empty. 'Another pint?'

'You wouldn't have any Drummond malt on the premises?'

'Drummond?' Mavis thought about that, then shook her head. 'I'm afraid not.'

Pity, Tommy thought. It would have been fitting to toast Gerald's departure with that.

'We've plenty others though.'

'No, it had to be Drummond. It's made in Dalneil where we both come from.'

He closed his eyes, again seeing Gerald fighting with the canopy and failing to release it. The long slow descent to the Channel and the final impact. A few minutes only, but they must have seemed like hours to Gerald. He shivered.

'Why don't you stay the night with me?' Mavis suggested softly.

Tommy stared blankly at her.

'Dan and his wife won't mind. I know they won't.' Dan Gilfeather was the owner of the Lamb and Flag.

'In your room?'

Mavis nodded. 'I have a double bed so we won't be cramped.'

Right then Tommy could think of nothing he'd like more. A warm body to hold and to hold him. 'All right,' he replied.

'Can you sneak back into camp in the morning?'

'That's isn't a problem. Some of the lads do it all the time.'

'Right then. Shall we go on up?'

Mavis stripped naked to stand in front of him. 'Well?' she smiled.

She was the first woman Tommy had ever seen fully unclothed. His mouth was dry, his pulse racing. 'You're gorgeous,' he said huskily.

Mavis gave a small laugh. 'Hardly that. I know I'm no great beauty. But I'm not too bad.'

'I think you're gorgeous.'

She came into his arms and he kissed her deeply. The smell of her was strong in his nostrils, the feel of her skin exciting in the extreme. He broke away, face red with embarrassment.

'What's wrong?' She frowned.

'There's something I have to tell you.'

She stared at him, waiting for him to go on.

He glanced down at the floor. 'I've . . . I've . . .' He coughed, this was awful.

Mavis smiled slowly as understanding dawned. 'Are you trying to tell me you've never been with a woman before?'

Still gazing at the floor, he nodded.

She should have guessed as much. 'That's all right.'

'I don't want to disappoint you. I know what to do but . . .' He trailed off.

'It doesn't matter, Tommy. Even if we don't do anything, I promise you. Now get those things off and come to bed before I freeze.'

He fumbled with his tie.

'Mavis?'

'What, Tommy?' she replied lazily.

'That really was wonderful.'

'For me too, darling.'

'Really?'

'Really.'

He snuggled up closer to her, marvelling at what had just taken place. How could you be prepared for such a thing? You couldn't.

'Are you sure that clock will go off?' he asked.

'Don't worry, it always does. It's never failed me yet.'

She caressed the inside of his thigh, and sighed. She'd had better lovers in her time, but that was where experience counted. Anyway, it was Tommy she'd wanted to sleep with, not Don Juan.

Minutes later she smiled, realising Tommy was fast asleep, she cradled in his arms.

Her last conscious thought was to hope he didn't dream of the CO.

'It's a letter from Tommy,' Hettie announced excitedly.

Jack sat upright in his chair. 'What does he say?'

'Hold on, Jack, I haven't even opened it yet.'

'Then hurry up, woman.'

Jack waited expectantly as Hettie swiftly read the single sheet of paper the envelope contained.

'Oh dear,' she whispered.

'What is it?'

'Gerald McTaggart, Barbara's brother, has been killed.'

Jack's lips thinned and whitened. 'But Tommy's all right?'

'Fine, according to this. Tired, but fine.'

Jack let out a sigh of relief. 'What else does he say?'

'Not a lot, there are only a few lines. All he's apparently got time for.'

Jack sank back into his chair, thinking about the McTaggarts. This would be a real body-blow for them. But at least Tommy was safe. It might be selfish on his part, but that was all he really cared about.

Hettie carefully refolded the sheet of paper and returned it to the envelope. 'I suppose a few lines are better than nothing,' she declared, trying to put on a brave face.

'Can I have the letter?'

She handed it to him.

'It seems like only yesterday he was a baby,' Jack said softly.

'Yes.'

Jack ran the tips of his fingers over the letter, trying to imagine the conditions under which it had been written. He knew only too well the sort of tiredness Tommy was referring to, appreciating the fact Tommy had actually forced himself, made himself find the time, to write.

'Would you like a cup of tea?' Hettie asked brightly.

'I'd love one.'

'And how about a piece of cake?'

'Even better.'

'I'll put the kettle on.'

Come home safe, son, Jack silently prayed. Please come home safe and sound.

'London's taking a right old pounding by all accounts,' Mavis declared to Tommy, placing a pint in front of him.

'Yes,' was the grim reply.

'It must be dreadful there.'

He'd seen the glow from the capital in the far distance during a night sortie. Bright red and orange, it might have been the gateway to Hell itself.

'You look exhausted,' Mavis stated.

'I am. I might even nod off right here at the bar.'

He reached for his glass, stopping his hand halfway on noting it was shaking. When he picked up his pint he spilled some.

'Is Dingo coming in tonight?' Mavis queried.

'Should be, a little later. He has something to do first.'

Mavis moved off to serve another customer.

They'd lost another member of the squadron that day, Tommy reflected. A replacement pilot who'd only joined them two days before. He hadn't seen the chap buy it, but several others had.

He'd been made up to Section Leader the previous week with Dingo flying as his wingman. They made a good team. And, so far, a lucky one.

Mavis returned. 'Did you ever write to the CO's parents as you thought you might?'

Tommy shook his head. 'I couldn't in the end. I did try but . . . just couldn't. I'll go and see them when I'm next in Dalneil.'

If he ever was, he thought to himself.

'How would you feel about Nancy taking meals with us?'

Andrew stared at Rose in astonishment. Really, this was going too far. 'Why should she do that?'

Rose shrugged, and glanced away. 'She's become almost part of the family.'

Anger flared in Andrew which he quickly brought under control. 'She's an employee, Rose, nothing more.'

'She is to me,' Rose stated defiantly.

Andrew recalled the small figure in the first painting Rose had done. There had been several paintings since, the same small figure in all of them. The face an amalgamation of his, Rose and Nancy's.

'Nancy brings me a great deal of comfort,' Rose said quietly.

'That's obvious.'

'We've become so close we're almost like sisters.'

Not sisters, Andrew thought, but mother and daughter. For that's what this was truly all about. Who would have foreseen when he brought Nancy into the house that this would be the outcome?

'The rest of the staff won't like it. They'll be jealous,' he said.

'That's their lookout.'

'And what does Nancy think about this?'

'I haven't mentioned it to her yet.'

'Then maybe you should.'

'I wanted to speak to you first, Andrew.' She shot him a pleading look that quite melted his resistance.

'It's very unusual to say the least,' he said gruffly.

'I know that.'

A few seconds ticked silently by. 'Do as you wish,' he growled eventually.

'And you'll be nice to her. Accept her at the table?'

'Of course I will.'

'Thank you, Andrew, I appreciate this.'

Rose got up and left the room, the last he saw of her that night.

The following morning a somewhat embarrassed Nancy joined them for breakfast.

Chapter 22

'David!'
Not caring what any of the others coming off shift might think, Bell flew across to where he was standing waiting and into his arms. 'Oh David,' she cried.

He squeezed her tight. 'Hello, darling. Surprise?'

A few passing female workmates giggled and tittered, but all were delighted for Bell.

'How long have you got?' she demanded throatily, not knowing whether to laugh or cry.

'Ten days. But I've already used up two of them.'

Bell frowned at him.

'I had to go to Auchgloan and see my folks. Now I've done that I can be with you.'

She took a step backwards to gaze him up and down. How handsome he looked in his uniform, quite the proper soldier. He'd lost a bit of weight, but it suited him. And his face had aged a little. The body that had embraced her had not only been leaner but tougher too.

'I presume you're not due back here till Monday morning?' he smiled, it now being Friday evening.

She nodded.

He encircled her waist and drew her off to one side. 'How do you fancy going away?'

Her eyes opened wide. 'Just the two of us?'

'That's right. I've managed to borrow a motor and enough petrol to see us through. There's a wee hotel I've heard of which I've booked us into. What do you say?'

Her mind was whirling. 'Are you suggesting a dirty weekend?'

He smiled lecherously. 'That's it.'

Bell caught her breath.

'I let slip to the owner that we're on our honeymoon. Which isn't true of course but they're not to know that. I thought it would make the whole thing easier.'

'You have got it all planned out,' she commented drily.

'I don't want to waste any time. Besides, I'm fed up going round the back of your house.'

Now she did laugh.

'It would mean we could actually go to bed together.'

The thought of that almost turned her legs to jelly. Anyway, why not? They'd made love together often enough, this was merely taking things one step further.

'Well?' he prompted.

'I'll have to pick up some things from home first.'

'Of course. I'll drive you.'

She hesitated. 'Will you mind waiting outside?'

He knew from his cousin Ronnie about Bell's parents and that she was deeply ashamed of them. The fact they were like they were didn't bother him in the least. He loved Bell which was all that mattered.

'Suits me.'

'Let's go then.'

'The car's over here.'

As they walked hand in hand towards the car she wondered what she'd tell her mother and father. By the time they reached her house she'd concocted a suitable story to explain her absence for the weekend. She'd say she was spending it with an old pal, as she occasionally did, who lived in a nearby village. Her parents wouldn't think to question that.

She asked David to park a little way further down the street before going inside.

Dingo yawned and then glanced at his wristwatch. It was ten past three in the afternoon and they hadn't been scrambled all day. 'Where the hell are the Jerry bastards?' he frowned.

'Don't complain. Enjoy the rest,' Tommy replied from the dilapidated armchair he was lounging in.

'I'm not complaining. Just curious, that's all.'

'Something's afoot,' Billy Moore commented from where he was sitting.

'Must be,' Dingo muttered.

When they were finally stood down they still hadn't been scrambled.

Andrew stared in concern into the contents of the toilet bowl. He'd passed blood, quite a lot of it too, which was worrying. He wondered if it was in any way connected with the intermittent pains he'd had in his stomach recently.

He was probably just run down, he decided. He hadn't had a proper break in God knows how long.

Maybe Dr Lesley had been right and it was an ulcer after all. But if so why hadn't it shown up in the hospital tests?

* * *

'It's a beautiful view,' Bell declared, looking out of the window of their double bedroom.

David came to stand beside her. 'It is that,' he agreed. 'But nowhere near as beautiful as you.'

'What a smoothie,' she teased.

He nuzzled the nape of her neck. 'Now we know what it's like to have a bed. Far more comfortable than the other, don't you think?'

'Oh yes,' Bell purred.

His hands covered her breasts causing her to moan. 'Stop that or we'll miss breakfast.'

'They'll understand if we don't show up in the dining room. We are supposed to be on our honeymoon, don't forget.'

'I'm not all that hungry anyway.'

'You should be after last night,' he chuckled.

'And you,' she retorted.

'We'll find somewhere to get a bite later on,' he said, one hand moving down to caress the swell of her buttocks.

They returned to the rumpled bed they'd just left.

'What's wrong with you?' Nancy demanded of Drew, back from school for the holidays.

He started, having been lost in thought. 'Nothing.'

'You had a face like fizz.'

'Had I?' he replied, pretending innocence.

'Are you bored, is that it?'

'No.'

'Then what?'

Drew shrugged. 'Why aren't you with Mum?' he queried, changing the subject.

'She's having an afternoon nap.'

He'd been thinking about his mother, guilt lying heavily on him. There were still times when he couldn't stare her straight in the eye.

'Are you bothered about something?' Nancy further probed.

He relented, and nodded.

'What?'

'I can't tell you.'

'I see.'

He turned away, desperately wanting her to remain with him, at the same time wanting to be alone. 'Things have changed quite a bit since I went away,' he commented.

She knew he was referring to her. 'Does it upset you?'

'Goodness no. I enjoy having my meals with you. Even if you don't say all that much. Only speak when spoken to.'

She blushed. 'I haven't got used to the situation yet if you want the truth. I don't want to . . . intrude I suppose.'

'Do you find Father daunting. Is that it?'

'Not really. He's kindness itself. And I owe him such a lot. Who knows what would have become of me if he hadn't come across me that day in Leithan.'

Drew reached out and touched her arm. 'I thought about you ever so much when I was at school. I had dreams about you.'

'Dreams!' she laughed, adding drily, 'I can imagine what sort.'

Now it was his turn to blush. 'I can't help dreaming, Nancy. Or what I dream about.'

'As long as they were nice dreams.'

'Oh yes,' he enthused. 'They were certainly that.'

She studied him for a moment, not for the first time trying to visualise the man he'd become. It was a pleasing picture.

'Can I come to your room tonight, Nancy?'

'No, you cannot,' she replied hastily.

'I'd like to talk.'

'And what else?'

'Nothing, I promise you.'

She smiled, knowing what his promises were like. Where she was concerned anyway.

'No, Drew, and that's an end of it.'

His disappointment clearly showed. 'I've changed my mind about what I said, Nancy. I would like to tell you what's bothering me. Why I had a face like fizz.'

She relented a little. 'Are you sure about that?'

He nodded.

It was asking for trouble. If Mr or Mrs Drummond were to find out . . . 'It's too risky,' she said.

'Please?'

The look in his eyes persuaded her. 'All right, but for no longer than half an hour. And, Drew, no funny business or you're straight out the door again.'

'You're a sweetie, Nancy.'

A fool more like, she thought.

Bell stood watching David walk down the street. That was it, his leave was over. Heaven knew when she'd see him again.

Thankfully there was a full moon which meant she could watch him for some distance.

Just before disappearing round a corner he turned and waved. She waved back, her mind crammed with the happy memories of the last week. Especially those spent in the hotel when they'd pretended to be on honeymoon. Memories that would stay with her for ever, no matter what.

And then he was gone from sight.

* * *

'Come in.'

Drew slipped silently into the bedroom and shut the door behind him. Once inside he stared around.

'It's certainly a lot nicer, and more comfortable, than the room you had before.'

It was Rose who'd proposed that Nancy move down into this bedroom which was on the level used by the family and guests. It was considerably larger than her previous one and, as Drew had rightly commented, far better appointed. For Nancy it was the very lap of luxury.

Drew crossed to the fireplace and gazed at the painting hanging above the mantelpiece. 'One of Mum's, eh?'

'She gave it to me.'

It was a landscape he recognised. What he failed to notice was the small figure almost obscured by foliage.

'Remember what I said, no more than half an hour.'

'Relax, Nancy, Mum and Dad are out as you know and won't be home for ages yet. We've nothing to worry about.'

'There's always Miss Campbell. She's often on the prowl at this time.'

'She's in the kitchen with Cook and the others. I checked.'

Nancy pulled her cardigan, a blue one she'd knitted herself, more tightly about her. It wasn't the best of fits. 'You wanted to talk, Drew?'

His face darkened. 'Yes,' he replied quietly.

'Then sit down.' She indicated a chair.

'And you?'

'I'll make do with the bed.'

'Can I bring the chair a bit closer? I don't want to have to shout across the room.'

She could see the sense in that. 'All right.'

Nancy perched herself on the edge of the bed and waited while he brought the chair over and placed it several feet from her.

He sat and lapsed into silence.

After a while he glanced up at her, his face filled with anguish. 'This isn't easy, Nancy.'

'Is it about me?'

He shook his head. 'No, Mum.'

'Your mother?' she queried softly, puzzled.

Drew took a deep breath . . .

'That's utter nonsense,' Nancy declared when he'd finally finished. 'You can't possibly have been responsible for your mother losing the baby.'

'But I *was*, Nancy. Didn't you hear me, I wished it to happen. And it did.'

'Pure coincidence, nothing more.'

'I can't believe that.'

'But it's true, Drew. Her miscarriage had nothing whatsoever to do with you. How could it possibly?'

'But I *wished* the baby away, Nancy.'

His newfound maturity of recent times had gone, vanished. He was again a little boy. And a terribly upset one at that. 'And you've been worrying about this ever since?'

'Yes,' he croaked.

She'd never heard anything so ridiculous. Poor Drew, what a burden he'd been carrying. 'I assure you, Drew, wishing the baby away didn't make it happen. As I said, it was just coincidence.'

'I blame myself, Nancy. I wished so terribly hard, you see. So terribly, terribly hard, and it came about.'

She slid from the bed to kneel in front of him, clasping one of his hands in hers. 'You're being silly, Drew.'

'No I'm not,' he replied defiantly.

'Oh yes, you are. You've got a guilty conscience about something that had nothing to do with you.'

His expression was one of utter wretchedness. 'Sometimes it hurts, Nancy, just thinking about it.'

'I agree you should never have made that wish in the first place, but in a way it was understandable. A new child was going to be born who'd put your nose out of joint, and so you were jealous. Right?'

He nodded.

'That sort of thing is common between brothers and sisters. Making that wish wasn't so awful, it was merely human. Millions of other boys and girls must have made the same wish.'

'But for *me* it came true.'

'Yes it did, but not because of your wish. What occurred was God's will and nothing else.'

Drew suddenly burst into tears. 'Oh, Nancy,' he sobbed.

'God's will,' she repeated.

Somehow, Nancy wasn't sure how, they were both on their feet, she holding him tight while he continued to cry.

His body shook in her arms.

'Nancy and I are going out after this,' Rose announced over dinner, speaking to Andrew but smiling at Nancy. 'There's a meeting in the village hall. We're discussing further ways of helping the war effort.'

'Very admirable,' Andrew commented with just a trace of sarcasm in his voice.

'We'll be gone for several hours at least. Won't we, Nancy?'

'I'd imagine so.'

'What sort of "further ways" do you have in mind?' Andrew queried, making conversation.

'Oh, I don't know. We'll just have to wait and see what's proposed.'

Andrew felt excluded at his own table which made him angry. It was Rose and Nancy, Nancy and Rose. He might as well have been a stranger. The barrier between him and the other two was almost tangible.

The rest of the evening stretched interminably ahead. He on his own. Not that it was all that different when it was just himself and Rose. Often it was as though she wasn't even there.

What were they talking about now? He forced himself to listen. Women's chat, nothing he felt he could contribute to.

Andrew excused himself before dessert was served. Rose wasn't put out in the least that he'd decided to leave them to it.

In fact, she seemed almost relieved.

'I had a letter from Irene this morning,' Bell said to Hannah McIlroy, working alongside her.

'How is she?'

'In the pink. Thoroughly enjoying life in the ATS which she says is enormous fun. The lucky blighter's been posted to London.'

'London!' Isa exclaimed.

'Trust her to get that posting.'

'But it'll be awfully dangerous there, what with the Blitz and all.'

'She's looking forward to it according to her. No matter what danger she might be in.'

'I hope she's going to be all right,' Isa frowned.

'Me too. There have been an awful lot of people killed there since the bombing started.'

'Ach, knowing Irene she'll probably have a whale of a time, bombs or not. You know what she's like, if she fell in a midden full of shite she'd come up smelling of roses.'

Bell laughed, that was true enough. And London would be full of men which would suit Irene down to the ground.

'You must miss her though,' Isa sympathised. 'The pair of you being best pals and that.'

'Aye, I do.' In fact she missed Irene even more than she'd thought she would.

They stopped talking abruptly when Balfour appeared, coming in their direction.

Tommy and Mavis were alone at the bar together, she having just locked up for the night. As was the custom that had grown up between them they'd have a few drinks to let Mavis catch up before going upstairs.

'I've been meaning to ask you.' Mavis smiled. 'What will you do when the war's over?'

If he came through it alive that is, Tommy reflected wryly. They'd lost another member of the squadron that morning to an Me110. His Section continued to be lucky without any fatalities.

'I suppose I'll go back to what I was doing before,' he replied thoughtfully.

'And what was that? You've never said.'

How strange war was, he mused. Mavis was right, she knew little about his life in Dalneil prior to joining up. Just as he knew little about her past, only that she came from Woking and was an only child. Neither of them had felt the need to exchange confidences, all that seemed to matter was the here and now. That's what war seemed to boil down to, getting through the day intact, not thinking about tomorrow, just staying alive.

He told her about his training as a traveller for Drummond's.

'That sounds a great job.'

'Well, it would have been when I got out on the road. If I'd stayed on that is. I'd have been well paid, had my own car and everything.'

He suddenly smiled.

'What is it?'

'Want a laugh?'

'I can always use one of those.'

'My burning ambition before the war was to be an African explorer and big-game hunter.'

She did laugh. 'You're joking!'

'No, that's what I desperately wanted to be. It was my dream.'

'Not a very practical one,' she commented drily.

'I suppose not. But I fantasised about it for years. I could just see myself with the gun and large hat.'

'Jungle Jim,' she teased.

'Something like that.'

'But why an explorer and big-game hunter?'

Tommy shrugged. 'I suppose it was the most exciting thing I could think of. Certainly a world away from Dalneil where I live.'

'A real hero, eh?'

'Oh yes. Carving my way through the undergrowth, rescuing fair damsels from killer lions, wrestling with man-eating gorillas, you get the idea.'

'As far as I'm aware gorillas are vegetarians,' she laughed.

'That may be so, but they're still dangerous beasties. Massive buggers.'

Mavis thought this a right hoot, but nice all the same. There was nothing wrong in having aspirations, after all. Even if they were daft ones.

'And what about you?' he asked.

She shook her head. 'I was just pleased to get a job when I left school. Being a barmaid was the first I was offered and that's what I've done ever since.'

'So why come to Laxworth?'

'No real reason. My mother started seeing another man and I felt in the way. I decided to move out of the area and eventually ended up here. No dreams in my case, I'm afraid.'

He finished his drink.

'Tired?'

'Aren't I always?'

She nodded her understanding. 'If you don't mind I'd like another before we go on up.'

'Have as many as you wish. I'm perfectly happy being here with you. There's no rush.'

She mustn't get too attached, she told herself. Not in the circumstances. That would be foolish.

But in the meantime . . . Well it was lovely having Tommy around – and in her bed.

Andrew gasped and bent over as pain exploded in his stomach. 'Christ,' he muttered through clenched teeth.

His senses swam, and for a few moments he thought he was going to lose consciousness.

'Mr Drummond. Mr Drummond!' Kelly exclaimed anxiously, hurrying over from where he'd been busy with some files.

Kelly grasped Andrew by the shoulders and manoeuvred him into his chair. 'What's wrong, sir?'

His stomach was on fire, a raging cauldron churning and bubbling. He'd had stomach pains in the past but nothing like this. It was excruciating.

'Would you like some water, Mr Drummond?'

Andrew nodded.

Kelly rushed from the office, swiftly returning with a glassful.

Andrew glanced up at the book-keeper, seeing the concern on the other's face. 'Thank you.'

He had a sip, then another. They didn't do any good. He took a deep breath and closed his eyes.

'What is it, Mr Drummond?'

'Indigestion,' he lied. If this was indigestion then he was a Chinese washerwoman.

Kelly nodded his sympathy, knowing Andrew had suffered from that in the past. 'Is there anything else I can get you?'

'No, thank you, Kelly.'

He'd gone weak as a baby, all his strength seemingly having drained from him. He'd also broken out in a cold sweat.

'I think you should go home, Mr Drummond, and have a lie-down.'

'There's a lot to do,' Andrew protested.

'Nothing that can't wait. Besides, look at the state you're in. You can't work like that.'

Kelly was right, Andrew thought. A lie-down was best. That and sleep if he could get it. Oh my God, but his stomach hurt. It was as if he'd swallowed a pint of acid.

'Help me up, Kelly.'

'Yes, sir.'

Kelly got Andrew to his feet where he swayed. He wasn't at all certain he could make it back to the house.

'You're going to have to come with me, Kelly.'

'Of course, sir.'

'Out the back way. I want as few people as possible seeing me like this.'

'I understand, sir.'

Andrew groaned when he took a step, sweat now running freely down his face. Lesley must have been right all along, he thought. This had to be an ulcer. Though it was still a mystery why it hadn't shown up on the tests.

It was a nightmare, Tommy's section and Red Section had been on a routine flight when they'd suddenly run into swarms of enemy fighters. The Jerry bastards were everywhere.

'I'm hit, I'm fucking hit!' Billy Moore screamed over the R/T.

Tommy was about to reply when an Me109 appeared behind him. He swore and took evasive action.

He glimpsed Dingo going into an attack, his cannons spurting flame.

'Coming to assist Section Leader,' Paul Wyborn announced calmly over the R/T.

Tommy threw his plane to port, and into a steep climb, hoping to shake off his pursuer. To no avail.

There was Paul Wyborn in his mirror now, lining up the Me109. Moments later the Me109 blew apart.

Relief surged in Tommy. 'Thank you, Paul,' he choked into the R/T.

'Waltzing Matilda . . . Waltzing Matilda . . .' Dingo started to sing.

Tommy almost laughed to hear that.

He pulled out of his climb and headed for cloud. But before he could get there an Me110 came into his sights. He instinctively fired, having the grim satisfaction of seeing the 110's fuselage become wreathed in black smoke and glycol.

He vanished into the cloud, only to almost instantly reappear again. The cloud had been a small one.

'Billy, where are you?' he queried.

There was no reply.

'Billy . . .'

'Billy's dead,' Dingo cut in. 'He got out but his chute didn't open.'

'Disperse, do the best you can,' Tommy instructed. If they remained where they were it would be curtains for all of them. The odds were simply too great.

And then it happened. His Hurry juddered and yawed as cannon shells ripped their way completely along its length. Tommy's right shoulder went suddenly numb and there was a spattering of blood on the sleeve of his flying jacket. Surprisingly, there wasn't any pain.

This was it, he thought, the plane hardly responding to the controls. He was a sitting duck.

And then he saw his attacker swooping in for the kill.

'Waltzing Matilda,' Dingo was singing again over the R/T. 'Waltzing Matilda . . .'

Chapter 23

'Let's get you into bed,' Elspeth Campbell said to Andrew, having taken over from Kelly.

'I think I can manage that by myself.'

Rose and Nancy were out, which was why Elspeth had assumed charge. It had given her a fright to see Andrew and the obvious pain he was in.

'Sit down,' Elspeth instructed in a strictly no-nonsense voice. When he had, on the side of the bed, she set about removing his shoes and socks.

'I'm going to send for the doctor,' she announced.

'No, I'll be all right. I promise you.'

She glanced up at him, her expression one of disapproval. 'That's plain silly, Andrew.'

It was too, he thought. Lesley should be fetched as soon as possible. That was the sensible thing to do. And yet he was reluctant, knowing that if an ulcer was confirmed then it probably meant an operation resulting in his being laid up for weeks.

'Now your collar and tie.'

Despite the pain he was enjoying being fussed over. It had been so long since a woman had done that to him. It gave him enormous pleasure, at the same time reminding him what he so missed from Rose. Not just lovemaking, but the day-to-day care and affection. The cherishing. How different it had all been before the last pregnancy and subsequent miscarriage.

Her hands were cool on his neck. He leant forward a little to give her better access to his back stud.

'That's better,' he declared, attempting a smile, when tie and collar had been removed.

'Now your jacket.'

'I told Kelly it was indigestion but I fear it might be an ulcer after all,' he said.

She paused to stare at him. 'I thought the hospital tests had disproved that theory?'

He shrugged. 'So did I. But what else can it be?'

She threw his jacket on to the floor, she'd tidy that away in a moment or two, then started on his shirt buttons.

'That's enough, Elspeth. Leave me my modesty,' he said when the buttons were undone to his waist.

'Get your trousers off.'

'Not while you're here!' he protested.

'You're acting like a big baby now. Get them off. I'll turn my back if you wish.'

It amused him to find he was embarrassed. Taking his clothes off in front of women, or having them taken off by them, had never bothered him before. Maybe it was because she was staff. There again, maybe not.

'Turn your back,' he said.

371

The pain had begun to ease he realised as he undid his flies. The trousers slithered to the floor and he scrambled under the bedclothes.

'You can look now,' he told her.

Elspeth quickly scooped up the trousers and jacket and put them away. 'Would you like a cup of tea?'

'No thank you.'

'Anything else?'

'A whisky I think.'

'Hardly the best medicine,' she commented drily.

He placed a hand on his belly and gingerly rubbed it. 'A whisky all the same.'

'No,' she stated emphatically. 'And I'll have no argument about that.'

'I'm your employer,' he reminded her. 'You'll do as I say.'

'Bully tactics, eh?'

He coloured slightly.

'You may be my employer but for now I'm your nurse, and nurse says no whisky.'

'What if I sack you?' he teased.

'Go ahead. You still won't get whisky.'

'Oh, all right,' he sighed. 'Now you're being the bully. The pot calling the kettle black.'

She grinned. 'Feeling any better?'

'A little.'

'Well, you stay there and rest quietly. I'm sending for the doctor.'

'I said not to bother.'

'And *I* said I'm sending for him.' She stared defiantly at Andrew. 'If it is an ulcer it isn't going away. At least not by itself. Ignore this and it might just happen all over again.'

She had another alarming thought. 'You don't think it's your appendix, do you?'

He frowned. That had never crossed his mind. 'Could be,' he admitted reluctantly.

'Then the sooner the doctor's here the better.'

And with that she swept from the room.

'Well, it definitely isn't appendicitis,' Lesley declared, having just given Andrew a thorough examination.

'What then? The ulcer you originally thought it was?'

Lesley shook his head. 'To be honest with you, Mr Drummond, I'm not sure. But it's hospital for you again, and this time you stay in until we find out what's what.'

'I can't do that. I—'

Andrew trailed off when Lesley held up a hand.

'I know you're a busy man, Mr Drummond, but certain things take precedence. We have to get to the bottom of this, no matter how inconvenient the process might be to you.'

Andrew stared hard at the doctor for a few moments, then slowly nodded, admitting defeat. 'When?' he asked.

'I'll get on the phone first thing tomorrow morning and then let you know. In the meantime stay in bed until this has completely passed. Understand?'

'Yes.'

'Good.'

Lesley packed away his bits and pieces, then stood. He had his suspicions but wasn't about to mention them to Andrew. This needed a specialist, not a local practitioner.

'Thanks for coming so promptly.' Andrew smiled.

'I'm glad I was able to. Another ten minutes and I'd have been off on another call.'

Elspeth Campbell met Lesley outside the bedroom and personally escorted him to the front door.

When she returned to Andrew's bedroom it was to find he'd fallen asleep.

'I'll be gone for a few days,' Andrew stated to Rose over breakfast later that week.

'Oh?'

It irritated him to see she'd hardly registered the fact. 'Business trip, that's all.'

'I hope you enjoy yourself, Mr Drummond,' Nancy said quietly.

Enjoy himself! He'd hardly be doing that. 'Thank you, Nancy,' he replied gruffly.

Rose began talking to Nancy about a paper drive she was organising for the war effort.

Andrew, as usual, felt totally excluded.

'Here, drink this.'

Jack gratefully accepted the hot toddy Hettie handed him. Albeit the fire was lit, he was sitting wrapped in an old travelling rug. He had a bad cold.

'This is the stuff for the troops,' he smiled.

'There's a good dollop of whisky in that so you can't complain.'

'As if I would,' he teased.

'Huh!' She then frowned when there was a knock on the outside door. 'Now who can that be?'

'Well, you won't find out unless you answer it,' Jack answered sarcastically.

She shot him a withering look. 'Very funny.'

Jack chuckled, sipping at his toddy as Hettie left the room.

My, that was rare, he thought appreciatively. It fair warmed the cockles of his heart. Something his mother had used to say about good soup.

'My God!' he heard Hettie exclaim.

There was the sound of excited voices and then Hettie bustled back into the room with Tommy in tow. 'Look who's here, Jack!'

'How can I look when I'm bloody blind, you daft eejit,' he retorted.

Hettie laughed, having momentarily forgotten Jack's disability. It had been a long time since she'd done that.

'Hello, Dad.'

Jack went absolutely still. 'Tommy?'

'Aye, it's me.'

The breath hissed from Jack's mouth. 'Welcome home, son,' he choked.

'He's wounded,' Hettie informed Jack.

'Wounded?'

'It's my arm, Dad. Nothing too serious. But it's put me out of commission for a bit.'

Tommy home, he couldn't believe it. 'Come here,' he rasped.

Tommy crossed over while a beaming and slightly tearful Hettie gazed on.

'Give me your hand, the good one.'

Jack clasped it. 'We wondered why we hadn't heard from you for a while.'

'Well, now you know. It's my writing arm that was hit.'

Wounded in the arm! Jack thanked God it hadn't been worse. 'Sit down while your mother fetches you a dram. I want to hear everything. And I mean *everything*.'

There was no chance of that, Tommy thought. Certainly not with his mother present.

'A dram sounds grand,' he replied.

Hettie hurried away to get it for him. She was excited fit to burst. All she wanted was a good cry.

McFarlane accepted Gypsy's reins from Rose. The horse had been ridden hard, but not cruelly so. And that's how it had been, more or less, since the beast's arrival. Much to his relief.

'A lovely crisp day to be out in,' he commented politely.

'It is indeed, McFarlane. I thought it might rain earlier but it's stayed away, thank goodness. I spotted some snowdrops which was nice. The first I've seen this year.'

'Aye, Spring isn't all that far off right enough.'

Rose patted Gypsy's flank. 'I want you to do something for me.'

'And what's that, Mrs Drummond?'

'Can we borrow a pony from somewhere?'

'A pony?' he queried, puzzled.

'I want to include one in my next painting. And I need a model.'

'You won't be riding it then?' McFarlane inquired craftily.

'Of course not. Why would I ride a children's pony? No, as I said, I only want it as a model.'

'I think I know where I can find a suitable Shetland for you. When would you want her?'

Rose thought about that. 'Is next week possible?'

'Oh aye, Mrs Drummond. The pony belongs to a lassie who's away at school, so I don't see any problem in having it whenever you wish.'

'Arrange it then, McFarlane. And agree payment if that's required.'

He touched his forelock. 'I'll do that.'

Rose left the groom and strode back towards the house. A pony with a child on it, she thought, smiling.

Mary.

'Yes, can I help you?'

The gaze was as fierce as Tommy remembered it. He hadn't been looking forward to this visit, but it was one he'd promised himself he'd make.

'I'm Tommy Riach, Mr McTaggart. I used to be a Sunday school teacher with Babs.'

Recognition dawned. 'Of course. The uniform quite changes you. Is it Babs you've come to see?'

'No, sir, you and your wife.'

Barney McTaggart frowned. 'And why's that?'

'May I come in?'

McTaggart stood aside and beckoned Tommy into the hallway. 'Anne, we've got a visitor!' he called out.

Tommy was ushered into the room where he'd previously met the family. He stood, cap in hand, feeling uncomfortable, while McTaggart vanished.

'Anne! Where are you, woman?'

Tommy noticed a silver-framed photograph of Gerald on top of the mantelpiece. Gerald whom he'd last seen being shot down in flames, struggling with a canopy that wouldn't open. He shuddered.

'Hello, Tommy.'

He turned to find Babs staring at him. 'Hello, I didn't hear you come in.'

'Fairy light feet, that's me.'

They both laughed.

'You're looking well,' she commented. 'Apart from the arm that is.'

'It's only a scratch.'

'I didn't know they put scratches in slings,' she retorted, slightly caustically.

'They got carried away.'

'Is that a fact.'

He hastily changed the subject. 'You're looking well yourself.'

'Thank you.'

How awfully young she seemed. A wee girl beside the woman that was Mavis Giddings. But it wasn't only that, it was him. His own youth had long since disappeared in the skies over southern England – and his innocence in Mavis Giddings' bed.

'You're here to see my parents?'

'That's right.'

'About what?'

He was about to reply when the elder McTaggarts appeared. Anne McTaggart's breath caught in her throat at the sight of Tommy's uniform. Then the moment was gone, and she'd regained her composure.

'I hope you don't mind me barging in uninvited,' Tommy apologised.

'Not at all,' Anne McTaggart replied. 'Will you stay for tea?'

Tommy shook his head. 'Thank you all the same.'

'Then please sit down.'

'I'd prefer to stand if that's all right.'

Barney glanced at his wife, then back at Tommy. 'So what's this all about?'

'I was in Gerald's squadron.'

Anne McTaggart sagged a little on hearing that.

'Did he ever mention me in any of his letters?'

'No,' Barney McTaggart replied quietly. 'Gerald wasn't a great one for letter-writing at the best of times. They became almost non-existent after the war started.'

This was the tricky part, where he had to tread carefully. 'I was there when he died.'

Anne McTaggart's eyes opened wide and a hand went to her mouth. Barney McTaggart's expression wasn't fierce any more, but grim in the extreme. He'd gone quite pale.

'How . . . how . . .' Anne McTaggart broke off, and sobbed.

'What exactly were you told?'

'Only that he was killed in action,' Barney answered.

Tommy nodded, it was as he'd thought. 'No more than that?'

'No.'

Anne McTaggart was staring intently at Tommy, her eyes full of pleading. He was about to tell her what she wanted to hear. That was why he'd come.

'It was instantaneous,' Tommy lied. 'He wouldn't have known anything about it, far less felt anything.'

Anne McTaggart started to shake, Barney putting an arm round his wife in support. 'Thank God,' he whispered.

'And you saw it happen?' That was Babs.

'Yes, I did.'

'Instantaneous,' Barney repeated. 'You hear such terrible stories. Pilots being . . .' he trailed off.

'I wanted you to know,' Tommy said. 'Now I'll leave you to it.'

'I'll see you out,' Babs volunteered.

Tommy was at the door when Barney called out after him. 'Thank you, son. We appreciate you coming here today.'

Tommy glanced back at them. 'Gerald was a brave man. I admired him tremendously. Brave, well liked and respected by his squadron. They don't come any better.'

Anne McTaggart managed to wait until Tommy had gone before collapsing, her husband catching her before she hit the floor.

Rose paused in her painting to glance over at Nancy who was staring into space. Nancy's brow was furrowed, her expression troubled.

Rose frowned. 'Nancy?'

She didn't answer, completely lost within herself.

'Nancy?'

Nancy started and turned to face Rose. 'Sorry. Did you say something?'

Rose placed her brush on the narrow indented ledge in front of the easel, and stretched slightly. She'd had enough for the moment.

'Are you all right?'

'Yes. Yes of course.'

'What on earth were you thinking about?'

Nancy coloured and dropped her gaze. 'Nothing really. Just the past.'

'You mean when you were a bondager?' Rose prompted softly.

Nancy nodded.

'A specific incident?'

Nancy sucked in a deep breath. 'A number actually. All bad.'

'Oh?'

'I was recalling one morning when I woke up feeling awful, really dreadful. My body ached and all my limbs were sore. I told Bill how I was and his reply was he didn't give a . . . well, that he didn't care. And I was to get out of bed right quick or it would be a leathering.'

'Oh, poor love,' Rose sympathised.

'Bill was like that, but then so were most of the men. Cruel as cruel. You had a day's graft to do and there were no excuses. He put his foot against my backside and kicked me on to the floor, telling me to get on with it and stop moaning.'

Nancy shook her head at the memory. 'I passed out three times that day, saved twice by my friend Annie McGillvary. She wasn't there on the third and I came round to find Bill about to hit me with his belt. I crawled away, pleading with him not to. But he still did.'

She paused, then said, 'You just don't forget things like that. They stay with you, haunting you, always.'

'It's he who should have been whipped,' Rose declared hotly.

'No, Mrs Drummond, that's just the way these men are. Bill was no worse than many. Though there are some with a kinder streak to them.'

'What sort of work were you doing at the time?' Rose asked, curious.

'Moving big boulders into place for a new dry stane dyke.'

'Dear God,' Rose muttered, thoroughly appalled. 'You shouldn't have been expected to do work like that.'

Nancy laughed bitterly. 'We women grafted as hard as any of the men, sometimes harder. There was nothing a man was asked to do that we weren't. That's how it is.'

Nancy dropped her gaze a second time.

'I'm so thankful to be here and out of all that. I can't tell you.'

Rose got up and went to Nancy, putting a comforting

arm round her. 'Well here you are now, and safe. There'll never be any more boulders and the like for you.'

Nancy shuddered. 'Thank you,' she croaked.

Rose decided to write a letter to the Secretary of State for Scotland. Ian Dalhousie was a personal friend of her father's. Something had to be done about this bondaging outrage, no matter how traditional it was in the Border counties. She would demand the situation be brought to the attention of the House.

Andrew emerged from hospital carrying the small case he'd taken in with him. It had been a far longer stay than he'd expected. Luckily he'd been able to telephone Rose with excuses about his continued absence. Not that he need have bothered, he thought bitterly, she hadn't seemed to care.

He went straight to the car and locked the case in its boot. It was a long drive home, he reflected. He only hoped he was up to it.

He stood for a moment and sucked in a deep breath. He felt so weak and wobbly on his feet and his head was spinning. That's what days in bed did for you.

There was a pub close by where he intended heading. He badly needed a drink.

Perhaps more than he'd ever needed one before.

'Are you alone?'

Tommy glanced up to find Bell Mathieson smiling down on him. He immediately rose. 'Sorry, I was lost in thought.'

'What happened to the arm?'

'Oh, it's nothing much. It'll soon heal.'

'It's nice to see you again, Tommy.'

'And you, Bell.'

'I'm with some friends over there.' She pointed to the other side of the pub. 'I noticed you and thought I'd come over to say hello.'

He gestured to the empty seat facing his. 'Will you join me for a bit?'

'I left my drink with the pals.'

'That's all right. I'll get you another. What's it to be?'

'Gin and orange would be lovely.'

'Coming up,' he declared, and strode off to the bar.

Bell watched his retreating back, thinking he was still as good-looking as ever. More so even. The uniform certainly suited him. It gave him a dashing air, reminding her of Errol Flynn in the pictures.

She recalled how she'd once been quite struck with Tommy Riach, even though he'd been younger than her. Still was, of course.

What a catch she'd considered him to be. Training as a traveller for Drummond's with excellent prospects in front of him. But that had never really been on. He was far too posh for the likes of her.

Anyway, she had David now. David who loved her and whom she was going to marry. It would be a fine life with David. Just dandy. She'd make sure of that.

Tommy returned with her drink, then went back again to the bar for his refill.

'So why are you in the pub? Is it an occasion?' he asked when he returned.

'Nope. We're just all fed up and decided to come out and get pished.'

He laughed at her bluntness. 'I know the feeling. I get it myself sometimes.' Only in his case it wasn't fed up but a combination of other things, not least fear and despair.

'How's Drummond's?' he queried.

'Ach, just the same. Well, not really. Some of the men have gone. A few called up, others joining. A couple of old fogeys have been brought out of retirement to help.'

'And Kelly, is he still there?'

'Oh aye, in all his glory.'

Bastard, he thought. That was how he always thought of Mister book-keeper Kelly.

'So why are you on your own?'

'Dad's got a cold and Mum won't let him out of the house. Otherwise he'd have been with me.'

'And so here you are.'

He smiled. 'So here I am.'

It was good being with Bell again, he'd always enjoyed her company. 'How's Irene?'

'She's in London.'

'London!' he exclaimed.

'With the ATS. She drives an ambulance for them. Having a whale of a time.' Bell giggled. 'Lots of men there, you see, which is right up Irene's street.'

'I can imagine.'

'That's why she went into the ATS in the first place. Said she wasn't doing that well round here where men were concerned.'

How at ease he felt with Bell, just as he did with Mavis. The two had a lot in common.

'How long are you back for?' Bell asked.

He shrugged. 'Depends on the arm. I'll rejoin the squadron when Lesley gives me the green light. Until then it's Mum's home cooking and the heady delights of Dalneil.'

'Will you go to the distillery? For old times sake, that is.'

He shook his head. 'I don't think so.'

'Pity, you're quite a smasher in that uniform. You'd have the lassies in bottling wolf whistling.'

Tommy grinned. 'Do you remember the Christmas party, when you and Irene had to walk me home?'

'Walk! We nearly had to carry you you were so far gone.'

'And we kissed. You and I.'

Bell blushed and looked away. 'I remember it fine. But that's a long time ago. There's a lot of water flowed under the bridge since then.'

'Aye, it has that,' he agreed.

There was a short silence between them. Then Tommy said, 'Tell me about your chap? I'd like to hear.'

Bell burbled on about David, their engagement, his conscription, and what their plans were when they eventually got married.

Tommy couldn't have been more pleased for her. A little wistful too perhaps. When they finally parted they'd spent nearly an hour together, an hour both had thoroughly enjoyed.

'Any idea where we are yet, Willi?'

The navigator of the Heinkel, poring over his maps, replied tersely into the R/T, 'None, Captain.'

Joachim Grüber swore and glanced out the side cockpit window. Nothing but blackness below, as far as the eye could see. Not even a single land light to give a clue as to their whereabouts.

They'd become separated from the others nearly an hour previously, going astray in thick cloud that had enveloped them. When he'd finally dropped below cloud level it was to find they were completely alone.

'So what do we do, Captain?' Wolf Kaplan, the co-pilot, casually inquired.

Joachim looked up at the heavy cloud layer high above the plane which totally obscured the night sky. It was that which was continuing to make it downright impossible for Willi to get a bearing.

'Another ten minutes, and then if we don't sight Clydebank we turn back.'

Wolf nodded his agreement.

The solitary Heinkel droned on.

Elspeth Campbell had been waiting for Andrew, certain he'd come and tell her what had happened at the hospital. She smiled when he appeared in the kitchen doorway.

'A cup of tea or cocoa, Andrew?'

He shook his head and produced a bottle of whisky from his dressing-gown pocket. 'I've been on this all evening. Far more appropriate.'

He collected a glass and then slumped on to a chair facing her. She watched as he poured himself a large dram.

'Are we celebrating?'

He barked out a short laugh. 'Hardly. The news was the worst possible.'

She frowned. 'How so?'

The smile he gave her was both tortured and strained. 'Not indigestion, not even an ulcer. I've got cancer of the stomach.'

She stared at him, appalled. 'Are they sure?'

'Oh aye. There's no doubt about it. I'm riddled with the damned thing. Well past redemption.'

'I'm so sorry,' she whispered.

He opened his mouth to speak, then shut it again without speaking. His eyes took on a misty look.

She knew instinctively that what she did next was the

right thing to do. Rising, she went to him and cradled his
head between her breasts, her arms encircling his throat.
'How long?'

'Six months, a year. A little more if I'm lucky.'

She didn't know what to say. What could she say?
Nothing

'Not long, eh?'

Elspeth didn't reply.

The warmth and affection radiating from her were
almost overpowering. Damn Rose, he thought angrily.
Damn her to hell.

He knew women, oh only too well. Elspeth was his for
the taking and had been for some time. What did infidelity
matter now? Not a jot.

'Could you kiss a dead man?' he joked.

'Try me.'

He got up and took her into his arms. No further words
were necessary.

'The ten minutes are up,' Wolf said.

Joachim grunted and glanced again out the side window.
Still nothing but blackness.

'Kurt, let them go,' he instructed the bomb aimer
through the R/T.

The Heinkel jerked as its deadly load fell free. Once it
was gone Grüber banked the plane, heading for home.

Andrew, hands inside Elspeth's nightdress fondling her
breasts, stopped on hearing a strange whistling sound. A
whistling that grew rapidly louder.

Several seconds later he and Elspeth were knocked
sideways as the first bomb landed on Dalneil.

Chapter 24

Andrew grabbed Elspeth before she fell over, while outside further explosions detonated.

'Jesus Christ, we're being bombed,' he exclaimed.

Elspeth's eyes went wide with fright. 'Bombed?'

He couldn't think of any other explanation. Besides, he'd heard bombs in Ireland though never the aerial variety.

His next thought was for Rose. Had the house been hit? He didn't think so. 'Wait here,' he commanded urgently, and dashed upstairs.

'Rose! Rose!'

She stumbled from her bedroom, hair dishevelled, nightdress gaping. 'What's going on?'

'Thank God you're all right,' he cried in relief.

'What's going on, Andrew?'

'We're being bombed.'

She stared blankly at him. 'Bombed?'

'That's right. Now get dressed while I see what's what.'

He ran along the length of that landing and then went up

another flight to the servants' quarters where several of them were anxiously milling around. If the situation hadn't been so serious he'd have laughed at the sight of Mrs Moffat in her night clothes. The large white cotton cap she was wearing, tied under her chin, was truly something to behold.

'Has anyone been hurt?' he demanded.

'I stubbed my toe,' Pattie Williams complained. 'It's sore.'

Andrew ignored that. Further inspection and inquiry revealed that everyone was fine and, as far as he could ascertain, there hadn't been any damage to the house.

He ran downstairs again.

Jack and Hettie had been fast asleep when the bomb landed in their back garden, blowing away the nearest wall. Their bedroom floor collapsed and the bed dropped through.

Hettie ended up half in and half out of bed. She was totally confused, coughing and spluttering from the swirling dust and plaster choking her throat.

'Hettie?'

She crawled over to Jack. 'What the fuck's going on?' he demanded.

'I don't know.'

There was a loud groan followed by a crash as their chimney stack toppled to the ground.

When Jack heard the following explosions he knew precisely what was occurring.

It was a sound he'd experienced only too often on the Western Front.

Bell too was fast asleep when the bomb crashed through their roof. She was still asleep when it exploded.

* * *

A distraught Rose was being cuddled by Nancy when Andrew rejoined her. 'Nancy?' he queried.

'Not a scratch, Mr Drummond. What's happened?'

Rose grabbed hold of Andrew. 'Stay here with me, Andrew. I need you.'

He shook himself free. 'We've been bombed I think, Nancy.' To Rose he said, 'The house doesn't seem to have been damaged. I'm going outside to see what I can.' He prayed the distillery hadn't been hit.

'No please, Andrew, stay with me.'

What a pathetic creature, he thought in contempt, then immediately regretted it. Rose was in shock which was completely understandable. 'You've got Nancy. She'll take care of you. I want to have a look at the distillery.'

'No, please stay, Andrew,' she pleaded.

'People will have been hurt in all this. I'll have to give what assistance I can. Now get everyone down to the kitchen and organise something. Do you hear me?'

Rose took a deep breath, then shook herself. 'Yes, Andrew,' she replied quietly.

There was a swift word with Elspeth, then he was out the back door. He stopped dead, appalled at the sight which greeted him.

The village was an inferno, at least half of it apparently on fire. Somewhere a woman was screaming. There was also an alarm bell of some sort clanging madly.

He turned in the direction of the distillery. 'Oh my God,' he croaked.

It was ablaze.

'We've got to get out of here before the whole damn building comes down,' Tommy said urgently to his parents.

'Is it that bad, son?'

'Worse than you can imagine, Dad.'

Jack cursed himself for his blindness. He felt so useless, so bloody useless.

Tommy picked up a coat that had been thrown on to the floor. 'Put this on, Mum.' He glanced around. 'I can't see your slippers.'

Jack, off the bed now, grimaced in pain as he stood on something sharp. He was still trying to take all this in.

He was one among many in what remained of Dalneil.

Andrew got as close to the distillery as he could, holding his hands in front of him to try and ward off the intense heat. The air was filled with the stench of burning materials.

The distillery was lost. There was no doubt about that. Drummond whisky had just been wiped off the map.

'Watch where you're going,' Tommy exclaimed as someone bumped into him.

'Sorry, pal. Didn't notice you.' And with that the figure was gone.

'My house, my bonny house,' Hettie whispered, staring in disbelief at the wreck which had been their home.

'Don't you worry, lass. We're alive and unhurt which is all that counts. I'll soon buy you another house,' Jack declared defiantly.

But it wasn't just the house, Hettie was thinking. It was many of the things in it. Personal items, mementoes of a long marriage. Keepsakes. They could never be replaced.

'Mr Drummond!'

Andrew turned to find Kelly there.

'You'd better get back in case the bond goes.'

Kelly was right, Andrew thought bitterly. If that went it would blow with the force of another bomb.

'Your house, Kelly?'

'A couple of broken windows, nothing more. And yours, Mr Drummond?'

'We escaped as well.' He stared again at the distillery. 'Which is more than can be said for here.'

'Aye,' Kelly agreed.

They both retreated to what they considered was a safe distance.

Andrew and Kelly stood helplessly by as the distillery continued to burn. At any moment they expected the bond to go up, but so far it hadn't.

'Listen,' said Kelly. Off in the distance was the clamour of a bell.

'Fire engine,' Andrew stated.

It was the first of many as every fire engine in that part of Perthshire converged on Dalneil.

Meanwhile Rose, Elspeth and Mrs Moffat had been busy. Masses of tea had been brewed, sandwiches made and the drawing room turned into a makeshift ward.

Christine had been dispatched to put the word round, and soon people began turning up at Drummond House, some injured, others, whose houses had either gone or were badly damaged, looking for a place to spend the rest of the night.

Rose and her staff did the best they could.

Andrew's mind was filled with memories. His own time running the distillery, the old days when it had been his father Murdo. He was in total despair.

He and Kelly glanced round when a fire engine came noisily towards them. It stopped and men jumped out.

Andrew didn't recognise the fire officer who came to stand alongside. 'This is Drummond's I understand?' the officer said.

Andrew nodded.

'And who are you?'

'Andrew Drummond, the owner. This is Mr Kelly, my book-keeper.'

'I see. Is the bond part of this building?'

'Yes it is.'

'Has it blown yet?'

'No.'

The officer's already grim expression became even grimmer. 'Where exactly is it situated, sir?'

Andrew told him, pointing it out.

The officer thought for a few moments. 'There's nothing we can do now. All I can suggest is we cordon off the immediate vicinity and wait for the inevitable.'

Andrew could only agree.

'Pity,' the officer said quietly, and with feeling, staring at the conflagration. 'I always liked a drop of Drummond's myself.'

Andrew had to smile.

'Hettie, Jack!'

Rose rushed across to them. 'Are you all right?'

'The house is a goner,' Jack replied with a tremor in his voice. 'But we're fine. Lucky I suppose.'

'Then you'll stay here for as long as it takes to get yourselves sorted out.' She held up a hand when Hettie started to object. 'You're as close as family, Hettie. I won't brook any argument.'

Tommy sat on a chair and held his head in his good hand. He was far more shaken than he'd realised. That was twice now he'd come within a whisker of death.

Rose called Jamesina Laing, the maid, over. 'Take the Riachs upstairs and put them in one of the bedrooms. See they get whatever they need.'

'Yes, Mrs Drummond.'

'I can help here,' Hettie protested.

'Later. Take care of Jack first.' She rounded on Tommy. 'What about you?'

He thought how magnificent she looked, remembering wryly that he'd fancied Rose Drummond rotten when younger. Still did, if he was honest. 'I'm OK.'

'Are you sure?'

'I might have only one arm functioning but I can put it to good use.'

Rose nodded her approval. 'Excuse me,' she said to Hettie and Jack, moving away as some ambulance men appeared at the door.

'I'll come up and see the pair of you shortly,' Tommy said to his parents as Jamesina began ushering them off.

'Mathieson . . .'

He rounded on the speaker who was Mrs Wilson, the local shopkeeper. 'What was that about Mathieson?'

'The Mathiesons, Tommy. They've all been killed.'

He went white.

'It was a direct hit apparently. The house and everyone in it went sky high.'

It was only a few short hours ago that he and Bell had been together, reminiscing, having a good laugh. And now she was . . .

'There's no mistake about that, Mrs Wilson?'

She shook her head. 'I'm afraid not, Tommy. I had it off

Mrs Farquharson who lives three doors down. There's just a hole where the house used to be.'

Tommy felt sick inside. This was a lot worse than losing his friends from the squadron. Far worse. This was personal in a way that that had not been.

He closed his eyes, picturing Bell as he'd last seen her. Recalling her hopes and aspirations for marriage with her David. Now she was gone; the marriage would never take place.

At least it would have been quick, he told himself. With a bit of luck she'd known nothing about it.

He was still thinking about Bell when the bond finally blew. It was the loudest explosion of all to occur in Dalneil that night.

Dawn had come and was long gone before Andrew returned home. He and Kelly had spent the last number of hours with firemen doing what they could. He was utterly exhausted, fit to drop.

Elspeth came hurrying over when she spotted him. 'You'd better have a seat and I'll get you some tea.'

'Whisky, Elspeth. Bugger tea, I want whisky.'

She didn't argue, but left him to find a bottle.

Andrew gazed around him. Rose and the staff had been busy right enough. The kitchen was filled with folk, others coming and going to various parts of the house.

He desperately wanted sleep, except that was impossible for the time being. There must still be a great deal to be done.

At least the house had survived, he thought. It would have been too much to bear to have lost that as well. And Rose was safe, another blessing to be thankful for.

'Mr Drummond.'

Andrew blinked, trying to focus. His eyes were stinging and watering from smoke. 'Tommy?'

'Aye, it's me. I wanted you to know Mum and Dad are upstairs. Mrs Drummond has given them a room.'

'They're all right then?' How often had he asked a variation of that question since this had started.

'It was a close shave but we weren't hurt in any way. The house is a wreck though.'

Andrew nodded his understanding, relieved to hear that Jack and Hettie hadn't come to any harm.

'I saw the distillery on the way here. I'm sorry,' Tommy said.

Andrew was suddenly too choked with emotion to reply. The distillery had been like an extension of himself.

Then Elspeth was by his side, holding out a huge whisky. He took it and swallowed half in one gulp. The stinging in his eyes increased but that didn't matter.

'I hear Clydebank outside Glasgow has been flattened by a Jerry raid,' Elspeth said.

'Clydebank?'

'They must have been after the shipyards there.'

What had happened to Dalneil must be connected in some way, Andrew thought, though how he couldn't fathom for the moment.

'Can I have a word, Mrs Drummond?'

Rose paused in what she was doing. 'Yes, Miss Campbell?'

Elspeth drew her aside and explained what she was proposing.

Andrew tapped on the door softly, then opened it a bit and stuck his head round. 'Can I come in?'

Rose glanced at him. This had been Elspeth's request,

that Andrew move back into her bedroom for the time being. His room was needed for Jack and Hettie.

'Of course.'

He slipped inside and closed the door again.

'You look terrible,' she commented.

'You don't look so clever yourself.'

They both laughed, and that broke the ice.

'I'm sorry about this,' Andrew apologised. 'But Miss Campbell says it's necessary. In the short term anyway.'

'She's quite right.'

'I'll use the spare quilt and sleep on the floor so as not to disturb you, Rose.'

She hesitated for a moment. 'You'll do no such thing,' she replied quietly. 'You'll sleep in the bed with me.'

He regarded her steadily. 'Are you certain about that?'

'Yes,' she snapped in reply.

Later, when they were lying side by side, she said, 'What are we going to do, Andrew?'

He considered that. It was a question he'd been asking himself. 'I honestly don't know, Rose.'

'Is the distillery completely destroyed?'

'Yes. Completely.'

Reaching out she took his hand and held it. 'I know how much it meant to you, Andrew. It was everything.'

He smiled. 'Not quite everything, Rose. You and Drew always came first.'

On hearing that Rose started to cry silently.

'Don't, Rose.'

'I can't help it,' she sobbed.

Pulling herself over she laid her cheek on his chest. And like that, they both fell asleep.

Outside their bedroom door Elspeth halted to stare at it. From inside came the faint sound of steady breathing.

Shoulders slumped she continued on her way to her own bed.

Mrs Wilson had said there was only a hole left where the Mathiesons' house had been, and that was exactly right. A hole filled with debris while other debris lay scattered around.

The bodies of the family, if found, had already been removed. The bodies or . . . Tommy swallowed hard . . . bits and pieces of them. Whatever had been left.

'Oh, Bell,' Tommy whispered, a huge lump in his throat.

He stood there for a good half-hour before retracing his steps to Drummond House.

Some of the rubble was still smoking as Andrew picked his way through the wreckage. He stopped in front of what remained of the pot-stills, unrecognisable now, just heaps of melted copper. Like all pot-stills they could never be replaced as such, each one being unique in shape and what it produced.

He remembered the first time Murdo had taken him into the distillery to show him round. He'd been a shaver then, quite uninterested in the goings on.

And that was how it had been through his youth and twenties. The distillery was to be his brother's one day after all. His future lay elsewhere.

And so it had been until Peter's death on the Western Front, and Murdo's on hearing the news. Then it had become his inheritance and his views towards the distillery had totally changed.

Andrew shook his head in disbelief. Yesterday at the same time the distillery had been intact, now it was a smouldering ruin. His, and his family's, livelihood had literally vanished in a puff of smoke.

What could he pass on to Drew now? Nothing. Oh, there was the house and capital in the bank. That remained. But the inheritance was no more.

He felt it was his fault somehow. And yet commonsense told him that was nonsense. He had no control over a German plane bombing the village, though why it should have done so was still unknown. The theory doing the rounds was that a plane *en route* to Clydebank must have got lost and jettisoned its load. Dalneil, wrapped in blackout, had just been the unfortunate victim.

Perhaps the lost theory was true, maybe it wasn't. He doubted they'd ever find out. All that was of concern was that the bombing had taken place with, for the village, catastrophic results.

He turned and stared out over Dalneil. How could it ever recover from this? That was something it was far too soon even to think about.

'Drew!' Rose exclaimed in astonishment.

He flew into his mother's arms. 'The headmaster called me into his office and told me what had happened. He said Dad had got a message through to him that you and he were safe and well, and not to worry.'

'So why are you here?'

'I wasn't going to remain in school after this. I wanted to come home and the headmaster finally agreed after I said if he didn't I'd run away anyway. I caught the train to Pitlochry and took a taxi from there. The driver wouldn't accept any money when he found out where I was going and why.' Drew paused, then stated, 'I'm home to help, Mum. To be with you and Dad.'

She held him close and stroked his hair. How thankful she was she hadn't become pregnant by Andy Somerville. That would not only have been cheating Andrew but Drew as well.

How selfish she'd been. She could see that now. Selfish and cruel out of morbid self-pity.

She felt truly ashamed.

'Hello.' He'd at last managed to corner her alone. How tired she looked, he thought. There were dark bags under her eyes while her hair had gone listless and dry.

Nancy smiled. 'Hello, Drew.'

He touched her, as though making sure she was actually there and not merely a figment of his imagination. 'I was worried sick about you. I knew Pops and Mum were fine, Dad sent a telephone message, but of course no mention was made of you.'

'It was terrible, Drew, really terrible,' she stated, tight lipped.

'I know. I've seen.'

'But you weren't there. It was as if the whole village was alight. I'll never forget it till my dying day.'

'I can imagine.'

Nancy ran a hand over her face. She'd hardly stopped during the past few days, and what sleep she'd had hadn't been good. Restless sleep disturbed by vivid dreams and nightmares was all she'd snatched.

'Come and sit down over here,' he suggested. They were in a small sitting room containing a sofa and chairs.

'I shouldn't really. There's so much to do.'

'Take a break, Nancy. If only for a few minutes at least. I insist.'

She smiled at the dominance in his voice. 'All right.'

He sat alongside her. 'I'm back to help out. Do what I can.'

'How long for?'

'As long as it takes.'

'But school . . .'

'Damn school,' he interjected vehemently. 'This is far more important. The family and you that is.'

She was touched by that. And surprised at just how pleased she was to see him. 'Have you had something to eat?'

He shook his head. 'I'm not hungry. I'll get something later.'

Nancy closed her eyes for a moment, feeling incredibly weary. There were still people in the house with nowhere else to go. People who had to be taken care of.

'I noticed the army's here,' he said.

'They've been terrific, organising all sorts. As have the other services. They've all been magnificent.'

'That's good.'

She named a few people. 'They were killed. Did you know them?'

He nodded.

'And others were maimed. One wee lassie lost both her legs. She's only six years old.'

Drew couldn't think what to say to that. It was appalling. How easily that could have been Nancy, or himself if he hadn't been off at school.

'You hear of the war,' Nancy went on. 'But it's all distant. Happening elsewhere. This brings home what it's really like. Not whist drives and coffee mornings, or knitting balaclavas and sweaters, but people you know, and are acquainted with, being killed and having their limbs blown off.'

'Aye,' he agreed softly.

Nancy took a deep breath. 'Now I must get on. I can't stay here chatting for ever.'

He smiled. 'I'll come with you. I'm here to help, remember.'

She matched his smile. 'If you wish.'

'I do, Nancy.'

He gazed deeply into her eyes and she into his. In that moment she knew their lives were inevitably intertwined. She'd considered it a bit of a joke before, a young lad with a crush on an older girl. But it was more than that, far more. Drew had been right all along.

'Let's get to it then,' she declared, rising.

They'd come in their many hundreds, folk from round about, and further afield, to pay their last respects to the dead of Dalneil. The church was crammed to bursting, those who couldn't get in standing outside, rank upon rank.

Tommy was there with Jack and Hettie, the three of them squashed together towards the front of the congregation. The service was the most heart-wrenching Tommy had ever heard.

When the names of the dead were read out he bowed his head when Bell's was mentioned. Bell from bottling who'd kissed him when he was drunk. Bell with the earthy sense of humour and ready laugh. Bell whom he'd never forget.

As the concluding words were being spoken there wasn't a dry eye in the church. With the exception of Jack Riach that is, for whom tears were impossible. But inside he was crying.

'Amen,' John McLean, the minister, solemnly intoned.

Outside a single army piper began to play 'The Flowers Of The Forest'.

The traditional Scottish lament, composed after the national disaster that was the Battle of Flodden.

Chapter 25

'Well, look who the cat dragged in!' Dingo Roberts exclaimed in delight when Tommy appeared in the Lamb and Flag.

Mavis beamed at Tommy from behind the bar.

'What are you having, sport?' Dingo queried as Tommy joined him.

'A pint would be nice.'

'It's on the house,' Mavis purred.

'Thank you.'

They stared at one another for a few seconds, then Mavis moved away to the pumps.

'How's the arm?' Dingo inquired.

Tommy flexed it. 'Good as new. Well . . . almost.'

They both laughed.

Tommy was pleased to be back, the last few weeks in Dalneil had been awful. A great sense of despondency had settled over the village as its inhabitants tried to gather up the pieces and get on with life.

'We heard about what happened,' Dingo said, his face creasing with concern.

'Not very pleasant,' Tommy mumbled.

'I can believe that. I take it you and your folks were OK?'

'We lost our house. A bomb landed in the back garden almost demolishing it.'

Dingo whistled softly. 'That was a bit rude of whoever dropped it.'

Rude, Tommy thought wryly. The understatement of the year. 'There was a lot of damage done. People killed. I doubt the village will ever really recover.'

Mavis placed his pint in front of him. 'You're a sight for sore eyes,' she declared.

'You too, Mavis.'

Dingo glanced away, allowing them to have a few private words together.

'Can you stay the night?'

He shook his head. 'Maybe tomorrow. I'll have to get settled in again first.'

'I understand.'

There was a yearning inside him for Mavis which had been with him all the way down from Scotland. Not just her body, though that would be more than welcome, but she herself. He'd missed her more than he'd realised.

She reached out and touched him lightly on the hand, her expression more eloquent than any welcome back speech.

'Are you serving, Mavis?' a customer called out.

'Excuse me.'

'Of course.'

Tommy looked round as he sipped his pint. There were many RAF uniforms, most of their wearers unknown to him.

'There have been quite a number of losses I take it,' he said quietly.

Dingo nodded. He reeled off a list of names that made Tommy blanch. 'Herbie too,' he muttered.

'Gone West with the others.'

Herbie Ootrove had been considered the best pilot in the squadron, a potential ace if ever there was. Now he too was gone.

Death was everywhere, Tommy reflected bitterly. So many pals, friends, acquaintances, flying off into the wild blue yonder never to return. When would that happen to him? It was surely only a matter of time.

Tommy shook himself. He mustn't think like that. Nothing was a foregone conclusion. His number might never come up. To believe it was inevitable was almost inviting it to happen.

'You'll be in charge of Green Section as I'm leading your old one,' Dingo said.

'Uh-huh.'

'No one in that section you're familiar with. They're all new boys.'

'Great,' Tommy muttered unenthusiastically.

He stayed for about half an hour before returning to camp where he found out he'd be flying in the morning just as he'd expected.

'What do you think?' Hettie asked Jack, having just read him a letter that had arrived in the morning post.

'Writing propaganda films?'

'That's what they say.'

'Based in Hertfordshire.'

'They'll provide accommodation close to the studios.'

Jack barked out a laugh. 'I wonder if they know I'm

blind? It's funny if you think about it, a blind man writing films.'

'No more than a blind man writing books and plays.'

She had something there, especially with the plays.

'Well?' Hettie demanded.

'It would certainly sort out our short-term problem of living with Andrew and Rose. It's kind of them to put us up but we can't go on accepting their hospitality for ever.'

'That's true enough,' Hettie agreed.

'How would you feel about living in England?'

She considered that. 'I don't really know. Their way of life is so very different to ours. There again . . .' She broke off.

'What, Hettie?'

'It would take us away from Dalneil for a while. I think that would be a good thing.'

'It would also mean we were closer to Tommy. Hopefully we'd be able to see him more often.'

'Aye, there is that advantage,' Hettie nodded.

They both lapsed into thoughtful silence.

'You can't keep moping around like this,' Rose chastised Andrew. 'You must find something to do.'

'Like what?'

'Something. Whatever.'

Every day he went to what remained of the distillery, stayed for a bit, and then came home again. He was still getting used to the idea that it was no more. He reached for the decanter.

'And you can cut back on that! It's only eleven in the morning, for God's sake.'

Andrew smiled inwardly. What did it matter how much he drank? It didn't in the slightest. The grim reaper was waiting no matter what.

He eyed Rose dyspeptically. He hadn't yet told her about the cancer, unable to bring himself to. And perhaps he never would. Keep it a secret.

He poured himself a dram.

'Andrew!'

He drank it off and immediately poured another.

Rose swept from the room in disgust.

'Propaganda films!' Andrew exclaimed.

'That's right.'

'Living in England. Hertfordshire,' Hettie added.

Andrew shook his head in bewilderment. 'When did this happen?'

'The letter came the other day and I've been thinking about it since then,' Jack explained. 'I've decided to accept their offer.'

'I hope it's not because you're staying here and feel in the way,' Andrew retorted. 'Because I'll be bloody angry if it is. You're welcome here for as long as you like. And that's both Rose and I speaking, not just me.'

Jack was deeply touched by that speech, knowing Andrew meant every word. 'Hettie says it would be good for us to get away from Dalneil for a while and I agree with her. That's the main reason for us going.'

'And because we'll be closer to Tommy,' Hettie added.

Andrew grunted. That seemed reasonable enough. 'As long as it is.'

'So when will you leave?' Rose asked.

'They want Jack there as soon as possible. So we thought next Monday.'

'So soon!' Rose exclaimed.

'It's high time I got back to work anyway. I don't like doing nothing.'

Rose glanced at Andrew who suddenly looked slightly uncomfortable.

'We can't thank you enough for what you've done,' Hettie said.

'As if you wouldn't have done the same for us if the boot had been on the other foot,' Andrew replied. 'You know you would.'

'And what about you, Andrew, when are you going to start rebuilding?' That was Hettie.

'Rebuilding?' he queried softly.

'Well, aren't you?'

He glanced down at the carpet so that none of them could see his expression. 'I suppose so,' he mumbled.

Jack frowned. 'Just suppose so. What kind of talk is that?'

Jack didn't know of his condition either, Andrew thought. No one in the room, apart from himself, did. There was a great black hole inside him which he felt he might tumble into at any moment.

'Well, Andrew?' Rose prompted.

'It's early days yet. There's lots of time to think about that.'

Jack's frown deepened. 'That's not like you, Andrew. Is it a case of money?'

Andrew shook his head. 'No, Jack, it's not.'

'Then what?'

Andrew was desperately trying to think of a plausible answer when he was saved by the appearance of Christine.

'Telephone for you, Mr Drummond.'

'Pardon me,' he muttered, and hastily left the room.

He used the telephone call as an excuse to absent himself from the house for a while.

'Why hello, Mr Drummond, you haven't been here for

ages.' McFarlane smiled when Andrew showed up in the stables. He noted Andrew was dressed for riding.

'How's Moonbeam?' Andrew queried, crossing to the gelding and scratching its ear. Moonbeam whinnied in recognition and appreciation.

'Just fine, sir. It took a bit for him to settle down after the bombing like, but that was only to be expected. He's his old self again now.'

'Good,' Andrew murmured. He fished some sugar lumps out of his pocket and gave them to an appreciative Moonbeam.

'You're taking him out I presume, sir?'

'Yes indeed, McFarlane. So if you'll saddle him up for me.'

'Of course, sir.'

Andrew gazed about him. He'd always enjoyed the smell of stables. There was something comforting about them. Something womblike in a way.

'Mrs Drummond hasn't been riding much recently,' McFarlane commented, heaving Andrew's saddle from its rack.

'No, I don't suppose she has.'

McFarlane was secretly pleased about that. He'd never forgotten what Rose had done to Strumpet. Neither forgotten nor forgiven her.

A sudden pain stabbed Andrew's stomach making him wince. He'd passed blood again that morning and he was losing weight. There were times when the thought of the cancer worried him almost out of his mind, other times when he felt quite ethereal about it. He'd considered confiding in Jack before he went off to England, then decided not to. Jack would leave unsuspecting they might never see one another again.

'The beast could do with a good long gallop, sir. I hope you'll give it to him.'

'I shall, McFarlane. I'm right in the mood for one.'

McFarlane nodded his approval. Such a gentleman Mr Drummond, a joy to work for.

'Right then,' Andrew said when Moonbeam was ready, and swung himself into the saddle.

'I'll be waiting for your return, sir.'

Andrew put all thoughts of cancer, and everything else, out of his mind as he urged Moonbeam forward.

It was over an hour later when Andrew came to a halt by the side of the main road leading to and from Dalneil. The weather was closing in, he observed, glancing up at a leaden grey sky. There would be rain before long. And heavy rain too by the looks of things.

He'd best get back, he decided. He didn't want to get caught in a downpour. Why add the possibility of a cold to the problems he already had? Besides, the ride had tired him out. A cup of tea and a lie-down was what he needed.

Off in the far distance lightning flickered. He waited for the sound of thunder which eventually came. A low rumbling, interrupted by another, larger, lance of lightning.

Not just rain but a storm, he concluded, as more thunder rumbled. A storm that could quite quickly be upon him if he was reading the signs correctly.

He was about to turn for home when a car came into view, one he recognised as belonging to Dr Lesley.

Lesley drew up alongside and rolled down his window. 'Hello, Mr Drummond.'

'Hello, doctor.'

'Thunder and lightning, we must be in for it.'

Andrew smiled. 'So it would seem.'

Lesley was staring keenly at Andrew. 'I've been expecting you to call on me.'

'You've had the results from the hospital then.'

'Oh aye. Several weeks ago.' He hesitated, then said, 'I really am very sorry.'

'A far cry from indigestion, eh?'

'A far cry,' Lesley agreed sympathetically. 'How do you feel?'

'So so.'

Lesley nodded. 'Much pain?'

'Some.'

'If it gets worse I can give you pills to ease it. And after that . . . I have a mixture that'll help.'

'Laudanum?'

'Old fashioned I admit. But it does the trick.'

'I'll bear the pills and mixture in mind, doctor.'

'How has Mrs Drummond taken it?'

'She doesn't know yet.'

Lesley frowned. 'When *are* you going to tell her?'

'When I decide to,' Andrew prevaricated.

Lesley wasn't really surprised. People dealt with these things in their own way. That was his experience. 'If you need me I'm always on hand. Day or night.'

'I appreciate that. Thank you.'

This time thunder cracked like a cannon discharging. 'I'd best be getting on then,' Lesley said.

Moonbeam was moving restlessly beneath Andrew, the noise both alarming and frightening him.

Andrew nodded and Lesley nodded in return.

Pills and mixture, Andrew reflected as Lesley drove away. There was clearly going to be a great deal of pain in the months ahead.

Of course there was always another way to avoid that altogether. It was certainly something to think about.

'Having a fly one then?'

Elspeth Campbell started and turned to find Andrew staring at her. She was at the rear of the house, not far from the kitchen door.

'It's my coffee break so I thought I'd come outside and watch the storm.'

A huge bolt of lightning zigzagged across the heavens followed almost instantly by a massive peal of thunder.

'That's close,' she commented, having another puff on her cigarette.

It was the first time they'd been alone since the night of the bombing and Elspeth suspected that Andrew had been purposely avoiding her. She searched his face for unease at her presence but couldn't detect any.

'How are you, Elspeth?' he asked softly.

She shrugged.

That told him a great deal. Although it didn't show, she was right, he had been avoiding her. What had nearly happened that night still troubled him.

'The Riachs are leaving tomorrow morning,' he said.

'So I understand.'

'I shall be driving them to the station and while I'm away you might arrange for my things to be moved back into the room they were using.'

She went very still inside, having wondered about that. She hadn't wanted to put Andrew and Rose together again but at the time it had made sense in the circumstances.

'I see,' she replied quietly.

The first drops of rain began to fall. Soft rain that was a prelude to what was to come.

'Have you . . . told her yet?'

Andrew smiled. That was the second time today he'd been asked that question. 'No, I haven't.'

'Don't you think you should?'

'When I'm ready, Elspeth. Whenever that might be.' If ever, he added silently.

She finished her cigarette, grinding it out on an empty matchbox and sticking the remains inside. 'Hiding the evidence,' she joked.

He noticed again those graceful hands of hers which so fascinated him. 'We'd better get in or we'll be soaked through,' he said.

'Can't you sleep?'

'No,' Tommy mumbled in reply.

Mavis reached out under the bedclothes and laid a hand on his shoulder. She was exhausted after their lovemaking and had actually dozed off only to waken again. 'What's wrong?'

Tommy twisted on to his back. 'I've been thinking about Dalneil and a girl I knew there.'

'Oh?'

'Her name was Bell Mathieson.'

'Was?'

'She was killed when one of the bombs scored a direct hit on her house.'

'I'm sorry.'

'I liked Bell. She was fun.'

Jealousy blossomed in Mavis. 'Did you know her well?' she asked casually.

Tommy laughed, having detected the jealousy. 'She wasn't a girlfriend, Mavis, though she did kiss me once when I was pissed.' He then related the story of the

413

Christmas 'do' and how Bell and her friend Irene had walked him home.

'And she worked at the distillery?'

'In bottling, the pair of them.'

There was a pause, then Mavis said, 'It sounds as if she was special to you?'

'Special?' Tommy mused. 'I suppose she was, in a way. She was part of my growing up. The period between school and the RAF. My youth, you could call it.'

'You're hardly an old man now,' Mavis teased.

'No? I certainly feel like one some days. War does that to you.'

'I can understand that,' she sympathised softly.

'You wake every morning whilst on active duty wondering if it's going to be your last. That takes its toll, Mavis, believe me.'

She ran a hand over his chest, thinking how much she'd come to care for Tommy Riach. She couldn't bear the thought of something happening to him.

'Bell was to be married,' Tommy went on. 'I never met the chap but they were daft on one another apparently. We spoke the night before she died and she talked about him and their plans together. It must have broken the poor sod's heart when he got the news.'

Tommy drew in a deep breath and closed his eyes. It was wonderfully safe here in bed with Mavis. Safe, and peaceful.

'Well, that's it then,' Andrew said as the train rattled into Pitlochry station. 'You've a long journey ahead of you.'

'We've got plenty of sandwiches and tea thanks to your Mrs Moffat,' Hettie said with a smile.

Andrew kissed her on the cheek. 'Don't forget there

are telephones in Hertfordshire. You can ring once in a while.'

'I won't forget. I promise.'

The train belched a great hiss of steam as Andrew turned to Jack. 'Don't let being a big film writer go to your head now,'

Jack laughed. 'I doubt it'll be quite Hollywood.'

'But knowing you, that's probably where you'll end up.'

'That'll be the day.'

Andrew had been prepared for this to be hard, but it was proving even more so than he'd expected. He and Jack had been friends a long time, bosom pals. Now it wasn't merely au revoir, but adieu.

Andrew startled Jack by wrapping his arms round him and squeezing him tight.

'Have you turned into a poof or something!' Jack exclaimed in alarm.

Andrew laughed and released him. 'Not on your life. Now get on board before you're left behind.'

Once that had been completed and their cases safely stowed on the overhead rack Andrew stepped back on to the platform and closed the carriage door. There was a lump in his throat the size of an egg.

Hettie let down the strap and leaned out of the window. 'Thanks again for all you've done, Andrew. You know how much we appreciate it.'

'Give my regards to England and all the Sassenachs,' he joked. 'And watch Jack round those actresses. We don't want him being led astray now.'

Hettie laughed, knowing there was about as much likelihood of that as there was of him regaining his sight.

The green flag was shown and the engine driver tooted his whistle. A sad, lonely sound, Andrew thought.

'Goodbye, Andrew!' Jack called out.

'Goodbye, old bean. Bye, Hettie.'

He waved till Hettie pulled herself back into the carriage, then dropped his arm.

'Goodbye, old bean,' he repeated in a choked whisper.

'What are you doing?' Rose demanded.

'Miss Campbell's orders, ma'am. Mr Drummond's things are to be returned to the room where the Riachs were.'

'Indeed,' Rose commented caustically, thinking she'd have a word with Miss Campbell about this.

And the sooner the better.

'Why, Andrew?'

Rose had purposely waited till after dinner to speak to Andrew, deeming that the most appropriate time.

He glanced across at her, having been thinking of Jack. 'Why what, Rose?' He knew precisely what she was referring to.

'I thought . . . Well, I thought . . .'

She was embarrassed, he noted, rather pleased in a way. He waited for her to continue.

'You've gone back to the other room, Andrew.'

'That's correct. Jack and Hettie have now left so it seemed the natural thing to do. Restore the status quo so to speak.'

Rose swallowed hard. 'I see.'

Andrew got up and crossed to the decanter from which he poured himself a dram. 'It's odd to think we'll soon run out of this,' he said. 'It's hard to imagine myself ordering cases of someone else's whisky, there being no more of our own available.'

Rose hung her head, shame and guilt strong within her.

They hadn't made love since sleeping together again. Once or twice she'd thought Andrew might attempt to do so, but he hadn't. As for herself, she hadn't been able to suggest it or make an advance of any kind in that direction, though, in truth, she'd wanted to.

She should apologise, she thought. Try and explain. But how could she explain what she herself didn't really understand. The loss of their baby, Mary, had played such havoc in both their lives.

'I hope Jack and Hettie are having a comfortable and speedy journey. It's such a long way,' Andrew commented casually.

'Yes.'

'With as little hold-up as possible. The train services have been dreadful since the war started. Understandable I suppose.'

'The war has upset and changed a lot of things.'

'Not least Dalneil,' he said softly.

'At least they'll be closer to Tommy where they're going.'

Andrew had a sip of whisky. His stomach had been playing up all day, and at one point he'd thought he was going to vomit. But thankfully the moment had passed.

He wondered what Rose's reaction would be if he told her about his cancer. Shock, horror no doubt. Maybe even hysterics. They had been married many years after all. And it had once been good between them.

He thought of Elspeth Campbell. Oh, what a temptation that was. A temptation to which he'd so very nearly succumbed.

What if he had, what then? He didn't know the answer to that.

'Drew will be home soon for Easter,' he said.

'Not long now,' Rose agreed.

What would become of Drew after he was gone? he wondered. What future now lay in store for the lad? What career? He had no idea.

He visualised the bombed-out rubble that had been the distillery, his heart sinking at the picture conjured up. Rebuild, Hettie had suggested. How could he do that when under the sentence of death? There simply wasn't time. Rebuilding was a long-term project, providing he could get hold of the materials which was doubtful in wartime. As for new pot-stills, securing the copper for those would be nigh on an impossibility.

And even if he succeeded in having new pot-stills made, adhering as close to the original shapes as he could, the whisky produced would be different. That was how it was with pot-stills. Each was unique and an individual which couldn't be re-created.

She deserved this, Rose thought. It was all her own fault. She had no one to blame but herself. The laugh was, she'd never stopped loving Andrew. Not for an instant. Even if she hadn't wanted him in her bed or being intimate with her.

'I think I'll go out for a walk,' Andrew declared.

'But it's late!'

Later than you realise, he thought wryly.

When he'd gone Rose remained staring into the fire. After a while she got up and went to her bedroom which now seemed an incredibly lonely place after Andrew's presence of the past few weeks.

Her own fault, she repeated to herself as she started to undress.

Mavis stopped and sucked in a deep lungful of air. 'Hmmmh,' she sighed dreamily on exhalation. 'That's good.'

Tommy, standing beside her, smiled. Her expression was almost beatific as the wind whipped her hair. 'A penny for them?'

'I enjoy working in the pub, but it's wonderful to get a day off and get out for a change. To be amongst the elements.'

'Even if it's raining?' he teased.

'It can rain and snow and chuck down hailstones for all I care. As long as I'm outdoors away from all that smoke and fug.'

He laughed. The pub did get that way at times, particularly later in the evening. There were occasions, with so many cigarettes and pipes being puffed on, you could hardly see from one end of the bar to the other.

He glanced up at the low, lowering sky. The rain had started a few minutes previously and from the looks of it was going to get a lot worse.

He took her hand in his and gently squeezed it, relishing just being in her company. How happy she made him, and, somehow, at ease with himself. If a coin has two sides then he was one, Mavis the other. Each different, yet part of the same whole.

'It's fortunate for me the weather's so bad today so I can spend it with you rather than flying.' All flying had been suspended until further notice.

She smiled her agreement.

The wind had brought colour to her cheeks, he noted. It suited her. She looked exhilarated.

'Do you mind getting wet?' she asked.

'Not in the least.'

She laughed. 'Me neither.'

The rain was getting heavier now, rattling against their coats like machine-gun fire. 'What are you thinking about?' he queried.

'Nothing. Nothing at all.'

Using his free hand he traced a line down her cheek. 'We're very lucky, you know.'

'How so?'

'To have found one another. Don't you think?'

'Yes,' she murmured huskily.

The wind suddenly gusted, making her stagger. Tommy immediately reached out and grabbed her in support. He drew her to him and held her close.

For almost a minute they remained like that, staring into each other's eyes. Neither stated what was in his and her mind. It was all too obvious.

It was hours later, the pair of them thoroughly drenched, before they returned to the Lamb and Flag. As days off went, it couldn't have been more of a success.

The sort of day that lingers in the memory for years afterwards.

Chapter 26

The clock in Andrew's study chimed midnight. The witching hour, he smiled thinly to himself.

He was drunk, the almost empty whisky bottle by his side bearing witness to that. And he didn't care. In fact, he didn't think he cared about anything any more.

Not true, he chided himself. Of course he did. He cared about Rose, and he certainly cared about Drew, both now fast asleep upstairs.

Andrew sighed, and ran a hand through his hair. The pain had been bad that day which was why he'd started early on the whisky, preferring that, for the time being anyway, to Lesley's pills. Besides, whisky was far more enjoyable than any pill he could imagine.

'Oh, Dad,' he whispered, thinking of Murdo. 'I wish you were here to talk to. Advise me what to do. How to cope with this thing.'

Murdo's death had been swift, instantaneous almost. One moment alive, the next dead of a heart attack.

Well, it wouldn't be like that with him. He wouldn't have such luck. His would be a long lingering death filled with agonising pain. The very thought of it made him break out in a cold sweat.

Pills, mixture, was that what it had all boiled down to? A life as rich and exciting as his ending with pills and laudanum. There was a certain irony about it really. Perhaps this was his punishment for all the bad things he'd done – murder included.

Murder that had happened so very long ago, reprisal for another murder, that of his beloved Alice whom he'd intended marrying.

Hers had also been a horrible death. Burning alive in a house engulfed by flames. He shuddered just thinking about it.

What a different life it would have been if Alice had lived. She instead of Rose would even now be the mistress of Drummond House. That would have meant no Drew of course, but undoubtedly there would have been other children.

Andrew shook his head. He couldn't wish away Drew. The wee laddie had been born and was his. Loved and cherished by him. His heir.

Andrew laughed mirthlessly. Heir to what? Oh aye, there was plenty of money in the bank, and the house of course. But the distillery was gone. The distillery that should have been passed on to Drew. As it had been passed on to him by Murdo before that. And his father . . .

How he bitterly regretted getting Rose pregnant the second time. Everything between them had been fine up until then. And might still be if the baby had been born. There again, the foetus had been that of another male child, while Rose's heart had been set on a girl. Mary, as she'd called her.

Who knew what knock-on effects a baby boy would have had? The answer to that was unknown, a mystery. But he didn't think it would have been as bad as losing the baby altogether. That had been a tragedy of immense proportions, for Rose and him. Immense.

He reached down for the bottle, holding it in front of him and studying the label. Drummond's Finest Malt, Best Speyside. Perhaps the best malt in all Scotland. Now defunct.

He swore volubly, emptied the remains of the bottle into his glass and tossed the bottle aside.

He recalled his ride out the day of the storm when he'd talked to Lesley. He'd told himself then there was an alternative to the pills and mixture, and there was. Release from all this in the length of time it took to pull a trigger.

Oh, it was an option all right. He had the means to hand. All it would take was to click the bullets into the chamber and point the barrel at his head.

Boom! For a fleeting second he might hear the noise, then nothing. Oblivion. Eternity.

He laid his glass aside and came to his feet. Crossing to the bureau he opened a drawer and there it was. The Webley revolver he'd brought back from Ireland as a souvenir. And beside it the box containing four rounds of ammo, just one of which would be sufficient.

He caressed the revolver with his fingertips, then grasped the butt.

Andrew smiled in memory. This was an old friend carried daily by him throughout his entire posting in Ireland. A friend who could now come to his aid if he so wished.

Don't, son.

Andrew started. He knew that voice. Knew it only too

well. The hairs rose on the back of his neck and he sucked in a deep breath.

Slowly he turned but there was no one there. He was alone in the study.

'Murdo? Dad?'

Silence.

'Is that you, Pa?'

Silence again.

And then he felt it, a pressure of some sort. Not alarming in the least, rather reassuring. A warm glow that seemed to encompass him. A presence and glow not of this world.

Don't, son, the voice said again. And still there was no one else present.

'Why not, Pa? It would be easier.'

That would be cowardly, son. Don't.

The glow had become a heat that was making him tingle from head to toe. He'd never felt more alive than he did at that moment.

'I won't, Dad. You have my promise.'

The heat abruptly left Andrew's body and the sense of a presence withdrew.

He shivered. Was he going mad? Had he imagined the whole thing? Too much whisky perhaps?

No, he thought with absolute certainty. Murdo had been with him. Returned from beyond the grave and whatever lay there.

He placed the Webley back in the drawer and shut it. Nor would he ever be tempted to open that drawer again.

He'd promised. A promise he'd keep.

Tommy was drained as he and Dingo entered the Lamb and Flag. Paul Wyborn had been shot down that afternoon during a sortie over France. Both he and Dingo had seen

Paul's parachute open so by now Paul would be a prisoner of war. In the bag for the duration.

At least Paul was out of it, Tommy thought. At least he'd survive. The conditions in the POW camps may be appalling, so rumour had it, but incarceration in one was preferable to the fate that so many of their comrades had met.

Ruffles, Dan Gilfeather's wife, was behind the bar polishing glasses. Ruffles was a nickname given to her years before on account of her fiery, and quick, temper. A local had said to her one night, Don't get your feathers ruffled, Gilfeather, and that's how the nickname had come about. She'd been Ruffles to all and sundry ever since.

'Hello, boys.' She smiled. 'What's it to be?'

'A couple of pints please,' Dingo retorted, heaving himself on to a stool.

Tommy looked along the length of the bar but there was no sign of Mavis, and it wasn't her night off.

'Upstairs in bed. She's feeling poorly,' Ruffles informed him when he inquired.

Tommy was immediately concerned. 'How poorly?'

'Flu I think. Or something similar. Came down with it earlier so I packed her off to her room.'

Ruffles smiled at Tommy. 'I was just about to take her up some soup. Would you like to instead?'

'Yes please.'

'Then come on through and I'll give it to you,' Ruffles said, serving Dingo.

'What about your pint?' Dingo queried of Tommy.

'I'll get it shortly. I won't be long.'

And with that Tommy followed Ruffles to the kitchen.

*   *   *

'Can I come in?' Tommy asked, poking his head round Mavis's door.

Damn! Mavis swore inwardly. What a sight she must look. She didn't want Tommy to see her like this. But the damage was already done.

Tommy entered the room without waiting for a reply. 'I've brought you a bowl of soup,' he explained.

She shook her head. 'I couldn't eat a thing.'

'But you must to keep up your strength.'

'I couldn't, Tommy. Honestly. I've no appetite at all. The very thought of food . . .' She trailed off and pulled a face.

Frowning, he set the tray he was carrying atop a chest of drawers, then crossed and sat on the edge of her bed.

'You shouldn't be up here this time of day. What will people say!' she admonished.

He shrugged. 'It's an errand of mercy. Quite understandable in the circumstances.'

'And I'm a mess!'

'Well, I hardly expected you to be all dolled up ready for a night on the tiles,' he joked.

She smiled at that.

Mavis was pale as anything, he noted, with dark smudges under her eyes. Her brow was dotted with perspiration.

'So how are you?'

'Weak.'

He grunted.

'And very hot.'

He felt her forehead which was burning. 'Ruffles says it's flu.'

'It could be.'

'Have you sent for the doctor?'

'Not yet.'

'Then why don't I go back downstairs and ring him.'

'I happen to know he isn't there just now. He's out delivering a baby and will be tied up for hours yet. I'll ring in the morning if I'm still bad.'

He stared at her, his anxiety clearly showing. 'Is there anything I can get you?'

'I could use some water. My glass is empty.'

He immediately rose, picked up the glass and went over to her washing jug and basin, filling the glass from the jug.

'Here,' he said, placing the rim of the glass against bloodless lips.

Mavis drank her fill then lay back on the pillow. 'This is quite unlike me. I just don't get ill very often.'

'Well, you are now. So you stay in that bed until you're better. Hear?'

'I hear.' What a truly lovely man he was, she thought. If only things had been different and there hadn't been a war on. There again, she'd never have met him if it hadn't been for the war.

'Could you take a hot toddy?' he asked. 'It would do you the world of good.'

She pulled her hand out from under the bedclothes and grasped his. 'That would be sweet of you.'

'Then a hot toddy it is, I'll go and fetch it. In the meantime don't run away.'

She laughed at that, the idea of her running anywhere in her present condition being so ridiculous.

'What are you doing!' Tommy exclaimed in alarm on returning with the toddy. Mavis was squatting by the side of the bed.

She coloured. 'I had to use the gazunder.'

'You should have waited till I got back.'

'I didn't want you to see. It's embarrassing.'

'Daft woman,' he chided, hurrying over. 'If you have to go you have to go and that's all there is to it. What if you'd fallen over, for God's sake!'

'Then I'd have got up again.'

'That's not the point.'

Her head was swimming and she felt even weaker than when she'd been tucked up. She swayed slightly.

Tommy instantly had her by the arm. 'Have you finished?'

She nodded.

'Then let's get you back under those clothes.'

He smoothed the quilt having first readjusted her pillows. 'How's that?'

'Better, thank you.'

Her hairline was damp he noticed, which, surprisingly, he found rather erotic.

'We're like an old married couple,' she joked.

Using his foot he pushed the gazunder out of sight. He'd empty it later. 'Nothing wrong in that.'

She didn't think so either. It was a most enjoyable experience. She wasn't used to being looked after. Certainly not by a man. And a lover at that.

'Let's get some of this toddy down you,' he declared.

She drank about half and then said she couldn't swallow any more. He laid the glass aside.

'What about your pals in the bar?' she asked. 'They'll be missing you.'

For some reason that angered him. 'I can be with them any night I want. I'm here now with you because you need me. And here I stay.'

That touched her deeply. 'What if I fall asleep?'

'I still stay. You may want the pot again. Or something else. Are you hungry?'

'Not in the least.'

'Have you had anything at all today?'

'Ruffles brought me a lightly boiled egg earlier that I managed to get down. But it was a struggle. I just don't have any appetite at all.'

He went back to the jug and basin, picking up the towel that was there. He used that to mop her forehead and neck.

'There,' he declared when he was finished.

'At this rate I'll lose pounds,' she smiled. 'Which is no bad thing.'

'Rubbish,' he admonished. 'You've got a lovely figure. Just right in my opinion. You don't want to get skinny with your bones showing through. Horrible.'

'You've quite cheered me up, Tommy. Thank you.' She smiled again.

'Have I?'

'Oh yes,' she breathed, wishing he was in bed beside her. Cuddled up close as they often were when they slept together. 'Do I really have a lovely figure?'

'Absolutely gorgeous.'

'My bottom's rather large.'

'Not so.'

'And my thighs . . .'

'Are a knockout,' he interrupted. 'Smooth as silk and shapely as can be.'

'You've got a nice body yourself,' she told him. 'With a beautiful bottom. Women like beautiful bottoms. It's a huge attraction in a man.'

'Well well,' Tommy murmured. He'd had no idea.

'And you always smell nice. Some chaps pong no matter what, but you never do.'

'I think this is a mutual admiration society,' he laughed.

'Well, if it is it's because we're so . . .' She trailed off.

'So what, Mavis?' he prompted.

She desperately tried to think of the correct word, not wanting to admit too much of what was in her mind. She didn't want to frighten him off. 'So compatible.'

He stared at her. Compatible? 'I suppose we are,' he replied softly. He hadn't thought of it like that before. But yes, they were.

'Tell me a story about Africa?' she requested.

'Africa! But I haven't been there yet.'

'That doesn't matter. You must know a lot about the place. Make one up.'

His mind raced, recalling Edgar Rice Burroughs whom he'd read years ago. Perhaps it was then the whole great dream had started. He wasn't sure. Edgar Rice Burroughs and, later, H. Rider Haggard.

'King Solomon, of old, had a fabled diamond mine whose whereabouts somehow became lost through the centuries . . .'

Mavis snuggled down deeper under the covers, closing her eyes to listen.

'Then, in Victorian times, a map was discovered . . .'

Tommy woke, sore and stiff. With a sudden jerk, realising where he was, he sat upright and glanced anxiously at the bedside clock, breathing a sigh of relief to see he hadn't overslept.

Pale morning light had invaded the room, it being not long after dawn. He rose and quietly stretched.

Mavis was breathing regularly, her eyes firmly closed. Just as she'd been before he too dropped off. He placed the chair he'd been sitting in back in its original position, then, ever so gently and lightly, touched her forehead.

It was warm, but no more than it should have been. He noted that the dark smudges under her eyes had disappeared.

Tommy smiled to himself. It seemed Mavis was on the road to recovery.

'Come in, Green Leader, this is Control.'

Tommy flicked on his R/T. 'Receiving you loud and clear, Control.'

'You are diverted to West Malling, Green Leader. We're fogbound here.'

Tommy frowned. Damn! he inwardly swore. This was a nuisance. He wanted to get back to Laxworth and Mavis.

'Is that certain, Control?' he queried.

'Quite certain, Green Leader. Please confirm.'

'Confirmed, Control. Am now making for West Malling.'

The R/T order had been heard by the rest of the section so Tommy didn't have to repeat it.

'Breaking right, chaps. Here we go.'

The section came on to its new course.

'I'm sorry, sir, I can't get through to that number.'

Tommy grimaced in disappointment. This was the third time he'd tried to phone the Lamb and Flag and the third time he'd failed.

'Thank you very much, operator.'

'You're welcome, sir. I'm sorry.'

Tommy hung up. He was desperate to know how Mavis was. Of all days to be diverted and then not be able to get through on the telephone. He just hoped Mavis was all right.

He returned to the Officers' Mess where a party was in progress, it being one of the West Malling-based pilots' birthday. A boozy, riotous affair which was bound to result in a few sore heads in the morning. He was determined he wasn't going to be among them.

Later, he attempted one more call, that too proving unsuccessful.

Tommy stared in disgust out of the window of the temporary billet he'd been allocated. It was a pea-souper which meant that West Malling was now also fogbound. He seethed with impatience, anxious about Mavis.

The 'drome remained fogbound for the rest of that day during which he attempted a number of times to ring the Lamb and Flag.

On the sole occasion the operator did manage to get a connection no one answered.

'Can I come in, Dad?'

Andrew smiled at his son, home for the holidays, standing framed in the study doorway. 'Of course.'

Drew closed the door behind him.

'So what can I do for you?'

'I thought we might talk.'

Andrew raised an eyebrow. 'About what?'

'The distillery.'

Andrew's face clouded over. That was the last thing he wished to discuss.

'Can I sit, Dad?'

'Aye, help yourself.'

There was a fine fire going which Andrew had positioned himself to one side of. Drew now pulled a chair across and positioned himself at the other side.

'It's a terrible loss,' Andrew stated quietly. 'I still haven't come to terms with it. As long as I can remember it's been there, and now it's gone. For ever.'

Drew's brow furrowed. 'For ever? Surely not?'

Andrew shrugged.

'Aren't you going to rebuild?'

Andrew became uneasy. He could hardly explain the reason why he hadn't considered doing that. Why it was impossible.

'Well, Dad?' Drew prompted.

'Some things are just meant to be, son, and there's nothing we can do about them.'

Drew couldn't believe he was hearing this. It was so unlike his father. 'But of course there is! You can rebuild.'

'With a war on? I'd never get the materials.'

'Surely from somewhere?'

Andrew sighed. The very guts had been knocked out of him, he thought. He was a shell compared to the man he'd once been. And, in a way, he felt ashamed.

He studied Drew. The lad was a credit to him and Rose. He'd been a bit of a tyke when younger. Spoilt if he was honest. But Drew had outgrown that. A young man was emerging, one of promise. He and Rose could be proud of themselves.

Andrew shook his head. 'Not a chance.'

'But you could try.'

'I'm telling you . . .'

'You must *try*, Dad,' Drew interjected hotly.

'Anyway, it's early days yet.'

'Not too early to start thinking about it, making plans. For the future if they have to be, but at least making plans. Doing something.'

There was a silence between them during which Andrew stared morosely into the fire.

'This is important to me, Dad,' Drew went on after a while. 'More than anything I want to carry on after you, just as you did after Grandpa Murdo. I've set my heart on it.'

'Have you indeed,' Andrew murmured.

'Yes I have. I've even got ideas of my own.'

That surprised Andrew. 'What sort of ideas?'

'We only distribute in this country, Britain that is. And even then not a huge amount into Southern England. When the war's over we can expand our market. First into Southern England, then abroad.'

'Abroad?'

'America to be precise. I'm certain the Americans would take as much as we could give them. We need the capacity of course, but we can acquire that by rebuilding on a far larger scale than the old distillery.'

Andrew stared at his son in amazement. Well well, he mused. It would seem he'd spawned a tiger.

Excitement gripped him. America! Now why hadn't he thought of that? The reason was obvious. Capacity, as Drew had pointed out. That had been his limitation. It had simply never crossed his mind to expand, being content to let things go on as they'd always been.

'What do you say, Dad?'

'Interesting premise, I'll give you that.'

'It's a golden opportunity we have here. One we should grasp with both hands.'

We? Andrew chuckled inwardly. Whatever else, the lad was certainly serious about all this. Particularly his own involvement.

'I was thinking earlier about a lecture you once gave me,' Drew stated, slightly changing tack.

'Oh?'

'About the people who work for us and our responsibility towards them. If you don't rebuild they'll be permanently out of a job. And think of the effect that'll have on Dalneil.'

Andrew blanched. That was below the belt. True, mind you, but still below the belt.

And yet, the fact remained, he was a walking, talking dead man. He just didn't have the time left to rebuild.

'But Drew did. Drew had a whole lifetime ahead of him.

'I'm worried about Dad.'

'In what way?'

Drew leant on the mantelpiece in Nancy's bedroom, having come to pay her a visit on leaving Andrew. Nancy had been reluctant to let him in, but had eventually been persuaded to do so.

'He doesn't look well. Have you noticed?'

Nancy thought about that. 'Can't say I have.'

'Well, I've noticed. I swear he's lost weight. And there's a tinge about his skin that isn't at all healthy.'

'Now you mention it,' Nancy frowned, 'his appetite isn't as good as it was. Your mother commented on that only recently.'

Tommy nodded. 'It's losing the distillery if you ask me. It's eating him up inside. That's what's bothering him and making him unwell.'

'Poor man,' Nancy sympathised.

'Well, I may have done something about that.'

'You?'

Drew smiled. 'The chat I had with him tonight has certainly given him a great deal to think about. He was quite bubbling with enthusiasm when I left his study.'

'So what did you say?'

Drew repeated the conversation he'd had with Andrew. When he finally finished Nancy was staring at him in admiration. Where was the boy of only a few years ago? This was a man talking. And an ambitious, far-sighted one at that.

'What do you think?' he demanded eagerly.

'It's a terrific notion.'

'And it'll work. Believe me. I just know it will. Oh, it'll take a long while to come to fruition, even if we started rebuilding tomorrow. Whisky takes time to mature before you can sell it to the public. It could be ten years from now, more, before the first bottle of Drummond's malt reappears in the shops and pubs. But reappear it must, and will.' His jaw jutted forward. 'I'm determined about that.'

'Why don't you kiss me,' she whispered.

He was smiling again as he moved towards her.

How many nights now had she waited for Andrew? Elspeth had lost count.

Sighing, she lit another cigarette. She'd hang on another half hour before returning to bed.

He hadn't come to the kitchen in the early hours since the night of the bombing, the night they'd come so very close to making love.

She would have to speak to him soon, she decided. She had to know where she was. She couldn't go on fretting like this.

Her heart leapt when there was a sound from outside in the corridor. Andrew?

But it wasn't. The kitchen door remained resolutely shut. Whatever had caused the sound, it hadn't been him.

The minutes continued to tick slowly by.

Chapter 27

Tommy and the section had been fogbound at West Malling for two days, then, on the third, had flown a sortie from there, returning at long last to Laxworth. At no point during this time had he managed to get through to the Lamb and Flag.

He now strode into the pub, coming up in surprise, and relief, to see Mavis busy behind the bar.

'Home is the hunter!' Dingo called out, giving Tommy the thumbs-up sign.

'How are you, mate?' Dingo asked as Tommy joined him. Dingo's section had landed considerably earlier than Tommy's which was why he was in the bar before him.

'Fine. And you?'

'Never better.'

Mavis served her customer and hurried across, eyes shining at the sight of Tommy.

'I thought you were at death's door?' he joked.

'Whatever it was I had passed quickly. I was up and about the afternoon after you left me.'

'I've been trying to ring but couldn't get through.'

Mavis nodded. 'There has been trouble with the phone lines, but I think it's sorted now.'

He wanted to take hold of her, clasp her in his arms. Tell her how much he'd missed her.

'I'm off to the dunny,' Dingo announced, deeming it polite to leave the lovers alone for a few minutes.

'Thank you for what you did,' Mavis said.

'It wasn't much.'

'Oh yes it was. It was appreciated I can tell you.'

He didn't know what to answer to that.

'Can you stay tonight?'

'I thought you'd never ask.'

She laughed and, reaching out, briefly touched his hand. A touch that was also a caress.

'I was worried about you,' he admitted.

'The doctor came but couldn't diagnose exactly what was wrong. It wasn't a cold, he said, or flu. Though the symptoms were similar to flu. He gave me some medicine and a few hours later I was back on my feet again.'

'Good medicine.' Tommy smiled.

'Maybe. But the best medicine was having you with me. That was an enormous comfort.'

There was a slight hiatus while they stared at one another. 'Now what are you going to have?' Mavis asked eventually.

'We should get married.'

Mavis went very still. Then, slowly, she turned to face Tommy. It was later that night and they were in bed together.

'Married?'

'I love you, Mavis.'

A thrill ran through her to hear those words. 'And I love you, Tommy,' she replied softly.

'If it wasn't for the war I'd propose here and now. There's no doubt whatsoever in my mind that I want you to be my wife. But how can we get married with a war on? We could be married one day, you a widow the next. I couldn't ask that of you. It just wouldn't be fair.'

She stroked his cheek, still damp from their recent lovemaking. 'How little you know of women, Tommy.'

'Is that so?'

'That's so,' she smiled. 'I'll happily marry you, no matter what.'

He sat up on an elbow. 'Are you serious?'

'Never more so. We love each other and that's all that counts.'

'But if I was killed . . .'

'Then it happens,' she cut in. 'There's no way of telling whether it will or not. But if it doesn't, think of all the time we'd have wasted.'

'We could go on just as we are for now.'

'We could. Except, what happens if you're re-posted?'

Tommy bit his lip. That was always a possibility. The war could drag on for years yet. The chances of his remaining at Laxworth indefinitely were very small if it did.

'If we were married I could follow you to wherever. There's always a need for barmaids.'

He studied her, thinking the last thing he wanted was for them to be parted. Even the few days he'd spent at West Malling had been torture.

'Are you absolutely certain about this?' he demanded.

'Absolutely.'

'No doubts . . . ?'

She interrupted him by laughing. 'None whatever.'

'Then will you marry me?'

'I'd be honoured to.'

A great whoof of breath escaped him. Then he was holding her tight, squeezing her against him. Now all that remained was the matter of where and when. The sooner the better they both agreed when he put that to her.

'Let's go and tell Ruffles and Dan,' she suggested. 'I have to tell someone.'

'But they're in bed.'

'So we'll wake them. They won't mind.'

Tommy released her and slipped from underneath the covers, Mavis getting out the other side. She put on her dressing gown, he trousers and shirt. They left the room hand in hand.

Ruffles and Dan Gilfeather were so excited by the news they insisted on opening a bottle of champagne, and a second bottle after that. As Dan commented, owning a pub did have its advantages. Like being able to lay your hands on champagne after closing time.

Andrew, hands deep in pockets, stood hunched, staring for the umpteenth time at the remains of the distillery. His mind was whirling, thinking about that conversation with Drew, wondering . . . wondering . . .

'Hello, Mr Drummond.'

Andrew started, and turned to find Kelly there. 'Why, hello, Kelly.'

'I was out for a constitutional and found myself wandering up here. It's something I often do.'

Andrew gave the book-keeper a wry smile. 'Me too.'

'It's a bit like visiting a cemetery I suppose,' Kelly said. 'Paying your respects, that sort of thing.'

Andrew nodded that he understood.

'Lovely day,' Kelly declared, glancing up at the sky. 'It promises to be a fine summer.'

'Let's hope it is.'

'And how are you, Mr Drummond?'

'Not too bad. And yourself?'

'Bored, if the truth were known. But I imagine that's how it's going to be from here on. No one else is going to employ me now. Too long in the tooth I'm afraid.' He sighed. 'When the distillery went so did my working life. I'm on the scrapheap now and there I'll stay.'

Andrew felt for the man.

'Still, it could always be worse,' Kelly murmured.

Aye, Andrew reflected, thinking of himself. It could be. 'Do you know the legend of the Phoenix, Kelly?' he asked.

Kelly frowned. 'Isn't that the bird who dies and then gets reborn again?'

'The very one. It literally rises again out of the ashes of its own funeral pyre. At least that's how I remember the story.'

Kelly regarded Andrew quizzically. 'Is there a relevance here?'

'Possibly,' Andrew mused. 'Let's go for a walk. I've something to discuss with you about which I wish your opinion.'

It was an enormous undertaking, Andrew reflected. He'd been doodling on a pad of paper, roughly sketching out how the new distillery might look. Of course he'd need an architect to do the job properly, this was just to give him some sort of idea.

A new distillery would have to be fully up to date which meant mechanisation wherever possible. The bottling department, for example, would be entirely updated, machines doing the bulk of work previously done by hand.

Naturally some processes couldn't change, they would be performed in the traditional manner. Had to be.

His thoughts were interrupted by a tap on the study door. 'Come in!'

It was Elspeth. He knew instantly from her expression what this was all about.

'I took the opportunity while Mrs Drummond and Nancy were out,' she stated.

He nodded. 'Take a seat.'

'I'd rather not, if that's all right.'

He laid his pencil aside and studied her. 'What's on your mind, Elspeth?' As if he didn't know.

'I want to know where I stand. About you and me that is.'

'And you have every right to,' he murmured. 'But please take a seat. I'm hardly the boss on this occasion.'

Elspeth hesitated, then crossed to a chair.

'Drink?'

She shook her head.

He decided he wouldn't have one either. His stomach was tender and he'd passed blood again that morning. Best leave well alone for the time being.

'I should have spoken before now,' he said.

'Yes, you should, Andrew.' Her tone was accusatory.

He dropped his gaze for a few moments, thinking about how he should phrase this. 'It's obvious I'm extremely attracted to you. Have been for quite some time. I certainly wasn't trying to simply take advantage of you.'

Tears came into Elspeth's eyes. 'You've made me feel so cheap.'

'I'm truly sorry about that, Elspeth. Honestly I am.'

'Then what happened? Why have you never approached me again since the night of the bombing? Is it me? Something I did? Something I said?'

Andrew shook his head. 'Attracted as I am, I realised it would be a mistake.'

'Why?'

'Because . . .' And here it was, the nub of the matter. 'Because I still, despite everything, love my wife.'

Elspeth jerked as though she'd been struck.

'That may sound ridiculous, considering how she's treated me, but nonetheless it's fact.'

Elspeth glanced away, tears now streaming down her face. 'How little you must think of me.'

'That's not so!' he exclaimed. 'I happen to think very highly of you. Very highly indeed. But I don't love you, I love Rose.'

Damn, he was going to have to have that drink after all. He got up and went to where he kept a bottle and glass. One of the last bottles of Drummond in the house. Galling as it might be, he was going to have to order a case or two of another brand.

'Do you want me to leave? My job that is?' she asked.

He thought about that. 'Not really. But I would understand if you did.'

He suddenly laughed. 'It's ironic really. I was quite the rake when younger, there were women galore. When it came to them I don't think I had a scruple in my entire body. It just shows you how we all change.'

'If that's how you feel why did you do what you did the night of the bombing? Was it because of what you'd been told at the hospital?'

He leant back against the bureau, feeling incredibly weary. Not just a physical tiredness, but a fatigue of the soul. 'I suppose so. I was full of self-pity that night. About my cancer, about my marriage. You were sympathetic. But more than that, I'd found something with you that I'd once had with Rose and which has been missing for years. Something I desperately needed, particularly that night of all nights.'

Elspeth didn't feel so bad any more. What he was saying made sense. She could understand it.

'It wasn't some kneejerk reaction,' Andrew went on slowly. 'At the time it seemed almost inevitable. But it would have been wrong, believe me.'

'I do,' she whispered.

He had a gulp of whisky, shuddering as it coursed its way down his throat. 'I should have spoken sooner, I know. You shouldn't have had to come and beard me literally in my den. Call it cowardice if you will. Call it whatever. I apologise.'

'You still haven't told Rose, have you?'

He smiled cynically. 'No.'

'Why not?'

He shrugged. 'I'm not certain I shall tell her.'

'But you must! You can't leave her in the dark. That's not fair.'

'I can do whatever I wish,' Andrew replied softly. 'Certainly where that's concerned.'

'But you said you still love her.'

'And I do. But Rose's affections for me have long since withered on the vine. Look at it this way, perhaps it's a case of what she doesn't know won't upset her. Anyway . . . I haven't decided yet. I may or I may not. I'll see.'

There were the beginnings of new lines on his face she realised. 'Are you in much pain lately?'

The cynical smile returned. 'It varies from day to day.

Whisky helps, though sometimes it gets too much for even that.'

Now Elspeth dropped her gaze. 'If there's anything I can do . . .'

'There is.'

'What?'

'Stay on until it's all over. I said I'd fully understand if you went, but I would like you to remain.'

'Why, Andrew?'

'Because . . .' He trailed off and frowned. 'I'm being selfish again, aren't I? Selfish and unfair. You must do what's right for you.'

Elspeth wiped away her tears, then snuffled into a hanky she produced from a pocket. 'Your Rose is a fool,' she said quietly. 'A bloody fool in my opinion. She doesn't realise what she's chucked away.'

'Compassion, Elspeth, remember the miscarriage. If anything's to blame it's that.'

She'd have to go to her room and wash her face, Elspeth thought. That and compose herself. 'You're a good man, Andrew Drummond,' she stated simply.

He laughed. 'Hardly that! Quite the contrary I should think.'

'But you are. And I wish you had fucked me that night. I'll always regret you didn't.'

Her using that word shocked Andrew. And yet, wasn't that, attraction or no, exactly what it would have been?

'I still go down to the kitchen in the early hours if you ever need companionship,' she said.

'No strings?'

'None. I still enjoy being with you, talking . . .' She bit her lip, and shrugged awkwardly.

'And I you.'

She hesitated for a few seconds, then said, 'I'll let you get on. I can see you're busy.'

'Thank you.'

She left him with a far lighter heart than she'd had on entering the study.

'My God!' Hettie exclaimed, reading the letter that had just arrived in the morning post.

'What is it?'

'Tommy's getting married a week on Saturday and wants to know if we can come!'

Jack was stunned. '*Married?*'

'So he says. A girl called Mavis Giddings. It's to be a civil ceremony.'

Jack was totally lost for words. He hadn't even known Tommy was courting, neither of them had.

'Well, I'll be buggered,' he managed eventually.

'Can we go?'

'Of course we'll bloody well go. Wild horses wouldn't keep me away.'

'I've got to sit down,' Hettie declared.

Jack rubbed his chin. Tommy getting married? This was a turn-up for the book. He just hoped it wasn't one of those fleeting wartime romances that would end in tears.

Please God it wasn't that.

'What are you and Kelly up to, locked away in your study hour after hour?' Rose demanded.

Andrew tapped the side of his nose. 'That's for me to know and you to wonder about.'

He was teasing her she realised. 'Oh come on, Andrew, spill the beans?'

'No,' he replied, shaking his head.

'*Pretty* please?'

He laughed. She was in as playful a mood as he. 'It's a secret.'

'Oh, one of those, eh?'

'Exactly.'

'But a man shouldn't have secrets from his wife.'

'And why not?'

'He just shouldn't, that's all.'

He wagged a finger at her. 'Are you saying you don't have secrets from me? Because if you do I won't believe you.'

Her eyes flew open in pretend innocence. 'Cross my heart and hope to die. Not a one.'

This was the Rose of old, he thought, smiling. How relaxed it made him feel.

'Come on,' she urged. 'Give.'

'It's a plan,' he declared.

'What sort of plan?'

'A plan I was asked to draw up by the War Office.'

That was obviously a lie. 'And when did they do this?'

'Some while ago. I had a telephone call from Winnie himself.'

Now it was becoming outrageous, but fun. 'I see.'

'Is that you, Andrew old chap, Winnie said. And then went on to tell me what he wanted.'

'Which is?'

Andrew leant forward in his chair and winked conspiratorially. 'A plan to bring about the downfall of Hitler.'

'Really!'

'Really,' he nodded.

'And how are you going to do that?'

'That's the secret.'

'And how did they get your name?'

'From Kelly. He's really a member of . . .' Andrew broke

off in apparent confusion. 'I can't say. I'm sworn not to.'

'Another secret?'

'That's right.'

Rose's lips were twitching with amusement. 'That makes you very important.'

'Indeed.'

'And Kelly?'

'Indeed again.'

'And you won't tell me?'

'Can't, Rose. Promised Winnie.'

Andrew thought he'd better get out of this while the going was good, while he was ahead. As an actor had once told him, important rule of the theatre, always know when to get off the stage.

A glance at the clock told him it was getting late. He rose, and stretched. 'It's bed for me.'

'I'll go on up shortly.'

Andrew turned to leave, then stopped. 'Oh by the way, I shall be spending a few days in Glasgow next week.'

She frowned. 'Glasgow?'

'On business.'

'But we don't have a business any more. It was blown up, remember?'

'Secret business, Rose. Winnie and the plan.'

What was he really up to? she wondered. It certainly had nothing to do with whisky. She was intrigued. And then she had a terrible thought, one that made her go quite cold inside. Was it another woman?

'Andrew?'

'What, Rose?'

'Can I come with you?'

That rocked him. 'To Glasgow?'

She couldn't hold his gaze, dropping hers to stare at the carpet. Had she left it too long? She didn't know. Perhaps she had.

'Rose?' he prompted.

'We had such a wonderful time when we last went there . . .' She swallowed, then added in a croak, 'Together.'

He couldn't believe he was hearing this. 'Is that what you want?'

'Yes,' she replied in a whisper he almost didn't catch.

Andrew took a deep breath, his mind whirling. 'What about the room accommodation?'

She looked up at him, her eyes bright. 'A double will do. If you wish it that is.'

A double, sharing a bed again with Rose. This time not merely out of convenience but at her request. Could it possibly be . . .' I haven't fixed a date yet. I'll let you know when I do.'

She nodded. 'Fine.'

'Do you have preferences?'

'No.'

'Because it doesn't matter to me.'

'Nor me, Andrew.'

'Probably the Thursday and Friday.'

'Whatever.'

'And the hotel, which do you fancy?'

'The one we went to before.'

He stared hard at her, still not believing he was hearing what he was hearing. 'All right then.'

She glanced away, aware that her face was slightly flushed. 'I'm looking forward to it.'

'Goodnight, Rose.'

'Goodnight, Andrew.'

He shook his head all the way upstairs to his room.

*   *   *

'So what do you think?' Mavis demanded of Ruffles. She'd been given the day off to go and buy her wedding outfit.

'Turn round.'

Mavis slowly did so.

'It's beautiful,' Ruffles breathed.

Mavis laughed. 'Hardly that, but the best I could do. With clothes rationing rumoured about to come in the shops are stripped bare. I was lucky to find anything at all.'

She was wearing a navy suit whose jacket had a nipped waist, rounded collar, short, slightly ruffled sleeves and a narrow cuff. There were neat covered buttons at the front.

The skirt was fitted at the waist, dropping to a slight flare at mid calf. The shoes were navy suede courts.

The entire ensemble was set off by a small navy hat, rayon-draped at the front, trimmed with feathers and perched at a jaunty angle.

'I still say it's beautiful,' Ruffles enthused. 'Tommy will be proud of you.'

'Do you really think so?'

'I'm certain of it.'

There was a warm glow inside Mavis as they began eagerly discussing accessories. And other necessities. Something borrowed . . .

'The Clyde by night and moonlight,' Andrew declared. He and Rose had been to Rogano's restaurant where they'd had a wonderful fish meal. After which he'd suggested they go for a stroll that had eventually brought them to the banks of Glasgow's main river.

The meal itself had been a somewhat constrained affair, as had their journey down by car. In a peculiar way they might have been strangers, or old friends thrown together after a terribly long time apart. Which, as Andrew had reflected earlier, was more or less what they were.

'Is it too late, Andrew?'

He didn't look at her, but continued staring out over the water. And he didn't reply.

Rose was finding this difficult, but had known she would. 'It's as if . . . I've been in another place. Of this world, but not of it. I've been hurt, confused and angry.'

He still didn't respond.

'I've treated you so badly, Andrew. What happened wasn't your fault, and yet I acted as though it was. I've been extremely cruel.'

'Yes,' he agreed.

Rose winced.

'And now?'

'It seems to have passed. At least I think it has. I'm seeing things more clearly. The anger and confusion have somehow lifted, gone away. I'll never get over Mary, that went too deep. But now I've come to terms with it.'

She hesitated, then said softly, 'I love you, Andrew. Even when I was hating you I loved you.'

'And I've never stopped loving you, Rose.'

The relief that washed through her then was almost tangible. 'Truly?'

'Truly.'

Her hand sought out his. 'So can we start again? A new beginning?'

'If that's what you want.'

'It's what I want more than anything, Andrew. I swear it.'

He turned to her and took her into his arms. How he'd so longed to hear these words, desperately craved to hear them.

451

'Just one thing, Andrew. I have to know.'

'What?'

'Is there someone else? I mean, I could hardly blame you if there was.'

'No, Rose,' he replied truthfully. 'There isn't.'

'Oh, Andrew.'

He held her close, her cheek pressed against his chest. For a while they remained like that, then he kissed her.

Later, they made love. Not the frenetic wild abandoned kind that had been their intermittent couplings since the miscarriage, but a tender, caring union that was far more fulfilling.

When they finally fell into a blissful sleep their bodies were intertwined.

'I now pronounce you man and wife.'

Tommy turned and gazed deep into Mavis's eyes, she into his. Beside him Dingo was beaming broadly. Ruffles, matron of honour and second witness, did the same.

Hettie, watching the ceremony, thought this one of the happiest moments of her life. She buried her nose in the already sodden handkerchief she was carrying.

Jack, who thoroughly approved of the match, having told Hettie he could tell from Mavis's voice that she was a good woman, was praying that the war would soon be over and Tommy would come out of it unscathed.

Chapter 28

That was it, Andrew thought, laying his pen aside. He'd written down everything he could think of about running a distillery, every piece of advice. All done for Drew's benefit when the time came.

He stared morosely at the almost filled ledger, the facts, figures, tricks of the trade. You name it and it was there. A dead man's guide, he reflected bitterly.

Drew would never be able to rebuild the distillery as the lad envisaged it. That might have been possible if the old distillery had been covered against acts of war, but it hadn't. Not one penny piece had come their way, or would come, in insurance money.

In due course an amount would be settled by the government by way of compensation, but nothing like the distillery's true worth. A gesture, nothing more.

He did have capital of his own of course, a considerable amount tucked away in the bank and various investments, but not nearly enough for an expanded rebuilding programme.

Another small distillery could be built, but not one incorporating modern methods.

Andrew sighed and closed the ledger. He would ensure that it was given to Drew when he was gone. A legacy of sorts.

Kelly had been brilliant, helping him with all manner of details a book-keeper specialised in. Together they'd been working incessantly for months now.

There was a tap on the study door. 'Andrew?'

'Come in, Rose.'

She entered carrying a cup of coffee with a biscuit on the saucer. 'That's the last biscuit for a while,' she announced cheerfully. 'They've become rarer than gold dust.'

He smiled at her, thinking how good it was between them again. Rose had asked if they could have a new beginning, and that's exactly what it had been.

'I'm finished for the day,' he declared as she placed the cup and saucer on his desk.

She regarded him with surprise. 'So early?'

He spread his hands. 'It's done. Completed.'

'Whatever that is,' she retorted, still in the dark as to what Andrew and Kelly had been up to week after week.

'You're looking particularly lovely this morning,' he said.

'Am I?'

'Most decidedly. You always look lovely. But today, for some reason, you look even more so. Has Nancy done your hair differently?'

'Not really. It's just a variation.'

'Whatever, it suits you.'

He went suddenly chalk white as the pain erupted in his stomach, pain far more intense than any he'd so far experienced.

With a groan he clutched himself and bent over till his forehead was resting on the desktop. It was sheer agony.

Rose was instantly by his side. 'Andrew, what's wrong? What's the matter?'

For the moment he couldn't answer. All his willpower was intent on coping with the raging hell boiling him alive.

She grasped him by the shoulders. 'Andrew?'

His vision was blurred and he was seeing double. Black spots were dancing before his eyes while her voice seemed to be coming from a long way off.

'Pills,' he managed to gasp at last. 'In the drawer.'

Pills, what pills? She frowned, tearing at the nearest drawer. The bottle revealed was brown, the writing on the label recognisable as Dr Lesley's.

'Two,' Andrew instructed through gritted teeth. 'With whisky. Quick, woman.'

She shook two pills on to the palm of her hand and then flew to the whisky bottle. Not their brand, the last of the Drummond having long since gone. She slopped out a huge one.

'Here,' she said, holding the pills to Andrew's mouth.

He swallowed them with a large gulp of whisky. Then he swiftly drank off what remained in the glass.

'More,' he croaked.

Rose didn't know what was going on, totally mystified by all this. Up until then Andrew had succeeded in keeping his attacks from her.

'I'll call the doctor.'

'No,' he jerked out.

'But you're ill.'

'No doctor,' he repeated, writhing on his chair.

His face was now covered in sweat, skin the colour of mud. His hands were pressed tight against his middle.

Rose was at a loss what to do. Ring for Miss Campbell? Ring for someone! And why wouldn't he let her telephone the doctor?

In that moment Rose knew something was terribly wrong. Terribly, terribly wrong.

'Leave me,' Andrew muttered.

'But, Andrew . . .'

'I said leave me!' he almost shouted. 'I'll be with you shortly.'

He was groaning horribly as she shut the study door behind her.

It was over an hour later before Andrew joined a distraught Rose. He was still in pain but the pills and whisky had taken effect, the spasms now nothing like they had been.

'I think you owe me an explanation,' she stated simply.

Yes, it was time for that, he thought. Time, because there wasn't all that much of it left to him.

'You'd better sit down,' he said.

An appalled Rose listened to what he had to say.

Rose was sitting at her vanity table removing her make-up. In the mirror she watched Andrew undressing.

Her mind was still numb from his news. Andrew with cancer, dying. She hadn't yet fully taken it on board.

'I'm tired,' he declared, undoing his tie. 'I feel I could sleep for a month.'

Rose blanched. According to him it would soon be for a lot longer than that.

He stared at her, and smiled. 'You took it well.'

'Did I?'

'I half expected hysterics or something of the like. But no, you were cool, calm and collected. I was proud of you.'

She glanced away, breaking eye contact in the mirror. Perhaps he might not be so proud of her when the shock wore off. She might well have hysterics then.

He hesitated, then said softly, 'Every moment left to us is precious, Rose. We must use them wisely.'

'Yes,' she agreed.

'Spend as much time as we can together.'

'Yes.'

He came across to stand behind her. Gently, he stroked her neck. 'At least we made up, Rose. We've that to be thankful for. I never thought we would.'

Her heart lurched inside her. Reaching up she took his hand and, bringing it to her mouth, kissed it.

Later, when Andrew was asleep, Rose began silently to cry.

'Well how about that!' Tommy muttered as he and Mavis left the village hall where they had been to the weekly pictures on Saturday night, the main attraction being *The Emperor's Candlesticks* starring William Powell and Maureen O'Sullivan. The B feature, a short, had been written by his dad.

'Talk about propaganda,' Tommy went on, referring to Jack's offering. 'That was laying it on with a trowel.'

'Probably what he was asked to do.'

'Probably,' Tommy agreed. The film had been about fighter pilots in the Blitz, the leading male a quite unbelievable hero who'd knocked Jerries out of the sky like ninepins.

'Do you think he had you in mind?' Mavis teased.

Tommy laughed. 'I hope not. For if that's the case he got it entirely wrong.'

'I enjoyed it nonetheless. I think it caught the spirit of the RAF.'

They talked about Jack's film until arriving back at the small cottage they were renting. A modest affair built of red brick, Peppercorn Cottage had a sitting room, kitchen, toilet/bathroom and two bedrooms. It had come fully furnished, the owner, a widowed lady, having decided to go and live with her sister in Oxfordshire for the duration.

Once inside Tommy closed the blackout curtains before switching on the lights. He gazed about him with satisfaction. It may not be much but for the present it was his and Mavis's. Their first home.

'It's lovely having a night off,' Mavis declared, turning on the gas fire. 'I wish I had more.'

'You don't have to keep on at the Lamb and Flag you know. I earn enough to keep us both.'

'Just about,' she laughed. 'Anyway, my money comes in handy. You can't deny that.'

'You still don't have to work there. I'd prefer you home every evening.'

'I'd get bored, Tommy. I'm used to working. Hanging around the house twenty-four hours a day would drive me crackers.' What she didn't say was that working helped keep her mind off the danger he was in daily while flying. To have dwelt on that wouldn't have done her any good at all.

'Would you like a cup of tea?' she queried.

'Love one.'

'Coming up.'

Mavis disappeared off to the kitchen and Tommy slumped into an easy chair. He'd ring his dad during the coming week, he decided. Let Jack know he'd seen the pic. Jack would be pleased about that.

Talk about Biggles, he thought, and chuckled. Biggles was tame compared to his dad's hero.

That idiot wouldn't have lasted five minutes in the real

Blitz. Heroes there had been a-plenty. But none, in his experience, as stupid and gung ho as that.

It was propaganda after all, he reminded himself. What was that expression? Theatrical licence. Yes, that was it. Theatrical licence.

He'd enjoy pulling Jack's leg.

'Mum, what's wrong with Dad?'

Rose went very still. 'Why do you ask?'

'I went to the toilet after him and there was blood in the bowl. It obviously hadn't flushed properly.'

Rose's mind was racing. She and Andrew had agreed not to tell Drew the truth for now. There was time enough for that when Andrew's condition became obvious.

'He's got piles,' she lied smoothly.

'Since when?'

'Drew!' she admonished. 'That's not the sort of question to ask. And don't mention them to your dad. It's a touchy subject.'

Drew grinned, thinking this highly amusing. 'I won't.'

Rose casually changed the subject.

'You're coming on really well.'

Nancy beamed at Drew who, during the long summer months, had been teaching her her letters. 'Am I?'

'You know you are, Nancy. Why, you read that entire page without hesitating or stumbling once. You've improved no end and are continuing to do so all the time.'

She laid the book to one side. 'At least I'll be able to read your letters when you go back to school.'

'*And* write a reply.'

She hugged herself with pleasure. She, Nancy Thompson, being able to read and write. Who'd have believed it!

She thought back to her early days and especially those with Bill McCabe. What a contrast to the life she now led. Chalk and cheese. Poverty and luxury. It still amazed her how she'd fallen on her feet. She owed the Drummonds, particularly Mr Drummond who'd hired her in the first place, everything.

And one day she'd be one of them, a member of the family. Drew swore that would be so. That they'd marry when he was old enough.

'I'll miss you so much when I go back to school,' Drew said.

'And I'll miss you.'

He stared at her, drinking her in. There would never be another woman as far as he was concerned. No one else but Nancy would ever interest him. They'd been born for one another. Soulmates.

'Now, let's have another page,' he declared.

She pulled a face. 'Do I have to?'

'Yes,' he replied, pretending to be stern. 'You haven't finished the day's quota yet.'

'Bully,' she teased.

'That's me. Now get on with it or else.'

'Or else what?'

'The strap. Across your bare bum.'

She squealed. 'You wouldn't do that to me?'

'Just try me, Nancy Thompson.'

She was giggling as she picked up the book again.

'Andrew!' Elspeth exclaimed in surprise. 'It's been ages.'

He rubbed a hand across a bristly cheek. 'I was lying awake and didn't want to disturb Rose. So here I am.'

'Just like old times,' she smiled. Though not quite.

'Any chance of a cup of tea?'

'Of course.'

Elspeth stubbed out her cigarette and then got up and crossed to the stove. 'I've missed our chats,' she said, her back to him.

He didn't respond to that, but instead sat.

'How are you?' she asked, aware of his silence.

'So so.'

'Is that good or bad?'

'It varies from day to day, Elspeth. Some are worse than others.'

She glanced at him in sympathy. 'I'm pleased you and Rose have settled your differences. You've told her I presume?'

He nodded.

'How did she take it?'

'Remarkably well, considering. She's been quite stoical. At least on the surface that is.'

'And underneath?'

'She cries at nights and thinks I don't know. But I do. I hear her.'

'I'm sorry,' Elspeth commiserated.

Andrew shrugged.

'So why couldn't you sleep?'

He gave her a wry smile. 'Memories running through my mind. Things that happened in the past. Conversations. Relationships. Places. Recalling things I've experienced.'

He paused, then added softly, 'They say that when you're drowning your whole life flashes before you. Well it was a bit like that with me tonight.'

'I see.'

The wry smile became somewhat disjointed. 'It wasn't that unpleasant. In fact I rather enjoyed lots of it.'

Elspeth poured the fresh tea into a cup, then brought it to him. Sugar and milk were already on the table.

Sitting down again she lit another cigarette. 'I'm smoking more and more of these damn things,' she commented.

'Even to the point of sneaking out for a fly one?' he jibed.

She knew he was referring to that day in the storm. 'Yes.'

'Oh well, if you like them why not. A little bit of what you fancy never does any harm. At least, that's always been my belief.'

She glanced away. That had struck home. She knew what she fancied all right, except that was now never to be. More than once recently she'd told herself she was mad to stay on here, why torture herself! The simple answer was Andrew wanted her to stay and so she would.

'And how are you?' he asked.

She knew precisely to what he was referring. 'Fine.'

Their eyes met and understanding flowed between the pair of them. How different things might have been if it hadn't been for Rose and Andrew's feelings towards his wife. But Rose, and his feelings, existed, and that was that. For the second time in her life she was a loser where love was concerned.

'I want you to order another couple of cases of whisky,' he stated.

Elspeth raised an eyebrow. She'd taken receipt of two cases only the previous week.

Andrew noted the raised eyebrow and smiled. 'It helps,' he explained.

She so wanted to comfort him. For it to be her in his bed instead of Rose. To care for him during what time remained. She nodded that she understood.

Andrew yawned. Strangely, he was dog tired but not at all sleepy. He sipped his tea.

'Is everything running smoothly in the house? No trouble with any of the staff?' he inquired.

'Everything's hunky dory, and no, there isn't.'

'Good.'

She stared at him through a haze of cigarette smoke. 'I know it's none of my business, but are things really all right between you and Rose again?'

He guessed she meant in bed. 'Yes,' he replied firmly. Elspeth flushed.

'In every respect,' he qualified.

'Then you did the right thing in not . . .' She trailed off.

'Whether or not Rose and I had made up it was still the right thing, Elspeth.'

'Then I'm glad it's worked out as it has for you.'

He appreciated how much it cost her to say that. 'Thank you.'

He suddenly didn't want any more tea. What he did want was to be back with Rose.

Andrew got up. 'It's been good talking again.'

'For me too.'

'Don't stay up too late. You've got an early rise.'

'I'm used to that. Staying up late and the early rise.'

He smiled. 'I suppose you are. Goodnight then, Elspeth.'

'Goodnight, Andrew.'

When he'd gone she went to the cupboard where the cooking sherry was kept and poured herself a glassful.

And when that was drunk she poured herself another.

Drew was curious, it was so unlike his father to ask him to go for a walk. Just the pair of them. He couldn't recall Andrew ever having done that before.

Andrew halted and sucked in a lungful of air. God, but the air was beautiful round here, he reflected. He was so used to it he normally never noticed how clean and pure it was. 'Shall we turn back now?'

'If you want, Pa.'

Andrew glanced sharply at his son. Drew normally called him Dad, Pa was what he'd always called Murdo. A different generation, a different mode of address. 'It's school again soon, are you looking forward to it?'

'You must be joking!'

Andrew laughed, he'd been none too fond of school either. 'Oh well, it's something that has to be done. A necessary evil we all have to endure.'

They began retracing their steps. 'Is there a reason for this walk today?' Drew asked.

Andrew considered his reply. 'I've always thought of myself as a reasonably good father. But up until the bombing I was a busy one. The distillery took up an awful lot of my time. Now I have plenty to spare it would seem to me a good idea if we get to know one another a little better. Do a few things together. What do you think?'

Drew was delighted. 'I'd like that.'

'As the saying goes, sometimes you don't see the wood for the trees. You forget what the really important things in life are. They get pushed to the background in the frantic day-to-day living and business.'

What an odd mood his father was in, Drew thought. He didn't think he'd ever seen him like this before. He'd always considered Andrew a slightly austere, even remote, figure. That appeared to have changed. He suddenly felt closer to Andrew than he'd ever done. It was an enjoyable experience.

'I thought we might take a ride out tomorrow,' Andrew suggested.

'In the car?'

'If you wish. Though it was the horses I had in mind.'

'You know I hardly ride.'

'You did when younger. Anyway, it's not something you forget. So, what do you prefer, car or horses?'

'Whatever. Either would be nice.'

'Then horses it is. And the day after that we'll go for a spin in the car.'

'Can I drive?'

Andrew smiled. 'I'll begin teaching you. How's that?'

Drew's face was radiant. He couldn't wait to tell Nancy. 'Great, Dad. Absolutely great.'

Andrew had the impulse to take the lad's hand, but of course Drew was far too old for that.

He felt an enormous sense of satisfaction and well-being as they continued on their way.

'Tommy?'

'Go back to sleep, love.'

It was still dark, but then it always was when Tommy got up to go to the 'drome.

'I was trying not to disturb you,' he said, shrugging into his flying jacket.

Mavis smiled lazily. They'd gone to bed early the previous night, but it had been hours before they'd actually got to sleep. Glorious hours that even now made her squirm with pleasure. 'Shall I make you breakfast?'

'You stay where you are. I'll get something there. If I'm smartish that is.'

'Come here, Tommy.'

He crossed to her, taking the hand she offered up to him.

'Be careful.'

'I always am.'

'Hurry back.'

'I always do.'

He bent and kissed her on the mouth, swiftly avoiding the arms that tried to encircle him. 'I must go. There isn't time for that.'

Once outside the cottage he started to hum a jaunty tune as he headed for the camp and 'drome.

'I need some of that mixture,' Andrew stated to Dr Lesley.

'The pain's worse?'

Andrew nodded grimly. 'It's with me all the time now. And past the whisky and pills stage. I require something stronger.'

Lesley rose and went to his medicine cupboard. 'You could always be admitted to hospital, Mr Drummond. You'd be more comfortable there.'

'No,' Andrew declared defiantly. 'I remain at the house. That's how I want it.'

Lesley shrugged. 'Suit yourself.'

Andrew had every intention of doing just that.

Lesley handed Andrew a large clear bottle filled with green liquid. 'One tablespoonful when necessary. It'll make you drowsy, and it is habit-forming, I have to warn you about that.'

Andrew barked out a laugh. 'I don't think I have to worry too much about long-term effects. Do you?'

Lesley smiled cynically. 'I don't suppose so. But I have to warn you nonetheless.'

Andrew slipped the bottle into a pocket. 'Thank you, doctor.'

'And if there's anything else don't hesitate to either ring or call in. I'll of course replace that bottle when it's empty.'

'Thank you again.'

En route home Andrew stopped the car and had a quick, surreptitious swig. It tasted foul. But what the hell, that didn't matter. All that did was it worked.

'I'm sorry, Rose, I really am,' Andrew said, pulling himself away from her.

'That's all right.'

'The mind is willing, very much so, but my body seems to have other ideas.'

She reached out and grasped his shoulder. 'Don't worry, Andrew. I understand.'

'I do love you, Rose.'

'I know that. And I love you.'

He'd lost so much weight these past few weeks, Rose was thinking. It was frightening. It wasn't so obvious when he was dressed, but stripped it was all too evident.

'Just cuddle me,' she whispered.

'It seems that's all I'm good for now,' he replied bitterly.

'No it's not.'

This sort of thing simply didn't happen to him. He never let a woman down, even drunk he was usually capable of performing. A great black cloud descended on him.

When Andrew made no move Rose shuffled over the bed and took hold of him. 'I said not to worry.'

It had never occurred to him this might happen. Stupid really, he should have realised it was a possibility. Laudanum did deaden the senses after all. Numb things. On the other hand, it might just be he was too ill, his body beginning to pack in.

'Maybe tomorrow night,' she said.

'Maybe.'

'Whatever, as I said, it doesn't matter. We have one another and that's all that does.'

He laid his cheek on her breasts and closed his eyes.

She began gently to rock him as though he was a baby.

Mavis had been ringing up at the till when Dingo entered the pub. Turning round again she found him at the bar staring at her.

'Hello, Dingo,' she smiled.

He didn't smile back while his grim expression became even grimmer.

'Mavis, can we be alone for a moment?'

Her own expression froze. 'Oh!' was all she could think of to reply.

She knew what was coming next.

Chapter 29

'He's dead, isn't he?' a wide-eyed Mavis asked. She and Dingo were in the Gilfeathers' parlour which Dan had said they could use. The look on their faces had told Dan this was bad news and he'd handed Dingo a bottle of brandy before they'd gone in.

Dingo nodded.

It was her worst nightmare come true. She felt as though she'd been hit full on the forehead by a hammer. 'How?' she croaked.

'It was over the Channel. We were escorting bombers back from a raid when we ran smack into several flights of Me109s and 110s.'

Dingo paused and sucked in a deep breath. He'd have given anything not to be saying what he was. 'The weather was foul, really bad. Visibility appalling and the rain hammering. It was some of the worst weather I've ever encountered out there.'

Mavis swallowed hard. Tommy! she was screaming inside her head. Tommy! She had to force herself to listen.

'There were fighters everywhere, absolute pande-monium. Pinky Smith saw it. Tommy's Hurricane disinte-grated, then blew up. There were flaming bits flying in all directions according to Pinky. But no parachute.'

Mavis sobbed.

'I'm so sorry, Mavis. Jesus Christ and all his Angels, I am.'

Dingo fumbled with the bottle and poured two large shots. 'Have this,' he urged, going to her.

Mavis's head was bowed. When she raised her face it was tear-streaked. 'Oh, Dingo,' she whispered.

'It would have been over in an instant, Mavis. You must remember that. And take comfort from it if you can.'

She could see Tommy as he'd been that morning before leaving her. Recall his words precisely. It just wasn't possible he was gone.

'Drink up,' Dingo croaked, thrusting the glass into her hand. Brandy spilled over the side of the glass as she raised it to her lips.

Mavis was a woman absolutely stricken. 'I loved him so much.'

'I know. And he loved you.'

'We had . . .' She sobbed. 'Such a short time together. No time at all really.'

'But you had it, Mavis. That's the main thing. It's something to treasure for the rest of your life.'

He threw brandy down his throat. The next moment Mavis had wrapped herself round him and was crying uncontrollably.

After a while he called Ruffles and they took her up to her old room where they put her to bed.

Mavis smiled as she came out of a deep sleep. She could

hear Tommy moving about, getting ready to go to the 'drome.

'Tommy?'

When she opened her eyes she found herself not in Peppercorn Cottage but in the Lamb and Flag. And Tommy wasn't there.

The room, apart from herself, was empty.

'You're doing really well,' Andrew enthused to Drew who was driving the Austin.

'Am I?'

'Top-class.' Andrew laughed. 'Give it a month or so and you'll be good enough for Monte Carlo.'

Drew knew he was being teased, but nicely so. Surprisingly he'd discovered Andrew to be a patient teacher having expected otherwise.

'Change down now,' Andrew advised.

Drew did so.

'Your clutch movement has improved tremendously. That was smooth as silk.'

Drew visibly swelled. 'Can we go out again this afternoon?'

Andrew laughed again. 'If you wish.'

'Driving's great fun, Dad. Even more so than I thought it would be.'

'Careful on the corner here. Concentrate . . . That's it, roll her round the bend.'

'Easy as pie,' Drew beamed.

'Just don't get overconfident, lad, or you'll start to make mistakes.'

'I won't, Dad. I promise.'

'Fine.'

Dalneil came into view, for which Andrew was thankful.

They'd be home shortly and he could have some more mixture. The last dose was beginning to wear off.

When they got in he'd have a sleep, he promised himself. Sleeping was something he was doing more and more of recently. He seemed to spend half his time in bed.

Sleeping . . . and dreaming.

Jack had his own office in the studios where he and Hettie worked together as they'd always done. It was nowhere as peaceful as Dalneil, continually being surrounded by hustle and bustle, but somehow they managed.

Jack was in the middle of dictating when the telephone rang. He sighed, another bloody interruption. Hettie laid her notebook and pencil aside and rose to answer it.

'Why hello, Dingo!' Hettie exclaimed in surprise.

Jack frowned. They only knew one chap with such an outlandish name, Tommy's best man. Now why should he be . . . A terrible sense of foreboding hit Jack with all the strength of a hammer blow.

'I see,' Hettie muttered, voice strained almost beyond belief. 'I see.'

Jack clasped and unclasped his hands. It took all his self-control not to demand there and then what was being said.

The exchange was brief, and then Hettie hung up, her eyes filled with tears. Slowly she turned to stare at Jack.

'Well?'

'It's Tommy . . . he's . . . he's been killed.'

Jack's expression remained impassive, but inside he was a tempest of emotions. 'Are they sure?'

'Yes.'

He swallowed hard, then swallowed again. 'Oh, lassie,' he choked.

Hettie flew to him, sank on to her knees and buried her face in his lap. Her entire body began to shake.

'Tommy,' Jack whispered. His son. Their son. Their wee boy.

He didn't want any details, not right now anyway. If indeed there were any. That was for later.

'Tommy,' he repeated, still in a whisper.

'Mavis couldn't ring herself, she's in too much shock,' Hettie wept.

At that moment they were two babes lost in the wood, clinging to each other for support.

Hettie continued to cry and shake. Jack didn't realise it, but he was shaking also.

He started to sob.

There was a full moon that night with millions of stars twinkling down. Mavis was sitting in darkness by the window gazing up at this panorama.

Someone had called earlier but she hadn't replied to their knocking. She presumed it to have been Dingo but hadn't wanted to talk to him. Not him or anyone else.

'I think I'll stay in bed for a while,' Andrew said to Rose, she having risen about ten minutes previously.

She was instantly by his side, trying, and failing, to keep the concern from her face. 'Shall I have some breakfast brought up to you?'

'No thanks. I'm not hungry.'

'But you hardly ate any dinner last night. It isn't good enough, Andrew.'

'Nag nag nag,' he joked. 'You're turning into a shrew, woman.'

'Sorry,' she mumbled. 'I'm only trying to do what's best.'

'I know.' He smiled weakly. 'And don't think I don't appreciate it. I'm just not hungry, that's all. No appetite whatsoever.'

'A slice of toast perhaps? Could you cope with that?'

He shook his head. 'I doubt it.'

There was a look in his eyes which caused her enormous pain. It was one of total resignation. Where was the dashing Andrew of yesteryear? The man in bed was a pale shadow of that.

'Why don't you come back and talk to me after you've eaten?' he suggested.

'I'll do that.'

'You could bring a cup of tea. That would be nice.'

'I shall, Andrew.'

He watched her do her toilet and dress, savouring every delicious moment of it.

When she did return with the tea he was sound asleep and remained so till early that afternoon.

Nancy's job was a great deal easier since Rose and Andrew had become reconciled, Rose no longer incessant in her demands of her. Life was far less arduous and considerably more pleasant.

She was *en route* to the kitchen for coffee and a natter with Cook when she passed an open doorway, glimpsing a pensive Rose inside staring into space.

'Mrs Drummond?'

Rose started. 'Yes, Nancy?'

'Is there anything you want done?'

Rose thought about that, and shook her head.

'Shall I join you for a bit?'

Rose's reply was to gesture to an empty chair which Nancy crossed to and sat on.

'Are you worried about Mr Drummond?'

Rose studied Nancy, and didn't reply.

Nancy flushed slightly. 'It's none of my business I know, but he obviously isn't well.'

'He's dying,' Rose stated matter of factly.

That shocked Nancy who'd had no idea. '*Dying?*' she whispered.

'Of cancer.'

'Oh, Mrs Drummond, I am so sorry.'

Rose glanced away. 'Yes, so am I.'

'Is there nothing can be done?'

'Nothing I'm afraid. It's only a matter of time.'

The rest of the staff had been talking for a while now, saying Mr Drummond wasn't his usual self, that he was peaky, listless, that he'd lost weight. They'd all put it down to the destruction of the distillery.

'Does Miss Campbell know?' Nancy queried, thinking that if the housekeeper did she hadn't let on to anyone.

'No. You're the only one. And I'd be obliged if you'd keep it that way, for now anyway.'

'Of course, Mrs Drummond. My lips are sealed.'

Rose gave Nancy an ethereal smile. 'You're a good lass, Nancy Thompson. I've often thought if my baby, Mary, had lived she might have grown up like you. A lass to be proud of.'

That embarrassed Nancy. 'Thank you,' she mumbled.

'Don't thank me, it's true. You'll make someone an excellent wife in time.'

Nancy hoped Rose still thought that when, one day, she became her daughter-in-law.

'I've been sitting here wondering about Drew,' Rose mused.

'Oh?'

'You see, he doesn't know either.'

Nancy was already aware of that. 'Shouldn't he be told?'

'That's what I've been mulling over. He'll have to be eventually of course, but now or later? That's the question.'

There were a few moments' silence while they both considered that. 'May I say something, Mrs Drummond?'

Rose nodded.

'Have you any idea how much longer Mr Drummond has?'

'That's the problem, Nancy, the doctor can't be specific. But it might be only a matter of weeks.'

'Then how would you feel, how would Drew feel, if Mr Drummond suddenly went without Drew having any inkling it might happen? That would be awful, surely? It seems to me it would be better to bring him back now, at least for a bit, to say his goodbyes. To be put fully into the picture. He is grown up after all. Not a little boy any more.'

Nancy was quite right, Rose thought. On both counts. She made up her mind there and then. 'I'll write to Drew later today,' she said. 'And his headmaster. I shall say there's a family crisis and he's needed at home. I'll then explain the situation when he gets here.'

Rose breathed a huge sigh of relief, glad that was settled. Better by far to be safe than sorry.

Poor Drew, Nancy was thinking. This was going to be terrible for him. She'd have to give him every support.

'What are you doing here?' Ruffles queried in surprise.

Mavis shrugged. 'I can't sit around the cottage moping any longer. I need to occupy myself. So I've come back to work.'

'But it's far too early for that.'

They were behind the bar and Mavis couldn't help but stare at the spot where Tommy had so often stood. A lump rose into her throat which she tried to swallow back.

'Mavis?'

'Sorry, Ruffles?'

'I said, it's far too early for that.'

'I have to come back sometime, so why not sooner than later? I need to keep active otherwise . . .' She took a deep breath. 'I think I'll go off my chump.'

Ruffles nodded her understanding. 'All right, if it's what you want.'

'It is.'

'Then you can start tonight. In the meantime, how about a cuppa?'

'Smashing.'

'And a piece of . . . wait for it, chocolate cake. Don't ask me how I came by the chocolate either. It's a secret.'

The evening shift was hard, so many of the customers sympathetic when that was the last thing she needed. But after a while, as the beer flowed, things became easier. By the end of the shift it was almost like old times. With one exception.

Tommy hadn't come in. Nor would he ever again.

'Are you cold?'

'Bloody freezing.'

Elspeth smiled. 'Let me put more logs on the fire for you.'

Andrew grunted his appreciation.

'Where's Mrs Drummond?'

'Gone out to one of her war effort meetings. She won't be long.'

It wasn't really chilly in the room but Andrew was

obviously feeling that it was. Elspeth squatted by the fire and began piling on logs. The wood was sweet-smelling apple.

'I've always admired your hands,' Andrew mused.

That took her aback. 'Really?'

'They're very elegant. Real woman's hands. It was one of the first things I noticed about you when you came for your interview.'

Elspeth gazed down at her hands which she'd never considered out of the ordinary. Elegant? It was a lovely compliment, though she didn't see them to be.

'How are you today?' she asked.

'Tired, but then I always am recently. All my energy seems to have disappeared.'

'What does the doctor say?'

Andrew barked out a laugh. 'What can he say! Nothing. It's merely a progression of what's wrong with me. Tiredness and inertia.'

She felt sorry for him, and tried not to show it. 'Would you like a rug round you?'

He shook his head. 'That's for cripples and the extreme elderly. I'm neither.'

'But you said you were cold?'

'I said no thank you, Elspeth.'

'Sorry, I was only trying to help.'

He sniffed. 'Now that I think about it, I could use a whisky. Nothing beats the cold better than that.'

She made a mock gesture of obedience. 'Your wish is my command O master.'

He laughed. 'Are you taking the michael?'

'Of course.'

He wondered yet again what it would have been like to . . . He thrust that thought from his mind. Those days were over, Rose could testify to that.

'Will you join me?'

'I'm working, Andrew.'

'And I'm still the boss who makes the rules and can break them when I so choose. Have a drink and keep me company.'

She smiled. There had been that ring of authority in his voice which had always brought her out in goose bumps. 'What shall we talk about?'

'Whatever. It's up to you.'

She couldn't help herself. As she walked past him she laid a hand lightly on his shoulder.

For a few minutes anyway she could pretend she and not Rose was his wife.

'Hello, Dad.'

Andrew opened his eyes and smiled at Drew. 'Hello, son. Good journey?'

Drew shrugged. 'All right I suppose.'

They stared at one another. 'Mum's told me,' Drew said eventually.

'Aye, well there it is.'

'Oh Dad,' Drew whispered.

'None of that now. I expect you to act the man who'll soon be taking my place as head of the family. Fortitude, as they used to say when I was young, you must show fortitude.'

Drew had been tense, wound up about this meeting, but now he suddenly relaxed and was completely at ease. 'I'll try.'

'Good,' Andrew growled, nodding approval. 'Now sit down. I want to tell you about a ledger I've been writing up as a notebook of sorts.'

Drew frowned. What was this? He listened intently as Andrew explained.

*   *   *

'Was it bad?'

Drew shook his head. 'Not really. I fully expected it to be but somehow it wasn't. If anything it was rather jolly actually.'

'Jolly!' Nancy exclaimed. Drew had come to her in her room directly after his conversation with Andrew.

'Sounds bizarre I know. But that's how it was. The old man just wouldn't let it get soppy or maudlin.' Drew's face crumpled. 'Oh Nancy. I still can't believe it.'

He went to her and she took him into her arms, holding him tight and then stroking the back of his head.

'Mum says he could go at any time,' Drew choked.

'I know.'

'It's so . . . horrible.'

'Death is something we all have to face up to eventually, Drew. I think we country folk are more aware of the fact, and accept it more readily, than others. It's part of the natural way of things.'

'I suppose it is.' He paused, then said, 'I'm so pleased you're here, Nancy. It makes it a lot easier for me.'

That pleased her.

'I shan't go back to school until it's over.'

'But he might last for some time, Drew. There's no knowing according to Dr Lesley.'

Drew's body stiffened. 'I don't care. I'm staying here and that's all there is to it. I shall tell Mum that.'

She eased his head back and stared into his eyes. She saw great sorrow there. And love. Love for her, love for his father now going through such a terrible ordeal. She'd promised herself she'd comfort him all she could. And that was a promise she'd keep.

'Come back here late tonight,' she said softly.

He stared at her in surprise. 'Here. What for?'

'You can sleep with me.'

Delight lit up his face. 'Can I?'

'But we have to be careful. Do you understand? We have to be very careful.'

'You have my word on that.'

'It would be a disaster if I fell pregnant. Especially now.'

'You won't,' he assured her. 'I have the means to make sure you don't.'

He trembled in anticipation.

As for Nancy, she was smiling knowingly.

The bar was empty, it being lunchtime. Mavis was polishing glasses and generally tidying up. Lunchtimes were usually slack, often passing without a single customer coming in. When she'd finished this she'd polish the brasses, she decided. Anything to keep her from thinking.

She stopped what she was doing when she heard a plane roar overhead, the engine unmistakably that of a Hurricane. The lead plane quickly followed by others.

Mavis thought of the lads up there, all of whom she probably knew. How many would be coming home again? All of them, she fervently prayed. Please God, all of them.

There was the hint of tears in her eyes as she bent again to the task in hand.

Ireland. For the past few days Andrew hadn't been able to get Ireland out of his mind. But mostly he was remembering that bastard McGinty, the Fenian he'd killed for murdering Alice and her family. An eye for an eye he'd decided, and so it had been. McGinty and his family for Alice and hers.

It was a deed he'd have to pay for, he'd always known that. But he didn't regret what he'd done. And never would.

No one had more deserved what had happened to him than McGinty.

Ireland with its green lushness and soft rain. Happy times, except at the end.

Faces from those long-ago days floated before him. Where were they now? How had they fared? He'd never know. All he could do was speculate.

Dublin was a fair city, as the song said. And the maids oh so pretty. He smiled in recollection.

One maid in particular, Alice Fortescue. His Alice. Alice who'd been burnt alive because she was a Protestant.

He shook his head, the dreams and memories continuing to flood through his mind.

'Can I come again tonight?' he whispered, having first glanced around to ensure no one was in hearing distance.

Nancy smiled at him. Truth was, there was nothing she wanted more. She'd forgotten just how good it could be. And with Drew, far better than anything she'd previously known.

She swelled inside with tenderness and love, wishing he was older and they could get married. But that would come in time. Meanwhile they just had to be patient.

'I'll be expecting you.'

Drew beamed at her.

'And don't forget to come prepared.'

'Cross my heart and hope to die.'

'Nancy!'

They both started. That was Rose calling.

'Tonight then,' Nancy crooned.

'You can count on it.'

'And make it late. I don't want anyone seeing you.'

'Late it'll be.'

'If you don't fall asleep that is,' she teased.

'No fears.'

'Nancy!'

He watched her hungrily as she hurried off.

'Why don't you go away from here?'

Mavis slowly laid her cup back on its saucer and stared at Ruffles. 'You mean Laxworth?'

'That's right. Far away. Make a new start.'

Ruffles glanced across at the clock. There were still five or six minutes left to opening time.

Mavis shook her head.

'Why not? It would surely be for the best.'

Mavis gave Ruffles a wry smile. 'I might, but not yet It's far too soon for that.'

Ruffles sighed. 'Well, at least move back into your old room. It can't be good for you being alone in that cottage. You've said yourself, all you do is mope when you're there.'

Mavis thought of earlier when she'd been packing up some of Tommy's things, a job she'd been putting off knowing how hurtful it would be. Well, she'd been right about that. Every item of clothing and personal effect she'd touched had been like a knife stuck in her.

And she'd re-read yet again the letter sent her by Hettie and Jack, the pair of them promising to come and visit when they could. They'd been as devastated as she, though, of course, in a slightly different way. They'd lost a son, she a husband.

'I prefer the cottage, Ruffles. But thank you all the same.'

Ruffles sighed again, sure that was a mistake.

Neither said another word until it was time to open up.

*   *   *

Mavis went over to where Dingo was sitting by himself in a corner. 'Can I join you? It's my break.'

'Surely, Mavis. Surely.'

Once seated she gazed quizzically at him. 'What's wrong with you tonight? You're unusually quiet.'

'Thinking of home, Mavis. That's all.'

'You mean Australia?'

'That's right. She's a beaut place, you know. Real beaut. I miss her like buggery.'

'Tell me about it.'

'I don't want to bore you, Mavis.'

She smiled. 'You won't. Tell me about it.'

His eyes took on an excited gleam. 'I was born on a cattle station in the Northern Territory. Born and raised there where the skies are blue and the earth red as rust.'

'Were you a cowboy?'

Dingo laughed. 'We call them stockmen. Or jackeroos. And yes, I have been one in my time. Now there's an exciting life. Lonely on occasion, but exciting too.'

When her break ended Mavis knew an awful lot about Australia, pleased as she returned behind the bar that she'd managed to snap Dingo out of his melancholy mood.

He was a good man Dingo, as Tommy might have said. One of the best. He couldn't have been kinder since . . .

Taking a deep breath she headed for a customer waving an empty pint pot at her.

'I'll take over here for a bit,' Dan Gilfeather announced gruffly to Mavis. 'There's someone in the parlour to see you.'

That surprised her. 'Me?'

'Yes, you. Now on you go.'

Mavis couldn't imagine who it might be. She was about to ask Dan if he knew who it was when he moved away from her to attend to a customer. Wondering, she left the bar.

The parlour door was ajar so she went straight in, coming up short in total shock when she saw the person standing there. Her jaw dropped open and her eyes bulged. It seemed to her that for several moments her heart stopped beating.

'Just call me Lazarus.' Tommy smiled.

Chapter 30

'What happened?'

'You fainted,' Tommy sympathised, stroking her brow. She was on the easy chair he'd half carried, half dragged her to.

She gazed at him in wonderment. 'Is it *really* you?'

'It's me all right, Mavis. In the flesh.'

'But you're dead. Dingo said you were.'

'And so I should be. It's little short of a miracle that I'm not. Now before I explain would you like a glass of water? Or a brandy perhaps?'

She grasped hold of him. 'No, don't leave me. I couldn't bear that.'

Already bent over he now squatted beside her, and resumed stroking her brow.

'How?' she asked simply.

'What did Dingo tell you?'

'That your plane exploded.'

Tommy nodded. 'That's right. It did. Or so I've

presumed anyway as I've no recollection of the actual event. I remember the plane being hit, then a God Almighty noise. The next thing I knew I was floating face upwards in the water with a bloody great submarine alongside.'

'Submarine?'

'Somehow I must have been blown free in the explosion.'

'But Pinky Smith said there was no sign of a parachute opening.'

'It didn't. It was still on my back when the sailors hauled me on board. Somehow, and it *is* incredible, I not only survived the explosion but also falling from that height. The impact when I hit the water alone should have finished me off, but didn't.'

Mavis was desperately trying to digest all this. As Tommy had said, it was little short of a miracle.

'The weather was appalling,' Tommy went on. 'Visibility dreadful, the rain coming down in sheets. That's no doubt why I wasn't spotted by our lads still in the air. I mean, who survives an explosion like that must have been? I certainly haven't heard of anyone doing so. And not only survive that but also the impact of hitting the Channel. And yet I did, on both counts.'

'So where have you been all this time?'

'To the Aegean. I'm not allowed to be specific.'

'The Aegean!'

'There and back. It was an amazing coincidence that the submarine was just where it was and that I came down so close to where it surfaced. If I'd been any further away chances are they wouldn't have seen me in that weather. The whole thing is miracle upon fluke upon coincidence.'

He broke off and laughed. 'Talk about luck! I must have used up ten lifetimes' worth that day.'

'But why the Aegean?'

'Ah, well the sub had surfaced for a reason. It was on a secret mission and the purpose of its surfacing was to send off its last radio message. From that point until returning to Portsmouth it was under strict radio silence. Hence the reason no one knew they'd picked me up.'

He took his hand away from her brow, lifted one of her hands and kissed it. 'We docked in Portsmouth yesterday and I came straight here. I didn't telephone or telegram because I thought it better this way. I haven't even been to the camp yet, though, by now, they know I'm on my way.'

She couldn't think what to say to all this, it was far too bewildering. All that really mattered was that Tommy was alive and well, and here with her.

'You could have given me a heart attack,' she chided gently.

'I'm sorry.'

'No, don't be. It's just . . . well . . . walking in and seeing you there.' She shook her head.

'I wasn't even hurt, neither in the explosion or fall into the Channel. Not a scratch.'

'And the submarine just surfaced beside you?'

'It was already coming up when I hit the water apparently. The officer on the periscope actually saw me go in.'

Mavis sucked in a deep breath. She could now desperately use that brandy Tommy had offered her but didn't want to let him out of her sight while he fetched it.

'Do you still love me?'

She smiled.

'You haven't taken up with anyone else thinking I was dead?'

'That deserves a smack, Tommy Riach.'

He was staring at her, hard. 'There was a Divine intervention that day, Mavis. What other explanation is there? You and I weren't meant to be parted just yet.'

'Kiss me, Tommy,' she whispered.

He encircled her with his arms and their lips met. For Mavis the world was suddenly a good place to be in again.

Andrew opened one eye and gazed at Rose sitting by his bedside reading a book. 'Let's have a party,' he suggested brightly.

Rose was astonished. 'A what?'

'You heard, a party.'

'But . . . why? You're ill.'

'Of course I'm ill, but that doesn't mean to say I wouldn't enjoy a party. In fact, I know I'll thoroughly enjoy one.'

Rose was flabbergasted. Andrew hadn't been out of his bed all week, and now this. It was ridiculous! 'And who do you intend inviting to this soirée?'

'The staff.'

'The staff!'

'That's right. Mrs Moffat can lay on a buffet and there'll be oodles to drink. I can't think of anything nicer.'

Rose laid her book aside. 'Are you sure you're up to it?' she queried quietly.

'You don't have to worry about me. I'll be there with bells on. Ring-a-ding-ding!'

She had to laugh, and did. 'Will we have music?'

'We'll use the gramophone, and you and I shall trip the light fantastic.'

She studied him, thinking how awful he looked. His face had become almost cadaverous. 'I can't exactly see you dancing, Andrew.'

'I'll dance,' he insisted stubbornly. 'You can bet your boots on it.'

She couldn't imagine why he wanted to give a party for the staff. It just didn't make sense.

'I shall wear black tie, you your prettiest gown and jewellery. It'll be a wonderful night.'

'I'm not so sure about this, Andrew,' she prevaricated.

'Well, I am. And that's an end of it.'

It was obvious how determined he was. 'And when shall we hold it?'

He frowned, considering that. 'Speak to Mrs Moffat and ask if this Saturday is all right? Tell her no expense is to be spared. And by that I mean if she has to pay out backhanders to get anything then she's to do it.'

'You mean the black market?'

'Precisely!' he beamed. 'Sod rules and ration books. Money talks, and we can afford it.'

'You're something else, Andrew Drummond,' she laughed.

'I should hope so. But then so are you, my darling. Something very, very special.'

Even after all she'd put him through, she thought bitterly. Well that was all over and done with. Forgotten. She hesitated . . . maybe not forgotten, but certainly in the past. An episode she'd always feel guilty about. And ashamed of.

'I'll have a word with her now,' Rose declared. 'If you're sure it's what you want?'

'I am. Completely sure.

'And decorations, Rose,' he added as she was about to leave..'Have Miss Campbell organise those.'

He wondered if there was any champagne in the house.

Saturday evening arrived, and Andrew and Rose came down together, arm in arm. He was wearing black tie as he'd said, Rose a stunningly simple black sheath without frills or fripperies that came to just above the knee. This was offset by a diamond choker and matching bracelet. Her hair, having been cut some while back, was equally simply styled, parted in the middle to fall curling into the nape of her neck.

Andrew's weight-loss was all too obvious, his clothes hanging on him. Nonetheless he was in a happy, buoyant mood as he and Rose entered the kitchen where they were immediately applauded by the staff.

The kitchen was hung with paper bells and streamers with lines of fairy lights sparkling overhead. Truly, a magical kingdom, Andrew thought on seeing it all.

The staff were in their Sunday best, for once not a uniform in sight. Mrs Moffat, resplendent in a brown concoction, reminded Andrew of a tea cosy.

'Speech!' Jamesina Laing called out, and blushed at her own forwardness.

'Quite right, a speech,' Elspeth Campbell seconded. She was smiling broadly, but secretly worried this was all going to be too much for Andrew, as indeed was Rose.

By now the staff knew the truth about Andrew's illness, all of them heartfelt in their sympathy. At Rose's request, not one of them had mentioned it to Andrew.

Andrew shook his head. 'This isn't a night for boring old speeches, I refuse to inflict one on you.' For a brief moment his expression changed. 'Except to say thank you for the hard work and loyal service you've given Mrs Drummond and me over the years. Now eat and drink up, and get that gramophone playing! I want to hear music.'

Andrew gazed about him, thinking how splendid this all was. For some reason he was reminded of his youth, though there had never been any such parties for staff that he could recall. Neither in the kitchen nor anywhere else.

Elspeth came forward and handed Andrew a glass of whisky. 'For you, Mr Drummond. I think you'll find it rather special.'

He raised a quizzical eyebrow, but Elspeth didn't elaborate.

'Drummond!' he exclaimed in delight on tasting it. 'Where on earth did you get this?'

'In the cellar. I found a bottle that had been mistakenly placed in a wine rack. It's goodness knows how old but still good. I tasted it just to make certain.'

Andrew laughed. Nothing could have pleased him more. This time he had a proper swallow, smiling as its mellowness warmed its way down his throat.

'Thank you, Miss Campbell.'

She gave him a small nod of acknowledgment.

Mrs Moffat had excelled herself with the buffet, having taken Rose's instructions to heart. Nothing but the best had been provided, and there was stacks of it.

'Now drink up!' Andrew called out. 'I want everyone to have a good time.'

Rose put an arm round Andrew and pulled herself even closer to him. Looking into his eyes she smiled, he smiling back. They were the very epitome of a happily married couple.

Pattie Williams cranked the gramophone and put on a record, filling the kitchen with lively dance music. To much amusement Jamesina Laing and Lena Johnstone, the latter already a bit tipsy, lacking male partners, got up together. Andrew clapped his approval.

'I haven't enjoyed myself so much in years,' he whispered a little later to Rose.

'Me neither.'

'Truly?'

'Truly.'

Not giving a damn about the others present he kissed her full on the lips.

Nancy appeared beside them when the kiss was over. 'I hope you don't mind, but I took the liberty of filling a plate each for you.'

'Why thank you,' Rose murmured. Nancy was about to move away again when Rose said, 'Stay with us for a bit. We'd like your company.'

Almost as though she was one of the family, Nancy thought. Which some day she would be. She obediently took her place at Rose's side.

The whisky was working wonders, Andrew reflected, as dram followed dram. He could feel all his old strength returning. Why, it was almost as if he was young again. His feeling of well-being continued to grow and grow.

It was shortly after that Andrew, having long since demolished the food given him, turned to Rose. 'Our dance I believe, my dear.' The record that had just started playing was 'The Anniversary Waltz'.

Nothing could have been more perfect, she thought, allowing him to take her hand and lead her forward into the centre of the kitchen.

Then they were in each other's arms and gliding round the floor. A couple completely in love.

For the space of a few minutes it was as though time stood still.

Andrew lay staring at the ceiling while beside him Rose was fast asleep. It had been a tremendous party, he reflected. All that he'd hoped for.

After Rose he'd danced with Mrs Moffat and then Elspeth, at the conclusion of which he'd given in and had to sit down.

And so the night had passed and midnight chimed, that, Rose insisting, being their cue to go on up and leave the others to it. Andrew hadn't objected, tired by then and wanting his bed.

Reaching out under the covers he touched Rose, gently running his hand up and down the swell of her buttocks, his mind filled with memories of their marriage.

How contented he was. How very complete. It struck him he couldn't have asked for a more perfect day. Or happier one.

He wasn't sure if he'd dozed off or not, but gradually he became aware that there was someone else in the room. A shadowy figure standing at the end of the bed.

Andrew frowned. Wondering who it was. Strangely he was quite unperturbed or afraid. Merely curious.

The figure shimmered and became clear. It was his father, Murdo, smiling at him.

'Hello, Pa,' Andrew whispered.

It's time to go, son. I've come to take you with me.

'Go?'

Aye, lad, go.

Andrew half turned to stare at Rose's outline. He touched her again, his hand lingering for a few moments before he withdrew it.

'Goodbye for now, my darling.' He smiled. 'But just for now.'

Darkness was giving way to light, light that quickly became brighter and brighter.

'Ready, Pa,' he said.

Postscript 1

1946

'That's it, we're away,' Tommy declared as the last line was cast ashore. He tightened the arm he had round Mavis, drawing her even closer.

'The start of your awfully big adventure,' Mavis replied teasingly.

'That's right. Destination Cape Town.'

Slowly the S.S. *Samson* began to get under steam, its decks crowded with passengers waving their goodbyes to those who'd come to see them off.

There was no one there to do that for Tommy and Mavis. Jack and Hettie had left for America the previous month, bound for Hollywood where Jack had been contracted to one of the big studios. To Jack's amazement Andrew's long-ago prediction had come true. The propaganda films he'd written during the war had made a big impression in the film capital and no sooner had hostilities ceased than a telegram had been winging towards Jack with an offer.

He and Hettie had discussed the matter long and hard. It meant totally uprooting themselves after all. In the end they'd agreed to take the chance, the sort, as Jack had put it, that only came along once in a lifetime. While they were gone their house in Dalneil would be rebuilt, ready for their return, should that either be for good or merely a holiday.

As for Tommy, shortly after his Aegean episode he'd been promoted and posted to Yorkshire as a flight instructor, and there, much to Mavis's relief, he'd remained till the end of the war.

Dingo was home in Australia, having also survived, the last letter they'd had from him promising he'd visit them in Africa when, and wherever, they eventually settled.

'I can hardly believe this is happening,' Tommy exclaimed. 'It's always been my dream and now it's about to come true.'

'Well, part of it anyway,' Mavis cautioned. 'Going to Africa is one thing, being an explorer and big-game hunter quite another. I'm not traipsing through the bush while you play at being Jungle Jim. That is simply not on.'

'I know,' Tommy sighed. 'You've made that clear enough.'

'I won't have you surviving the Jerries only to be eaten by a hungry lion or swallowed whole by a monstrous snake.'

'Stop nagging, woman,' he teased.

The ship's horn hooted its farewell, a sad sound, yet, conversely, a joyful one too. A door was closing, a new one opening.

They stayed on deck until, at long last, there was nothing remaining to be seen of England.

'Let's go below and get unpacked,' Mavis suggested.

'But first we stop off at the bar.'

She smiled. 'If you insist.'

'I insist. This calls for a celebration.'

The toast was to absent friends, and the exciting future that lay ahead.

In Africa. Land of Tommy's dreams.

Postscript 2

1953

There had been many despairing times when Drew had thought this day would never arrive, but arrive it finally had. The re-opening of Drummond's Distillery. The new, far larger building rising, Phoenix-like, from the ashes of the old.

His grandfather Willie had been their saviour. On learning of Drew's plans from Rose, and the lack of money to carry these plans properly through, Willie had made a gift of a large amount of capital to Rose, telling her it would have come to her anyway on his death. Rose had promptly made it available for the rebuilding.

The next great stumbling block had been materials, extremely difficult, and sometimes nigh on impossible, to get in post-war Britain. But somehow, by fair means and occasionally foul, the materials had been acquired and workmen set to their task.

Kelly, the book-keeper, had been an invaluable help to Drew, assisting him every step of the way. Kelly and the detailed ledger Andrew had left.

And so the new Drummond's Distillery had been born, everything that Drew had envisaged. A modern building filled with modern machinery and a potential output far exceeding the previous one.

There was still a long way to go of course, years before the first bottle of Drummond appeared back in the shops and other outlets. But for now that was irrelevant. All that mattered was that the distillery was up and running again.

'Pleased?' Nancy queried with an amused glint in her eyes, knowing only too well that he was.

'What do you think?'

'That today's the second happiest of my life.'

'And the first?' he teased.

'Our wedding day.'

He paused, then said softly, 'That's exactly how I feel.'

All about them people were milling, village folk and assorted worthies. Those who'd been employed previously had been rehired, breathing life back into a Dalneil shattered by the bombing. The village was alive again, the distillery's not the only rebuilding to have taken place.

Rose broke away from Willie and Georgina to come over. Holding her hand was Mary, Nancy and Drew's daughter. Nancy was pregnant again, and this time they were hoping for a boy whom they'd agreed to call Andrew after his father and paternal grandpa. A male to carry on the long Drummond tradition of malt whisky-making *par excellence*.

Drew bent and scooped up the youngster. 'Are you enjoying yourself, angel?' he asked.

Mary nodded.

'Have you had something to eat?'

'Yes, Daddy.'

'Good.'

Rose glanced about her, then back at Drew and Nancy, the latter whom she'd welcomed into the family with open arms. Her eyes were bright, the hint of a tear glistening in them. 'I want to say something,' she said huskily.

'What's that?' Drew queried.

'Your father would have been proud of you this day. Proud fit to burst.'

'Thank you,' Drew choked in reply. That meant an awful lot to him.

'And so am I.' She looked at Nancy. 'Of both of you.'

'What about me?' Mary demanded.

Rose chucked her under the chin. 'We're all proud of you, my poppet. Wee Mary.'

For a moment Rose's face clouded, then cleared again. If only Andrew had been here to see this, she thought.

And then a strange feeling took hold of her. And she knew, without doubt, with absolute certainty, that he was.

WILD
STRAWBERRIES

Chapter 1

The wind blowing in off the Lizard was as cold and sharp as a witch's nail.

Christian Le Gall switched off the car engine, leant back, and sighed. He was lost, hopelessly so, thanks to the damned mist swirling everywhere. He could just about make out the front of the bonnet of the Morris Eight Tourer he was driving.

Christian fumbled for his cigarettes and lit up. What to do next?

There had been a signpost a few miles back which had been completely unhelpful. The name on the sign was nowhere to be found on the map of Cornwall he'd brought along.

He was certain he was fairly near his destination, the fishing village of Coverack, which he reckoned to be only a few miles away. But in which direction?

Damn these narrow twisting Cornish lanes! Most of them were in existence long before the combustion engine had been invented. In places the hedges were so high he had no idea what lay beyond on either side.

He sniffed. Was that the tang of the sea or merely his imagination? He couldn't be sure.

His stomach rumbled causing him to make a face. On top of everything else he was starving, having thought he'd reach Coverack long before now. And he would have too if the weather hadn't closed in. One moment the road ahead had been perfectly clear, the next, or so it had seemed, an impenetrable wall.

He drew on his cigarette, then shivered. What were his options? Get out and walk? Well he could do that, trudging on till he came to a house where he'd perhaps find help. Perhaps even be lucky enough to get a warming cup of coffee and a bite to eat. .

The other option was to sit tight and wait until the mist cleared. But who knew how long that would take? It might remain for the rest of the day and continue on through the night till the following morning.

What a beginning to a leave, he reflected ruefully. A leave he'd been so desperately looking forward to. The fulfilment of a dream he'd had for years now.

Christian wound down his window and flicked the remains of his cigarette away. At least he had plenty of those on his person so he wouldn't be going without tobacco.

He was about to wind up his window again when he saw a movement straight ahead. Something dark shimmered, was lost to view, and then flickered again. A figure loomed, black as pitch against the whiteness of the mist.

The hairs on the back of his neck sprang to attention and he was suddenly covered in goose flesh. What was this? A ghost! Without realising he was doing so he shrank down into his seat, startled eyes popping. He swore quietly in his native French.

The figure slowly approached, what might have been small wings flapping on either side. Christian hastily crossed himself and began muttering a prayer. He was completely transfixed.

The figure appeared to float alongside the car where it stopped and stared in. The face gazing directly into his was pale, the eyes a piercing green.

The face smiled. 'Are you having trouble?'

Relief whooshed through him, for the voice was friendly and that of a woman. This was no ghost but as earthly a being as himself.

'I'm lost,' he admitted.

The woman took in the strangeness of his uniform, and frowned. 'You're not English,' she accused.

'No. French. An ally.'

The expression softened. 'Ah!'

'I'm trying to find Coverack.'

'Are you indeed?'

He nodded.

'And why's that?' There was still suspicion in the voice.

'I plan to stay there for a while. I'm on leave.'

'I see.' She paused, studying him further, then queried, 'So where have you come from?'

Inquisitive, he thought. But then country folk usually were. They liked to know the ins and outs of a cat's backside. 'Plymouth. I'm stationed there.'

The woman digested that.

'Can you help me?'

'Of course. Couldn't be easier.'

She was wearing a cloak he now noted, the hood drawn over her head. What he'd imagined to be wings were merely the sides of the cloak. 'You gave me a terrible fright,' he confessed.

She arched a plucked eyebrow. 'Really?'

'Don't laugh, but I thought you were a ghost.'

She did laugh. 'A ghost!'

'Appearing out of the mist as you did. You scared me half to death.'

Rather handsome, she mused inwardly, thinking she mustn't stay chatting too long. She was already late for the meeting.

Something screeched near by causing Christian to start. 'What was that?'

She almost laughed. He *was* jumpy. 'An animal of some sort. A bird possibly.'

A rather aquiline nose and sallow skin, she further reflected. The hair straight and somewhat lank. She judged him to be somewhere in his early twenties.

She pointed back the way she'd come and gave him clear instructions that involved two turnings. 'That'll take you down the hill into Coverack,' she stated.

'Thank you. Do you know the Paris Hotel there?'

This time her expression was quizzical, the gaze penetrating in the extreme. 'Yes, I do.'

'Where will I find that?'

'When you get to the bottom of the hill turn right when you can go no further. It's at the far end of the village. You can't miss it.'

During the past few seconds he'd become aware she was concealing something under her cloak, a metal object she was holding. 'Thank you again.'

'Do you intend putting up there?'

'If there's a room available.'

'Oh, I'm sure there will be, it being October and a war on.' She gathered her cloak about her. 'Now I must be getting along.'

It seemed strange to him that she, a lone woman, should be out in such weather. It crossed his mind she must be well familiar with every inch of the terrain thereabouts.

Christian reached for the key and restarted the engine, the latter bursting into a satisfying growl that rumbled under the bonnet.

Her glance flicked round the inside of the car, then settled again momentarily on his face. 'You'll be all right now.'

'I'm most obliged.'

As though by magic she disappeared, vanishing in the opposite direction from which she'd come.

Christian shivered, and not entirely from cold. Thank God the woman had happened by when she had.

As he was slowly driving off it suddenly struck him that the metal object she'd been holding might have been a pistol. There had been that shape and familiarity about it.

He shook his head in bewilderment. A pistol? Surely not. Why would a woman be wandering around in the mist carrying a gun? It simply didn't make sense.

He must have made a mistake, he decided.

'Hello! Is anyone here?'

Christian glanced round the bar of the Paris Hotel where a large cheery fire was blazing in a grate. He laid down his case and strode over to the hearth, standing in front of it and vigorously rubbing his hands.

Taking a deep breath, he leant against the mantelpiece, smiling in contentment as the warmth began seeping into him.

His stomach rumbled again, reminding him how hungry he was. But first he'd have a drink. If not several. He was not only hungry but dog tired. The journey had taken a lot out of him.

A piece of wood crackled and spat, narrowly missing his trousers. He moved back several feet; the last thing he wanted was for his uniform to be burnt.

'Hello?' he called out a second time. Again without response. The bar was deserted apart from him.

Christian rubbed his leg which was more painful than it had been for several weeks. He put that down to the journey and damp in the air.

'Hello?'

The only reply was the chime of a clock at the far end.

He was beginning to wonder if he was the only one in the hotel.

'Can I help you, sir?'

He twisted swiftly towards the woman who'd spoken. Now where had she come from? It was as if she'd appeared out of nowhere.

'I'm after a room. I wish to stay for a while.'

The woman, tiny with a wizened face and short cropped hair, nodded. 'Plenty of rooms available. In fact they all is.'

She looked him up and down, taking in his uniform. 'You're foreign I take it?'

'French, madam.'

'Army?'

He brought himself to attention. 'Second Lieutenant Le Gall at your service.'

The woman sniffed. A Frog, she thought. She might have guessed.

'I was wondering if I might have a drink? I've been on the road for hours.'

'I don't see why not. We is a pub after all, the only one in Coverack.'

'You're very kind.'

She gave him an odd, sideways look, as though she didn't quite know what to make of him, then suddenly chuckled. 'What's your poison, my lover?' she queried, going behind the bar.

He frowned. Her lover? What sort of address was that? 'Would you have a cognac?'

She was so tiny only her head and the top of her shoulders were visible. 'I don't usually serve behind here,' she informed him, struggling to reach a glass. 'I's in the kitchen normally.'

'You're the cook then?'

'Dogsbody more like. Though I does cook when necessary.'

Christian sank on to a stool, thankful to get the weight off his leg. He'd change the dressing before going to sleep.

'There you are,' she declared, plonking the charged glass before him. 'Will you pays for it now or shall I put it on your bill?'

He decided the latter would be more convenient. 'On my bill please.'

'Right you be.'

He sipped the cognac to discover it wasn't cognac at all but a rather inferior brandy. But it was warm and relaxing which was all that mattered. 'Is there any chance of some food?' he inquired.

'Lunch is past. We don't start serving dinner till half seven.'

'Oh!' He couldn't mask his disappointment.

'Hungry, my lover?'

'Starving.'

Her expression became sympathetic. 'I'll tells you what. I could make you a sandwich.'

'That would be wonderful.'

'Cheese and pickle is all we got.'

'Lovely.'

'Then I shan't be long.'

He watched her bustle away.

My lover? he mused. Obviously a local expression. He rather liked it. He had another sip of brandy and reached for his cigarettes.

How peaceful it was in here, he reflected a little later. The only sound, apart from his own breathing, was the steady tick of the wall clock that had chimed earlier.

Turning round on his stool he gazed out over the Channel, as the English called it. All he could see was mist; the water was totally obscured.

Beyond that mist lay France, he thought, a lump coming

into his throat. *La Belle France* and Hennebont. His country that was now occupied by the hated Boche, his city crawling with the jackbooted bastards.

What an evil day that had been when France had fallen. A day of great infamy. The memory of it made him feel sick inside.

Well, France wouldn't stay occupied for ever. Another day would dawn, the day of liberation. And he would be there taking part in it. He swore that by all that was Holy.

He wondered what had become of Marie Thérèse, his girlfriend before he had joined up. There had been a few letters, and then everything had happened so quickly. There had been no way to get in touch with her before his evacuation at Dunkirk. Even if he'd tried it would have been impossible, the Germans having already overrun Hennebont.

He thought of Marie Thérèse with enormous affection. He hadn't been in love with her, though she'd been with him. They'd slept together on a number of occasions, the last one of which he now recalled quite vividly.

It had been his farewell, and a frantic emotional hour it had been. Marie Thérèse had cried non-stop, in near hysterics when they'd actually parted. And the lovemaking itself, how intense that had been, particularly on her part. He'd felt as though he was being swallowed whole into her body.

He wished she was with him now. And wondered again where she was and what she was doing.

'There you are, Lieutenant. Best English cheddar. A real treat.'

He turned again to smile at the tiny woman. 'Thank you.'

'You don't get better cheese than that. Not nowheres.'

He didn't contradict her, thinking there was many a Frenchman would disagree with her statement.

The bread was brown, and when he lifted the top slice the

pickle she'd promised, also brown, was revealed. He'd been expecting something different.

'Right tasty,' she said.

'Do you have a name, madam?'

'Here, less of the madam! That's the second time you've called me that. I'm no madam. I'm Alice, pure and simple. No frills or fripperies with me. Just plain Alice.'

He smiled. 'Then Alice it shall be. Thank you, Alice.'

She noticed his glass was empty. 'Another of thae?'

'Please. What sort of summer did you have?' he inquired as she poured his refill.

'A total disaster. Hardly any trade at all. But then, what could we expect in the circumstances. Though we did hope we'd do better than we did.'

'There is a war on after all,' he commiserated.

'And don't we know it. At this rate Mrs Blackacre might well have to close down part of the hotel for the duration. The accommodation that is. Just leave the bar for the locals.'

'Mrs Blackacre?'

'She owns the place. Well, she and her husband do. But he's off at sea in the Merchant Navy doing his bit like.'

'I see.'

Alice's expression became conspiratorial, and when she next spoke her voice was softer. 'Sam Blackacre fell on his feet all right. A fisherman all his life and then a few years back a relative of his dies in New Zealand and leaves him plenty. He used the money to buy the Paris and gave up fishing, though his heart's still at sea, I say. He couldn't wait to get into the Merchant Navy when the war started. Went off with a smile on his face as big as a cow's arse.'

Christian laughed at the image conjured up.

'And a right good go they were making of the hotel too until the war came along. Now she's left to run the place all on her ownsome, which is quite a responsibility I can tells ee.'

Christian nodded that he understood.

'There's hardly an able-bodied chap left in the village. So what happens when she needs repairs and the like? Why, we had a blocked drain only last week and not a plumber to be found for love nor money.' Alice squared her thin shoulders. 'In the end we sorted it though. She and me the gether. We wuz proud of that.'

Christian lit another cigarette, thinking he would never get used to English tobacco. He would have given anything for a Gauloise or Gitanes. 'I can imagine.'

Alice snorted and nodded.

'And where is Mrs Blackacre? When do I get to meet her?'

'Oh, she's out on business at the moment. Don't ask me where. She said business but it could be she's visiting a relative. There's an old aunt she drops in on a lot. Keeps her company like and makes sure she's all right.'

Alice regarded him keenly. 'Is that your car out front?'

'It is indeed.'

'Lucky to get petrol. It's hard to come by nowadays.'

Christian winked. 'Being in the army does have its uses, if you understand.'

Alice became conspiratorial again. 'If ee wants more I knows someone who can oblige. At a price, mind you. 'Tain't cheap. But if you knows how to keep your mouth shut and has the cash then he's your man.'

'I'll remember that,' Christian answered. He should be fine for petrol, he thought, having several large containers of the stuff in the boot. Still, it was useful to know he could get more if required. And money was no object. Within reason that is.

'Here!' Alice exclaimed suddenly, eyes narrowing. 'I thought ee was starving hungry?'

'And so I am.'

'Then why hasn't ee started on the sandwich? Instead you're smoking again.'

He smiled inwardly. She seemed quite incensed. 'Because I was taught that it was impolite to eat in front of a lady when she isn't and I'm in conversation with her.'

Alice positively preened. Lady! Oh my my, that was rich. One for the book. She flushed slightly and lowered her gaze.

'That satisfy you?' he teased.

'Oh yes indeed. I'd best be getting back to the kitchen then and leave you to it.'

'Could I have some beer before you go?'

'Of course. Best bitter?'

'Please.'

'Pint or half?'

'A half will do nicely.'

She poured the beer, bursting to tell someone, anyone, of the compliment this handsome Frenchie had paid her. No matter she was old enough to be his grandmother, he'd called her a lady. Her. Alice Trevillick!

'I'll return shortly to see if you wants anything else. In the meantime you tuck in.'

He distinctly heard her giggle as she scuttled away out of sight.

It was pandemonium, chaos. Soldiers were retreating as far as the eye could see. Thousands of them.

'Come on, lads, keep up!' a British sergeant barked near by.

Heavy gunfire sounded in the distance, only a few miles away, Christian calculated grimly. He must make the coast where they said the British were being evacuated. He couldn't even begin to contemplate being captured by the enemy; the shame would be too much to endure.

They'd somehow become separated from the rest of their unit during the night – hardly surprising considering the dark and general confusion.

'I'm desperate for a shit,' Jean Van Rose, also a Second Lieutenant, grumbled beside Christian.

Christian grinned. 'I wouldn't recommend it. Not with the Boche hard on our heels. I'm sure they'd find it amusing to discover you with your trousers down round your ankles.'

'True enough,' Jean agreed ruefully. 'But I'll have to go soon or I won't be able to contain myself any longer.'

Christian marvelled that someone could be worried about a bodily function in their present desperate situation.

'I've got an upset stomach,' Jean explained.

'Oh!'

Jean pulled a face. 'And it's bloody murder.'

'You can go first opportunity we get.' Though God knew when that would be.

Christian glanced round. There were eighteen of them left in the unit that had started out forty strong. He hoped and prayed the others were safe and sound.

'Messerschmitt!' an English voice shouted.

Christian and Jean simultaneously glanced skywards. There it was, a dot coming swiftly in their direction.

'More of them!' another voice screamed.

Those were coming in at a forty-five degree angle to the first, a flight of six in all.

'Holy Jesus!' Jean muttered, and crossed himself. 'With any luck they'll pass on by.'

Christian was now looking round for cover, but there wasn't any. They'd been caught out in the open.

Bright flashes of flame suddenly spurted from the first plane, their excited chatter clearly heard by the two Frenchmen. Christian watched spurts of earth flying upwards where the shells hit the ground.

'All down!' he bellowed, and promptly threw himself flat.

Moments later they were being strafed by the flight of six which had closed incredibly fast. Christian's ears were filled with the deadly hum and zing thudding all around them.

It lasted only a minute, maybe a little longer, but it seemed an eternity. Christian was dimly aware that during the entire attack he held his breath.

His body sagged with relief as the sound of the planes faded coastwards. That had been close, too bloody close. It would be a miracle if no one had been hit.

'Are you OK, Jean?'

There was no reply. Jean continued to lie with both hands clamped over his head.

Christian sat up. 'Jean?'

He crawled the few feet separating them and shook his friend by the shoulder.

'Je—'

Christian abruptly broke off on seeing the blood staining the far side of Jean's uniform. It had only taken a single bullet but that had proved enough.

The stench assailing his nostrils told him that Jean's last wish had been granted.

Christian blinked awake, shivering. How often had he had that dream, and others, leading up to the actual evacuation at Dunkirk itself? Too often.

His mouth was tacky and his leg hurt even more, albeit he'd changed the dressing before lying down. He still suffered pain despite the wound being almost healed. The doctor who'd attended him in Plymouth had warned him this would be the case. Even when fully better and in no need of further dressings the leg would pain him for some while.

A glance at his bedside clock told him he'd slept longer

than he'd intended. He'd have to get a move on if he wasn't to miss dinner.

He sighed with satisfaction and pushed his plate away. The main course, plaice, chips and vegetables, had been excellent. The fish had been served with a thin crust on top and a pat of butter on its middle. Extremely fresh of course, which was only to be expected from a fishing village.

English chips amused him; so different to the *pommes frites* he was used to. At least these hadn't been soggy like so many he'd encountered since coming to England.

The vegetables had been glazed carrots and a green he couldn't identify. He would later discover it to be curly kale.

'Are you finished, sir?'

The waitress was a young girl of no more than fourteen or fifteen, her skin literally glowing with health and well-being.

'Yes, thank you.'

She collected up his plate. 'Will you want a sweet, sir?'

'What's on offer?'

'Damson pie, sir, with cream.'

'Clotted cream?' He smiled.

'Of course, sir. The genuine article. Made right here in Cornwall.'

He'd heard of clotted cream but never tasted it. He was looking forward to the experience.

The framed faded photograph hung on a side wall and was of a large ship stuck fast on rocks. Ted had mentioned the photo to him several times when talking about Coverack.

The ship he knew, because Ted had told him, had a clipper bowsprit and a classic counter stern. It boasted three tall funnels.

It was on Whit Monday, 1899, that the ship had run

aground on the Manacles, an infamous reef just off Coverack which had claimed many vessels in its time.

But on this occasion the ship had been saved. It had stayed aground for three weeks until finally being released after compressed air had driven out the water, allowing vast holes in her hull to be cemented over by a German salvage team.

The ship was the SS *Paris* whom the hotel was named after, and at one time had held the Blue Ribbon for the fastest crossing of the North Atlantic.

A fine ship, Christian mused. And one with not a little history attached. According to Ted she'd run aground again on the Cornish rocks, this time in 1914, near Rame while steaming for Plymouth, and again had survived. According to Ted the ship had finally been broken up in Genoa in 1923.

Christian pulled out his cigarettes and lit one, remembering how amused he'd been to hear of a hotel called Paris in a Cornish fishing village. It had seemed quite absurd somehow. And yet there was a rational explanation for it as this ancient photograph bore out.

On finishing his meal he'd wanted to take a walk, but that was out of the question as it was still thick with mist outside. Perhaps he might venture across to the nearby quay where, even if he couldn't see much, he'd at least get a breath of fresh air.

He'd wait till he'd finished his cigarette, he decided, before making a move. He'd have to return to his room first and get a coat.

'Good evening, Lieutenant.'

He turned to find himself staring at a woman whose face was familiar. And then the penny dropped.

'I see you found your way here.'

He nodded. 'Your directions were quite explicit.'

The green eyes filled with amusement. 'I'm Mrs Blackacre by the way. The owner of the hotel.'

Chapter 2

'I'm curious. How did you come to hear about the Paris Hotel?' Mrs Blackacre asked, placing a brandy in front of Christian who was now sitting at the bar. They were the only two in the room.

He regarded her steadily, thinking what a coincidence it had been to encounter her in particular back there on the road.

'A friend of mine, a painter, once spent a summer here. He thought Coverack the most wonderful place.'

She raised an eyebrow, inviting him to go on.

'And he stayed in this hotel. He said that summer was one of those very special occasions that sometimes happen in your life. Or hopefully happen anyway.'

For some reason she looked wistful on hearing that.

'According to him the sun never stopped shining and the sea was always blue. Perhaps the fact it was his honeymoon had something to do with it,' he added drily.

Mrs Blackacre smiled. 'How long ago was this?'

'Many years. Twenty or more. Would you have been around then? I don't mean as owner of the hotel, but living in Coverack.'

She pursed her lips. 'Not really. I mean yes and no. I come from Porthoustock, which is close by.'

'And what's that like?'

'Oh, smaller than this. It's a beautiful spot, mind you. But lonely, especially in winter. There again, so too is Coverack.'

'Ted has a painting of Coverack in his sitting room that has always fascinated me. It was one he painted when he was here that year and decided never to sell because it meant so much to him.'

'The honeymoon?'

'I suppose so.' Christian grinned.

'And is this Ted a professional painter?'

'Very much so. He lives in Hennebont where I come from.'

Mrs Blackacre paused to listen. 'There's a wind coming up which should blow away the mist. Can you hear it?'

Christian listened also. 'Can't say that I do.'

'Well, I can. It's not much at the moment but it'll probably get stronger. They usually do this time of year.'

She was an attractive woman, he thought. If she had one fault it was that she was too wide-hipped. He didn't know it but that was a common trait amongst Cornish women.

'What's his surname?' she queried, returning to the subject of Ted.

'McEwen.'

'That's hardly French!'

Christian shook his head. 'Ted's English of Scottish descent. But he's a real Bohemian by nature.'

'And his wife?'

'English as well. She's called Petula. Pet for short.'

Christian lit a cigarette, thinking how cosy it was with just the pair of them, and the fire, as earlier, blazing in the grate.

'So how do an Englishman and his wife end up living in France?'

'Ted prefers it there. Says the way of life suits him. He does come back quite regularly, mainly for business reasons. He's quite successful, you see.'

Mrs Blackacre's face clouded. 'Where is he now? Still in Honne . . . What did you call it?'

'Hennebont. And I hope not. I trust he and Pet got out before the Germans arrived. Otherwise who knows what'll have happened to them.'

Christian became morose and introspective. He worshipped Ted like a second father. The thought of Ted and Pet falling into German hands was just horrendous. The Germans would hardly take kindly to him, an Englishman of his temperament.

Christian saw off his brandy, the wall clock chiming as he did.

'Another?'

'Please. And won't you change your mind and have one? I hate drinking on my own.'

She decided she rather liked this young Frenchman, now out of uniform and dressed in civilian clothes. The latter made him appear even more French than before.

'Thank you, I will. A glass of wine, I think.'

Christian watched her opening a bottle of red, noting with mild surprise that the seal on top was French. He wondered about that.

'Cheers!' she toasted.

'Cheers. *À votre santé.*'

She had a sip then refilled his brandy.

'I told Ted that one day I'd come to Coverack and see it for myself,' Christian stated quietly. 'And now here I am.'

'Though so far you haven't seen much.'

He laughed. 'Nothing at all.'

'But you will come morning.'

'I'm looking forward to it.'

Christian closed his eyes, recalling the picture that had fascinated him for years. There was an extraordinary wild beauty about it, yet also a profound feeling of tranquillity. In a strange way the scene portrayed was timeless. Of this world and not of this world. It had drawn him, mesmerised him, right from the very first.

'I noticed you limping coming through here,' Mrs Blackacre probed softly. 'Do you have a bad leg?'

He blew a long stream of smoke away from her. 'I was wounded at Dunkirk.'

'Oh?'

'Nothing serious. It's nearly healed. That's the main reason I was granted leave. To recuperate.'

'Was it awful? Dunkirk I mean?'

Christian glanced down at his drink, his mind churning with memories. 'Pretty awful. A lot of good men died there. I lost a few myself from what remained of our unit.' He paused, then reflected sadly, 'If it hadn't been for the Royal Navy and other British sailors none of us would have escaped. Myself included.'

'How were you wounded?'

'We were strafed by a plane. I'd just lost a good friend a few hours before that to the same thing. I was fortunate and survived. Poor Jean didn't.'

'I'm sorry.'

He stared at her and could see she meant it. 'The bullet went straight through the fleshy part of my leg. Straight in and straight out again. A crew member aboard the frigate that picked us up gave me first aid. Then it was a hospital in Plymouth.'

At this point they were interrupted by the door banging open and a group of older men coming in, the atmosphere in the bar instantly changing.

'Good evening to you, Denzil!' Mrs Blackacre cried out.

'And to you, Maizie, me lover,' the grizzled chap in the lead replied. It was clear from what they were wearing that these were all fishermen.

'Get thae pints poured, Maizie. We be dry as dust.'

Mrs Blackacre laughed and moved to the pumps, the men clearly regulars and favourites of hers.

'Why, it never ceases to amaze me what a fine-looking woman you be, Maizie Blackacre. I hope that Sam of yours appreciates the fact, the jammy bugger!' a third proclaimed with a mischievous twinkle in his eye.

'You never change, John Corin. Always the flatterer,' she retorted.

''Tis true. 'Tis true. But where's the harm in that?' He heaved himself on to a stool. 'There again, how can it be flattery when it's God's Gospel.'

The group started to banter amongst themselves and with Mrs Blackacre, their dialect so strong that Christian found most of it unintelligible.

After a while more people arrived and the hum of conversation increased. The only further time Christian managed to speak to Mrs Blackacre was when ordering another drink.

Eventually he left and returned to his room, the bar still buzzing with Mrs Blackacre continuing to pull a steady stream of pints, some beer but mainly cider.

A lump came into Christian's throat as he stared out over Coverack from the quay, more or less positioned on the spot from where Ted had painted his picture.

It was a raw day, clouds scudding across the sky, with a hint of rain to come. But the mist had gone completely and gave him an uninterrupted view.

The same qualities were there as were in the picture. The tranquillity, the wild beauty. Timelessness. All of it.

He glanced across at the hotel instantly to spy a face staring down at him from an upstairs window. Mrs Blackacre, there was no doubt about it.

The face abruptly vanished when she realised she'd been spotted, lace curtains falling back into place.

Christian had been about to give a friendly wave, but couldn't do that now. With a shrug he returned his gaze to the sprawl of the village.

The air he sucked into his lungs was as heady as strong wine.

'You're the Froggy, ain't ee?'

Christian roused himself from his reverie to glance at the stranger who'd addressed him. He was sitting on a bench looking out to sea, and the man had come up silently from behind.

'I'm French, yes.'

The older man grunted. 'No mistaking ee but for a foreigner. If nothing else thae clothes gives ee away.'

Christian stared at the shiny hook dangling from the man's right cuff, where a hand ought to be.

'Lost it in an accident aboard a boat when I tweren't more than a nipper,' the man explained. 'Can I join ee?'

The last thing Christian wanted was company, especially that of a stranger, but thought it rude to say so. 'Please do.'

'The name's Wesley Repson,' the man stated on sitting. 'But most folk call me Hookie for the obvious reason.' He extended his remaining hand which Christian shook.

'And I'm Christian Le Gall. Tell me, how did you know I was French and not some other nationality?'

Hookie gave a throaty chuckle. 'It don't take long for things to get round in Coverack. One knows, we all do within hours. That's how it be.'

Christian had to smile at that. Alice would be the culprit, he decided. She would have put the word about.

He dug in a pocket and pulled out his cigarettes. 'Would you care for one?'

Hookie shook his head. 'None of thae for me, lad. I'm a pipe man. Can't beat a pipe, I always says.' He produced a briar and they both lit up. 'Army, I heard?'

Christian nodded.

'Lieutenant?'

'Not quite, a Second Lieutenant. Or *Sous Lieutenant* as it's called in the French Army.'

'A sous, eh? I thought that was some kind of chef.'

Christian laughed. 'Same idea. *Under* chef, *under* lieutenant.'

Hookie drew heavily on his pipe and sighed with satisfaction. 'You arrived in the mist last night, I believe.'

The man would tell him what sort of underwear he had on next, Christian thought. 'I got lost, but fortunately I bumped into Mrs Blackacre who directed me here.'

'Aah, Maizie Blackacre. Out gadding about, wor she?'

'I wouldn't know about that,' Christian replied, eyes narrowing. 'But she was on the road and kind enough to help.'

'Lucky for you, eh?'

'Indeed.'

'Wouldn't fancy spending the night out in the mist meself,' he said, adding wryly, 'but then I wouldn't be lost hereabouts, would I?'

'I suppose not,' Christian grinned, still not certain about this Hookie Repson.

Hookie tamped down the contents of his pipe with a gnarled, yellow finger. 'I'd fight in this war too if they'd let me. But what use is a cripple, eh?'

Christian wasn't sure how to respond to that, so said nothing.

'At least that's how they sees it. But 'tain't stopped me working all me life. By God it ain't.'

'You're a fisherman I take it?' He presumed that to be the case, as Hookie had said he'd lost his hand on a boat.

'That be so. And a grand life she be.'

'I can imagine.'

Hookie fixed him with a beady, calculating eye. 'You likes cognac I'm told.'

That startled Christian. 'Yes, I do.'

'I can get ee a few bottles if you're interested. For the right price, that is.'

Christian stared hard at his companion. 'Can you really?'

'That be so.'

'And how's that?'

Hookie used the implement he was nicknamed after to tap his nose. 'That's for me to know and you to wonder about. Now, me lad, are you interested?'

'That depends how much you're asking.'

Hookie named a sum Christian thought more than reasonable. 'Fair enough.'

'How many bottles then?'

'I thought you said a few?'

'Few is few. Half a dozen!'

'All at the same price?'

'That's so.'

'Then I'll buy them.'

Hookie beamed. 'We have a deal. Now when do you want them?'

'Whenever's suitable.'

'Meet me here at four this afternoon and I'll have them with me. And make sure you bring the cash, mind. No cash, no cognac.' Hookie came to his feet. 'I'll see you later, Monsewer Le Gall.'

Christian winced at the man's atrocious accent. 'Till then.'

Hookie strolled away, humming a tune to himself.

Christian had a sudden thought. 'Hookie?'

Hookie stopped and turned, his expression a frown.

Christian hurried to his side. 'I don't suppose you can get any French cigarettes?'

Hookie shook his head. 'Not at the moment. But how long's you staying in Coverack?'

'I'm not certain. Two weeks probably. Perhaps more.'

'Then speak to me again about it at the end of next week. I's always around. You'll see me. How many would you want?'

'As many as you can supply.'

Hookie laughed. 'A couple of thousand?'

Christian gaped. 'Can you really do as many as that?'

''Tis possible. There again, I might not be able to get any. It all depends.'

Depended on what? Christian wondered as Hookie continued on his way. He'd heard of Cornish smugglers, but surely they were a thing of the past? And if they did still exist it was inconceivable that they were going over to France with a war on.

Or was it?

'A very nice young man, for a foreigner that is,' Alice Trevillick declared, busy peeling potatoes for the evening meal.

Maizie Blackacre glanced up from her paperwork which was the bane of her life. She loathed the administration which seemed to have proliferated since the war started. 'You mean Lieutenant Le Gall?'

'Who else? 'Tain't no other foreigner in Coverack at the moment. Leastways not that I knows of.'

Maizie pursed her lips. 'I suppose so.'

'Well, he impresses me and no mistake.' Alice paused to smile in recollection. 'Called me a lady, he did. That fair made my day, I can tell ee.'

Maizie smiled. She could have replied that Christian was only being polite, but why should she spoil Alice's pleasure?

'You had a good old chin wag with him at the bar last night, you mentioned earlier.'

Maizie nodded. 'Till Denzil and his cronies arrived.'

'And what did ee learn?'

'Not a lot.'

Alice let out an exasperated sigh. 'Come on, Maizie Blackacre, ee's as nosy as me and no mistake. Ee must have learnt something.'

Maizie told Alice about Ted and his wife Pet.

'So that's why he came here. I knew there had to be some reason. I mean, few people come down all this way in October unless there's a reason for it. 'Tain't exactly the height of the holiday season.'

Maizie didn't mention she'd been watching him on the quay that morning, still embarrassed at being spotted.

'Is he married? He don't wear no ring.'

Maizie considered that. 'There wasn't any mention of a wife. Nor does he have that married air about him, so I think it's safe to say he's a bachelor.'

'Good catch for some maid, handsome bloke that he is. It's true what they say about Frenchmen, they do have a certain way about them. They oozes charm and romance.'

Maizie laughed.

'Well, 'tis true, Maizie, 'tis true! He's like someone out of thae romantic novels. Something written by Daphne Du Maurier.'

Maizie immediately thought of Daphne Du Maurier's newly published book, *Frenchman's Creek*, which she'd not yet read. That was set in Cornwall she believed.

Alice pointed her peeler at Maizie. 'Well! Don't ee agree?'

'He's certainly handsome,' Maizie acknowledged slowly.

Alice cackled. 'He's probably a right proper lover too. The sort who gives you flowers and chocolates and the like. Who makes a right fuss of ee.' Her expression changed. 'Unlike the men round here. 'Tain't one of them got a romantic bone in his body.'

Maizie thought of her husband Sam to whom that description certainly applied. Sam's idea of romance was sex, sex and more sex. And selfish with it too. Selfish to the core.

'Wasn't your husband romantic, Alice?' Henry Trevellick had been lost at sea sixteen years before when his boat had gone down in a sudden storm. Three good men had gone down with him.

Alice paused to smile. 'He tweren't romantic in the least. A fine provider mind, and never looked at another woman that way after we married. But romantic?' She shook her head. 'Never. Not in a thousand years.'

Maizie regarded her employee and friend with sympathy. 'Do you still miss Henry? You rarely mention him.'

'Of course I does. 'Tis right lonely being on your own with your one and only child flown the nest. There's manys a night I wish Henry was there, sitting opposite like he used to, me knitting or whatever, he usually just gazing into the fire thinking God alone knows what. In bed too, maybe there more than anywhere. Even now I sometimes stretches out my hand thinking to touch him, and then I comes awake and remembers. Those be the loneliest times of all.'

'Sally should visit you more often,' Maizie said, a hint of criticism in her voice. Sally was Alice's daughter.

'She's busy with her own family. And Padstow's a fair ways away. She comes when she can. Bless her.'

They lapsed into silence for a few moments, Alice continuing with her peeling, thinking what a misery life had become since Henry's death. She'd have gone out of her head long ago if it hadn't been for her job at the hotel to keep her occupied and feeling useful.

Maizie threw down her pen, her concentration now well and truly disturbed. 'Shall I put the kettle on?'

'Do you need to ask?'

Both women laughed. 'And we'll have a chocolate biscuit,' Maizie added. 'Though Heaven knows, they're getting harder and harder to come by nowadays. I was lucky to get the last packet.'

'Then we'll just keep them for ourselves, like the little piggies we be.'

Christian came into the bar to find it deserted. He sat on a stool, lit a cigarette and waited.

It was a full five minutes before Mairie Blackacre appeared carrying a large cardboard box.

'Do you want some help with that?' Christian offered.

'I can manage, thank you very much. Are you after a drink?'

'If it's possible.'

Maizie glanced down at the box, then back at Christian. 'Just help yourself. You'll find your tab in the till, add whatever to it.'

Trusting, he thought. He rather liked that. 'How about you, will you join me when you're finished whatever you're doing?'

'It's far too early for me. But maybe later.'

He watched the swing of her hips as she left the room. Pity about their size, he thought. Slimmer hips would have made all the difference. That and a more chic dress. Any decent French woman would have despaired of Maizie's shapeless grey woollen garment that had neither style nor appeal.

He'd noticed that in Plymouth, he reflected as he poured himself a brandy. English women just didn't seem to bother about looking smart. It surprised him that their men let them get away with it.

He couldn't help but think of Marie Thérèse. She would have knocked these frumpy English women sideways.

Opening the till he carefully added a brandy to his bill.

Christian's face registered his surprise when he saw the brand of cognac Hookie had brought along. He hadn't expected such quality.

'All right?' Hookie demanded.

'I'll say.'

'Then where's your cash?'

Christian pulled out his wallet and extracted some notes. 'You'll find that's correct,' he declared, handing them over.

'I'll still count them if you don't mind,' Hookie replied drily.

'Please do.'

He grunted when he'd finished. 'Pleasure doing business with you, Monsewer Le Gall.'

'And with you.'

'I won't forget thae cigarettes. Though no promises, mind.'

'I understand.'

Christian picked up the box containing the cognac. He couldn't wait for a glass; it would be such a treat after the stuff Maizie Blackacre was selling.

A huge boom of thunder brought Christian awake. Rain was rattling against the window panes and now a great streak of jagged lightning lit up the sky. That was followed seconds later by another peal of thunder.

He wondered what time it was and reached for the switch of his bedside lamp. Nothing happened when he pressed it. He tried again, to no avail. The electricity was off.

What a storm, he thought, glad to be tucked up in bed. Thunder cracked again.

He'd have a cigarette now he was awake, he decided, swinging his legs out of bed. He was reaching for his packet when he heard a distinct cry of distress coming from below.

Instantly he was up and shrugging into his dressing gown. The cry had to have come from Mrs Blackacre as he and she were the only ones in the hotel.

He wished he had a torch as he groped his way towards the door. Outside he stumbled his way along the landing.

'Mrs Blackacre?' he called from the top of the stairs.

'Down here,' a small voice replied.

He found her at the bottom, sitting on the hall floor and nursing an ankle. 'What happened?' he demanded, squatting beside her.

'I fell, stupid bugger that I am,' she grimaced.

'Are you badly hurt?'

'I think it's just a sprain.'

He realised he'd left his lighter behind and wished he'd brought it with him. That would have given a little light at least.

As though reading his mind Maizie said, 'There are candles under the bar. It was those I was going for when I fell. The electric's off.'

'Yes, I know. I'll get the candles. You wait here.'

She couldn't help but laugh. 'I'm hardly likely to be rushing after you, am I?'

He smiled, sharing the joke. 'I won't be long.'

Maizie was sitting on the stairs, a candle burning brightly beside her, when he eventually returned from the fuse box.

'I've rewired them twice and still no luck. It isn't the fuses,' he announced.

Maizie swore. 'The whole village must be out then.'

'No, it isn't. I glanced out a window and saw lights, so it isn't the entire village. It's the hotel it seems.'

Maizie shook her head. 'The wiring is pretty bad. Sam and I have been planning to do something about it for ages and never quite got round to it. Then he was off and . . .' She broke off and sobbed. 'Christ, there isn't an electrician for miles around. The usual chap's off in the Forces with the rest of them.'

Christian's heart went out to her and he began to realise just how hard it was for a single woman to run a business on her own. Particularly in wartime with all that that entailed.

'It's best I get you back to bed. Come morning I'll have a look at things for you.'

She stared at him. 'Do you know anything about electricity?'

'A bit.'

'Then you can fix it?'

He held up a hand. 'I never said that. But I'll certainly do what I can.'

'Thank you,' she whispered.

Maizie started when the loudest peal of thunder yet banged, seemingly, directly overhead. 'God help all men out at sea in a night like this,' she said quietly.

Christian crossed himself. 'Amen.'

She smiled at him, pleased he was there and that she hadn't been in the hotel by herself. His presence was a distinct comfort.

'Now let's get you back upstairs,' he declared, carefully lifting her to her feet.

He blew out his own candle, and laid it aside. Then he picked up hers. 'Put your arm round my shoulder and up we go.'

It took a while but finally he got her back to her bedroom where she collapsed on the bed.

He noted the smell of perfume in the room, a very womanly smell that was extremely pleasant. He didn't take much else in.

'Is there anything you want?' he queried.

She shook her head.

'I'll be up early and send Alice to you when she arrives in. OK?'

'OK,' she nodded with a smile.

'I'll leave you to it then.'

He closed the door softly behind him.

Chapter 3

'How are you getting on?' Christian glanced round from the ladder in surprise to find Maizie Blackacre standing below him in the cellar, where he was attempting to trace the electrical fault.

'You should be in bed,' he admonished.

'My ankle's a lot better this morning. The swelling has gone right down and there's only a twinge of pain. I couldn't have sprained it after all.'

'That's good news. I'm pleased.'

She'd never noticed before what an elegant figure he had. Slim and lithe but well muscled with it. 'Are those tools Alice dug out all right?' she inquired.

'Fine. Everything I need, thank goodness. There's little I could have done without them.'

'I've brought you some coffee,' she declared, proffering a steaming mug.

He sighed, stretching his arms which ached from working above his head. 'The very job. I could use a break.'

He stepped down off the ladder and accepted the mug which he balanced on a tread. He then fumbled for his cigarettes.

'Can I have one?' she asked.

'Of course. I didn't know you smoked.'

'Only occasionally. Sam doesn't approve of women smoking,

you see, so I have to do it surreptitiously when he's around.'

'Which he isn't at the moment.'

'No,' she smiled.

They both lit up and he returned the packet and lighter to his pocket.

'Hmmh!' she murmured. 'That's good.'

'I'm hoping to get some French ones.'

Maizie raised an eyebrow. 'From where?'

'A Mr Hookie Repson. I've already bought six bottles of cognac from him.'

She frowned. 'What did you pay for those?'

He told her.

'Trust Hookie. That's well over the odds.'

'I thought the price fair.'

'I would have got them for you for less than that. Why do you want cognac anyway?'

That embarrassed him. 'I . . . eh . . . Well, to be honest, I prefer it to the brandy you sell.'

She laughed. 'I see. Mine isn't good enough for you, eh?' The last was said teasingly.

'No no no,' he quickly replied, not wishing to give offence. 'It's just I prefer cognac.'

'You should have said. I have some in stock. All you had to do was mention it. I'll see it's on the bar later. That way you can save most of what you bought and take it back to Plymouth with you.'

'Thank you, Mrs Blackacre.'

She wiped a stray wisp of hair from her forehead. 'I think we can dispense with the formalities. Why don't you call me Maizie? Everyone else does.'

'Only if you call me Christian.'

'So be it.'

'So be it,' he repeated with a large smile.

He sipped his drink, which was nothing like French coffee.

Like the cigarettes, he missed decent coffee a lot. Suddenly he wondered if Hookie could get him that as well.

'I'll speak to Hookie about the cigarettes,' Maizie declared. 'And see you don't pay more than you should.'

'Thank you.' He hesitated. 'Tell me, is Hookie a smuggler?'

All expression instantly vanished from her face and her eyes filled with innocence. 'What makes you say that?'

He shrugged. 'It just seemed likely, that's all.'

'I think you have been listening to too many tales about us Cornish folk, Christian. Anyway, how could anyone smuggle with a war on?'

'That's what I thought.'

She gazed up at the overhead wiring. 'How are you getting on? Can you fix whatever?'

She'd changed the subject, he noted. Nor was he fooled by the bland expression and suddenly innocent eyes. He knew women better than that. 'Perhaps, I don't know yet.'

'What happened?'

'I think, only think mind you, there was a power surge that came back on the hotel. A sudden overload.'

'And that blew things?'

'If I'm right it did. But to what extent I've still to discover.'

She drew heavily on her cigarette, savouring the effect and taste. It made her feel quite wicked.

'What did you do before the war?' she inquired, curious.

'I was at university in Rouen. I'm learning to be what you call a surveyor.'

'That's interesting,' she enthused.

'I enjoy it.'

'And you'll return to university when the war's over?'

'If I'm still . . .' He caught himself in time, he mustn't say that. It could be unlucky. 'Of course.'

He ground out the remains of his cigarette on the cellar's stone floor. 'Now I'd better get on. I don't want to be down here all day.'

She took his empty mug and ground out the remains of her cigarette as he had. 'I'll leave you to it.'

He was climbing the ladder again when he became aware of a smell tingling his nostrils. The same scent as the night before.

Maizie's perfume.

Christian offered up a silent prayer, crossed his fingers, then pulled the main switch. To his great relief the lights snapped on.

'Hooray!' Maizie and Alice greeted him when he entered the bar. 'You did it!'

He was hot and sweaty, badly in need of a bath.

'You managed to get the electric on again.' Maizie beamed.

'It seems so.'

'The least I can do is give you a drink.'

'Beer, please. I'm thirsty.'

Maizie went behind the bar and pulled a pint which she placed in front of him. 'I can't thank you enough, Christian.'

'I'm only glad I was able to help. If it had been anything more major I'd have been out of my depth. Electricity isn't exactly something you want to be fiddling around with if you don't know what you're doing.'

'I quite agree.'

'I knew a chap once blew himself right across a room,' Alice chipped in. 'Silly sod had forgotten to turn the power off.'

'Was he hurt?' Christian queried.

'Only his pride.'

'He was lucky.'

'That's for you,' Maizie said, placing a small glass beside the first.

He guessed its contents right away. 'Cognac?'

'That's right. I got a bottle out while you were busy.'

He had a sip. 'Excellent,' he pronounced.

'You've got a large streak of dirt right down your face,' Alice informed him.

'I'm not surprised. It's filthy down there. I'll have a bath shortly, if that's all right?'

Maizie nodded. 'Leave your clothes out and I'll wash them for you.'

'Oh, I can't have you do that!'

'They're mucky on my account, so I'll wash them.' She held up a hand. 'I won't have any further argument.'

'Thank you,' he smiled.

She decided she'd do all his washing and ironing during his stay at the hotel. One good turn deserved another, after all. And with business as slack as it was she was hardly run off her feet.

'Can I ask ee a question?' Alice queried.

Christian turned his attention to her. 'Fire away.'

'How comes ee speaks such good English? I mean, there's an accent there but that's all. So how comes?'

He laughed, and finished his cognac. Maizie immediately moved to refill the glass. It was something she too had wondered about.

'I began studying English early on at school and discovered I had an aptitude for languages. But what really helped was the fact I was friendly with an English painter called Ted . . .'

'Maizie mentioned him,' Alice interrupted, nodding.

'When he and I were together, which was often, we always spoke English. In the end I became fluent.'

'And fluent you most certainly are,' Maizie praised, sliding the recharged glass in front of him.

'Do you speak other languages then?'

He gave Alice a wry smile. 'German as well. Though I'm not so good at that as English.'

'No equivalent of Ted?' Maizie said.

'Precisely. But I speak it fairly well nonetheless. I also have a smattering of Spanish. Though a smattering only. Enough to get by if I had to.'

Maizie shook her head in admiration. 'You are clever, Christian. People this side of the Channel just don't pick up languages the way you Continentals do. I suppose it's because we expect everyone to speak English.'

'We French are very similar in that respect expecting others to speak French. I've always considered it to be rather arrogant, for both nations, but there we are.'

He was quite something, this Christian Le Gall, Maizie reflected. The more she knew about him the more she warmed towards him. And he was such easy company. Why, after only a few days she felt as though she'd known him for years.

Christian suddenly became aware of Maizie staring at him in a strange, quizzical way. When he returned the stare she hastily glanced away, her face colouring slightly. Now what was that all about?

'Well, I must get back to the kitchen. Things to be done and we's all behind this morning like the proverbial horse's backside,' Alice declared, getting up from where she was sitting.

'Me too.' Maizie smiled. 'So we'll just have to leave you to it, Christian.'

She gestured at the bottle of cognac situated under the gantry. 'Just help yourself if you want more.'

He shook his head. 'Perhaps later.'

'Have a nice bath,' Maizie added before following Alice who'd already bustled away.

'Thanks again!' she called out before disappearing round a corner.

What a stunning view, Christian thought. Sheer picture postcard. He'd climbed a hill behind Coverack and could now see over the surrounding countryside and out across the Channel.

There was a ship off in the far distance, a big one too from what he could make out. But whether merchant or otherwise wasn't clear.

Gulls cried and screamed raucously overhead, wheeling first this way and then that. They always seemed extremely angry, he mused, deciding that must simply be the nature of gulls.

He glanced at his wristwatch. Another ten minutes and he'd start back. He'd walked far enough for one day. Which was considerable in view of his wounded leg. He didn't want to overdo things.

He was about to rise from the boulder he was perched on when he noticed a figure crossing open ground to his left. About a quarter of a mile away, he judged. Maybe less.

The black billowing cloak told him it was Maizie, unless there was another woman in Coverack with a similar garment, which he doubted. He wondered where she was going as the direction she was taking didn't seem to be leading anywhere.

He watched her vanish behind a rise in the ground and waited for her to emerge again.

After a while he frowned. Where was she? He continued to wait expectantly, but she didn't reappear.

His frown deepened. This was odd to say the least. He decided to investigate.

Christian gazed about him in astonishment. No Maizie. Nothing at all except wind and rustling grass. It was as though a wizard had waved his magic wand and, hey presto!

He must have made a mistake, he thought. Come to the wrong rise in the ground. But he knew he hadn't. He'd kept his eye firmly on his objective all the way there.

Nor had she emerged without his seeing her. He'd been

able to observe both entrance and exit point during his walk over.

He shook his head in disbelief. Incredible. One moment she'd been there, the next gone.

Christian laughed. Had he been imagining things? Seen someone or something that he'd thought was Maizie when it wasn't? A trick of the light perhaps. A day dream?

Nonsense! What he'd witnessed had been real all right. Flesh and blood in a black cloak. So where was she?

His bemused reverie was interrupted by rain. Slowly, reluctantly, with several backward glances, he began his return to the hotel.

'I thought I saw you earlier,' he stated to Maizie who was serving behind the bar. He had just come through from the dining room.

'And where was that?'

'You were walking alone over that way.' He pointed in the general direction of where he'd been.

Again that blank expression and innocent eyes. 'Oh?'

'I recognised your black cloak.'

She smiled. 'I didn't see you.'

'So you were there!' he exclaimed triumphantly. He knew she'd been.

Maizie bent down to rearrange some glasses that, as far as he could make out, didn't need rearranging. 'I was visiting a friend,' she said over her shoulder.

'You went behind a rise in the ground and never reappeared.'

She laughed. 'Of course I must have done. You just missed me, that's all.'

'I was watching very carefully.'

Maizie shrugged. 'Not careful enough it would seem.'

He sighed. The last thing he wanted was to argue about this. And yet he knew what he'd seen.

There was silence between them for a few moments, then Maizie rose again to her feet and abruptly left the bar.

How curious, he thought. How very curious. He could only think she must be hiding something. But what? And then there was the matter of that suspected pistol on the day of his arrival . . .

Next morning Christian ran into Maizie in the corridor outside his bedroom, carrying a supply of fresh linen. 'Oh, Maizie, I was just coming to look for you. Don't expect me for lunch today. I've decided to drive up to Helston as I'm short of a few things.'

'Helston!' she exclaimed. 'Can you possibly take me?'

He hadn't expected that. 'I'd be delighted to.'

'The bus is only once a week and the journey takes for ever because there are so many stops *en route*. A lift would be far more convenient.'

He glanced at his watch. 'I intend leaving in half an hour. Would that be OK?'

'Perfect. I'll naturally pay my share of the petrol.'

'You'll do nothing of the sort!' he retorted.

'But I insist.'

'You can insist all you like, I'm not taking a penny piece. Like it or lump it.'

She laughed. 'All right then, I'll like it.'

'Where shall we meet?'

'Downstairs.'

'I'll be waiting.'

'And I'll be ready.'

What an unexpected treat, he thought. It would be lovely having Maizie's company.

He noted she'd done herself up for the occasion. Underneath the smart navy blue gabardine coat he could see a floral blue and white dress topped by a jaunty, pointed collar. She was also wearing more make-up than usual, her lipstick a vivid red that could easily have appeared tarty but didn't. Her smart court shoes were black.

He opened the door for her. 'Your carriage awaits, madam.'

Her eyes twinkled with amusement. 'Why, thank you, kind sir.'

He helped her into the car, making sure she was quite comfortable, before making his way round to the driver's side. 'Let's hope this weather keeps up,' he smiled, sliding alongside her. It was a fine, if somewhat blustery day.

'I think it will.'

'You're the local, you should know.'

Maizie settled back as he started the engine. 'Do you remember the way?'

'If I get it wrong I'm sure you'll be quick to tell me. Like you did that day in the mist.'

She regarded him quizzically. 'Did you really think me a ghost?'

'You frightened the life out of me. It's a wonder I didn't have a heart attack.'

'Just as well you didn't,' she teased. 'I still might not have any electric at the hotel if you had.'

He thought that amusing. 'True enough.'

'Nor would I be having this lift into Helston. For which I'm most grateful.'

'What do you intend doing there?' he queried, coming on to the hill that would take them out of Coverack.

For a moment she hesitated. 'Shopping.'

'Oh?'

'I do get a regular delivery from there as it's the nearest town. But there are times when I like to go in personally to see what's what. That's also when I usually pay my accounts.'

'I see,' he murmured, wondering why she'd hesitated. Her reasons were straightforward enough.

'And you?'

'Socks.'

'Socks!'

'I need some more. Besides, I'd like to have a look round Helston while I'm down this way. Ted once told me it was worthwhile spending a couple of hours there and recommended a pub called The Pixie Inn which, according to him, does wonderful steak and kidney puddings. A great favourite of Ted's.'

'I know The Pixie Inn,' Maizie nodded.

'And?'

'It's nice enough. Very olde worlde with lots of bits and pieces dangling from the ceiling. It's popular with the tourists during the season.'

The smell of her perfume was strong within the car. He guessed that she'd dabbed some on before joining him. As before, it was a scent he liked.

'Is there anyone back in France?' Maizie asked coyly.

He glanced at her. 'How do you mean?'

'A special girlfriend.'

The question, coming as it had out of the blue, caught him by surprise. He didn't know he wanted to discuss Marie Thérèse with Maizie, though there was no reason why he shouldn't.

He thought of Marie Thérèse and their last meeting together and smiled in memory. 'There was someone,' he admitted reluctantly.

'And?'

'And what?'

'What was her name?'

'Marie Thérèse.'

'Marie Thérèse,' Maizie repeated. 'Pretty. Was she?'

Christian found himself discomfited. 'I thought so.'

'Dark haired or fair?'

He laughed. 'You'll be wanting to know what size bust she had next.'

Maizie coloured and glanced away. 'Sorry, I was being nosy.'

'Why the interest?'

She shrugged. 'Just wondered, that's all.'

There was silence between them for a few moments. 'Did you meet her at university?' Maizie further probed.

'No, she lives in Hennebont. Latterly I only saw her during the holidays.'

'She was special then?'

'In a way.'

Maizie frowned. 'What does that mean?'

'You are nosy, as you put it,' he said tartly.

She coloured again. 'Sorry. I'm being rude.'

He suddenly relented. What the hell! Why shouldn't he tell Maizie about Marie Thérèse. 'We've known each other for years. Grew up together, you could say. She works in a shop selling lingerie.'

'So tell me more about her.'

Christian sighed. 'She's a year younger than me. Dark haired, good figure, lots of fun. She makes me laugh.'

'That's always a good sign.'

'I suppose so.'

'Do you miss her?'

Now he was becoming irritated. Why this harping on about Marie Thérèse? 'I certainly think about her from time to time and wonder what's happened to her. It can't be easy for people in Hennebont at the present, not with the town overrun with Nazis.' His expression became grim. 'The very thought is quite odious.'

'I can well understand that.'

The hands holding the steering wheel tightened until their knuckles shone white. Who knew what the Nazis were capable of? There were stories, rumours, about Poland and Czechoslovakia, not to mention Finland. Murder, rape, torture . . . He began to sweat as his mind ran riot.

'Christian?'

He blinked, suddenly aware he couldn't remember anything of the last few minutes' drive. That was dangerous.

'Christian? Will you have finished your business by lunchtime?' she asked.

'I, eh . . . suppose so.'

'Then why don't we meet up at The Pixie Inn for lunch? We could try the steak and kidney puddings, if they still do them.'

'That's a wonderful idea. I'd love to.'

'Shall we say one o'clock?'

He groped for his cigarettes, trying to put Hennebont and what might be going on there out of his mind.

Christian was pleased with himself. He'd called in at the hospital where a doctor had examined his wound. From now on he could dispense with dressings, he'd been informed. There would be a scar, but he didn't care about that. A scar was nothing.

He'd also managed to buy three pairs of socks, civilian ones that he'd been short of. So all in all it had been a successful trip.

He glanced at his watch. Almost one o'clock, and there was The Pixie Inn straight ahead. He couldn't have been more spot on.

Once inside he looked around but there was no sign of Maizie. She'd probably be late, he reflected. In his experience women usually were. Most of them seemed to be so as a matter of course.

He ordered a pint and asked about food. To his disappointment steak and kidney puddings weren't on the menu. Further inquiry revealed there had been a change of management since Ted's day.

It was twenty past when he finished his pint and ordered another. He hoped Maizie wouldn't be too much longer, he was getting hungry.

And then, through a window heavily etched with an advert for a brand of Cornish beer, he spotted Maizie deep in conversation with an older man, the pair of them standing across the road. Whatever they were discussing, passions appeared to be running high on both sides. Maizie violently shook her head and the man threw up his hands in exasperation.

The conversation continued for a few minutes more, then they parted, the man striding angrily away, Maizie crossing the road towards the pub.

Christian turned his attention back to the bar and wondered what that had been all about. It had certainly been a heated exchange.

'Hello.'

He smiled at her. 'Hello. No steak and kidney puddings, I'm afraid.'

'Oh dear. I was rather looking forward to that. I haven't had one in ages.'

'So, what can I get you?'

She thought about that for a moment. 'A gin and tonic would be rather nice.'

'Large?'

'No, I . . .' She broke off. 'Oh why not. I always think of a day away from the hotel as something of a holiday.'

'Then a large one it is. Now why don't you find a seat and I'll bring the drinks over.'

He placed his order while Maizie selected a quiet table situated in a corner.

'Do you think I could have another of your cigarettes?' she asked when he rejoined her.

'Of course.'

They both lit up.

'I've brought the menu as you can see. We can choose shortly.' He smiled

Maizie inhaled deeply and sort of shuddered.

'Something wrong?'

That startled her. 'No. Why do you ask that?'

'You seem a little . . . agitated.'

'Do I?'

He nodded.

'There's no reason why I should be,' she replied, and gave a brittle laugh.

A lie, he thought. She was agitated after what had taken place outside. And yet she wasn't mentioning the man or incident.

'Meet anyone you know in town?' he inquired casually.

Maizie had a gulp of her drink, and sighed. 'Only the shop owners I spoke to. They're all acquaintances of long standing.'

He didn't reply to that, just smiled wryly.

'And how about yourself, did you get the socks?'

Christian could only wonder, both during lunch and the drive back to Coverack, why Maizie was being secretive about her meeting.

Chapter 4

Christian lowered his *Express*, in which he'd been reading the latest war news, and frowned to hear the raised voices through in the bar. What was going on?

Maizie suddenly appeared, eyes blazing with excitement. 'Have you ever seen a shark?' she queried.

Christian shook his head.

'Well, now's your chance to see hundreds of them if you wish.'

'Hundreds!' he exclaimed.

'Just offshore. Basking sharks, huge blighters. I'm going out in Hookie's boat to get a proper look. Do you want to come?'

He threw the paper aside, the tranquillity of the morning gone. He couldn't help but be infected by Maizie's excitement. 'Count me in.'

'Let's go then.'

'I'll have to get a coat.'

'Don't worry. Hookie'll have something on board if you get cold. We won't be out that long anyway.'

They strode into the bar where Hookie and Alice were waiting. 'Is he on?' Hookie demanded.

Maizie nodded.

'Good for ee, Froggy. Good for ee. It'll be some sight I can tells ee.'

'Are you coming, Alice?' Christian inquired.

She pulled a face. 'Not me, me 'andsome. I ain't going swanning around no sharks. Besides, someone's got to stay behind. We can't just shut up shop you know.'

'Come on then, you lot!' Hookie declared, leading the way out of the door, Maizie and Christian hurrying after him.

They were swiftly down to the quay where Hookie's and several other boats were bobbing in the water. Within seconds the lines had been cast off and they were under way.

'Are basking sharks common round here?' Christian queried of Maizie.

'We see them from time to time. But a whole shoal is almost unheard of.' She shook her head. 'Though why on earth they've suddenly congregated like this here I can't think. Hookie!'

'No idea, Maiz. Just one of these odd things that happen I suppose. There must be a reason mind, though what it is is beyond me.'

The boat's engine was a muffled growl and Christian noted there was sailing gear in evidence. The boat could therefore run on either engine or sail. He could not help but think that must be useful if Hookie was a smuggler, as he suspected.

'There!' Maizie exclaimed, pointing ahead.

There were hundreds of them too, Christian marvelled, their fins quite visible. Beside him Maizie had started snapping with a box camera she'd brought along.

'There'll be another picture here for the bar,' she said. 'I'm bound to get one really good one.'

There were two crew members in addition to Hookie. Christian recognised John Corin but the identity of the other man was unknown to him.

'Pity 'tain't pilchards,' Hookie said, coming to stand alongside Maizie and Christian.

'Pilchards?' Christian queried.

'At certain times of the year we used to make a grand living out of thae,' Hookie informed him. 'They'd come in their millions and all you had to do was scoop them up. It was money in the bank when the pilchards were running.'

Christian frowned. 'Does that mean they don't any more?'

'Sad to say,' Hookie nodded.

'What happened?'

'You tell me. There's those say we overfished them, though I can't believe that's right. Maybe the water conditions changed. Who knows? But it's years since the pilchards ran round here.'

'There used to be a special lookout for them,' Maizie informed Christian. 'And when he spotted them he rang a bell. When that bell rang all pandemonium broke out. Every fisherman hared for his boat.'

'And they just stopped running?'

'For generations Coverack men fished the pilchards,' Hookie stated ruefully. 'And then it just stopped. A bad day that was right enough.'

'Look at the size of him!' Maizie gasped, pointing.

Merde alors! Christian thought. That wasn't a shark, it was a whale. It was enormous.

Hookie's eyes had narrowed. 'You have to watch them. They can capsize a boat if they has a mind to.'

'Capsize the boat!' Christian choked.

'That so. Even the smaller ones.'

Christian hadn't realised this would be dangerous, thinking he'd be quite safe on the boat.

Hookie laughed. 'Don't ee worry, monsewer. They won't eats you, thae's not that type of shark.'

Christian thanked God for that.

'I still wouldn't want to be in the water with them,' Hookie went on. 'Thae's real ugly bastards.'

For a moment Christian had a clear view of a head. Hookie

wasn't exaggerating. They were ugly. And very frightening, even if they wouldn't eat you.

'Ahoy!' Denzil Eustis called out from his boat about thirty yards off the port side.

'Ahoy!' Hookie yelled back.

'You take a photo for me, Maiz. I want one of those.'

Maizie waved that she'd comply.

'Never seen nothing like it in all me born days,' Denzil further shouted.

Hookie agreed by shaking his head in wonderment.

Christian shivered. He was cold and getting colder. A quiet word with Hookie and he disappeared to return with an old and battered reefer jacket that smelt strongly of fish and salt.

'Put that on. Ee'll warm you up,' Hookie declared.

A bath when he got back, Christian decided, slipping it on. He couldn't help but wrinkle his nose in disgust.

'You're a proper fisherman now,' Maizie teased.

He was about to reply he undoubtedly stank like one, then thought the better of it. That would be rude.

'I wanted to ask you something,' Christian said quietly to Hookie.

'What's that?'

'Is there any chance you could get me some real French coffee from the same place you might get those cigarettes?'

Hookie ran a hand across his bristly chin. ''Tis possible.'

'I'd be most obliged.'

'How much ee want?'

Christian had a quick think. 'A couple of dozen bags?'

''Twould cost ee.'

Christian remembered what Maizie had said. 'Maizie will do my negotiating for me.'

Hookie's face fell. 'That's the way of it, is it?'

'I'm afraid so.' Christian didn't really care what he paid

as long as he got the coffee. But why pay over the odds if he didn't have to? That would be silly.

'That's the way of it, Hookie,' Maizie suddenly interjected, having overheard the conversation.

Hookie slowly nodded. 'I ain't making no promises, mind. No matter the price.'

'I'm sure you'll do your best,' Maizie smiled sweetly, adding, 'I owe Christian a debt in case you're wondering.'

'I see.'

Hookie broke away when John Corin, at the wheel, called for him to come over.

'Thanks,' Christian said to Maizie.

'Don't mention it.'

They went back to watching the sharks.

'I got hot coffee for ee. I reckoned you'd need it!' Alice greeted them on returning to the hotel.

Maizie's face was flushed from cold, wind and pleasure. Christian was rubbing his hands.

'The very thing, Alice.'

Alice had laid out some cups and saucers and now began pouring. 'How was it?' she asked.

'Amazing. Truly amazing,' Maizie answered, wrapping her hands around one of the already filled cups.

'Maizie took lots of pictures so you'll be able to see for yourself,' Christian smiled.

''Twas a sight eh?'

'And a half,' Maizie responded.

'I think I'll have a cognac as well,' Christian declared, eyeing the bottle. 'Would you care to join me, ladies?'

Ladies! Alice preened to hear that. 'Not for me, thank you very much. I'd keel over this time of morning.'

Christian laughed. 'Maizie?'

'Do you know, I believe I will. It was a bit chillsome out there.'

Christian was amused to watch Alice get the bottle which was slightly out of her reach. She solved the problem by going on tiptoes and then sort of lurching forward. He reflected yet again how incredibly tiny she was.

Maizie and Christian had both plonked themselves on to adjoining stools. 'I wouldn't have missed that,' Christian enthused.

'Me neither. I doubt we'll see anything like it again in my lifetime.'

'Big buggers, eh?' Alice probed.

'Huge, Alice. Some of them fifty feet I'd say. Christian?'

He nodded. 'That's right.'

'Fifty feet!' Alice marvelled, and shook her head trying to imagine such a phenomenon.

'They're the second largest fish in the world,' Maizie commented knowledgeably.

Christian lifted an eyebrow. 'I didn't know that.'

'Neither did I till Hookie told me.'

'Well well,' he mused.

Maizie had a quick sip of the cognac Alice placed in front of her, closing her eyes in appreciation as its warmth coursed through her insides. She'd been even colder than she'd realised.

'Thank you for asking me along,' Christian stated quietly.

She reopened her eyes and stared at him, seeing him, somehow, in a totally different light which, momentarily, both jolted and confused her. 'You're welcome.'

Reaching across he briefly touched her hand. She felt as though she'd been scalded. 'I appreciate it. Today will be something to tell my children whenever they come along.'

Maizie's lips pursed and she turned away. Christian was

puzzled, then it dawned on him Maizie didn't have any. He berated himself for being so unthinking.

Maizie swallowed the rest of her cognac and rose. 'Things to do. I'm way behind now.'

'What about your coffee?' Alice queried.

'I'll take it with me.'

Christian gazed after her retreating figure. He was finally roused out of his reverie by Alice. 'Another of thae congacs before I joins Maiz?'

He was surprised to see his glass was empty, having no recollection of drinking the contents. 'Please.'

'What's Sam Blackacre like?' he found himself inquiring.

Alice shrugged. 'All right.'

'Just all right?'

'Typical chap from hereabouts. No different to many. Older than Maizie.'

'Oh?'

'By eight or nine years. I can't remember which. It's his second marriage.'

That was interesting. 'Really?'

'First wife died. Pleasant maid she was too. That was a loss.'

'What did she die of?'

'In childbirth. The baba also. Sam was right broke up afterwards. Had proper black moods for a long time, which is understandable. Then he eventually took up with Maiz.'

She was talking too much, Alice suddenly thought. Gossiping. 'If you wants anything else just help yourself,' she declared.

And hurried after Maizie.

Maizie picked up the letter that had just landed on the front door mat, her heart sinking when she recognised Sam's handwriting.

Don't be so silly, she chided herself. She should be delighted to hear from him. It was just . . .

Read it now or later? She decided she'd take herself off to the far end of the dining room and open it there.

There were only two pages, but then Sam had never been much of a writer. He was in Liverpool where his ship was having a quick turnaround. He'd then be back to sea for at least another couple of months. He was due leave when he returned from that voyage and all going well he'd be down to see her.

He mentioned a few locals, asking how they were. And he hoped she was coping all right with the hotel. At the end of the second page he mentioned briefly he'd been to New York, but didn't elaborate.

Maizie dropped the letter into her lap, and sighed. He was a good man, she reminded herself. She had no complaints. So then why wasn't she pleased to hear from him? Or at the prospect of seeing him again before too long?

She gazed out over the Channel. Was this to be it for the rest of her life? Married to Sam Blackacre and living in Coverack?

She loved Coverack and the surrounding area. It was in her blood and bones the way it was with all the locals. Yet still she yearned for more.

Marriage to Sam had seemed the right thing at the time, Sam being keen on her. He had turned out to be an even better catch than she'd imagined. After all, who would have guessed he'd be left all that money? There had been much envy when that had happened. A few spiteful things had been said that were best forgotten about.

So were Coverack and this hotel her lot till the end of her days? It could be worse, she reflected. A lot worse. There were many who would have given their eye teeth to be in her position. So what did she have to complain about or regret? Nothing, nothing at all. And she should never forget that.

There was just one flaw in this argument, she thought bitterly. She didn't love Sam and never had.

When he'd proposed she'd imagined she'd come to love him in time. But that had never happened. Nor could she accuse herself of not trying; she had. It was simply that Sam wasn't a very loveable man.

He didn't give the affection she so craved. The little things – the touching, caressing, the cherishing. Things women need and she so longed for.

Maizie took a deep breath. This would get her nowhere. As the saying went, she'd made her bed and now she had to lie in it.

But a cold bed it could be. Even when Sam was in it with her.

Christian had been lying awake for over an hour. He'd been dreaming of Dunkirk again and it was that which had awakened him.

He thought of Hennebont and wondered for the umpteenth time what was happening there. Were his parents all right? He prayed with all his heart they were.

Dear Maman, she was the one to worry about. That fiery temper of hers could land her in all sorts of trouble with the Boche if she wasn't careful.

He smiled, picturing her in his mind. Seeing her as she'd been years ago when he was little. A tall, proud woman who'd idolised him, her only child. Idolised maybe, but that hadn't meant she'd spoilt him. Not one bit of it. She'd been strict, without being overly so. And always, always fair.

And then there was Papa. Philippe Le Gall, owner of a small, but very successful, engineering factory employing over twenty people. Papa, who'd been dreadfully disappointed when Christian had announced he had no interest in the factory and intended pursuing an entirely different career.

Philippe may have been disappointed, but had never made a meal of that disappointment. On the contrary, Philippe had encouraged his son to do as he wished. To follow his heart.

Please God they hadn't come to any harm, nor would. That they'd see the war out safely and be waiting for him when he finally returned home. When the nightmare was over and the Germans had been kicked out of France.

Christian glanced at the bedroom window, wondering if he should shut the curtains as the darkness might help him to drop off again. It was a clear night with a full moon high in the sky. He decided to get up and have a cigarette while sitting by the window. There was no need for his lamp; the glow from the moon allowed him to see perfectly.

He slipped into his dressing gown and padded across to the window. Pulling a cane chair over from where it stood beside the wardrobe, he then sank into it, and lit up a cigarette.

What a strange place England was, he reflected. So very different to his beloved France. The sights, smells, people, were all quite, quite different, but despite those differences he liked it here. Especially Coverack.

He was still mulling over the English traits when he noticed a movement in the darkness below. Not an animal, it was too large for that, and completely the wrong shape.

Suddenly, for the briefest second, Maizie's face was illuminated by moonlight, gleaming palely against her black cloak which was wrapped tightly about her. And then she was gone.

Christian frowned. What on earth was she doing out and about at this time of morning? A secret meeting perhaps, a rendezvous?

He sighed, and dragged heavily on his cigarette. Maybe there was a man involved somewhere. Could that be it? She was having an affair? That could explain why she was out in the mist the day of his arrival. But not why she was carrying a pistol.

At least he'd thought she was carrying one, but couldn't be entirely sure. Then there was the time she'd vanished behind the rise in the ground. Was that connected with all this?

Christian shook his head, not knowing what to make of it all. It was a mystery. Mystery upon mystery.

And none of his business, he reminded himself. What Maizie got up to was her own affair. Even if that's what it was, an affair.

He sighed again, wondering why he was feeling as he was. There was a whole medley of emotions playing through him, many of which he couldn't analyse.

Whatever, it had nothing to do with him. Nothing at all. He was merely a guest at the hotel. Nothing more.

And yet . . .

Maizie cradled the telephone. 'Damn!' she swore vehemently.

'What's wrong?'

She glanced over at Christian sitting at the bar where he'd elected to have his after-lunch coffee. 'There's a meeting been called for tonight in the village hall and that was someone who works for me saying she can't come in because she's down with flu.'

'And you want to go to this meeting?'

'I should.'

'What about Alice?'

Maizie shook her head. 'Alice loathes bar work. Probably because she has trouble reaching everything. Though no doubt she'll cover for me if I'm absolutely desperate. But I hate to ask her. Besides, she'll want to go to this meeting too.'

Christian had an idea. 'If that's the way of things, then how about me?'

'You!' Maizie exclaimed.

'Why not? I'm available and only too happy to lend a hand. I've worked a cash till before and it shouldn't be too difficult to draw a pint. Also the prices are clearly marked, so what about it?'

Maizie slowly smiled, bemused by the suggestion. It would certainly solve her problem. 'Under different circumstances I could easily find a replacement but they'll all be at this meeting – it's been called as a matter of urgency. Everyone will be there.'

'In which case I probably won't have to serve anyone!'

That was true, she thought. It was doubtful he would. And she'd be straight back directly the meeting was over. 'You're a gem, Christian.' She beamed at him.

'I take it that means yes.'

'Indeed it does.'

'What time do you want me on duty?'

'A quarter to eight all right?'

'I've no plans to be anywhere else,' he joked. 'A quarter to eight it is.'

The door flew open and Maizie came hurrying in. 'There's a whole pile of folk behind me gasping for a drink. How did you get on?'

She was flushed, which Christian decided rather suited her. 'Absolutely fine. A couple turned up asking for accommodation and I've installed them in number five. I told them what the tariff was, showed them round and they pronounced themselves quite satisfied. They inquired about food and I said they were too late for that. A main meal that is. However, if they came down later I was sure you'd make them a plate of sandwiches. Was that OK?'

She gaped at him. 'You have been busy. I'm impressed.'

He shrugged in that special Gallic way, secretly pleased

to hear her say that. 'It was nothing. They're a Mr and Mrs Vanstone, by the way. Down from Exeter. They wish to stay a week.' He paused, then winked salaciously. 'I don't think they're really married.'

'How do you make that out?'

'I don't know. They didn't quite act as a married couple should. Why, is that a problem?'

Maizie shook her head. 'Not in the least. We get more of those than you might imagine.'

'But I thought the English didn't go in for such things?' He was testing now, watching her reaction.

'Don't you believe it! We just happen to be more discreet than other nationalities about such matters.'

'Ah!' Now that was interesting.

'Four pints there, Maiz!' Denzil shouted, barging through the door with others crowding at his heels.

'Shall I stay on here?' Christian queried. 'At least while you're busy?'

'It would be a great help.'

What a kind man, she thought. And lovely with it. Perfectly charming.

'Yes, Mr Repson?' Christian smiled a few moments later, the bar rapidly filling.

Hookie blinked. 'What you doing there, Monsewer?'

'Serving, as you can see.'

Hookie snorted. 'Whatever next. A Froggy barman!'

Christian didn't take offence as he knew there was none intended. It was only banter. 'So?'

'A pint of best bitter then.'

'Coming up.'

Maizie snicked the last bolt home, straightened, and swept a strand of hair from her eyes. 'I'm glad that's over.'

'How did I do?'

'As though you'd been a barman all your life. You can have a job here any time you like.'

He laughed. 'I wouldn't mind taking you up on that.'

She regarded him quizzically. 'Are you serious?'

It surprised him how tired he was now that the excitement was over. He hadn't realised bar work was so strenuous. And his leg ached, which he wasn't going to mention in case it upset her. 'Not really, I suppose. It's just that Coverack is like a dream you can easily be caught up in. What is the English expression? Land of the Lotus Eaters, I seem to recall. Yes, it's a bit like that. A dream, a fantasy. But, for me anyway who doesn't live here, hardly reality.'

'Well well,' she murmured. 'You are waxing lyrical. That was a Frenchman speaking.'

'I should hope so. I am French after all!'

He had been good behind the bar, Maizie reflected. And the villagers had taken to him. That Gallic charm again. 'Now, what about a drink on the house? You certainly deserve one. We both do.'

'Everyone seemed to be talking about children tonight. Was that what the meeting was about?'

Maizie slid a generous cognac in front of him. 'We're about to have two dozen or more Plymouth children descend on us, evacuees. They're being sent here on account of the bombing there.'

He nodded. 'It's bad.'

'Terrible by all accounts.'

'Many people killed. A lot of property destroyed and damaged.'

Maizie had a gulp from the glass of cognac she'd poured for herself. 'Bloody Germans!' she swore. 'Anyway, we'll be looking after these children for the foreseeable future.'

'We?' he queried.

'I've agreed to take two of them. Well, why not? I have plenty of room after all, which others don't.'

He smiled. 'They'll keep you busy and no mistake.'

'I've no doubt. But we'll cope, Alice and I that is. Between the pair of us we'll manage somehow.'

'They'll certainly disrupt your life.'

Her expression became wistful. 'I haven't been blessed with any of my own so far, as you know. It'll be nice having some youngsters about. Liven the place up a little. Sometimes in winter it can be like the grave in here.'

'I'm sure you'll do very well and they'll enjoy their stay. I'm certainly doing so.'

'You're hardly an evacuee or child,' she retorted.

He looked down into his drink, suddenly troubled. His good humour vanishing. 'Evacuee? Perhaps I am, considering the circumstances.'

She realised then the *faux pas* she'd made. 'I'm sorry, Christian. I wasn't thinking.'

'It's all right.'

They spoke for a little while longer about the imminent arrival of the children, and then both went to bed.

His last thought before drifting off was to wonder if she actually had gone to bed or had sneaked out again to meet up with her lover. And if so, had that lover been in the bar earlier?

Chapter 5

'Here they come!' Alice exclaimed excitedly. She and Christian were standing just outside the hotel watching the arrival of the bus from Plymouth that was bringing the evacuees.

'A boy and girl from the looks of it,' Christian observed.

Alice glanced up at the heavy grey sky. 'I hopes it don't rain. 'Twould be a pity that. Give thae mites the wrong impression of Coverack.'

Christian laughed. 'I hardly think so considering the amount of rain we've had recently.'

''Tain't been that bad!' Alice protested.

He tickled her under the chin. 'I was only pulling your leg, little one.'

Maizie, who was in the main welcoming group, waved to them.

'I wonder what they'll be like?' Alice mused.

'We'll soon find out.'

'I hope thae's hungry. We've prepared enough grub to feed an army.'

Christian thought of Maizie and Alice who'd been bustling around madly all morning. You'd have thought Mr Churchill himself was coming to stay.

The boy had a surly look to him, Alice noted as Maizie

and her charges got closer. Please God he wasn't going to be trouble.

'Let's go inside,' Christian suggested.

'I's ever so nervous,' Alice confessed.

'Why? They won't be living with you.'

'I's nervous all the same. I will have a lot to do with them after all. I's also nervous for Maizie. 'Tis a big step taking on two youngsters. Especially when you've no experience in the matter.'

'I'm sure you'll keep her right,' Christian commented drily.

'This is it, children,' Maizie declared as the threesome came through the door. 'The Paris Hotel. Your home from home for the time being.'

The boy glanced about him, and sniffed.

'Alice, come and meet Bobby and Rosemary Tyler. They're brother and sister.'

Alice could see that now. There was no mistaking they shared the same parentage. 'Hello,' she beamed, crossing to them.

'And children, this is Alice Trevillick who works here and is also my good friend. You can call her Mrs Trevillick.'

'Hello, Mrs Trevillick,' the girl said pleasantly enough.

'How was your journey, my lover?'

Rosemary giggled. My lover indeed! How funny to be called that. 'Fine, Mrs Trevillick.'

'I want to pee,' Bobby suddenly announced.

'Ah!' Maizie exclaimed. 'Come with me and I'll show you where the gents is.'

'Why don't I do that,' Christian interjected, thinking a boy Bobby's age would prefer a man to accompany him.

'Good idea,' Maizie agreed, cottoning on. 'Children, this is M'sieur Le Gall. He's French and a guest here.'

Rosemary's eyes opened wide. 'French. Gosh!'

'At your service, mam'selle.'

Rosemary giggled again and covered her mouth with both hands.

'Come along, Bobby,' Christian said, and led the way.

They were both so filthy, Maizie was thinking. That had been something of a shock to her. And their clothes! Little better than rags, to say the least. They were going to have to be kitted out from scratch.

Maizie had another thought, and eyed Rosemary's hair suspiciously. She couldn't see anything but that didn't mean the hair wasn't lousy.

'Are you hungry?' Alice asked Rosemary.

'Starving.'

'Then I'll serve up.'

'After which it's a bath for you and Bobby,' Maizie stated firmly, desperately wondering where she could get some clothes to fit the pair of them.

Her troubles were only just beginning.

Christian laughed at Maizie's expression. 'Regretting it already, I take it?'

Maizie sighed wearily. 'Not really. But they are a handful. And to top it all they've both got nits.'

Christian frowned. That wasn't a word he knew. 'Nits?'

'Head lice. They're crawling.'

That was enough for someone who'd always been fastidious about his personal hygiene. 'I'm going out. I'll leave you to it.'

'Coward!' she teased.

'Not at all. They're hardly my responsibility. That's yours as you offered to have them.'

'I know. I'm well aware of the fact,' she replied quietly.

He took pity on her. 'Is there anything I can do?'

Maizie shook her head. 'But I might ask you to open up the bar later, if that's OK?'

'I don't mind. It'll be a pleasure.'

'Thanks, Christian,' she smiled. 'You're a gentleman.'

He had the sudden impulse to reach out and touch her, to stroke away the lines that had appeared on her face. Instead, he said, 'I'm off out then.'

'Enjoy yourself.'

'I'll try.'

Outside he checked the sky. The threat of rain had passed and it looked like staying that way. Several boats were heading into the harbour, one of them Hookie's, he noted.

He hoped they'd had a good catch.

Christian found himself walking towards the same rise in the ground that Maizie had disappeared behind. A good trick that, he reflected, wondering how she'd managed it.

Maizie had said she'd emerged from the other side and he just hadn't seen her. But he couldn't understand how that was possible. From his original vantage point, right up until he'd reached the rise, he'd had a clear view in all directions.

On reaching the rise he went behind it and then stopped. Rise in the ground was the wrong description, he thought. That was how it had appeared from where he'd been. In fact the ground rose and then fell away steeply, exposing a rockface with many pieces of broken boulders scattered about. It was a common enough sight in the area.

He hadn't approached the actual rockwall itself during his previous visit there and decided to do so now. It was about seven yards high, he reckoned, sheer in parts, sloping in others. And the length? About thirty yards or so.

He laughed out loud. This was silly! Maizie had to have been telling the truth. She'd simply re-emerged without his spotting her. That had to be the case. There was no other explanation.

He was turning away from the rockface when he noticed that one section seemed to jut out in front of another. Worth investigating, he decided, moving towards it, treading carefully over the debris underfoot.

He peered behind the jut and caught his breath. It was an entranceway of some sort. It didn't stop as he'd imagined it would, but went on into the rockface itself.

Was this where she'd gone? And if so, where did the entranceway lead?

Darkness closed round him as he went inside. He groped for his lighter and flicked it into life. A tunnel was revealed, a natural phenomenon by all appearances, about six inches higher than himself. He continued on, wishing he had a torch with him.

He could hear a drip of water somewhere, a steady plop plop plop. The air was clammy and had a musty, dank earthy smell about it.

After a bit he halted, thinking he daren't go any further in case his lighter ran out. He shivered, not from cold but because he found it all rather spooky.

Enough for the moment. Regretfully he began retracing his footsteps, wishing he could have followed the tunnel to its end.

Back outside he clicked shut his lighter, which was almost red hot, and sucked in a deep lungful of fresh air. Intriguing, to say the least. Fascinating actually.

An old smugglers' tunnel perhaps? It was a possibility. Then, thinking about Hookie, maybe one still in use by those selfsame people.

Which begged the question: was Maizie tied in with them in some way? Was that what all these mysteries were about? It would be an explanation. With the exception of that pistol, that is. There again, that could also be tied in in some way but he just couldn't see how.

One thing was certain. He was coming back. And next time he'd have a torch with him.

'There you are, Mr Vanstone,' Christian smiled, placing a port and lemon beside the pint he'd already poured. Going to the till he marked the drinks up on the Vanstones' bill.

Maizie appeared and slipped behind the bar. 'Thanks, Christian. I'll take over now.'

'How are things upstairs?' He was referring to the children.

'Alice is with them, the three of them playing Snakes and Ladders. That should keep them quiet for a while.'

'How about the nits?'

'Sshhh!' she retorted fiercely, but quietly. She glanced over at the Vanstones, the only customers present, then back at Christian. 'We'll keep that to ourselves if you don't mind.'

He grinned. 'I understand.'

'It's in hand. I cut their hair and then liberally applied black soap. In the morning I'll use a nit comb to get rid of the dead bodies and then wash their hair again.'

'You cut Rosemary's hair as well?'

'She wasn't best pleased, I can tell you. But it was the only thing to be done.' Maizie sighed. 'They're so wild the pair of them, and cheeky with it. Especially Bobby. There have been a couple of times today I've almost slapped him.'

Christian raised an eyebrow. 'That bad, eh?'

'Worse. They have no manners whatsoever. You should see them eat! It's disgusting.'

Maizie had taken on a lot more than she'd bargained for, Christian sympathised. 'How did you get on about the clothes?'

'Alice managed to scrounge suitable ones, I'm happy to say. Secondhand of course, but perfectly adequate.' Maizie shook her head. 'You should have seen the state of the bath after they'd been in it. It took Alice ages to get it clean again.'

'They'll settle down in time. They're probably frightened half to death if you think about it. Taken away from their parents and where they were brought up, dumped here in a strange place with a woman they'd never seen before today. We should try to see their side of things.'

'You're right,' Maizie agreed. 'I hadn't thought of it that way.'

They both glanced upwards when there was a crash from upstairs. 'What now!' Maizie exclaimed angrily.

'It sounds like they've broken something. You go on up again, I'll stay here.'

Muttering to herself Maizie hurried off to investigate.

'An *Express* please.' It had become Christian's daily morning habit to stroll down to the village shop and pick up a newspaper. Maizie had said she could have it delivered but he preferred to collect it himself.

And a weird and wonderful shop it was too. Christian had never before come across the like. There was merchandise stacked everywhere, to such a degree it was difficult to move up and down the passageway. A lot was old stock too by the looks of it. Some of the boxes were quite ancient.

'And what can I be doing for ee?' Mr Ayres, the proprietor, leered, pretending he hadn't heard. He always leered at Christian, eyes laughing, as though he was party to some private joke. Christian disliked the man intensely.

It was the same every morning, Christian sighed inwardly. Ayres asked him what he wanted and he replied an *Express* newspaper. You'd think Ayres would have learnt by now. There again, and he knew he was right, Ayres was, as the English say, taking the piss. Christian couldn't help but wonder if he was like that with all his customers. Probably only outsiders to the village, he'd decided.

'An *Express* please,' he repeated.

Ayres grunted, picked up the requested paper and placed it in front of Christian. 'Anything else?'

'Do you have such a thing as a torch?'

Ayres blinked. This was new. A break in the pattern. 'A torch you say?'

'That's right.'

Ayres eyed Christian suspiciously. 'What ee want a torch for?'

Christian fought back the urge to tell Ayres to mind his own damned business. 'It's to keep in the car,' he lied. 'I lost the one I had.'

Ayres grunted again. 'Why does ee keep a torch in the car?'

The man was simply infuriating, not to mention nosy in the extreme, and impertinent with it. 'In case I break down at night-time. Keeping a torch for such purposes is quite common practice.'

Ayres nodded. 'Makes sense I suppose.'

'So do you have one?'

'Oh yes.' Ayres scratched his thinning hair. 'Somewheres that is. Now let me think.'

'Would you like me to call back tomorrow?' This was delivered ever so slightly sarcastically.

'No no, I'll finds it. Just give me a moment, that's all.'

This could take for ever, Christian thought, picking up his newspaper and glancing at the headlines. The main story was about the ongoing Battle of the Atlantic; another that Roosevelt had denied he planned going to war.

Ayres came out from behind his counter and shuffled off down the shop. It amused Christian to see he was wearing carpet slippers that were trodden down at the heel. The slippers might have belonged to Methuselah.

Ayres studied a stack of boxes, scratched his head again, then moved further off down the passageway. Minutes passed before he collected a small set of steps and placed them in front of a stack. He laboriously climbed the steps.

'Small torch or large one?' he called out.

'Large.'

A box was removed, rummaged in, and a torch produced. 'How's this?' Ayres queried, waggling the torch at Christian.

'It'll do.'

Ayres grunted, replaced the top and put the box back where he'd taken it from.

'That's thirty shillings,' he declared eventually when he was again behind the counter.

That was an outrageous price! Well over what it should have been. 'Rather expensive, wouldn't you say?'

Ayres shrugged. 'Maybe. But you'll have a long ways to go before ee can buy another.'

Christian would have loved to have got hold of his scrawny neck and squeezed. 'I'll need batteries as well.'

'Ee never mentioned batteries!'

'The torch isn't much good without them,' Christian retorted tartly.

'But ee never mentioned them all the same.'

Patience, Christian counselled himself. Patience. He didn't reply.

Ayres glared at him, a glare Christian recognised to be quite false, then came out from behind the counter once more and shuffled off down the passageway.

When he finally emerged from the shop Christian was seething. But he had his torch and batteries which was all that mattered.

*   *   *

He'd return to the tunnel after lunch, Christian thought, as he strode along the road towards the hotel. That would give him the entire afternoon in which to explore.

He came up short when he spotted Bobby sitting on some rocks that bounded the quay. Now what was he doing down there? Fortunately the tide was out and he was in no danger of a soaking.

Bobby looked up as Christian approached him. 'What do you want?'

It certainly wasn't his day for encountering good manners, Christian reflected. The boy's tone left a lot to be desired.

'I thought I'd join you. Do you mind?'

'Yes I do. I want to be alone.'

Christian ignored that and stared out over the Channel. 'France is just beyond there,' he declared, pointing. 'I get quite homesick thinking about it.'

That caught Bobby's attention. 'Do you?'

'Oh yes. And one day I'll return to help kick out the Germans. It's a day I can hardly wait for.'

'How you going to do that then? You're no soldier.'

'Oh but I am. A Second Lieutenant in the French Army.'

'Then where's your uniform? All soldiers wear uniforms.'

Christian was studying Bobby's face. A pug face, was how he'd have described it. And definitely cheeky. He had a small upturned nose and bright, inquisitive eyes. There was a faint spattering of freckles on both cheeks. A proper little town urchin, Christian decided. He'd seen many similar in Rouen. 'Mine is at the hotel. I'm wearing civilian clothes because I'm on leave. I was wounded at Dunkirk.'

Bobby's expression changed to one of respect. 'How badly wounded were you?'

'I was hit in the leg. Nothing serious. It's more or less

healed now. I'll be going back to rejoin my unit shortly.'

'My dad's in the army. The *British* Army,' Bobby announced proudly.

'Really!'

'He's out in the Far East somewhere. He couldn't say exactly where in his letter because he wasn't allowed.'

Christian nodded that he understood. 'Has he always been a soldier?'

'Naw. He was a coalman before the war.' There was a choke in Bobby's voice when he said that.

'As I mentioned earlier, I'm homesick too,' Christian stated quietly. 'It's perfectly normal.'

'I don't want to be here. I want to be back in Plymouth,' Bobby declared, a firm set to his jaw.

'No doubt. But you've been sent to Coverack out of harm's way. For your own good.'

Bobby snorted.

'The bombing there is terrible.'

'I'm not scared of that!' Bobby retorted fiercely. 'The bombs don't bother me nothing.'

'You could be killed. Or worse . . .' He trailed off.

'How do you mean, *worse*?'

'Have your legs or arms blown off. Have you thought about that?'

Bobby went white.

'Or you could be blinded. That would be awful.'

Bobby swallowed hard, and didn't reply.

'So you see, you're safe here. Your mother did the wise thing in sending you.'

There was a pause, then Bobby said softly, 'I miss her. Even if she is hardly ever home. At least that's how it's been since Dad went off.'

'She leaves you alone quite a lot then?'

'She goes out with other blokes you see. Dad will knock

her block off if he finds out when he gets back. There'll be a right barney. She'll be in for a good hiding.'

Bobby didn't have to say any more, Christian had the general picture. How sad, he thought, remembering his own childhood which couldn't have been more caring and loving. His heart went out to the lad.

'Lots of other blokes?' Christian inquired softly.

Bobby nodded. 'I wish she wouldn't.'

Christian produced his cigarettes and absent-mindedly took one from the packet.

'Can I have a fag?'

Christian was shocked. 'No, you certainly can not. You're far too young.'

Bobby shrugged. 'Suit yourself. I'll get some somehow.'

'How long have you been smoking?' Christian queried, curious.

'Years and years.'

Christian smiled. He doubted that. 'Do you inhale?'

'Not much point if you don't, is there?'

The smile became a laugh. 'All right, take one. But for God's sake don't tell Mrs Blackacre. She'd be furious with me.'

Bobby accepted a light from Christian. 'Ta. These are better ciggies than I normally get. Willy Woodbines are smaller too.' He took a deep drag. 'She wants me to go to school. Well, I ain't going.'

'She?'

Bobby jerked a thumb in the direction of the hotel. 'Mrs Blackacre. She says Rosemary and I have to start Monday. Well, she can stuff that for a start. School's boring.'

Christian was frowning. 'But surely you went in Plymouth?'

'Naw. Mum thinks I did, but I didn't. Anyway, our school was hit early on in the bombing so nobody really knows where anyone is nowadays. To do with school that is.'

'But you'll have to go here,' Christian stated firmly. 'You mustn't neglect your education.'

'I don't need no more education. I can read, write and count well enough. The rest is all baloney.'

'Hardly baloney! You need an education to get on in life.'

'Not to be a coalman which I'm going to be when I grow up. A coalman just like my dad.'

There was a certain logic to the boy's argument Christian had to admit. Especially if he could already do what he said he could. 'Well you'll have to go while you're here and that's all there is to it.'

'I'll run away if they try and make me.'

'Where to?'

Bobby blinked. 'Away. Just away.'

'Not so easy, I'm afraid. Think about it. You saw the countryside during your drive down on the bus. Beyond the hill into Coverack there's miles and miles of moorland and farmland. And it's dark, very dark at night. You'd end up wandering around lost. Cold, hungry, and probably wet through. You wouldn't last long.'

Bobby digested that.

'It's not like Plymouth out there. No houses, or very few anyway, and no shops. You could well die from exposure which would be the end of Bobby Tyler. Such a waste, don't you agree?'

'I could make it,' Bobby replied, putting on a show of bravado.

'It would be extremely silly to even try. And whatever else you are, Bobby, you're not a silly lad. You're far too intelligent for that.'

Bobby glanced sideways at Christian, his expression one of cunning. 'You could take me? I'd be safe then.'

'But I won't. I'm not taking you back to all that dreadful

bombing. And even if I did, what about your sister? Would you abandon her?'

'She could come too.'

'But she might not want to. Look at what you've got here. A nice place to stay, a comfy bed, lots of good food. Not to mention beautiful surroundings. Oh yes, I think Rosemary would see things differently to you. Anyway, it doesn't matter for I'm certainly not taking either you or her.'

Bobby flicked the remains of his cigarette on to a patch of wet sand. 'I hate school,' he hissed.

'I always enjoyed it when I went. I thought it fun.'

'Fun!' Bobby snorted. 'That'll be the day.'

'Well, a lot depends on what you put into it. Just like life really. The more you put in the more you get out. That's what my father used to say, and he's right.'

This was clearly a new concept for Bobby who fell to thinking about that.

'It's almost lunchtime and I'm starving. How about you?' Bobby nodded.

'It's this sea air. Does wonders for the appetite. And Mrs Blackacre is such a good cook, don't you agree?'

'She's all right,' Bobby admitted reluctantly.

'Is your mother a good cook?'

'My mum's good at everything,' Bobby declared proudly.

I'll bet, Christian thought wryly, knowing what she was probably best at. 'Of course she is.'

The hint of a tear appeared in Bobby's eye which he swiftly dashed away. 'She said she'll write.'

'Then I'm sure she will. In the meantime, why don't you write to her? Tell her what it's like here. I'm sure she'd want to know.'

That enthused Bobby. 'I'll do so later.'

'And in the meantime it's stargazy pie.'

Bobby frowned. 'What's that?'

'A fish pie with the fish heads sticking out the top.'

Bobby was incredulous. 'You're pulling my leg!'

'That's what Mrs Blackacre told me. I must admit, it sounds a bit odd to say the least, but she assures me it's a local delicacy.'

'Fish's heads sticking out the top?' Bobby laughed. 'Do we eat those?'

'Well I shan't.'

'Me neither.' He made a face. 'Uuggg!'

'Shall we go on up then? And after we've eaten you can ask Mrs Blackacre for some paper and a pen.'

Bobby jumped to his feet. 'OK!'

Together, side by side, laughing and joking, mainly about stargazy pie, they made their way back to the hotel.

Christian felt he'd been walking for miles but was certain that was only his imagination playing tricks. Nonetheless, he had come a fair distance, and still the tunnel stretched ahead.

He stopped and sniffed. There was no doubt about it, he could smell the sea, which meant he must be getting close to the end.

A little further on the tunnel broadened out considerably for a number of yards, creating a space the size of a small room. In this space was a wooden table with several canvas-wrapped bundles on top, two lanterns and a wooden box stencilled WD. There were four chairs set round the table.

WD Christian knew meant War Department. Now what was this?

He picked the top bundle off the pile and squatted next to the table. When he unrolled the bundle a gleaming brand-new .303 Lee Enfield rifle was revealed.

Christian whistled softly to himself. More mystery. Why on earth would an army-issue rifle, and others presumably, be down here? Were the smugglers dealing in arms. Was that it?

'Has ee had a good look then?'

Christian whirled round to find a grim-faced Denzil Eustis staring at him from about a dozen feet away. Denzil was holding a pistol pointed straight at his belly.

'What is ee, a spy of some sort?' Denzil demanded in a harsh, grating voice.

Christian swallowed hard and, rising, started to explain.

Chapter 6

'In the tunnel!' Maizie exclaimed in horror.

'That's right. Claims ee followed you there.'

'I did. I even told you about it,' Christian interjected hurriedly.

'You never mentioned the tunnel.'

'Because I hadn't found it then. I did later and decided to investigate. I simply wanted to know how you'd managed to disappear that day the way you had.'

Christian gestured towards Denzil's pistol. 'Does he have to keep pointing that thing at me? It's been on my back all the way here.'

'You shuts your mouth,' Denzil snarled. 'You's lucky I didn't shoots you there and then.' He glanced at Maizie. 'I thought I'd best have orders before I did that.'

Orders! Christian wondered. 'Are you the leader of these smugglers then?' he queried of Maizie.

She frowned. 'Smugglers. What are you talking about?'

'Well, it seems to me that's what's going on. Smuggling arms in some way.'

Maizie laughed drily. 'You've got quite the wrong end of the stick, Christian. The tunnel has been used by smugglers in the past which is how we knew about it, and why it's so useful to our plans.'

Christian was lost. 'Well, if you're not smuggling, what are you doing?'

'We wuz told to kill anyone who found out about us, Maiz. They were quite plain regarding that.'

She sighed; this was indeed a quandary. One thing was certain, she wasn't going to sanction Christian's death. That would have been ludicrous. Though she was perfectly entitled to do so.

Christian had been fearful before, now he was even more so. 'Will someone please explain what's going on?' he pleaded.

Maizie made a decision. 'Put that pistol away, Denzil.'

'But, Maiz—'

'I said put it away.' This time her tone was steely. 'And you, Christian, sit down.'

She crossed to a cupboard, opened it and took out a bottle of whisky. 'I don't know about you two but I need a drink.'

'Please,' Christian croaked.

Denzil glared at Christian and, unlike Ayres the shopkeeper, this glare was for real. The pistol disappeared underneath the oilskin top he was wearing.

Maizie poured three large tots and handed them round. 'To the downfall of the Germans!' she toasted.

'May they all rot in hell for ever more,' Denzil added.

Christian had a quick swallow, grimacing slightly as the fiery liquid burnt its way down his throat. He'd much have preferred cognac.

Maizie perched herself on the edge of a worktop and studied Christian. 'You certainly have complicated matters,' she stated softly.

'I'm sorry.'

'Denzil's right, I should have you executed. Those are the orders. On the other hand you're a member of the French Army, allies. I just don't believe the orders apply to you.

At least, that's my interpretation of them. Of course it all depends on your swearing to keep your mouth shut.'

Christian nodded. 'You have my word. I swear by the honour of *La Belle France*.'

'That's good enough for me.'

Christian stared into his glass, then back at Maizie. 'So, are you going to tell me what this is all about?' he asked yet again.

'What I don't understand is why you were so interested in me in the first place?'

He laughed, a laugh that trembled a little at the thought of how horribly close he'd come to being killed. Thank God Denzil had chosen to speak to Maizie first.

'It was all the mysteries.'

'Mysteries?'

'The first time we met you were out in all that fog which seemed strange. Also the fact I thought I spotted you had a pistol. I wasn't certain about that, but it did appear to be one.'

Maizie regarded him thoughtfully. 'Go on.'

'Then there was you sneaking out at nights. I came to the conclusion you had a lover somewhere.'

A smile broke over her face. 'Did you indeed!'

'It seemed the obvious explanation. Then you just disappeared the way you did that day. That really made me curious.'

'And so you decided to investigate?'

'Exactly. I couldn't believe that I wouldn't have seen you re-emerge from behind that rise in the ground. And so I found the tunnel.'

'And then Denzil found you.'

'Examining one of thae Lee Enfields,' Denzil chipped in.

'Which led me to think you must be smuggling arms.' He pulled out his cigarettes and lit up.

'Quite the contrary,' Maizie replied. 'That's the beginnings of our cache.'

'Cache?'

There was a knock on the kitchen door which normally stood always open. 'You in there, Maiz?' Alice's puzzled voice queried.

'I'm having a private conversation, Alice. I'll be out again shortly.'

There was a pause, then Alice said, 'Are ee all right, maid?'

'I'm fine, thank you. I shan't be long.'

'Cache?' Christian repeated.

Maizie took a deep breath. 'This may sound like something out of a B-movie but Denzil and I are members of the British Secret Army.'

Christian slowly nodded.

'We're unofficially known as Auxiliary Units, unofficial because we don't officially exist. We've been formed to cause mayhem and havoc amongst the Germans should they succeed in invading.'

Christian finished off his scotch. He was fascinated. B-movieish yes, but it did make sense.

Maizie went on. 'We're formed into bands or cells, each operating locally. There are quite a number of us all along the Cornish coast where it's feared the invasion could take place.'

'It was Winston Churchill hisself who thought up the idea,' Denzil explained.

Christian held out his now empty glass. 'Could I have another please?'

'Denzil.'

The fisherman, whose glass was also empty, took Christian's, glanced at Maizie who shook her head, and then went to the bottle.

'We're to be well armed,' Maizie said. 'Sten guns, plastic explosive, timers, everything we may require. Those Lee Enfields are the first consignment to reach us.'

'A sort of Resistance, eh?'

'That's it. An underground movement.'

He nodded. 'Now I understand.'

'Each of us has pledged to fight to the death if needs be. And so we shall,' Denzil declared over his shoulder.

'We've signed the Official Secrets Act,' Maizie continued. 'That's required of every member.'

'And you've to kill anyone who finds out about you?'

'In the event of an invasion there might be collaborators. Horrible to think, but it could well be. Collaborators who would betray us. And so we've been sanctioned, in the name of secrecy, to kill anyone who does find out.'

'Which *you* have,' Denzil growled, giving Christian his refill.

'I'm hardly a collaborator!' Christian protested.

'Quite,' Maizie responded. 'Hence my reason for letting you live.'

Christian was seeing Maizie in an entirely new light, for he had no doubt she would have ordered his execution if she'd thought it was required. There was a ruthlessness in her he hadn't before suspected.

'Can I have one of your cigarettes?'

'Of course.' He hastily rose and went to her, offering his packet. Her eyes never left his as he helped her to a light.

'And just who did you think was my lover?' she queried softly.

'I honestly had no idea.'

Her gaze flicked to Denzil. 'I think that's that then. You may as well be on your way.'

Denzil saw off his whisky. 'I got nets need repairing before I goes out again. That'll keep me busy for a while. Until tonight as arranged?'

'I'll be there. As will the others I'm sure.'

'You're a lucky Frog,' Denzil declared to Christian. 'You could have been fish feed by now.'

Christian blanched. 'Thank you for consulting Maizie. And I mean that sincerely.'

Denzil grunted and departed, leaving the kitchen door wide open.

'You must never mention this,' Maizie warned Christian.

'I gave my word. I won't.'

'See you don't then.' Maizie suddenly smiled. 'I must say I'm flattered.'

'About what?'

'You thinking I had a lover. That quite tickles my fancy.'

'It seemed an obvious explanation.'

'Yes, I can understand that.' She took a deep breath. 'I'll finish this fag and then I must be getting on. I have a hotel to run.'

A curious Alice appeared. 'Have you finished your conflab then?'

Conflab wasn't a word Christian knew but he could guess its meaning. When he looked again at Maizie that innocent expression was back in her eyes. An expression he was coming to know rather well.

'I got thae pheasants to pluck. Shall I start on them?' Alice asked Maizie.

'Go ahead. I'll cook them tomorrow.'

'Right.'

'And where's Rosemary?'

'Gone to bed saying she was tired. Though I don't sees how the maid could be.'

'I'll go and tell her to come down and help you. You can show her what to do with the pheasants.'

'Oh she'll love that!' Alice cackled. 'She being a city girl and all. She'll probably run screaming.'

'And when you've finished with the pheasants you can gut and dress the salmon that arrived earlier.'

Alice slapped her thigh. 'Even better. I can't wait to see her face. It'll be a proper picture.'

'No doubt,' Maizie commented drily, stubbing out her cigarette.

A rather shaken Christian wandered through to the bar where he poured himself a cognac. One good thing had come out of all this. He'd learnt that Maizie didn't have a lover after all.

For some reason that pleased him enormously.

'That's them off,' Denzil announced, rejoining the others in the tunnel. 'I certainly don't envy them the drive to Helston. It's chucking down outside.'

Maizie surveyed the many boxes that the lorry had brought them and which they'd just finished lugging to what had become their command centre, the place Christian had discovered.

'I think we've done enough for now,' Maizie declared wearily. 'We'll start sorting things out tomorrow night.'

Cyril Roskilly, a local farmer and member of the group, turned to Maizie. He was a middle-aged man with a slightly florid complexion and a body prone to corpulence. 'I wants to speak to ee, Maizie.'

She groaned inwardly, knowing this was trouble. It always was where Roskilly was concerned. He'd never got over the fact she'd been elected head of the group and not himself, he thinking that as a farmer and the most prominent person amongst them that honour should have been his. It was also obvious he absolutely loathed taking orders from a woman.

'And what's that, Cyril?'

'Denzil here has been telling me about the Frenchman staying at your hotel finding this tunnel.'

'That's right.'

'You should have shot him out of hand. Orders is orders.'

Maizie gave Denzil a reproving glance. Trust him to go and open his big mouth. Still, it was only to be expected. For Denzil too disapproved of what she'd done. He hadn't mentioned so since meeting up with her again that night, but it was obvious that was how he felt.

'It was my decision,' she replied firmly.

'And the wrong one in my opinion.' Roskilly looked round the others for support.

'What's this then?' John Corin demanded.

Maizie explained.

'Bloody Ada!' Charlie Treloar, another fisherman, exclaimed.

Roskilly puffed out his chest, an irritating habit he had when opining. 'I says he should still be killed. Those were the orders from London.'

'He's a French soldier and officer, an ally,' Maizie pointed out. 'He's no danger to any of us. Anyway, in a short time he'll be gone, back to Plymouth and his people there.'

Roskilly saw this as a possible way of deposing Maizie as leader. 'And what if he talks to them. Or anyone else come to that?'

'He won't. He gave me his word.'

'His word,' Roskilly sneered. 'Who'd believe the word of a Frenchman?'

'I would,' Maizie snapped back. 'I know the man. He'll keep his mouth shut and that's an end of this.'

'*Know* him?' Roskilly said slyly, voice filled with innuendo. 'And what exactly does that mean?'

Maizie coloured. 'Get your mind out of the gutter, Cyril Roskilly. That's uncalled for. Shame on you.'

'I said nothing,' he answered, pretending surprise.

'You insinuated.'

'Did I indeed?'

'Yes you did. And I won't have insinuations like that. If I was to tell Sam when he gets home he'd be calling on you.'

Fear tinged Roskilly's face for he was scared of Sam Blackacre who'd have made mincemeat of him. 'There's no need for that,' he protested.

'The Frenchman lives and that's final. He's no threat to either us or the movement. I'm not having a decent chap killed for fuck all. Understand?'

Her swearing shocked all of them. Especially the use of that particular profanity.

Roskilly glanced down at the ground, highly embarrassed 'As you say, Maiz, it's your decision. The responsibility lies with you.'

'Agreed.' Her eyes swept all present. 'Agreed, Denzil?'

'Agreed, Maiz,' he replied sheepishly.

'If that's all then let's be getting on our way. It's been a long night,' Phil Carey declared. He was another fisherman who also kept sheep on a smallholding that had come to him through marriage.

Maizie took a deep breath. Damn that Cyril Roskilly, he was a born troublemaker always moaning on about something. She wished he'd never joined the group.

'That was telling them, Maiz,' John Corin whispered to her as they were returning along the tunnel.

At least that made her smile.

Maizie turned slightly to get a better look at herself in the full-length mirror. It was no use, she thought in despair. She'd been born with a big bum and, no matter what she did, that was how it remained.

In the past she'd tried diets, exercising, in fact everything she could think of, all to no avail. Her bum remained stubbornly big.

Sam liked it, mind you, said it gave him something to hold on to. The sort of thing he would say. He also enjoyed smacking it, a practice that had at first horrified her when he'd suggested it. No, suggest was the wrong word, he'd more or less insisted. Still, he didn't do it every time, just once in a while when the mood took him. She hated when he did that to her, feeling quite humiliated. And it hurt. No light, playful taps from Sam, but a right hearty whack, occasionally with his full force behind the blow. Once he'd bruised her so badly the marks had remained for nearly a fortnight. Afterwards he'd promised never to be that heavy-handed again. A promise he'd, thankfully, so far kept.

Maizie put her rear, the bane of her life, out of her mind and crossed to the window. There were Christian and Bobby on the quay, the pair of them fishing with rods she'd supplied.

Maizie smiled. Christian had promised to teach Bobby how to fish even though he knew nothing about it himself. If they managed to catch anything it would be down to sheer luck rather than skill.

Now was the time, she told herself. Christian would be on the quay for another half hour at least, probably longer. Striding from her bedroom she walked to his, which she opened using her master key.

She didn't care much for what she was about to do, but it was a necessity. She had to be absolutely one hundred per cent certain Christian was who he said he was. He had arrived in a French uniform, but so what? She could have put on a nun's habit but that wouldn't have made her one.

She started with the drawers, carefully going through each one, ensuring that she left each one looking undisturbed. In the last she found documents that confirmed his identity.

They seemed perfectly genuine and in order to her.

It was with relief that she replaced them exactly as they'd been, before closing the drawer again. She then moved to his suitcase which he'd stored on top of the wardrobe.

She found the photograph in a stretchy material pocket. It was of a young woman about Christian's age smiling into the camera. She guessed correctly this must be Marie Thérèse whom he'd once mentioned.

The girl was pretty, very much so, with masses of thick curly hair. There was no mistaking her to be French; there was something about her features that made them undeniably so.

Maizie sighed as she studied the photograph which was of head and shoulders only, feeling quite old and plain by comparison. She'd have bet anything Marie Thérèse didn't suffer from the drawback of having a less then petite bum!

Enough, she told herself, replacing the photograph. She'd seen everything she needed to. Christian was who he said he was, the proof of the documents verifying that.

She slid the suitcase back on top of the wardrobe, glanced round the room to make sure everything was as it should be, then left, relocking the door behind her.

For the rest of that day she couldn't get the image of Marie Thérèse out of her mind.

'So how was school today?' Christian inquired of Bobby as he and Rosemary burst into the hotel.

Bobby pulled a face.

Christian laughed. 'Go on, I'm sure it wasn't as bad as that!'

The truth was that Bobby, much to his amazement, was rather enjoying the local school. This was entirely down to his teacher, Miss Hitchon, who had the gift of making any type of lesson interesting, even those that were normally tedious and boring. Bobby had become quite a fan of Miss Hitchon.

Bobby shrugged. 'It was all right, I suppose.'

Alice appeared as though from nowhere. 'Come and help in the kitchen, Rosemary, I got some things for ee to do.'

'I have homework, Mrs Trevillick,' Rosemary replied glibly, hoping that would excuse her from kitchen chores.

'Don't matter, my lover. Plenty of time left over for that later.'

Rosemary giggled; she'd never get used to being called 'my lover', no matter what. Her pals back in Plymouth would roar when she told them about it.

'Have you got homework too?' Christian asked Bobby, who nodded affirmation.

'I'm starting to learn French next week,' Bobby suddenly announced.

'*Français. Très bien!*' Christian exclaimed, delighted.

'I thought you might help me when I do. You being French that is.'

'Ahh!' Christian sighed. 'I'd be only too happy to. But I shan't be here much longer.'

Bobby's face fell, for he'd become quite attached to Christian in the short time they'd known one another, considering him fun. 'Do you have to go?'

'I'm afraid so, Bobby. I'm a soldier, don't forget, and there's a war on.'

'I know that but . . .' Bobby trailed off.

'I don't want to leave. I love it here. But unfortunately that doesn't come into it.'

Bobby turned away so Christian couldn't see his face. He tried to speak, but couldn't, the words clogging his throat. Hurrying past Christian, he fled upstairs.

'*Merde,*' Christian whispered to himself. That had been nasty, knowing that the boy had come to see him as something of a big brother. He felt quite wretched.

'Hey, Frenchman, I've got something for you.'

Christian hadn't been aware of Hookie entering the hotel, but there the man was coming towards him carrying two cardboard boxes with a large paper bag balanced on top.

Hookie placed the boxes and bag on Christian's table. 'The coffee, two thousand cigarettes and more cognac if ee wants it.'

Christian swiftly opened the bag to discover a jumble of Gitanes packets. With a hoarse cry he reached for one.

'Thae all right?' Hookie queried with an amused twinkle in his eyes.

'Absolutely perfect. I can't thank you enough.'

Christian lit a Gitanes and inhaled deeply. *That* was more like it, what he was used to. A smile of contented satisfaction wreathed his face.

Hookie named an overall price that was apparently only a fraction over what he'd have charged the locals. Surely Maizie wouldn't disagree with that?

'There you are,' Christian declared, placing notes on the table. 'And I won't take offence if you count it.'

Hookie grinned. 'I thinks I can trust ee. All the same, old habits die hard.' He picked up the notes and flicked through them, nodding at the total.

'Pleasure doing business with ee, monsewer.'

'And you, Hookie.'

A disappointed Christian replaced the telephone on its cradle. That was that then. He'd tell Maizie later when he could get her on her own.

That proved to be when Maizie closed, locked and barred the door, after serving a steady trickle of customers all night long.

Christian gestured to the stool beside his. 'Will you join me for a moment?'

Maizie sat, brushing away a stray lock of hair as she did so. 'You look proper down in the dumps,' she commented.

'Do I?'

'Your face has been tripping you all evening.'

He laughed. 'I'm sorry.'

'Something wrong?'

'Very much so I'm afraid,' he replied slowly.

She regarded him with concern.

'I have to leave in the morning. Go back to Plymouth.'

She glanced down at the carpet. 'I see.'

'I hate to go.'

'We'll miss you. You've become almost part of the furniture.'

What a quaint language English was at times, he reflected. Part of the furniture indeed! Still, it was most expressive. 'Yes,' he agreed. 'That's exactly how I feel.'

She would miss him too, Maizie thought. Which was unusual for her where a guest was concerned. Mostly they just came and went and were soon forgotten. Not so with Christian; it would be a long time before he was just a dim memory.

Reaching out he touched her hand, then swiftly moved his own away again. He attempted a smile but somehow it didn't come out quite right.

'Wait here,' Maizie said, and hurried off.

Christian lit a Gitane; sheer bliss! He wondered why she'd left. A few moments later she returned brandishing a bottle of champagne.

'I too bought some stuff from Hookie including a case of this. I think we should crack one now.'

'What a wonderful idea!' he exclaimed. 'I am honoured.'

'It's pink champagne, is that all right?'

'Fine.'

She smiled rather wickedly. 'I've never had pink champagne before. I thought it rather decadent.'

He laughed. 'Here, let me.'

Maizie went behind the bar and produced two flutes which she set in front of Christian. 'I hope it's cold enough.'

'Just right in my opinion. It spoils champagne if it's *too* cold.'

He could have removed the cork without popping it, but decided the latter way was better for the occasion. It popped splendidly, the cork flying off in a great arc.

'Let's hope you return one day,' Maizie toasted when she'd raised her glass.

'Let's hope so. I'd certainly like to.'

She could tell by his tone he meant that. She couldn't help herself blushing slightly.

'Hmmh,' he murmured. 'Delicious.'

Maizie closed her eyes. 'It has a definite taste about it. Like something . . . something I can't quite put a name to.'

'Try,' he urged.

Her eyes snapped open. 'I have it. Wild strawberries! Not cultivated ones, that's a different taste entirely. But yes, wild strawberries.'

He thought that was a brilliant description, and quite apt. He was about to comment on that when their eyes suddenly locked and what might have been a charge of electricity surged between them.

Maizie broke the spell by glancing away. 'I'll have your bill made up for you first thing as I presume you'll be having an early start?'

'Directly after breakfast, I'm afraid.'

He stopped the car on the brow of the hill so he could look back down over Coverack spread out below. His gaze fastened on to the white building with blue trim that was the Paris Hotel. There was a lump in his throat that felt the size of an egg.

The goodbyes had been difficult. With Bobby it had been bad; Maizie was a lot worse. And everything so trite between the pair of them. All show and pretence.

Yes, he would come back. If that was possible. But, as he'd said to Bobby, there was a war on and he was a soldier. So who knew what lay in store?

He'd hoped for one last glimpse, that she'd remained outside watching his departure. But there was no sign of her.

He remained there for a short while, sunk deep in thought and memory, before restarting the engine and continuing on his way.

Overhead a weak winter sun was shining brightly.

Chapter 7

'Maaiizz!'

The familiar voice stopped her dead in her tracks. She swung round, her jaw dropping open in astonishment.

Sam thundered across the floor and swung her into his embrace, his face alight with excitement. 'I'm home, me darling!'

His lips pressed against hers, his tongue hot, urgent and probing. He was squeezing her so tightly she could hardly breathe.

Breaking off from the kiss he held her at arm's length. 'By God, but you're a sight for sore eyes.'

'This is a surprise,' was all she could think of to say.

His barrel chest heaved with laughter. 'That's the way I wanted it. To surprise ee.'

Sam, home at last. Her feelings were mixed. 'Well I'm certainly that. Here, let me catch my breath. You've all but squeezed it out of me.'

'A sight for sore eyes,' he repeated. 'You can't imagine the times I've thought of ee.' He waved a hand. 'And here. The hotel and Coverack. And now here you be, you and thae. If I was a dancing man I'd do a jig I'm so happy.'

'You look well, Sam.'

'I am. In the pink, as they says. And so do you. Slimmer than I recall.'

That pleased her. 'Do you think so?'

'Most definitely. Not that I'd mind one way or t'other. You's always perfect for me.'

Flattery! What had got into him? He certainly had been away a long time.

He delved into the pocket of his black reefer jacket. 'I got ee a present, Maiz. Call it a Christmas one if you likes, though that's well past.'

He produced a maroon-coloured rectangular jewellery box which he handed her. 'Tell me what ee thinks of that.'

She gasped on opening it. 'A gold wrist watch, Sam!'

'All the way from Times Square in New York. It's a Waltham. The chap who sold it me swore it was one of the best money can buy. But there we are, nothing's too good for my Maizie.'

She was quite astounded. Sam was not normally a gift-buying person. Nor was he known for his generosity. 'It must have cost a small fortune, Sam.'

He nodded. 'Try it on. You can adjust the bracelet if she don't fit.'

But it did fit, and perfectly. It was the most beautiful, and expensive, personal item she'd ever owned. Receiving it hadn't exactly left her speechless, but she was the next best thing.

'How did you get to Coverack this time of week?'

'I took a private hire from Helston. We only docked at Liverpool early yesterday morning, and now here I be. Good eh?'

'You really are putting your hand in your pocket,' she teased.

'I only have ten days so I've got to make the best of them. Anyways, you can't spend cash away at sea where I mostly am.'

A hard gleam came into his eyes that she recognised of old.

She knew then what was coming next. 'Are you hungry? Shall I make you something to eat?'

'I's hungry all right, maid, but not for food. For ee.'

She managed to smile.

'Shall we goes upstairs?'

There was no refusing him in the circumstances. Besides, if she was honest, there was a need in her also. 'Let me have a word with Alice. Meanwhile you collect your duffel bag and I'll follow you up.'

'How is the old girl?'

'Right as rain. Never better.'

He took her by the chin. 'Now don't ee be long. You hear?'

'I won't, Sam. Quick as wink.'

He gave a throaty chuckle and went to where he'd tossed his duffel bag on entering the hotel. He paused for a moment to look at her once more, then bounded up the stairs.

Maizie lay staring at the ceiling while Sam snored beside her. She was dreadfully sore down there, her thighs aching from the pounding she'd taken. She felt bruised and raw inside.

Why couldn't he learn to be a little tender, treat her gently? Think of her and not just himself?

But that was Sam all over for you. Straight to the point and drive as hard as he could. Treating her as though she was no more than . . . well, a receptacle. Something, not even someone, to be used for his own satisfaction.

Love? That never came into it. Not as she understood the word anyway. It was shagging, pure and simple, and brutal shagging at that. She could have wept from self pity.

Reaching under the clothes she touched herself, and winced. She'd have a steaming bath later and soak till the water ran cold. A little cream on her thighs wouldn't go amiss either.

God, he was an animal. Were all men like that? It was a question she'd asked herself a hundred times. She couldn't believe it was so. Surely not? There had to be some who'd treat her body with respect if nothing else.

It wasn't that she was made of porcelain. Hardly that. She wasn't going to break in two. But all the same. He'd treated her, as he always did, as if she was some bought tart in a brothel. A nobody, there to provide a service. God, how she hated their laughingly called lovemaking. That was a joke where Sam was concerned.

At least he hadn't spanked her on this occasion. She had that to be grateful for, though no doubt he'd get round to that soon enough. It was guaranteed. Her bottom contracted in dread.

She'd never understood what pleasure he got out of that. How could he possibly enjoy hurting another person, his wife in particular?

She'd tried to get him to explain once but all he'd said was that it made him excited. Really got him going. There was a name for such a thing, sadism. Thankfully, in his case, spanking was as far as it went.

The watch was beautiful, and totally unexpected. Though, in truth, she'd have gladly traded it for one loving, caring cuddle. A genuine show of appreciation and affection. Cows would fly first, she thought bitterly.

Reaching out she picked up the watch and glanced at the time. With a sigh she swung herself out of bed.

'Where are you going?' Sam demanded as she wriggled into her skirt.

'I thought you were asleep.'

'Well, I'm awake now. So where are you off to? I ain't finished yet.'

'I'm afraid that's all there is for you, Sam. The children will be home shortly from school and I'll have to see to them.'

He sat upright. 'What children?'

She explained about the evacuees being sent to Coverack and how she'd agreed to take in two of them, a boy called Bobby and his sister Rosemary.

His face clouded with what might have been anger.

'I had to do it, Sam. They're no bother, honestly. A bit rough round the edges, I have to admit, but that's only because of the sort of home they come from. Underneath they're really good kids. I'm becoming quite attached to the pair of them. As I'm sure you will.'

'I didn't expect no kids,' he grumbled.

'Why don't you get dressed and come down and meet them?'

'I'd much rather be here with you.'

'And I with you,' she lied glibly. 'But needs must.'

'How old are they?'

'Bobby's ten, Rosemary twelve, soon to be thirteen.'

He digested that. It could have been worse, he thought. They might have been nippers forever running and screaming round the place. At those ages they should be reasonably quiet.

Maizie was fully dressed now. She crossed to a chest of drawers and checked her face. A few deft dabs with her powder puff, a fresh application of lipstick, and she was ready to take on the world.

'So are you coming down, Sam?'

'In a minute or two. I wants a pint.'

She left him sitting thoughtfully in bed gazing after her.

As is the way in villages, word had got round almost immediately that Sam Blackacre was back, so that evening a steady procession of cronies and friends showed up in the bar to celebrate the fact.

Maizie was delighted for they were doing their best business in ages. Pint after pint had been served, and now some of the men were on shorts. The night's takings were going to be excellent.

'Some of thae will be crawling home,' Trudy Curnow remarked to Maizie. She was a casual employee who helped Maizie out when necessary, mainly during the summer months when the holiday season was on. Trudy's husband was one of those sitting round Sam.

'Pissed as newts,' Maizie commented.

'Farts more like,' Trudy added, and laughed.

Sam was regaling those listening with tales of foreign ports he'd been to, including ones in America, and incidents that had occurred there. Although drunk, he was still being careful not to say anything incriminating. Nothing that would land him in trouble with Maizie.

Some of those present had also been in the Merchant Navy with stories of their own to tell. But for the most part it was Sam's night.

Maizie wiped a few beads of sweat from her brow, wondering if she dared nip into the back and have a cigarette from the packet she'd hidden earlier.

Her thoughts were interrupted by Denzil lurching up to the bar. 'A pint of scrumpy and a scotch please, Maiz,' he slurred.

'How are you doing, Denzil?'

'Thoroughly enjoying meself, Maiz. It's good to see Sam back again. And in one piece.'

She nodded as she began pulling his cider.

Denzil glanced about him to make sure they weren't being overheard. 'What about the Movement while Sam's here?' he queried quietly.

Her eyes flicked, also checking. 'I can't come out of an evening, Denzil, he'd want to know the whys and wherefores if I did.' Sam was completely unaware of her involvement with the Movement as it was strictly forbidden to tell anyone, even your nearest and dearest, about it.

'I understand, Maiz.'

'I can always be spoken to during the day, mind. Take any decisions that have to be made.'

'How long's he here for?'

'Ten days.'

'He'll be gone again before we knows it.'

Maizie placed the pint in front of Denzil. 'Just keep an eye on Cyril for me. You know what he's like, he'll try to cause trouble if he can.'

'I'll do that, Maiz. And I'll let ee know if he tries to start anything.'

'We're due to get more plastic explosive and timers soon, but so far I haven't been given a delivery date. I'll pass on the details when I do.'

Denzil chuckled. 'We're beginning to get quite an arsenal down that tunnel, Maiz. There's part of me almost wishing the Gerries do invade.'

She gave him a reproving look. 'You don't mean that, Denzil. Let's just hope and pray we in the Movement are never called into action.'

Despite his weather-beaten face he clearly blushed. 'Right you are, Maiz. I's talking daft.'

'When's the food coming up, Maiz? We're all starving here!' Sam called out from where he was sitting.

She glanced at the wall clock. Alice should have it ready by now. She'd go and see.

'My stomach's rumbling so much it sounds like a fog-horn,' Sam added, which drew a great deal of raucous laughter.

They'd decided earlier to lay on food as it was a special occasion, agreeing on sandwiches and baskets of chips. It was those Alice had been preparing.

'Hold the fort, Trudy,' Maizie instructed, and slipped away.

Before going into the kitchen she went to where she had her cigarettes hidden, frowning when she opened the packet to discover there were two fewer than she'd thought. She must have made a mistake she decided, and hastily lit up, thinking she'd have to be quick about this. Sam would be furious if he caught her, although it was unlikely, he being well ensconced in the bar. Still, there was no harm in being careful. Sam had a terrible temper and so disapproved of women smoking, having often declared it was both unfeminine and unladylike.

Through in the bar old Jim Corin, John's father, struck up on his accordion and the company began to sing a rousing sea shanty.

This could go on for hours yet, Maizie thought. Something she was only too pleased about as it meant all the more money in the till.

Maizie came out of a deep sleep to find Sam on top of her, pumping for all he was worth. She twisted her head to one side as the smell of his breath hit her, the result of his drinking earlier.

Her nightdress had been pulled up round her waist and her legs parted. She wondered how long he'd been at it before she'd wakened.

He suddenly grunted loudly and his body jerked. He continued to stay on top and inside her for a few more moments, then rolled off.

'It was a grand party. I thoroughly enjoyed meself,' he mumbled.

She didn't reply.

Soon he was snoring again.

Twice more that night she was awakened by his demands,

alcohol didn't make any difference to Sam when it came to that. He was always capable.

He had her again in the morning just before she got up.

'What's wrong?'

Bobby and Rosemary were sitting at either ends of the kitchen table doing their homework. He glanced up when Maizie spoke.

'You've nearly chewed that pencil to pieces,' she added with a smile.

'It's this French,' he groaned. 'It's terribly difficult.'

'Maybe that's because you're stupid,' Rosemary jibed.

'I am nothing of the sort!'

She stuck out her tongue at him.

'Enough!' Maizie declared sternly. 'I won't have any of that. Rosemary, mind your manners. And Bobby isn't stupid. Far from it. He has an excellent brain in his head.'

'See,' Bobby retorted to his sister.

Rosemary snorted and got on with her work. She knew full well Bobby was bright which irritated her. Far brighter than she, though she'd never have admitted that.

'I'd help if I could but I don't speak a word of French,' Maizie sympathised with Bobby.

'I find maths and everything else easy. It's just this,' Bobby sighed. 'I wish Christian was still here.'

A little jolt ran through Maizie to hear that name mentioned. She'd often thought of Christian, wondering about him. 'He'd certainly be the one to help you,' she agreed.

'I miss him,' Bobby said wistfully. 'He was fun.'

And a real gentleman, Maizie thought. Terribly handsome too. But there had been more to him than both these things. A lot more. She couldn't resist comparing him to Sam, the latter coming off a bad second best.

'I must get back to the bar,' Maizie declared. 'Will you be all right?'

'I suppose so.'

'You must tell Miss Hitchon about the difficulty you're having. I'm sure she'll give you extra attention until you grasp the fundamentals.'

Rosemary frowned. 'What's that?'

'It means the basics,' Maizie explained.

'Fundamentals,' Rosemary repeated. It was an awfully big word.

Maizie glanced from one child to the other, sad that they hadn't yet heard from their mother despite Bobby having now written three times. What on earth was the woman thinking about? Honestly, some people! They just didn't deserve to have kids.

'Right then,' Maizie smiled, and left them to it.

'*Entrez!*'

Christian opened the office door and stepped inside. He closed the door again before saluting.

'Take a chair, Capitaine,' Commandant Duclos instructed, indicating one in front of his desk.

A puzzled Christian slowly dropped his arm. 'You mean Sous Lieutenant, don't you, sir?'

Duclos grinned. 'No, Capitaine's quite correct. You've been promoted. Congratulations.'

Christian was stunned, there had been no hint of this whatsoever. He couldn't have been more delighted.

'So, how did you find the manoeuvres?' Duclos asked when Christian had sat down.

'Salisbury Plain isn't exactly the most pleasant place to be this time of year. But we survived well enough,' Christian replied, still trying to come to terms with his promotion. He'd jumped two whole ranks which was most unusual.

There again, it was wartime and many officers had been lost getting out of France. Not to mention those left behind in circumstances that didn't bear contemplating.

Duclos smiled. 'I can well understand that. It sounds inhospitable to say the least.'

He regarded Christian thoughtfully while smoothing down the pencil-thin moustache he sported. There were those who said it made him look like Ronald Colman, the film actor, which never failed to please him whenever it was mentioned.

'I haven't just asked you here to inform you about your promotion,' he stated slowly.

Christian's brow creased. 'No, sir?'

'I have a proposition to put to you, Capitaine Le Gall. One I think will be of interest.'

'I'd always heard the food in England was awful, and I can only wholeheartedly agree,' Sous Lieutenant Roland Portevin declared to Christian. 'That dinner we just had will undoubtedly give me indigestion.'

'Ssshh!' Christian warned. 'Someone might hear and take offence.'

'We're speaking French.'

'That doesn't matter. We still might be understood.'

Roland took a sip of his wine and leaned further back in his chair, a brown leather dimpled one. They were in the lounge of a smart Plymouth hotel having just dined there. They were celebrating Christian's promotion.

'*Capitaine* Le Gall,' Roland mused, shaking his head. 'Some people have all the luck.'

'It rather caught me by surprise, I can tell you.' He thought of the conversation he'd had with Commandant Duclos, the proposition the Commandant had made him. He had twenty-four hours to mull it over before giving his decision.

'So what shall we do for the rest of the evening?' Christian queried. 'I thought we might go dancing.'

Roland's eyes took on a predatory glint. 'I have a better idea.'

'Oh?'

He dropped his voice a little, the tone conspiratorial. 'Don't look now, but there are two women sitting by themselves in the far corner.'

'What about them?'

'Both are wearing wedding rings, yet I get the distinct feeling they're approachable.' Roland winked. 'If you get my meaning.'

Christian did, only too well. He waited a few moments, then let his eyes drift sideways.

'So? How about us introducing ourselves?'

The women were in their mid-twenties, Christian judged. Both were well dressed and wearing jewellery. One was a smallish redhead, her companion dark-haired and of medium height. Each had a cocktail in front of her.

'Not bad,' he murmured. And yes, Roland was right, they did, somehow, appear approachable. 'Perhaps they're waiting for their husbands?'

'I doubt it. They dined alone, I spotted them when we went in, and now they're still alone. My guess is they're officers' wives whose husbands are away. Royal Navy maybe.'

Christian lit a cigarette while he considered the matter, wishing he had some Gitanes left, those, sadly, long since finished. 'What would we say?'

'Ah, you're interested then?'

Was he? Christian wasn't sure. He would certainly have appreciated some female company, but no more than that. He wasn't after sex, not even fresh from four long hard weeks on Salisbury Plain. 'I don't know,' he demurred.

'You can have your pick.'

Christian laughed. 'It isn't that.'

'What then?'

For some inexplicable reason a picture of Maizie Blackacre popped into his mind. Maizie of fond memory who'd saved his life when others would have killed him for discovering that tunnel. 'I don't think I have the energy,' he lied.

Roland regarded him with incredulity. 'You're joking, *mon ami!*'

'I really am tired after the manoeuvres.'

'But you mentioned dancing?'

'That would be all right. For a short while anyway.'

Roland shook his head, 'I don't believe I'm hearing this. A Frenchman too tired to pursue a beautiful woman! You've been in England too long, my friend. Far too long.'

Christian smiled at his friend's teasing. 'Perhaps you're right.'

'Well, I can't make a move without you. And I find the redhead fascinating.'

'I thought you said I could have my pick?'

Roland shrugged. 'The other is just as pleasant on the eye. With a better figure too I'd say.'

Christian had another casual glance. There was no denying the dark-haired one did have a lovely figure.

'Well?'

Christian was about to reply when there was an almighty explosion. The entire room shook, dislodging pieces of plaster from the ceiling.

'Air raid!' Roland exclaimed as sirens began wailing.

That had been close, Christian thought. Extremely so. There was the sound of more explosions. The Luftwaffe was giving Plymouth yet another pasting.

Bedlam had broken loose, people appearing from every-where to mill around. The air filled with the babble of frightened voices.

'Your attention please!' a waiter shouted, waving his arms above his head. 'Will you please proceed to the basement. The entrance is clearly marked just round to the left in the corridor.'

Another near miss dislodged more plaster, sending clouds of white dust swirling round the lounge.

The two women were forgotten as Christian and Roland joined the mêlée heading for the basement, which they discovered to be situated, thankfully, deeply underground.

'Bloody Gerry bastards!' a middle-aged man declared apoplectically, standing alongside Christian and Roland in the positions they'd taken up. Overhead a naked lightbulb swung at the end of its cord.

Christian glanced about him, but there was no sign of the two women. If they were down there he couldn't see them.

Half an hour later when they emerged into the night it was to see huge fires blazing all around.

'Look at that!' Roland urged, grabbing Christian's arm with one hand and pointing with the other.

Just up the street a massive building was slowly collapsing in on itself in a great cascade of sparks and leaping flames.

An ARP man hurried past, his grim features streaked with dirt. He was muttering to himself but Christian couldn't make out what.

Searchlights were still traversing the sky even though the German planes were long gone. Perhaps they were hoping to pick up a straggler.

'I've had enough for one evening,' Christian said softly.

Roland nodded his agreement. 'Let's go.'

Mercifully they found Christian's car unmarked and undamaged where he'd parked it.

Sam was down at the quay having come out for a breath of

fresh air. He stared out over the Channel, thinking about the basking sharks Maizie had told him of the night before. He would have loved to have seen that. It must have been quite a sight.

He turned round as Bobby and Rosemary were coming out of the hotel on their way to school, the pair of them running off down the road skylarking together.

He found Rosemary disturbing. For some reason she reminded him of the Chinese girl he'd had in New York's Chinatown. About the same age too.

Not that Rosemary looked anything like her, there was no resemblance whatsoever. And yet remind him she did. Perhaps it was the age similarity.

He smiled, remembering the experience. To begin with he hadn't been keen on that particular girl. But his mates, thinking it funny, had goaded him into it. It wasn't that she was a whore, after all that was why you went to a whore house. It was simply that she'd been so damned young.

He recalled the room, small and depressing, the only light coming from a bedside lamp. She'd been wearing a wrap, as she'd called it, with nothing underneath. Once he'd paid she'd simply removed it and smiled at him.

Sam swallowed hard. Her breasts had been mere buds, her pubic hair a faint fluff, her hips only slightly rounded.

Somehow the combination had excited him, it was as if ... as if ... He didn't know what it had been as if. But it had excited him enormously.

He'd spent an hour with the girl and returned three more times before his ship had sailed.

Her name was Xi Wang.

'I don't know why I ever let you talk me into this, it's a right load of nonsense,' Maizie declared. She and Alice were sitting facing one another across the kitchen table, Alice busy laying out the Tarot cards Maizie had picked from the pack.

'Get on, ee knows ee enjoys it.'

'It's ages since we last did this.'

Alice nodded. 'Well, it's best that way. There should be a good while between readings.'

Maizie sipped her tea as Alice studied the cards now face up before her.

'Death,' Maizie commented, focusing on the first card which portrayed the grim reaper. She laughed nervously.

'It only means the end of something, the finish,' Alice reassured her. 'At least . . .' she hesitated. 'Most times anyway.'

Alice studied the spread, her features slowly forming into a frown. She'd been reading for years and was much in demand by the women of the village, especially in times of trouble and personal crisis. She had the reputation of being extremely accurate.

'Well?' Maizie demanded. She didn't really know whether or not she believed in all this. If nothing else, she usually told herself, it was a bit of fun. A giggle.

'Interesting,' Alice murmured. 'Very interesting.'

Maizie was suddenly filled with dread and apprehension. 'Someone *is* going to die, aren't they?'

'Possibly,' the older woman demurred. 'There again,' she added, and shrugged, 'it might be nothing of the sort, but the end of something, like I said.'

Alice made a decision. Some things were best left unspoken, unforetold.

Chapter 8

Christian stared out of the carriage window, listening to the rhythmic clickety clack of the train's wheels on the railway line. It had been a long journey from Euston, the carriage freezing the entire way. He hadn't once removed his greatcoat.

What did Scotland have in store for him? he wondered for the umpteenth time. And what would the others be like?

It started to snow, large thick flakes sticking to the window abruptly reducing visibility.

He groaned as the train ground to a halt. Yet another delay. How long for this time? He would have given anything, paid any price, for a cup of hot French coffee and an equally hot *petit pain* dripping butter. He was ravenous.

The train suddenly jolted and continued on its way. Thank God for that, he thought. This delay had lasted only a few seconds. The last one had been forty minutes.

He glanced round the carriage. There had been other passengers occupying it intermittently during the long journey north, but for the present he was alone. He much preferred it that way.

He wished he knew more about Scotland, his scant knowledge being limited to visions of bagpipes and men in skirts.

Kilts they called them. That and some abomination called haggis that they ate. He'd once had the contents of haggis described to him and it had sounded disgusting. How could anyone actually willingly eat such a thing!

Three months he was to be here. May, June and July. The training would be hard, he'd been warned. And there was a great deal to learn. He only hoped he could cope.

The officers would be British and he would be under their direct command. And while there his rank meant nothing. He would simply be one of a group.

Were there others in that group aboard the train? Probably. But who they were he had no idea. There had been no plan for people to meet up beforehand. He'd been given a ticket and instructed which train to catch and where to get off.

He peered again out the window. Bleak and inhospitable, that was his initial impression of Scotland.

He hoped he wasn't going to regret volunteering.

Bobby dragged heavily on his cigarette, well hidden from view behind the school toilets. It was midway through the morning playtime break. Out in the playground other boys were playing cowboys and indians, as they did every day, the girls either talking or skipping rope.

'If a teacher catches you doing that you'll be for the high jump.'

He swung round in alarm to face the speaker, a girl from the class above him. 'Well they haven't yet,' he replied, affecting an air of bravado.

'You're Bobby Tyler.'

'What of it?' He took a nonchalant drag, showing off.

'I'm Emily Dunne.'

'I know.'

'Do you now?'

He shrugged. 'I suppose I heard it somewhere.' He suddenly regarded her suspiciously. 'Are you going to tell on me?'

'I might.' She paused. 'There again, I might not.'

'What does that mean?' he snapped.

'It all depends.'

'On what?'

She came closer, her shrewd eyes fixed on his. He began to feel uncomfortable. He didn't normally talk to girls. Not alone that is. Now he'd had the chance to have a proper look at her he thought Emily rather pretty. Not that he was interested in girls. They were all soft and talked about daft things.

'Have you any more of those?'

He blinked, that having caught him off guard. 'One more.'

'Let me have it and I'll keep my mouth shut.'

He grinned. 'Bugger off.'

'Then I'll tell on you.'

'I'll say you're lying. Trying to get me into trouble.'

'Why would I do that?'

'I don't know. But I'll say so anyway.'

Her mouth set into a firm line. 'I've always wondered what it's like to smoke. But I've never had the chance to try.'

'Well you're not having one of mine. So there.'

His defiance interested her. She knew she had an overbearing presence which usually made even bigger boys wary, but Bobby wasn't frightened in the least. 'It'll be detentions for you,' she threatened.

'No it won't. Because it'll only be your word against mine.'

'They'll believe me because I'm a local not an incomer,' she parried.

'You could still be a liar.'

'They're far more likely to take my word.'

'We'll see.'

She played her trump card. 'And you know why? Because when they smell your breath it'll pong of tobacco.'

She had him there, that was obvious. He could just imagine the look of disappointment on Miss Hitchon's face when she found out. Or worse still, Sam Blackacre's when he was informed as he was bound to be. Truth was, Sam scared him. There was just something about the man.

Bobby dug in a pocket and produced the second cigarette. 'I was going to give it to you anyway,' he lied.

Emily laughed as she accepted it from him. 'Have you got a light?'

'Sure.'

He handed her a box of matches and watched in amusement as she struck one. Next moment it was his turn to laugh as she coughed violently.

'Serves you right,' he muttered gleefully.

Emily glared at him and had another tentative puff. 'It's quite nice really when you get used to it.'

'Huh!'

She puffed again, but didn't inhale. 'What's Plymouth like? I've never been there.'

'Terrific.'

'In what way?'

'In every way.'

'I'd love to see it one day,' she sighed wistfully. 'I just can't imagine a place with so many houses. Thousands and thousands of them.'

'Oh, more than that.'

Her eyes widened. 'Really?'

He nodded.

'Gosh.'

Bobby spoke about Plymouth, Emily listening avidly, until the bell rang for them to return to their classrooms.

'Thanks, Bobby,' she smiled as they parted.

He felt quite buoyant, uplifted somehow. She wasn't so bad, he told himself. For a girl that is.

'I'm going to Helston tomorrow to pay the bills and do the ordering. Do you want to come?'

Sam sat on the edge of the bed and began removing his shoes. That meant Maizie would be away for the entire day, a Saturday. Here was his opportunity.

'I don't think I'll bother,' he replied casually.

That surprised her, as she thought Sam would have jumped at the chance. 'Suit yourself.'

'I want to ring through to the company to find out what's what.' The company he referred to was the Anchor Line, his current employer.

'Why would you do that?'

'They were having trouble with the ship's engines before I left. Who knows? If they haven't yet managed to fix them my time ashore might just be extended.'

'Is that likely?' she frowned.

''Tis possible. The engineers weren't at all sure what the problem was. If they haven't been able to sort it then sailing could well be delayed.'

'I see,' she murmured.

'So I'll hang on here.'

That night was the first since his arrival home that he didn't lay a finger on her, not even in the morning before she got up.

That puzzled her, but she certainly wasn't complaining. For whatever reason it was a welcome relief.

Maizie stopped outside the pub where she and Christian had

had lunch, smiling at the memory. That was the day she'd had business with Tim Lambrick, the Movement's overall Area Commander. They'd argued on the pavement opposite, she recalled. Tim was another not too keen on dealing with women.

Oh well, that was long over and done with, the matter discussed then resolved to her satisfaction.

On sudden impulse she entered the pub and went up to the bar where she ordered herself a drink and some food.

She sat at the same table as before.

'Are you all right, Rosemary? You look awfully pale.'

It was that evening and Maizie had returned in time to make supper which she was now dishing up. She frowned at Rosemary, waiting for a reply.

Rosemary mumbled something she couldn't hear. 'What's that?'

'I'm fine, thank you.'

'Well, you don't look it. And why are you squirming like that? Have you got ants in your pants?'

Bobby giggled.

'She seems OK to me,' Sam said slowly.

'So why is she squirming?' Sam's expression became black and thunderous.

'I fell over earlier,' Rosemary said very quietly.

'Fell over?'

'On the stairs. I tripped and landed on my bottom. It's bruised.'

'Idiot!' Bobby snickered, thinking that hysterical.

Rosemary shot him a venomous glance.

Maizie sighed, remembering the occasion she'd fallen down the stairs and hurt her ankle. It was easily done. 'Would you like some cream for it later?'

Rosemary dropped her gaze and shook her head.

'It might help.'

'No thank you,' Rosemary croaked.

'I've got some news for ee,' Sam declared to Maizie, abruptly changing the subject.

'What's that?'

'I was right about thae engines. There's proper flap on. Anyway, the upshot is that sailing's been delayed a further week. 'Tain't that grand?'

Maizie's heart sank, but she instantly rebuked herself for being churlish. 'I'm so pleased.'

Sam briskly rubbed his meaty hands and beamed at all present. ''Tis a proper break now and no mistake.'

He smiled benignly at Rosemary. 'And no mistake.'

Maizie switched the bedside light off and waited for Sam to make a move. But, to her utter amazement, he didn't.

'Night, Maizie.'

'Night, Sam.'

Hardly able to believe her luck she felt him roll over, away from her.

Truly, miracles would never cease!

Christian flopped on to his cot. Every inch of him ached, every bone felt as if it had been broken. 'The man's a sadist,' he groaned. The man in question was Sergeant Major Jock Thompson of the Scots Guards.

Gilbert Du Bois, who shared the room with Christian, sat on the single chair provided. 'I won't disagree with you there.' Gilbert was another Frenchman by the rank of simple *soldat*, or private. Normally a member of the other ranks would never have shared with an officer, but here at Craiggoyne, amongst the group, ranks were irrelevant.

'I don't think I can take much more of this.'

Gilbert laughed hollowly. 'Of course you can. It's just a case of getting fit, that's all.'

'But I *am* fit!'

Gilbert gave Christian a jaundiced look. 'Not to the good Sergeant Major's standards obviously. None of us are.'

'What I don't understand is how the women do it.' There were two in the group, both civilians.

'Well, you can't accuse him of not being as hard on them as he is on us. That simply isn't true.'

Christian sat up and reached for his cigarettes. 'I suppose we'll have to go and eat some of that slop they call food now.'

Gilbert grinned ruefully. 'Stew and dumplings tonight I believe.'

'I wouldn't feed it to pigs.' He sighed wistfully. 'I'd give my right arm for some of Maman's cooking. I actually dreamt about it last night.'

Gilbert laughed. 'Well, we've no choice, stuck out here in the middle of nowhere. God alone knows how far it is to the nearest restaurant. Nor what they'd actually serve up if we actually got there.'

A gong boomed, echoing round and round the mansion house that was Craiggoyne.

'At least there's plenty of it. That's something,' Gilbert mused.

It turned out Gilbert was wrong about the beef stew. The offering was spam fritters, chips and processed peas, which was even worse.

'I think that maid is sickening for something,' Alice commented to Maizie.

'You mean Rosemary?'

''Tain't herself at all these past few days. Maybe she's got a cold or the flu coming on.'

Maizie stopped what she was doing. 'She has been peaky and out of sorts. Perhaps I should take her to the doctor.'

'I would if I were you. A good iron tonic might do her the world of good.'

Maizie resumed buttering bread. 'I did ask her and she says she's fine. Though I have to admit she did seem a bit odd about it when I asked.'

'How odd?'

Maizie thought about that. 'I don't know, sort of uneasy. It was as if she couldn't wait to get away from me.'

'I thought you and she got on well?'

'We do. At least I thought we did.'

'Maybe something at school is bothering her, Maiz. Could it be bullying?'

'I wonder,' Maizie mused.

'Does go on you know. And not only amongst the boys either. Some of thae maids who look as though butter wouldn't melt can be right little tormenting buggers.'

It was certainly a possibility, Maizie mused. Rosemary was an outsider after all. She'd have a quiet word with Bobby later and find out if he knew anything.

Maizie realised what Sam had in mind the moment the back of her dress was lifted. 'For Christ's sake, Sam, not here. Someone might come along,' she hissed.

He chuckled. 'Makes it all the more exciting, don't it? Now you just bend over that banister, girl.'

Despite what she'd said they and Alice were the only ones in the hotel, the bar being shut while the three guests in residence were out. Even though!

'I'm carrying all this bed linen,' she complained.

'I'm sure ee won't drop it. Not that it matters if ee does.' He pushed her shoulders, forcing her to do what he wanted. 'That's right. Just bend over.'

Maizie closed her eyes as her knickers were tugged down. This was the last thing she felt like. And certainly the last place to do it.

It was all so cold, and clinical, and . . . well downright humiliating. Nor was there any tenderness involved. Not one iota.

'Hello again.'

Bobby quickly glanced round to see who was watching. 'Not in the playground, Emily. The lads will laugh at me.'

She smiled mischievously. 'Will they now?'

'You know they will.'

'But I want to talk some more about Plymouth. You promised me we could.'

'Yes, but not here.'

'Then where?'

'Behind the toilets during the afternoon break.'

'Have you any more cigarettes?'

He shook his head.

'Are you certain about that? You're not holding out on me?'

'I'm absolutely certain. Now scoot off. Please!'

'I'll be waiting, Bobby.' She winked, and walked away.

He exhaled a huge sigh of relief, pleased to see that their private conversation hadn't been noted. If the lads thought he was getting chummy with a girl they'd make his life a misery.

A completely naked Rosemary gasped as Maizie came into her bedroom, hurriedly snatching up her nightie from the bed and covering herself. But not before Maizie had glimpsed the massive bruising on her backside.

'I'm sorry,' Maizie apologised. 'I thought you were in the bathroom. I was going to pick up your washing.'

'It's Bobby in the bathroom,' Rosemary choked, eyes wide.

Maizie's expression became grim. 'That's a terrible bruise, Rosemary. Are you all right?'

Rosemary nodded.

'I didn't realise it was so big.'

'I gave myself a hard thump, Auntie Maiz. I came down with my full weight.'

Maizie was full of sympathy thinking how painful that must be. 'Here, let me have a proper look.'

'No!' Rosemary exclaimed, backing away.

'Don't be shy. We're both women after all. I've seen female bottoms before.' She smiled disarmingly. 'Including my own which is rather difficult to miss.'

'There's nothing you can do, Aunt Maiz. It was my own stupid fault for not looking where I was going anyway. It'll soon disappear. Mum used to always say I was a quick healer.'

'Well, if you're sure?' Maizie frowned.

'Honestly, I'm OK.'

Shy and modest with it. Well, what did she expect from a girl that age? Still, it was an appalling bruise all the same. 'I can let you have some cream which you can put on yourself,' she proposed.

Rosemary desperately wanted rid of Maizie, knowing she was close to tears. Maizie would be even more reluctant to leave if she burst out crying.

'I'll put it on tonight then.'

Maizie nodded. 'Now you'd better hurry up, you don't want to be late for school. Unless . . .' She hesitated. 'You'd prefer to stay at home today?'

Rosemary vigorously shook her head. 'I don't want to miss my lessons. And we have a test this afternoon.'

'Right then, breakfast in five minutes. I'll collect the washing later.'

Poor mite, Maizie commiserated as she returned down-stairs. It must have been a hard thump right enough.

Maizie turned round in alarm as Bobby was propelled into the kitchen, swiftly followed by an irate Sam. 'What's going on?' she demanded.

'I found the little bastard smoking in the back,' Sam explained, throwing a packet of cigarettes on to the table. 'And those were in his pocket – he must have stolen 'em.'

'I didn't!' Bobby stuttered.

'Of course ee did. No one here would sell 'em to ee. And Mr Ayres in the shop certainly wouldn't. So ee stole 'em.'

Rosemary was watching these proceedings, her face tight with fear.

'I found them out the back,' Bobby lied.

'My fucking arse you did, boy!'

'Language, Sam,' Maizie quietly admonished. For a moment she'd started when Bobby had claimed where he'd found them, except the packet wasn't hers; she didn't like Pasha.

Sam reached for his belt buckle. 'Well, I'll sorts ee out so ee'll never steal again. I'll teach ee a lesson you won't ever forget. I won't have no thief in my house.'

Bobby whimpered while Rosemary went deathly white. She gulped when Sam's belt snaked free.

Maizie knew she had to do something. Sam's temper was renowned. If he thrashed the boy with the belt he'd half kill him.

'Please?' Bobby pleaded.

Sam was smiling as he cracked the belt. Slowly he began advancing on Bobby.

'The cigarettes are mine,' Maizie stated firmly.

Sam came up short and blinked at her. 'You what?'

'The cigarettes are mine,' she repeated. 'Bobby must have found them like he said.'

'But ee don't smoke, Maiz.'

'I took it up again while you were away.' She decided a little soft-soaping was in order. 'Sometimes it was so lonely without you, Sam. Those long nights all by myself. Smoking gave me comfort. I'm sorry, I know you hate women smoking, but it was comfort, nothing else.'

Bobby sagged with relief.

Sam was staring hard at Maizie. 'So the boy *didn't* steal them?'

She shook her head. 'I had them hidden. But obviously not well hidden enough.'

Bobby opened his mouth to speak, then thought the better of it. All he wanted was out of that room, away from Sam Blackacre.

'I see,' Sam breathed.

Maizie guessed what was going through Bobby's mind. 'Hop it, Bobby,' she instructed.

Bobby didn't need to be told twice. He fled the kitchen for the sanctuary of his bedroom.

'He was still smoking,' Sam pointed out, eyes narrowed.

'And I'll punish him for that. And not with a belt either.'

'I—'

She held up a hand, cutting Sam off. 'Come on, what he was doing wasn't that bad. Most young lads have a cigarette at some time or another. It's part of growing up. Why, I'll bet you even did yourself.'

Sam glanced away, his expression confirming that to be so.

'He's a normal lad, Sam, not an angel. You can't be too hard on him.'

'I'd have leathered him if he had been stealing.'

'But he hadn't. He simply came across the packet and decided to have one.' She suddenly smiled. 'You should have left him alone. If he'd got through the whole cigarette he'd probably have been sick.'

Sam smiled also. 'True enough.'

'So you leave his punishment to me. I'll think of something suitable. OK?'

'OK,' he agreed. And began fitting his belt back again.

'So what have you got to say for yourself?'

'Thanks, Auntie Maiz.'

She regarded him sternly. 'But you did steal them, Bobby. And from us no doubt.'

He didn't reply.

'Well?'

He nodded.

'Like Sam, I won't countenance stealing. Not from us or anyone else. Is that understood?'

'I won't do it again, Auntie Maiz. You have my promise.'

'Then see you keep it.'

It was clear to Maizie how wretched Bobby was, and how pathetically grateful that she'd lied for him. She'd certainly made a friend here. 'Have you smoked before?' she asked.

'Yes,' he croaked.

'Often?'

He nodded.

'That really is awful, Bobby. You're far too young.'

'That's what Christian said. But everyone my age smokes in Plymouth. Especially the boys.'

'And how did Christian find out?' she queried, curious.

He told her about the time down by the quay, and Christian giving him a cigarette. 'Christian was all right,' he mumbled.

Maizie couldn't disagree with that, though she didn't approve of what he'd done. 'Well it stops here and now.' Adding pointedly, 'Or else.'

Bobby got the message.

'In the meantime you still have to be punished.' She had a think about that. 'For the next three nights you're confined to this room except at mealtimes.'

'Yes, Aunt Maiz.'

That seemed fair to her, and to him too apparently judging from his expression.

'I'll leave you to it.'

Out in the corridor she halted, thinking of Sam whom she still had to face regarding her own smoking. That wasn't going to be pleasant.

Maizie locked and barred the front door then crossed to Sam sitting morosely in a corner. He'd been drinking heavily for most of that evening.

'Are you coming up?' she asked.

He regarded her blearily. 'Sit down a moment, Maiz.'

She sighed inwardly, knowing what was coming next. 'Yes, Sam?'

'This smoking thing.'

'You mean me or Bobby.'

'You, Maiz. Is I being too harsh on ee?'

That surprised her to say the least. 'Not exactly harsh, Sam. I can well appreciate you don't like the idea and the reasons you give. But lots of women smoke nowadays. It's quite accepted.'

He grunted.

'You see it in here all the time.'

'I know . . . I know . . . I . . .' He trailed off. 'Is it really that lonely without me, Maiz?'

It would seem her soft-soaping had had some effect. 'What do you think? Locked in here night after night by myself. It's worse in winter with the wind howling outside and me the only soul in the building. Of course I miss you.'

'And 'tis a comfort to ee?'

'Cigarettes, yes.'

He picked up his pint and drained the glass. 'So be it, Maiz. I'll soon be gone again anyway. I can't deprive ee of a little comfort. Not in the circumstances. Not when I can't comfort ee myself.'

She smiled. 'Thanks, Sam.'

'Then enough said. Let's go to bed.'

She took his arm as they went upstairs, thankful that Bobby had been spared the leathering, and she wasn't going to suffer as a result of her lie and confession.

Chapter 9

'The car's here!' Alice announced, turning away from the bar window.

Sam nodded. He was all ready to go, having brought down his duffel bag a little earlier.

He gazed about him, sorry to be leaving. The trip home had been even better than he'd anticipated, an added bonus being the extra week the company had given him thanks to the trouble with the ship's engines. Now it was back to sea and the ever present dangers lurking there.

A smiling Maizie appeared. 'At least you've got a nice day for the journey,' she said. She was walking stiffly as a result of the previous night when Sam, even by his standards, had been unusually energetic.

'Let's have a last drink, eh? There's no telling when I'll be here again.'

She went behind the bar. 'What would you like?'

'Brandy I think.'

That momentarily startled her for Sam never drank brandy. She bypassed the cognac and went for the cheaper stuff. 'I'll join you in that,' she declared over her shoulder.

'Well, Maiz, what to say, eh?' He smiled as she placed his glass in front of him.

'There's nothing much to say, Sam, except stay safe.'

'I'm glad I went crabbing with Denzil yesterday. 'Twas good to be in a fishing boat again and not one of those bloody great things I'm usually on nowadays. 'Tis proper sailing that.'

The driver interrupted them to inquire for Mr Blackacre and Sam replied he'd be right out. 'Will you see me to the car, Maiz?'

'Of course.'

'I'll try and write, girl, but you know me.'

'I know you all right, Sam,' she acknowledged softly. 'Pen and paper were never exactly your forte.'

'As long as you understand.'

'I do.'

'I'll be thinking about you though. You can be sure of that.'

'And I'll be thinking of you.'

He sighed and got off his stool. ''Tis time.'

She came round from behind the bar and joined him. Together they went out to where the car was waiting.

He stopped and looked over Coverack, then out across the Channel. 'God knows when I'll see this lot again.'

'Maybe sooner than you imagine.'

He shook his head. 'It could be anything up to a year the way things are going. Perhaps even longer. You will be all right though?'

'Of course I will. I'm quite capable.'

'You are indeed that, Maiz. I did the right thing when I married ee and no mistake.'

She wished she could have said the same about him, but it wouldn't have been true. It had seemed a good idea at the time, but she'd changed since then. Come to expect more out of life. Something she'd never have. As the saying went, she'd made her bed and now she'd have to lie in it. And that, for better or worse, was the way of it.

The elderly driver took Sam's duffel bag and put it in the boot. It was the first time he'd been to Coverack and thought it a lovely place. He decided to bring the missus there during the summer.

'Goodbye then, Sam. Take care.'

'And you, Maiz.'

He kissed her deeply, his hands tight about her waist. Then he climbed into the front passenger seat and pulled the door shut behind him.

Maizie smiled and waved as the car drove off. When she turned again to the hotel it was with mixed feelings. Sam was her husband after all, a huge part of her life.

At least she'd be able to get a decent night's sleep again, she told herself.

As chance would have it Rosemary was in the playground by the railings as Sam's hired car went by with him clearly visible. Her face went still, her eyes expressionless as she watched both it and him.

She continued watching the car until it disappeared from view.

'Can I go out, Aunt Maiz?' Bobby asked eagerly. It was a Saturday morning.

'Have you done all your work?' she queried, wiping her hands on her pinny. Things were looking up at the hotel, six guests having arrived the previous evening, the most they'd had at once for some while.

He nodded.

'Then off you go.'

'Thanks, Aunt Maiz!' he cried, and hurried away.

Out with his pals, she presumed. Off somewhere to play no doubt. Well that was what a boy should be doing on a Saturday. She only wished Rosemary would do likewise but recently all the girl seemed to do was mope sullenly round the place. She put it down to the difficulties of growing up. It was undoubtedly something she'd eventually snap out of and become her old cheery self again.

'You're late,' Emily accused Bobby.

'I had work to do. I got away as soon as I could.'

Emily sniffed. 'I've been waiting fifteen minutes and I don't like being kept waiting.'

'I'm sorry, Emily. I ran all the way.'

That mollified her somewhat. She sat on a large rock and patted a spot beside her indicating Bobby should do the same. They were on Lookout Point where tradition had it lookouts had been posted during the various wars with the French and Spanish.

'I hope we're not going to talk about Plymouth again,' Bobby sighed.

'And why not?'

'I've told you everything I know.'

'I'm sure there's more.'

'There isn't, Emily. Believe me.'

That made her cross; she'd been looking forward to talking about Plymouth, the city having become something of an obsession with her. She'd already decided to go and live there one day when she was grown up and the war was over.

'You never mention your parents,' she stated suddenly.

That startled him. It was a subject he'd intentionally kept off. 'What do you want to know?' he asked reluctantly.

'What they're like. You know.'

'There's not much to tell really. They're pretty ordinary.'

'Well, what does your father do?'

'He's a coalman. Which I'm going to be. He's in the army now. Away in the Far East somewhere.'

'That's interesting. And your mum?'

Despair filled Bobby. 'She's just a housewife. Nothing more.'

'I suppose she writes to you while you're here.'

That was like a knife to the heart. All these long months and not a single letter despite the ones he'd sent. 'Of course. All the time.'

'And what does she say?'

'Oh nothing, this and that. Pretty boring really.'

'And you reply?'

'Of course.'

Emily nodded. 'It must be hard for her. You and your sister being here and her there. She must miss you both awfully.'

'Yes,' Bobby choked.

'No doubt she'll come down and see you sometime. When she can.'

'I suppose so. When she can.'

He thought of the men she'd be going out with, men who clearly meant more to her than her children. Why else hadn't she written? Why else had she seemingly abandoned him and his sister? Despite himself, his emotions got the better of him and tears started to flow.

'Bobby?'

He quickly turned away.

Emily was frowning. 'Bobby, what's wrong?'

'Nothing.'

'Yes there is.'

His shoulders were heaving now, his face awash. He shook himself free when Emily tried to put an arm round him.

'Go away,' he sobbed.

She didn't know what this was all about but she wasn't going to leave him in this state. 'Is it something to do with your mum?'

Suddenly he had to tell her, confide in her. Be comforted in his wretchedness. 'Promise you won't let on to anyone?'

'I promise.'

'I mean it, Emily.'

She made a motion with a finger. 'Cross my heart and hope to die. Now what's this all about?'

It all came tumbling out in a rush of words.

'That's terrible,' Emily said softly when he'd finally finished.

'My dad will knock her to bits when he comes back.'

If he can find her, Emily thought grimly. It sounded to her as if Mrs Tyler might not be around. 'I'm so sorry, Bobby. Really I am.'

'I thought she might be ill. I thought . . . well all sorts of excuses. But I know in my heart of hearts none of them are true. She just doesn't want to know me and Rosemary any more. We were in the way. And now we're not.'

Emily's arm went back round Bobby's shoulders and this time he didn't shrug it off.

'Oh, Emily,' he whispered.

'Let's look on the bright side, Bobby. You've got Mrs Blackacre to take care of you and she's smashing, everyone says so. And you've also got me as your friend.'

At that moment he valued her friendship more than almost anything. 'Thanks, Emily.'

She held him close and, using her free hand, brushed away his tears. 'I've got something that'll cheer you up.'

'What?'

She was about to say her mum had given it to her, then thought better not as that might upset him even more. 'A whole bar of chocolate for us to share. How about that?'

'I love chocolate.'

'So do I. It's ever so yummy.' She groped in a pocket and produced the bar. 'See, here it is. Just for the two of us.'

Bobby managed a weak smile.

'That's better.'

She undid the wrapping and broke the bar in halves, giving Bobby one. She was about to bite into her own when she suddenly had a horrible thought. What if all this was nonsense and the real reason for Mrs Tyler not replying to Bobby's letters was because she'd been killed in the bombing. Hundreds of people had, maybe even thousands. It was clear that possibility had never crossed Bobby's mind.

There again, if she had been, surely Bobby and Rosemary would have been notified through Mrs Blackacre.

'Let's go for a walk along the beach,' she suggested when the chocolate was finished.

'OK.'

As they made their way down the path that led to the seashore she slipped a hand into his. And was pleased when he let it remain there.

'Your turn, Le Gall. Now don't forget what you've been taught.' The speaker was Captain Smith of the Parachute Regiment, one of a number of instructors at Craiggoyne.

Christian glanced at Gilbert who pulled a sympathetic face. He was to be next.

Captain Smith helped Christian into the harness, watching carefully as Christian fixed the various fastenings that held it in place. When he was satisfied all was in order he raised a hand to the winchman and made an upwards motion.

Christian gritted his teeth as his feet left the ground. The main thing was not to panic, he reminded himself. He could easily get hurt if he did. He swiftly went through the landing procedure in his mind.

Christian felt ridiculous hanging there with everyone watching him. Ridiculous and . . . apprehensive, if not downright scared. He'd never been a great one for heights.

Eventually he came to a halt. My God, he gulped. It didn't

look nearly so high from the ground. But from up here the drop was terrifying.

'When you're ready, Le Gall!' Captain Smith called out.

His instinct was to close his eyes, but he couldn't do that. Tentatively he gave the signal to be released.

Seconds later it was all over and he was picking himself up off the ground.

Gilbert ran over to assist him. 'You all right?'

Christian grinned. 'I rather enjoyed it, actually. It was fun.'

And it had been too. He was actually looking forward to going up again.

'Why so morose?'

Gilbert turned and smiled at Christian. They were in the small bar that Craiggoyne boasted, the pair of them sitting at the window table. Christian was drinking brandy because unfortunately they didn't stock cognac and Gilbert nursed a pint of beer. They'd both learnt early on that the wine on offer would have been a good substitute for vinegar.

'Sorry.'

'Something bothering you?'

'Only what lies ahead.'

'Do you mean the course or—'

'No, afterwards,' Gilbert interrupted. 'When we're back in France.'

'Ah!' Christian sighed. 'So that was it.'

'It's being captured that worries me. And the torture that'll go with it.'

'You'll have a pill to prevent both.'

'But what if I don't get a chance to take it? It does happen, I understand.'

It was something that had been preying on Christian's mind too. They'd eventually be shot of course, that's what happened when you wore civilian clothes. It was the bit between being captured and shot that didn't bear thinking about. He'd heard the Germans did terrible things to you to make you divulge what you knew. Forcibly tearing out your nails, both fingers and toes, one by one for example.

'Yes,' Christian replied softly.

'There again, if faced with it would I have the guts to swallow the pill?'

'You'd be a fool not to. Better a quick death than a long drawn-out, excruciatingly painful one. I shall have no compunction.'

Gilbert had a sip of warm beer. 'Well, this is a cheery conversation, I must say.'

Christian laughed. 'Too true. But one has to be prepared for the worst after all. It's not as though we're walking into this without knowing what might lie at the other end.'

'Amen,' Gilbert whispered, his eyes taking on a faraway, slightly haunted look.

'Aren't you hungry?' Maizie queried of Rosemary who'd been pushing her food round the plate.

Rosemary shook her head.

'But you must eat. You'll get ill otherwise.'

'I'm sorry, Aunt Maiz. I just don't have an appetite.'

More and more Rosemary was worrying Maizie. She decided there and then that a visit to the doctor was in order. Get the iron tonic perhaps that Alice had suggested.

'I'll have it if she doesn't,' Bobby volunteered.

There was nothing wrong with his appetite, Maizie thought. It was as healthy as could be.

'You've had more than enough already,' Maizie replied.

'Aww!'

Rosemary leered at her brother then, swift as a striking snake, stuck out her tongue at him.

'We'll have no more of that!' Maizie snapped.

'Can I get down?'

'No, young lady, you'll stay where you are until we're all finished.'

Bobby giggled.

Rosemary glared at him. 'Bobby's got a girlfriend,' she announced to Maizie.

Bobby went very still, swearing under his breath.

'Really?'

'Her name's Emily Dunne.'

Maizie was amused. He was very young to have a proper girlfriend, but it was good he was showing an interest in girls. Even if it might have been a little premature. 'Is this true, Bobby?'

'No.'

'Liar!' Rosemary accused.

'I am not a liar!' Bobby retorted hotly.

'The whole school knows about it. You and Emily Dunne.'

Maizie knew the Dunne family of course. They were good people. She remembered Emily in her pram. God, she thought with a sinking heart, she really was getting old.

For two pins Bobby would have smacked Rosemary, sister or not. How could she humiliate him like this? What he didn't know was that Rosemary was turning the attention away from herself.

'Well, girlfriend or whatever I think that's strictly Bobby's business,' Maizie declared.

If the entire school knew then he was in for it, Bobby thought in despair. The other lads would have a right go at him. He could already hear the teasing and taunting. What he couldn't understand was how he and Emily had been found out. They'd been so careful not to be seen together, but clearly they had. And by someone with a big mouth.

'Now, who's for pudding?' Maizie inquired.

Rosemary declined.

The moorland reminded Christian of parts of Cornwall, but if anything it was even more bleak and forbidding.

'Right, Le Gall,' Sergeant Major Thompson barked. 'Dig yourself a hole and when you've done that get in it. Understand?'

'Yes, Sergeant Major.'

'You will then stay in that there hole until I come back and tell you to get out. Do you understand that?'

'Yes, Sergeant Major.'

'And when you're in it I don't want to be able to see you, so it had better be a deep hole.'

'Yes, Sergeant Major.'

Christian cursed inwardly when, as if on cue, it started to rain, which really made Thompson smile. The damned man was enjoying every moment of this, Christian thought.

'Get cracking then, Le Gall. Get cracking!' And with that Thompson left him, striding out over the heather.

Christian shrugged off his pack and undid the spade strapped to its front. He began to dig.

Christian started awake to find himself staring into the wrong end of a sten gun.

'Had a nice little nap then?' a prostrate Sergeant Major Thompson inquired mildly.

It was the middle of the night, hours after Christian had climbed into the hole. Overhead a myriad of stars shone brightly down.

'You're a fucking disgrace, Le Gall. A fucking disgrace!' Thompson suddenly screamed. 'What are you?'

Christian swallowed hard. 'A fucking disgrace, Sergeant Major.'

'What if I'd been a prowling Gerry, eh? You know what you'd be, son?'

'What, Sergeant Major?'

'Dead fucking meat, that's what.'

Christian didn't reply to that.

'Now I'm going to leave you – and stay awake this time! Because if I return and find you asleep again you'll regret it, me lad.' He chuckled evilly. 'Oh yes, you'll regret it all right because I'll take your clothes, every last stitch, and leave you here stark bollock naked. How would you like that?'

'I wouldn't, Sergeant Major.'

Thompson rose to his feet and stared down at Christian in disgust. 'I'll make a proper soldier of you before I'm finished, Le Gall. A proper soldier and no mistake.' Adding with a dismissive sneer, 'If that's at all possible.'

'Yes, Sergeant Major.'

Thompson abruptly wheeled and strode away.

Bastard, Christian thought. Absolute bastard!

It was nearly noon before Thompson came back. Christian was whacked, out on his feet which were paining him dreadfully. Thompson walking towards him was the most welcome sight Christian had seen in a long time. He knew better than to scramble out to meet the Sergeant Major; he'd wait until he was told.

Thompson arrived at the side of the hole and grinned grimly down. 'You had three cigarettes last night, Le Gall, I counted.'

Oh shit, Christian thought.

'Or was it four?'

'Three, sir,' Christian admitted with a catch in his voice.

Thompson nodded. 'Need I say more?'

Christian shook his head. 'No, Sergeant Major.'

'That was very careless, laddie. Very careless indeed. If I'd been Gerry . . .'

'I'd be dead meat,' Christian finished for him.

'Precisely!' Thompson roared. 'Now get your arse out of there.'

Christian was only too grateful to oblige him.

The Sergeant Major's belligerence abruptly vanished to be replaced by a friendly smile. 'Tired?'

'Yes, sir.'

'Hungry?'

'Yes, sir.'

'You'd like some breakfast I take it?'

'Yes, sir.'

'And breakfast you shall have.' He swivelled and pointed into the distance. 'See that hill over there?'

Christian groaned inwardly. The indicated hill was at least a mile away. 'Yes, sir.'

'Well you're going to run to the top of it and from there back to Craiggoyne where breakfast will be waiting. Understand?'

'Yes, sir.'

'Then hop to it, laddie. Hop to it.'

Christian swiftly gathered up his pack, refastened the spade to its front, put it on and started off.

'I'll be watching to make sure you don't cheat!' Thompson bellowed after him.

Christian had no doubt about that.

'I'm not going to the doctor!' Rosemary declared defiantly.

'Oh yes, you are.'

'I'm not ill.'

'You're losing weight and won't eat. Besides which you're pasty faced and lacking energy. I want the doctor to have a look at you.'

'I'm not going!' Rosemary shrieked, and fled the kitchen, banging the door shut behind her. They heard her go clattering upstairs.

'Well,' Alice murmured softly, glancing at a furious Maizie.

'Of all the . . .' Maizie trailed off, her hands clasped into tight fists from a combination of anger and frustration.

'She must go,' Alice stated matter of factly.

'I know that. And she shall, if I have to drag her kicking and screaming. Which I'm quite prepared to do.'

'I've never seen the maid so upset,' Alice said thoughtfully.

Neither had Maizie. Normally Rosemary was very even tempered, placid almost, though of late that hadn't been quite the case.

'Can I say something, Aunt Maiz?'

Maizie turned to Bobby. 'What is it?'

'Why don't I go up and speak to her? Try to make her see sense.'

Maizie considered that. If she went up there would only be another shouting match. Bobby might have more luck. 'On you go.'

He slipped quietly from the room.

'What a to-do,' Alice commented, shaking her head. 'Children nowadays. What do you make of them?'

Maizie had no answer to that.

Bobby tapped her bedroom door. 'Can I come in?'

'Go away!'

'Aw, Rosie, it's only me.'

'Go away all the same.'

He could hear her sobbing her heart out which distressed him no end. Taking a deep breath he twisted the handle and stepped inside.

Her eyes were inflamed, tears streaming down her face. She was completely distraught. 'What's the matter, Rosie?'

'Nothing,' she gulped.

He crossed to the bed and sat beside her. 'It's only the doctor. Where's the harm in that?'

'I just don't want to go.'

'But why?'

'Because there's nothing wrong with me.'

He placed a comforting hand on her arm. 'Aunt Maiz is right, you haven't been yourself of late. All nervy and twitchy and the like. She's also right about you not eating, I've noticed that myself.'

'Oh, Bobby,' she whispered.

He put an arm round her just as Emily had with him that day on Lookout Point. 'Is it something to do with Ma. Is that it?'

She shook her head.

'Then what?'

She desperately wanted to unburden herself, but couldn't. That was something she'd never do. Not to anyone. 'Just go and leave me, Bobby. Please?'

'Not till you promise about the doctor.'

Suddenly all the defiance drained out of her and her shoulders slumped. If only she could get rid of these images in her mind that haunted her day and night. The awful dreams were the worst.

'Well?' he prompted.

She was being stupid, she told herself. But there was nothing the doctor could do for her. She knew that. It would be an entirely wasted visit.

'Well?' he prompted a second time.

She thought of Maizie downstairs and the scene they'd just had. A scene that had been totally uncalled for and which she now bitterly regretted. Maizie had been nothing but kindness itself. The last thing Rosie should be doing was causing her grief.

'OK,' she replied, attempting a smile through the still flowing tears.

He kissed her wet cheek. 'I'll nip down and tell Auntie Maiz.'

'And I'll be down shortly. Say I'm sorry.'

'I'll do that.'

It was a full hour before she'd pulled herself together enough to venture out of her bedroom. Her apology was accepted and hugs were exchanged. All was forgiven.

Chapter 10

Dr Renvoize had long since retired but had been drafted back into service when the local doctor had gone into the Forces. He was a man in his eighties but still fully fit and capable. He was known for his bedside manner.

Renvoize removed the tip of his stethoscope from Rosemary's chest. 'You can do yourself up again,' he instructed as he folded the stethoscope and put it away in his bag.

Maizie was anxiously looking on, waiting for the verdict. They were in the church hall which the doctor came to every Thursday morning, to use a small room at the rear for consulting.

Renvoize cleared his throat. 'Because you are an evacuee, Rosemary, I have no medical notes to go on so I have no idea about your history.' He regarded her keenly through bleary eyes. 'Is there anything you can tell me? Past illnesses?'

'I had chickenpox a few years ago.'

'Uh-huh,' he nodded, jotting that down.

'And German measles before that.'

He wrote down rubella. 'Anything else?'

Rosemary shook her head.

'I see,' he murmured thoughtfully, tapping the end of his pen on the makeshift desk.

'Oh, and I get a sty from time to time. But I haven't had one for ages now.'

He smiled, nothing unusual there. 'I take it you've started having periods?'

Rosemary blushed bright red and lowered her gaze.

'Answer the doctor, Rosemary, there's nothing to be ashamed of,' Maizie urged. 'Periods are quite natural after all.'

'Yes,' Rosemary muttered.

'When was your last one?'

The blush became scarlet. 'A fortnight ago.'

'And was it normal?'

'Yes, doctor,' she whispered.

Renvoize turned to Maizie. 'Has she had any flu symptoms recently?'

'No.'

His next question surprised both Rosemary and Maizie. 'Do you have a boyfriend, Rosemary?'

She shook her head.

He grunted in disappointment; that more or less ruled out glandular fever. Or it appeared to anyway.

'I can't find anything wrong with the maid, Mrs Blackacre,' he declared. 'I think she's simply run down.'

Maizie heaved a great sigh of relief.

'So my advice is for her to get plenty of rest and not overdo things. Which means no sport or physical jerks at school for the foreseeable future.'

Maizie nodded that she understood. She'd write a letter to Rosemary's teacher when they got back.

Renvoize had another thought. 'Has anything been bothering you, Rosemary? Perhaps there's something you're worried about?'

There it was, the one question she wouldn't, couldn't, answer. 'No,' she lied.

'Are you certain?'

'Yes, doctor.'

He pulled a pad towards him. 'I'm going to write you a prescription. It's a tonic and some pills. The dosage will be on the labels, make sure you take both accordingly. All right?'

'Leave that to me,' Maizie assured him.

Maizie smiled at Rosemary when they were again outside.

'See, it wasn't so bad.'

Rosemary matched Maizie's smile but didn't reply.

'When we get back to the hotel I'm going to make a big pot of soup. The kind that sticks to your ribs. And you're going to have some whether or not you're hungry.'

To Maizie's delight Rosemary devoured two bowls of the soup when it was dished up, declaring it the best she'd ever tasted.

Denny Herbert was older than Bobby, and a lot bigger. He was also the school bully.

'So have you felt her titties yet?' Denny leered. The other lads with him, his cronies, burst into raucous laughter.

Bobby, trapped against the school railings, didn't reply.

'Perhaps she doesn't have any yet. Is that it, evacuee?'

Bobby had never liked Herbert, now he positively hated him. How dare he!

'But she must have a fanny. Have you felt that? Had a finger in?'

A red mist began to descend on Bobby. He didn't want to let Miss Hitchon down, or Aunt Maiz, but this was too much. 'Fuck off, Herbert,' he hissed.

Denny glared at him. 'Don't talk to me like that, shrimp.'

'And don't talk about Emily as you've just been doing.'

'I'll do and say what the hell I like, Tyler,' Herbert retorted, jabbing a rigid finger into Bobby's chest.

That was the last straw. Bobby didn't care how many of them there were, or what happened to him.

The next moment his fist smashed into Herbert's face sending the bigger boy reeling.

'So who started it?' Mr Brookfield, the headmaster, demanded sternly. Bobby and Denny stood before his desk.

'He did, sir, he attacked me,' Herbert replied, a picture of innocence.

That surprised Brookfield. 'Did you, Bobby?'

'I hit him first, sir, if that's what you mean.'

Brookfield took a deep breath, his steady gaze alternating between the two. He knew Herbert's reputation, and personally couldn't stand the lad, considering him a bad lot. Just like his father.

As for Bobby, until now he'd behaved himself impeccably since arriving at the school. Miss Hitchon, whose judgement he highly respected, had nothing but good to say about him.

Now why would Bobby attack someone the size of Herbert? There had to be a reason, it was hardly credible otherwise. Inwardly he smiled to himself. From what he could see Bobby had certainly got the better of Herbert in the short time the fight had lasted before the pair of them had been pulled apart by Mrs Greenwood on playground duty.

The answer had to be provocation but of what sort he had no idea. But provocation enough for this to happen.

'You'll both have to be punished,' he stated.

Herbert gave Bobby a filthy look. 'But he attacked *me*, sir.'

'And why did he do that, Denny?'

'Don't know, sir.'

'No?'

'No, sir. I swear.'

'He just came up and attacked you, is that it?'

'Yes, sir.'

'While you were with your mates.'

'Yes, sir.'

Brookfield paused, then said softly, 'That seems highly unlikely, wouldn't you say?'

'It's what happened, sir.'

Brookfield opened a drawer and took out a well-worn slipper. 'Both of you bend over my desk.'

He started on Herbert, giving Denny a right tanning which he considered well overdue. 'You can go now,' he declared when he was finished. A sniffling Herbert headed for the door.

'And if there are any more fights there'll be a lot worse than that,' Brookfield added.

When it was Bobby's turn Brookfield was far gentler, more of a token punishment than anything else.

That was why he'd dealt with Herbert first and then sent him from the room. There was no need for Herbert to witness his leniency where Bobby was concerned.

'Bobby, wait up!'

Emily came running down the road. 'I heard about the fight,' she gasped, wide-eyed, on reaching him.

He glanced about, noting they were being seen by a number of other children returning home. Well, that hardly mattered any more as they all knew about him and Emily anyway.

'And that you had to go to the headmaster.'

Bobby continued on his way, Emily walking beside him. 'Did you get the slipper?'

He nodded.

She pulled a face. 'Was it sore?'

He shook his head. 'Not really.'

'That Denny Herbert is nothing but a big brute!' she declared angrily. 'And he always picks on smaller boys too. That's a coward if ever there was.'

She was flushed, her eyes filled with concern. Bobby rather liked that as it was on his behalf.

'So what was it about, Bobby?'

'The fight?'

'Well, of course, silly.'

He kicked a stone to send it skidding across the road. A great many seagulls were screeching and crying overhead which probably meant some of the boats were back and unloading. 'Can't say.'

She frowned. 'Why not?'

'It's personal.'

Her lips set in frustration. 'But I want to know.'

'There's lots of things I want and will never get,' he jibed. How could he tell her about the titties and fanny remarks? She'd be mortified. Besides, he couldn't mention such things to a girl. It would be disgusting.

'Bobby!'

'No,' he declared emphatically, vigorously shaking his head.

'Please?'

'I think I'll go down to the quay and watch the unloading before going in. Do you want to come?'

'Stop changing the subject.' She grabbed him by the arm, forcing him to stop. 'Was it about us?'

He didn't reply.

'It was, wasn't it?'

'Sort of.'

Emily was furious. 'Was he making fun?'

'In a way.'

Her fury evaporated and she suddenly beamed. 'You were defending me weren't you, Bobby Tyler?'

He blushed.

'My hero.'

'Oh, for cripes' sake, Emily!'

The beam became the widest of smiles. 'That's what you are to me from now on, Bobby. My hero!'

'If you don't stop it I'll throw up.'

She laughed, a feeling of warm well-being pervading her. 'Let's go watch the boats unload then.'

She considered taking his hand, then thought the better of it. Not here in public anyway.

When she got the chance she was going to kiss him. The kind of kiss grown-ups have.

Her hero.

'You're improving, m'sieur. Your receiving has come along by leaps and bounds,' Miss Sampson-Hardy declared to Christian. He was in the wireless class, practising receiving and sending messages, which she presided over.

Miss Sampson-Hardy was an upper-crust Englishwoman somewhere in her fifties. A large bouncy lady with more than a trace of moustache, she was popular with everyone. She was a civilian who'd never married and was reputed to be able to drink even the Sergeant Major under the table.

'R/T isn't my strong point I'm afraid,' he apologised. He had had terrible trouble with it but during the last week things that had previously been beyond him had started to fall into place.

Miss Sampson-Hardy might be a spinster but that didn't mean she didn't like men. Quite the contrary. Her only problem was she'd never been proposed to by one, which fact she put down to having always been well overweight and by no stretch of the imagination good looking. But she had had her moments in the past.

She smiled at Christian, whom she considered to be a hot piece of stuff. A beautiful young man whom, given half the chance, she'd have whisked off to bed. Sadly though, that was never to be. But it made for a lovely fantasy.

'Your touch has become quite delicate,' she praised. 'That's what's required. What the best operators have.'

He didn't think he had a delicate touch at all, but didn't contradict her.

'Keep up the good work, m'sieur.' And with that she moved to the next trainee.

Christian paused for a moment, thinking about when he'd be doing this for real. It sent goose bumps coursing up and down his spine.

Maizie opened the front door to find Hookie Repson standing there. 'Can I have a drink?' he asked.

'At this time of the morning?'

'I'm desperate and I've nothing at home.'

'Certainly, come on in, Hookie. A pint of cider?' It was hours before she should be serving alcohol but who was there to know?

He slumped on to a stool, his face grey with fatigue. 'I've just come back from over-by,' he stated.

She knew that meant France.

'I'm sorry, but I can't fill your order. Not yours or any-one else's.'

He took a deep breath which he then slowly exhaled. 'Something wrong?'

'There was last night. I nearly ran into a Gerry E Boat. The bastard would have had me if I hadn't spied him first and there hadn't been fog around. It gave me the fright of my life I can tell you.'

She placed the cider in front of him. 'That's awful, Hookie.'

'It's me own fault. I been stupid continuing to go over there with a war on. I was bound to run into trouble sooner or later.'

'You didn't land then?'

He shook his head. ''Twas impossible, Maiz. That E Boat must be new in the area, certainly since I was there last. But I wasn't taking no chances. I turned tail and headed straight for home. A cargo ain't worth getting my head blown off for or losing me boat over.'

He picked up his pint and drank half of it in one go, wiping his lips with the back of a hand as he replaced the glass on the bar. 'Fair gave me the shits and no mistake.'

'I would have thought you'd have heard it before you saw it? Especially in fog.'

'The bugger had its engines off and was just wallowing there, riding the swell. But 'tweren't broken down or nothing. I had just brought *Snowdrop* about when she burst into life. What a clatter that was! I thought she were after me, but no. I could hear her quite clearly for minutes afterwards. She must be patrolling that section of the coast.'

'You were lucky, Hookie.'

'Don't I knows it. I go cold thinking of how narrow an escape I had.'

'What about your own engine?'

'I always go in that close under sail so she never heard me. Thank God!'

Hookie swallowed the rest of his pint and asked for another which Maizie was only too willing to give him. 'Have that one on the house,' she said.

He acknowledged her generosity with a nod.

'And see you don't try to go over there again.'

'Don't you worry. I learnt my lesson. Smuggling is out for the time being.'

He gazed morosely into his cider. 'Fair gave me the shits it did.'

'Watch out, look who's coming over,' Gilbert hissed. Their training had finished earlier that day and now the group were celebrating before dispersing next morning. Christian and Gilbert had been ordered to London.

Sergeant Major Thompson was carrying two bottles of whisky which he plonked on the table Christian and Gilbert were sitting at. His sharp gaze ranged over the group.

'I've trained better in my time, and I've trained worse. You lot will do.' He gestured at the bottles. 'That's for you.'

The group were stunned into silence.

'That's very kind,' François Legrand managed to say at last.

'You hate my guts now but the day might well come when you thank me for being so hard on you. That's not an apology by the way, but an explanation.'

'I think we always knew that, Sergeant Major,' Christian replied softly. 'Though I have to admit, speaking on everyone's behalf, there were occasions when we'd happily have stuck some plastic up your arse, lit the blue touchpaper and retired.'

Thompson guffawed, thinking that very funny. 'No doubt. Now enjoy yourselves. You've earnt it.'

He left them to return to the bar where he was drinking with Miss Sampson-Hardy.

'Not a bad old stick really, as the English put it,' Henri Coudurier commented.

In fairness, they all had to agree.

They all got gloriously drunk and sang French songs for most of the night, ending with *La Marseillaise.* Not a few tears were shed during the rendition of that.

'Here, lookee what I found,' Alice said to Maizie. ''Twas down behind the tallboy in one of the guest bedrooms. 'Twas all covered in dust so must have been there for a while.'

Maizie accepted the small object which she now saw was a cufflink. An expensive one too, she noted. Gold and enamel.

'What's that?' Alice queried, pointing to the emblem engraved on the enamel.

Maizie smiled. 'The Cross of Lorraine.'

'You what?'

'The Cross of Lorraine, Alice. That's the cross the French use.'

'It must be that Christian's then. We ain't had no Frogs here since cc.'

Indeed it must, Maizie thought, wondering why he'd never mentioned that he'd lost it. Perhaps he hadn't realised.

'You could forward it to him, I suppose,' Alice suggested.

'I could if I had an address. Unfortunately I don't.'

'Pity that. 'Tis a pretty thing. He'd be sad to lose it.'

'I'll put it by in case he ever returns,' Maizie smiled. 'He did say he'd like to come back sometime. So who knows?'

Alice was no fool. She'd known there was an attraction between Maiz and Christian, though she doubted it had gone any further than that. Maiz was a married woman after all, the sort to keep her vows. A decent upright maid not to be led astray, no matter how tempting the attraction. Anyway, that was none of her business and certainly not to be commented on. She knew her place.

'Who knows?' Alice echoed, aware of the gleam that had come into Maizie's eyes.

Several times during the rest of that day Maizie took the cufflink from her pocket and stared at it.

It brought back happy memories.

Maizie paused on the landing outside Rosemary's door. There could be no mistaking what she was hearing. Rosemary was crying.

The girl had gone up to bed early saying she was tired. It would now seem that wasn't the truth. Or not the full truth anyway.

'Rosemary?' she said, lightly tapping the door.

The sound of crying abruptly ceased.

'Rosemary, I'm coming in.' When there was no reply she opened the door and went inside.

Rosemary, fully clothed, was sitting on the side of her bed. The look she gave Maizie was one of sheer anguish.

'Oh, my angel,' Maizie whispered and went straight to sit alongside her. 'What is it?'

Rosemary shook her head.

'It must be something?'

Rosemary bit her lip. 'I don't want to say, Aunt Maiz. Please don't press me.'

Maizie didn't know what to think. The medicine Dr Renvoize had given the maid had worked, or appeared to anyway. She'd regained her appetite and put back the weight she'd lost. To all intents and purposes she'd been back to normal. And now this.

'But I want to help.'

'You can't.'

'Are you certain about that?'

Rosemary nodded. She closed her eyes briefly for a second. If only the memories would go away, the dreadful nightmares. But they never would. They'd be with her as long as she lived.

'Is it . . . well, are you ill in any way?'

'No, Aunt Maiz.'

'Then what?'

Rosemary knew she was going to have to lie, there was nothing else for it. It had gone on too long without some sort of explanation. 'Plymouth,' she said.

'Plymouth?'

'I miss my mum and friends. Sometimes it just . . . overwhelms me.'

'Ah!' Maizie breathed, so that was it. What she'd more or

less suspected all along. But why had the girl taken so long to tell her? Homesickness was perfectly natural after all.

As though reading her thoughts Rosemary said, 'You've been so kind to Bobby and me. I didn't want to seem ungrateful.'

Maizie laughed. 'I wouldn't have thought that. Not at all. I'd have perfectly understood.'

She gently smoothed down Rosemary's slightly rumpled hair. 'I enjoy having you and Bobby here. It gives me great pleasure. Don't forget, I haven't children of my own. Having you two, if only for a while, kind of makes up for that. It's not all one-sided you see.'

Rosemary glanced sideways at Maizie. 'Can I ask you a personal question, Aunt Maiz?'

'Of course, sweetness.'

'Why haven't you had children? Is there something wrong?'

Maizie smiled sadly. 'No, there's nothing wrong. At least, not that we know of. There's no reason why Sam and I don't have children, it's simply never happened that's all. But perhaps sometime.'

'You'll make a smashing mother.'

Maizie couldn't have wished for a nicer compliment. 'Why, thank you, Rosemary.'

Rosemary thought of her own mother who wasn't a patch on Maizie, at least not in that way. There was a large part of her wished things had been different. But only where Maizie was concerned. Sam was an entirely different situation.

'Now why don't you get changed and into bed, eh?'

Rosemary nodded.

'Shall I bring you up a hot drink?' She winked conspiratorially. 'I've got some choccy biscuits hidden away. You might like one of those.'

'Oh, yes please.'

'And when you're finished I'll tuck you in. Just as if you were a little-un. How about that?'

Rosemary gave her a beaming smile. 'That would be nice.'

It was with a heavy heart Maizie went downstairs to put the kettle on. If only there was something she could do to alleviate the distress. And why didn't the damned mother write?

Then she had an idea.

'Of course I'll look after the hotel for ee, Maiz. We'll get Trudy Curnow in and whoever else we need. So don't ee fret.'

'Thanks, Alice,' Maizie smiled.

'I think ee's doing the right thing, Maiz. Though I'll worry about ee up there with the bombing still so bad. They say 'tis terrible.'

'It'll be all right, Alice, never fear. The Gerries won't be blowing me up just yet.'

Maizie's defiant tone caused Alice to laugh. 'So when will ee go?'

'Day after tomorrow. And let's keep it to ourselves where I'm off to. Just in case.'

'I understand, Maiz. I quite agree.'

'Adam Daw is taking his truck to Helston early on that morning. He'll give me a lift. But it'll have to be a hired car back.'

Alice sighed. 'That's settled then.'

'I'll see if I can get hold of Adam now,' Maizie declared, and headed for the telephone.

Maizie was enjoying her train journey, relishing being out in the wide world again. She loved Coverack and would never have wished to live anywhere else, but it was nice to escape for a while.

The naval rating sitting opposite was very young and from the looks of him suffering from a severe hangover. Probably been out half the night celebrating before returning to duty, she guessed. His complexion had a definite green tinge about it. They were the only ones in the compartment.

How different this part of Cornwall was to the Lizard, she reflected. Far lusher and greener. More civilised somehow. She began working out how long it had been since she'd last visited Plymouth.

The rating pulled out a packet of cigarettes and lit up, his umpteenth since leaving Helston. He and Maizie had exchanged a few pleasantries but no more than that.

His eyes suddenly hardened while his jaw dropped slightly open. 'Bloody Ada!' he exclaimed. Next moment he was across at the window peering skywards.

Maizie followed the direction of his gaze, the breath catching in her throat when she saw what he'd spotted – a huge wave of low-flying German planes, the markings on their sides clearly visible.

The rating glanced at her, then again out the window. 'Returning from a raid,' he muttered.

She realised, according to the direction they were taking, that he was right. From Plymouth no doubt.

'Gerry bastards,' he murmured, then was instantly apologetic. 'Sorry, missus.'

'That's all right. Do you think they'll . . .' She swallowed hard. 'Shoot at us?'

He made a face. ''Tisn't likely. If they'd wanted to bomb this line they'd have done so long ago. 'Tain't important enough you see. They won't have any bombs left aboard anyway, and precious little ammo either which they'll want to save in case they're attacked going back over the Channel. No, I think we're safe enough.'

And so it proved, the planes droning on their way without breaking off to strafe them.

Maizie heaved a sigh of relief when the planes finally disappeared. 'Good riddance,' she declared.

The rating grinned at her. 'To bad rubbish right enough.'

A few minutes later they witnessed a flight of Hurricanes go screaming after the Germans. From a compartment close by a great rousing cheer went up.

Chapter 11

Maizie had heard of the devastation caused by the bombing, and read about it in the newspapers, but actually to see it first hand took her breath away. Plymouth was a ruin, parts of the city still smoking as a result of the recent raid. Somewhere in the distance a fire engine's bell was furiously clanging.

It took her a while but, with the help of directions from a friendly policeman, she eventually found Chapman Street, knowing the address from Bobby's letters. Number thirty-four was a small, mean-looking terrace house.

The woman who answered her knock was roughly the same age as herself and appeared to have just got out of bed, despite the fact that it was mid-afternoon.

'Yes?' the woman frowned.

'Mrs Tyler?'

The woman nodded.

'I'm Maizie Blackacre from Coverack. Bobby and Rosemary are staying with me.'

'Oh!'

'Can I come in?'

'Yes, yes, of course. Please forgive the mess, I haven't had time to do any housework.'

The room Maizie was ushered into was a tip and smelt

of sweat and cheap perfume. There were bits and pieces, including empty bottles, lying strewn everywhere. Through a partially open doorway Maizie glimpsed an unmade bed.

'This is a surprise.' Shirley Tyler smiled, nervously pulling at the collar of the Chinese-patterned dressing gown she was wearing. Maizie couldn't help but note it had stains down its front.

Maizie took in the fact Mrs Tyler still had on the previous night's make-up, deep red lipstick and lots of rouge, now badly smudged, while her hair was a tangled bird's nest. A slapper through and through if ever there was, Maizie decided. It was more or less what she'd expected.

'I'm Shirley by the way,' Mrs Tyler said, extending a hand which Maizie shook. 'Bobby has often mentioned you in his letters. How are they both?'

'Well, I'm happy to say. Living in a village by the sea seems to agree with them.'

Shirley nodded. 'I had to get them away from here, you understand. The bombing . . .' She shook her head. 'It just goes on and on.'

'I did get quite a shock when I came out of the railway station.'

'Terrible. It's just terrible.' Shirley tugged at her hair. 'I sleep late because I don't get home till the small hours. I work in a club as a hostess.'

And looked every inch the part, Maizie thought snidely. She would have bet that Shirley Tyler did more than pass out drinks and be nice to people.

'Can I offer you a cup of tea or coffee?'

'No thank you,' Maizie replied quickly. God alone knew what state the kitchen was in. 'I had one in a café on my way here.' That was a lie, but a reasonable excuse to refuse.

'So why have you come, Mrs Blackacre, if there's nothing

wrong with the kids?' She was aware Maizie hadn't returned the compliment of exchanging Christian names.

'I had to be in Plymouth on business,' Maizie further lied. 'And thought I'd take the opportunity of looking you up. I was sure you'd want to hear how Bobby and Rosemary are getting on.'

'Of course. Of course. Do you mind if I smoke?'

'Please do.'

Shirley picked up a packet and opened it. 'How about you?'

'No thanks.'

Shirley inhaled deeply, then blew out a long stream of smoke, after which she coughed. 'Sorry, first of the day,' she explained.

What a horrible woman, Maizie thought. It pained her to think this was Bobby and Rosemary's mother. Both deserved better than the sad creature before her.

'Why don't we sit down?'

Shirley swept some debris off a chair and indicated it to Maizie, taking up a position opposite. Both chairs were dilapidated in the extreme. The one Maizie was occupying had several bad burn marks on its right arm.

'The children are concerned they haven't heard from you,' Maizie stated bluntly.

Shirley glanced away. 'I keep meaning to write, but you know how it is?'

Maizie wanted to reply no, she didn't. Instead she didn't reply at all, waiting for the other woman to continue.

'I just never seem to have any time. The hours at the club are long and when I do get home I'm utterly exhausted. No excuse really, but there we are.'

Maizie still didn't reply but continued staring directly at Shirley.

'I must get down to it.'

'They'd appreciate a letter. Rosemary in particular, she's been quite homesick recently.'

'Well, there's nothing here for her right now,' Shirley said hastily. 'I'm out all hours and there aren't any of her pals left. They've all been evacuated same as herself.'

Maizie wasn't sure whether or not she believed the latter. It was clear Shirley Tyler didn't want her children back, for now anyway. It was easy to guess why. They'd be a nuisance. In the way.

'I see,' Maizie murmured.

'But I will write, and soon. You have my word on that.'

'Good,' Maizie said tightly. That was all she'd really come for.

She stayed another ten minutes before taking her leave, hurrying away from Chapman Street and Shirley Tyler as fast as her legs would take her. The woman had disgusted her. The woman and the conditions she lived in. Not to mention what Shirley did for a living.

She had a bite to eat at the station prior to catching the train back to Helston, from where she took a hired car to Coverack.

She stood on the quay for a bit, sucking in lungful after lungful of clean sea air, before going into the hotel.

It had been a long long day. And a most disturbing one.

The flat Christian and Gilbert had been allocated was just off Sloane Street in Chelsea. It came fully furnished, though somewhat spartanly so, had two bedrooms, combination toilet and bathroom, small kitchenette and a lounge. There was also a telephone.

Gilbert yawned. 'Do you want to go out for a drink?'

Christian, who'd been dozing in the chair until a few minutes ago, considered that. 'Could do.'

'Unless you can think of something better?'

Christian shook his head.

'I wonder if that girl will be in the Eight Bells again tonight. I thought she was gorgeous.'

Christian grinned. 'She was also with somebody if you remember. A great hulking brute of a chap.'

Gilbert shrugged. 'He wasn't necessarily her boyfriend. He could have been a brother or cousin even.'

'The way he was staring at her? Some hopes.'

Gilbert ran a hand through his hair. 'I'm getting sick and tired of all this hanging about waiting for orders. It's boring with nothing to do except go to the barracks every day for training.' The barracks he was referring to were Chelsea Barracks, not far away.

Christian came to his feet; if they were going out he needed a shave. 'Our time will come soon enough. You'll see.'

Just then the telephone rang. A summons for Christian to see Colonel G next morning at nine.

That could only mean one thing.

Operations Centre for the Executive was situated in Portland Place and Christian duly presented himself there at five to the hour. A pleasant WRAC whom he'd met previously informed him he'd be taken through directly.

'Ah, Le Gall, please be seated,' Colonel Galbraith, known in the Executive as Colonel G, said when he entered the latter's office. Also present was Major Hammond, second in command.

Christian sat on the wooden chair placed in front of the Colonel's desk and waited.

Colonel G studied him intently, his eyes reminding Christian of a bird of prey. He found them quite unnerving. 'Fancy a spot of action, Captain?' Colonel G suddenly smiled disarmingly.

'Yes, sir.'

'Good. Because I have something here that's right up your street. You were a surveyor before the war according to your records?'

'Studying to be one, sir. I wasn't fully qualified.'

Colonel G grunted. 'Nonetheless, you should be able to manage the task we have for you. You're from Brittany, I understand?'

'That's correct, sir. A place called Hennebont.'

Colonel G put on a pair of spectacles and stared at a map spread before him. 'Come round this side, Captain.'

His finger jabbed at a section of coastline. 'Gerry is up to something here. We've had reports that they're building defences of some kind. At least we presume them to be defences. What we want you to do is go there and take a look see.'

Christian studied the indicated coastline. 'I understand, sir.'

'If they are defences we want to know everything we can about them. Intended size, construction, et cetera. Can you do that?'

'Yes, sir.'

'Excellent.' Colonel G beamed.

Major Hammond spoke for the first time. 'These defences are in the early stages of being built so I would imagine part of your report, possibly a large part, would have to be speculation?'

Christian nodded. 'Probably, sir. But I shall be able to surmise a great deal from whatever foundations have already been laid. They should give us a fair indication of what Gerry has in mind.'

Colonel G's gaze bored into Christian. 'A set of plans would be most beneficial, if it was possible to acquire them.'

'Difficult, sir.'

'I appreciate that. But they could be of immense value. However, that is not your primary objective. When you return we will want a full written report detailing what is fact and what speculation.'

'How do I get there, sir?'

Colonel G gestured to Hammond. 'That's your department.'

'Right,' declared Hammond. 'I thought we'd take you in and drop you off by MTB. Time to be decided. The navy have assured me they can lay one on for us.'

Christian frowned; he wasn't at all keen on that. 'Aren't Motor Torpedo Boats very noisy, sir?'

Hammond regarded him steadily. 'True enough. But they're extremely fast. The landing will be over and done with before Gerry has an inkling we're about.'

'May I speak openly, sir?'

'Of course.'

Christian shook his head. 'It's an awful risk, sir. Fast or not, they'll hear the MTB coming for miles. What if we're unlucky and there's a battery emplacement there? Or what if Gerry, alerted by the noise, is waiting to pick me up the moment I step ashore? It's too risky in my opinion, sir.'

Hammond glanced at Colonel G. 'He has a point,' the Colonel said.

'Then perhaps I can arrange something else. Something quieter.'

Christian bent again to the map, a grin lighting up his face when he studied the English coastline opposite. 'May I make a suggestion, sir?'

Colonel G nodded.

Christian explained what he had in mind.

*   *   *

'A letter for me!' Bobby exclaimed, having just come down to breakfast.

Maizie brandished an envelope. 'And Rosemary. It's addressed to the pair of you.'

His hands were trembling when he accepted it from her. 'It's Mum's writing,' he whispered, his voice choked with emotion.

'I thought it might be.'

'What's up?' Rosemary demanded, coming into the kitchen.

'A letter from Mum,' Bobby informed her.

Next moment he was tearing open the envelope.

'I think it's ever so exciting your mother's coming to visit,' Emily said to Bobby, as the pair of them sat on rocks at the shoreline. The tide was far out and the air was strong with the smell of stranded seaweed.

'She didn't say when. But she'll come when she can.'

'It'll be great fun,' Emily enthused.

'She'll stay at the hotel of course. Though for how long I don't know. As long as possible I suppose.'

'I hope I'll get to meet her?' Emily smiled.

Bobby had sudden misgivings. His mother was a little different to the people of Coverack after all. Maybe they wouldn't like her? Think her odd.

'Well?' Emily demanded.

'We'll have to wait and see,' he prevaricated.

'Is Rosemary pleased?'

'Ever so much. It seems such a long time since we left Plymouth. Absolute ages and ages.'

'And since you last saw your mum.'

He nodded.

'Have you replied yet?'

'I shall do that tonight after homework. And Rosemary's going to put in a page as well.' His face clouded. 'I just wish she'd written before now. But she's been ever so busy she said. She can't help that.'

'Wartime,' Emily commented sagely.

'There was no word about my dad though. Mum says she hasn't heard since we left home. I only hope he's all right.'

'I'm sure he is. He's probably in a jungle somewhere where there aren't any postboxes.'

'Yes, that's it,' Bobby agreed. 'Has to be.'

Bobby closed his eyes. He couldn't wait for his mum to arrive in Coverack so he could tell her all the things he'd been up to. You could only put so much in a letter after all.

Oh, it would be great when she got here. A real red letter day. That was an expression his dad had sometimes used.

A real red letter day.

'Maiz, come and listen to this!' Alice called out.

'What is it?'

'Come and listen.'

Alice was standing at the hotel door where Maizie joined her.

'Do you hear it?'

'What?'

'Guns, Maiz. Out over the Channel somewhere.'

Maizie could hear them now. A faint sound, but clearly of big guns firing.

'If it 'tweren't so foggy we might be able to see something,' Alice commented. Close to shore the fog was quite light but further out it became dense and impenetrable.

'Do you think it's a battle, Maiz?'

She considered that. 'Unlikely in the Channel. It's just not the place for a full-scale battle. But something's going on, that's certain.'

The wind changed direction and the sound of firing

became even more faint so that they had to strain to hear it.

'God bless and protect our boys whoever they are,' Alice said softly.

'Amen.'

'No doubt we'll learn what went on sooner or later.'

'No doubt,' Maizie agreed.

Then a different sound cut through the air, that of her telephone ringing. She hurried back inside.

It was Tim Lambrick, the overall Area Commander of the Movement.

'How do you feel?' Gilbert asked casually.

Christian glanced at him, and smiled. 'Truth?'

'Truth.'

'Nervous as hell.'

Gilbert laughed. 'I'd be surprised if you were otherwise.'

Gilbert knew Christian was off on assignment, but not what the assignment was, or where. That was none of his business. Nor would Christian have told him if he'd inquired. The matter was secret.

'When do you leave?'

'First thing in the morning. Early.'

'Any idea for how long?'

Christian stared at him, not wanting to divulge even that information.

Gilbert shrugged. 'Suit yourself. Just don't complain if you come back and find me with some popsy installed.'

'You'll be lucky!' Christian teased.

'Maybe, maybe not. But if there's any luck going then I hope it's with you.'

Christian was touched, his expression reflecting that. 'Thanks.'

'Shall we have a last drink before you disappear? That girl might be in the Eight Bells.'

Why not, Christian thought. He could certainly use one. A very large one come to that. For who knew what lay ahead?

'Can I have a cognac, please?'

'Coming up, sir,' Maizie replied, brow furrowed in concentration, busy with pencil and paper with her back to the bar.

She laid the pencil and paper aside and reached for a glass. 'Large or small, sir?'

'Small, I think.'

Her face registered shock and surprise when she turned to face the customer sitting smiling at her. 'Christian!' she gasped.

'Hello, Maizie.'

'By all that's . . .' She trailed off, delighted to see him again. 'Here, have that on the house.'

'Why, thank you.'

'What brings you down here?'

'I missed the Paris Hotel, what else?'

'And how long are you here for?'

'That depends,' he replied slowly.

'On what?'

Not yet, he told himself. Give it a few minutes first and hope no one else came in. He wanted to enjoy their reunion. 'You look wonderful,' he said, changing the subject.

'On what, Christian?'

He shrugged. 'This and that.'

'Are you on leave?'

'Why don't you join me, Maizie?'

She laughed, amazed at the sheer joy she felt at his return. He really was a sight for sore eyes. 'Wait till I tell Alice and the children when they get in from school.'

She poured herself a gin and tonic and came round to sit beside him. 'You look well,' she stated. 'But thinner. Haven't you been eating properly?'

He stopped himself from making a crack about her sounding like his mother. 'Oh yes. It's simply that I'm fitter than I was. Very much so as a matter of fact.'

'It suits you.'

'Thank you.'

She self-consciously touched her hair, wishing she'd known he was going to appear. She'd have tidied herself, perhaps worn different clothes. The skirt and sweater she was wearing were long past their best. 'Are you booking in?'

He nodded.

'How long for?'

'That depends. One night, two, maybe more. As I say, it all depends.'

She regarded him seriously. 'You are being mysterious.'

'Am I?'

'You *know* you are.'

'Perhaps I'm just teasing.'

She couldn't get over how pleased she was to see him, what a thrill it gave her. 'We've often spoken about you,' she confessed.

'Really?'

'Especially the children,' she added quickly. 'Bobby in particular. You were a big hit with him.'

'How is the little rascal?'

'Fine. He's even got a girlfriend.'

'At his age!'

Maizie pulled a face. 'Children seem to be growing up faster nowadays. Her name's Emily and they spend a lot of time together.'

'Well well well,' Christian murmured. 'And Rosemary?'

'Rosemary's different. I've had a bit of trouble with her.'

'Oh?'

'Homesickness, it made her act very strangely for a while until I got to the bottom of it.' She went on to tell Christian about going to Plymouth and having a confrontation with Shirley Tyler.

'Well, at least she's written and is coming here,' Christian commented when Maizie finished.

'Rosemary has bucked up a lot since that letter. Though she still has her moments. Hopefully she'll be even better after Mrs Tyler has been.'

'And Alice?'

'Oh, Alice is the same. She never changes.'

'And you, Maizie. How have you been?'

She dropped her gaze. 'Fine, I just soldier on.' She wondered whether to mention Sam had been home, then decided not to.

'You don't seem too certain about that?'

'I am. I assure you.'

He produced his cigarettes. 'You?'

'Yes please.'

He assisted her to a light, their faces coming quite close together as he did. He noted she was still wearing the same perfume.

'Oh by the way, Alice found something of yours.'

He couldn't think what and shook his head.

'A cufflink with the Cross of Lorraine on it. At least we presumed it's yours.'

'It's mine all right!' he exclaimed excitedly. 'I knew I'd lost it but had no idea I'd done so here. I can't tell you how relieved I am to have it back. The set was a birthday present from my parents.'

'I'll give it to you later then. After we've had supper.'

He noted the *we*. So he was to eat with the family and not alone in the restaurant.

She noticed his glass was empty. 'Will you have another?'

'Only if you do.'

She laughed. 'It's early for me, Christian. I'll get drunk.'

'That's what I was hoping.'

There was a hiatus between them after he'd said that, broken only by her glancing away. She was horribly aware that her neck was flushed.

'Well, it is a reunion,' he added lamely.

She got up from her stool and returned behind the bar. 'Of course I'll join you. I'll put it on your tab.'

'I think I'd better pay for everything up front this time, Maizie.'

'But why? Your credit's good.'

Christian ground out the remains of his cigarette. 'Is it true this pub doesn't close till a minute past midnight,' he said slowly and emphatically.

Maizie almost dropped the glass she was holding. That was it, the passphrase Tim Lambrick had given her over the telephone. The one to be used by a stranger to whom she and the Movement were to give every assistance they could.

'You?' she queried, her face a picture.

'Yes, Maizie, me.'

She was utterly flabbergasted.

'Christian!'

'Bobby!'

The boy thundered towards Christian and threw himself at the Frenchman who, laughing, caught him and swung him round and round.

'I do believe you've grown a foot since I saw you last,' Christian declared.

'Hardly that, Christian. But I have grown.'

'To become quite the young man.'

'How long are you here for?'

'I'm not quite certain yet.' He glanced at Maizie. 'But a couple of days at least.'

'Do you want to come out to play?'

Christian laughed. 'I'm a bit tired for that. I've motored all the way down from London today.'

'You leave him alone,' Alice scolded Bobby. 'He didn't come down here to play, me lad, but to enjoy hisself.'

'Perhaps tomorrow,' Christian promised. He turned his attention to Rosemary. 'How are you?'

'Fine, thank you.'

'You've grown up as well. I see a big difference.'

Something momentarily flashed in her eyes which Christian noticed. Something he couldn't quite make out. Something puzzling.

'Now you children run and get washed while I dish up supper,' Maizie declared.

'And I'm off home,' Alice said. 'I'll just get me coat.'

'It's stargazy pie,' Maizie informed Christian, almost coyly. 'With the heads sticking out.'

They both laughed.

It was as if he'd never been away, he thought as he followed her through to the kitchen.

'Can you do it?'

Denzil Eustis lifted his gaze from the sea chart to stare at Christian. It was late that night, the bar long closed. He'd been summoned earlier by Maizie and the situation explained to him after the last customer had gone.

'I can doos it all right,' Denzil replied slowly. 'But in the dark you say?'

Christian nodded.

'That makes a difference.'

'How so?'

'I don't know these waters close in all that well to be truthful. 'Twould be easy as anything in daylight and following the proper channels. But in the dark and . . . well the Gerries are bound to be watching the usual approaches which means keeping away from thae.'

He shook his head. 'To be honest I sure as hell wouldn't like to attempt this under the circumstances.'

'But don't you smuggle from there? You must be used to it.'

Denzil gave a dry laugh. 'I don't do no smuggling. The family did years back along, but not me. There's only a few does that any more, and none of them are in the Movement.'

'What about Hookie?' Christian suggested.

'He's your man right enough. But he ain't in the Movement. His name was mentioned but we rejected him on account of his being a cripple.'

'He seems to manage his boat all right despite that,' Christian replied drily.

'One of the best seamen round here. And he knows thae French waters like the back of his hand. Or hook as the case may be,' Denzil added with a chuckle.

Christian looked at Maizie. 'What do you think?'

'I think we'll have to speak to Hookie. But best we don't mention the Movement. The story will simply be that you came to us to get you over there. OK?'

'OK,' Christian nodded.

'I'll help crew. That's the least I can do,' Denzil offered. 'And we'll use others from the Movement to make the full complement. Hookie's lads can stay at home that night.'

'Agreed,' Maizie said. 'We'll speak to Hookie in the morning.'

Chapter 12

Hookie was a bachelor who, despite that, lived in a cottage as neat and tidy as any house-proud woman could boast. It was the first time Maizie had been in there and she was impressed. She couldn't help but compare it with the squalor of Shirley Tyler's house.

'What is this, a delegation of some sort?' Hookie queried, ushering them into the kitchen. 'I got the kettle on so who wants tea?'

They all said they'd love a cup.

'So, monsewer, you're back again like the proverbial bad penny,' Hookie declared, taking his caddy down from a shelf.

'That's right, Hookie. Only on this occasion I'm here on business.'

Hookie eyed him shrewdly. 'Why have I got this awful feeling it somehow involves me?'

'Because it does.'

'Can I help?' Maizie offered.

'You sits yourself down, Maizie Blackacre. I can manage what's necessary.'

She realised she'd offended him. 'Sorry.'

'So what's up?'

'You'll have to keep quiet about what you hear next, Hookie, whether you help us or not.'

He regarded her keenly. 'I understand.'

'It's army business, Hookie. Top Secret, hush hush.'

He laughed. 'I can't imagine what the army wants of me. Or why you lot is involved.' His gaze fixed on Christian. 'You're behind this, I take it? Being you're the only one with army connections.'

'That's right.'

Hookie grunted. 'Well, let's have it then.'

'Christian has come to us asking to be taken to France,' Denzil explained. 'Drop him off ashore like in the middle of the night. I could try of course, but you're the obvious answer.'

Hookie barked out a savage laugh. 'Me! You can forget that. The bastards nearly caught me last time I was over by. Remember I told you, Maiz?'

'I remember,' she confirmed. 'But this is really important, Hookie. Vitally important, otherwise we couldn't come to you.'

He set out fine bone china cups and saucers. 'And why would that be?'

'The army, your British Army, want me over there on a job, Hookie. I need to be dropped off and then picked up again at a later date to be agreed upon.'

'I see,' Hookie murmured. 'Did Maiz tell ee about the E Boat I nearly ran foul of? Gave me the fright of my life it did.'

'Maiz did mention it on our way here,' Denzil nodded.

'‘Tis patrolling that section of the coast. And maybe others like it. 'Twould be madness going over there again knowing thae things are lying in wait. You'd either end up blown to smithereens or in a Gerry prison, neither of which I fancies.'

'The first time we met you said you'd fight in this war too if they'd let you,' Christian reminded him. 'Well, now's your chance.'

'I didn't mean no cloak and dagger stuff!' Hookie protested. 'That was never in me mind at all.'

'It wasn't in my mind either when I joined up. And yet here I am.'

Hookie regarded Christian dyspeptically. 'You Frenchies are all alike, smooth-talking buggers.'

Christian laughed. 'I'll take that as a compliment.'

'Well, 'tweren't meant as one.'

'So what about it, Hookie?' Maizie prompted. 'Are you ready to do your bit for King and Country?'

He didn't answer that as he filled their cups. 'There's sugar and milk on the table. Help yourselves.'

Having completed that task Hookie crossed to a coat hanging behind the door from which he produced his pipe and tobacco pouch. He took his time about filling the former before lighting up.

'Where exactly would you want to be dropped?' he asked casually.

Christian pulled out the sea chart. 'I'll show you.'

'I don't need no chart,' Hookie snorted. 'Just tells me.'

Christian did.

'And who suggested there?'

'Some chap in the Admiralty.'

'Well, he's talking shit. Excuse the language, Maizie. There's tides, eddies and currents round there that I wouldn't go near this time of year. Are you being met, monsewer?'

Christian shook his head.

'Then there's a tiny cove I know about half a mile away. Would that suit just as well?'

'It would,' Christian replied.

'It's well screened by rocks with a high rockwall behind it. But there is a path leading up which I can tells ee how to find. I'll drop you there, how's that?'

Christian beamed. 'Excellent.'

Hookie scratched his head. 'I must be off my chump agreeing to this. If that E Boat sights us it's all over and no mistake. One way or t'other.'

'They wanted me to go in by MTB, which is our equivalent of their E Boat, but I said it was far too noisy. That's when I had the idea of asking Denzil, thinking then that he was a smuggler too,' Christian explained.

'So this is all your doing, eh?'

'I'm afraid it is,' Christian smiled.

'Serves me right for getting ee fags and cognac. I does ee a favour and this is how ee repays me. Putting me in a situation where I could get me head blown off.'

'You're a good man, Hookie Repson,' Maizie said quietly.

Hookie's weatherbeaten face coloured ever so slightly. 'There's no need to go soft there, Maiz. I's only doing me duty when called to do so.'

His eyes became reflective. 'I'll have to ask me crew. Explain things. 'Tisn't fair otherwise.'

'I'll crew for you, Hookie, and Charlie Treloar. Charlie hates the Germans. Your lads can stay here safe and sound.' Denzil had named Charlie because he was a member of the Movement, but Hookie didn't have to know that.

Hookie grunted. 'Sail with ee, Denzil? Only if I's skipper.'

'It's your boat, Hookie. No argument about who's skipper. You'll be strictly in charge.'

Hookie turned again to Christian. 'How long is ee going to be there?'

Christian considered that. 'Three days should be about right.'

'Then three days it is. I'll be back on the third night after I drops ee. And make sure you're there, monsewer. Because if you're not then tough luck. I ain't making a second trip. I'll risk me neck, but only so far.'

'I understand,' Christian replied quietly.

'Another thing. Is ee going inland or staying there on the coast?'

Christian couldn't understand why he'd asked the question. 'Does it make a difference?'

'If ee's staying on the coast I has friends in a village close by where you'll be landing. Give them my name and they'll look after ee while ee's there.'

Christian frowned, going over the pros and cons. 'I'd rather not contact anyone, Hookie. If the Germans were to capture me it would mean torture and . . . Well, you get my drift.'

Maizie had gone white at the mention of his being captured and tortured. That was something just too awful to contemplate.

'You're probably right,' Hookie acknowledged. 'We'll leave them out of it.'

'That's settled then,' Denzil declared.

'When do you want to go, Frenchman?' Hookie queried.

'As soon as possible.'

Hookie nodded. 'Well, I got to think about that. Work out the tides and study the forecasts. Tell ee what.' He looked at Maizie. 'I'll come down the Paris this dinnertime and tell ee what I decided. How's that?'

'It'll be however you say, Hookie,' she replied.

'So be it.'

He had a long draw on his pipe, and then laughed. 'I must be stark raving mad to be doing this. Stark raving!'

Maizie placed the lamp she was carrying on the table. 'There are our stores, Christian, all clearly marked. Help yourself.'

Maizie had brought Christian along to the tunnel to select those items he needed. It had been decided in London it was better this way rather than he be issued with them there and then have to bring them down with him.

'Thanks, Maizie.'

The cave wall, lit by yellow lamp light, danced with Christian's shadow as he set about opening various boxes.

'This is going to be very dangerous, isn't it?' she said quietly.

He paused to look at her. 'Don't worry, I shan't be taking any unnecessary risks.'

'But it's still dangerous.'

'Yes,' he acknowledged gruffly, removing a small wrapping of plastic explosive similar to that he'd been trained to use. Several more units of PE followed the first into his coat pocket. He then moved on to another box containing the pencil timers.

'Have you heard from Sam recently?' he asked suddenly.

That startled her, coming so unexpectedly as it did. 'Why yes. In fact he was home not that long ago.'

Christian glanced sideways at her. 'Oh?'

'On leave. Which was extended due to their having trouble with the ship's engines.'

Christian forced himself to say the next bit. 'That must have been nice for the pair of you.'

'Yes it was.' Now why had he brought up the subject of Sam? She'd hoped to keep away from it. 'He brought me this gold watch,' she said, holding her wrist in his direction.

'I noticed that and wondered if it was new.'

'Sam got it for me in New York. A surprise really as he's not normally one for buying presents.'

Christian didn't reply to that. Instead he hefted a sten gun that had already been cleaned ready for use. He'd strip it later to ensure everything was in perfect working order.

'What exactly are you going to do over there?' Maizie asked with a catch in her voice.

'You know I can't tell you that.'

'No, I suppose not,' she mumbled, dropping her gaze. She felt quite wretched.

He stared at her. 'It'll be all right, Maiz. I promise.' He was saying that to cheer her up as much as anything. He had no idea whether he'd be all right or not.

'You came to Coverack as a guest, Christian, then became more than that. A friend to myself and the children. We care a great deal about you.'

'And I about you,' he whispered in reply.

Her instinct was to fly into his arms, to comfort him and herself at the same time. But she couldn't do that. It was out of the question.

'I shall be thinking about you all the time you're away,' she said.

He opened his mouth to reply, and then changed his mind.

'Do you have a cigarette?' she asked quietly.

He smiled. 'I don't think that's a good idea with all this ammo in here, Maiz. Do you?'

She coloured. 'No, of course not. How stupid of me.'

'But we'll have one as soon as we get outside again. Can you wait?'

She noted the tease in his voice and managed a smile to match his.

'I won't be long,' he declared, and returned his attention to the piled-up stores.

'How did you get on with Mr Blackacre when he was here?' Christian asked Bobby, as the pair of them were strolling down the quay. They'd been speaking French together and Christian was delighted with the boy's progress.

Bobby immediately became defensive. 'He was . . . OK.'

'Just that, OK?'

'Well . . . he wasn't as nice as you. He could be awfully grumpy. I don't think he likes children very much.'

'Indeed,' Christian mused.

'Rosemary loathed him. I don't know why, she's never said. But I could tell. If she came into a room when he was there she'd leave. I saw her do that often. Also . . .' Bobby trailed off.

'Also what?' Christian prompted.

'He always had his hands on Aunt Maiz. Always touching her. I found that embarrassing.'

Christian turned away so Bobby couldn't see his expression. A green flame of jealousy surged through him. 'They are man and wife after all,' he heard himself saying. 'It's quite natural.'

'I don't see other men touching their wives like that all the time. Do you?'

Christian took a deep breath. 'We'd better go in. It's cold out here. And I could use a drink.'

Maizie stared hard at herself in her vanity mirror. Thirty-two years old and looking every day of it, she thought in despair. How she wished she could go somewhere and be pampered like some of the women she'd read about in magazines. A face and full body massage for starters, creams, oils, potions, hot scented baths. A top-class hairdresser followed by someone to put on make-up for her expertly, something she'd never been terribly good at doing herself.

She sighed, running a hand through her hair. That was one of the penalties you paid for living beside the sea – it not only played havoc with your complexion but also with your hair. Once, years ago, hers had been lovely and silky with a glorious sheen to it; now it was coarse and dull, thanks to constant exposure to the salt that permeated the air. She started when there was a tap on the door.

'Come in!' she frowned, thinking one of the children

must have woken up and couldn't get back to sleep. A nightmare perhaps. Her face reflected her surprise when Christian entered.

'Are you decent, Maizie?'

'Just about,' she smiled, pulling the lapels of her dressing gown a little tighter.

'I hope you don't mind this intrusion, but I've come to ask a favour.'

'Of course, Christian. What is it?'

He crossed over to her vanity table and placed a sealed envelope on it. 'I know I told you I'd be all right, and I'm certain I will, but just in case . . .' He broke off and cleared his throat, steadfastly avoiding her gaze. 'When the war ends, as it will one day, would you see that gets posted. It's to my parents in Hennebont.'

'Oh, Christian,' she whispered, turning pale.

'I'd like them to know what happened. Or something of what happened anyway. I know such a letter would be a great comfort to Maman.'

She stared at the envelope as though it was a snake about to strike her. 'Nothing will happen,' she stated emphatically. 'There'll be no "just in case". You'll be back.'

She was still transfixed by the envelope when the bedroom door clicked shut behind him.

It was the foulest of afternoons, the sky grey and so low you felt you could reach up and touch it. Cold rain pelted down.

Hookie, Denzil and Charlie Treloar were already on their way to the *Snowdrop*, Christian having lingered behind to say his goodbyes to Maizie. He was dressed in oilskins borrowed from Hookie.

'I'll come to the boat with you,' Maizie said, reaching for an old mac that hung just inside the hotel door.

'No, you stay here. I don't want you getting soaked.'

She hesitated. There was sense in that. But maybe she should go all the same.

'Please, Maiz?'

She understood then; he didn't want her there. 'OK, Chris.' It was the first time she'd ever called him that.

'Wish me luck.'

'You know I do.'

'I'll be back before you know it.'

She smiled at him, a glint of tears in her eyes. 'You'd better get on then. Hookie won't take it kindly if you keep him waiting.'

'Right.'

He didn't move.

On impulse she went to kiss his cheek but, somehow, he turned his head slightly at the last moment and her lips landed full on his. Then his arms were around her, pulling her tight.

She broke away with a gasp, but didn't say anything. Neither did he, just simply wheeled about and strode off into the rain.

A few minutes later Charlie Treloar cast off and the *Snowdrop* began chugging out of the harbour.

Tears streamed down Maizie's face mimicking the falling rain.

'Has ee any experience of small craft, monsewer?' Hookie casually inquired of Christian.

'None, except that day we all went out to watch the basking sharks.'

Hookie smiled knowingly, his eyes twinkling. 'If ee's going to be sick make sure you do it overboard. And hang on to something, we don't want to lose ee.'

'I won't be sick,' Christian replied defiantly.

'We'll see,' Hookie said, and moved away to join Denzil in the wheelhouse. Charlie Treloar sat aft, hunched miserably.

The smell aboard was revolting, a combination of fuel, oil and fish. The movement of the boat itself was both ceaseless and pitiless. Up, down, roll to the side, a shuddering yaw. Already Christian was wishing the journey was over and he was back on dry land.

It took him a while but eventually he managed to light a cigarette which he held in a cupped hand. A couple of drags and he felt the bile rise in his throat. He quickly threw the cigarette over the side.

A little later Denzil appeared with a mug of tea. 'Here, gets that down ee. It'll warm ee a bit.'

Christian gratefully accepted the mug. 'Thanks, Denzil.'

'How's ee feeling?'

'Fine.'

Denzil raised an eyebrow before returning to the wheelhouse.

Christian's stomach was heaving now and he'd gone quite lightheaded. His legs had somehow turned to jelly.

He managed to finish the tea and staggered over to the wheelhouse. 'How are we doing?' he asked.

'It'll be slow on account of the weather. But that's to our advantage,' Hookie replied.

'It keeps visibility down,' Denzil added.

''Tis supposed to be a moonless night, but this here's better than that. 'Tis fortunate weather for us, monsewer.'

There was a small, partially shielded light showing in the wheelhouse with a chart laid out below. The stink of fuel, oil and fish was even more cloying and nauseating in these confines.

'I'll take ee in as close as I can, then Charlie will row ee ashore,' Hookie explained. 'That all right?'

'Whatever you say.'

'At least you won't mind getting your feet wet after this,' Hookie laughed, thinking that was very funny.

The boat seemed to stand on its end, throwing Christian backwards right out of the wheelhouse. He desperately grabbed a stanchion to hold on to. My God, but this was awful.

He knew then he was going to lose the large lunch Maizie had cooked, a special one to see him on his way. He desperately scrabbled over to the side and, hanging on for all he was worth, voided the contents of his stomach while his face was spattered by flying spume.

'I'm amazed he lasted so long,' Denzil commented drily to Hookie.

'Me too. 'Tis a rough passage right enough.'

Christian continued to retch although nothing was left to come up. He felt he must surely die.

A few miles off the French coast Hookie cut the engine and ordered the sail to be hoisted. The weather had abated a little, but not by much. Hookie was drawing on years of experience to calculate exactly where they were, praying he was right. Many vessels had foundered or been wrecked on nights just like this.

'I'm glad you're at the wheel, Hookie, and not me,' Denzil commented when he rejoined him.

'How's the Frenchman?'

'Wishing he'd never been born.'

Both men laughed.

Christian looked up when Denzil materialised by his side. 'Listen,' Denzil instructed.

Christian stood up, having been sitting on a coil of rope. 'It's a ship's engines.'

'You're right there. The E Boat, Hookie says. 'Tis out there somewhere on its patrol.'

Christian listened more closely. The sound was far more

powerful and noisy than the one the *Snowdrop* made. There was also a definite whine to it.

'It's not as close as ee thinks,' Denzil said quietly. 'That sort of engine sound carries, even in this weather. You can be thankful you're not going in on that MTB that was suggested. Why, you may as well send up flares and rockets to announce your presence.'

Christian nodded his agreement as the *Snowdrop* silently continued on its way.

'This is as far as I dare go,' Hookie announced to Christian as Charlie Treloar dropped anchor.

'I understand.'

'You'd better give me thae oilskins.'

Christian quickly divested himself of the waterproofs and handed them to Hookie. Underneath he was wearing typical French working man's clothes. He then picked up the canvas duffel bag containing the sten gun and other bits and pieces he was taking along.

'Now remember, monsewer, three nights from now. Be waiting, because if you're not I shan't be returning. Not with that E Boat prowling about I won't.'

'If I'm still alive I'll be there, Hookie. You can count on it.'

Hookie smiled. 'I don't envy you your job, monsewer, whatever it is. You're going amongst a nest of Gerries, may their souls all rot in hell. You're a brave man, I'll say that for ee.'

'Thank you, Hookie.'

While they were talking Charlie had pulled the small boat alongside. 'I'll get in first and you follow,' he instructed Christian.

Christian eyed the heaving rowing boat. One slip and he'd be swimming.

'Good luck to ee, monsewer,' Hookie said gruffly, extending his hand.

Christian shook it. 'Thanks.'

'Same from me,' Denzil added, joining them.

Christian took a deep breath. This was it. Denzil and Hookie both helped him over the side.

It was no use, she just wasn't going to get any sleep that night. Maizie sighed and snapped on her bedside lamp. She may as well get up and dressed.

She reached for her cigarettes and lit one. It was worrying about Christian that was keeping her awake. Had he landed yet? Had the *Snowdrop* run into any trouble on the way across? Had . . .

She shook her head. All she could do was wait for the *Snowdrop*'s return and find out exactly what had happened. Hopefully that meant nothing more eventful than Christian being put safely ashore.

She shivered; it was freezing in the bedroom. Slipping from under the covers she reached for her winter dressing gown and shrugged into it. She'd go downstairs and have a milky drink. That might help calm her a little.

Oh bugger that, she decided. She'd have a proper drink. Maybe even two.

A glance at the bedside clock confirmed the earliness of the hour. It would be a long agonising time yet before the *Snowdrop* could be back. Providing it did get back.

'Maizie!' Alice exclaimed. 'What's ee doing here at this hour?'

'Can I come in?'

'Of course, my lover. Now what's to do? Is it Christian?' Alice was party to the fact that Christian was going to France on a mission for the army, but, like Hookie, was completely unaware of the Movement's existence. She'd been sworn to secrecy about Christian and given her solemn word, which Maizie knew she'd keep. Alice could be as big a gossip as the best of them, but could also be trusted to keep her mouth shut when required.

Maizie removed her sodden mac and the hastily tied head scarf she'd thrown on. 'Do you remember that reading you did for me back along?'

Understanding dawned in Alice's eyes. She nodded.

'You said someone was going to die but couldn't say who. Could you say now?'

'That all depends on the cards,' Alice replied uneasily. 'I can only tell what I sees in them.' Or wants to tell, she thought.

'Will you give me another reading now?'

Alice, newly woken, wasn't in the mood for that at all. 'I'll have to wash my face and have a cup of tea first. But I'll do it for ee if ee insists.'

'Please, Alice.'

Maizie's anguished expression left Alice in no doubt at all about her concern for Christian. 'Sit ee down and I'll put kettle on,' she said.

'I need to get back before the children wake so I can get them out to school.'

'I'll see you get back all right,' Alice promised.

Maizie waited anxiously while Alice put the kettle on and then went off to wash her face.

Alice's reading was the same as previously. There would be a death but she didn't know who. Even Maizie's anguish wouldn't make her divulge that.

Christian had made good time, keeping to the fields and pathways and avoiding the roads. From his vantage point he could now dimly discern what must be the installations under construction. He'd come far enough for the present and would wait for first light before deciding what to do next.

Thankfully the rain had stopped but the temperature had fallen even further. He chittered with cold and briskly rubbed his hands together.

Sleep or not? He decided that he would not risk it until he knew exactly what was what. There might well be Gerry sentries about. If one of them came across him his mission would be over before it had even begun.

He rubbed his stomach which thankfully was settling down again. He felt he could eat a few mouthfuls of the iron rations he'd brought along. It was a pity about Maizie's special lunch, he thought ruefully. That would have kept him going for some time. Well, he only hoped the fish had enjoyed it as much as he had.

He snuggled down to wait.

Chapter 13

The cold light of dawn revealed the beginnings of massive constructions that stretched as far as the eye could see. Already some sections were starting to take shape while others remained at the foundation stage. Concrete was apparently the main material being used. Mountains of huge bags were everywhere in evidence.

There were also some temporary wooden huts, each with smoke spiralling from a chimney. As he watched, two grey-uniformed soldiers emerged from the nearest. Billets it would seem.

Half an hour later scores of open-topped trucks arrived, each jammed with civilian men. The workers, he correctly guessed. Which meant the soldiers were undoubtably there as guards.

By nine o'clock the area was a hive of activity, transformed into an enormous building site where the workers toiled under the watchful eye of the Wehrmacht.

He was going to have to get down there, Christian decided. Move amongst the site so he could see and judge exactly what was what.

But first of all he'd bury his duffel bag and its contents. Using a long-bladed, black-painted killing knife he began to dig a hole.

* * *

Maizie, who'd been keeping a look-out all morning, was on the quay when the *Snowdrop* docked. She jumped aboard without waiting for it to be moored up.

'Well?' she demanded of Denzil standing by the wheel-house.

'No problems, Maizie. He went ashore safe and sound.'

A great sigh of relief whooshed from her. Now all that remained was for Christian to return safely.

'The weather was foul,' Denzil went on. 'Otherwise we'd have been home hours ago.'

Hookie joined them. 'We heard the bloody E Boat but never saw it. Nor it us, thank God.'

Denzil suddenly grinned. 'Sick as a pig he was. Honking away like a good un.'

'Give him his due though,' Hookie said. 'He held on for a while before letting go.'

'Poor Christian,' Maizie murmured. She'd never experienced sea sickness herself but knew from others how awful it could be. 'But he's all right, that's the main thing.'

Denzil yawned. 'It's bed for me after that. I'll sleep well, I can tell ee.'

'I thought you might like to come up to the hotel and have some breakfast. It won't take Alice and me a jiffy to get it ready for you.'

'That's handsome, Maiz,' Hookie beamed. 'Bacon, egg and the full shebang, eh?'

'The full shebang,' Maizie promised. 'With lashings of tea or coffee to wash it down.'

'Just what the doctor ordered,' Charlie Treloar smiled, having secured the mooring before coming over.

'Let's go then,' Maizie declared.

She knew the next three days and nights were going to seem interminable.

*   *   *

'I'll be waiting for you after school,' Emily said to Bobby, as the pair of them met in the playground during the morning break.

'All right.'

She smiled at him, then moved away.

When Bobby turned round he found Denny Herbert and a few cronies staring at him. He stared right back.

'Come on, lads,' Denny growled, and they also moved off.

Bobby hadn't had any trouble with Herbert since the fight and subsequent visit to the headmaster's office. Like many bullies, Herbert didn't like a victim who fought back. Certainly not one who could punch as hard as Bobby.

He liked the Head's slipper even less.

'We haven't spoken for a couple of days,' Emily said to Bobby as they began making their way through the village.

'I know.'

'I was wondering if you'd heard again from your mum?'

His face fell. 'No.'

'I thought you would have done by now.'

'Me too. I have written again but still no reply.'

Emily felt so sorry for Bobby about this. He'd been so full of his mother's forthcoming visit, enthusiasm that was now clearly on the wane.

'Never mind,' she sympathised.

'She'll come,' Bobby declared through clenched teeth. 'She promised.'

'Of course she will. Mums don't break promises. They always keep them.'

That bucked Bobby a little.

'I'm having a birthday party in a fortnight's time. Consider yourself invited. You're the first person I've asked as you're my best friend.'

The first! Best friend! He couldn't have been more pleased. 'I'll be there, Emily,' he promised.

'You'll enjoy yourself. There's going to be ice cream and jelly, lots of sandwiches and sausage rolls. We've even got balloons from Mr Ayres in the shop.'

Balloons, jelly and ice cream! This was going to be a treat.

'And we'll have games,' Emily went on. 'Blind man's buff, musical chairs, postman's knock, all those.'

'Sounds smashing.'

'It will be now I know you'll be there.'

Bobby blushed bright red.

The pair of them halted at the point where Emily had to leave him. 'I'm sure your mum will be in touch soon,' Emily said.

He desperately hoped so. 'See you tomorrow then.'

Part of him was depressed by his mum not writing again, as he continued on towards the hotel. But another part was excited at the thought of the forthcoming party.

Now *that* was something to look forward to.

Christian had changed his mind about going down on to the site for now. The fewer times he did that the less chance there was of being caught. For the rest of that day he'd observed the comings and goings, trying to work out, as well as he could from a distance, what the Germans were aiming for.

A defence system of some sort, he'd concluded, which is what they'd guessed at the Executive. And one that clearly stretched for quite some distance.

Another long cold hungry night stretched ahead. In the morning, when the workers started to arrive, he'd make his move.

*   *   *

It was easier than he'd imagined. The workers outnumbered the guards by about twenty to one. The guards themselves were all apparently fairly old men, or oldish anyway, and quite lax in their attitude, which was unusual for Germans. That was probably because they didn't consider there to be any danger, either from the workers or any other source.

Once on the site Christian picked up a plank of wood and strode purposefully off, giving the impression he was heading somewhere in particular, the truth being he simply wanted to eyeball as much as he could.

It wasn't long before he'd taken on board that the workers consisted of a number of nationalities. Many were Polish, at least he thought that's what they were, others sounding similar to him but not Polish, perhaps Czech. There was a variety of regional French accents, a few Belgian voices, plus a smattering of Europeans who might have been absolutely anything.

All these men were thin, haggard and drawn, their expressions universally one of defeat.

He passed one of many German engineers shrieking at a work detail who weren't doing things exactly as he wanted. Also some black-uniformed SS. He kept well away from the latter.

He walked a good mile before coming to a stop, the construction still stretching far ahead. He laid down the plank, did a little detour round a small unattended excavation, picked up the plank again and started back. All the while he walked he was taking in as much detail as he could.

At noon a klaxon sounded, as it had the previous day, and the workers lined up for food. He joined a queue and was eventually given a plate of fatty grisly stew and a tin cup of the most horrible coffee he'd ever tasted. No matter, both were welcome as they were at least hot if nothing else.

He sat close to some other Frenchmen and listened in on the conversation. They were located in a camp about five miles inland, one of a number of camps in the area. Conditions there were appalling from what he could make out. To his amusement he discovered these particular men were convicts from the prison at Morlaix.

The klaxon sounded again, plates and cups were handed back, and work resumed. His biggest fear was that he'd be attached to a gang or work party from which he couldn't extricate himself before it was time to go off site. Luckily that didn't happen.

There was a wooden site office not too far from the original vantage point he'd taken up. Engineers were constantly going in and out.

There was bound to be a set of plans in there, but were they taken away at night or left over? That was the question. His own experience of site offices told him they'd be left over.

Colonel G had wanted plans if possible. But how could he contrive to get his hands on them?

During another walking expedition, all the while trying to memorise what he'd seen, he came across what transpired to be a fuel dump. That gave him an idea.

He waited till mid-afternoon before making his escape from the site. As tricky a business as he'd imagine it would be. For one dreadful moment he thought he'd been spotted and would be challenged, but it seemed he'd been lucky and got away with it.

His heart was pounding nineteen to the dozen, his body and face covered in cold clammy sweat, when he returned to the spot where his duffel bag was buried.

He offered up a silent prayer of thanks.

It had been one of those unexpectedly busy evenings when

people turn up for no apparent reason. It had started about seven thirty, since when she'd hardly stopped.

Bobby had come out about eight to say he'd finished his homework and could he help? She'd asked him to act as potman and also to wash and dry the glasses.

Cyril Roskilly and his horrible wife Elizabeth were there, Cyril putting away pint after pint and getting redder and redder as a result. Every so often she caught him glaring at her.

Elizabeth Roskilly was one of those folk with a face like a permanent thundercloud. She wasn't popular in the village but it had never seemed to bother her. She was also known to be incredibly mean even in a community where money had always been tight, and people were used to watching their pennies.

God, she could have used another pair of hands behind the bar, but it was too late now to summon anyone. Maizie smiled to herself remembering Christian helping out the night she'd gone to the meeting about the imminent arrival of the evacuees. She would certainly have welcomed his assistance now.

She'd been trying not to think, and worry, about him over there in France. Or the fact he might never return. The very thought made her feel sick.

'There you are, my lover,' she declared, placing yet another pint on the bar. 'Four and six if you please for that little lot.'

She rang the money up on the till and gave Albert Giddings, a dairyman, his change of a ten-bob note. She would have loved a drink herself but there wasn't time for that. She moved swiftly to another customer, one who rarely came in.

'It's good to see you, Mr Brock,' she smiled.

He sniffed. ''Tis me birthday so I'm treating meself.'

'And how old are you then?'

'Too bloody old, and that's the truth. Every morning when I wakes I pinch myself to make sure I's still alive.'

She laughed.

'And one of thae mornings I won't be. Lord save the day.'

'It comes to each and every one of us, Mr Brock. That's something we can all be certain of.'

He sniffed again causing a large wart on the end of his nose to tremble. 'Maybe so, but hopefully not yet.'

'Amen to that.'

She glanced at Bobby, expecting him to appear tired, but he didn't. Nonetheless she'd pack him off to bed soon, he had school in the morning. She'd slip him a tanner for helping out. He'd earnt it.

Christian couldn't face another night out in the open, the previous one having been sheer hell. According to his wristwatch it was approaching midnight. There had to be some place not too far away where he could be more comfortable.

He crept up on the barn, waiting for a dog to start barking at any moment. Farmers always kept dogs, usually outside.

His luck was in. If there was a dog about it didn't detect him. The small torch he carried revealed the interior of the barn to be filled with hay and straw. Absolutely perfect for his purposes. Minutes later he was concealed and warmly bedded down.

He must be up early, he warned himself. Before dawn, the farmer and anyone else. There was no guarantee, and he hated admitting this about a countryman, that the farmer might not turn him over to the Boche.

He switched off his torch and lay back in the darkness. He would make his play to get the plans the following night when he was also due to be picked up by the *Snowdrop*.

He began to plan exactly how he was going to go about it.

Maizie was exhausted, yet knew if she went to bed she wouldn't sleep. The whisky in front of her was her fourth, the cigarette she was smoking her third since locking up.

She wondered where Christian was and if he was safe. Christian who'd come to mean so much to her in such a relatively short time. Christian whom she'd kissed before he left.

She smiled at the memory and, not for the first time, wondered what it would be like to be made love to by him. A stupid fantasy – it would never happen. She was a married woman and besides he was far younger. But all the same, there was no harm in dreams.

'What's this name on the top of your party list?' Mabel Dunne, Emily's mother, demanded with a frown.

'It's Bobby Tyler who's at school with me.'

Mabel's expression became one of disapproval and distaste. 'Isn't he one of thae evacuees?'

Emily nodded.

'Well, I ain't having none of thae ragamuffins in my house. I couldn't trust them. Who knows what would be missing after they left. Sticky-fingered blighters, no doubt.'

Emily was appalled. 'Bobby's no thief! It's unfair of you to suggest he is.'

'He's from Plymouth, 'tain't he? And a gutter rat at that from all accounts. He and all the rest. Well, not one is stepping foot over my door and that's that.'

Tears welled in Emily's eyes. 'But I've already invited him, Mum.'

'More fool you then. You'll just have to disinvite him.'

'But Mum!'

'I've spoken and that's an end to it.'

'He's ever so nice, Mum, honest. You'll like him.'

Mabel snorted her disbelief.

'You will!' Emily protested. It had never crossed her mind that her mother would take objection to Bobby coming to her party. What a nightmare!

'Well, I'm not going to find out. Now you hurry and get ready for school. That clock is ticking away and I don't want you getting a black mark for being late.'

How could she possibly tell Bobby he wasn't welcome after all? He'd be mortified. As upset, maybe even more, as she was now. This was cruel of her mother. Nor was there any point in appealing to her dad; he was ruled by Mabel.

'Please think about it again, Mum?'

'No!'

'There hasn't been any trouble with any of the evacuees since they arrived here. And if other people can take them into their homes then why can't I invite Bobby to my party?'

'What other folk does is their business and none of mine. I think they're mad, all of them. And you mark my words, they'll live to regret harbouring these townie brats. Why, some of them were infested with nits when they arrived, and that's gospel.' Mabel shuddered. 'Filthy beggars.'

'They are not!' Emily shouted, losing control.

'Don't you dare talk to me like that, young lady. I won't have it, you hear?'

'It's so unfair,' Emily sobbed.

''Tis nothing of the sort. I don't want ee consorting with the likes of thae.'

Emily whirled round and rushed from the room.

'You've still got school to go to!' Mabel yelled after her.

'What's wrong with you, Maiz? You've been standing staring at that carrot for the past few minutes.'

Maizie brought herself out of her reverie. 'Sorry. I was, eh . . .' She trailed off.

'Is ee worried about Christian?' Alice asked shrewdly.

Maizie nodded.

'He'll be all right. You'll see.'

'I hope so,' Maizie whispered.

Alice put the potatoes she'd been cleaning into a colander and then rinsed them under the tap. 'He'll be back before ee knows it.'

Maizie sighed. 'It's just . . . well he's become like family, Alice. If anything happened to him it would be like losing a brother.'

'A brother?' Alice queried softly. 'Are you sure about that?'

Maizie couldn't look the older woman in the face. 'What do you mean?'

'It seems to me it might be becoming more than that.'

Panic blossomed in Maizie. Was it so obvious? 'I've no idea what you're talking about.'

'Don't you?'

'Alice, mind your tongue!' Maizie snapped.

Alice coloured slightly. 'I apologise, Maiz. It's got nothing to do with me. I should have kept my big trap shut.'

Maizie was instantly contrite; that outburst had been quite unlike her. She valued Alice's friendship enormously and normally wouldn't have done anything to hurt her. But she had hit a sore spot.

'There's nothing between Christian and me if that's what you're insinuating,' Maizie stated.

Alice didn't reply.

'I take it you think there is?'

Alice shrugged.

'I'm a married woman, Alice, for God's sake. I don't do things like that. It would go against everything I believe in and the way I was brought up.'

'He's certainly a personable chap,' Alice murmured, her back to Maizie.

'And young, don't forget.'

'There is that.'

'And I enjoy his company. Where's the harm in that?'

'None,' Alice agreed drily.

'As do you.'

'He's a charmer, right enough. But then all these Frenchies are, I'm told. There's certainly nothing disagreeable about him.'

'So don't you go seeing something where there isn't. You'll make me cross.'

Alice smiled to herself; what was that saying about the person protesting too much? Maizie might fancy Christian but it had gone no further than that. She believed Maizie there. Still, temptation was temptation, and they were all weak. 'Twas human nature after all. Sam Blackacre couldn't be the easiest of men to be married to, and he was away.

'Christian called me a lady, bless him. I'll never forget that,' Alice said over her shoulder, and laughed.

Maizie knew the moment of tension had passed. 'It's natural for me to worry, Alice. It would be the same if it was you in danger over there.'

Not quite, Alice thought. Not quite.

Emily stared at Bobby whom she could see across the playground. He was talking to one of the other lads, another evacuee.

How could she tell him he wasn't invited to her party after all? That was going to be terrible. She could just imagine how hurt he'd be. And rightly so.

She couldn't believe her mother could be so cruel, but there again, her mum was a snob through and through. Always had been for as long as she could remember. Mabel Dunne thought herself a cut above the rest because her husband worked for the electricity board. Though why that should make him, and her mum, better than other people she failed to understand.

One thing was certain, the party was spoiled for her now, and she wished the idea had never been suggested in the first place. But there was no use telling her mum she didn't now want a party. Mabel wouldn't hear of that. She'd insist it go ahead.

When school was over Emily was one of the first out the gate and off down the road in case she bumped into Bobby. She'd have to face him at some point, but not yet.

Despite the freezing cold, Christian was sweating profusely due to sheer nerves. There were two guards at the site office where he'd been hoping there would be only one. The men were standing alongside a small brazier which glowed redly.

Christian had smeared his face and hands with dirt while over his shoulder was slung the sten. His poison pill was in a pocket within easy reach. If things went wrong they wouldn't capture him alive. Better a quick death than one after long agonising torture.

The night was still with a smattering of stars in the sky. Hardly ideal. At least the moon was in its quarter phase which was something of a help.

He went forward slowly, moving from cover to cover as he'd been taught. He could almost hear Sergeant Major Thompson instructing him.

There would be other guards out further down the site, but they didn't concern him. Only the pair outside the site office he'd selected mattered.

Eventually, after what seemed an eternity, he reached the

fuel dump. Squatting low he placed his duffel bag in front of him and groped inside for the plastic.

It was the work of moments to fix a wodge of plastic to a drum, then he removed a pre-set pencil timer from his top jacket pocket and inserted it into the plastic. A twist of the fingers and the timer was live.

He skirted round to the other side of the dump and repeated the procedure using a second pre-set timer. Another twist of the fingers and that too was alive. He'd given himself twenty minutes to be on the safe side.

He flitted silently back to a position relatively close to the site office, concealing himself behind bags of concrete. A glance at his luminous wristwatch told him there were six minutes to go.

One timer went off several seconds after the other, both explosions igniting the fuel which banged and then blazed spectacularly. Christian grinned to himself as all hell broke loose.

Men erupted from the huts, shouting, screaming, issuing orders. He watched with satisfaction as *en masse* they rushed towards the conflagration.

To his delight one of the two guards went also, leaving only one to be dealt with.

The remaining guard's attention was fixed on the blaze when an arm clamped round his throat and the killing knife was thrust home. He was dead when Christian lowered him to the ground.

His nerves had disappeared now, his entire being focused on what had to be done. As he'd expected, the office was heavily padlocked.

He attached a tiny amount of plastic to the lock and inserted the timer set for thirty seconds. A twist of the fingers and he ran round behind the office.

The resulting explosion sounded deafening to him but he

knew that was just his imagination. He waited till he was absolutely certain it hadn't been heard over the bedlam round the dump and then he was inside the office itself.

He flipped on his small torch to reveal several desks and drawing boards. There wasn't time for the luxury of examining the drawings pinned to the boards and scattered over the desks. He simply grabbed everything in sight and stuffed them into his duffel bag and pockets. Enough, he told himself. He had enough. Now get out of there and away.

But first he had one final thing to do. A wad of plastic on the nearest desk and another pre-set timer. He didn't want the Germans to know their plans had been stolen.

He ran as fast as he could, sten at the ready. He was off the site when the office went up.

He paused for a moment to look back, smiling in satisfaction, then continued on his way to rendezvous with Hookie and the *Snowdrop*.

'*Halt!*'

That single word stopped him in his tracks.

'*Halt!*'

'*Ich bin ein Kamerad!*' he yelled, twisting round in the direction of the voice. '*Ich bin ein Kamarad!*'

He could make out two figures which he walked slowly towards, the sten at arm's length pointing downwards.

He sensed the two Germans relax slightly which was his cue. He swung the sten up and squeezed the trigger.

Maizie woke with a start and a muffled cry, her face contorted, eyes staring. She hadn't thought she'd sleep that night, but eventually she had.

'Oh, Chris,' she whispered.

She'd seen him clearly, lying stretched on the ground, awash with blood, body riddled with bullets.

Her hands knotted into fists, one of which she jammed into her mouth. He was dead. She'd had a premonition, or a vision, or whatever you wanted to call it. Chris was dead.

Maizie was standing on the quay when the *Snowdrop*, engines already cut, glided into harbour. Only Charlie Treloar was visible, busying himself with mooring lines. Fear and dread were clutching at her heart, squeezing it tight.

There was a low murmur of voices coming from the wheelhouse as the *Snowdrop* gently bumped alongside. The door opened and Denzil stepped on deck, followed by a grim-faced Hookie.

And then, as though by magic, for she'd have sworn the wheelhouse was now empty, Christian appeared, to smile and give her a wave.

The overwhelming sense of relief was so intense and profound she almost fainted.

Chapter 14

As Maizie had done after the first trip, she gave them all a hearty breakfast. Filled with warm contentment, she watched Christian wolf down his. She'd already established that his mission had been successful.

'Some more?' she asked him when he'd finished well ahead of the others.

He smiled gratefully at her. 'I wouldn't mind.'

It was obvious he'd hardly eaten while away. She'd soon make up for that. She refilled his coffee before returning to the frying pan.

'Well, I'm right glad that business is over,' Hookie growled.

'Amen with knobs on,' Charlie Treloar muttered, causing them all to laugh.

'So what happened, monsewer? Surely you'll tell us now,' Denzil asked.

Christian shook his head. 'I'm sorry. I can't.'

'I know, hush hush,' Denzil grumbled.

'I would if I could, honestly. You fellows put your lives on the line for me after all. But I'm sure you understand.'

Hookie hadn't noticed the stain on Christian's trousers before, now he did. A long dark red smear of it. 'That blood?' he inquired casually, pointing with his fork.

Christian glanced down, and nodded.

'Yours?'

'No.'

Denzil took a deep breath. 'Did you kill him?'

'I killed three, actually. But that's all I'm saying.'

Maizie swallowed hard, remembering all too vividly the premonition she'd had. Thank God it had been wrong. Her hand holding the spatula was trembling, she noted.

What had occurred in France wasn't discussed any further. When they'd eaten their fill Hookie and company thanked Maizie and declared they'd be off.

Christian walked them to the front door where he told them again how grateful he was for what they'd done and the risks they'd taken on his behalf.

'Don't mention it, monsewer,' Hookie replied gruffly.

Christian returned to the kitchen where he found Maizie clearing up. Alice wasn't due for another half hour yet.

'You're a mess,' Maizie smiled. 'Face all covered in dirt and your clothes torn.'

He shrugged and didn't reply.

She wanted to go to him and take him in her arms. Tell him what a relief it was to have him back safe and sound. How much she'd worried about him. How scared on his behalf she'd been.

'I'm getting the children up shortly,' she said instead. 'Can you wait until they've gone to school before having your bath?'

'Of course.'

'You look whacked.'

'I am, believe me. I didn't get a lot of sleep while I was over there. And none at all last night.'

'Not even on the boat?'

'I tried but the rolling motion kept me awake.' He suddenly grinned. 'At least I wasn't sick this time.'

'I heard,' she commented sympathetically. 'The lads thought

you did well holding off as long as you did. They said the conditions were horrendous.'

'They were. Luckily coming back was nowhere like the journey over. I'll remember that as long as I live. I thought I was going to die.'

She nodded. 'I've been told how bad sea sickness can be. I think everyone who goes to sea experiences it at one time or another.'

He was tempted to ask if Sam ever had, then thought the better of that. 'After my bath I must ring London to report in,' he said. 'And then I'll drive up.'

She stopped what she was doing to stare at him. 'That's daft.'

'Why?'

'Well, let me ask you this, is it that important for you to return straight away?'

He considered that. 'I don't suppose it is.'

'Well then. Look at it this way. You're so tired, and it's such a long drive, you'll probably fall asleep at the wheel and crash the car. Now that's no good to anyone.'

He couldn't help but agree. 'An extra day wouldn't make all that much difference really,' he conceded.

Triumph flared in her. The last thing she wanted was for him to leave immediately. Besides, what she'd said was true. He was in no fit condition to drive to London.

'You can leave early tomorrow morning,' she stated firmly in a no-nonsense tone.

He smiled. '*Oui, mon colonel.*' He pronounced the latter word in the French manner.

She laughed at that. 'Don't be so cheeky. I'm not bossy.'

'No?' He raised a disbelieving eyebrow.

'Well, perhaps in some instances. But not normally.'

He reflected how wonderful it was to be with Maizie again. There had been times over there when he'd doubted he'd ever make it back. But he'd been lucky, and now here he was, and there she was. 'I took something along for good luck,' he informed her.

'Oh! What?'

He dug in a trouser pocket till he found what he was after. He held out a closed hand and slowly uncurled it. Lying on his palm was the Cross of Lorraine cufflink.

'Why that?' she queried softly.

'I don't know. Ridiculous I suppose, but I just thought it might bring me good luck.'

Maizie lowered her gaze, feeling there was a reference in there to her. That somehow she was connected to the cufflink. It pleased her enormously.

'Something else,' he said.

'What's that, Chris?'

He didn't fail to note she'd called him the more intimate Chris and not Christian. 'Is it possible to have a cognac? I have been up all night after all. And through quite a bit if I say so myself.'

Including killing three men, she thought grimly. He deserved a cognac. A whole bottleful if he wished.

'You know where to find it. Help yourself while I get on here.'

She started to sing softly when he'd gone. Right then the world couldn't have been a better or happier place.

All the fear, dread and terrible anxiety she'd gone through over the past few days and nights had completely evaporated.

'Mum, won't you please change your mind about Bobby Tyler coming to my party?' Emily pleaded.

Mabel stared hard at her daughter. 'Does that mean you haven't told him he's not welcome yet?'

'Yes,' Emily whispered.

Mabel snorted. 'Well, if you don't I will. I'll go down to the school gate and tell him when he's coming out.'

Emily was appalled. That would be awful. And so humiliating, for her and Bobby. She cringed inside.

'You wouldn't do that, Mum.'

'I most certainly would. Just you try me.'

Emily's shoulders slumped. Her mum wasn't going to change her mind. She was going to have to face Bobby with this after all.

'Well, young lady?'

'I'll do it,' she mumbled.

'And today. Best get it over and done with. No time like the present, I always say. And by the by, it was difficult but I've finally managed to get all the ingredients for the cake. It's going to be a smasher. You'll be the envy of every child at the party.'

No matter how lovely the cake she was going to hate it, Emily thought.

The cake and party.

'Bobby, will you stop day dreaming and pay attention!' Miss Hitchon snapped. 'It's most unlike you.'

Bobby coloured when the rest of the class laughed.

Miss Hitchon picked up a ruler and rapped it on her desk. 'We'll have none of that, thank you.'

She turned again to the blackboard. 'Now where were we?'

Bobby had been thinking about Emily's forthcoming party and what he could get her as a present. He had some money saved up which he'd use, cash given him by Maizie as either pocket money or for helping round the bar.

The trouble was, what did you buy a girl? Something nice, something she'd appreciate and treasure. A diamond bracelet would have been ideal but he could hardly run to that. Not even a single solitary diamond. Anyway, even if he'd been rolling in it there were no such bracelets to be had in Coverack.

He'd have to go into the shop and see what he could get there. And then he had another idea. The Women's Institute was having a jumble sale for the war effort that weekend. He might be able to pick up a present from the white elephant stall. You never knew. You found all sorts on that particular stall.

He'd have a look round the shop first but wait for the jumble sale before deciding.

Whatever he bought he was certain Emily would be delighted.

A present and a card, he must have one of those as well.

'Come in!'

Maizie entered Christian's bedroom carrying a tray. 'I heard you moving about and thought you might like a cup of coffee and one of Alice's jam tarts.'

'Why thank you, Maizie,' he beamed. 'As you English say, just the dab.'

She laughed. There were times when you could almost believe he wasn't a Frenchman at all. And then all you had to do was look at his face to see it there. His face was as Gallic as the Gitanes he loved to smoke.

Maizie placed the tray on his rumpled bed which was covered in papers. 'What are these?' she asked. 'They look like plans of some kind.'

'That's exactly what they are, Maizie. And one of the reasons I went over there. Getting them was a bonus you might say.' He began gathering them together.

'How do you feel now?'

'A lot better,' he nodded.

'You certainly look it.'

'Nonetheless I'll sleep well again tonight.'

He was wearing a dressing gown under which she could see he was naked. That sent a shiver up and down her spine. Did he always sleep that way? she wondered. Sam wore pyjamas, top and bottoms. Hardly romantic but practical. She also noted that his chest appeared devoid of hair. Sam's on the other hand was covered with it. A race horse, she suddenly thought, that's what Christian was compared to Sam's lumbering cart animal.

She wasn't being fair, she chided herself. You shouldn't, couldn't, compare men like that. She flushed slightly, wondering what he made of her big bum, the despair of her life.

'Maizie?'

'What?'

'Something wrong? You've gone all peculiar.'

'No, nothing's wrong. I'd better leave you to have your coffee and get dressed. I'll be downstairs.'

'I shan't be long. Oh, and, Maizie. I'm glad you talked me into staying over the extra day. As you said, it would have been daft to try to drive up the way I was.'

'I've got Trudy Curnow helping out tonight,' she said a trifle coyly. 'We can have a drink together.'

'I'll look forward to that.'

'Now what about those dirty clothes? I'll wash and press them for you.'

'You won't have time for that. I'll take them back as they are.'

'You'll do nothing of the sort!' she protested. 'Bring them down with you and I'll have them ready for packing in the morning.'

The clothes were unimportant, but he wasn't going to argue the point. Let her do them if she wanted to.

'Right then,' he agreed.

Maizie bustled away, stopping at the top of the stairs to catch her breath. For a brief second she visualised him without his dressing gown, then, scandalised at such a thought, and the instant effect it had had on her, quickly put it from her mind.

It had reminded her of a picture of the Boy David sculpture she'd once admired in a book.

Bobby's face had gone white as milk. He stared at Emily, feeling sick to the very pit of his stomach.

'I'm so sorry,' Emily whispered, voice quavering. 'But it's not my fault. I wanted you there more than anything. Please believe me.'

He knew if he tried to speak he wouldn't be able to, disappointment and humiliation wrenching him apart inside. He turned and ran.

'Bobby!'

He continued running as fast as he could, anything to get away from there and Emily.

'Bobby!'

He ended up down by the quay, wedging himself between two rocks as though trying to make himself invisible.

That was the end of his friendship with Emily Dunne, her fault or not. He wasn't good enough to be her friend. Her mum said so.

Suddenly he hated Coverack.

Hated it . . . hated it . . . hated it.

'Where have you been?' Maizie demanded. 'Your meal will be ruined by now.'

'I'm sorry, Aunt Maiz,' he replied quietly.

She studied him. 'Is everything all right?'

He nodded.

'Are you sure?' Christian queried.

Bobby nodded again. 'I'm not hungry anyway. I think I'll just go on up to my bed.'

'What about your homework?'

'I don't have any tonight,' he lied.

Maizie thought that was unusual, but it had happened, if very occasionally, in the past. 'You should eat something though.'

Rosemary stared at him in concern. She'd drop in later and see if she could find out what was the matter. Something clearly was; she knew Bobby only too well.

'Are you ill?' Maizie frowned.

He just wanted to be alone again, secreted away in his room. 'No, I'm fine.'

'I'll bring you up a tray later on.'

'Thanks, Aunt Maiz,' he mumbled, and hurried off.

'If it isn't one thing it's another,' Maizie sighed, wondering what all that had been about.

Christian had already brought the Morris round to the front of the hotel and was now packing his things into the boot. A little earlier he'd returned to Maizie those items he'd borrowed from the Movement and torn up the sealed envelope addressed to his parents he'd given to Maizie before he'd left on the *Snowdrop*.

'I wish it could have been longer,' he said to Maizie, standing beside the car when he was finished.

She glanced up at the sky. 'At least you've got a good day for it. Coldish, but clear.' She brought her attention back to Christian. 'I'll miss you. We all will.'

'And I'll miss all of you.'

There was a pregnant, uncomfortable pause between them. 'Bobby seemed a bit down going off to school this morning,' he commented.

'If there's anything wrong I'll find out. He's probably just had an argument with someone.'

'Probably.'

Maizie pulled her cardigan more tightly about her shoulders. 'I'm glad it all went well and you achieved what you were after.'

The light caught her hair, giving it a glow, an aura almost, that quite mesmerised him. He moved to kiss her on the cheek but she deftly stepped away.

'It's a village, Christian. There are eyes everywhere. We don't want to do anything that might be misconstrued. There's enough general gossiping going on as it is.'

'I understand.'

She wished he'd kissed her inside where they'd been alone. On the lips as had happened when he'd gone to France.

'Will you keep in touch?' she asked casually.

'I'll try. But I can't promise anything.' He shrugged. 'I could be sent anywhere at a moment's notice. It's difficult, Maizie.'

'Well whatever, you take care of yourself. And remember, there's always a bed and welcome here for you whenever you want it.'

'I appreciate that, Maizie,' he replied softly, deeply touched.

'Bye then, Chris. You'd better be on your way before I catch my death.'

He said something very quickly in French, then climbed hurriedly into the car.

'What was that?'

He'd already switched on the engine and his window was up. Tapping his ear he pretended he couldn't hear. He waved and drove off without further ado.

Maizie was left speculating as to what he'd said.

Christian was bone weary as he let himself into his Chelsea

flat. It had been a long and arduous drive up from Cornwall, not helped by a flat tyre *en route*. That had taken him ages to change as the nuts had been tightened as if by a gorilla with superhuman strength. Somehow he'd got them off in the end but it had been a mighty tussle. Unfortunately for him he'd had the puncture miles from civilisation and the nearest garage.

The lights were on but the lounge was deserted. He doubted Gilbert had already gone to bed so reasoned he must be down at the pub. He wondered whether or not to join him.

There was a muffled exclamation and when he turned round there was a totally naked woman staring at him. He recognised her instantly as the girl from the Eight Bells with whom Gilbert had been so enamoured.

Clutching herself, trying to hide what she could, the woman vanished back into Gilbert's bedroom.

His flatmate had been busy during his absence, Christian reflected with a wry smile. Well, good luck to him. The woman was certainly a looker. Even better with her clothes off than on.

An embarrassed Gilbert appeared wearing a hastily thrown-on dressing gown. 'Sorry about that,' he apologised. 'You gave Madeleine quite a start.'

'Is there anything to drink in the flat?'

'Wine and whisky.'

Christian decided on whisky, needing something stronger than wine after the wearying drive. 'Where is it?'

'In the kitchenette.'

'I'm sorry to have interrupted. I had no idea.'

Gilbert pulled a face. 'And I had no way of letting you know.' His expression changed. 'Everything go OK?'

Christian nodded.

'You were successful then?'

'Completely.'

'That's good.'

Both men stared at one another. Christian couldn't elaborate further, nor did Gilbert expect him to. The mission had been successful, that was all that mattered. That and the fact Christian had returned unharmed.

'Madeleine, come on out here!' Gilbert called.

A somewhat sheepish Madeleine came into the room, now wearing a chenille wrap. 'You must be Christian,' she smiled.

'I'm pleased to meet you.'

'I'm sorry about that. We never heard you arrive.'

'Don't worry, Madeleine. It's forgotten as far as I'm concerned.'

'Madeleine is a shorthand typist for the Air Ministry,' Gilbert explained. 'She lives just round the corner.'

'With three others,' Madeleine added.

That explained why they were using the flat. The opportunity of being alone. Up until now that was. 'We've seen you in the Eight Bells.'

'Yes, it's my local.'

'I'll get you that whisky,' Gilbert declared to Christian, and headed for the kitchenette.

'Gilbert said you were away for a while and didn't know when you were coming back.'

'I didn't know myself. It's that sort of a business.'

'With the Free French, same as Gilbert?'

'That's right.' He wondered precisely what Gilbert had told her. Whatever, it wouldn't be much. Still, he didn't want to say one thing if Gilbert had said another.

Gilbert returned with the whisky. 'There you are. *À votre santé!*'

'I'll have this and then go straight through. I'm worn out.'

'And how are the men in Plymouth?'

Christian's expression didn't change. 'Absolutely fine. A little bored when not on exercise perhaps, but OK apart from that.'

Christian sipped the whisky, wishing it was cognac. He would have given anything for that and a Gitanes right then. He hadn't smoked a Gitanes since the last of those Hookie had got for him.

Madeleine used a hand to sweep back her hair that had been unpinned to tumble about her shoulders. 'I should be going.'

'Please don't on my behalf,' Christian said quickly. 'Just carry on as you were.'

Madeleine went bright red, for it was obvious what they'd been up to. She'd hardly have been naked otherwise.

Christian yawned. 'I'll sort my things out in the morning, and meanwhile take this drink to bed with me. Goodnight then.'

'Goodnight,' Gilbert and Madeleine chorused in unison.

Christian waited to smile until after he'd closed his bedroom door behind him. Lucky old Gilbert. He was jealous as hell. Or was he?

Later he was wakened by a rhythmic thump against the wall adjoining their bedrooms. When he drifted off again it was to dream that he too was with a woman. Though one whose face he couldn't quite make out.

'Well done. Splendid effort!' Colonel G enthused.

'Congratulations,' Major Hammond added.

'These are everything we could have wished for,' Colonel G went on. The plans, which he and the Major had been studying before Christian had been admitted to his office, were spread over his desk.

'Thank you,' Christian replied modestly.

'Did you have much trouble?' That was Colonel G.

'Not really, sir.'

'A piece of cake, eh?'

Hardly that, Christian thought. There had been one or two moments, especially when challenged by the German patrol, when it seemed his luck had run out. He smiled, but didn't answer.

'We'll get these off to the appropriate boffins for an evaluation,' Colonel G continued. 'In the meantime you'll write up that report I told you I wanted. Put down every last detail from landing to leaving again. The full facts plus speculations. Understand?'

'Perfectly, sir.'

Colonel G glanced again at the plans. 'Gerry is putting on quite a show here. Far bigger than we'd imagined. This is going to cause a lot of interest further up, I can assure you.'

Again Christian didn't reply.

'So you'd better get on with it, Captain. And I shall expect that report as soon as possible. But don't skimp or rush. Clear?'

'Yes, sir.'

'Dismissed then.'

Christian saluted and turned for the door. It was a good feeling to know you'd succeeded to such an extent. Colonel G wasn't one known to be lavish with his praise, so what he'd received had been approbation indeed.

Bobby pulled the lapels of his coat up against the cutting wind that was blowing in off the Channel. His ears were red and aching with cold. His feet, despite the heavy socks he had on, were frozen through.

He hadn't meant to come, told himself he wouldn't, but despite all that here he was at Emily's house listening to the party going on inside.

He'd positioned himself behind a hedge from where he could see but not be seen. He felt wretched, an outcast, as he listened to the sounds of revelry and shrieks of laughter coming from within.

He hadn't spoken to Emily since she'd told him he wasn't invited any more. Several times she'd tried to approach him but he'd either snubbed her or moved away. He missed her dreadfully, not having fully realised just how good friends, and close, they'd become.

Through the large front window he could see some children in paper hats. As he watched, one of them, he couldn't quite make out who, raised a toy trumpet type thing to his mouth and blew a loud blast. In the same room someone was playing a piano.

Emotion was clogging his throat as he turned away, walking off disconsolately in the direction of the cliffs. Dusk was falling, but he didn't care about that. In fact he'd welcome the darkness.

He'd never felt so lonely, or miserable, in his life.

Maizie cradled the telephone. Well, she certainly hadn't expected that. Not so soon anyway. She could have whooped with pleasure.

'Are you serving, Maiz?' John Corin called through from the bar where he'd been patiently waiting.

'I'll be right with you.'

'Another pint of cider, Maiz.' He scrutinised her face. 'What are you so happy about?'

'Am I?'

''Tis writ all over ee. Plain as anything.'

'It's just the mood I'm in,' she lied.

'I think ee must have been at the cider yourself. Has that effect on some people.'

She laughed. 'Well, it isn't cider, John. I can assure you.'

''Tis something though.'

It was a few more minutes before she could get out to the kitchen where Alice was working. 'Well, there's a turn up for the book,' she declared.

'Oh, and what's that, maid?'

'Christian just rang. He's been given leave and is coming back down in a few days' time to spend it here.'

Alice was delighted. 'Just leave and nothing else?' Maizie realised she was referring to the mission in France.

'Nothing else.'

'My my,' Alice muttered, she too having noted how happy Maizie was to have received that news.

'I'll make up his room later on,' Maizie announced, eyes sparkling.

Alice's face clouded as she remembered what she'd read in the Tarot cards.

Something she'd never told Maizie about. Something she fully intended keeping to herself.

Chapter 15

C hristian entered the Paris, his smile of pleasure fading when he discovered a distraught and thoroughly agitated Alice behind the bar. 'What's wrong?' he demanded.

'Oh, Christian, 'tis good you're here. It's Bobby, he's gone missing.'

'Missing?'

'Three days now. Maiz came down in the morning to discover the front door unlocked then later, when she went to call him, he'd gone.' Her eyes misted with tears. ''Tis feared the boy has drowned,' she whispered.

Christian sucked in a deep breath. This was awful. Absolutely appalling. 'Why do you think he could have drowned?'

'They've searched the village and surrounding area high and low. Scoured everywhere could be thought of. The likely places and unlikely ones. But he hasn't been found anywhere.'

'That still doesn't mean he's drowned.'

'Where else could he be but in the Channel? He couldn't get far from Coverack on foot. And if he was out on thae moors they'd have come across him by now. There's no place else but the water.'

'Sweet Jesu,' Christian whispered. 'Where's Maizie now?'

'Down by the shoreline. The tide's coming in, you see,

they're thinking perhaps his body will be washed ashore.'

'But . . . why? Are you saying it might not be accidental if, heaven forbid, he is dead?'

Alice shook her head. 'He's been proper out of sorts recently. Well, you know that yourself. And Maizie never did discover what it was all about. Nor could Rosemary, his own sister. She tried as well but Bobby was saying nothing. What's so worrying is that he's been spotted a number of times on the cliffs of late. On the last occasion old Mrs Trethowen was out walking her dog, which she does every night faithfully be it hail, shine or a Force ten. She saw Bobby and spoke to him, saw he was upset, but thought no more of it till he went missing.'

He had to get to Maizie, lend what support he could. She must be beside herself. 'Any idea which way she went?'

'None at all, Christian. Thae's all strung out like. Volunteers from the village, the Home Guard. I tell ee, there's been a right proper to-do over this.'

Christian had already dumped his luggage in front of the bar. 'Keep an eye on that for me,' he said, indicating it. 'I'm going to look for Maizie.'

'Pray God they find the lad,' Alice choked.

Pray God indeed, Christian thought, heading back for the door.

'Maizie!'

Her eyes were swollen from crying, her cheeks puffed. She wasn't wearing even a smidgin of make-up and her hair was badly tousled by the wind. 'Oh, Christian!' she exclaimed, and fell into his arms.

'*Ma chérie*,' he mumbled. He held her trembling body tight.

About thirty yards further up the shoreline Denzil Eustis was watching them.

'Alice explained.'

'They haven't found him yet. Denzil says if he doesn't come in on this tide then he might not at all. He could have been swept right out.'

'Are you certain that's what's happened. That he's not on the moors somewhere?'

'They've been over every inch. Locals, farmers, they've been out in their dozens. If he was on the moors they'd have found him by now.' She shuddered. 'He certainly couldn't have made it across them. A little boy like that in weather like this. He wouldn't have had any chance. That's why they're certain he must have fallen in the water. Or . . .' She broke off, unable to say the next word.

Suicide, Christian thought grimly. 'I take it he still hasn't heard from his mother?'

'No.'

'And what about school?'

'He never turned up.'

'I mean, you thought something had happened there to upset him?'

Maizie shook her head. 'No one there knows anything. Neither Miss Hitchon, Mr Brookfield the headmaster, nor anyone.'

Maizie, suddenly aware of Denzil watching them, disentangled herself from Christian's embrace. 'I feel so guilty,' she said.

'You've nothing to feel guilty about.'

'I must have failed him in some way.'

'That's being ridiculous, Maiz, and you know it.'

'He was in my care, Chris, my responsibility. What else am I to think?'

'You didn't fail him, Maizie,' he stated emphatically. 'The only one who's done that is his mother. The blame rests entirely with her, not you.'

They were interrupted at that point by a loud halloo! Mr Ayres, the shopkeeper, came striding towards them.

'Have they found something?' Maizie queried, a catch in her voice.

''Fraid not, Mrs Blackacre. I imagined you could use some hot tea so I brought ee a flask. You and Denzil yonder.'

Maizie didn't know whether she was relieved or not. 'Thank you, Mr Ayres.'

''Tis a bad business,' Mr Ayres declared sympathetically. He'd left his wife in charge of the shop so he could assist in the search.

'No news of any kind?' Christian asked.

'None at all. 'Tis as if the lad has vanished in a puff of smoke.' He looked out over the Channel. 'She don't always give up her victims that one. There's many she keeps. There's a lot of fishing families along this coast can testify to that.'

'Will you stop sobbing like that. It's getting on me nerves!' Mabel Dunne scolded Emily.

'I can't help it.'

'Of course ee can. Pull yourself together, girl. And I'll tell you this, it's back to school for you tomorrow. I'm having no more of this being off ill when there's nothing wrong with you.'

Emily glared at her mother, thinking how hard-hearted she was. Bobby was missing, feared drowned, and no sign whatsoever of either sympathy or remorse from Mabel.

Emily had said nothing up until then, but now she snapped. 'It was not coming to my party that probably did it,' she accused.

Mabel stared at Emily in astonishment. 'Don't be silly. That's utter nonsense.'

'Is it? Think how he felt, Mum. I might as well have slapped him in the face.'

Andy Dunne, Emily's father, came into the room. 'What's all this then?' He was home for his tea after having been out searching with the others.

Emily explained about the party and how badly Bobby had taken the rebuff.

Andy's face darkened with rage. 'Is this true, Mabel? For 'tis the first I've heard of it.'

'Of course it's true. I wasn't having a little guttersnipe like that in my house. Heaven forbid!'

'You're a snob, Mabel, the worst kind. And 'tis certainly not a quality I admire in ee. Me or anyone else.'

Mabel gawped in amazement. Andrew never spoke to her like this. How dare he criticise! 'Why . . .' she spluttered.

'If I'd known what you'd done I'd have gone to the Paris myself and invited the boy again.'

'You'd have done no such thing.'

'I bloody well would!' he almost roared.

Mabel took a step backwards. 'You're shouting at me,' she gasped.

'And about time too. I've kept my trap shut all these years for an easy life, letting you away with blue murder. 'Twas wrong of me and no mistake.'

'Andrew, I—'

'Don't call me Andrew,' he interjected hotly. 'Everyone else calls me Andy. This Andrew nonsense is just another one of your high falutin affectations. I really don't know who you think you are, but you're certainly not some grand lady and that's for sure. You're just a villager like the rest in Coverack. No more, no less. So remember that.'

Mabel was reeling from shock. At long last the worm had turned. And with a vengeance it seemed.

'Bobby's my best friend, Dad,' Emily said quietly.

'Is he, girl?'

'He's ever so nice. You'd like him.'

'A townie who came here with nits. Imagine that, *nits!*' Mabel protested.

'Shut up!' Andy yelled.

Mabel flinched as though he'd struck her.

'I don't know if this party thing has anything to do with the lad being missing, but if it has then it's on your conscience. Especially if they fish him out the sea.'

Mabel gulped, and gulped again, knowing that the hold she'd had over her husband was lost for ever. She could clearly read that in his eyes.

'Now get my tea and be quick about it,' Andy said, making a dismissive gesture.

A thoroughly cowed, and chastened, Mabel hurried off to the kitchen.

'Do you think Bobby really is dead, Dad?' Emily sobbed.

Andy went to her and took her into his arms. 'I don't know, girl. I honestly don't.'

'I'm getting fed up to the back teeth with these meetings,' Cyril Roskilly declared. 'All we do is come here to the cave and talk. We don't do nothing and I say we should.'

Maizie ran a hand over her forehead. It had been a long emotional day and now this. It was the last thing she needed.

'Patrols for example,' Roskilly went on. 'We should mount a nightly one.'

'The Home Guard already do that,' Denzil pointed out.

Roskilly snorted. 'The Home Guard. Thae duffers! That's a joke.' He laughed raucously in what he thought was scorn.

'I would remind you, Cyril,' Maizie said quietly, 'that doing nothing is exactly what we've been ordered to do. We're here to act only if, and when, the Germans invade.'

'Then why have these meetings? Total waste of time if you ask me. I got better things to do than come along here every so often for bugger all.'

'We should remain in contact and make regular inspections of our stores,' Maizie countered.

'Well, we'd certainly run things differently if I was in charge, and that's a fact,' Roskilly leered.

'Which is probably why you aren't,' she snapped in reply, her temper beginning to get the better of her.

'Don't you speak to me like that, Maizie Blackacre. Useless bloody woman.'

Maizie paled.

'Watch your tongue, Mr Roskilly,' Christian growled.

'And what are you doing here, Frenchman? You've no right.'

'Christian already knows about us,' Maizie reminded Roskilly. 'And he's here to see me coming and returning. It's a bad night out there.'

'The weather's never bothered you before,' Roskilly sneered.

'May I remind you that the boy in her charge has gone missing,' Christian said. 'Mrs Blackacre's been under terrible strain. It was against my advice that she came at all tonight.'

'*Your* advice!' Roskilly exploded. 'And who the fuck are you to be giving anyone advice?'

'Calm down, Cyril,' Phil Carey warned.

Roskilly stepped forward and jabbed a meaty finger into Christian's chest. 'You just keep your Froggy mouth shut from now on. Understand?

'Understand!' This time the jab to Christian's chest had Roskilly's full force behind it.

That was enough for Christian. Next moment Roskilly was flat out, unconscious, on the ground. He could as easily have delivered a killing blow.

'Holy shit!' Denzil exclaimed in admiration. 'How did you do that?'

Courtesy of Sergeant Major Jock Thompson, Christian thought. And his course in unarmed combat. 'Are you OK, Maizie?'

She nodded.

Christian glanced round the others present. 'Isn't someone going to help him?'

Charlie Treloar and John Corin gathered round the fallen man. 'He asked for it,' Charlie muttered.

'He did that,' Denzil agreed, thinking he'd never seen anyone move so fast, and effectively, as Christian. He was more than impressed. Especially as Christian was so slightly built.

Roskilly groaned as he started to come round.

'Shall we go?' Christian asked Maizie.

Her expression said it all. 'Yes.' She turned to the others. 'But before we do is there anyone else thinks we should discontinue these meetings?'

There was no reply.

'I remind you all again, our orders are to do nothing unless the Germans invade. Then, and only then, do we become operational. For now it's as though we don't exist.'

Roskilly's eyes fluttered open. 'What happened?' he croaked.

'You were hopefully taught some manners,' Maizie replied acidly.

Roskilly, assisted by Charlie and John Corin, was coming to his feet as she and Christian started back along the tunnel.

'I'm drunk!' Maizie declared.

'I'm not surprised.' Christian smiled. It was over an hour since they'd returned from the tunnel. What had begun as a nightcap had developed into quite a session, particularly on Maizie's part.

'Am I still making sense?'

'Just about.' He couldn't help but think how lovely she was like this. Most women looked ghastly when drunk, sloppy somehow. Unfeminine. But this certainly didn't apply to Maizie.

'I think you should go to bed now though,' he prompted.

She screwed up her eyes, trying to focus. 'You're a strange one, Christian Le Gall.'

'In what way?'

'I don't know. Just strange, that's all.'

'Nice strange?' he queried.

'Oh yes. Very nice strange.' She leant forward slightly on her stool. 'It's lovely you've come back so quickly. I was pretty certain you would come back, but not so quickly.'

'Oh?'

She hiccuped. 'You're such a pretty man. Everyone thinks so. Even Alice.'

'Do they indeed?' He didn't think he liked being thought of as pretty. Handsome maybe, if he was flattering himself, but not pretty. That smacked of the effete.

'Pretty and ever such good company. You make me laugh, Chris. You're a joy to be with.'

He glanced down at the floor, suddenly embarrassed. 'Thank you.'

'No, I mean it. The whole place lights up when you're here.'

He couldn't resist the jibe. 'And doesn't it with Sam?'

Maizie closed her eyes and a pained expression came over her face. 'No,' she whispered. 'It doesn't.'

He realised then just how unhappy she was in her marriage. He'd had inklings before, but now it was confirmed. He felt sorry for her, sorry and sad. Maizie deserved better. A whole lot better.

She hiccuped again. 'You're right about bed. I'm beginning to see double. I know I'll regret this in the morning.'

She fastened him with a steady, if slightly unfocused, stare. 'Thank you again for what you did earlier. With Cyril Roskilly that is. It was high time he got his comeuppance.'

'He's not a very nice person.'

'And a woman-hater. Thinks we're all inferior. That none of us has a brain in our head.'

'Well, you certainly do, Maizie. I can vouch for that.'

She smiled at him. 'You're so sweet, Chris. And a proper gentleman if ever there was. I admire that in you.'

Maizie eased herself off the stool. 'Let's go. Will you put out the lights?'

'Of course.'

He found her waiting for him at the top of the stairs clutching the banister. 'I haven't been so drunk in a long while,' she said.

He thought it had probably done her the world of good considering what she'd been through during the past few days. If nothing else it had taken her mind off Bobby.

He walked her to her door. 'Goodnight then, Maiz.'

'Goodnight, Chris.'

They stared at one another for a few seconds, then she opened her door and disappeared inside.

He took a deep breath, his emotions mixed. He'd never before in his life been so attracted to a woman as he had to Maizie Blackacre. But he continued along the corridor to his own room.

Maizie appeared in the restaurant carrying his breakfast. 'How do you feel?' he asked as she placed the plate in front of him.

'Don't ask.'

'That bad, eh?'

'Worse.'

She clutched her forehead.

'It's as if I have a troop of heavy cavalry charging around in here.'

He fought back the urge to laugh, as there was nothing funny in a hangover. 'You did have rather a lot,' he commented.

Maizie coloured. 'Unusual for me. The Roskilly business on top of Bobby . . .' She trailed off and pulled a face. 'I suppose it all just suddenly got to me.'

'Understandable, Maiz. Now, have you taken anything?'

'A couple of aspirins. They should sort me out. I only wish I didn't have to be in the kitchen though. The smell of frying isn't doing me any favours at all.'

'Then get out of there. Leave it to Alice.' He had a thought. 'Tell you what, when I've finished this we'll go down to the quay for a breath of fresh air. That should help.'

'I'm all for that.'

She turned to go, then hesitated. 'I hope I didn't say anything untowards last night, Chris.'

He feigned innocence. 'How do you mean?'

'I can remember some of it, but not all. I wasn't too . . . overfriendly I hope?'

'Not at all,' he smiled. 'Nothing untowards, as you put it, was said. I promise you.'

Her relief was evident. 'I'll meet you in the bar when you're ready.'

He watched her walk away, feeling a tremendous warmth towards her.

'No, nothing at all,' Hookie answered in reply to Maizie's questioning look. Which was what she'd expected.

She gazed out over the Channel's dull grey and choppy water, unable to bear the thought of Bobby's body swirling somewhere in its depths.

Christian lit a cigarette, with difficulty in the wind.

'I wish there was something more we could do,' Hookie sympathised, speaking to Maizie.

'Everything that could be done has been. All that's left now is to notify his mother.'

'Talking of her, I've been wondering,' Christian mused.

'What?' Maizie queried.

'If he hasn't gone there—' He held up a hand as Maizie opened her mouth to protest. 'I know what you're going to say, that Bobby could never have made it across the moors on foot at this time of year. But suppose, just suppose, mind you, that he has. And he's now in Plymouth?'

Hookie shook his head in disagreement.

'Even if he got to Helston, how would he get to Plymouth from there? He hasn't any money. At least none to speak of,' Maizie replied.

'He's a resourceful lad is Bobby, at least that's how he struck me. Who knows? He might have found a way.'

'He could have hitchhiked on to Plymouth,' Hookie volunteered.

Christian frowned, it wasn't a word he knew. 'That again is possible,' he said, after Maizie explained it to him.

'One thing 'tis certain, the only way to find out is if someone goes there to see,' Hookie declared.

Which was precisely what Christian intended to do.

'We could contact Constable Fowler and ask him to get the Plymouth police on the job,' Maizie suggested. Constable Fowler was the local officer.

'I think it's better we do this ourselves. One of us anyway. As I have the car I'll drive up there. You have his address, don't you?'

Maizie recalled the squalor of Bobby's home and her meeting with Shirley Tyler. 'Yes, I have it. And I'm coming with you. Unless you object that is?'

'Shouldn't you stay here, Maizie?'

'How long will the whole thing take?'

Christian considered that. 'We can be up there by this evening and back again sometime tomorrow.'

'Then I'll definitely come. I'd rather do that than wait around here worrying myself half to death. Alice can stay over for the night, she won't mind.'

'That's settled then,' Christian nodded.

'Leave in about an hour?'

'Suits me,' he agreed.

Despite the circumstances Maizie was delighted that she'd be alone with Christian for a while. Just the pair of them.

She was looking forward to that.

Miss Hitchon sighed and put down the chalk she'd been using. She simply couldn't concentrate. Every time she looked over the class Bobby's empty desk and chair mocked her.

The children were listless, devoid of any interest or enthusiasm. And who could blame them? One of their number was gone, feared drowned. It was perfectly understandable for them to be both shocked and upset.

'Class, rise!' she instructed.

They did, wondering what this break in routine was all about.

'You have an extra playtime today. I'll call you in when I'm ready.'

This was greeted with silence, followed by a ragged cheer. There was a mad scramble to be first out.

She'd go to the staff room and make herself a cup of tea, Miss Hitchon decided.

Bobby had been something of a favourite. The cheeky monkey.

Maizie, with Christian standing beside her, gently tapped Rosemary's bedroom door. 'Can I come in?'

When there was a muffled sound which she took to be an affirmative she opened the door and went inside.

Rosemary was standing by the window staring out. She was still in her night things and dressing gown.

'You haven't been down for breakfast,' Maizie admonished.

Rosemary shrugged.

'You must try to eat something. I don't want you being ill.'

'Maybe later, Aunt Maiz.'

Rosemary hadn't been to school since Bobby's disappearance, spending most of the time either helping the searchers or else in her room. Sometime during the previous afternoon she'd given up hope of ever seeing her brother alive again. Since then she'd been remembering – memories, good and bad, of their childhood.

'Chris and I have decided to go to Plymouth. To your house,' Maizie stated. 'There's just the vaguest possibility, and I don't even think it's that, Bobby's there. Also your mother has to be told of what's happened. Do you want to come?'

Rosemary turned to stare at Maizie, her eyes large and round. There was a quality about them Maizie found most disturbing. 'Plymouth?' she repeated with a frown.

'That's right. Your house. Do you want to come?'

'No,' Rosemary declared emphatically.

'I thought you would want to, having been so homesick.'

The homesickness had been an exaggeration, a lie. For some reason the thought of returning to Plymouth, to her previous life, repulsed her. She found that quite curious. 'I want to stay here until there's something certain about Bobby,' she said.

Maizie glanced at Christian, both aware that if Bobby had been swept out into the Channel there might never be anything definite.

'All right,' Maizie replied softly with a smile.

Christian went to Rosemary and placed his hands on her shoulders. 'Is there anything we can . . .'

What happened next astounded him. Rosemary wriggled out of his grasp. 'Don't ever touch me again!' she shrieked. 'Don't ever!'

Maizie was as taken aback as Christian who'd immediately retreated a few steps. 'Rosemary?'

'I don't want him touching me. Do you hear?'

A dumbfounded Maizie nodded.

'I didn't mean anything,' Christian protested.

'Just leave me. *Please*,' Rosemary pleaded, her face having contorted into a horrid mask of loathing.

Maizie thought that might be the best thing to do. 'Chris?'

Once out in the corridor Maizie closed the door again.

'What was that all about?' a thoroughly shaken Christian queried.

Maizie shook her head. 'I've absolutely no idea. None whatever.'

'I only took hold of her shoulders. You saw that. It wasn't as if I touched some place I shouldn't.'

'She's upset,' Maizie said. 'Not quite rational. Not herself. Just forget what happened. Let it pass.'

Inside the room Rosemary had crawled into her bed and pulled the clothes over her head.

She shouldn't have done that, reacted so violently. Christian had never been anything but kind to her.

But hands, male hands . . . She shuddered with a loathing that came from the very core of her being.

They spotted the smoke before Plymouth itself came into view. The city had been bombed again. Christian swore under his breath. Damned Boche!

They located Chapman Street without any difficulty, Maizie remembering how to get there from her previous visit. They parked outside number thirty-four.

'Not a very attractive area,' Christian declared grimly. 'What's left of it anyway.' Somewhere in the distance a siren began to wail. They didn't know whether that was announcing another attack or what it might be.

They were hoping Shirley Tyler would be at home as she worked nights. If not they planned to find the club employing her and try there. Someone thereabouts was bound to know the name of the club and its location. They got out of the car and walked the short distance to the front door.

Their knock was answered almost immediately by a pale-faced Bobby whose expression mirrored his disappointment when he saw who it was.

'Dad's dead,' he said. 'I thought you might be Mum.'

Chapter 16

For a brief moment Maizie thought she was going to faint from a combination of shock and relief, then she swept Bobby into a tight embrace. All too swiftly her euphoria turned to anger. 'Do you know what trouble you've caused running away?' she accused harshly. 'The entire village has been hunting for you. We all thought you drowned.'

Bobby didn't reply. He just stared blankly back at her.

'Do you hear me!' she cried, shaking him.

'Enough of that, Maizie,' Christian intervened. 'I suggest we go inside.'

Once in the house his nose wrinkled in disgust at the smell assailing him. The place stank.

The living room they entered was as bad a tip as Maizie remembered. 'Well?' she demanded of Bobby.

'Wait a minute,' Christian intervened again. 'Did you say your father's dead, Bobby?'

Bobby nodded.

'How do you know that?'

Bobby pointed to a telegram perched on the mantelpiece which Christian swiftly crossed over to and read. The telegram, dated several weeks previously, was from the War Department stating with regret that Private Robert Tyler had been killed in action. Christian took the telegram to

Maizie, her anger evaporating as she scanned its contents.

'Where's your mum?' Christian asked.

'I don't know. She wasn't here when I arrived and hasn't shown up since. I've been waiting for her.'

'Oh, my poor angel,' Maizie whispered. 'I'm so sorry for that but you must realise how worried we've all been. We thought you too were dead. Fallen into the sea or . . .' She didn't finish the comment.

'Have you any idea where your mother is?' Christian queried.

'No, I thought it best just to wait until she got back.' Tears welled in his eyes. 'But she hasn't come.'

What a bloody awful mess, Maizie thought. Where was the damned woman? 'First things first, are you all right?'

'I'm hungry, Aunt Maiz. I haven't eaten anything. There was nothing in the house and my money is all finished.'

'And what money's that?'

'The pound I found on the cliffs. It paid for my train fare.'

'You found a pound?'

'Up on the cliffs. A pound note was stuck on a piece of gorse. It must have been there for ages because it was all faded and torn at the edges. But it was still a pound note. The ticket man gave me a funny look when I handed it to him, but took it all the same.'

'I guess it's been lost by a holidaymaker at some point,' Maizie said to Christian. 'I can't imagine anyone from Coverack losing a pound. They simply don't do that kind of thing.'

'A piece of gorse stem was stuck right through it,' Bobby explained. 'That's why it didn't blow away.'

'And you caught the train at Helston?' Christian probed. Bobby nodded again.

'You walked across the moors all by yourself?' an incredulous Maizie queried.

'No, I hid on the fish truck.'

'The fish truck?'

'One of those that come twice a week to pick up the catch and deliver it to Helston. The driver went off for a cigarette before leaving and that's when I managed to get on. I snuggled down behind some crates.'

Maizie wanted to laugh. Of course! Why hadn't anyone thought of that? The fish trucks arrived and left early in the morning to make the Helston market and London rail connection. That was how he'd got safely across the moors. There was one question left. 'But *why*, Bobby?'

He frowned at her.

'Why run away?'

'Because of Emily's birthday party.'

Emily's birthday party? This was new.

Bobby slowly explained, his face colouring with embarrassment, the words stumbling from his lips. 'I wasn't good enough to go,' he ended miserably.

Maizie knew who was behind this nonsense. That bitch Mabel Dunne, the pretentious cow.

'They invited you then withdrew the invitation?' Christian said.

'I didn't want to be in Coverack after that. I wanted to be home here in Plymouth amongst my own kind.'

God help Mabel Dunne when she got hold of her, Maizie vowed. She'd read her the bloody riot act! She swore it would be a meeting Mabel wouldn't forget in a hurry. If ever.

Now she knew why Bobby had been so upset the night Mrs Trethowen had spoken to him while out walking her dog. Two and two had been put together and they'd come up with five.

'We'll have to let Alice know so the hunt can be called off,' Christian declared, wondering where the nearest telephone might be and if it would be working.

'Yes of course,' Maizie agreed. Turning again to Bobby she said, 'And your mother hasn't been home at all since you arrived back?'

He shook his head. 'It's been days.'

Maizie couldn't understand that. But there must be some explanation for it. Then she had a thought. 'Which is your mother's bedroom?'

Bobby pointed it out.

'Wait here, the pair of you.'

Maizie went into the bedroom and glanced around. It was in an even bigger mess than the living room. The top of a chest of drawers, which had a free-standing cracked mirror on it, was awash with face powder, some of the latter having spilt on to the floor. There were also several old lipsticks and an empty pot of something or other beside the mirror.

Maizie went to the already open wardrobe. One look inside confirmed her fears – only a few odd items of clothing remained.

'Well?' Christian demanded when she reappeared in the living room.

'I think Mrs Tyler has gone away for a while.'

Bobby's face crumpled and the tears returned. He didn't comment.

Maizie spread her hands in a gesture of being at a loss as to the real situation. Gone away for a while, but how long?

'I think what we should do now is get something to eat,' she declared.

'I'll attend to that. You remain here with Bobby,' Christian said.

She smiled at him. 'Anything will do, as long as it's filling. Whatever you can get hold of.'

'Right.'

Christian hesitated, then crossed to Bobby, going down on one knee before the lad. 'You mustn't worry, we're here now. Everything's going to be all right.'

On impulse Bobby threw his arms round Christian. 'She said she would come and visit and never did. She only ever wrote the one letter in all the time Rosie and I have been in Coverack.'

'I know,' Christian crooned. He couldn't think of what else to say.

'It's cold in here,' Maizie declared, shivering. 'Is there any coal?'

'A bit,' Bobby answered over Christian's shoulder.

'Then let's you and I get a fire going while Christian sees to the food, eh?'

'Yes, Aunt Maiz.'

Maizie stopped Christian as he was about to leave. 'Tell Alice that Bobby's father has been killed which is why he ran away. That should stop any repercussions when we get back to Coverack.'

Christian nodded. 'I understand.'

'Then on you go.'

Maizie turned and smiled at Bobby. 'Let's you and I get started on that fire, shall we?'

Christian emerged from the telephone box which, thankfully, had been working. It had taken ages to be connected to the Paris Hotel but eventually the operator had succeeded and he'd spoken with Alice. She'd been ecstatic on hearing the news. Christian had emphasised that Bobby had run away because his father had been killed. Alice hadn't thought to ask how Bobby had found out.

There was a pub facing the box which, just round the corner from where Shirley Tyler lived, must be her local. He decided to go in.

The pub was quiet, the busty barmaid brassy as a bedstead. He judged her to be in her sixties.

'What are you having, me love?' she asked with a smile.

He was thirsty after their long trip and decided a pint would be in order. He waited patiently while she poured it.

'That's ten pence ha'penny,' she declared, placing the brimming glass in front of him.

He counted out the correct money. 'I wonder if you could help me?' he queried.

Her eyes flicked over him with new interest. 'Depends what you want?'

'Do you know a Shirley Tyler?'

The barmaid considered that before answering. 'What's she to you?'

'I'm a friend. So you do know her then?'

The barmaid nodded.

'I've just been round to her house and she's not in, so I'm presuming she's at the club where she works. Would you happen to know its name and address?'

'Sure. It's the Singapore in Octagon Street which runs off Union Street. Doesn't open till later though.'

'Thank you.'

'Only she won't be there.'

'Oh?'

Christian pulled out his cigarette and offered her one.

'Ta, don't mind if I do.'

He lit hers then his own.

'Good friend, are you?'

'I don't wish her any harm if that's what you mean,' he prevaricated. 'I only want a few words.'

'Well, she's a regular here all right. Port and lemon usually. Sometimes gin. Can't half pack it away when she's in the mood and has the cash, I can tell you. A good customer.'

'So why won't she be at the club?'

'Because she's gone. Packed her bags and hopped it with her new chap. A bloke, businessman he said, down from Blackpool. Quite respectable too.'

Christian's heart sank. Poor Bobby and Rosemary. 'To Blackpool?'

'That's right, me darling. Or at least so they said. He's something to do with naval supplies, I believe. Real chummy they were, all over one another.'

The barmaid winked. 'Love's young dream, eh?'

She was being sarcastic, Christian realised, and smiled.

'I hope that don't put you out too much?'

'Not really. It wasn't very important.'

The barmaid looked round when a group of drunken sailors came into the pub. 'Here's trouble,' she muttered. 'I can smell it a mile off.'

The sailors were rowdy and had clearly been drinking for some time. Christian had to agree with the barmaid, they did look trouble. He quickly drank his pint and left.

'Fish and chips!' Christian announced to Bobby who answered the door.

Bobby beamed.

There was a nice fire going in the living room which cheered it up considerably. 'Well, that saves me cooking,' a relieved Maizie declared, for the kitchen was filthy and she wouldn't have wanted to risk using anything.

'I bought an extra one for Bobby as he's so hungry,' Christian explained.

'We may as well eat them straight out of the paper,' Maizie said. 'Tastes better that way.'

Bobby was already tearing at the first of his parcels and immediately began wolfing down the contents.

Christian manoeuvred Maizie away from the lad. 'We have to talk privately,' he whispered.

'Found out something?'

'And it isn't good.'

She nodded. 'Leave it to me.'

In the event Maizie didn't have to organise anything. Bobby

excused himself after he'd finished his meal saying he was going to the toilet. That was situated outside, and so they had a few moments alone.

'So give?' Maizie demanded as soon as Bobby had left the room.

Christian related his conversation with the barmaid.

'Shit,' Maizie swore. They could hardly tell that to Bobby. What a slag Shirley Tyler was. Her husband only recently dead and she'd run off with someone else, effectively abandoning her children. The rope was too good for a woman like that.

'So what do we say?' Christian asked.

'I'll think of something. Just give me a few minutes.'

Bobby returned, feeling a lot better now his stomach was full. He joined Maizie and Christian sitting by the fire.

'Chris met a neighbour of your mother's at the fish and chip shop,' Maizie lied. 'It seems she's found a better job up north and has gone to work there.'

Bobby digested that. 'Where up north?'

'The neighbour had no idea,' Maizie further lied. 'It could be Manchester, Liverpool, anywhere.'

Bobby's expression had become one of dejection. Gone away? And again without writing. He screwed his hands into tight fists.

'So you'll have to come with us in the morning as we can hardly leave you here,' Maizie went on.

'You mean Coverack?'

'We all want you back. Me, Rosemary, Alice. We love you. And forget this silly party business. People like that aren't worth bothering about.'

'That's very true,' Christian added.

'They said I wasn't good enough,' Bobby muttered.

'That's a load of baloney. You're as good as anyone else. There's absolutely nothing wrong with you. Chris?'

'Absolutely.'

'So let's forget that nonsense. Tomorrow you'll be home and it'll be as though you'd never been away.'

Bobby gazed around him. 'But this is my home.'

'Well, the hotel's your temporary home shall we say. While this dreadful war's on.'

'And what if I want to stay here?'

'You can't, Bobby,' Christian stated emphatically. 'You're far too young to be on your own. You'll be unable to look after yourself.'

His expression became stubborn.

'What'll happen is the authorities will find out and take you away,' Maizie continued. 'Now you don't want that, do you? They'll simply place you with another family in the country, or worse still put you in an orphanage.'

'Mum wouldn't allow that!' Bobby exclaimed. The thought of an orphanage terrified him.

'There's no forwarding address for your mother so they won't be able to contact her,' Maizie explained. 'They'll just do with you as they wish. If you take my advice you're far better off at the Paris with myself and your sister. Surely you can see the sense in that?'

Bobby's resistance crumpled. 'Yes,' he whispered.

'Good, that's settled then. Now come here.'

Bobby reluctantly went to her. 'We do love you, angel. No one more than I. I can understand how upset you've been, something of what you've been through, and that includes losing your father. I remember how I felt when mine died. It was awful. Truly awful. Unfortunately those of us left just have to pick up the pieces and carry on. That's how it is.'

Christian watched as she took him into her arms and hugged him. 'Everything will be all right, Bobby. I promise,' she whispered.

Bobby didn't reply, he was too choked to do so. His shoulders heaved several times.

'I think I'll go to bed,' he said eventually in a tight, strained voice.

She smoothed his hair, and kissed him on the cheek. 'It's hard growing up, isn't it? But it's something we all have to do. And as I said, don't you worry about that party business. It was their loss not yours, I'd be proud to have you at any party of mine. Very proud indeed.'

'Me too,' Christian smiled.

Bobby pulled himself free. 'Thanks, Aunt Maiz. You too, Christian. I only wish . . . I'd seen Mum again.'

Outwardly Maizie was smiling, inwardly she was cursing Shirley Tyler to hell. 'Would you like me to tuck you in?'

He nodded.

'Then off you go and I'll be through directly.'

Nothing was said between Maizie and Christian for a few minutes after Bobby had left, then she glanced across at him. 'Can I have a cigarette?'

'Of course.'

He noted the hand taking it from his packet was shaking.

'He's off,' Maizie announced.

Christian had banked up the fire with the remainder of the coal. 'Are you having the woman's room?'

Maizie's mouth wrinkled in distaste. 'Have you seen it? The sheets haven't been changed in God knows how long and are covered in . . .' She broke off. 'Marks,' she added lamely.

Christian got the message.

Maizie gestured to the couch, ancient and dilapidated but still in one piece. 'I'll sleep on that. What about you?'

He certainly wasn't going to get into a bed as disgusting as Maizie had described. He supposed they could always change it, but didn't know where the spare bedding was kept, besides which, it would be too much of a bother. They were both dog tired. It had been a long and wearisome day. 'I'll take that chair,' he replied. 'It'll do me fine.'

'I'd love a cup of tea,' she sighed. But there wasn't any in the house, she'd checked earlier.

'I'll go out and get some things in the morning,' he said. 'We'll need breakfast before starting off.'

Maizie was suddenly uncomfortable, unsure of herself. She'd never bargained to be sleeping in the same room as Christian. There again, neither of them had considered what the arrangements would be.

'Why don't you go out for a drink and I'll stay here?' she suggested. 'There's still time.'

'You could come with me?'

She shook her head. 'I won't leave Bobby. No, you go and I'll remain. A drink will do you good.'

Suddenly that appealed to him. He'd pay the local another visit and hope the drunken sailors were gone by now.

When he returned Maizie was fast asleep on the couch having covered herself with her coat. She was gently snoring.

He placed the guard in front of the remains of the fire and settled himself down in the chair. He sat watching Maizie's face reflected in the firelight until he too dropped off.

'What!' Maizie came awake with a start. 'What's that?'

'Bombs. It's an air raid,' Christian answered across the pitch-black room. The blackout curtains at least were in good repair.

She sat up when there was another explosion followed by another and then a third. 'That's close,' she whispered.

'Yes.'

There was a whole series of explosions, some near by, others far off. They could both hear the drone of aeroplanes.

'I hate to admit this but I'm scared,' she said.

'Me too.'

'Are you really?' That somehow cheered her, made her feel less inadequate.

'I'm afraid so. Though perhaps not so much as I'd have been in the past. I used to dream a lot about Dunkirk and the time leading up to it, but haven't in ages. I think fear is something you eventually come to terms with. I thought I'd be terrified when in France, but wasn't. Apprehensive, yes, but not deep-rooted fear. The sort that can numb and paralyse you.'

He stopped when there were more explosions, and now ack ack had come into play. He decided to try and lighten the atmosphere. 'Do you know you snore, Maizie?'

That horrified her. 'I do not!'

'Oh but you do, I assure you.'

Her face flamed. 'How embarrassing.'

'Don't be. It's rather nice actually. Reassuring in a funny sort of way.'

'But it's awful for a woman to snore. So unfeminine.'

Sam had never mentioned it, she thought. And she was certain he would have done. It must therefore, unless Chris was pulling her leg, be a recent phenomenon.

'I don't believe you,' she declared.

He laughed. 'It's true. Honestly!'

She hung her head. 'I'm mortified. Through and through.'

'I enjoyed listening to you.' He was about to add that his mother snored, then thought the better of it. Maizie wouldn't appreciate his drawing comparisons between herself and his mother.

This time the explosion was a tremendous roar that almost deafened them.

'Dear God,' Maizie croaked. 'What was that?'

'Something's received a direct hit,' Christian conjectured. 'Perhaps a munitions factory or dump.'

'My ears are still ringing.'

'I'm used to being kept awake recently,' he said casually.

'Why's that?'

'My flatmate Gilbert has a girlfriend and the pair of them are at it nightly like rabbits. Thump thump thump against my bedroom wall. It's most upsetting.'

Maizie smiled. 'I can imagine.'

'No shame, either of them. That's one of the reasons I came back to Coverack so quickly. To get away from the noise.'

She could just make out the outline of his shape. 'And what were the other reasons?'

He wanted to say *you*, but didn't. 'I've told you, I like it there. Coverack and the people. It's so peaceful.'

She bit back her disappointment. 'I see,' she said quietly.

'But I've told you that before.'

More ack ack batteries opened up while the drone of planes increased in both volume and intensity.

'I think the whole of the Luftwaffe must be up there,' he joked drily.

'It certainly sounds that way. I just hope it doesn't wake Bobby.' She shook her head. 'I feel so sorry for that lad. A father killed in action and a mother who doesn't give a damn.'

'I think I'll have a look,' Christian declared, rising from his chair and padding over to the window. Cautiously he opened the curtains a few inches and peered out.

Long lines of white light were criss-crossing the sky and fiery red tracer shells were spitting upwards. He could quite easily make out the shapes of many planes.

Maizie joined him, placing a hand on his shoulder. 'It's quite a sight,' she declared softly.

He was only too aware of the hand and closeness of her presence. All he wanted to do was fold her into his arms and kiss her. No, more than that. Fondle, caress, lift up her skirt and . . . His breathing became short and sharp.

'They've got one!' Maizie exclaimed.

Sure enough, one of the planes had been hit, flames streaming from the fuselage as it plummeted earthwards.

'I wouldn't like to be beneath that when it smacks,' Christian stated grimly.

He turned a fraction to discover her eyes staring into his, their faces only inches apart. He found himself aching with desire.

'Let's hope it doesn't last too long,' Maizie murmured huskily, breaking away and returning to the couch.

'No.'

He remained at the window for about another minute, more to regain his composure than anything else. He marvelled again at the effect she had on him. An effect no other woman had ever had.

Taking a deep breath he went back to his chair. 'We'll make an early start,' he said.

'Good idea.'

Maizie wanted to ask him over to the couch, to hold her, cuddle her till the raid was over. But she was afraid of what might occur if she did. It would be all too easy there in the dark with an air raid taking place to succumb. Oh, all too easy indeed.

Rosemary came rushing out when they pulled up in front of the Paris, grinning broadly to see Bobby waving at her from the rear. Then he was out of the car and standing beside her.

'Dad's dead,' he stated bluntly.

'I know. Alice told me.'

'And Mum's gone north somewhere to a better job. She didn't leave a forwarding address.'

Rosemary understood the full implication of that. She was older than Bobby after all and more experienced. 'We thought you drowned,' she said.

Bobby blanched. 'I didn't mean to cause bother. Upset everyone.'

'Well, you did. There's been a terrible to-do here since you disappeared. The entire village was out searching, including me.'

'Well, I'm back now,' was all he could think of to reply.

'Are you hungry?'

He nodded.

'Alice has some soup on in the kitchen. Come in and I'll give you a bowl.'

'Thanks, Rosie,' he said softly.

She touched him gently on the cheek. 'I want to hear all about it over the soup.'

'So put the word round, will you, Hookie. Bobby ran away because his father had been killed. That should stop any resentment about the trouble he caused. Alice will do the same.'

'Understood, Maiz. Is he all right?'

'Right as rain, Hookie. Somewhat chastened, mind you, but fine all the same.'

She hadn't told Hookie about Shirley Tyler, and certainly wouldn't be letting on that she'd run off with a man. The story would stand as it was.

Maizie emerged from the school. Mr Brookfield had been most sympathetic and declared he was looking forward to having both Bobby and Rosemary in class again the following Monday.

So that was sorted out satisfactorily, Maizie thought. Now for Mabel Dunne, the pretentious bitch. Oh, but she was looking forward to this.

Chapter 17

'**B**obby!'

'Go away!' he replied crossly.

Emily hurried to catch up with him and fall in alongside. 'I told you it wasn't my fault, Bobby. I had nothing to do with it.'

He was hoping his embarrassment wasn't showing. Since returning to school he'd continued studiously to avoid Emily.

'I want us still to be friends,' she pleaded.

'Huh!'

She grabbed him by the arm. 'Will you stop and talk to me?'

He came to a halt and glared at her. 'We've nothing to say to one another.'

'I missed you dreadfully at the party, Bobby. You not being there completely spoilt it for me.'

'I'll bet!' It was on the tip of his tongue to say it hadn't sounded that way to him when he'd stood outside listening. The party couldn't have been jollier.

'Mrs Blackacre went to see my mum about it.'

That surprised Bobby. 'She did?'

'Mum was in a dreadful state when Dad got home that night. He told her it was all her own stupid fault and she'd deserved what she'd got. Mum burst out crying and went to bed after he'd said that. Dad had to make his own tea.'

Bobby grinned. Good old Aunt Maiz. That was one in the eye for snooty Mrs Dunne. He'd love to have been present when Maizie was there. It must have been something to hear.

'Would you like a boiling?' Emily produced a bag and offered its contents to Bobby. 'They're awfully nice.'

'No, thank you.'

'Go on, Bobby, you like sweets.'

He sniffed in disdain.

Emily thrust the bag into his hand. 'You have all of them. Please?'

'I can't take your—'

'Please?' she interjected.

He suddenly relented. And it had nothing to do with the sweets either. 'It's true you wanted me there?'

'More than anything. We're best pals.'

'And it was just your mother?'

Emily nodded. 'Dad was furious when he found out. He shouted at her. I've never heard Dad do that before. He said she should be ashamed of herself.'

Bobby digested that.

'Dad's been quite different since that day. He doesn't let Mum bully him any more.'

Bobby liked the sound of that. It was funny somehow. He extracted a boiling from the bag and gave the bag back. 'One's enough. You keep the rest.'

'Does that mean we're friends again?'

He was terribly fond of Emily, and had missed her company something awful. 'Yes,' he nodded.

Emily squealed and pecked him on the cheek. 'That's wonderful!'

Bobby was horrified. Kissed by a girl! He quickly glanced

around praying no one had seen. He didn't think they had.

'Come on then,' he growled.

Emily was so happy she began to skip.

'It's a good day for that,' Christian commented. He'd come into the courtyard at the rear of the hotel to find Maizie pegging out.

'It's certainly windy enough,' she smiled. 'These clothes will be dry in no time.'

'I'll need my stuff ready for the day after tomorrow.'

She paused and a frown creased her face. 'Is that when you'll be off?'

'I'm afraid so, Maiz.'

She resumed pegging out, her heart suddenly heavy within her. 'Will you . . . be going over to France again?' she asked casually.

'I don't know. At least I don't know if I'll be going right away. But I will be going. That's what I'm trained for after all.'

'I suppose so,' she muttered. Her heart had now started thumping.

'I wish I could stay on here,' he stated softly.

Maizie momentarily halted to wipe hair away from her face. She'd make him a special meal the following night, she decided. She had some fillet steak in the larder that she'd come by, they'd have that.

'I say this every time, but we'll miss you, Chris.'

'I'll return as soon as I can.'

'I know,' she teased. 'You find it peaceful here.'

'Christ!' he exclaimed as a seagull dropping splattered directly in front of him. 'That was close. Bloody birds!'

Maizie laughed. 'It would have been better if it had hit you. That brings good luck.'

'Does it indeed?'

'So they say.'

He extended a foot and stood on the mess. 'There, will that do?'

'Don't you go tramping that into my hotel, Christian Le Gall. We have more than enough cleaning as it is.'

Now it was his turn to laugh. 'But will it bring me luck just as if it had fallen on me?'

Suddenly she was very serious, all humour disappeared. 'I hope so, Chris. I truly do.'

So did he, he thought. So did he.

He'd missed London, Christian realised driving down the King's Road. Even in wartime there was a vibrancy about the place that he enjoyed. He wished Maizie was with him so he could show her round.

He'd given Maizie his telephone number before setting off, instructing her to ring at any time. It didn't have to be important, he'd emphasised. A chat would be nice if that's all she wanted.

He parked in front of the flat and got out. The nearby hovering barrage balloon was still there, he noted. Grey and menacing, it loomed above him as a deterrent to enemy aircraft.

He opened the door to find the flat in darkness, so he presumed Gilbert had gone out. The note was on the table.

It was brief and somewhat jocular. Gilbert was on assignment (at long last!) and didn't know when he'd return. A postscript informed him there was a present on his bed.

Christian tore the note into small pieces and disposed of them. He wondered if Gilbert was already in France, and where, if he was. He offered up a silent prayer for Gilbert's safety.

His face broke into a huge grin when he saw what the

present was. Three packets of Gitanes and three of Gauloises. Now where had Gilbert managed to get those!

Moments later he'd lit up. Sheer heaven! he thought. Sheer heaven.

'Bless you, Gilbert, wherever you are,' he muttered.

'Captain Le Gall reporting as ordered, sir,' Christian declared, giving Major Hammond a salute.

'How was your leave?'

'Fine, sir.'

'Did you go away?'

'Down to Cornwall, sir. As you may recall I have friends there.'

Major Hammond leant back in his chair. 'Of course, the fishermen who helped us out.'

'And others, sir.'

Hammond studied Christian thoughtfully for a few moments. 'I want you to work in the R/T Section for a while. How do you feel about that?' R/T meant receive and transmit on a wireless.

Christian couldn't mask his disappointment. 'I was hoping you might have another field assignment for me, sir.'

'Not yet, Captain. In the meantime you may as well be doing something useful. I wish you to run two "joes" for us.' A 'joe' was what an operative in the field was called.

'I see, sir.'

'One of them will be of particular interest to you. He's your flatmate, Private Du Bois.'

'Gilbert!'

'Codename Umbrella on this occasion. He's been sent over to organise a resistance cell outside Beauvais. When that is up and running he'll have a number of sabotage targets to deal with before returning. You'll be his contact here.'

Christian nodded. 'I understand, sir. And the second?'

'Her real name needn't concern you. Her codename is Tumbril.'

'When do I start, sir?'

Major Hammond smiled. 'That's the spirit, old boy. Why don't you toddle off to R/T Section right now and get yourself acquainted with procedure there.'

The interview was clearly at an end. Christian saluted again. 'Thank you, sir.'

Well, at least there was a consolation to all this, Christian thought as he left the Major's office. Gilbert *was* in for a surprise!

'Women can't throw. They're hopeless at it,' Bobby declared. He and Emily were down at the shore chucking pebbles out to sea.

Emily knew he was right. She personally couldn't throw for toffee. 'We can do other things well that boys can't,' she retorted sniffily.

'Such as?'

That flustered her. 'I don't know. But other things.'

Bobby laughed. 'You can't think of anything, can you?'

She was furious because she couldn't.

He laughed again.

'Don't you laugh at me, Bobby Tyler! That's horrid of you.'

She really was quite funny when angry, Bobby thought. Especially when she went red in the face. That was highly amusing. 'I was only teasing.'

'Well don't.'

He picked up a large flat pebble. 'Watch me make this skip,' he boasted. The pebble completed six hops before sinking.

'You're very clever,' she commented sarcastically.

He heard the sarcasm in her voice and it annoyed him. 'I think we should go back,' he said. 'It's getting cold.'

She shrugged her shoulders. 'If you want.'

'I was only thinking of you,' he protested.

That cheered her. 'Were you?'

'Of course I was. Anyway, look at that sky. It's going to snow.'

Emily glanced upwards and had to agree. There was definitely snow in the offing. She was pleased she had on her thickest woollen gloves, even if they were past their best and one had a small hole in it.

'Let's be off then.' Bobby turned to go.

'Wait!'

He stopped. 'What is it?'

She was suddenly shy, unable to look him directly in the eye. 'There's something I want to say,' she mumbled.

He frowned. 'Go on?'

'I've been meaning to for ages but somehow never got round to it.' She prodded an empty crab shell with her foot. This was difficult.

Bobby waited patiently.

'I know how upset you've been which is what made it hard. I should have said it when we made up, but didn't.'

'What is it, Emily?' he queried softly.

'I'm ever so sorry about your father. It must be terrible for you.'

He quickly glanced away to stare out over the Channel, digging his hands deep into his pockets. 'Thanks,' he managed in a choked voice.

'Is there anything I can do?'

Bobby shook his head.

'Do you want to talk about it?'

'No,' he stated emphatically.

'It must be terrible,' she repeated.

'I remember the last time I saw him,' Bobby said, picturing

the scene in his mind. 'He gave me half a crown and told me not to spend it all at once. Now he's dead.'

'You've still got your mum though. Don't forget that.'

Had he really? Bobby wondered. She'd only written once and never visited like she'd promised. Then she'd gone away up north without letting him and Rosemary know. She could at least have done that. In his heart of hearts he was beginning to believe he'd never see her ever again, that she too was gone for ever. For a moment he thought he might cry, but didn't.

'Bobby?'

'Let's go,' he declared, taking Emily by the hand. He found great comfort in that.

They walked hand in hand till they reached the road, when he dropped hers in case they were seen.

Maizie glanced at the clock. Ten past two in the morning of New Year's Day. She slumped on to a stool at the bar and wondered about getting herself a drink. She'd only had a couple of glasses of wine during the entire evening.

It had been hectic earlier on, but then many of the revellers had left to celebrate the new year in their own homes. The last stragglers had departed only a few minutes previously.

It had been a strange night, she reflected. The merrymaking had seemed forced. The war was to blame, of course; it governed and affected everything people did nowadays. The war and worry about those who were off fighting it.

The only casualty of the evening had been old Jim Corin, John's dad, who'd suddenly passed out while playing his accordion. He'd gone right in the middle of playing a tune. One moment he'd been as lively as the rest of them, the next fast asleep over his instrument.

What was 1942 going to bring? God alone knew. The war wasn't going too well, that was certain. Only last month, the

Japanese had attacked Pearl Harbor. Nearer to home points rationing had come into force. There were those who said Pearl Harbor was a blessing in disguise as it brought America into the war, which must surely turn the tide in their favour. As for points rationing, that only affected her marginally where food was concerned. She could easily get what she needed, as could all the villagers. She pitied the poor souls living in towns; they'd really be up against it.

Hong Kong had been captured. Other bad news had been that the *Repulse* and *Prince of Wales* had been sunk off Malaya with the loss of many lives. Luckily no one from Coverack had been serving aboard either.

She thought about Sam and wondered where he was. At sea or in port? If the latter then he'd certainly be drunk. That was guaranteed. She hadn't heard a word from him, but then, had she really expected to? And uppermost in her thoughts there was Christian – she smiled thinking of him – where was he? Probably at a party somewhere, bound to be. She hadn't heard from him either, which was disappointing. There again, she could have rung but hadn't liked to. Once she'd almost done so only to shy off at the last moment, the telephone actually in her hand. He'd turn up again in time.

Then she had an idea which made her smile even more. It was appropriate for the new year after all. There was still one more bottle of the champagne she'd shared with Christian, which she'd described as having the taste of wild strawberries. She'd get the bottle, take it up to her room and drink it there.

Yes, that's exactly what she'd do. Drink it and dream of what might have been if she'd been younger and not a married woman.

Christian laid down his pencil and studied the latest message from Gilbert which he'd just decoded. It was routine enough, nothing unusual in it to be concerned about. And yet . . . there was something, something between the lines that nagged him.

Things weren't going the way they should. Gilbert was unhappy, uneasy perhaps, and he didn't know why. Any other operator wouldn't have picked it up but he did because he knew Gilbert so well.

Christian wondered if he should mention this to Major Hammond, but eventually decided not to. He didn't want to be accused of an over-active imagination, of reading something into Gilbert's transmissions that wasn't really there.

So far he hadn't quizzed Gilbert about any of this. But maybe the time had now come when he should.

He made up his mind to tack an addendum of his own to the next outgoing transmission.

Christian was shivering as he entered the Eight Bells, for it was a raw March night, bitterly cold with an evil wind whipping along the street. The pub had been out of any type of brandy for the previous week but the landlord had told him there might be some in that evening.

He was in luck! He ordered one together with a half pint of beer, during which exchange the landlord informed him he was limited to two small measures. No more.

His face screwed up when he tasted the brandy. It was awful. Now he knew why the landlord's eyes had been twinkling when he'd been served. The brandy was Spanish and complete *merde* as far as he was concerned. With the best will in the world he couldn't even begin to pretend it was the cognac he so relished.

'Hello.'

He glanced up in surprise, then immediately stood. The speaker was Madeleine whom Gilbert had been seeing. 'Why, hello,' he smiled.

'Do you mind if I join you? I was supposed to meet a girlfriend but she hasn't turned up. Probably some flap on in her part of the Ministry and she's had to stay on. And I don't exactly like being in a pub on my own.'

'Be my guest.' He pulled out a chair and she sat alongside. 'So how are you?'

'Not too bad. Yourself?'

He shrugged. 'Same as that I suppose. Not too bad.'

She regarded him quizzically. 'I haven't seen you in here since Gilbert went away?'

'I've been around. We must have come in at different times, that's all.'

'And how is Gilbert? I haven't heard.'

He had to be careful here, he cautioned himself. What had Gilbert told her to explain his absence? 'Me neither I'm afraid.'

She frowned and began rubbing the rim of her glass to produce a squeaking sound. 'I was hoping he'd be back by now. Though in all honesty he didn't know how long his course would last.'

Course, that was a clue. 'I was on leave when he left so I don't know the details either.'

Madeleine had a sip of her gin and tonic. 'If it's cold like this in London what must it be like in Scotland? The poor love must be frozen through most of the time.'

Scotland, another clue. He now had a fair idea of the story Gilbert had given her. 'Rather him than me.'

Madeleine opened her handbag to produce a packet of Senior Service. 'No, here, have one of mine,' Christian said hurriedly, digging for his own cigarettes. It was nice to have female company, even if it was a trifle awkward on account of Gilbert.

'Now what about you, Christian, have you found a girl-friend yet?' she queried after they'd both lit up.

The change of subject, and directness of the question, slightly threw him. He shook his head.

'Pity, you're such a good-looking chap. I'm sure there must be hundreds of women who would love to meet you.'

He laughed. 'I'll take your word on both counts.'

'I'll tell you what. I've a few friends at the Ministry who might interest you. Why don't I bring one along some night?'

He was tempted, very much so. Life had become lonely since Gilbert had gone off on assignment. He spent too many nights by himself in the flat with nothing to do. 'I don't think so,' he replied reluctantly.

'Whyever not?' she queried in surprise. Her eyes suddenly opened wide. 'You're not . . . you know?'

What was she on about? 'I'm not with you, Madeleine.'

She coloured. 'One of . . . *those?*' She dropped her hand in a limp gesture.

That stunned him. 'No I'm not!' he exclaimed emphatically. 'Whatever gave you that idea? I don't look like that, do I?'

'Not at all. It's just . . . well sometimes it's hard to tell. I didn't mean to offend you.'

'You didn't,' he lied. 'Forget it.'

'Most men would jump at the chance of being introduced to a pretty girl. Unless . . . is there someone else? Gilbert said there wasn't. That you were completely unattached.'

'There's no one,' he smiled, thinking that was only half true. There was Maizie but how could he explain that situation? He couldn't, perhaps not even to himself.

'Then come on, let me arrange something. There is a war on, who knows what tomorrow might bring? We might all be blown to smithereens during a raid.'

Or killed on duty in France, he thought grimly. Considering that, he was being silly denying himself. He too wanted to make a wall thump a few times more in his life. He was only human after all. And young, with all the urges and needs that went with that.

'Do you prefer blondes or brunettes?' she asked mischievously.

'Darkish hair usually.' With auburn highlights, he thought, picturing Maizie.

'I've got just the girl. Smashing figure too. You'll like her. And I'm sure she'll like you.' Madeleine giggled. 'She got quite jealous when she learnt I was going out with a romantic Frenchman. She'll think you a right dish.'

Christian finished his brandy, grimacing as it went down. 'Will you have another?' he said, gesturing to her glass.

'Please.'

'I shan't be long.'

Should he or shouldn't he? he wondered as he went up to the bar. Where was the harm? And as Madeleine had pointed out, with a war on who knew what the future held. He should enjoy himself while he had the chance. It would be stupid not to. He was still mulling it over when he returned to their table with the drinks.

'When are you in here again?' Madeleine queried.

'Maybe Friday.'

'At what time?'

'I said *maybe*, Madeleine.'

'And I *said*, what time?'

His lips curled in wry amusement. 'Quite persistent, aren't you?'

'Uh-huh,' she agreed. 'Now what time?'

He put Maizie from his mind. 'Eight o'clock?'

'Eight o'clock it is. We'll be here,' she declared triumphantly.

It was only an hour since he'd said goodbye to Madeleine and he was already regretting the arrangement, doubts beginning to assail him shortly after they'd parted.

What on earth had he let himself in for? A blind date, he believed the Americans called it. He couldn't believe the girlfriend would be horrible. Surely Madeleine wouldn't do that to him. There again, you never knew with women. They didn't view their own sex the way men did. Quite the contrary.

'Damn,' he muttered, and worried a nail. Nor could he not turn up. That would be ungallant. He had to go through with it now.

Of course he knew what the real trouble was – a feeling of guilt where Maizie was concerned. Now that really was ridiculous. There was nothing between Maizie and himself, nothing concrete anyway. He fancied Maizie and was sure Maizie fancied him. But that was as far as it went.

He glanced over at the telephone, experiencing a great urge to pick it up and ring Maizie. Talk to her, though certainly not about Friday night.

Why was life always so complicated, never straightforward? At least that's how it seemed to him.

He lit a cigarette, telling himself he was smoking too much nowadays. And cigarettes weren't the easiest things to come by. Luckily for him he had a sympathetic tobacconist, what the English called a Francophile, who'd promised to keep an eye out for any Gitanes or Gauloises he might be able to get hold of, though the tobacconist doubted he would.

It would be lovely to hear Maizie's voice and hear her recount what she'd been up to. He also wanted to know how Bobby and Rosemary were. Yes, the latter was his excuse if he did ring.

'Damn,' he muttered again.

He decided to take the bull by the horns. Why the hell not! What did he have to lose? It was a bad time to ring as she might well be busy at the bar and not able to speak for long. Even so, just to make contact again, hear her voice, for however short a period, would be a treat.

Rising, he crossed to the telephone and when the operator came on gave her the number of the Paris Hotel which he now knew by heart. That same heart was banging in his chest as he eagerly awaited to be connected.

The operator kept him hanging on for ages and he became more and more impatient as the minutes ticked past.

'I'm sorry, sir, we can't seem to get through to that part of Cornwall tonight. I don't know what the problem is but all the lines to the lower section of the county are dead.'

His disappointment was intense. 'Thank you,' he replied.

'I'm sorry, sir. Perhaps in the morning?'

Perhaps, he thought as he cradled the phone. Though he doubted he'd be trying. He had work to go to and would probably have had second thoughts by then anyway.

He tried to read instead. A novel by Trollope in French that had amused him previous nights. But he couldn't concentrate, his mind kept drifting off.

All he could think of was Maisie and Coverack.

Gilbert was worried. Should he tell Christian what he suspected or not? So far he'd denied any problems when prompted by Christian because he had no proof, none whatsoever. There had been a number of little things, all intangible, elusive wills o' the wisp that disappeared before you could grab hold of them.

He sighed and scratched his backside. It could be his nerves were simply getting the better of him. Everything seemed all right on the surface, and yet . . .

He sat in front of the wireless set, switched it on and waited for it to warm up. When he judged it ready he placed the headphones over his ears and tapped out his callsign. Almost immediately Christian responded that he was being received loud and clear.

His message contained no reference to what was bothering him.

Maizie instantly recognised the back of the solitary man sitting at the bar. It wasn't opening time for another twenty minutes.

He heard her footsteps and swivelled round to smile at her. She was shocked by his appearance for he'd aged dramatically. His hair had gone totally grey. He might have been fifteen years older than when she'd last seen him.

'Hello, Maiz.'

'Sam.'

A tic jumped in his right cheek. 'I was torpedoed.'

Chapter 18

They'd come up to their bedroom for privacy, Alice hastily summoned to take care of the bar in the meanwhile. Sam crossed over and sat on the end of their bed as Maizie closed the door behind them.

'It's good to be home. I never thought I'd see you or Coverack again,' Sam said. There was a strange glint that Maizie didn't recognise in his eyes.

'What happened, Sam?'

He took a deep breath. 'We were on the Malta run, a fair-sized convoy with an armed escort. It was the fourth time we'd made that run, each trip worse than the one before. We lost two of the crew to strafing on the first run, four on the second, barely escaped being bombed on the third, and nearly everyone on the last. There were only three survivors including me.'

The glint vanished from Sam's eyes which now took on a faraway look. His fingers were entwined, restlessly moving against each other. When he next spoke his voice had gone thick with emotion.

'I'd been down below, in the engine room actually, and had just come back up on deck when I spotted the torpedo heading directly amidships. If I'd stayed below, hadn't come up when I did . . .' He broke off and shook his head.

'Go on, Sam,' Maizie prompted after a few moments' silence.

'A lookout yelled a warning at the same time I did. Whoever was at the wheel tried to alter course but by then it was too late. There was another merchantman off on our starboard side already engulfed in flames. We were next.

'I froze, Maizie, froze with fear as that damned thing came hurtling towards us. And then it hit.'

Sam shuddered.

'I'll never forget that till the day I die. Boom! The most horrendous explosion followed by a great sheet of flame that swept the stern.

'I was thrown up in the air and then fell heavily on deck. The noise was incredible. I can't even describe it. When that passed away all I could hear were the shrieks of the dying and badly wounded. One chap, burning from head to toe like a torch, raced by me and threw himself overboard.

'The ship was broken in half, Maiz, both parts already beginning to sink. I knew I had to get off of there, into the water. And then we began to sink.'

Sam paused to take another deep breath.

'Shall I get you a drink, Sam?'

He shook his head. 'Later maybe.'

Sam rose from the bed and went to the window to stare out.

'German planes appeared and started to strafe us, those still aboard and those already in the water. Escaped fuel oil caught alight, whipping and dancing over the water where men were trying to keep afloat. I saw Jacksy Johnstone, a good mate of mine, ignite from the shoulders up. He was screaming like a stuck pig. The pain must have been awful.'

'So what did you do?' Maizie asked quietly when it appeared he was going to fall silent again.

'I went to the port side, away from the burning sea,

scrambling over the hull as our part of the ship was starting to roll. I slipped and fell several times, cutting myself on barnacles, and then I was in the water.

'That was when there was a second explosion and suddenly debris was flying everywhere. I think I got hit on the head by a bit of it 'cos when I came to again I was underwater entangled in a piece of rope that was attached to something heavy.

'I was sinking like a stone. I desperately tried to free the rope but couldn't. It was wrapped round both my legs and all of a tangle. I knew then I was going to die. That this was the end.

'Further down I distinctly saw the shape of the submarine that had got us continuing on its way. The water was so clear I could even make out the Italian markings on the side.

'And then . . . and then . . .' He turned to stare at Maizie. 'A miracle happened, nothing else would explain it. The rope simply fell away of its own accord and released me.

'I was heading upwards again, the surface of the water sparkling above me. I was choking from lack of air at that point, my head feeling as though it was about to burst. I closed my eyes and began to pray. Our Father, Who art in Heaven, hallowed be thy name . . .

'Suddenly I was gasping in air and floundering on the surface. Both sections of the ship had gone under and the flames were still raging on the water, but luckily a good hundred yards or so from me.

'German planes were everywhere, strafing other members of the convoy, the armed escort answering back with everything it could throw at them. One plane received a direct hit and blew up in mid-air and all I could think was take that, you bastard.'

Maizie lit a cigarette. She'd never heard such a harrowing story. It had made her blood run cold. No wonder Sam had aged. Anyone would after that.

'A frigate came bearing down on me but I knew better than to imagine it would stop. They were under orders not to as that would make them a sitting duck. I watched the faces of the RN blokes as it steamed on past – they aware that if their ship had been sunk they too would have been left behind.

'One of them had the presence of mind to grab a rubber dinghy and sling it in my direction which I managed to reach and scramble on to. A few minutes later I was joined by one of our officers, the Second Mate, and shortly after that by an AB, that's Able Seaman, called Trick.

'There were no paddles on the dinghy so all we could do was drift. We did that for the rest of that day, that night, the following day and the following night.

'Can you imagine, Maiz, there was no food, no drinking water, just us drifting helplessly. Then the second miracle occurred. A small cargo ship flying the Swedish flag appeared and hove to. The Swedes are neutral as you know. They hauled us aboard and went on their way, eventually putting us ashore at the Pool of London.'

He ran a trembling hand over his face. 'And that's it, Maiz.'

She stubbed out her cigarette, went to him and took him into her arms. 'Poor Sam,' she whispered.

His body was tensed tight, but as she continued to hold him he began to slowly relax. '*Two* miracles, Maiz, most men don't even get one.'

'Yes,' she agreed quietly.

'And now I'm home. Never thought I'd see it again. It or you.'

'Poor Sam,' she repeated. 'Can I get you anything?'

'Nothing, Maiz, just being here with you is enough.'

That touched her deeply. 'Why don't we go down and

have that drink? I could certainly use one after what I've just heard.'

'Then a drink it be,' he replied. ''Tis a long while since I had a pint of cider. And I have a fancy for cheese. Fresh cheese. A bloody great wedge of the stuff.'

She laughed. 'Cider and cheese coming up. A bloody great wedge of it.'

In all her married life she'd never felt so well disposed to Sam Blackacre as she did at that moment.

Christian was wondering what to do with the rest of his Saturday afternoon, when the telephone rang.

'Hello?'

'Christian, it's Madeleine.'

He knew what this had to be about. It had been the previous evening that he'd met up with her and her friend Jill Simpson, a pleasant enough woman as far as he was concerned but there had been no attraction on his part.

'Are you still there?' she queried.

'Sorry. Yes, of course I am.'

'I thought last night went rather well, didn't you? And what did you think of Jill? I'm dying to know. She was most taken with you.'

Oh God! 'I considered it to go very well too,' he prevaricated. 'And Jill's very pleasant company.'

Warmth crept into Madeleine's voice. 'I'm glad you feel that way. So, are you going to get in touch with her? I can give you the telephone number.'

Christian sighed, this was difficult. He didn't want to upset anyone. 'I don't think so, Madeleine, thank you very much.'

'Oh?'

'I said she was pleasant, and she was. But not my type, I'm afraid.'

'I see.' The voice had turned cold.

'I'm sorry.'

'She'll be terribly disappointed, Christian. As I mentioned, she was most taken.'

'I'm very flattered, truly I am. But that's how it is.'

'What exactly didn't appeal?' The tone had become slightly puzzled.

She was persistent, Christian inwardly groaned. Why couldn't she just let the matter drop? 'I don't know really.'

'Oh come on, there must have been something?'

An image of Maizie floated into his mind, making him smile. 'I suppose there simply wasn't any chemistry. That magical something that attracts one person to another. It wasn't there for me.'

'She *is* good looking, you have to admit,' Madeleine continued to persist

'Oh yes, extremely.'

'With a lovely figure.'

'It was indeed, Madeleine. She's just not my type, that's all.' He suddenly guessed that Jill was with Madeleine right now which made this even worse. Well, that was just too bad. The arrangement to meet up hadn't been his idea, Madeleine had instigated the whole thing. It wasn't his fault he hadn't been attracted to her friend.

He knew what he was passing over – a romp in bed. Or as many romps as he liked. Other men would have jumped at the chance, had Jill between the sheets quick as a wink. The latter was a favourite expression of his old friend Ted McEwen. It wasn't as if he didn't want sex. He did. But not with Jill.

'When are you in the pub next?' Madeleine probed.

'I've no idea.'

'How about Monday night?'

'I'm busy I'm afraid,' he lied.

'All right, Tuesday?'

'I shall probably be working late.'

She sighed in exasperation. 'You're not making this very easy, Christian.'

He didn't want to be introduced to any more of Madeleine's friends, certain that was what she had in mind. There was another pub not far away he'd been into a few times, The Chelsea Potter. That's where he'd go in future when he wanted a drink. That way there was less likelihood of bumping into Madeleine again.

'I'll have to go, there's someone at the door,' he lied again. 'Goodbye, Madeleine, and thanks for ringing.'

'You will let me know if you hear anything from Gilbert?'

'Of course. That's a promise.'

He hung up and stared thoughtfully at the phone, realising he wouldn't be able to get in touch even if he wanted to as he didn't have either her number or address. Oh well, hopefully Gilbert would be back before too long.

Rosemary's eyes widened in surprise when Sam walked into the kitchen, just after she returned from school. As they stared at one another he slowly smiled.

'You're looking in the pink,' he declared affably.

'Thank you.'

'Is Maizie about?'

'Somewhere I imagine. I haven't seen her yet.'

Rosemary was shocked by his appearance. She'd considered him an old man before but now he looked positively ancient. And smaller somehow, definitely smaller.

'I only got in this morning,' he said.

'Oh?'

'I'll be here for a while. A few weeks at least, though I'm hoping for longer.'

Her heart sank to hear that.

He rubbed his hands together. 'I'm starving. How about you?'

Any hunger she'd felt had vanished on seeing him. She shrank away when he moved closer. If Sam noticed this he didn't give any indication.

'Shouldn't be long till we eat,' Sam commented, still smiling. 'Unless Maizie has changed the order of things which I doubt.'

'Excuse me,' Rosemary said, and hurried from the room.

Sam tugged at his beard which badly needed trimming. He'd ask Maiz to do that for him later after the bar was closed.

Maizie was nervous knowing what Sam had been like in the past when she'd told him what she was about to do now. Furious was as good a word as any. She watched him pull on his pyjama bottoms followed by his top.

'Sam?' she said quietly.

He turned to her.

'I know you've been away a long time and what it must be like for you, what you must be expecting tonight. But I can't. It's that time of the month.' Having spoken she waited for the outburst.

He frowned.

'There's nothing I can do about it, Sam. And I'm really heavy.'

The frown disappeared. 'Well, if 'tis so then 'tis so. As you say, there's nothing you can do about it.'

She couldn't believe her ears. 'You don't mind?'

'Of course I mind. But I'll just have to wait a little longer, eh?'

Relief washed through her. It was incredible he was being so reasonable. Here was a turn-up for the book. 'Thanks, Sam.'

He shrugged and yawned. 'I's dog tired anyhow. 'Twas a long journey down. Sleep's probably best.'

On impulse she went over and kissed him on the cheek.

'Can't ee do better than that, maid?'

She kissed him on the mouth and he tenderly drew her to him. He ran a hand up and down her back as they continued to kiss.

'I'll take that on account,' he declared when the kiss was over.

She couldn't help but smile.

'But there'll be a full reckoning when you're ready, mind?' he joked, wagging a thick stubby finger at her.

'I don't doubt it.'

He stroked his beard. 'Ee did a fine job with this, Maiz. I was beginning to feel like the wild man of Borneo.'

'Hardly that!'

''Tis how I felt, I say.'

She hesitated. 'Sam, I usually have a cigarette before I get into bed nowadays. A sort of wind down after the day. Is that OK?'

'I don't approve of smoking as you know, filthy habit, but you do as you will. 'Twon't bother me none.'

What a change there was in him, she thought. It was the same Sam, only mellower. What a difference it made. She could only hope and pray the change was permanent and he wouldn't revert to how he'd been before.

'There, that's the last one,' Maizie declared, laying the dish she'd just washed on the draining board. She and Rosemary were alone in the kitchen. Sam and Bobby were off elsewhere, though not together.

Rosemary finished wiping a plate and placed it on the pile in the cupboard. It was the perfect opportunity, she decided. She could only hope neither Sam nor Bobby returned too soon to spoil it.

'Aunt Maiz?'

Maizie glanced over at her. 'What is it?'

'I've been thinking recently about Alice,' she said, innocent as any cherub.

'Oh?'

'She must get terribly lonely living by herself.'

'I suppose so,' Maizie mused.

'I feel so sorry for her. Going back to her place every night with no one to talk to and pass the time with there.'

Maizie took off her pinny, deciding what she was going to do next. 'She's used to it by now I daresay.'

'Even though, it isn't very nice.'

Maizie smiled at Rosemary. 'It's very kind of you to be concerned for her welfare. I must ask her to hang on for a meal one night. It's been ages since she last did. Maybe after Sam's away again.'

'I thought . . . well I thought I might stay with her for a while.'

'Stay with her!' Maizie exclaimed.

'Just for a while. I'd enjoy that and I know she would too. It would be a nice change for her to have some company of an evening.'

'I'm sure it would. But I don't know about you staying with her. Alice may not be agreeable. Despite what you say she is rather set in her ways.'

'Oh, but she is agreeable. I've already asked her.'

Maizie stared at Rosemary in astonishment. 'You have?'

'Earlier. We were chatting and it came up. She said she'd be delighted, providing you didn't mind.'

This had caught Maizie rather on the hop. She wasn't sure what she thought about the idea. Rosemary was in her charge after all, her responsibility. There again, where was the harm? And it would be good for Alice, liven up her life a little. A life she knew to be dreary outside the hotel.

'What do you say, Aunt Maiz?'

'When would you think of moving in?'

Triumph flared in Rosemary. She'd done it. Aunt Maiz had no objections, that was obvious. She wouldn't now have to come out with the arguments she'd prepared if there had been.

'How about tomorrow? I'll come back here from school and then when Alice is ready I'll go along home with her.'

'You'll need to take some clothes.' Maizie frowned.

'That isn't a problem, is it?'

Maizie couldn't see that it was. 'How long is a while?'

Rosemary pulled a face. 'A couple of weeks. Maybe a bit longer. It'll cheer her up no end.'

'And Alice is really agreeable?'

'She thought it was a smashing idea. But it's all up to you of course. *Please*, Aunt Maizie?'

'If you want. Tomorrow after school then.'

Rosemary turned away so Maizie couldn't see her expression. She offered up a silent prayer of heartfelt thanks.

Maizie was staggered. Was this the same man she'd married? He'd made love to her in a way he never had before. In the past he'd always been somewhat rough, insistent, not caring about her needs. And then there had been the spanking, his pleasure at inflicting pain on her.

But this . . . He hadn't exactly treated her as if she was made of porcelain, nor would she have wanted him to, but the roughness had gone, replaced by a sort of tenderness. And he'd actually tried, even if he hadn't been too successful, to think about her and her satisfaction and not only his own.

Wonders would never cease, Maizie reflected. Sam was a changed person altogether. Not only in his day-to-day attitude but in this respect as well.

She smiled as he began stroking her flank. This too was

new. He'd never touched her afterwards. It had usually been straight to sleep and that was that.

She was glowing inside, she realised. And somehow feeling far more womanly. She sighed with contentment.

'Maiz?'

'What, Sam?'

'Are you awake?'

'What does it sound like?' she teased.

He laughed, a low throaty rumble. 'Daft question I suppose when ee's already answered.'

'Mind you, I might be talking in my sleep,' she further teased.

He laughed again. ''Twas good, Maiz. As good as ever there's been.'

She considered pointing out to him why it had been good, special even, then decided not to push her luck. 'Yes,' she agreed.

His hand moved to the inside of her thigh. 'Like silk she be there. Pure China silk.'

Compliments now! And sincere by the sound of it. He truly was a changed man for the better. If that's what nearly dying did for you then she heartily approved. She immediately chided herself, that was a terrible thing to think. He'd nearly died in the most horrible way, a death suffered by so many of his shipmates. And yet, it had to be said, the experience seemed to have been beneficial where he was concerned.

'What are you thinking of, Maiz?'

'Nothing much,' she lied.

'Me neither. Or if I am, it's how pleased I is to be here with you. Just the pair of us, all snuggled up in our bed like two rabbits down a burrow. Warm and snug as can be.'

Maizie thought that was a lovely image.

'I's so happy, Maiz. I don't think I's ever been happier, and that's the God's honest truth.'

She felt quite overwhelmed by that statement. It was as if
. . . backalong had never been. It was a rebirth, she thought.
A rebirth of their marriage. No, more than that. The birth
of what their marriage should have been all along, what she'd
always wanted and dreamt of.

His arm crept round her shoulders and he drew himself
even closer to her, his groin pressing against her bottom.

Maizie's smile was almost beatific when she eventually
nodded off.

Gilbert poured himself a glass of red wine while he contemplated the latest signal from London. The designated target
was the largest and most ambitious yet. The entire cell would
have to be involved, all six of them. And it was going to take
a great deal of planning.

He sipped his wine, wishing this was all over and he was
back in London. The niggle remained with him, the doubt,
though there was still nothing concrete to base that on.

An informer in the cell. A traitor? If so, who? Jacques
the schoolmaster? Surely not. He'd lost a brother to the
Germans. What about Louis the baker? Louis was quiet
and never said very much, a person who kept more or
less to himself. Louis was a bachelor who lived with his
parents and didn't seem to have much time for women.
Was he the imaginary weak link? If he was, there had been
no indication so far.

Then there was Juliette, sweet, beautiful Juliette who
adored him and slept with him most nights. It was absurd
to think it might be her.

Gilbert shook his head. He just couldn't believe she
was other than she appeared and behaved. They were too
intimate for her not to have given herself away at some point
or another.

He finished the first glass of red wine and poured himself

another while he continued to reflect on, and dissect, each member of the cell.

'I'm going to marry you when you grow up.'

Bobby gaped at Emily. The pair of them were down by their favourite haunt, the quayside. Out in the Channel a solitary boat was chugging its way towards harbour, the usual mob of seagulls ganged overhead. 'What?'

'I'm going to marry you when we both grow up,' Emily repeated with determination in her voice.

He laughed. 'That's nonsense.'

'No it's not!'

'Of course it is. We won't be grown up for years and years. Ever so long. You probably won't even remember me by then.'

Her expression became steely. 'It isn't that far off, Bobby Tyler. And I certainly shan't be forgetting you, no matter where you are. If you're in Plymouth I'll come and find you and then we'll get married. You'll see!'

His mood changed to one of moroseness. Plymouth! Where his home was. His home and . . . He corrected himself, his mum wasn't there any more. She'd gone up north to another job. At least that's what she'd said.

Bitterness welled inside him. How could she treat him and Rosemary as she had? It was one thing to send them away from the bombing, he could understand that, it made sense, what a good parent would do, but to send them away and then never get in touch apart from one rotten letter. On top of which she'd left Plymouth without a forwarding address. Just upped and gone with no thought for either him or his sister. It made him feel sick. Sick and worthless.

'Bobby?'

'Why would you want to marry me, Emily?'

She suddenly went coy. 'Because.'

'Because what?'

'Don't you want to marry *me*?'

'I've never thought about it. Marrying you or anyone else.'

'Well, we women think about these things. And I've decided that you're the man for me.'

Man! Oh he liked that. Not boy, but man. 'Where would we live?'

'I don't know. We'd find a house I suppose. Or a cottage.'

'And what would I do? I want to be a coalman same as my dad.'

'There are coal merchants in Helston. Perhaps you could get a job there. Though I have to say I wouldn't want to leave Coverack.'

Neither would he, Bobby realised. The Paris Hotel and Coverack had come to mean more to him than Plymouth did now. Plymouth had become a dream, a memory. Especially since learning that his father had been killed.

'Well, maybe I might stay on here,' he conceded, looking away.

Emily beamed. 'That would be wonderful.'

'But what would I work at?'

'We'll find something. There's always the hotel for a start. I'm sure Mrs Blackacre would give you a job.'

That was true, Bobby mused. He'd enjoy working in the hotel. He could become a chef or head barman. All sorts of things. And it would be great fun living permanently at the seaside. Especially in summer when the place was thronging with holidaymakers.

'Is it agreed then?' Emily queried.

He blinked. 'Is what agreed?'

'That we'll get married.'

Bobby glanced down at the water gently lapping against

the quay wall. He could see various fish slowly undulating this way and that. He simply couldn't imagine himself being married with . . . He gulped. Children of his own.

'Well?' Emily demanded.

He nodded.

'Is that yes?'

'Yes,' he croaked.

Emily took a deep breath. That was that then. Settled. 'We'll have to keep it a secret for now, mind?'

'OK. I think that's best.'

'This makes us engaged you know.'

His mind was whirling. 'I suppose so.'

'You should be giving me a ring. But I doubt you have one?'

'I'm afraid not, Emily.'

She thought about that. 'They used to show a movie picture here once a week before the war started, and there was one I saw which has given me an idea.'

He feared the worst. 'Oh?'

'It was a western. Well, anyway, this white man and this Indian became blood brothers. Do you know how they did that?'

Bobby shook his head.

'They each cut their wrist and put the bloody bits together. That made them blood brothers. We could do the same. It's as good as getting engaged.'

He didn't like the sound of this at all.

'All right,' he agreed reluctantly.

Her smile turned to a frown. 'How shall we do it?'

'I have a penknife.'

'Then we'll use that.'

Bobby dug in a trouser pocket to produce the knife, an old one of his father's that was a prized possession. He pulled out the single blade.

'Scared?' she teased.

'Not in the least.'

'Neither am I.'

He stared at the blade, then at her. 'Who's first?'

'Me as it was my suggestion.' She held out a wrist. 'Go ahead.'

He held his breath as he made the nick, not too deep but deep enough to draw blood. Emily grimaced as he cut.

'Now your turn,' she declared, taking the knife from him.

It surprised Bobby that it didn't hurt. Well, hardly, anyway.

'Now we hold our wrists together so the blood mingles,' Emily stated.

They did that.

'That's us engaged,' she smiled, eyes shining bright as any stars. 'You'd better kiss me.'

He first made sure no one was watching, then placed his lips on hers. One thought above all else was racing through his mind. His mum might not want him any more but Emily did.

He felt on top of the world.

Chapter 19

'What's got into ee of late? Ee's like a dog with two tails.'

Maizie, at the kitchen table doing her accounts, glanced up at Alice. 'I beg your pardon?'

'You heard me, Maizie Blackacre. Sitting there humming away and occasionally laughing to yourself. I never seen ee like this afore.'

Maizie laid down her pen. It was true enough, she thought. She was incredibly happy. 'It's having Sam home,' she replied guardedly.

Alice raised an eyebrow. 'Well, ee do surprise me.'

'And how's that?'

'You didn't act like this last time he was here. Nor before he went off in the Merchant Navy.'

Maizie dropped her gaze. She was bubbling inside and had been since getting up that morning. The transformation in Sam was amazing. Previously he'd been gruff, surly, given to black and very unpleasant moods. Now he was almost sunshine itself. 'It's funny what war can do to some people,' she replied mysteriously.

Alice stared blankly at her. 'What's that supposed to mean?'

'Haven't you seen the change in Sam?'

'He's older-looking.'

'No, I don't mean that. His personality, his attitude to things. You must have noticed it.'

Indeed Alice had. 'He's treating you more kindly then?'

That shocked Maizie. Had it all been so obvious before? She supposed it must have been. Especially to Alice who spent every working day at the Paris. 'Yes,' she replied quietly.

'Good.'

'I've never known him be so tender or thoughtful.'

Alice couldn't help but wonder about Christian. This would put a spoke in that wheel. Which was right and proper after all, Maizie being wed to Sam. 'I'm right pleased for you, Maizie. You deserves it.'

Maizie smiled at her employee and friend. 'Thanks, Alice. Now tell me, I've been meaning to ask, how are you getting on with Rosemary? I hope it's not proving too much for you?'

'Not at all! She's grand company is Rosemary. Some nights we sits and listens to the wireless. Other nights we plays cards.'

'Cards!'

'A quick learner that maid. Smart as paint. I'm also teaching her to knit.'

How cosy it all sounded, Maizie thought. 'As long as she isn't any trouble.'

'Quite the contrary. I shall miss her when she comes back here. Truly I will.'

It had surprised Maizie how much *she* missed Rosemary. She'd become used to the maid being about the place. That and caring for her. In many ways she'd come to look on both Rosemary and Bobby as her own. She couldn't bear to think of them leaving, should the highly improbable happen and their mother turn up to claim them.

Maizie sighed. 'I'd better get on with this bookwork.

Believe me, it's tedious in the extreme. But it has to be done I'm afraid.'

Alice smiled to herself when a few minutes later Maizie started humming again.

Christian let himself into the flat. *Merde*, but he was drunk, as drunk as he'd ever been. Tumbril, his other 'joe', was back in England which accounted for the celebration. She'd been picked up by a plane the previous night and that morning had reported in to Colonel G.

He'd met her, a rather stout lady of middle years and not the pretty young thing he'd imagined. Together, the pair of them, plus several others from the Executive, had gone to a seedy all-day drinking den in Soho where they had proceeded to try to drink the club dry.

Christian fell into a chair and clutched his spinning head. He was going to pay for this, nothing was surer. But what the hell, it had been worth it. Tumbril, real name Ginette Verney, had been his responsibility, just as Gilbert still was. The relief of her homecoming had been profound.

Christian fumbled for a cigarette and lit up. Closing his eyes he savoured the smoke in his lungs and the peace of the room. A peace that reminded him of Coverack.

He smiled, thinking of Maizie. He really should have phoned before now, kept in touch. He wouldn't be able to go down there again until Gilbert was also back in England and he had no idea when that might be.

A glance at his watch told him it was only a little after eight o'clock. The way he felt it might have been midnight.

'Maizie.' He said her name aloud, tasting it, enjoying the sound of it. 'Maizie,' he repeated.

He wanted to tell her about Tumbril, share his relief and delight with her. And why not! There was nothing stopping him, the phone was there to be used after all.

Christian hauled himself to his feet, groaning at the sudden sharp pain that lanced from ear to ear. Unsteadily he made his way over to the phone hoping this time the lines wouldn't be down, or out of order, or whatever.

'Putting you through now, sir,' the operator declared a few moments later.

'Hello, Paris Hotel. Sam Blackacre speaking.'

The smile froze on Christian's face, and suddenly, as if by magic, he felt very, very sober.

'Hello?'

He hung up.

'There ee are, me dear, a nice hot cup of cocoa.'

Rosemary accepted the steaming cup. 'Thanks, Alice.'

Alice moved to her chair and sat down. 'I always used to have a biscuit with me nighttime cocoa but you can't get biscuits nowadays for love or money. Even Maizie can't get hold of any and she's in the trade.'

'You look tired, Alice.'

'Oh, I be that all right. It's me age I suppose, I'm not getting any younger. But then none of us is, eh?'

Rosemary smiled. 'Does Mr Blackacre know when he's returning to sea yet?' she asked casually.

'Not that I heard.'

A disappointed Rosemary gazed into her cocoa. One thing was certain, she was staying put until he'd gone. Wild horses wouldn't get her back to the Paris while he was there.

'It must be soon though,' she went on.

'I expects so. 'Tis nearly three weeks after all. 'Tis a good leave that, even if it does follow him being sunk.'

Sunk, Rosemary reflected wryly. How she wished . . .

Gilbert glanced over at Juliette stretched out on the sofa like a cat. Her husband had been one of those in the area rounded up by the Germans and taken off to a labour camp somewhere, possibly on the Polish border, rumour had it. She hadn't heard from him since the day he'd been taken.

'Why don't you come over here and join me?' she said, patting the sofa.

'I'm thinking.'

She laughed. 'I've never known a man think as much as you, Gilbert. You seem to spend half your life doing it.'

'Maybe so, but there's a lot to think about.' He was silent for a few seconds, then said, 'I heard from London this afternoon.'

She was instantly alert. 'Oh?'

'The drop's in three days' time.'

'That's wonderful!' she exclaimed, swinging her feet to the floor. 'Where?'

He couldn't help but look at her ankles which he found incredibly sexy. There was just something about them.

'I'm keeping that secret,' he replied. 'I won't be telling anyone till we set off.'

She frowned. 'Even me?'

'I treat everyone the same, Juliette.'

'Oh really! Does that mean you're screwing all of them?'

He laughed. 'Don't be ridiculous.'

She pouted. 'I thought I was different. That I wasn't just one of the others.'

'You're not.'

She rose and undulated across to sit on his lap. Her natural body odour was suddenly strong in his nostrils. 'I should hope so,' she whispered, and nibbled his ear.

He knew how this was going to end up. It was inevitable. 'Will you stop that.'

'Why?'

'Because . . .'

A hand snaked inside his shirt. 'I simply adore strong men,

Gilbert. That's what attracts me so much about you. Strength of character just oozes out of you.'

Despite himself he was flattered. He liked to think of himself as the strong type. His hand brushed an armpit and he could feel the hair beneath the material of her blouse. English women shaved their armpits which he'd found rather strange. He much preferred them *au naturel.*

'And how was your friend Christian?'

'There was nothing personal in either message. It was a straightforward exchange. He told me when the drop was to be made and I told him where. We'll be fully supplied again after this with more than enough explosive to do the job required. There will also be a top-up of ammunition for our weapons as we're getting low.'

She caressed his bare chest. 'Will we get to kill Germans?'

'I hope not. I want us to blow the junction and be gone before any Germans show up.'

'So it's the railway, eh?'

He didn't mind her knowing that. 'A very important one that'll completely disrupt the main line through the entire district. If we do the job properly it'll take the Boche weeks to effect repairs. And in the meantime the line will be out of action which will inconvenience them considerably. In fact, when they realise the repercussions, they'll be hopping bloody mad.'

'Oh I like the idea of that,' she purred, continuing to caress his bare chest. 'But I am disappointed we won't be killing any of the bastards. Now that I really enjoy.'

He regarded her with amusement. 'Bloodthirsty little beast, aren't you?'

'Only where Germans are concerned.' Her face darkened. 'And I have every cause to be.'

'Do you still miss him?' Gilbert asked softly.

She turned her face away. 'Of course I do. We were happily

married. I've never pretended otherwise. But . . .' She took a deep breath. 'He may well be dead by now. That's something I've had to come to terms with. Who knows how long this war will go on for and with every passing day his chances of survival, if he is still alive, become more and more remote.'

'I'm sorry,' Gilbert apologised. 'I shouldn't have brought it up.'

When she turned to look at him again her face was streaked with tears. 'We can't change what's happened, no one can do that. But we can avenge ourselves and I have every intention of doing so. That's why I joined your cell in the first place.'

He kissed her tears. 'Dear lovely Juliette,' he said huskily, genuinely moved. Both with passion and sympathy.

'Now take me to bed and let's forget this conversation.'

'It's early yet.'

'So?' she teased.

It was a Sunday morning and Rosemary had come back to the Paris for some clothes she wanted. Also a schoolbook she needed. She was coming out of her bedroom when Sam appeared in the corridor. She sucked in a breath and froze on the spot. She'd thought he was out somewhere. Or so Bobby had said.

'Hello, Rosemary.' He smiled thinly, coming to stand in front of her.

She didn't reply.

'I've wanted to have a quiet word with you alone and this is the first chance I've had.'

She still didn't reply.

'Are you being a good girl?'

She knew precisely what he meant by that, and nodded.

'Aahhh!' he slowly exhaled. 'Are you sure?'

'I'm sure,' she whispered.

'Then everything's all right.'

She shrank back a little when his gaze travelled over her from top to toe.

'You've grown a bit I'd say.'

'I suppose I have.'

He grunted his approval. 'Now why don't you run along to wherever you're going.'

Rosemary didn't run, she fled.

'I'm afraid the price of your meat has gone up, Maizie.'

She stared at Cyril Roskilly in a combination of surprise and distaste. 'I don't buy my meat from you,' she pointed out.

His smile was one of smug satisfaction. 'That be so, Maizie. But now you do, in a manner of speaking. You see, us local farmers have got together and decided to raise our prices.' He shrugged. ''Tis the war, it's put extra demand on us and we're having to pay more for feed and the like.'

Maizie knew that to be a lie. The animals in the area were grass-fed in the main. Grass and hay.

'I still don't buy from you,' she repeated.

'As I said, we've got together like and I'm their spokesman.' What he didn't mention was that he'd organised the entire thing. They'd met at his instigation and once he'd got them to agree had more or less elected himself as leader.

'What's going on here?' queried Sam striding up to them. The look on Maizie's face had told him something was wrong.

Cyril, a little nervous now that Sam was present, repeated what he'd already told Maizie.

Sam glared at Cyril. 'All the farmers?'

'All,' Cyril confirmed. That wasn't entirely true. There was one who'd refused to go along with this but he wasn't going to mention either that or the farmer's name.

'How much of a rise?' Maizie queried.

Cyril named various prices for beef, lamb and chickens.

'Christ Almighty, man, that's more or less double,' Sam protested.

''Tis the war, Sam. 'Tain't nothing we can do about it. We've got to make a living same as everyone else.'

Maizie nearly laughed to hear that. This was a lot more than a living. 'You know what you're doing is called?' she queried softly.

'What's that, Maizie?'

'War profiteering.'

Anger glinted in Cyril's eyes. ''Tis nothing of the sort. 'Tis only us adjusting prices to the present-day situation. Nothing more.'

'Bollocks,' Sam snarled.

Cyril hastily retreated a few steps. He was terrified of Sam Blackacre. The man's temper and physical prowess were well known. Sam was one of those extraordinary strong men.

'Well, that's the way of it. You've no choice. The new prices start as from today.'

'I think you'd better be on your way,' Maizie stated, fury bubbling inside her. How she loathed Cyril Roskilly.

'As you wish.'

'I do. And quickly.'

Cyril took his leave of them with as much dignity as he could muster. He waited till he was outside before allowing a broad smile to light up his face.

The idea of raising prices was a cracker. He was going to make pots out of it.

'Do you mind if we don't tonight, Gilbert? I'm not feeling very well.'

He was immediately filled with concern. This was most unlike Juliette. 'No, of course not. What's wrong?'

She shook her head. 'I don't know. I just feel . . . awful. Sort of drained and shivery.'

'Perhaps you're worried about tomorrow night?' That was the time of the drop.

'I don't see why. It should be fairly straightforward after all.'

He frowned. 'Perhaps you've got a cold coming on. There's a lot of it about at the moment.'

'Maybe you're right.'

She went to the bed and crawled under the sheets. 'I'll be better in the morning, darling.'

He liked her calling him that. 'Would you prefer if I slept in the other bed?'

'Would you?'

He crossed over and kissed her on the forehead. 'You get some sleep. And if you need anything in the night just call out. I'll hear you.'

'Thanks, Gilbert. You're sweet.'

He kissed her forehead again before leaving her to it.

'Here you are, angel, coffee,' Gilbert declared the next morning, sitting on the bed where Juliette was sleeping.

She groaned.

'Juliette?'

One eye slowly opened, then the other. 'Oh Christ,' she mumbled.

'What is it?' He laid the coffee aside and placed his hands on her shoulders.

'I've been awake most of the night. In dreadful pain.'

Alarm flamed in him. 'What sort of pain?'

Her face contorted grotesquely. 'It's a migraine. I haven't had one in ages. Years. That's why I didn't realise.'

'Can I get you anything?' he asked anxiously.

'No. Just don't open the shutters. I must have darkness. There's nothing else for it. All I can do is lie here and wait till it passes.'

'Oh, Juliette,' he crooned sympathetically. He knew a little about migraines. Someone had once described one as the worst headache you can imagine magnified a hundred times.

She brought a hand from under the clothes and touched his arm. 'Better to leave me alone. And be quiet round the house. As quiet as you can.'

'I will. I promise.'

'I'm so sorry,' she croaked.

'Don't be. It's not your fault. It's just one of these things.'

She managed a faint smile. 'Thanks for being so understanding.'

'Are you sure there's nothing I can do or get you?'

'All I need is to be left alone in peace and quiet. That's all that can be done.'

'I'll look in later to see how you are.'

She groaned again, a pitiful sound that tore at Gilbert. Her eyes drooped shut.

Picking up the coffee cup he tiptoed from the room.

Christian glanced at the wall clock. It was hours yet before he was due to hear from Gilbert so his being there was really a waste of time. However, he'd wanted to be early. Just in case. You never knew. Things didn't always go according to plan.

He lit a cigarette and sat back in his chair to wait.

Sam, just off the telephone, was scratching his beard as he came into the kitchen where Maizie and Alice were busy preparing lunch plus doing some baking.

'Well?' Maizie demanded.

'I has to report into Liverpool a week today to pick up a ship.'

Maizie had been expecting something like that. Sam's leave had gone on far longer than either he or she could have hoped.

'Where's she bound?' Maizie inquired casually.

'No idea, Maiz. No idea at all. And there was no use asking, they wouldn't say if I did. I won't know till we clear harbour. None of the crew will.' He shook his head. 'Anything but the Malta run. I don't want to go through that hell again.' He thought of the mates he'd lost. Good men all.

Maizie crossed her fingers for him.

'Any tea in the pot?'

'I'll get it for ee, Sam. You sit down and take a load off,' Alice volunteered.

He smiled gratefully at her. 'I'll miss the Paris when I go,' he said.

His gaze met Maizie's and she knew he meant more than the Paris. She flushed with pleasure.

'Listen!' exclaimed Jacques the schoolteacher. 'I can hear it.'

There it was, faint yet unmistakable. The drone of an approaching plane.

'Get the torches lit,' Gilbert instructed. 'Then spread out in the circle as I showed you.'

There were only five of them there for the drop instead of six, Juliette having been left home in bed still suffering from her migraine. She'd remained there the entire day, the only thing she'd been able to take being a few sips of water. She'd managed to wish Gilbert a weak good luck before he left.

The torches, made of wood, rags and oil, were soon alight. The circle they now formed was the marker for the drop. A visual sighting for the pilot.

There was a slight wind blowing which made the torches flicker and occasionally flare sideways.

The site chosen by Gilbert was a clearing in the middle of

a wood. An ideal spot, he'd decided. There wasn't a German for miles around.

He glanced from figure to figure, some of their faces illuminated by the torchlight. Guilliame was the youngest of them at only sixteen years of age; Nicole the only other woman in their group.

The plane banked to make its approach, the sound of its engines now loud and clear. Gilbert watched anxiously as, just before flying over the circle, two bundles were pushed clear. The parachutes opened immediately.

One bundle landed right in the middle of the circle, the other slightly outside it. The plane banked again on its return flight.

The bundles would be too heavy and cumbersome to carry as such. They'd both be opened and the contents split up. What they couldn't take with them, if anything, they'd come back for the following night.

Guilliame and Jacques were tearing at the first bundle when the Germans opened fire.

For a split second Gilbert stood frozen with shock, the message hammering in his brain that this was a trap. The Germans must have known about the drop, otherwise why were they there.

Guilliame gave a cry and pitched over his bundle, blood spurting from his neck where an artery had been severed. Nicole was thrown sideways as she too was hit.

It was pandemonium, bedlam. German small-arms fire spat from all directions. Gilbert spun while clawing for his sten which was slung over his shoulder.

Louis, screaming like a banshee, charged the nearest Germans to be almost instantly cut down. He lay writhing horribly on the ground.

Only one person other than himself knew where the drop was to be. Juliette, the bitch, she'd wheedled it out of him in bed that night. He'd thought her safe, the only one he could totally trust.

Something smacked into his shoulder, sending him spinning to the ground where he must have lost consciousness for a few moments. When he came to again it was to silence. The firing had stopped.

'Damn you, Juliette,' Gilbert muttered, tears in his eyes. How could he have been so stupid? He'd sensed there was something wrong, that there might be a traitor in their midst. But never her. He'd trusted Juliette.

He was reaching for his sten which had flown from his grasp when he was clubbed on the back of the head with a rifle butt.

Christian glanced again at the wall clock and frowned. Gilbert was late. But not late enough to worry unduly yet. He lit another cigarette and continued to wait patiently.

Sam was drunk. Pint after pint of cider had vanished down his throat while he sat brooding in a quiet corner of the bar. Somewhere during this time he'd decided what he was going to do.

'Sam, where are you going?' Maizie called out anxiously as he lurched towards the door.

He didn't reply but continued on out into the night where he sucked in a deep breath of air that helped clear his head a little. Then he set off purposefully along the street.

Elizabeth Roskilly answered Sam's knock, her face registering surprise on seeing him there.

'Cyril home?' Sam growled.

'Yes.'

He didn't wait to be invited in but brushed on past her.

He found Cyril sitting in front of the fire. 'I want to speak to you, *alone*,' he stated gruffly.

Cyril came hesitantly to his feet trying not to show how scared he was. 'Elizabeth?'

'I'll leave the pair of you to it,' she said, and vanished swiftly from the room.

'What can I do for ee, Sam?' Cyril asked jocularly.

'I was sunk last trip,' Sam stated, brow furrowed, eyes gleaming darkly.

'Yes, I know. A terrible thing to happen.'

'A lot of good men went down with that ship. Many with families. And do you know why they died, Cyril?'

Cyril shook his head, not daring to state the obvious.

'They died for their country and the folk in it. Doing their duty, Cyril. What do you make of that?'

'I don't know what to say, Sam.'

'Doing their duty to keep our country free from thae Gerry bastards. And while they're dying you're doing a bit of war profiteering, cashing in on their sacrifice. Lining your own pockets at their expense. At they and their families' expense.'

Cyril was now thoroughly alarmed. 'It's not quite like that, Sam. You've got the wrong end of the stick.'

'Shut up, you cunt!' Sam roared. 'And listen to me. You can forget any idea of raising the price of meat round here. You'll continue selling at the going rates.'

'Touch me and I'll inform the police,' Cyril squeaked.

'Oh, I ain't going to lay a hand on you, Cyril. I won't be giving you the thrashing you deserve. Instead I'll make you a promise.' He paused, then said, 'Unless the prices come down again you're going to lose your barn and outbuildings. All of them and what's inside.'

Cyril went white.

'I might be going back to sea but it won't be difficult to

arrange. People don't like war profiteers, especially when it's one of their own that's screwing them. So one night, when you're least expecting it, the whole sodding lot will go up in flames. And if you're really unlucky, who knows? The house might just catch fire too.'

Sam pulled himself up to his full height. 'That's all I got to say to you, Cyril Roskilly. The decision is yours. Just don't for one moment think I's bluffing because I'm not. I've never been more serious in my entire life.'

And with that Sam strode from the room, a speechless and shaking Cyril staring after him.

Juliette had stayed in bed to keep up the pretence just in case, by some miracle, Gilbert escaped and returned. It was where Major Kemmel found her, having let himself in.

Kemmel was a short, thin man with the air of a born bureaucrat, or civil servant, about him. He gazed balefully at Juliette.

'It's over,' he announced. 'We captured Du Bois alive as we hoped. The rest are dead.'

Juliette let out a sigh of relief and slipped from the bed to shrug into a dressing gown. 'I've kept my part of the bargain in full, now you keep yours and release my husband as you promised.'

Kemmel's smile was one of amusement. 'Ah yes, that was what we agreed in return for your betrayal. Unfortunately it can't be done.'

'Why not?' she queried hesitantly.

'Because your husband is already dead. He died months ago.'

She watched in sudden horror as he reached for his holster. 'Dead, as are you, Madame Noguellou.'

He was still smiling as he shot her through the forehead.

Chapter 20

'Did you really say that!' a delighted Maizie exclaimed after Sam had recounted what had passed between him and Cyril Roskilly. She stared at her husband in admiration.

Sam grinned. 'I did indeed. You should have seen his face, Maiz. It was a picture. A sight to behold.'

Maizie had to laugh; she could just imagine the scene.

''Twas a conversation he won't forget in a long time, that's for certain.'

'Burn his barn and outbuildings,' Maizie mused. It was inspirational. 'You weren't really serious though? I mean, it was only a bluff?'

Sam shook his head. 'I meant every word of it. 'Twould be easy to organise before I leave. Roskilly is hardly the most popular man around, and there's many must be deeply resentful of what he's trying to do.'

Maizie lit a cigarette. She was smoking more of late. It was no longer only the occasional one but a full packet a day.

''Twas thinking of me shipmates that made me do it, Maiz. The likes of Roskilly should be hung, drawn and quartered as far as I'm concerned. They're despicable beyond words. The scum of the earth.'

Maizie went to Sam and put her arms round him. 'You did the right thing.'

'I has your approval then? I wasn't sure.'

'You have my approval. Let's just hope it doesn't come to an actual burning, though.'

'Naw, not if I'm any judge. Roskilly won't risk his property, you can bet on it.'

She kissed him lightly on the lips, thinking yet again what a changed man he was. He'd succeeded in finding a place in her heart where he never had before.

'Do you mind taking that cigarette away from my face. The smoke's going up my nose.'

'Sorry,' she laughed, and broke away. 'Would you like another drink before going up?'

'Only if you has one with me.'

'All right.'

He watched her walk behind the bar, an enormous warmth washing through him. He too was seeing his spouse in an entirely different light to previously.

'Make mine whisky. I've had enough pints for one night,' he smiled.

Maizie had the same.

Something was definitely wrong, Christian just knew it. He worried a nail while staring at the R/T set in front of him, desperately willing it to burst into life.

He glanced at the wall clock for what might have been the thousandth time. Gilbert was now hours overdue.

The drop had gone ahead as planned, that had been confirmed by the pilot radioing back to base and the information had been forwarded to Portland Place.

So where the hell was Gilbert?

Gilbert grimaced with pain as he came to. He remembered

the exchange of fire, the realisation of betrayal, being hit and going down. His last memory was of reaching for his sten.

He brought himself into a sitting position and gazed around. He was in a cell, that much was obvious. A not very large one either, smelling strongly of damp. The floor he was sitting on was flagstoned.

He gingerly felt his shoulder, grunting in agony at the even fiercer pain that produced. From what he could ascertain the bullet had passed clean through.

Anger raged in him at the thought of his stupidity with Juliette. The trouble was she'd been so plausible; right from the first contact she'd been that. But why would she betray him to the Germans after what they'd done to her? It just didn't make sense. Beyond him for the moment.

He knew what had to be done and recalled a conversation he'd once had with Christian about it. Well, the Nazis weren't going to torture him, for he had the means of ensuring they didn't.

He fumbled for the suicide pill neatly sewn into the back of one of the lapels of his jacket. His probing fingers found nothing except what felt to be the tiniest remnant of a thread.

Juliette, she'd betrayed him even there. Who else would have known about the pill and more importantly where he kept it? The bitch must have somehow removed it before he and the others had set out for the drop.

Gilbert closed his eyes and conjured up a picture of Juliette. Lies, lies, everything she'd said and done was lies. If he'd been able to get hold of her right then he'd have killed her without the slightest of qualms.

His body sagged. They'd come for him in the morning sometime. Then what? They wouldn't execute him right away, oh no. They'd kept him alive for a reason.

Information of course. It had to be. Dear God, please let him be strong enough not to give them what they wanted.

To keep his mouth shut no matter what they did to him.

He shuddered at the prospect of what lay ahead.

Maizie was smiling as Sam lay snoring beside her. It was time to get up but she'd let him lie in for a while till breakfast was ready. He could come down then.

What a night it had been! Drunk or not, Sam had been more than capable. Four times he'd woken her to start all over again, each bout lasting longer than the one before.

The last time she'd thought he wouldn't manage, but he'd stopped, turned her over and spanked her hard before continuing again with renewed vigour. Her bottom still tingled but for once she didn't mind. It had given Sam pleasure, which was enough for her.

Maizie knew she was going to have trouble walking when she got out of bed. At least for a while anyway. And again, she didn't mind. On the contrary, the entire experience had been most satisfactory. Far more so than she'd previously ever known.

She touched him gently on the face, thinking of his exchange with Cyril Roskilly. His recounting of that had amused her greatly.

Why had it taken so long for their relationship to get to this stage when it should have been right from the beginning? Thank God for his ship being torpedoed and his subsequent deliverance.

She was desperately sorry for the men who'd died of course, but the incident, and the repercussions it had had on Sam, had proved to be their personal salvation. For that she could only thank God.

He actually cared for her now and, more than that, loved her. She couldn't ask for more. All was forgiven.

She was right about having trouble walking.

*   *   *

Christian sighed and lit his last cigarette. Dawn had come and gone hours ago and still the R/T remained stubbornly silent. He blinked weary eyes and scratched his slightly stubbly chin. Neither mattered. Only Gilbert did.

Where the hell was he?

The two men who eventually came for Gilbert wore the uniform of the hated and dreaded SS. No words were uttered, they simply gestured for him to get up and go with them.

'Ah, Umbrella!' Major Kemmel breathed when Gilbert was bundled into his office. 'And how are you today?'

Gilbert didn't reply.

'That's a nasty wound you have, I can have it seen to shortly. In the meanwhile, would you care for a cup of coffee?'

Kemmel lifted a silver flask and poured steaming coffee into a cup. 'Milk and sugar?'

Gilbert gazed longingly at the coffee, his throat dry and clogged. He put temptation aside.

'And a cigarette?' Kemmel flicked open a leather-bound case in that particularly irritating way Germans have.

'I don't smoke.'

'Ah so,' Kemmel beamed, and snapped the case shut again.

Standing as straight as he could, Gilbert recited his name, rank and serial number.

Kemmel studied him, his expression one of seeming pity. 'I already know who you are, Private Du Bois. Unfortunately, for you that is, these matters are irrelevant. You were captured in civilian clothes and are therefore a spy to whom the niceties of the Geneva Convention don't apply.'

Gilbert now noticed there was a woman in the room. Late twenties, he judged. Possibly early thirties. Fair hair, blue eyes and a reasonable figure. She was sitting quietly to one side watching him intently. She was wearing a white blouse, black skirt and a swastika armband. She, like Kemmel, made his flesh creep.

'I could have some breakfast brought in if you wish?' Kemmel went on.

Gilbert shook his head.

'Pity. And the coffee?'

Gilbert shook his head a second time.

'Another pity.'

Kemmel sighed and sat back in his chair.

'Perhaps you're wondering why we've allowed you to remain alive?'

Here it comes, Gilbert thought.

'I'm quite prepared to let matters stay that way, if you'll cooperate, that is. When we've concluded our business I'll have you taken to a camp where you shall spend the rest of the war. You won't exactly be living the life of luxury there. I must admit, conditions are a little trying, but you will survive the war. And afterwards, return home again.' He paused. 'I would say that is an excellent offer, wouldn't you, Du Bois?'

'You speak very good French, m'sieur,' Gilbert replied.

'Why thank you! And the offer?'

Gilbert swallowed hard, then shook his head.

'You do realise the alternative, I presume?'

Gilbert didn't answer.

'And you will talk eventually. I promise you that. It is inevitable.'

'Go fuck yourself!' Gilbert spat.

Kemmel laughed. 'Anatomically impossible.' He glanced at his wristwatch. 'I will give you five minutes to reconsider. After that, well you have only yourself to blame.'

While Kemmel busied himself with paperwork, the woman's eyes never left Gilbert, a fact he was only too well aware of. Behind him the two SS guards stood motionless. The seconds continued to tick on by, stretching out to what seemed an eternity.

Finally Kemmel laid down his pen. 'Have you reconsidered?' he asked softly.

'No.' The single word came out harsh and grating.

Kemmel's lips tightened into a thin slash. 'Ingrid, it's up to you.'

The blonde, her eyes still not leaving Gilbert, took out a packet of cigarettes and lit one.

Slowly she rose to her feet.

'You've been here all night I understand.'

Christian nodded. 'Yes, sir.'

'How do you feel?'

'Tired, sir.'

'Do you wish to be relieved?'

'No, sir.' Christian gazed up at Major Hammond. 'Du Bois is not only my "joe" but also my friend, sir. I'll sit here for as long as it takes.'

Hammond nodded his approval. Christian had always impressed him. Not a bad sort, for a Frenchman, that is. He'd never been particularly keen on the French. 'Carry on then.'

'Thank you, sir.'

'Have you eaten at all?'

'No, sir.'

'I'll have a meal brought to you.'

'Thank you, sir. And some cigarettes, if that's possible.'

Major Hammond smiled. Producing an almost full packet of Senior Service he laid them in front of Christian. 'That should keep you going for now.'

'Thank you very much, sir.'

The R/T set kept its silence.

*　　*　　*

Gilbert hit the flagstones with a sickening thud. Behind him the metalled door clanged shut.

His torso from the waist up was on fire from tiny burn marks everywhere. Next time it would be his buttocks and legs, Kemmel had promised.

Ingrid, whoever she was, hadn't rushed matters. First she'd had his jacket and shirt removed, then instructed he be held firm by the SS guards.

He'd lost count of the number of times her cigarette end had seared into his flesh. But it had seemed like hundreds.

He'd thought it would never end. That he was already dead and in hell. He'd come to see her as a female version of the devil incarnate.

Not once had she spoken, only pausing in her task when Kemmel occasionally interrupted yet again to ask if he'd cooperate. Why go through all this when he didn't have to? Kemmel had said. He was going to talk eventually. Why not save himself all this pain?

The worst bit had been when Ingrid pressed the cigarette end to the entry point of his bullet wound. A black gaping hole that the cigarette had sizzled into. He didn't know how he hadn't passed out then.

Amazingly he hadn't screamed, not once. He was proud of that. They weren't going to break him. Never, he swore it. He wouldn't betray as he'd been betrayed.

As for being sent to that camp? Nonsense! If he did talk he'd never see any camp. He'd be summarily shot when he'd told them all they wanted.

They already knew a few facts about SOE and Portland Place. But they wanted more, a great deal more. Some of which he could have given them.

He groped for his shirt which, along with his jacket, had been thrown in with him. He somehow managed to get it round his shoulders even though it was excruciating to do so. His wounded arm was also hurting beyond belief.

Alone, scared witless, he broke down and sobbed uncontrollably while his damaged body shook.

After a while a tray was put into the cell. On it was a tin plate containing an evil-looking mess, and a tin cup of water.

He drank the water so quickly he immediately threw it up again.

'That's over twenty-four hours on duty, Captain. You must break off and get some rest.'

'That's an order,' Major Hammond added firmly, but not unsympathetically, when Christian started to shake his head.

Christian knew the Major was right, he was out on his feet. Much longer and he'd nod off where he sat.

'Go home, have a bath and a sleep. Report back when you're ready. In the meantime, if Umbrella comes through we'll ring and let you know.'

'Thank you, sir,' Christian replied wearily.

'I shall be sitting in for you till you return,' a hearty female voice boomed.

Christian hadn't noticed this newcomer's arrival. He smiled when he saw who it was. 'Hello, Miss Sampson-Hardy.'

'Hello, Captain. Nice to run into you again.'

'It's Du Bois, remember him?'

Miss Sampson-Hardy's features softened. 'Of course I do, Captain. I remember all my pupils.'

'Why aren't you at Craiggoyne?'

Her eyes twinkled mischievously. 'Taking a spot of hols away from that ruddy Scottish wilderness. I have a fortnight here in town to enjoy myself. Which I have every intention of doing.'

He couldn't help but notice her moustache to be even fuller than he recalled.

'Now you shove off,' Miss Sampson-Hardy declared. 'Let me take over.'

Christian knew he couldn't have left his R/T set in better or more capable hands.

'The pubs are open. Let's you and I have a stiff drink before you toddle away to bed,' Major Hammond said to Christian.

'It doesn't mean Du Bois is dead or captured,' he said when he and Christian were ensconced at a table.

Christian blinked at him.

'All manner of things might have occurred. It's quite possible he's on the run, that somehow the drop went wrong. That's happened several times since we started sending over operatives.'

Christian nodded he'd taken that on board.

'Your zeal and diligence do you proud, Captain.'

'As I mentioned, sir, he's a friend.'

'Quite.'

Hammond pursed his lips and bent a little closer. 'I'll let you into a secret.'

'Oh?'

'I have another agent in place not that far from where Du Bois is located. If, at the end of another twenty-four hours, we still haven't heard anything, I'll have him see what he can find out. How's that?'

'At least it would be something.'

'Good.' Major Hammond pointed a warning finger. 'But keep this strictly to yourself. In our line of business it's often best not to let the left hand know what the right is doing.'

Christian smiled. 'That makes sense to me.'

They only had the one drink, then Christian made his way back to the flat where he didn't bother with a bath but fell straight into bed.

When he finally woke again it was with the realisation that the telephone hadn't rung.

It was the same two guards as before who took Gilbert to Kemmel's office.

He was hardly through the door when a stony-faced Ingrid lit up.

'Sam's gone fishing with Denzil today,' Maizie informed Alice when she arrived for work.

'That's nice.'

'He misses it, the fishing I mean. He says that being on a merchantman just isn't the same.'

'He'll be away all day then?'

'I imagine so. Unless the weather turns really foul, which I doubt it will. They've gone crabbing.'

'So where do you want me to start?'

'The tats I suppose. How's Rosemary?'

Alice glanced sideways at Maizie. 'Fine.' Alice hesitated. 'She mentioned something last night that maybe I should tell ee. 'Tain't confidential or nothing, but I thought perhaps you should know.'

Maizie was intrigued. 'What is it?'

'She says she's leaving school at the end of term and wants to come and work here full-time with ee.'

Maizie did a rapid mental calculation. 'She will be old enough by then. If only just.'

'What do you think?'

Maizie shrugged. 'I'm not quite sure. She'd certainly be a help about the place.'

'The maid's keen, Maiz. I got the impression she believes she owes you and wants to start paying ee back.'

'That's nonsense!' Maizie exclaimed. 'Neither she nor Bobby owe me anything. I've only done what had to be done. Besides, and I have to say it, it's been lovely having them here. They've somehow become the children I never had.'

Alice stared at Maizie in concern, having noted the regret in her voice. 'The good Lord moves in mysterious ways, Maiz. Anyway, it's still not too late for you to have one of your own. There's plenty of time for that.'

Maizie thought of her new and improved relationship with Sam. 'I'd give anything to have a baby, Alice. And that's the truth.'

At which point Bobby rushed in eager for his breakfast and the conversation was ended.

'Well, that's it then,' Sam declared. He and Maizie were standing in front of the hired car that was to take him to Helston.

'You will be careful?'

'As much as I can be, Maiz. I promise ee that.'

She had to keep a brave face, she told herself. Getting all emotional and weepy wouldn't do any good. 'I just hope it's not the Malta run again,' she said.

He scowled. 'You and me both, girl. Anything but that. Even the Rusky run ain't so dangerous.'

'Try to write, Sam.'

'Now, Maiz, ee knows what I'm like where that's concerned. But I will try, I promise ee.'

'That's all I ask.'

He took a deep breath. 'It's goodbye then.'

'For now.'

'That's right,' he replied softly. 'For now.'

Sam started to move towards the car. 'Aren't you going to kiss me!' she chided.

'Out here in the open? What will folks think?'

'Bugger folk, I'm your wife, damnit. What they would expect.'

He gathered her into his arms and kissed her. Then he was in the taxi and slamming the door.

She waved, thinking he'd turn round and look through the taxi's rear window. Perhaps even wave back.

She was disappointed.

The two guards stripped Gilbert naked and then bound him securely to a chair, tying his hands behind his back. Ingrid made a gesture and one of the guards pulled a large black box into view which Gilbert, through swollen eyes, recognised as a battery. When the battery had been placed in front of him he watched in horror as Ingrid began attaching leads to it.

When the leads were in place she reached up and cupped his testicles, smiling serenely as she stared at them. Gilbert winced as the leads were then attached, one to each testicle.

'Will you cooperate now?' Kemmel asked softly, his brow furrowed in a frown.

'Go to hell.'

Kemmel nodded and Ingrid threw a small red switch on top of the battery.

Gilbert's neck bulged as the scream shredded his throat.

'It's lovely to have you home again,' Maizie declared to Rosemary.

'It's lovely to be here. I was wondering if I could talk to you later. In private that is?'

'Of course.'

Well, she knew what that was all about, Maizie thought.

'Still nothing?' Miss Sampson-Hardy asked Christian, having come to do her shift. She and Christian were alternating twelve hours each per day.

Christian had inquired if this wasn't interfering with the fun she'd come to London to have, and she'd replied that it wasn't at all. He could only marvel at her fortitude and stamina.

Christian shook his head.

Miss Sampson-Hardy sighed. 'It doesn't look good, does it?'

'No,' he murmured disconsolately.

'Still, you never know.'

A thoroughly dejected Christian left her to it. In his heart of hearts, or perhaps it was a sixth sense, he didn't believe they'd ever hear from Umbrella again.

If Gilbert had been captured he hoped he'd managed to take his death pill. The alternative was too awful to contemplate.

Time had no meaning for Gilbert any more. Day or night, they were all the same. The one constant was pain. Dear God, let me die, he prayed for the umpteenth time. Please God, let me die.

'We've lost patience with you, Du Bois. This is your last chance, agree to cooperate or die.'

Gilbert stared down at the shattered remains of his broken hands, mangled thanks to Ingrid, the merest hint of a smile twitching the corners of his mouth. That was what he wanted, had so often prayed for, to die. The sooner the better.

'Well?' Kemmel demanded harshly.

Gilbert didn't reply. To have tried to do so would have been agony in itself. The continual screaming had brought that about.

Kemmel glanced over at Ingrid sitting where she always sat. There was an angry glint in her eyes. She didn't like being beaten, something that happened only rarely. She hated Gilbert for being one of the exceptions.

Kemmel shrugged, Du Bois was close to death anyway. It

was clear the man was never going to capitulate which left only execution. It was a great pity; Du Bois's information would have been so useful.

He rose from behind his desk and strode towards the door. 'Bring him,' he instructed the guards.

The room was bare with the exception of several large hooks protruding from the ceiling. Although Gilbert didn't notice them there were also a number of smaller hooks screwed into one wall.

The guards positioned him under one of the hooks with Kemmel grimly watching on. Ingrid set down the leather bag she was carrying and opened it. What she took out was a large coil of piano wire.

Smiling angelically, but with the anger still in her eyes, she slowly fashioned a noose using one end of the wire. When she was ready she slipped the noose over Gilbert's head, dropping it to rest round his neck.

What she did next startled Gilbert and filled him with revulsion. She kissed him lightly on the lips after which she reached down and caressed his charred testicles. He wanted to spit in her face but had no saliva with which to do so.

Ingrid flipped the wire over the hook above and then walked to the wall where she half wound it round a hook there. Slowly, ever so slowly, she began tightening.

The wire digging into his flesh caused Gilbert to rise until he was balanced on the balls of his feet. When he was in that position Ingrid tied off the wire.

His eyes were bulging as the Germans left the room, Ingrid the last to go.

'*Au revoir, mon cher*,' she murmured from the door, the only time she'd ever spoken in Gilbert's presence.

She closed the door softly behind her.

Chapter 21

C hristian was thinking about his youth in Hennebont, smiling at memories that drifted lazily through his mind. In front of him the R/T set remained obstinately silent.

There was a summer's afternoon when he and his parents had gone for a picnic on the banks of Le Blavet, the river that ran through Honnebont. He could vividly recall the hot steamy haze that hung everywhere, his father talking to his mother, telling jokes, reminiscing. Delphine's laughter had tinkled in the still air.

What happy times those had been, times he'd foolishly thought would go on and on for ever. There had been a girl round about then, a pretty little thing called Françoise. They'd thought it daring to hold hands and even more daring to kiss. It had never gone beyond that stage, they'd been far too young. But what sublime bliss it had all been.

Françoise, he wondered what had become of her. She and her family had moved away to another town, which one he couldn't remember, and that had been that. Out of his life for ever. Wherever she was now he wished her well.

'Captain?'

Christian started and snapped out of his reverie to find Major Hammond staring down at him. 'Sir?'

'Leave that and come with me, will you?'

'But, sir . . .'

'Just leave it, Captain, there's a good chap.'

In that instant Christian knew what this was all about. Hammond had news of Gilbert. And telling him to leave the set unattended could only mean one thing.

The room Hammond took Christian to was one he'd never been in before. There was a table with a green velvet cloth over it, several club armchairs and a comfy sofa.

'Colonel Galbraith's private day room,' Hammond explained wearily.

'It's about Gilbert, sir, isn't it?'

Hammond turned to face Christian, staring him straight in the eye. 'Bad news I'm afraid, old boy. He was captured and taken to the headquarters of the local Gestapo.'

Christian blanched. '*And*, sir?'

'He was eventually executed there. I'm afraid I have none of the details, only that he was captured and executed.'

Hammond was lying. He knew exactly what had been done to Du Bois, but had no intention of relating any of it to Christian. Christian was still a field operative after all. Details of the sort he possessed might make the man lose his nerve. Or, in certain field conditions, his judgement. No, best the gory facts were kept from him.

'I'm sorry,' Hammond added softly.

Christian ran a hand over his face, feeling suddenly old, drained and very tired. 'I wonder why he didn't take his pill?'

Hammond shrugged: 'I've no idea. Perhaps he was knocked unconscious and never had a chance to swallow it before capture. We'll never know.'

'Poor Gilbert,' Christian muttered.

Hammond crossed to a sideboard and opened it to reveal an array of bottles. 'I could certainly use a drink. How about you?'

'Please, sir.'

'There's gin, whisky, brandy . . .'

'Brandy, sir.'

'Good choice. I'll join you.'

Hammond poured two hefty measures and handed Christian one. 'It's a rotten business,' he declared.

Christian nodded his agreement.

'I hate asking, but do you think, when you can get round to it, that you'd pack up his stuff. I'll have it collected and put into storage. It'll be sent on to his next of kin when the war's over.'

'I'll do that, sir,' Christian mumbled, thinking that was going to be a bloody awful task. 'Do you mind if I smoke?'

'Carry on. Here, have one of mine.'

The brand, Passing Cloud, was one Christian had never come across before. Instead of being round, the cigarettes were oval-shaped.

'Take the rest of the day off and go home,' Hammond said. 'In fact you can stay there till we contact you.'

'Thank you, sir.'

'There's a field mission coming up shortly that we have you in mind for. What do you say to that?'

'It's what I'm trained for, sir.'

'Good chap.'

Suddenly Hammond and his English manners were irritating Christian. How he wished he was back on the banks of Le Blavet during a hot, sultry summer's day.

'Another?' Hammond inquired when Christian had finished his glass. Christian was tempted, but decided against it. He'd go to a pub instead where he could be on his own and grieve for Gilbert.

'No thank you, sir.'

'You toddle off then. And may I say again, Le Gall, I am sorry. Du Bois was doing a damned fine job. I shall be recommending a decoration.'

Christian smiled cynically. What use was a decoration to a dead man?

Christian couldn't stay in the flat any longer, he needed to get out for some fresh air and company. At least to be in the presence of others, to hear voices even if he didn't talk to the people concerned. As he left the flat he knew he was going to the Eight Bells and not The Chelsea Potter. And he knew why.

He'd been there half an hour when Madeleine came in with a group of female friends, all of them chatting noisily and laughing as they went to the bar.

'Madeleine?'

She turned to him in surprise. 'Christian! Why, hello, stranger. How are you?'

'I'm fine. And you?'

'Couldn't be better. We're out celebrating Helen's birthday. Say hello to Helen.'

Helen was a rather vacuous brunette who'd evidently once had bad acne. 'Hello, Helen,' he said, forcing a smile on to his face.

'Christian is a Frenchman,' Madeleine declared. 'As you can probably tell from his uniform. A friend of Gilbert's whom you've heard me speak about.'

Christian exchanged pleasantries with Helen and a few of the others who asked him to join them.

'Come on, let your hair down,' Madeleine urged when he hesitated. He could now tell from the sparkle in her eyes that she'd already had a couple before coming into the pub.

'Actually I wanted a word with you in private,' he replied.

'About Gilbert?' she queried quickly.

'As a matter of fact, yes.'

'He's back then?' She glanced round the pub as though expecting to spot him somewhere.

'Not exactly.'

Her face dropped a little. 'But he will be soon. Is that it?'

'In private, Madeleine. It'll only take a few minutes.'

'Be with you shortly,' she said to the others as Christian ushered her away.

They went to the table where he'd been previously. 'So what is it?' she demanded eagerly as they sat.

Christian cleared his throat. 'I'm afraid I have some bad news, Madeleine. Gilbert won't be coming back.'

She frowned. 'Has he been posted elsewhere?'

There was no easy way to say this. 'He's dead, Madeleine. He was killed while on active duty.'

Her face crumpled, her expression one of disbelief. 'Dear God.'

'I'm sorry.' Reaching across the table he laid a comforting hand over hers.

'There's no . . . mistake. No doubt?'

'None whatsoever, Madeleine.'

Tears sprang into her eyes. With a muttered apology she fumbled for a handkerchief.

'I only found out today which is why I came looking for you,' he explained gently. 'I thought you should know.'

'Thank you,' she croaked, reaching for her drink which she downed in one.

'Can I get you a refill?'

'Please.'

When he returned from the bar she tried to get him to elaborate, but he refused to be drawn. Not that he knew that much anyway.

He lit a cigarette while she continued trying to come to terms with what he'd told her. She was completely distraught, shaken to the core.

'I don't want to stay here. Let's go somewhere else,' she said at last.

'If you wish.'

'Oh, Christian,' she whispered, eyes puffy, cheeks washed free of make-up and now red.

'I know.'

Madeleine made her excuses to the others explaining she'd just received some bad news and would tell them about it at work in the morning. They were sympathetic and concerned, for it was obvious the state she was in.

'Don't bother about me. You girls have a good time,' she muttered croakily, and hurried off with Christian following.

'I'm pissed as a rat,' Madeleine slurred.

It wasn't an expression Christian knew, but its meaning was clear. He was none too sober himself.

'I had hopes for us, Christian, Gilbert and myself I mean.' She shrugged. 'Stupid I suppose with a war on when everything's so bloody uncertain.'

He couldn't have agreed more with the latter comment. He studied Madeleine, thinking what an attractive woman she was. Gilbert had been lucky.

Madeleine staggered, Christian catching hold of her arm to steady her. 'My head's spinning,' she hiccuped.

'What you need is some coffee.'

'No, another drink.'

'Coffee, Madeleine.' He didn't want her throwing up, that would be so undignified. Not to mention unfeminine. 'Now what's your address?'

She mumbled something incomprehensible.

'Say that again.'

This time he caught it. The street was quite some distance from where they now were, whereas his flat was relatively near.

He decided to take her there to sober up before she collapsed entirely.

'Sure,' she mumbled when he suggested it.

He was none too clever on his feet either, he noted. They really had put away an awful lot. But then it wasn't every day you had the sort of news they'd had.

'Wibbly wobbly,' she said, and giggled.

'What does that mean?'

She giggled again. 'Me, I'm all wibbly wobbly.'

He held her even tighter.

'Home sweet home,' she declared rather too loudly as they entered the flat. 'Yours that is, not mine.'

'Would you like to go to the toilet?'

'Please.'

'Do you remember where it is?'

She drew herself up to her full height. 'Of course I do. I've used it often enough.'

'Then I'll put the kettle on while you're there.'

About five minutes later she emerged from the toilet crying again. 'I'm sorry. I'm sorry,' she choked.

He took her into his arms. 'There's nothing to apologise for. It's perfectly normal.'

She moulded herself against him and he was acutely aware of her firm breasts pushing into his chest. It seemed the most natural thing in the world when they kissed.

Two people consoling one another in their mutual grief.

For a brief moment he wondered who was lying beside him when he woke next morning. Then he remembered.

'Oh Christ!' he muttered to himself. What had he done? What on earth had possessed him? Gilbert hardly in his grave and he'd gone and slept with his girlfriend. Remorse and revulsion swept through him.

He twisted on to an elbow to stare at Madeleine. It had been a frantic coupling, she so eager he'd thought she was trying to devour him. He recalled how her nails had raked his back as they'd bucked and heaved together.

What to do now? How to face her? That was going to be awful. Not that it was entirely his fault, what had happened had, if anything, been more at her instigation. She'd almost ripped the clothes from him before they'd even reached the bedroom.

His head was hurting; well what else could he expect? He could only be thankful it wasn't hurting even more than it was.

She was due at the Ministry later, she'd mentioned that in the Eight Bells. So he was going to have to wake her. He slid from the bed and reached for his dressing gown.

He'd do it with coffee.

Her embarrassment was acute. She muttered that she didn't know what had come over her, then snatching up her things had rushed off to the bathroom.

Christian listened to the sound of running water as he lit his first cigarette of the day.

'Goodbye then, Christian.'

'Goodbye, Madeleine.'

Since getting up she'd studiously avoided looking him in the eye. Even now, standing at the door, she was doing the same.

'I think it best we forget last night,' she mumbled.

'Yes.'

'I'll run into you again sometime no doubt.'

'Probably.'

She shifted from one foot to the other. 'I'd better hurry if I'm not going to be late.'

'I understand.'

'I, eh . . .' She trailed off and hung her head.

'You'd better go then.'

She left him without another word.

Since getting up neither had mentioned Gilbert.

'Le Gall?'

Christian instantly recognised Major Hammond's voice. 'Speaking, sir.'

'Do you remember that job I mentioned?'

'The one coming up?'

'That's right. Well, it's to be sooner than we anticipated. Take ten days' leave and then report back here. You'll be off shortly afterwards.'

'Understood, sir.'

'Good.'

'Thank you, sir.'

Christian cradled the phone and stared thoughtfully at it. His feelings were mixed. The only good part was that he'd be returning to his beloved France. That the Germans were there was the bad aspect.

He knew exactly what he wanted to do with his leave.

'Christian will be arriving later today,' Maizie announced casually to Alice who sat cleaning the silverware.

'That's nice,' Alice replied, equally non-committal.

'He rang last night to ask if we had a free room. As if we haven't had a free room since this war started.'

Maizie thought back to the conversation. After a few minutes of his oblique probing she'd realised he wanted to know if Sam was there. Now how had he known that Sam had been home? Maybe he didn't and had simply been checking.

For a moment she'd been tempted to say Sam was about,

hoping that would put Christian off. Only a month ago she'd have welcomed his arrival with open arms, but that was before she and Sam had at long last found happiness and love together.

It wasn't as if she and Christian had done something they shouldn't, she reminded herself. Well hardly anyway. But a warmth had been there, an attraction. The understanding that something could happen and might. All that was changed now of course.

Maizie sighed. Life could be so difficult at times. Nothing was ever straightforward and easy.

He'd be here for just over a week he'd said, eagerness in his voice. Eagerness that had faded when she hadn't been so enthusiastic in her response.

Damnation, she thought to herself.

'Christian!'

He laughed and dropped his case as Bobby came charging towards him and into his arms. 'How are you?'

'I'm fine, Christian. It's marvellous to see you. Will you take me fishing while you're here?'

'Of course I will.'

Bobby extricated himself and beamed at the older man. He then spoke several sentences in French which delighted Christian, who replied in his native language.

'I'm coming on, aren't I?'

'You are indeed. Now where's Maizie?'

'Aunt's in the kitchen. Shall I tell her you're here?'

'Please.'

Bobby went careering off again.

Christian glanced round. It was good being back in Coverack. In fact it was a lot more than that. He couldn't wait to see Maizie whom he'd missed dreadfully.

A picture of him and Madeleine popped into his mind,

which he instantly banished. That had been a terrible mistake, an aberration when they were both drunk. To be forgotten about. He felt guilty as hell about it.

Maizie appeared wiping her hands on a pinny. 'Hello, Christian.'

'Hello, Maizie.'

'How was your journey down?'

'Not too bad. I rather enjoyed myself.'

She smiled. 'It must be a familiar route to you by now.'

'Indeed it is. I know every signpost along the way.'

Maizie half turned. 'Bobby!' Then to Christian, 'He'll show you to your room. It's the same one you had last time.'

'Then I don't need to be shown. I'll just go on up.'

'If you'll excuse me, Christian, I'm rather busy. Come on down and help yourself to a drink at the bar if you want one. No cognac I'm afraid, but there is brandy.'

'That'll do.'

His own smile disappeared when she'd gone. That had been cool, somewhat offhand to say the least. He'd expected a far warmer welcome.

He was halfway up the stairs when it dawned on him that she'd called him Christian and not the familiar Chris.

Something was wrong, but what? Christian wondered as he tackled the dinner he'd ordered. Why was he in the dining room and not eating with the family as he'd become used to?

Had he said something last time here, done something to offend? Been amiss in any way? He didn't think so.

So what was going on?

'Anything been happening since I've been away?' Christian asked Bobby. It was the following day, Saturday, and he'd decided to take the lad fishing as he'd promised. They were down at the quay trying for sea bass.

He still hadn't had a proper conversation with Maizie. It might have been his imagination, though he didn't think so, but it seemed she was avoiding him. And her attitude, when they had spoken, was definitely cool. Pleasant enough, but cool nonetheless. The old intimacy that had existed between them had gone. In fact, it was almost as if it had never been.

Alice too. She'd been cheery enough, but reserved, almost withdrawn. A barrier had been set between them. The whole thing was quite baffling.

Bobby shook his head. 'Nothing really. It rarely does in Coverack.'

Christian reeled in and re-cast, watching the spinning silver lure fly majestically through the air.

'Did I hear someone mention Mr Blackacre was here?' Christian queried vaguely.

'Oh he was here, all right. He was torpedoed.'

Christian glanced at the boy. 'Torpedoed?'

'In the Mediterranean he said. He was one of only a few survivors apparently.' Bobby frowned. 'He was a lot nicer this time. He even gave me money for sweets which he'd never done before. Oh, and Rosemary went to live with Alice for a while.'

Christian wasn't interested in the latter. 'Tell me more about Mr Blackacre.'

'Not much to tell except he was a lot nicer. He laughed quite a bit, which is unusual for him. And he made Aunt Maiz happy. That was easy to see.'

A chill went through Christian. 'Happy in what way?'

Bobby shrugged. 'I don't know. Just happy. I saw them kissing once, a real smacker of one. Then went upstairs.' He smirked knowingly at Christian. 'Guess what they were going to do?'

The chill had become an ice-cold sensation. 'Well well,' he murmured.

'You've never met him, have you?'

'Never.'

'He can be a bit scary.'

'Oh?'

'You know, the way some people can. We had a neighbour in Plymouth who was the same. Always fighting and getting thrown into jail. Drunk too half the time.'

Christian digested that. 'Are you saying Mr Blackacre drinks a lot?'

'He can do. But he's a sailor and all sailors drink. So my mum once said, and she knew many sailors.'

Out of the mouths of babes, Christian thought. 'Have you eh . . . heard from your mum at all?'

Bobby's face darkened, a look of terrible sorrow in his eyes. He silently shook his head.

At that point their dialogue was interrupted by Christian getting a bite.

Maizie glanced surreptitiously sideways at Christian sitting by himself. She'd come across to join a group of locals celebrating a diamond wedding anniversary. It was late and normally she would have been shut by now but had made an exception because of the party.

This was the third night running she'd managed to evade getting into a proper conversation with Christian. She knew she should invite him over, include him in the merrymaking. But she didn't want to do that.

She was being unfair, horribly so. But somehow she just couldn't bring herself to explain to him. For the umpteenth time she reassured herself nothing had gone on between them and therefore an explanation wasn't required. But in her heart of hearts she knew it was.

A few minutes later Christian got up and, without even waving goodnight, went upstairs to his room.

Maizie heaved a soft sigh of relief, then quickly brought her attention back to the table when she realised she was being addressed.

Christian stood on the cliffs overlooking Coverack, the fierce wind whipping and tearing at his clothes. When he returned to the hotel he'd ask for his bill and settle up. This was his last ever visit to Coverack, he knew that now for a certainty.

He could only guess at what had happened from the scant information he'd been able to glean. Something had occurred between Maizie and her husband, a sea change in their relationship. Maybe it had been because of his being torpedoed, but whatever, it was a change that now excluded him from her affections.

He should have said goodbye to Bobby that morning, but simply couldn't bring himself to do so. No doubt Maizie would come up with something to account for his sudden departure. He was going to miss the little lad. Bobby had become quite a favourite of his.

Christian didn't stop and look back over Coverack as he left it for the last time.

Even if he had he wouldn't have seen Maizie watching him from behind the curtain of an upstairs window. She bit her lip as his car disappeared from view.

She'd handled all this badly, she berated herself, and had no doubt she'd hurt Christian. She should have spoken to him, told him the truth. She'd owed him that. Oh well, what was done was done, she rationalised. It was all over now. Christian had gone and judging from his attitude as he'd paid his bill she doubted she'd ever see him again.

Maizie smiled, thinking of Sam and their nights together. But more than the nights, the days when he'd been so kind and considerate. A completely reformed character.

And Sam was her husband. Nothing would ever alter that. For better or worse. Well, the worse was now over and the better had arrived. The future was nothing but rosy.

Providing he survived the war that is. Please God, let him do that. Let him come home again when it was all over.

She'd miss Christian though. She had to admit that. He'd been fun and . . . there when she'd needed someone.

She'd always think kindly of him.

It had been a bumpy ride due to a great deal of air turbulence. Christian had felt queasy the entire way. A glance at his wristwatch confirmed it was almost time.

The plane's navigator appeared and gestured to the door in one side of the fuselage. Christian helped him remove the door, then hooked up ready for the jump.

'You OK?' the navigator smiled.

Christian nodded.

'Remember the drill. Go when the red light turns green.'

Christian's reply was the thumbs-up sign.

'Good luck, chum. Happy landings.'

The navigator moved away as Christian positioned himself by the edge of the door. Below him, shrouded in darkness, lay his beloved France.

When the light turned to green he launched himself into space.

Chapter 22

Bobby had been invited to join in the game of football now taking place in the playground but declined when he realised Denny Herbert and some of his cronies were playing. He wasn't one to court trouble when it could be avoided, and who knew what Denny might get up to. Denny had a reputation as a dirty tackler.

'Bobby?'

He turned to find Emily smiling at him. It still made him uneasy, which she was aware of, when she spoke to him in the playground. Albeit their friendship was hardly a secret, he didn't like flaunting it at school.

'What is it, Em?'

'I'll meet you at the gates when school's over this afternoon. There's something I want to tell you.'

He couldn't imagine what.

'You will be there?'

'I'll be there,' he replied cautiously. 'What's it all about?'

Her eyes twinkled mischievously. 'You'll have to wait. I'll tell you then. Don't forget now.' And with that she walked away.

Bobby stared after her, somewhat disconcerted. They nearly always went home together so why go out of her way to make sure he'd be there that particular day?

His attention was brought back to the game when a great shout went up as a goal was scored.

'What are you doing this Saturday afternoon?' Emily asked coyly.

He had to think about that. 'Nothing special. I'll help Aunt Maiz at the hotel for a bit as I usually do. But nothing after that.'

'Then how would you like to come to tea?'

'You mean to your house?'

'That's right.'

Bloody hell, he thought. 'But your mother doesn't approve of me. You've admitted so yourself.'

Emily had the grace to blush. 'That's in the past, Bobby. It was Mum who suggested it.'

What Emily didn't know was that it was really her father who'd had the idea and that there had been a row between him and his wife before Mabel had capitulated and agreed. She'd then been warned to be on her best behaviour, or else.

'I don't know,' Bobby said slowly, completely thrown by this turn of events. He hadn't forgotten the birthday party to which he'd been disinvited, or standing outside the house listening to all the children having fun. He still thought bitterly about that from time to time.

'Oh please, Bobby, please. For me?'

He kicked a stone, sending it skittering across the street. What if he let himself down in some way? He could just imagine being too embarrassed to even speak. And what about Emily's father? What was he like? The man might be an ogre who looked down his nose at him. He could feel himself starting to panic.

'Bobby?'

He then had a brainwave about how to defer his reply. 'I'll have to ask Aunt Maiz,' he said.

'Oh!' She was clearly disappointed, having expected an answer there and then.

'It's up to her. She might not want me to go. I don't think she and your mum are the best of friends.'

'I think Mum's trying to make up for the party,' Emily said, having guessed something of what was going through Bobby's mind.

Bobby remembered the humiliation and his subsequent flight to Plymouth. He'd hated Coverack then because of the party. But not any more. He'd gone back to loving the place.

'I still have to ask Aunt Maiz,' he declared stubbornly.

'Well, let me know tomorrow then.'

He didn't reply to that. Instead he kicked another stone, this one far harder than the previous.

'Invited to tea!' Maizie exclaimed. Now there was a turn-up for the book. Clearly her 'chat' with Mabel Dunne had had an effect.

'I don't want to accept.'

Maizie frowned. 'Why not?'

Bobby shrugged and didn't answer.

Maizie could understand his reaction only too well. 'I think you should,' she said softly.

He scowled. 'I won't feel right there.'

'Why not?'

He shrugged again. 'You know.'

Maizie sighed and leant against the sink to gather her thoughts. 'Sometimes in life it's best to let bygones be bygones, Bobby. It's part of growing up. We adults do it all the time. It's even more important in a village where you see the same people day in day out. Where we're all sort of confined in a relatively small place. Can you understand that?'

He reluctantly nodded.

'I'm sure Mrs Dunne will go out of her way to make you feel relaxed and at home. She's the one admitting the mistake, after all. You were entirely blameless in the whole affair. It was her in the wrong which she's now acknowledging.'

'I suppose so,' he admitted grudgingly.

'Then I think you should go.'

Bobby was squirming inside. All that Maizie said was true and made sense, and yet . . .

'Well?' she queried with a smile.

'What if she's rude to me? Makes me feel awful?'

God help Mabel Dunne if she did that, Maizie thought. She'd go round there and tear the bitch's hair out.

'There he is!' Emily exclaimed excitedly as the doorbell rang.

'You'd better go and let him in, maid,' Andy Dunne said from the comfy chair where he was sitting.

He fastened his gaze on Mabel when Emily was gone from the room. 'Remember,' he growled. 'You behave as ee should or you'll have me to answer to.'

A thrill ran through Mabel. This new dominant Andy, whom she still wasn't used to, excited her far more than the previous Andrew. They still had a clash of wills on occasion with her invariably caving in.

'Do you hear me, woman?'

'Yes, Andy,' she answered meekly.

'Right then.'

Mabel rose from where she was sitting and put a smile on her face. When a nervous Bobby came in Andy also got to his feet to extend the hand of welcome.

'I have to say I was pleasantly surprised,' Mabel declared to Andy as Emily was showing Bobby out. The lad had been politeness itself. And impressive too with his impeccable table manners. Nor had he belched once when eating as she'd half expected he would.

She had found herself occasionally glancing at his hair, wondering . . . Then good sense had told her that Maizie Blackacre would have long since attended to that problem. Besides, Bobby wouldn't have been allowed to attend school with head lice. He'd have been sent home instantly they'd been discovered.

'I liked the boy,' Andy said. 'Emily could do a lot worse than him for a friend.'

'I'll just do the dishes,' Mabel declared, and bustled dutifully away.

'So how did it go?' Maizie queried anxiously as Bobby came bursting into the kitchen.

'I had a great time.'

She immediately relaxed. She hadn't thought Mabel would be nasty, but you never knew. 'Did you get lots to eat?'

He nodded. 'And afterwards Mr Dunne took me out to his shed and showed me all his tools. He's got hundreds of them.'

'Has he indeed,' Maizie replied drily, delighted at how enthusiastic Bobby was.

'After his shed he showed me the inside of his van where he's got lots more. Those ones are all to do with his job. He explained quite a few to me and what they were for.'

Men together, Maizie smiled. Show Bobby his tools! Wasn't that just like the thing.

'Mr Dunne has spikes he puts on his feet for climbing telegraph poles. He's promised to let me try them sometime.'

Maizie laughed. 'It sounds to me like Mr Dunne was a great hit and the pair of you got on really well together.'

'We did,' Bobby enthused. 'He also puts ships in bottles. He showed me how he does that as well.'

'I suppose you'll be wanting to try that next?'

'There's a trick to it, you see. It's to do with the masts. But I don't think I could make ships like his. It must be awfully difficult. Mr Dunne's been doing it for years and years, ever so long.'

'And what about Mrs Dunne?' Maizie probed.

'She couldn't have been nicer. You were right about her making me feel at home. She really went out of her way.'

'So all's well that ends well,' Maizie declared with satisfaction.

'Aunt Maiz, can I invite Emily here to tea sometime?'

'I don't see why not. But let's leave it a while, eh? A month at least. That would be appropriate.'

'You don't mind then?'

'Not in the least. I'll look forward to it.'

Bobby beamed. What he hadn't told Maizie, and had no intention of doing so, was that Emily had kissed him when saying goodbye. A proper kiss this time.

She had ever such lovely soft lips.

'Surprise!' Maizie and Alice exclaimed in unison.

Rosemary's eyes opened wide to see a beautiful iced cake with a single candle on top that was placed in the centre of the table.

'For your leaving school,' Maizie explained.

It was a smashing cake, Rosemary thought. She certainly hadn't expected this.

'It's only sponge I'm afraid,' Alice apologised. 'We had hoped to make you a fruit one but couldn't get hold of the ingredients for love or money. It's this blessed war as ee'll understand.'

Rosemary felt quite choked. It was a big thing to leave

school after all and go out into the adult world. Going through the school gates for the last time she'd felt as if she was leaving her childhood behind. Which, in a large way, she had.

'Thank you both.' She went to Maizie and kissed her on the cheek, then did the same to Alice.

'We'll cut it as soon as Bobby gets here,' Maizie declared.

Rosemary put her school bag in the corner where she usually dumped it on arriving home. 'Good riddance to bad rubbish,' she said, glaring at it. 'I'll never have to carry that thing again.'

She then tore the tie from round her neck. 'Or wear that.' The tie landed on top of the bag.

'I thought a celebratory glass of wine would be in order,' Maizie smiled 'Alice?'

Alice poured three glasses out of the already opened bottle and passed them round.

'Here's to your future. May it be a happy one!' Maizie toasted, and the three of them drank.

'I can't say I never enjoyed school, but it's great to be out of it,' Rosemary said.

Maizie recalled the day she'd finished school and the fantastic feeling of freedom she'd experienced. A long time ago now. 'Don't forget you start here in the morning,' she reminded Rosemary.

'I know. I'll be up bright and early.'

Not only had Maizie agreed to give her a job but she would pay her as well. Not a lot, as there was her bed and board to account for – her lodge as Maizie had called it – but enough for her to put something by every week.

Her plan was to save until she had enough to leave Coverack and head back to Plymouth where she'd find another job. Maizie had been good to her, still was, and she would have stayed here if it wasn't for . . .

Rosemary took a deep breath. Would she ever forget that nightmare? She doubted it. She was safe for the time being, and more or less till the war ended. Occasionally staying with Alice when the need arose would see to that. But in the long term . . . That was something else entirely.

Hatred bubbled inside her. That and loathing. She had to turn away so neither Maizie nor Alice saw the expression on her face.

'We haven't been here for ages,' Emily said to Bobby, staring round the small sandy cove they'd come to. Behind and around them the sheer cliffs rose skywards.

It was a gorgeous summer's day, the sun scorching down, the Channel peaceful and a deep blue colour. The air was still and heavy, the only sound, apart from their voices, the buzz of insects.

Bobby flopped on to the sand and sighed with contentment. This was his idea of paradise. All it needed was a couple of palm trees and they might have been somewhere in the South Seas.

Emily sat beside him. 'A penny for them?'

'I was just thinking how lovely all this is.'

'Nicer than Plymouth?' she teased.

'Oh, much.'

'I still want to go there one day though. It must be ever so exciting.'

Bobby thought back to his last visit. 'If there's anything left standing when you get there.'

'How do you mean?'

'The bombing, Em. Half the city's already been blown to bits, and they're still bombing. If it goes on like that there'll only be a pile of bricks and stone at the end of it.'

'At least we're safe here,' she commented, closing her eyes, enjoying the sun beating against her face. 'Bobby?'

'What, Em?'

'Can I see your willy?'

He thought he hadn't heard her properly. 'What's that?'

Her voice had gone all shy. 'I said, can I see your willy?'

He sat bolt upright, shocked to the core. 'No you can *not*. Whatever made you ask such a thing?'

She giggled. 'They call it that as well. A boy's thing.'

Bobby felt himself go red, and quickly looked away.

'Please, Bobby?'

'No, and that's *final.*' He hesitated. 'Why do you want to see it anyway?'

'Because I've never seen one, only heard about them. I suppose it would have been different if I had a brother, but I don't.' She regarded him quizzically. 'Have you seen Rosemary's fanny?'

His red turned to beetroot. This was awful, embarrassing in the extreme. He muttered something she couldn't make out.

'Say that again?'

'I must have done when she was younger but can't remember now.'

'Rosemary's must have hair on it. I have too.'

He wanted to jump to his feet, run away. But he stayed exactly where he was.

'Do you?'

'Do I what?'

'Have hair on it?'

Oh God! He was literally squirming. 'No,' he croaked.

'I'm not surprised. I'm told boys get that later than girls. You probably will soon though. I started my periods at the end of last year.'

He knew about periods; they'd been a constant source of irritation and bad temper to his mother. 'That's nice.' What a daft reply to make, he inwardly groaned.

'If you show me yours I'll show you mine.'

He swallowed hard.

'I'll go first if you like.'

Had the girl no shame? Despite himself he was curious. Very curious in fact.

'Well?'

He didn't trust himself to speak, so nodded instead.

Emily came to her feet, glanced around to make sure they were entirely alone, then reached under her skirt and pulled down her knickers. She next lifted her skirt waist high. 'There.'

He peeked out the corner of his eye, the breath catching in his throat when he saw what was revealed. She hadn't been lying, she did have hair, though not too much of it. A strange excitement took hold of him.

'Do you want to touch it?'

He simply didn't have the nerve, thinking it might bite him. That was ridiculous of course, it didn't bite. But that's what kept going through his mind.

'No,' he choked.

She dropped her skirt and wriggled back into her knickers. 'Now it's your turn.'

'I can't, Em. I can't.'

'But I showed you! That's cheating, Bobby Tyler.'

He ground his teeth, knowing he was going to have to do it. How humiliating! And yet, there was also part of him that wanted to.

'Come on,' she urged, eyes gleaming in anticipation.

He slowly stood and fumbled with his buttons. When they were undone he allowed his shorts to drop to the sand.

Emily held her breath, waiting for him to continue. She was fascinated.

His mouth had gone dry, his throat constricted. He wished

they'd never come to this cove which was so isolated. His hands hooked into his underpants and slid them over his bottom.

Emily wriggled closer to get a better look. 'It's awfully small,' she declared.

'Em!'

'I expected something bigger. But then you're not fully grown, not a man yet. Can I touch it?'

She may as well, he thought. He'd gone this far. 'On you go.'

She reached out and gently placed the tips of her fingers on him. 'It's like a mole,' she breathed. 'A small white mole. I wouldn't be afraid of that at all.'

'Afraid?' he frowned.

'You know. If you were to put it inside me. That's too small to hurt.'

'Have you finished, Em?'

She cupped it in the palm of her hand and stroked it with the other, a large smile on her face. 'I'm trying to imagine it with hair,' she said.

That was it. He jerked away and hastily reached for his underpants. Seconds later they and his shorts were back in place. 'Happy now?'

'We'll see each other naked all the time when we're married, Bobby. At least I presume we will.'

Somehow, and he didn't know why, that made it all right. For one day they would be married.

'What do you want to do now?' she asked.

'Go for a walk.'

'All right.'

She stood and kissed him lightly on the lips. 'Not too far as I'm getting hungry,' she said.

As they started off she slid a hand into his. 'It's a lovely willy,' she whispered. 'Just like a little white mole.'

He couldn't bring himself to return the compliment and say she had a lovely fanny.

But that night he dreamt about it and in his dream his willy was huge and covered in hair.

'Rosemary, go and give number four a knock. They asked to be wakened especially early. They'll be first in for breakfast which is almost ready.'

'OK, Aunt Maizie.'

Maizie stared at Rosemary's departing back. Having her working full time was proving a blessing. What a help she was, easing her and Alice's load considerably. Then she turned her attention again to what she'd been doing.

Rosemary hummed happily to herself as she made her way along the corridor. Number four was the last door on the end and the best guest room in the hotel. The couple, a Mr and Mrs Quigley, were down from Bristol.

She paused outside the door and was raising her hand to knock when she heard the unmistakable sounds coming from within. She felt as though she'd been hit by a sledge-hammer.

Mrs Quigley was moaning loudly and Rosemary could quite distinctly make out the slap of flesh on flesh. It was that which did it, made her remember.

Rosemary hastily turned away, and for a few moments thought she was going to throw up. Her forehead was suddenly beaded in sweat while she'd gone chill all over. Her stomach was heaving.

Mrs Quigley cried out as if in acute pain.

Rosemary quickly retreated.

'Are ee all right, maid?' Alice inquired with a frown when Rosemary returned to the kitchen.

She'd stood outside for a couple of minutes to try to regain her composure, though clearly she hadn't quite managed that. She nodded.

'Ee sickening for something?'

Rosemary shook her head. 'I just came over funny for a moment.'

'You'd better sit down,' a concerned Maizie advised.

'I'm fine, Aunt, honest. It'll soon pass.'

'Would you like a cup of tea?' Alice asked.

'No thanks.'

'You might feel the benefit of it. I always swears by a good cup of strong tea I does.'

'Did you give number four a knock?' Maizie queried.

'No, I could hear them. They were already up and about.' Well, part of that was true anyway.

'No matter, you should still have knocked. They might think we've forgotten otherwise and that doesn't reflect well on the hotel.'

'Sorry, Aunt Maiz,' Rosemary apologised.

'Are you sure you don't want that cup of tea?' Alice persisted.

'I'm OK now. Whatever it was it's past.'

'Well, you'd better go back up and knock this time,' Maizie said.

Thankfully, when Rosemary reached the door again it was now quiet inside. A little later when she served the Quigleys their breakfast she couldn't look either in the eye.

'I want to quit,' Cyril Roskilly stated, when he and the others next gathered at their command centre in the tunnel.

''Tis all a load of nonsense anyway,' he went on. 'We don't do nothing. Just meets up occasionally and yaps. What's the use of that?'

Maizie was tempted, oh so tempted. It would be so much easier without Cyril's presence. 'You can't leave, Cyril, and that's that,' she replied emphatically. 'You know the rules, once in it's for good. Which means until we're officially disbanded.'

His face, already florid from quite a few drinks earlier that evening, became even more flushed. 'And what if I say bugger the lot of you!' he roared.

This was all because she was the leader, Maizie knew that. Another attempt to make life difficult for her. She glanced at Denzil, and then at the others present. Charlie Treloar was wearing a silly, probably nervous, grin.

'Then you become a loose cannon, Cyril, and we can't allow that,' she said slowly. 'You'd be shot.'

He laughed and smacked his thigh. 'You wouldn't shoot me. Don't talk stupid, woman.'

'Oh, but we would, Cyril. Or, to be more precise, I would. I promise you. Rules are rules and we all have to abide by them.'

He glared at her. 'You ain't got the guts to shoot me, Maizie Blackacre.'

That angered Maizie. 'Don't I? Well there's certainly one way for you to find out.'

Perhaps it was her tone, perhaps her expression, but suddenly Cyril wasn't sure any more. 'I still wants to quit,' he declared stubbornly.

'That's entirely up to you. But if you do you'll have to pay the penalty.'

Denzil scratched an unshaven cheek. 'Is there no alternative, Maizie? Some sort of compromise?'

'Surely there's something,' John Corin murmured.

Maizie's gaze flicked from one to the other, then back to Roskilly. How she loathed the man, a born troublemaker if ever there was. He'd known the rules when he joined the group, they'd been explained explicitly enough, and now here he was trying to renege. And no doubt all just to spite and upset her. Maybe he hoped she'd resign as leader and offer him the job to stay on. Well, if he thought that he certainly had another think coming. She'd be damned if she would. She was leader and leader she'd stay.

'Compromise?' She frowned.

'There must be something. A way round this without Cyril getting a bullet in the head.'

Cyril swallowed hard on hearing that.

And then Maizie had it. Of course, the perfect solution. One that would let them both off the hook and was very much to her advantage. The more she thought about it the more it appealed.

'Tell you what,' she said. 'How about if Cyril is excused coming to these meetings from here on? He remains one of us, and will do what has to be done should the Germans invade, but in the meantime just doesn't attend. What do you all think of that?'

Denzil nodded. 'Sounds good to me, Maiz.'

'And me,' declared Phil Carey and Charlie Treloar almost in unison.

'John?'

'Me too, Maizie.'

She took a deep breath. 'Do you agree to that, Cyril?'

'I's still a member but don't come along to these bloody stupid pointless meetings?'

'That's it.'

He didn't really believe Maizie would carry out her threat. And yet, somehow, she'd convinced him she would. Whatever, it was too much of a gamble to risk. 'I agrees,' he growled.

'Settled then.'

Maizie felt an enormous sense of relief. Without Cyril forever trying to put a spoke in her wheel leading the group would be relatively easy.

'Just remember, Cyril. You never mention anything about us or the organisation. Your mouth is shut on the subject.'

He glared at her again. 'Can I go now?'

'If you wish.'

He turned and stamped off back along the tunnel.

'Would you really have done it, Maiz, shoot him, I mean?' Charlie Treloar asked after Cyril had gone.

She didn't reply. Her expression said it all.

Hookie Repson was heading for harbour after an all-night fishing trip when he saw the four German Focke-Wulf 190s coming in almost at sea level heading for Coverack.

Enemy aircraft in the vicinity was nothing new, but there was something about these four that caused his eyes to narrow. Then he realised they were on an attacking run.

'Jesus Christ!' he exclaimed as the first bomb fell.

Chapter 23

Maizie was busy doing her accounts and bringing her books up to date when the bomb fell near by, the ensuing blast lifting both her and her chair off the floor and hurling them across the room. She found herself under the sink amongst all the paraphernalia there.

She was dazed, bewildered, not knowing what had happened. Then another bomb went off, quickly followed by the rattle of machine-gun fire.

Was she all right, hurt in any way? She didn't know. Gingerly she felt herself as the realisation dawned that the village was under attack. When she peered out from under the sink it was to see a fine cloud of dust and powder gently floating down from the ceiling.

Alice burst into the room. 'Maiz! Maiz, where is ee, maid?'

'Over here, Alice.'

Alice, her eyes wide with fear and shock, scuttled to the sink and helped her to her feet. They both jumped a fraction when another bomb exploded.

'Is the hotel hit?' Maizie spluttered, throat choked with dust.

'I don't know. I don't think so.'

She must look a sight, Maizie thought, also acknowledging

how irrelevant that was in the circumstances. She noted her skirt had been ripped.

'Get the guests and everyone else down into the cellar,' she instructed. 'I'm going outside to see what's what.'

Alice clutched her arm. 'That's too dangerous, Maiz.'

'I'm going anyway. Now round up the guests.'

She doubted the hotel had been hit, it just didn't feel as if it had. She staggered out of the kitchen after Alice and headed for the main door.

Rosemary was coming out of the Post Office, having been sent there on an errand by Maizie, when the first bomb hit. Seconds later a German plane went hurtling overhead.

She stood rooted in shock and horror at the sight of the flames leaping from Granny Hunter's roof. What had been a cottage was now a raging inferno.

There were screams from everywhere, and not too far away a man, she couldn't make out who, was shouting orders at the top of his voice. She also had a clear view of the harbour where the water was bubbling from machine-gun fire.

'German planes!' Bobby exclaimed to Emily, pointing out over the Channel. They were on one of the hills overlooking Coverack where they'd gone to enjoy a picnic packed by Maizie. Their jaws dropped open when they saw a bomb detach itself from the leading plane. Mesmerised, they watched the bomb all the way to its impact.

'Fucking bastards! Fucking German cunts!' Hookie yelled, waving his only fist in the general direction of the German planes. He was so incensed he was almost dancing on the spot.

As he continued yelling the Germans peeled away to regroup for another run, one leaving a white, milky vapour trail behind it. It was this plane that took a wider arc than the others, an arc that brought Hookie's boat *Snowdrop* directly into its sights.

Hookie's heart leapt into his mouth and he fell silent as the plane headed towards him. Then its machine guns opened up.

One pass was all that was needed. The fuel tank was hit and instantly exploded.

The *Snowdrop* disintegrated in an orange fireball.

Everything was unreal, time seemingly standing almost still. Each ticking second had become an eternity for Maizie.

It was pandemonium, chaos. People were running about like headless chickens, their faces contorted.

Graham White, an evacuee from London, was only yards away from the house where he lived when he was raked and killed by gunfire.

Graham was five years old.

'Should we go on down?' Emily asked Bobby, her voice a tremulous whisper.

'Are you mad? We're staying right here until this is over.'

She started to shake, thinking of her mother and father. 'Hold me, Bobby, please. I'm scared.'

He took her into his arms and, like that, they continued to witness the carnage being wreaked below.

'You'll all be OK here,' Alice said to the six guests she'd ushered into the cellar. All were middle-aged holidaymakers.

A Mrs Barron suddenly burst into hysterical laughter. 'We came to Coverack to get away from the blitz, and now this!' Her laughter rose in pitch to become maniacal, but it ceased abruptly when her husband slapped her across the face.

Alice chewed a thumb, wondering what to do next. She

was worried sick about Maizie and the children. She decided to go and try to find Maizie.

'You lot stay put. I'll return shortly,' she declared. 'OK?'

When that was agreed she hurried up the stairs.

Bullets whacked into the stonework of the hotel wall where Maizie was standing. Chips of stone flew in all directions, but luckily she remained unscathed.

She stared uncomprehendingly at the marks left by the bullets. How she hadn't been hit by either them or the flying chips was a miracle.

Alice was in such a hurry to find Maizie that she was careless and tripped, badly spraining an ankle.

Her language would have done an angry Irish navvy proud.

And then, as though a magic wand had been waved, it was all over. The German planes zoomed off back across the Channel leaving a pall of smoke over Coverack and a number of raging fires.

Time flowed normally again. A thoroughly shaken Maizie walked out into the street and went in search of Rosemary whom she knew had to be somewhere between the hotel and Post Office, a relatively short distance.

She came up short, tears springing into her eyes, when she saw the maid lying prostrate, a large chunk of something or other covering her back.

As she ran she vaguely took in that the front of the Post Office was gone, part of which proved to be what had hit Rosemary.

'Rosemary?' she gasped, sinking to her knees beside the girl. Rosemary's eyes were closed, a thin trickle of blood coming from her mouth.

The large chunk of something turned out to be a piece

of the cob of which the Post Office was constructed. Maizie grabbed hold of it and strained to push it away. Normally she'd never have been able to move such a weight, but somehow she did, cutting a hand in the process.

Swallowing hard she bent and listened for the sound of breathing. It was there, though faint.

'Can I help, Maizie?' The speaker was old Jim CorIn, John's dad.

'She's unconscious.'

Jim knelt alongside Maizie. 'Best to leave her be till the services get here. We might do further damage if we shifts her without knowing what we's doing.'

That made sense to Maizie, though God knew how long it would be before the services, as Jim called them, arrived. 'Can you nip back to the hotel and get me a couple of blankets and a pillow, Jim?'

'I'll be as quick as I can, Maizie.'

'Bless you.'

Jim hurried away as fast as his old and very spindly legs would take him.

'Oh, my angel, my poor angel,' Maizie crooned, stroking Rosemary's cheek. She noted the girl's pallor was a dirty grey which didn't look at all promising.

She checked Rosemary's breathing again.

'Here you are,' Jim said, handing the blankets and pillow to Maizie who immediately draped the blankets over Rosemary, then carefully raised her head so she could slip the pillow underneath.

From utter pandemonium a hush had now descended on the village. Somewhere a baby started to cry.

'What's wrong with the maid?' Alice demanded, hobbling up with the use of a walking stick.

Maizie explained what had happened.

'Is she going to be all right?'

'Your guess is as good as mine, Alice. What have you done to your leg?'

''Tis me ankle. I sprained the bugger which is a right nuisance.' Alice glanced down the street. 'Any sign of Bobby yet?'

'No, but I'm not too worried about him. He and Emily were off on a picnic and should have been out of the village.'

Jim Corin returned having absented himself for a few minutes. 'Someone managed to telephone Helston during the attack so the services should be on their way.' His face crumpled. 'Granny Hunter's dead, blown to smithereens. She and I were of an age you know. She was a grand old lass was Clara Hunter.'

ARP Warden Hargreaves came striding over. 'We're setting up a dressing station at Wyndleshore. I'll arrange for this girl to be taken there.' Wyndleshore was a large house in the village.

'I don't think she should be moved,' Maizie replied.

He frowned. 'What exactly is the matter with her?'

Maizie pointed at the chunk of cob. 'She got hit in the back by that.'

'Hmmh,' he murmured thoughtfully. 'Is her back broken?'

'I can't say. She's still breathing, if only just. That's why I don't think she should be moved for the present.'

Hargreaves nodded his agreement. 'Dr Renvoize is around somewhere. I'll find him and send him to you.'

'Thank you.'

He took a deep breath and gazed about him. ''Tis a proper nightmare and no mistake. I never thought to see the like.'

A few minutes later Bobby appeared which was a huge relief to

Maizie, even though she hadn't been overly concerned about him. Still, you never knew.

'What's wrong with Rosie?' he queried, bottom lip trembling.

Again Maizie explained.

Tears welled in his eyes. Kneeling beside his sister he took one of her hands in his. 'Don't die on me, Rosie. Don't die. You're the only family I got left.'

Maizie wanted to assure him Rosemary wouldn't die, but couldn't. She simply didn't know one way or the other. And it would be awful to mislead the lad, give him false hope.

Dr Renvoize, even blearier-eyed than usual, emerged from round a corner and came across.

Maizie explained yet again what had happened.

Renvoize pulled down the blankets and gave Rosemary the best examination he could in the circumstances.

'Is the maid's back broken?' Alice queried.

'Can't rightly say. But I don't think so.' His fingers resumed probing.

'Well?' Maizie demanded when, with a sigh, he came again to his feet.

'Difficult to tell, Maiz. I'm pretty certain she's got internal injuries, and she's certainly concussed. The skull hasn't been broken but could be fractured. You were right not to move her. When an ambulance arrives I'll have her taken straight to Helston General. That's where she should be in my opinion.'

'Is there nothing you can do for the moment?'

He shook his head. 'Not really. Just see she remains wrapped up and as comfortable as possible until the ambulance gets here. Now, if you'll excuse me I have other patients whom I must attend to.'

He stopped beside Alice. 'What's all this then?' he queried, indicating her stick.

''Tis me own blooming fault for being so clumsy. I's sprained me ankle. Nothing to worry about.'

'Are you sure?'

'I'll be all right, doctor. Now you gets on your way and sees to those who need you.'

He smiled thinly. 'Right you are, Alice Trevillick. I've had my orders.'

Maizie's mind was whirling. If Rosemary was to be taken to Helston General Hospital then she was going also, which meant she would need a few things while there. For surely she'd be in Helston for several days at least. Possibly longer.

'Alice, stay with Rosemary until I return. Will you do that?'

'Of course, Maiz. Of course.'

'I'm staying too,' Bobby choked.

Off in the distance, at the top of the hill leading out of Coverack, appeared the first of many vehicles coming to their assistance.

'Careful now, careful,' the army doctor instructed as the two male volunteers lifted Rosemary's stretcher prior to putting it into the ambulance. There were already other badly injured casualties inside.

'Telephone us and tell us what's what,' Alice said to Maizie.

'I will. Later tonight if I can.'

'I want to go too,' Bobby declared.

Maizie didn't consider that wise. 'You remain with Alice and look after the hotel for me. There's a good lad.'

His expression became stubborn. 'She's my sister.'

'I know that, Bobby. But hospitals aren't a place for someone your age. Not unless you're ill that is, which *you* aren't. So you remain with Alice.'

He opened his mouth to protest further but Maizie silenced him by holding up her hand.

'Now give me a cuddle before we're off,' she said.

He did, clinging to her for all his worth. 'Don't let her die, Aunt Maiz. Please.'

She couldn't think of anything to reply to that. Instead she pried herself free and passed her suitcase to the nurse in the ambulance. Then she climbed aboard, the nurse closing the doors behind her.

The ambulance's bell started to clang noisily as it moved away.

'Mrs Blackacre, could you please come into my office.' Maizie had been waiting patiently for well over an hour in the corridor outside the ward where Rosemary had been taken. She now rose from the hard wooden bench she'd been sitting on and followed Sister O'Hagan through the swing doors.

A doctor who was reading notes in Sister's office glanced up and smiled when Maizie entered. 'I'm Mr Mallory,' he announced. 'Please take a chair.'

Mallory perched himself on the edge of Sister's desk as Maizie sat.

'How is she?' Maizie asked quickly.

'She'll be taken off to X-ray shortly. Until I receive those I can't diagnose precisely what damage has been done.'

'Is she still unconscious?'

'I'm afraid so.'

He glanced at the notes. 'Now let me just go over a few of these details you gave us. I want to ensure everything is absolutely correct.'

They spoke for a few minutes longer and then the doctor left.

'Would you like a cup of tea?' Sister queried kindly.

Maizie shook her head.

'Have you eaten at all?'

Maizie had to think about that. 'Not since breakfast.'

'Then why don't you go and get something. As the doctor said, we won't know anything further until he's seen the X-rays, and that could be some time yet. They have to be taken and developed. You'll only be hanging around for nothing.'

The idea of leaving didn't please Maizie at all. 'But I want to be here. To be on hand when she wakes up.'

'I understand your feelings, Mrs Blackacre. And please stay on if you wish. But if you take my advice you'll have a bite to eat. She won't be back on the ward for an hour or more. Maybe a lot longer.'

Maizie slumped a little. She wasn't hungry in the least, but realised what the Sister had said was good advice. She suddenly felt desperately tired.

'Is she going to die, Sister?'

Sister's tone became completely professional. 'It's too early to say, Mrs Blackacre. We just don't know the extent of her injuries until those X-rays come back.' Her tone softened a little. 'One thing though, the doctor is pretty certain her spine isn't broken.'

Maizie sighed with relief. That was something.

'So what are you going to do?'

'I'll have a meal and book into a hotel I know.'

Sister nodded her approval. 'Do you wish to leave that suitcase here?'

Maizie considered the option. 'No, I'll take it with me. But thank you anyway.'

'When you return ask to see me.'

Maizie gave her a wan smile. 'You're very kind.'

The food dished up in the café she found was terrible, the coffee afterwards quite disgusting. Maizie paid her bill and from there walked to the hotel which was only a few streets away. She and Sam had once attended a dinner dance there on one of the rare occasions they'd gone out together. She booked a single room with bath.

'Maizie! Thank God you've rung. We've all been on tenterhooks. How's the maid?'

'Her back isn't broken, Alice, but she will have extensive bruising there. The bad news is her skull is fractured.'

Alice digested that. 'Is she still unconscious?'

'Unfortunately so. The doctor has no idea how long that will last. She could come out of it at any time, or it could go on for days. It's just a matter of waiting.'

'And what about thae internal injuries Dr Renvoize mentioned?'

'There aren't any. She's been very lucky really. If you can call having a fractured skull lucky, The doctor at the hospital assures me that's not as terrible as it sounds though. So all in all we have a lot to be thankful for. Now, how's Bobby?'

'Extremely upset and desperate to hear about his sister. Emily's here keeping him company which is a blessing. The pair of them are playing snakes and ladders up in his room. At least that's what they said they were going to do.'

'And Emily's parents?'

'They're fine. They lost a chimney stack, mind, but that can be soon mended. Emily came over as soon as she heard about Rosemary.'

Maizie manoeuvred herself round so she could sit on the bed. She wouldn't be long out of that, she thought. She was totally exhausted. 'How's your ankle?'

'Sodding painful. I strapped it up which has helped. Serves me right for being so bloody clumsy. I was in such a hurry I tripped over me own two feet I did. What about your hand?'

'Oh, that's OK. They put some antiseptic on it at the hospital and then bandaged it for me. It's very minor.'

Maizie hesitated for a moment, forming a question she was reluctant to ask. 'Do you know who was killed during the attack, Alice?'

She listened in grim silence as Alice reeled off a list of names, ending with Hookie Repson.

'Hookie!' Maizie exclaimed in consternation. 'Not him.'

'One of thae planes went after his boat which blew up. There was only matchwood left of it apparently.'

Dear Hookie, Maizie thought. An odd character in many ways, but a friend nonetheless. It was hard to believe he was gone.

'There's to be a communal service a week today,' Alice went on. 'I imagine the whole village will be there. It's going to be awful.'

Maizie could just see the scene in her mind, and shuddered. 'I'll be there too,' she promised.

'Trudy Curnow turned up to help out by the way,' Alice said. 'Though I doubt we'll be doing much business for the next few days.'

'What about the guests?'

'They've all left. I didn't charge them, Maiz. Wouldn't have seemed right somehow.'

'You did the correct thing, Alice.'

'Have you any idea how long you'll be in Helston?'

'None at all.'

'Well, don't ee worry about us here. We'll manage no bother. Especially as there aren't any guests and it's likely to remain that way for a while at least.'

'Will you be staying over?'

'Of course, Maiz. I'll be here as long as I's needed so don't you fret none about that.'

'You're a treasure, Alice.' Maizie smiled. 'I don't know what I'd do without you.'

'Oh, you'd get by, Maiz. I'm sure about that.'

Maizie had a thought. 'I'd forgotten to ask, I take it the hotel is OK?'

'You mean damage? I's been right round it and the only damage is some bullet holes at the front. Nothing apart from thae.'

Maizie went cold recalling how close she'd been to the spot where the bullets had hit. She could so easily have been killed or badly injured herself.

'Good,' she muttered.

'If that's all, you ring tomorrow and tell me how the maid.is.'

'I'll do that, Alice.'

After she'd hung up she lit a cigarette and thought about those who'd died, all of whom had been well known to her.

Later she fell asleep the moment her head touched the pillow.

That night Maizie dreamt she was being made love to by Sam. The new Sam who was tender, caring and cherishing. Who didn't inflict any pain on her.

Somehow during the dream Sam's face changed to become Chris's, and now it was he making love to her. His hands on her body, he deep inside her.

In the dream she wasn't surprised at this happening, it just seemed natural. Smiling up at Chris she continued enjoying herself.

In the morning when she remembered, and thought about it, she wasn't at all upset.

The assignment had been easier than he'd thought, Christian reflected with satisfaction. Everything had gone like clock-work. Thank God.

He put these thoughts from his mind when he heard the

distant drone of a plane. The RAF was right on schedule.

He crossed swiftly to the first of the four oil-soaked torches he'd planted in the ground and lit it. When all four were ablaze he went to one side and waited.

The Lysander touched down and bumped over the field Christian had chosen. As soon as it came to a halt he ran towards it.

The pilot kept his engine running as Christian climbed up the specially fitted metal ladder attached to the fuselage and into the rear seat. Christian tapped him on the shoulder to signal he was properly in and the pilot closed the canopy.

He'd be back in England before it was dawn, Christian thought in delight as the Lysander became airborne again.

The assignment was a job well done and he was proud of that.

Sister O'Hagan was again on duty. 'We've had to put Rosemary into a side room as she was crying out and shouting during the night which was disturbing the other patients,' she explained.

Maizie frowned. 'That sounds bad?'

'Not necessarily. What it probably means is that she's regaining consciousness. With a bit of luck she'll come round today.'

Maizie still didn't like the idea of this, and continued to frown as she followed Sister to the side room where Rosemary had been taken.

She stopped short inside the doorway at the sight of Rosemary's heavily bandaged head. But of course, she should have expected that.

'In the old days we would have shaved her, but now we don't,' Sister smiled. 'So much better, don't you think?'

Maizie nodded her agreement. It would have been dreadful

for such a young girl to come round and find she'd lost all her hair. Upsetting to say the least.

'If she isn't conscious by this evening we'll put her on a drip,' Sister went on. 'That's standard procedure.'

Sister consulted the watch pinned to her chest. 'Now if you'll excuse me I must get on.'

'Of course.'

'If there's anything you want just let one of my staff know.'

'I'll do that, Sister, and thank you.'

Maizie took off her coat when Sister had gone and draped it over the bottom of the bed as there weren't any hooks in evidence. She next pulled the single chair round till it was level with Rosemary's face.

Time passed and every so often someone would pop in to see how she and the patient were. At one point Mr Mallory appeared, had a good look at Rosemary and pronounced everything to be satisfactory. He promised to return later.

Sitting doing nothing for someone used to being always on the go was tedious in the extreme. Also the atmosphere was soporific which made Maizie sleepy. On several occasions she nearly nodded off.

'No, no,' Rosemary suddenly said in a weak voice.

Maizie, whose mind had been drifting, instantly gave the girl her full attention.

'No, please no,' Rosemary went on.

Maizie wondered what she was talking about or referring to. Was it the attack?

Rosemary's features contorted. 'No, please, Mr Blackacre,' she pleaded, voice now strong.

That shocked Maizie. Why was Rosemary thinking about Sam?

'It's painful, Mr Blackacre. Please don't hurt me any more.'

Maizie went very still and cold all over. Hurt? When had Sam ever hurt Rosemary?

Rosemary whimpered, and her body shook. 'You can't, Mr Blackacre. You can't.' She raised her hands as though fighting off an assailant. 'Oh . . . oh . . . oh . . .' she moaned.

Maizie couldn't believe what she was hearing. Didn't want to believe it. It simply couldn't be true. She was putting the wrong interpretation on this, had to be.

Rosemary muttered on and off for the next five minutes or so. When she finally finished and again lapsed into silence Maizie was sitting weeping, her insides heaving with revulsion and disgust.

'Damn you, Sam Blackacre,' she muttered at last through clenched teeth. 'Damn you to hell, you bastard.'

Chapter 24

Christian was roused out of a deep sleep by the persistent ringing of the telephone. He fumbled for the bedside light, switched it on then glanced at the clock. Who on earth would be trying to contact him at this time! It had to be headquarters, he thought as he groggily shrugged himself into a dressing gown.

He padded through to the lounge, put on the light there, yawned loudly, and picked up the phone. 'Hello?'

'Christian, is that you?'

The Cornish overtones and cadences to the voice were unmistakable. 'Maizie?' He came fully awake. She was the last person he'd expected to hear from, especially at this outlandish hour.

'I'm sorry, have I woken you?'

There was a tremble to her voice which puzzled him. 'That's all right. What's wrong, Maizie?'

She started to sob. 'Oh, Chris, something terrible has happened.'

'What, Maiz?'

She couldn't come right out and tell him about Sam. She'd only be able to do that face to face, certainly not on the telephone.

'The village was attacked by German planes,' she choked.

'People were killed including Hookie Repson.'

'Hookie!' God Almighty.

'His boat was blown to pieces with him on board. He was coming in to harbour.'

Christian shook his head trying to digest this news. 'Are you OK?'

'I'm fine, Christian. And so's the hotel. There were four of them. They dropped bombs and machine-gunned the village. Rosemary was hurt.'

'How badly?'

'A fractured skull. She's still unconscious in hospital.' Maizie broke down and began to cry.

He waited for a few moments before asking, 'What hospital's that?'

'The Helston General. I'm staying in a hotel not far away.'

'What about Bobby?'

'He and Emily were away having a picnic when the attack took place, so they missed it.'

That was a relief.

'Christian . . .' She trailed off.

'Yes, Maizie?'

'It's an imposition I know. But . . . but . . .' She hesitated.

'But what?' he prompted.

'I need a friend, Chris. Someone to talk to. There's more you see.'

'More?'

'I can't say right now, Chris. I can only tell you when we're alone.'

What a state she was in, he thought. Alone? 'Are you asking me to come down there?'

'Can you, Chris. Please? I'd be ever so grateful.'

He heard her take the phone away from her ear and then

blow her nose, meanwhile continuing to cry.

'Are you still there, Chris?'

'Of course I'm still here.'

'Can you come?'

The timing was impeccable. If she'd rung the previous night she wouldn't have had a reply as he'd been on the way back from France. 'As chance would have it I'm due some leave. I'll sort that out first thing in the morning and then start off. What hotel are you in?'

She gave him the name and address.

He couldn't imagine what else she had to tell him. Something pretty awful by the sound of things.

'You're still my friend, aren't you, Chris?'

He found himself smiling. 'Yes, Maizie. I'll always be that.'

'I thought maybe . . . after . . .'

He knew she meant his last visit when she'd more or less given him the cold shoulder. Well, that was in the past, she needed him now and he'd go, no matter what.

'What do your doctors say about Rosemary?' he queried.

'They finally admitted there was the possibility of brain damage, but wouldn't know until she regains consciousness. I'm dreadfully worried about her, Chris.'

'Has anyone tried to contact the mother?'

'The Helston police contacted their counterparts in Blackpool, but so far they've drawn a blank. They can't locate her anywhere. There again, they don't have much to go on.'

He wished he was with Maizie now, could put his arms round her and comfort her. It was clear she was distraught in the extreme. Well, she had to be to ring him like this in the small hours.

'I can't speak to anyone in the village, Chris,' she cried. 'Not about what's happened.'

He frowned. 'You mean the attack?'

'No, the other thing.' There was a few seconds' pause. 'Oh Chris!' she wailed.

'I'll be there as soon as I can, Maizie. You have my word on that.'

'Come to the hospital. I'll probably be in Rosemary's room.' She then told him the name of the ward and which floor it was on. He jotted all the details down on the small pad he kept beside the phone.

His mind was racing. Major Hammond wouldn't be at his desk before 9 a.m. Providing that was the case and he got straight through he could be on his way by half past. He quickly calculated how long it would take him to drive to Helston. He would be packed and ready to leave prior to ringing the Major.

'I've been such a fool, Chris. I trusted him, never thought, never dreamt . . .' She broke off, realising she'd already said too much.

Christian was bewildered. Who was she talking about. Sam? Had to be. So what had Sam been up to and what did it have to do with the attack on Coverack?

'I'd better go,' Maizie whispered.

'Will you be all right until I get there?'

She didn't answer that. 'Just come as soon as you can, Chris.' And with that she hung up.

Christian replaced the telephone to stand staring at it. Maizie was beside herself, a woman literally crying out in need.

And it was him she'd rung. Asked for help. That pleased him enormously. Though he was worried sick about what was going on.

He returned to bed and tried to sleep but couldn't. He was up long before his alarm clock went off.

*　　　*　　　*

'Aunt Maizie.'

Maizie, sunk in thought, looked up in surprise to discover Rosemary smiling at her. 'You're awake then.'

'I've got an awful headache.'

Maizie reached out and took her hand which she gently squeezed. 'How else do you feel?'

Rosemary thought about that. 'Weak. Very weak.' She glanced about. 'Where am I?'

'In hospital. You were knocked unconscious during the attack.'

Rosemary's expression became one of non-comprehension. 'During what attack?'

'I'll explain it all shortly. Now you just hold on a minute while I find Sister. I promised to do that as soon as you came round.'

A puzzled Rosemary watched Maizie swiftly cross to the door and vanish out of the room.

Try as she might she couldn't recall an attack of any sort.

Maizie looked round when there was a tap on the door. It opened to reveal a smiling Christian carrying a large bunch of flowers.

'Can I come in?'

'Of course.'

She rose as he approached the bed, her delight at seeing him evident. 'I didn't expect you for a while yet,' she said.

'I made good time.' That was true, the reason being he'd put his foot down the entire way.

He turned to Rosemary. 'And how's the patient?'

'Covered in bandages.'

He laughed. 'Not quite covered, only your head.' He was about to kiss her also on the cheek when he remembered the last occasion he'd touched her and the violent reaction he'd got.

'These are for you,' he declared, handing her the flowers.

She gratefully accepted them. 'Thank you, Christian. Aunt Maiz said you were coming to see me.' She smelt the flowers. 'They're gorgeous.'

'I wanted to buy some grapes but couldn't find any for sale. The war I suppose.'

'Aunt Maiz?'

Maizie took the flowers and laid them on top of the bedside table. 'I'll ask for a vase when a nurse appears.'

'So how do you feel?' Christian queried.

'Not too bad. Still a bit woozy though. And I have a headache.'

He nodded his sympathy.

'I don't remember anything at all about the attack. Aunt Maizie has been telling me about it. Sounds dreadful. All those poor people killed and injured.'

'It could have been worse,' Maizie stated grimly.

Christian was thinking about Hookie Repson whom he'd liked enormously. He was a sad loss.

'Still,' Maizie declared. 'That's over and done with now. What we have to do is get you better, Rosemary. That's the main thing.'

Rosemary closed her eyes for a moment.

'Are you tired?' Maizie asked softly.

'A little.'

'Then perhaps you'd better get some sleep. Why don't you do that while Chris and I go out and get a cup of tea somewhere.'

'Do you mind?'

'Not in the least. I could certainly use a cup of something decent.' To Christian she explained, 'The tea and coffee in here are foul. Heaven knows what they're making it from. But one thing's certain, it isn't proper tea or coffee.'

Christian thought back to France and the coffee he'd been

drinking there. That too had been terrible. Ersatz it was called. An abomination compared to what he'd been used to.

'Thanks again, Christian,' Rosemary smiled.

Maizie fussed over her for a few moments, smoothing the top sheet and fluffing up her pillows. 'There, my darling. You have a lovely sleep. We'll see you again later.'

Out in the corridor they ran into a nurse whom Maizie told about the flowers, the nurse promising to attend to them.

'Have you booked into the hotel yet?' Maizie asked as they went downstairs.

'No, I came here first. I'll book in later.'

'I know I mentioned tea, but there's a nice pub near by. We could go there if you wish.'

'That sounds a far better idea.'

They made small talk until they reached the pub which was quiet at that time of day. He sat Maizie at an out-of-the way table and then went up to order. Maizie had asked for whisky, but there wasn't any. Nor was there wine or brandy. It was gin, beer or cider. Again the privations of war. He bought Maizie a large gin and a pint of beer for himself.

'So,' he said as he sat facing her. He pulled out his cigarettes and offered her one.

'Gitanes!' she exclaimed. 'One of your favourites.'

He decided not to mention his being in France, that was irrelevant at the moment. 'I was lucky to lay my hands on a few packets,' he prevaricated.

'Thank you for coming and so quickly too. I'm afraid I was rather emotional when I rang this morning.'

'You were upset.'

She dropped her gaze to stare into her drink. 'Yes.'

He waited patiently for her to go on.

Maizie spoke at length about the attack. How old Jim Corin had helped her with Rosemary and the fact Alice had sprained an ankle.

'I see you've been wounded yourself,' he stated, pointing at the bandage on her hand.

'Hardly wounded. I cut it that's all when heaving the cob off Rosemary.'

'Cob?'

She explained that was a west-country building material composed mainly of mud, straw and virtually anything else lying about.

The idea of a building made of mud tickled Christian. A mud hut was the expression that sprang to mind.

'It's very durable,' Maizie stated earnestly. 'Keeps interiors warm in winter and cool in summer. There's a lot of it down here.'

He had a swallow of his beer. 'You mentioned there was something else. Something you couldn't tell me over the telephone.'

Maizie flushed.

Again he waited patiently. When there was still no reply he said, 'Is it about Sam?'

She glanced quickly up at him. 'How did you know?'

'I guessed.'

'Well it is,' she whispered, and had a heavy draw on her cigarette. 'It's so difficult, Chris. So shaming.'

A silence ensued that became a full minute or more. Finally she said, 'Rosemary started to talk yesterday while she was still unconscious. She was pleading with Sam not to hurt her. Not to . . .' She trailed off.

Christian had a horrible suspicion of what was coming next. 'Go on, Maiz.'

She started to cry, her shoulders heaving. 'He raped her, Chris. The bastard raped her.'

Christian slowly ground out his cigarette, having suddenly lost the taste for it. 'She said that?'

'While unconscious. She spoke of him . . . forcing her to . . . Well you know what.'

Christian was outraged, furious, but did his best to hide the fact. 'Are you sure about this? That it wasn't some sort of . . .' He groped for the English word. 'Fantasy on her part?'

'It was real all right. I knew as soon as she mentioned . . .' Maizie took a deep breath. 'There's something Sam likes to do which he did to her. That was conclusive proof it wasn't her imagination.'

Christian was intrigued. 'And what's that?'

'It's so embarrassing, Chris.'

'Then don't say.'

Maizie saw off the remainder of her gin and shuddered. 'He likes to spank,' she whispered. 'Not just in fun either. But to hurt. Really hurt. There have been times in the past when my bottom has been nearly red raw. At least that's how it felt. Rosemary couldn't have known that unless she too had experienced it.'

Christian was thinking of Rosemary's age, and the fact Sam was forty or something years old. What Maizie was describing was sadism. And to a mere child! Even if that child did have a woman's body.

Maizie shook her head. 'The thing is, if he was unfaithful with Rosemary then how many others have there been? That's what I've been asking myself. Now that he's in the Merchant Navy he must have plenty of opportunity.'

'I take it you haven't said anything to Rosemary?'

'Not a word, and I won't. Not unless she comes and tells me herself.'

'I doubt that,' Christian mused. 'I suspect Sam must have threatened her in some way to keep it secret.'

'Poor baby,' Maizie choked. 'I pity her. I really do. It must have been horrible.'

'Was it more than once?'

'That I don't know. It might well have been.' She attempted

a smile that didn't quite come off. 'Can I have another gin please, Chris?'

He picked up her glass. 'I won't be a moment.'

'And another of your cigarettes. I don't have any with me.'

He lit that for her and then returned to the bar. No wonder she was so distraught. What a bombshell it must have been. Especially as she'd had no suspicions whatsoever. He tried to put himself in Maizie's place, and couldn't. Embarrassing, she'd said. Well, it was far more than that. Apart from anything else he suspected she must feel a proper fool.

'There you are,' he declared on rejoining her.

'Thanks, Chris.'

She'd stopped crying now, got a hold of herself. Well almost, inside she was heaving. 'We got on so well together last time he was home too,' she went on. 'He was a totally changed man. Being torpedoed must have done that. Given him a sense of his own mortality if nothing else.'

She smiled cynically.

'Now I understand why Rosemary went to stay with Alice when he was last with us. She didn't want a repeat of what had happened previously.'

'Will you divorce him?'

She frowned. 'On what grounds? I can hardly cite Rosemary. I simply couldn't do that to her. The maid was blameless, don't forget.'

'You could have him prosecuted if Rosemary agrees?' he suggested.

'Think of that, Chris. Appearing in court, saying she was raped. The publicity. Her life would be ruined. No, it's best to leave things as they are.'

'Will you confront him when he gets back next?'

Her eyes blazed. 'You're damned right I will. This is something I can't just ignore.'

'There's always me, Maiz,' he said softly.

She stared at him. 'How do you mean?'

'I think you know how I feel about you. We could try and make a go of it together as you English say.'

Maizie glanced away. 'Without getting divorced?'

'Why not? It's been done before.'

'Live in sin,' she mused. She couldn't imagine herself doing that.

'No one need know. I present you as my wife and that's that. Who's to guess we aren't married?'

Maizie didn't answer.

'You haven't said how you feel about me?'

'I . . . eh . . . I'm very fond of you, Chris,' she prevaricated. 'You must have realised that.'

'Is it my age? Being younger than you?'

She considered that. 'It does come into it I suppose. There is quite a difference.'

'I'll tell you something, Maizie. War matures men beyond their actual years. It certainly has me. I don't feel younger than you. Not at all. In fact in some ways I feel older. To me, anyway, the difference wouldn't matter.'

She hadn't been expecting this. She'd wanted a shoulder to cry on and instead she'd got a proposal. It needed careful thinking about. She could hardly be expected to make up her mind there and then.

'I don't know how I came to fall in love with you, Maizie. Or when. But I did.'

She gazed into his eyes and saw the truth of that.

'Well, say something?' he prompted.

'How can you love someone with a bum my size?' she suddenly blurted out.

He couldn't help laughing. What a thing for her to come out with. Typically female. 'I think it's lovely,' he said.

'No it's not. It's far too big. Enormous.'

'Hardly that,' he admonished. 'Besides, we French are known to like curvy women. All the ladies depicted in French paintings have large *derrières*. We consider it very sexy.'

'Well, the English don't,' she mumbled.

He took her hand and clasped it in both of his. 'It's you I'm in love with, Maizie. *You*. Which means all of you including your bottom.'

A tremendous sensation of warmth swept through her. Warmth and much more.

'Will you consider it?' he asked.

She nodded.

It had just gone midnight, Chris having said goodnight to Maizie about half an hour previously, when there was a knock on his bedroom door. He instantly knew who it was. It couldn't be anyone else.

Maizie's expression was a combination of guilt and sheepishness. 'I've run out of cigarettes,' she lied.

He ushered her inside. 'I've got plenty as long as you don't mind French.'

'That'll be fine.'

'I enjoyed tonight,' he said as he crossed to his suitcase. He was referring to the meal they'd had downstairs which had been a somewhat subdued affair, the earlier proposal not referred to.

'So did I.'

He found what he was looking for. 'One packet enough?'

'I only need a couple.'

'You'd better take the packet. Just in case you don't sleep.'

'But I can't,' she protested. 'Your French ones are so hard to come by.'

'A couple then,' he smiled.

'Thank you,' she said as he handed her two.

'Don't mention it.'

Maizie made no move to go.

'I'd offer you a drink but I haven't any.'

'That's all right,' she replied nervously. 'I've had enough for one day.'

Her personal scent was strong in his nostrils. He desperately wanted to reach out and touch her. Stroke her hair. Kiss her.

She dropped her gaze to stare at the floor. 'I didn't really come here for cigarettes,' she confessed in a small voice.

'I guessed that.'

'Can we just . . . cuddle? Be together but not do it.'

Now he did reach out and place a hand on her arm. 'If you wish, Maizie.'

'I've . . . I've never done anything like this before, Chris. I swear.'

'I know.'

'I was a virgin when I married Sam. He's the only man I've ever been with.'

'Well, there's one thing I can promise you, Maizie,' he said, hoping to lighten the mood a little.

'What's that?'

'I don't spank.'

She burst out laughing. 'Thank God for that!'

Somehow she was in his arms and they were kissing, the blood pounding in their veins.

'My bottom is still too big,' she whispered when the kiss was over.

'And I say it's not. Besides, bottoms are a matter of personal taste and I find yours most attractive.'

Her eyes glistened. 'Oh, Chris.'

He led her towards the bed.

It was a wonderland of many sensual delights he'd taken her

to. He'd done things to her she'd never dreamt men did to women. Things that had had her gasping with pleasure.

And all the while he'd been tender, as gentle as a mother with a new-born babe. His hands, mouth and tongue had been everywhere. She'd simply never known lovemaking could be like that.

She was positively glowing with satisfaction. Every fibre of her being was relaxed and replete. Beside her he lay fast asleep.

Maizie touched the curve of his buttock, a little shiver snaking through her. What had taken place between them had been a complete revelation.

It was as if she was truly alive for the first time ever. And how good a feeling that was. Better than anything she could have ever imagined.

French men had a reputation for being excellent lovers. Well, as far as she was concerned, it was all true. Compared to Sam ... She mentally shrugged. There just was no comparison.

Maizie sighed with contentment as a drowsiness settled over her. This was a night she'd never forget. A memorable night. A night of sheer and utter magic.

What abandonment he'd induced in her. At times she'd acted like a slut, and a greedy demanding one at that. Revelling in what they were doing together.

And he loved her. Christian loved her. Just as she loved him. A love she'd never admitted even to herself up until this moment.

'Oh, my darling. My sweet, sweet darling,' she whispered in the darkness.

For the second time that day she began to cry. Only now the tears were of pure joy.

It was their second visit of the morning to the hospital. On arrival earlier Sister had told them Mr Mallory was with

Rosemary giving her tests and could they please come back later. So here they were again.

Sister O'Hagan appeared and bustled towards them. 'If you'll come with me, Mr Mallory would like to speak to you privately in my office.'

Fear clutched at Maizie. That, despite the fact Sister was smiling, sounded ominous. 'Of course.' Chris took her by the arm as they followed Sister through the swing doors on to the ward.

Mallory was again perched on the edge of Sister's desk reading notes. 'Good news,' he beamed.

Profound relief flooded through Maizie to hear that.

'As far as I can ascertain, Rosemary hasn't suffered any brain damage. I've put her through a number of rigorous tests and all have proved satisfactory. She's a very lucky young lady indeed,' Mallory declared.

'Does that mean we can take her home?' Maizie asked quickly.

'I'd like to keep her in for further observation, just to be on the safe side. But hopefully I'd say she can leave here a week today. How's that?'

'Wonderful,' Maizie enthused.

'I'll put her through further tests and in the meantime she can certainly use the bed rest. She has been through a rather harrowing experience, after all. But all being well she'll be discharged on the day I specified.'

'I can't thank you enough, doctor,' Maizie said gratefully.

'I'll arrange for your local doctor to attend to her from now on. And I'll want her back at some point to ensure everything's as it should be.'

'I'll drive her home to Coverack in my car. That should make it easier for her,' Christian volunteered.

Mallory stared at Christian's uniform which he didn't recognise. 'Are you Mr Blackacre?'

'No, a friend of the family.'

'I see. Well, going home in a car will certainly be beneficial. Just take it carefully. The last thing Rosemary needs is to be jolted.'

He held up a hand when he saw Christian's expression. 'I'm not criticising your driving, but referring to the state of the roads that far down in Cornwall. They leave a lot to be desired.'

Christian nodded that he understood. Slow and careful it would be.

'Has Rosemary been told yet?' Maizie asked.

'I thought you might like to do that.'

'Oh, yes please.'

'Right then,' declared Mallory, sliding from the desk. 'I'd better get on.'

Rosemary was thrilled to bits when Maizie gave her the news.

'Are you ready?'

Maizie, dressed entirely in black, replied in the affirmative. She wasn't looking forward to this at all. For they were about to set off for the communal memorial service in the church.

Christian was wearing his uniform with the addition of a black armband. A pale-faced Bobby had on his best clothes with a black tie. Alice hadn't come in that morning and would be going directly from her cottage.

Bobby took Maizie's hand, wishing it was Emily's. She and her family, indeed the entire village, would also be there. Those who couldn't get a seat had been instructed to cluster round the front door and join in the service from there.

Maizie locked up before they started off down the street to the melancholy peal of a single church bell. From all directions folk were streaming towards the church to pay their last respects.

Chapter 25

'I wish you didn't have to go back to London tomorrow,' Maizie murmured lazily. They'd come for a picnic to the tiny secluded cove at the end of the tunnel where the Movement held its secret meetings. Maizie had suggested it because it was so secluded. The only way into the cove from land was the tunnel. They were surrounded on three sides by towering cliffs that overhung the cove. As long as they stayed relatively close to the tunnel entrance they were in no danger of being observed.

Not wishing to be seen leaving the village together, Christian had set out alone in his car with the picnic Maizie had packed in the boot. She'd followed a little later on foot. This subterfuge was to ensure that tongues wouldn't wag.

'So do I, Maiz. So do I,' Christian answered. He'd been on the phone to Hammond who'd informed him he had to do another stint in the R/T Section starting the following Monday.

Although it was now early September, the weather was still glorious, the sun cracking in a robin's egg blue sky, the temperature sweltering. They'd just finished eating and had drunk most of the two bottles of white wine Maizie had included in the hamper.

They were lying side by side on a tartan rug, soporific from plenty of food and the sun's sultry heat.

Christian turned on to his side to stare at Maizie, thinking how wonderful the nights had been since their first together in the Helston hotel.

'A penny for them?' she queried.

'I was just wondering if you'd ever been to London?'

'I haven't I'm afraid. I've always wanted to go but somehow never got round to it. In fact I've never even been outside Cornwall.' She laughed softly. 'I suppose that makes me a real country yokel.'

He frowned. 'Yokel?'

She explained the meaning of the word.

'Never, Maizie. You could never be a yokel. Why, you don't even speak like the others. The accent is there but you always use proper English and not dialect.'

'I can do, you know. But when I was at school one of my teachers came from Sussex and always insisted we use the King's English at all times. I suppose I just got used to doing so.'

'Why don't you come up and stay with me for a while? I could show you the sights.'

She laughed. 'Fat chance. I have the hotel to run, remember. I can hardly go swanning off to London and leave it.'

'You could for a few days if you really wanted.'

She was certainly tempted. The thought of a trip to London appealed very much indeed.

'Well?'

'I can't while Rosemary is still recuperating.'

'And afterwards, when she's fully recovered?'

'I'll see,' Maizie demurred.

'You'd love Chelsea. A lot of artistic people stay there. Writers, poets, painters and suchlike. Though I have to admit there's little evidence of artistic endeavour at the moment with the war on. But the atmosphere's unchanged. At least so I'm told.'

'Endeavour?' she teased. 'That's a big word for a foreigner to use.'

'Ah, but my vocabulary is expanding all the time due to my living here and constantly speaking the language.'

As always she felt so relaxed with him. It was going to be a wrench, even more so now that they were lovers, when he went away. Still, he'd promised to return as soon as he could. That was something to look forward to. The lonely nights in between would be another matter entirely.

'You haven't answered my question you know,' he said casually.

'About London?'

'No, about living in sin with me.'

She didn't answer.

'Maizie?'

'I'm still thinking about it,' she prevaricated.

'You'd adore France, especially Hennebont.'

She pushed herself up on to an elbow. 'So we'd go to France, would we?'

'It seems logical, don't you think? You would be Madame Le Gall, my wife.'

'And what about your parents?'

'I'd explain matters to them. They'd understand. After all, living in sin would only be a temporary arrangement. We'd apply for an English divorce, which could hardly be refused if we were living together, and then get married someplace else when that came through.'

She smiled. 'You've got it all worked out, haven't you?'

'We Bretons are very much like you Cornish, you know. In fact, historically speaking, many of us originally came from Cornwall. That's what Brittany means, little Britain. There are many differences between the two people, but many similarities too. It wouldn't take long for you to feel right at home there.'

'And what would I do in Hennebont?'

'Look after the house, cook, clean, and bring up babies.'

'Babies?'

'Naturally there would be those. Lots and lots I hope.'

Maizie took a deep breath. 'Sam and I have never had children. He had one who died by his previous marriage so the fault's not his. Perhaps I'm one of those unfortunate women who can't have any.'

Christian thought about that. 'I understand a little of these things. It might be that you and he aren't right to have them. That there isn't a fault with either of you, but together it simply doesn't happen. If that was the case then you might well conceive with another man. No?'

'It's possible I suppose.'

'And you'd wish to have children?'

'Oh yes,' she breathed. 'Very much so.'

'Then that's another argument for you coming with me.'

Maizie smiled. 'You're very persuasive, Chris. A real silver tongue. I do believe you could charm the birds down off the trees.'

'Silver-tongued maybe, Maizie, but sincere with it. I mean what I say.'

She knew he did. 'Tell me more about Hennebont.'

'Our summers are warmer than here, and longer. Often we sleep in the afternoons because of the heat. And the food! Ah, that is magnificent. There are many restaurants that I will take you to, *en famille* when the children come along.

'The houses are designed to be very cool inside because of the heat. Darkish you might think, but that's welcome during the summer months. The town itself is quite lively with lots of bars and other places of entertainment. The folk there are extremely friendly.'

It sounded idyllic, Maizie thought. Madame Le Gall? She smiled at the idea of that.

'We have an open market every Saturday which is a lot of fun,' Christian went on. 'You can buy all sorts of local produce there. Fish, cheese, fruit, clothes, you name it and you'll find it in the market. Maman goes every Saturday. At least she did before the Germans invaded.'

'I'd miss the Channel,' Maizie reflected out loud. 'I've always lived near open water.'

'We do have Le Blavet, the river. That can be most pleasant. And whenever you wished to see the sea I would drive you there. It's not too far, quite close actually.'

Maizie reached out and drained the wine left in her glass. 'And what would you do for a job?'

'I would have to finish my studies of course, but as I'm near the end that wouldn't take long. Then I would start a practice in Hennebont.'

She shook her head. 'You've given this a great deal of thought, haven't you?'

'A great deal, Maizie, believe me. And I can promise you, if you do agree to come with me, you'll never regret it. I swear that.'

She sucked in a breath as his hand came to rest on her naked thigh.

'Maizie?'

'What?'

'Have you ever made love out in the open?'

She quickly glanced away, her heart pounding. The question had caught her completely by surprise. 'No,' she whispered.

Christian was pleased to hear that. It was the perfect day for such an adventure, particularly if it was her first time.

'Sam would never do such a thing,' Maizie said huskily. 'He'd think it . . . well, I don't know what he'd think about it but he'd just never do it.'

Christian's hand travelled up her thigh to the hem of the swimsuit she was wearing. 'Why don't we do it right here and now. Would you like that?'

She dropped her head a little, her mind whirling. She was terribly aware of his hand and the pressure of it on her flesh. She could feel herself responding.

'I know I would,' he crooned.

His other hand caught hold of the zip at the back of her swimsuit and began to slowly tug it.

'Oh,' she exhaled as the entire front of the suit fell away exposing her breasts to the sun's caress.

Maizie knew they couldn't be seen, that they were entirely safe there. A delicious thrill ran through her.

'Stand up,' he instructed.

She did, closing her eyes as he eased the swimsuit to the ground. She felt completely exposed and vulnerable. It was intensely arousing.

Christian used a foot to flick away his trunks. He was all too obviously as aroused as she was.

'I love you, Maizie.'

'And I love you, Christian.'

'I want to be with you always.'

He kissed her deeply, his hands flitting all over her body.

'Lie down,' he instructed.

He took his time after that, teasing, caressing, probing, till finally she was begging him to enter her.

And then the angels started to sing.

Alice hastily gathered up her Tarot cards when she heard Maizie's distinctive footsteps. She'd been frowning at what she'd seen in them. Death still lurked.

Maizie breezed into the kitchen, a beatific smile on her face. 'Hello, Alice.'

'What's ee so happy about then, maid? It's fair oozing out of ee.'

'Oh?' Maizie replied casually. 'It's a beautiful day. Why shouldn't I be happy?'

Alice had earlier watched Maizie make up the picnic, a picnic that was clearly for two. Christian had driven off with it, and then shortly afterwards Maizie had announced she was going out. What did they think she was, a fool? And now here was Maizie back with a smug, self-satisfied smile plastered all over her face, the sort of smile Alice remembered only too well. In her case it might have been a long while, but she remembered it nonetheless. Ah well, it was none of her business. She knew her place. But Maizie had better be careful. Nothing went by unnoticed in a village, or precious little anyway. And if Sam got wind . . . That didn't bear thinking about.

'There was a telephone booking while ee was out,' Alice declared. 'A couple coming down from Birmingham next week.'

'That's good,' Maizie replied, only half taking in what Alice had said, still thinking about the cove and what had happened there. Her stomach rippled at the memory.

Maizie began humming as she busied herself with a sauce she had to prepare for that evening's menu, wishing she could have stayed at the cove with Christian for ever.

Alice put her cards away, a cold dread lingering from what she'd read in them.

'I've brought you a cup of tea,' Maizie announced as she entered Rosemary's bedroom.

Rosemary was sitting up in bed with a large pad of paper in front of her and a pencil in her hand.

'What are you up to then?'

'I thought I'd do a bit of sketching to pass the time. It gets awfully boring up here all by myself.'

'Sketching, eh? Let's have a look.'

The likeness to Bobby was amazing, Maizie thought. In fact the sketch was so lifelike she almost expected it to open its mouth and speak.

'What do you think?' Rosemary asked coyly.

'It's terrific. Where did you learn to sketch so well?'

'Oh, I don't know. I've been doing it off and on for ages now.'

'It's Bobby to a T. I'm impressed, truly I am.'

'I'll do one of you if you like?'

'Would you? That would be lovely.' Maizie took the pad from Rosemary and studied the sketch more closely. The likeness was uncanny. 'You've got talent, Rosemary.'

The girl blushed. 'Not really.'

'Well, I think you have. Do you always sketch portraits?'

'Usually. I have done a few landscapes and city scenes, but the portraits are better in my opinion. I also get more enjoyment doing them.'

She handed the pad back to Rosemary. 'Would you like that framed?'

Rosemary's expression was one of pure delight. 'Do you think it's that good?'

'I most certainly do.'

Rosemary stared hard at the portrait, then again at Maizie. 'Yes please, when it's finished.'

'Then framed it shall be. I'll put it in next time I go to Helston.'

Rosemary was a lot better, Maizie thought as she made her way back downstairs. Dr Renvoize was calling the following morning and she'd ask if Rosemary could now get up, at least for meals.

Who would have guessed the girl to be so talented? she mused. It just went to show you never really knew people.

*   *   *

'Are you awake?'

'Uh-huh.'

'I can't sleep either.'

All night long Maizie had been horribly aware of the bedside clock ticking away the time. They only had a few hours left together before Christian returned to London.

'I'll miss you,' he whispered.

'And I'll miss you.'

His groping hand found hers. 'You mean everything to me, Maizie. Honestly you do.'

Suddenly she wanted to cry, but managed not to. She couldn't bear the thought of his driving off and the lonely nights that were to follow.

'You will think on what I asked you?'

She knew he meant their going to France after the war.

'Of course I will.'

'I want so much for you to agree, Maizie. You and I are right for each other. As right as a man and woman can be.'

'Oh, Chris,' she choked.

He slipped an arm under her neck and drew her close. With the other hand he stroked her hair. 'My darling. *Chérie.*'

'Make love to me again, Chris. Who knows how long till the next time.'

Who knew indeed, he reflected bitterly. And what if they sent him back to France in the meanwhile?

What remained of the night passed all too quickly.

Maizie laid Rosemary's sketch pad on the bedside table and then began stripping the bed. Rosemary was downstairs gossiping with Alice in the kitchen.

The girl was coming on by leaps and bounds, Maizie thought with satisfaction. Dr Renvoize was terribly pleased with her and had declared only the previous day that she was almost as good as new. An appointment had been made to see Mr Mallory at the hospital in a week's time. Rosemary hoped he'd give her the go ahead to resume work.

Maizie kicked the dirty linen into a corner and placed fresh on the bed. It was then she had the idea of peeking into Rosemary's sketch book. Rosemary was in the middle of doing a portrait of her which so far the girl had refused to let her see. Naturally she was curious.

Picking up the pad again she began leafing through it, her expression one of total shock when she came to the fourth sheet.

Sam leered out at her, his face the very embodiment of evil. He had fangs and short horns sprouting from his temples. The eyes were hideous and bloodshot.

'Dear God,' Maizie whispered to herself. Was that how Rosemary saw her husband? Evidently so. It was horrible.

She quickly closed the pad and replaced it on the table. The poor girl, the poor, poor girl.

She could have wept for her.

'Hello, my lover.'

Maizie laughed at Christian's use of the Cornish expression. It sounded so completely wrong and false coming from him. 'Hello, Chris.'

'What are you laughing at?'

'You, you idiot. My lover indeed.'

Now he laughed into the telephone. 'How are things in Coverack?'

'Quiet.'

'And Rosemary, how's she?'

'Tip top. She's back at work, though I'm making her stick to light duties for the present. I don't want her overexerting herself. Just to be on the safe side.'

'I understand. I should have rung before but . . . Well I thought it best not to. It would only have made things even more difficult hearing your voice. You being there and me here that is.'

'Yes,' she agreed. She'd guessed why he hadn't been in touch.

'And Bobby, how's he?'

'Fine. Doing well at school.'

'Still seeing Emily?'

'Of course. The pair of them are thick as thieves.'

'And Alice?'

'The same. She never varies.'

'How's business?'

'Terrible. But it always is this time of year. You know that.'

Christian smiled to himself. 'Did you remember this is our anniversary?'

Maizie was baffled. 'What are you talking about?'

'It was two years ago today that we met. You gave me directions in the mist.'

She laughed. 'To be honest I'd forgotten. Is it really two years?'

'To the very day, Maiz. So happy anniversary.'

'And you, Chris.'

'Happy anniversary to us.'

She thought it ever so romantic that he'd not only remembered the exact date but had rung her on it. A warm glow filled her.

'So,' he went on. 'If business is as bad as you say why don't you come to London like we discussed?'

That threw her into temporary confusion. 'I can't.'

'Why not?'

'I just can't, Chris.'

'Do you mean you can't, or won't?'

Maizie heaved a sigh. This had really caught her on the hop.

'Maizie?'

'Can't, Chris. I've the hotel to run.'

'What's there to run with business like it is? Alice can take care of things for you. She's done so before.'

'But London . . .'

'Please, Maizie,' he interjected. 'I desperately want to see you.'

She thought to reverse the situation. 'Why don't you come here?'

'That's impossible. I'm unable to get away right now and I haven't any leave coming up in the foreseeable future. I'm afraid I'm stuck in London. But you're not stuck in Coverack.'

Suddenly she made up her mind. He was quite right, there was absolutely no reason why she couldn't go. 'OK,' she agreed. 'But only for a few days. I mustn't be away longer than that.'

His voice was jubilant. 'Good! You find out the times of the trains and I'll ring back night after next. I'll be there at Paddington to meet you.'

'You won't let me down, Chris? I don't know a soul in London apart from you. I'd be lost.'

Christian laughed. 'I'll be there, Maiz, don't you worry about that. I can't wait to see you again.'

'Or me you.'

'I love you, Maizie.'

'And I love you, Chris. With all my heart.'

They spoke for a few more minutes and then hung up. Maizie leant against the wall by the phone to gather her wits and generally compose herself.

Now what was she going to tell Alice and the children? Whatever she came up with, it couldn't be the truth.

Christian was fretting. The train was over an hour late and still no sign of it. He'd already been into the bar twice for a drink to pass the time. 'Oh come on,' he hissed through clenched teeth. He was in a fever of impatience to hold Maizie again. Just to be with her.

And then, as if by magic, there it was on the board. The train was due to arrive at any minute.

Maizie stepped down on to the platform, overawed by her surroundings. She'd never imagined a station could be so huge. And the masses of people; it was teeming!

'Maizie!'

She followed the sound of the shout and there was Christian hurrying towards her, his face alight with excitement.

He swept her into his arms, hugging her so tight he almost squeezed the breath out of her. 'At last,' he whispered.

She pulled her lips away when he attempted to kiss her. 'Not in public, Chris. Not in front of all these people.'

He chuckled. 'You're in London now, Maiz. No one would give a damn. To them we'd be just another couple in love. No more, no less.'

She glanced back up the platform, wondering if there was anyone on the train she might know. It wasn't impossible. Though there hadn't been anyone getting on board at Helston whom she'd recognised. Still, you couldn't be too careful.

Christian understood immediately when she voiced this concern. Taking her case he ushered her down the platform and out of the station to where his car was parked.

They did kiss as soon as they were inside, Maizie matching his passion.

Maizie gazed about her, thinking it was precisely as she'd expected a bachelor flat to be. 'It smells in here,' she announced. 'When did you last give it an airing?'

'Smells?' a puzzled Christian queried.

'It most certainly does.' And with that she crossed to the nearest window and threw it open. 'And talk about untidy,' she went on. 'This place is a tip.' She strode to the kitchen and went in. As she'd thought, there were dirty dishes piled in the sink while the top of the cooker was encrusted. 'I'll get started right away. The whole flat needs a proper clean.'

Christian caught her round the waist, delighting in the warm smell of her. 'You can do that later. Afterwards.'

'Afterwards?' she repeated, pretending she didn't know what he meant.

His hands went under her coat to her blouse which he started unbuttoning. 'First things first, Maiz, I want you so badly I'm almost bursting with it.'

She laughed throatily as her bra came loose. 'You are impatient.'

'Very.'

The truth was she felt the same. During the journey images of the pair of them together had kept flashing through her mind. In particular the day at the cove when they'd made love naked under the sun.

'You'd better show me your bedroom,' she commanded.

He took her hand, kissed her lightly on the lips, and propelled her out of the kitchen. 'Come to my boudoir.'

'Men don't have boudoirs,' she corrected him. 'Only women do.'

'Then call it what you like. It's where my bed is.'

Once inside the bedroom they became almost frantic, tearing each other's clothes off. There was nothing slow or subtle about what happened next, their immediate need was too great.

It was hours later when, both now satiated, Maizie positively glowing, they emerged from the flat to go for a drink and hopefully find something to eat.

*   *   *

After Christian had departed for work next morning Maizie set about cleaning the flat from top to bottom. When she finished that she decided to go for a walk along the King's Road. Christian had left her a key that had once belonged to Gilbert so that she could come and go as she pleased.

The shops she encountered were a wonderland to her, far superior to anything to be found in Helston. She was thankful she'd brought along her clothes rationing coupons.

Her first purchase was a two-piece slacks suit, or so the assistant called it. This was tailored in durable cotton suiting, the shirt long with a double yoked back. The slacks had cuff bottoms and a two-buttoned waistband and buttoned placket. The inside seams were pinked. Its colour was navy with white stripes.

Her second was a cream coloured culotte dress made of cotton seersucker, the under section having a zip closing. It was a one-piece style with a set-in belt.

The final item of clothing was a dress of snowy polka dots on rayon French-type crêpe accented by a sailor-style collar and contrast buttons. The shirred jacket waistline gave it a slim fitting line. The skirt had the popular three-gore panel. As she'd already chosen navy for the slacks suit she opted for what was described as luggage brown.

She found a darling South American style pair of shoes with a two and a half inch Cuban heel. There was a bow at the front of each shoe, which were fashioned in white crushed kid leather.

She couldn't wait to show all this to Chris when he got home and hoped he would approve. As it turned out Chris did and was full of praise and admiration for her new chicness.

The few days had turned into a full week, but now Maizie definitely had to return to Coverack. She'd had a wonderful time, thoroughly revelling in the experience.

As for their lovemaking, that had been memorable to say the least. They fell into bed at every possible opportunity.

But now the time to leave had finally arrived. They'd hardly spoken during the trip to Paddington, the occasional glances they gave one another more eloquent than words.

They'd found an empty compartment on the train and Chris had placed her case on the rack above the seat. He'd lowered the window for her so she could lean out, which was what she was now doing.

They stared at each other in silence, hearts heavy as stone. There was a glisten of tears in Maizie's eyes.

Christian looked round desperately when the guard blew his whistle, following that by waving his flag.

'Goodbye for now, Maizie.'

'Goodbye, Chris.'

'I love you.'

'And I love you.'

The train jolted into movement.

He blew her a kiss and she smiled.

'I'll come down as soon as I can.'

'I'll be waiting.'

He raised a hand in forlorn salute as the train slowly pulled away.

Maizie pulled up the window, secured it by its leather strap, and sat down. When she tried to light a cigarette her hands were shaking so badly it took her several attempts.

Chapter 26

'I'm going to work for the electricity people,' Bobby announced casually over breakfast.

Maizie looked down the table at him. 'What on earth makes you say that?'

'Mr Dunne told me I'm very practical and good with my hands. When I'm old enough he's promised to get me a job alongside him. I'm to be his apprentice.'

This was the first Maizie had heard of the idea. Bobby had become well in with the Dunne family and was forever over at their house – when Emily was not at the hotel. 'Would you enjoy that?'

'Oh yes. It would be terrific.'

Rosemary eyed him dyspeptically. 'And what about Plymouth? We'll be going back there one day.'

'Not me. I love Coverack and this is where I want to stay.' Adding hastily, 'If that's all right with you, Aunt Maiz?'

'Of course it is.' Truly it was, for she'd come to think of both children as her own. Nonetheless, there was their mother Shirley to consider. Or was there? She hadn't been heard of since leaving for Blackpool. Nor had she been located by the police when Bobby had gone missing. It would appear she and Christian had been right in surmising she'd abandoned Rosemary and Bobby.

'What about Mum?' Rosemary asked softly, voicing what had been going through Maizie's mind.

'She doesn't want us. You know that. Even if she did turn up I wouldn't go back with her. My life's here now.'

'An apprentice,' Maizie mused. 'You could do a lot worse than that.'

'The pay's good too,' Bobby enthused. 'I wouldn't get much to start with, but that would change when I was qualified. Mr Dunne has already showed me lots of things to do with electricity and how it works.'

Rosemary lowered her eyes, jealous of her brother. If things had been different she too might have stayed in Coverack. But they weren't different, the war would end one day and Sam Blackacre would come home. She shuddered inwardly at the thought. She'd be long gone before then. He'd never again put her through that awful ordeal.

'What qualifications will you need?' Maizie queried.

'Only those I get from school here. I'll also have to do one day a month at college in Helston. Mr Dunne says that can be easily arranged.'

'I suppose you're doing all this because of Emily,' Rosemary commented waspishly.

Bobby stuck out his chin. 'What if I am?'

'It just seems daft to me that's all. You're still a baby.'

'He's hardly that,' Maizie broke in. 'He's almost a young man.'

That delighted Bobby. 'See!' he declared triumphantly to his sister.

'Huh!'

'Anyway, don't start having a go at me just because you can't find yourself a boyfriend.'

Rosemary went pale.

'Enough of that, Bobby,' Maizie snapped, horribly aware of why Rosemary might not want one.

'Well, it's true.'

Rosemary carefully laid down her knife and fork, then rose. 'Excuse me,' she said, and walked in as dignified a manner as she could from the kitchen. Once outside she fled to her room.

'I didn't mean to upset her that much,' Bobby apologised to Maizie.

Maizie thought about going after Rosemary, but decided not to. That remark must have cut the maid to the quick. Maizie could only hope Sam hadn't put Rosemary off men for life.

She would have understood if he had.

Nineteen forty-three and still no end of the war in sight, Maizie reflected in despair. It was dragging on endlessly.

To cheer herself up she decided to tidy her chest of drawers. It was late at night, the hotel was closed and she wasn't tired in the least. She was also restless and moody, something she'd suffered a great deal from of late. She put it down to long winter nights and interminable grey skies during daylight.

She was on the third drawer when she came across the folder, recognising it immediately. It contained their wedding photographs.

She stared at it for ages before picking it up and flicking it open. The first photograph was just her and Sam, the pair of them looking radiantly happy.

Bastard, she thought. Adulterer and rapist. Bastard. What ill star had shone to cause her to marry such a man? Closing her eyes she recalled the ceremony, hearing again the words spoken.

Laying the folder, still open, on top of the chest she reached for her cigarettes and lit up. In her mind she was recalling Sam's last visit home, and how different it had been between them. That visit had really given her hope, hope that had been blasted to smithereens when Rosemary had spoken from her hospital bed.

She could never forgive him. Never. If it had simply been a fling with another woman then perhaps she could, given time. But to force himself on a maid Rosemary's age was completely beyond the pale. May his rotten soul burn in hell for evermore.

But what to do? That was the thing. The question had been haunting her all these months. What to do?

It should have been easy, but somehow wasn't. Nothing in life was ever black and white and this was certainly no exception. She couldn't stay in Coverack and divorce him; that would mean citing Rosemary which she had no intention of doing. To divorce Sam she'd have to go off with Christian, which she dearly wanted. Except that meant leaving Coverack and living in a foreign country.

There was one other option. Confront Sam, have it out with him and then carry on. Not as if nothing had happened, oh no, certainly not that. It would be a sham marriage from there on, in name only, for she'd never let him touch her again. She swore it. How could she possibly make love to a rapist and abuser of children? The very idea was repugnant in the extreme.

She could hear the vicar's words as she took her vows before God. In sickness and in health ... for better or worse ... There it was, her duty was to stand by him no matter what.

Maizie shook her head. Her heart was with Christian, there was no doubt about that, but her duty was with Sam.

Picking up the folder again she snapped it shut and threw it back into the drawer.

Her vows had been before God. Was she prepared to break them, no matter what the provocation?

Then it dawned on her she'd already done so by sleeping with Christian.

'I'm going out for a while, Alice,' Maizie announced.

'In this rain? You must be mad.'

Perhaps she was, Maizie reflected. There were times recently when it certainly seemed so.

'Where ee off to then?' Alice queried.

'I'm going to church.'

Alice stopped what she was doing and turned to stare at Maizie in amazement. ''Tis a Tuesday morning, what's ee going to church for?'

'To pray.'

'Pray!'

'Anything wrong with that?' Maizie answered defensively.

'No. Nothing at all. It just ain't like ee. I mean, ee might pray but I's never knowed ee go especially to church to do so. Not when there ain't no service taking place.'

'Well, I'm going anyway. The peace and quiet there is just what I need.'

'Suit yourself.'

Alice arched an eyebrow after Maizie had gone. This had to be tied up with Christian in some way, she correctly guessed. She'd have bet her life on it.

Now what exactly was going on?

It was the first decent day they'd had in Coverack for a fortnight. Maizie had decided to take advantage of it and go for a walk. She hadn't intended heading for the cove where she and Christian had made love; but that was where she ended up.

She lit a cigarette and stood staring out over the Channel, tortured by the ongoing problem she still hadn't resolved. It was all beginning to wear her down, really get to her. The previous night had been another disturbed one; she'd kept waking every few hours to toss and turn. Edgy, fidgety, tired and yet not tired.

Maizie sighed. Looking in the mirror that morning she'd been horrified to see the bags under her eyes. Blue puffy ones that aged her terribly.

If she left it would mean saying goodbye to the children whom she loved dearly and who'd come to rely on her. Coverack was their home now, she their mainstay and provider. To leave would be utterly selfish on her part.

But could she put up with years of Sam, seeing him day in and day out, knowing what he'd done? Hating him. Being his wife in name only?

She could well imagine what it would be like. How long before Sam started pestering her for sex? For pester he would. Sam Blackacre wasn't a man to go without. A new thought struck her which made her go ice cold inside. What if at some stage Sam lost control and raped *her*. What then?

And if he got away with raping her once he'd go on doing so. She'd fight of course but she was no match for Sam. He'd caused her physical pain in the past, so what would it be like under those circumstances? It wouldn't only be her bottom he hit. For there was a mean, vicious streak in Sam. God help her if it was directed towards her.

Nor would she be able to say anything. A man had his married rights after all, she wouldn't get any sympathy if it became known she was denying him his.

And again there was Rosemary. How could she make such a thing general knowledge without also giving her reasons for denying him?

Maizie swore. Then swore again. It was tearing her apart.

'What's up with ee, Maiz?'

Maizie glanced at Denzil in surprise. 'How do you mean?'

'Ee's been a misery all night. I even saw you snap at the maid which is most unlike ee.'

The maid referred to was Rosemary, and Maizie *had* snapped at her. Quite unfairly so.

'Has ee got something on your mind like? If so I'm a grand listener.'

Maizie smiled her gratitude. 'I have got something on my mind, Denzil, but it's nothing I want to talk about.'

'Private, eh?'

'Yes,' she agreed, handing him the pint of cider she'd been pouring.

'I've noticed it this while back along. You just ain't been yourself.'

Maizie reached across the bar and patted him on the hand. 'You're a good friend and I appreciate your concern.'

'Well, if ee changes your tune ee knows where to get in touch with me.'

'Thanks, Denzil.'

He picked up his glass and went to rejoin the other fisherman he was with.

Had it really become so noticeable? It must have done for Denzil to mention it. Well, she was just going to have to get a grip of herself. Hide her inner turmoil. Present a face to the world.

She had been bad tempered recently, she'd been aware of that. In the afternoon she'd given Alice a right old telling-off for a matter so inconsequential it should hardly even have been commented on. Alice had been hurt, though she hadn't said anything. The incident made Maizie ashamed now she thought about it.

Sam and Coverack, Christian and France. God or her heart.

She looked over at Denzil talking with his cronies, all men she knew and liked. That was another thing, if she left Coverack she'd be leaving all her friends behind. That in itself would be a horrendous wrench. People she'd known for years who, in a way, were part of an extended family.

But first things first. She'd go and find Rosemary and apologise for snapping. There had been absolutely no need for that.

'Come in!'

'Captain Le Gall reporting as instructed, sir.'

Colonel G was sitting behind his desk, Major Hammond standing alongside. Christian was hoping this was going to be another assignment. He was tired of R/T Section and wanted to see action again.

'At ease. Take a seat. Smoke if you wish to.'

'Thank you, sir.'

Christian sat and lit up, Colonel G producing a battered old briar and doing likewise. The latter puffed contentedly for a few moments before going on.

'As you've probably guessed, Le Gall, I have a mission for you.' He glanced at Major Hammond and smiled. 'One that's literally right up your street.'

Major Hammond laughed. 'Very good, sir.'

Colonel G focused on Christian through a haze of blue smoke. 'Let's start at the beginning. Gerry has devised a revolutionary new fighter plane which, if it lives up to expectations, and there's every reason to believe it shall, will knock anything we've got clean out of the skies. What do you make of that?'

'Revolutionary in what way, sir?'

'It's powered by rocket.'

'Rocket!' Christian exclaimed, eyes wide.

'We've been working on the same thing but haven't had any luck so far. It appears the Nazis have. The prototype has already been tested in eastern Germany and now they're making certain modifications before going into full production.'

Colonel G's eyes slitted. 'It's possible this plane could swing the whole balance of the war. It could certainly prolong it if nothing else, which would mean even more lives lost.'

Christian digested that. A rocket plane on the German side was a terrifying prospect.

'Most of the plane is being built in Germany itself, with several exceptions. One is the gyroscope which is an integral and necessary part of the system. In other words, the gyroscope is so important the damn plane can't fly without it.'

'I see, sir,' Christian murmured.

'A factory in France has been taken over to produce this gyroscope. Why in France the reasons aren't clear. But the factory has been commandeered nevertheless. It's the only place where this gyroscope is being made.'

Colonel G paused to puff on his pipe. 'Now, Captain, if this factory was to be destroyed it would put production behind by many months, possibly even years.'

Christian nodded. 'I understand, sir.'

'That's why we want you to go over there and blow the damn thing up.'

Christian was puzzled. 'You mentioned it was right up my street, sir? Any SOE operative could do that job. It's hardly a specialist one.'

'Agreed, Captain. But why you're particularly qualified is because you know the factory and locale. I presume you've been inside the place many times, are familiar with the layout, et cetera, et cetera.'

'Where exactly is this factory, Colonel?' Christian asked slowly.

'Why, Hennebont of course. It's your father's.'

Bobby ran into the kitchen where Rosemary and Alice

were working. 'Christian's arriving tomorrow,' he declared excitedly. 'Aunt Maiz just told me.'

Maizie followed him in. 'That was Christian on the phone. He's been given a week's leave and will be spending it with us.'

'How lovely,' Alice replied, watching Maizie's face closely. What she saw there was a mixture of emotions.

'Will you prepare the room he usually has, Rosemary,' Maizie instructed. 'You'll have to make up the bed as it's stripped down.'

'Do you want me to go on up now, Aunt Maiz?'

'No, later'll be fine. After you've finished doing that.'

'Wait till he hears how well my French is coming along,' Bobby enthused. 'He's in for a surprise.'

Maizie smiled indulgently. Bobby was doing extremely well in that subject according to his last report.

This turn of events had caught her on the hop, for she hadn't yet made her decision.

She knew the next week was going to be a difficult one.

It was just after midnight when Maizie slipped into Christian's bedroom. He was lying wide awake with the side light on. 'Hello,' he smiled.

She padded over and sat on the edge of the bed. 'Hello.'

'I wasn't sure you'd be coming.'

'Oh?'

'You've been a bit . . . shall I say standoffish since I got here. Has something happened?'

Maizie shook her head. 'Nothing's happened. And I didn't mean to be standoffish.' The latter was a lie.

'That's good then.' He took her hand, raised it to his lips and kissed it. 'I've missed you so much, Maizie.'

Up until that point she had not known whether or not she'd sleep with him; now she did. Her body ached for his.

'Take those off and get in beside me.'

She stood, shrugged free of her dressing gown, her night-dress quickly joining it on the floor. 'This what you want?' she teased.

'Oh yes.'

She blanked everything else out of her mind. All that mattered was that Christian was here, the pair of them alone.

And that they loved one another.

He came awake to find a fully dressed Maizie placing a cup and saucer on his bedside table. 'Your coffee,' she smiled.

'You're up early.'

'Not really. At my usual time. Besides, I have to be careful, don't forget. I don't want either of the children to know I spent the night with you.'

He grunted as he pushed up on to an elbow. 'How are you?'

'Absolutely fine. Quite buzzing actually.'

'Buzzing?'

She raised an eyebrow. 'That was quite a session we had. I feel on top of the world.'

He laughed. 'I understand.'

'And you?'

'No complaints. None at all.'

Maizie's expression became mock stern. 'You committed a terrible sin during the night.'

That surprised Christian. He couldn't think what. 'Did I?'

'You snored. Very loudly too.'

'I'm sorry.'

'And so you should be,' she teased.

'Anyway, you're hardly one to talk. You snore too.'

'I do not!'

Now he was teasing. 'Oh yes you do. I first noticed it

that night in Plymouth at Bobby's house. Like a little pig snuffling around for food.'

'Pig!' She was outraged.

He imitated a pig snuffling. 'But I don't mind. It's very appealing. Quite attractive really.'

'I do not snore, Christian Le Gall.'

'But you do, Maizie Blackacre. So you can hardly criticise me for doing the same.'

They both laughed. 'It's wonderful having you back, Chris,' she suddenly stated quietly. 'You don't know how much.'

'I'm sure it's no more wonderful than it is for me to be here.'

They stared at one another.

'I love you, Maizie.'

'And I you, Chris. Now I must be getting on. It's time to give Rosemary a knock.'

At the door she hesitated. 'Do I really snore?'

He nodded.

'Bastard,' she riposted. But her eyes were twinkling.

He wouldn't tell her about France till he was due to return to London, not wanting to spoil the week for her. She'd only worry. He had considered not telling her at all, then decided that wouldn't be fair in case the worst occurred while he was over there. So just before leaving it would be.

In the meanwhile . . . He smiled broadly at the prospect.

Maizie hadn't laughed so much in a long time. Her sides were positively sore from it. The four of them were having supper when Christian had started telling jokes, ones he'd heard in the R/T Section where usually a new joke went the rounds every day. Because the children were present he was being careful only to tell clean ones.

'Stop it, Chris. Stop it!' Maizie protested, holding up a hand. 'Any more and I'll be ill.'

He grinned, delighted to see her enjoying herself like this. 'Are you sure?'

'Oh yes,' she gasped.

'I want to hear more,' Bobby pouted.

Christian winked at him. 'Later. How's that?'

'You won't forget?'

'I won't forget,' Christian declared solemnly. 'I promise.'

'You're very good at telling jokes,' Rosemary commented.

'Why, thank you.'

She'd been somewhat morose before they'd sat down, but she had now perked up considerably.

Maizie gazed at Christian in open admiration. What fun he was. A complete joy to be with. She could easily imagine spending the rest of her life with him. It would be no hardship at all.

'Where do you hear them all?' Rosemary queried.

'At work. My colleagues are forever coming out with them.'

'You mean in the army?'

'That's right.' Well that was only half a lie. Many of his colleagues were in the Services, albeit others were civilians.

'Now who's for sweet?' Maizie queried, rising to her feet. 'It's ice cream and jelly.'

'Yes please!' Bobby and Rosemary chorused in unison.

As Maizie moved away from the table all Christian could think about was later that night when she joined him in bed.

If anything their lovemaking just got better and better. He would not have thought that possible considering how good it had been before. But it did.

It was a mild day for winter, the temperature unseasonably

warm. There had been a wind earlier but that had now died right away. Christian stared out over the Channel from a position on the quay, thinking how tranquil it looked.

He still couldn't believe he'd soon be home in Hennebont, seeing his mother and father again, back in the house where he'd been brought up. A shiver of anticipation ran through him.

What a shock it had been when Colonel G had announced it was his father's factory he was to destroy. He couldn't imagine what Philippe's reaction was going to be. Horror most likely. His father was a realist however, and would understand why it had to be done. After all, what were lives compared to bricks and mortar? The factory could always be rebuilt after the war. But a single life lost was gone for ever.

Christian took a deep breath, enjoying the salt tang stinging his nostrils. Tomorrow was his last full day in Coverack, when he'd inform Maizie about France. Sometime in the afternoon was probably about right, he decided.

Closing his eyes he pictured images of his mother and father as he'd last seen them and a surge of emotion swelled through him. Had they changed at all? Bound to have done under an occupation.

And Hennebont, what about it? Times past and images of familiar scenes tumbled through his mind bringing a warm glow of contentment.

Maman and Papa.

Rosemary flinched when Christian's hand accidentally brushed hers. The glance she shot him was one of anger and loathing.

'Sorry,' he instantly apologised. 'How clumsy of me.'

'That's all right,' Rosemary forced herself to say. Without realising she was doing so she rubbed the part of her hand where it had been touched as though wiping clean the point of contact.

Christian stared after Rosemary as she hurried off about her duties. If Rosemary didn't come to terms with what had happened then her life, where men were concerned, was ruined.

Sam Blackacre had a lot to answer for. A lot to answer for indeed.

'That's that then,' Maizie declared, locking the front door after seeing out the last customer. She turned to Christian at the bar, dreading what was to follow.

'Would you like a nightcap?' she asked.

He was impatient to go upstairs. 'Only if you're having one.'

'I am.'

'Then I will.'

'Go over to the fire and I'll join you there.'

He settled himself into an easy chair and lit up. Moments later Maizie had handed him a glass of brandy and sat facing him.

'To us!' he toasted.

Maizie half raised her drink, then dropped it down again. 'Christian, I want to talk.'

'What about?'

'Us.'

His expression became expectant. 'You've decided?'

She nodded.

'And?'

Maizie took a deep breath. God, but she was hating this. 'I've been thinking all day about something my mother once said to me. And that was, you can't have everything you want in life. It simply doesn't work out that way.'

His heart sank. 'Go on, Maiz.'

'I won't leave Sam or Coverack, Christian. I'm sorry.'

He was stunned. 'But why? I thought you loved me?'

'I do, Christian. Believe me, I do. But there's a lot more to this than just you and I.'

'Like what?' he queried harshly.

She recited all the reasons she'd gone over a hundred times in her mind. Her vows, for better or worse. Vows made in the eyes of God. The children, Coverack itself and the surrounding area of the Lizard – all she'd ever known – her many friends.

As he listened Christian could hear the finality and determination in her voice. No argument on his part would sway her otherwise. He'd lost.

'I see,' he murmured when she finished.

'I know I'm doing the right thing. I just know it. And I'm sorry for hurting you. But don't forget, I'm just as hurt. I suppose it all boils down to a sense of responsibility. At least that's how I see it.'

There was no need to tell her about France now, he thought. That would be pointless. It was over between them. This time when he drove out of Coverack it *would* be for good.

'Christian?'

He laid the remainder of his drink on the table and got to his feet. 'It's best I go on up. See you in the morning.' And with that he strode away.

Maizie didn't see Christian in the morning. When she came down she found a letter waiting for her saying he'd gone early and thank you for everything. He'd always remember her. He enclosed money for his stay along with the single sheet of paper.

Maizie didn't know how she got through the rest of the day.

Chapter 27

'Who's there?' a suspicious and anxious Philippe Le Gall demanded in response to an insistent tapping on the front door. It was well past curfew.

'It's me, Papa. Christian.'

Philippe shot a startled backward glance at his hovering wife, and then swiftly twisted the key already in the lock. Christian, boasting a different hairstyle, newly grown moustache and wearing plain-lens glasses, the combination an effective elementary disguise, slipped silently inside while Philippe hastily relocked the door.

'My God,' Philippe breathed, eyes shining. 'It really is you.' Both men fell into each other's arms.

Then it was Delphine's turn, tears in her eyes, as Christian hugged her tight. 'It's a miracle. A miracle,' she whispered.

'Why are you here?' Philippe queried, mind racing. If the Boche were to find out they'd all be shot.

'In a moment, Papa. Can we sit down first.'

'Of course.'

Christian shrugged out of his rucksack and took it with him through to the kitchen where he placed it out of the way against a wall. He looked round the room, a thousand memories flying through his mind.

Delphine was in a daze. The last thing she, or Philippe, had expected was this, the answer to all her prayers. She commented on his appearance which he explained, then asked, 'Are you hungry?'

Christian shook his head, a little shocked at how old his parents had grown. His father's hair was now completely white where there had only been traces of grey before. His mother was smaller somehow, and stooped. 'Do you have any coffee?'

'I'll get you some,' Delphine replied instantly. 'And wine, we will have wine.'

Christian laughed. 'It's so good to be back. In this house. I've missed the pair of you and it so very much.'

'Come, sit down and tell us everything,' Philippe instructed.

Christian slumped on to a chair by the table while Delphine fussed at the stove. Philippe had opened a cupboard to produce a bottle of red wine.

'There,' said Philippe, placing a glass in front of Christian. 'Drink up.'

The wine, the local vintage, brought back memories of long and lazy family mealtimes. 'This is good!' Christian sighed appreciatively. 'I've been existing on inferior brandy and warm beer in England.'

'Ah!' Philippe exclaimed. 'So is that where you've been? England?'

'Yes, Papa. I escaped there from Dunkirk with many other French soldiers. And that's where I've been ever since.'

Philippe's face clouded. 'We knew nothing, whether you were alive or dead. Your maman . . .' He trailed off.

'I couldn't get in touch, Papa. It was impossible.'

'I understand. It's just been such a worry. Have the English treated you well?'

'Yes, Papa. I have made good friends there.'

Philippe nodded.

'Coffee,' Delphine stated, voice quavering slightly as she laid a large white cup and saucer before Christian.

Philippe had taken out a packet of Gitanes. 'Here, have one of these.'

Christian put his own cigarettes away and then lit up, closing his eyes in enjoyment, savouring the oh so familiar taste.

Delphine brought over two more cups of coffee and joined the men at the table. Her eyes were fastened on Christian. Pray God this wasn't some dream from which she'd wake at any moment. It certainly seemed real enough.

Christian exclaimed at his first sip of coffee. 'It's real! Just as I remembered.'

'We can still get real coffee and other things if you know the right people and have enough money,' Philippe informed him. 'And I qualify on both counts.'

Christian placed a hand over Delphine's, but said nothing. The gesture itself was self explanatory.

'Now how did you get here and why?' Philippe demanded.

'I parachuted in from an RAF plane,' Christian explained. 'Another will pick me up again when I wish to leave.'

Philippe nodded. 'That was dangerous. The whole area is crawling with Boche. They're everywhere, poking, prying.' He barked out a laugh. 'I sometimes think they'd look up your arse if they thought about it.'

That made Christian smile. 'I did see quite a few on entering the town. But knowing Hennebont as I do it was relatively easy to make my way without being caught.'

'It was still dangerous.'

Christian shrugged. 'Everything in war is that, it seems. It was a risk that had to be taken.'

Philippe glanced at Delphine, then back at Christian. 'And the reason for that risk? I presume you're not here simply to pay us a visit.'

'Hardly, Papa,' Christian replied softly. 'I'm here to destroy the factory. Your factory.'

Philippe's eyes went wide. 'You're what!' he exploded, aghast.

'You heard me, Papa. I'm here to destroy your factory.'

Philippe swore vehemently, and thumped the table with a fist, making the glasses and crockery jump. 'I won't allow it, you hear! I won't allow you to do that.'

'It will save many lives, Papa. French as well as Allied.'

Philippe drew heavily on his cigarette, telling himself to calm down a little. 'How so?'

'First of all, are you still in charge?'

'I am. With most of my original workforce under me. We're supervised by German engineers of course. I can't even fart without their permission.'

'I see. Now what about keys, do you still have those?'

Philippe nodded. 'As do the Germans.'

'Another thing, are there guards present during the night? Or watchmen?'

Philippe shook his head. 'I've often wondered why not. Probably because there is a guard post about fifty metres away from the main entrance. They patrol the streets every hour.'

'At exactly the same time?'

'Always.'

Christian smiled inwardly. That was German efficiency for you. It helped a great deal when matters were predictable. This was going to be easier than he'd thought.

'Do you know what you're producing?' he asked.

'Gyroscopes. The Germans arrived at the factory one day, said they were commandeering it, and replaced a couple of the machines and adapted the others. Within a month we were turning out these gyroscopes which have been modified again and again since the originals.'

'It's the gyroscopes that are important, Papa. You see, they're an integral part of a system the Germans have developed for a new fighter plane, one that's powered by rocket.'

Philippe whistled. 'Rocket! I had no idea. Is such a thing possible?'

'Apparently so. The British have been trying to do the same but the Germans have beaten them to it. The British believe that once these rocket planes become operational they'll be able to knock their existing planes right out the sky. That would prolong the war and swing the outcome in favour of Germany.' He paused. 'Your factory is the only known one making these gyroscopes, without which the rocket planes can't function. Destroy the factory and its machinery and you ultimately destroy the planes. At least for the time being.'

Philippe poured more wine. 'The only factory?'

'To our knowledge. Why they chose to make the gyroscope in France, and in your factory in particular, is unknown to us.'

'Probably because of the existing machinery we had,' Philippe said slowly. 'We are, or were, specialists in our field. We had new machines, and any adaptation of the old ones was minimal.'

'That would explain it then.'

His factory destroyed! Philippe was finding it hard to take that on board. And with his agreement, that would be the most incredible aspect. The factory was part of his life; after Delphine and Christian, the most important. So much of himself was invested in it. Why, losing the factory would be like having an arm or leg cut off. Worse. But lose it he must. For France. That's how he must think about it. For France. The sacrifice would be for his beloved country.

'So, how do you plan to go about this?' he asked.

'Why, Maman, it's just as I left it!' Christian exclaimed in delight. They were in his old bedroom where he'd spend the night.

'That's how your papa and I wanted it. In case you returned one day, which is precisely what's happened. And here you are.'

His childhood was in this room, Christian thought. There were the model cars he'd once collected. The kite he used to fly propped in a corner. He'd literally walked through a doorway into the past.

'How long do you think you'll be with us?' Delphine casually inquired.

'No more than a few days. After I've carried out my orders I'll leave Hennebont straight away and hide in the country. I thought I might stay with Aunt Sophie for a bit. Her farmhouse is well out the way, remote almost. I imagine I'd be safe there.'

'But why not return to us?' Delphine protested.

Christian sat on the edge of his bed and indicated his mother should do likewise. 'I'm going to try to do this so that it appears to have been an accident. An electrical fault, that sort of thing. I certainly don't want it to appear as sabotage. If the Germans thought that, who knows what reprisals they might take. It stands to reason that you and Papa would be the first to fall under suspicion, the workforce next.' Christian thought of the stories he'd been told of other reprisals the Germans had carried out. Only a few months previously they'd lined up thirty French people picked at random, including some children, and shot the lot. He couldn't, wouldn't, risk the same sort of thing happening in Hennebont.

'I understand,' Delphine nodded.

'Good. Once I leave that night you must ensure there's no trace of my having been here. Is that clear?'

'Perfectly, Christian.'

He smiled and took her into his arms.

'Are you sure the RAF will pick you up again?'

'Don't worry about that, Maman. I have a wireless with me to contact them and make the arrangements. I concealed it outside town as I didn't want to bring it in with me. Now what about Aunt Sophie, will she agree?'

'I'll visit her tomorrow and explain the situation. She'll agree all right. I have no doubts about that. Sophie is a patriot.'

Delphine reached up and gently touched his cheek. 'My baby. How much I've thought about you since you went away. Every single day without fail.'

She rose and wiped her nose with a tiny lace handkerchief. 'I'll leave you to get some sleep. Do you want waking in the morning?'

'Not too early. But not too late either.'

She smiled. 'Are you still awful to get out of bed?'

He matched her smile. 'No, Maman. The army cured me of that.'

'I'll bring you coffee like I used to.'

'Goodnight, Maman.'

'Goodnight, son. Welcome home.'

Philippe reached out under the bedclothes and grasped Delphine's hand. 'Quite an evening, eh?'

There was no reply.

'Are you crying?'

'No.'

He squeezed her hand. 'Our boy is back and safe. Nothing else matters.'

'Nothing,' she agreed.

'I think he looks well.'

Again she didn't reply.

'Don't you?'

'Yes, Philippe, he does.'

'It will be a dreadful thing to lose the factory. But I suppose one must put these things into perspective. It's the only way.'

'It has meant so much to you,' she sympathised.

He certainly couldn't disagree with that. 'I'll rebuild it after the war. That's a promise I made myself as I was getting undressed.'

She was pleased to hear that. It would give him hope, a goal to aim for during the long months, and maybe years, that lay ahead under the occupation. Everything would be fine just as long as Christian survived unscathed. That was all that truly counted. That he survived all this.

Philippe began to hum *La Marseillaise*, smiling in the darkness.

Early the following afternoon Christian decided to do an exterior recce of the factory, to refresh his memory and to see if anything had been altered. He also wanted a good look at the guard post his father had mentioned.

Philippe had been right in saying there were Germans everywhere. He couldn't even begin to guess how many were billeted in the town. At one point a German staff car went by, the officer, about his own age, sitting in the rear. Because the car was open topped he was able to get a good look at the man who, to him anyway, appeared to typify Germans as a whole.

Arrogance oozed out of him, that and superiority. He boasted a duelling scar on his cheek which did nothing for his blubbery-lipped appearance. He was smoking a cigarette using a hand encased in a black leather glove.

Bastard, Christian thought to himself as the car moved off down the street.

The factory was exactly as he remembered it. No change

there. The guard post was closer to the main entrance than the fifty metres his father had said. He walked past the post, scrutinising it closely without appearing to do so.

He wasn't too worried about being stopped and asked for his papers. The British had provided him with an immaculate forgery which declared him to be Jean-Marc Aupied, employed by the town cleansing department. The forgery was so good it appeared as though it had been in someone's pocket for years.

He was surprised when a tank rattled into view, followed by another and another. Clattering and clanging they veered off to the right, ten in all, one after the other. He wondered why there were so many of them.

His biggest worry was running into someone he knew. Twice he spotted a familiar face and hastily changed direction to get away from the person. One was a neighbour, the second the daughter of a family friend.

It distressed him to see how dispirited and downtrodden the people looked. But then what did he expect in the circumstances?

In the Place Marechal Foch he paused to stare at the Nazi flag flying over the mayor's building. His face was expressionless but inside he was raging to see it there. A number of German officers came striding down the mayor's steps as he watched, as arrogant and full of themselves as the young man in the staff car. The word he uttered under his breath was a lot stronger than bastards.

Sickened, he decided he'd had enough and would return home. But before he did there was one place he wanted to go, the nearby cathedral. The Basilique Notre-Dame de Paradis was a haven of peace and tranquillity, and it was as if all his cares and worries dropped from his shoulders the moment he stepped into its cool interior.

A quick glance round assured him he was alone. It would

have been dreadful if there had been Germans present. He dipped his fingers into holy water, bent his knee and made the sign of the cross. Then he went over to where the votive candles were, some white, some red.

He lit two of the more expensive ones, said a brief prayer then retired to a pew behind which he got down on his knees to pray further.

When he'd finished he opened his eyes again but stayed where he was for a short period of reflection.

There, in the silence of God's house, under the gaze of the Virgin Mary, with many candles flickering before the altar, all he could think about was Maizie and Coverack.

'There,' Philippe declared, laying down his pencil. 'That's the interior of the factory as it's laid out at the moment.'

Christian had been studying the drawing as it progressed, occasionally asking a question for clarification. 'Thank you, Papa.'

'This is the location of the main junction box you inquired about. The entire building's electricity is supplied through that.'

Christian nodded.

Philippe picked up his pencil again. 'Here, here, here and here are combustibles.'

'Chemicals?'

'This one is and this one. The others are flammable materials that'll be easy to ignite.'

Again Christian nodded.

'Now I have a suggestion to make?'

Christian eyed his father. 'Go on.'

'You intend entering and leaving by the main door, correct?'

'That's right.'

'Which is risky.'

'Not if the guards are as regular as you say.'

'Risky nonetheless. Any German soldier might just happen along, purely by chance, and that'll be the end of it.'

'True,' Christian agreed.

'Well, I have a far better, and safer, idea. It came to me this afternoon when I was in the storeroom. There's a window there that even I had more or less forgotten about. It's certainly never used. At present it's hidden by crates.'

'A window?' Christian frowned.

'Only a small one, and extremely filthy as I doubt it's been cleaned in years. In fact it's so dirty you'd hardly even notice it even if it wasn't behind crates.'

'You say small. How small?'

'You can get through it. And it'll open. I worried it might not after all this time so I tried it, I had a bit of trouble but it did open in the end.'

'And that's accessible from the rear?'

'Better still, a little cul-de-sac that runs off the alley at the back. It couldn't be better.'

Christian beamed at his father. 'You're right, this is far safer than going in the front.'

'I've locked the window again for now but I'll unlock it before leaving work the night you intend breaking in.'

Christian passed his father a Gitanes. 'Thanks, Papa. You're a genius.'

Philippe laughed. 'Hardly that. Just trying to be of help.'

Christian knew it was stupid to go out and about when it was unnecessary but who knew when he'd return to Hennebont. If ever? For that was always a possibility. He might not come through the war.

It was lunchtime; more people than usual were on the streets. He considered going in somewhere for lunch himself then decided against that. He'd eat at home with his parents. Why heighten the foolhardiness he was already indulging in?

And then he saw her. He stopped short in surprise. There was no mistaking it was Marie Thérèse. He quickly turned to face a window when she began walking in his direction on the opposite side of the street.

Her reflection was quite clear in the window. He noted that, like Philippe and Delphine, she too had changed. Where was the chic young woman of yesteryear? Gone it would seem. Her clothes were dowdy, her beautiful dark hair pulled back and tied with something or other. A sideways glance confirmed that her complexion had become sallow and slightly mottled.

Oh, Marie Thérèse, he thought sadly. So this is what war has done to you. She'd become as defeated and downtrodden as the rest of the townsfolk. Where was the sparkle he recalled, the bounce in her step, that radiant face? She too had grown older than her years.

He wanted to cross the road and say hello, take her for coffee, hear all that had happened to her. But of course that was impossible. She mustn't know he was back in Hennebont. That would only lead to questions he couldn't answer.

It was silly, but he decided to follow her, see where she was going. As he resumed walking, now in the direction she was taking but staying on his side of the street, his mind was filled with memories, particularly of the last time they'd made love.

Was it really only a few years ago? It seemed an eternity. So much had happened in between. He certainly wasn't the same person she'd known. He was far more mature, far more experienced in life. He wondered if they would have anything left in common or would they both be so changed as to be almost strangers to one another?

He soon realised they were heading for the river, unless

she intended stopping somewhere *en route* along the way. She didn't, and shortly she was standing on the bank of Le Blavet staring out over it.

Marie Thérèse. He'd often thought about her, wondering where she was, what she was doing. And now there she was, just as out of reach as when he'd been in England.

He wondered if she had a lover. And if so was it someone he knew? Why, she might even be married with a family. He doubted the latter, she simply didn't look married. There again, what did a married person look like?

She lit a cigarette and then crossed to a bench and sat, continuing to stare out over the river. What was she thinking about? Work? Domestic problems? Her lover?

He suddenly had the insane idea he could trust her. He'd be gone by morning so why not have just a few words?

No, he rebuked himself. What if, for some reason, she was questioned? Nothing was impossible after all. It might be a million to one chance but it could happen. If he revealed himself then there was a clear connection with his parents and who knew what that could lead to. It was just too risky.

He was pleased he'd seen her, even if they hadn't been able to speak. He could only wish her well.

He smiled in memory. Then, turning, he quickly retraced his steps.

It was a moonless, starless night. Perfect for his mission. Christian located the window without any trouble and eased it open. He paused for a few moments to listen, but heard only welcome silence. He swiftly clambered inside having pushed his rucksack through before him.

There was no need to rush, he reminded himself. He could take as long as he wanted or needed. He snapped on his torch and glanced about.

He couldn't recall the last time he'd been in the storeroom, or indeed if he ever had. No matter, he now had a clear picture of it in his head, and where everything was, thanks to Philippe's drawing.

He padded towards the door that would take him into the main shop floor where the electrical junction box was located. That was his first port of call.

'Have you finished tidying?'

Delphine nodded. 'If the Boche do search they won't find anything to tell them Christian has been here. I'm certain of that.'

Philippe let out a sigh of relief.

'I could use a glass of wine. Something to steady my nerves.'

He knew exactly what she meant. He too was jittery, to put it mildly. 'I'll get us both one.'

Delphine glanced at the wall clock, wondering if Christian was in the factory yet, wondering . . . God but this was awful. There wouldn't be a wink of sleep for her that night. How could there be with Christian in danger?

Philippe reappeared with two glasses of pastis. 'Here, try this instead,' he said, handing her one, wishing it had been brandy or cognac. But they had neither of these, or any other spirit, in the house.

'We must carry on as we'd do normally,' Philippe counselled. 'Nothing must be different or unusual.'

'Of course.' Her lips thinned. 'I'm so scared, Philippe. Not for myself but for Christian. If they catch him they'll—' She broke off and shuddered, unable to say the word torture. Naturally the Gestapo were present in Hennebont, and it was they who'd deal with him should he be taken alive.

Philippe ignored that, not wanting to think about it. 'It's ironic,' he mused. 'I've worked so hard to build up my business and now here I am actively helping to destroy it. It makes me want to laugh.'

'There's nothing funny about it,' Delphine replied slightly crossly. 'It's a sacrifice that has to be made. I'd give up ten businesses, more, just as long as Christian's safe.'

He swallowed his pastis, then took her into his arms. 'You're right, I wasn't saying otherwise. Only that life has a habit of throwing nasty surprises at you.'

The wall clock chimed the hour, making them both start. 'It's going to be a long night,' Philippe stated softly.

One more to go and he was finished, Christian thought with satisfaction. The amounts of *plastique* he was using were tiny compared to what he would have used if he'd intended blowing the place sky high. These would cause small fires in strategic places that would, hopefully, result in one great conflagration. The timers were set to give him plenty of opportunity to make his escape.

Finally all was completed, everything in place and activated. He ran through in his mind exactly what he'd done and how he'd done it. He couldn't find fault with anything.

He returned to the storeroom, rucksack again going through the window first followed by himself. Outside in the cul-de-sac he paused to listen, hearing nothing to worry about.

He pulled the window shut, wishing he could relock it, then shrugged on his rucksack. All that now remained for him to do was get out of Hennebont and make his way to Aunt Sophie's.

It was a piece of cake, as the English would say. Knowing Hennebont as he did, he flitted from one dark alley to another. Twice he halted when he heard the sound of German voices, but neither occasion came to anything.

He was thankful the town was blacked out; that made

matters a great deal easier. Before long he was on the outskirts of the town and heading into the countryside.

His wireless was where he'd left it. Collecting it he started up a hill that had once been a favourite haunt of his and Marie Thérèse's. From the summit one could see all of Hennebont spread out below.

It was nearly an hour later when he spotted the flickering flames standing out starkly against the darkened background. As he watched the flames swiftly grew in size and intensity.

The job was done, successfully he hoped. Now all he had to worry about was getting back to England.

Chapter 28

Where was she? An agitated Christian peered anxiously, for the umpteenth time, down the track that led from the farmhouse but there was still no sign of Aunt Sophie. She'd gone into Hennebont that morning, as she did every Friday, for supplies. It was now three days since he'd arrived at her house and so far there had been no word about the fire or what damage had been caused.

He'd expected this. In the circumstances his parents were hardly likely to make a visit, and the remoteness of the farmhouse ensured that Aunt Sophie rarely had callers, even from her nearest neighbours.

He and Sophie had discussed the matter and decided that her regular weekly trip into town was the ideal way to gather information without arousing any unnecessary suspicion.

Christian paced up and down. Had something gone wrong? Or was she merely later than she'd said she'd be? He simply didn't know.

'Damn!' he muttered.

It was almost nightfall when he heard the approaching sound of a horse and cart. She was back at long last, thank God. He ran to the door and flung it open just as Sophie was alighting to the ground.

'Relax,' she called out. 'Everything's fine.'

He crossed to her side. 'Maman and Papa?'

She smiled. 'I never knew Philippe was such a good actor. I tell you, even the Boche feel sorry for him.'

'The factory was destroyed then?'

She began unharnessing the horse. 'You certainly did a good job there. Not only the factory but half the street as well went up in smoke. The Germans believe it was an accident and are blaming it on inferior French wiring and workmanship.'

She laughed. 'I liked that bit. *Les merdes.* Inferior indeed.'

A great sense of relief washed through Christian. The factory and half the street! A bit excessive perhaps, but there was nothing he could do about that now. 'What happened on the night?' he demanded.

'It wasn't the Germans who came to tell Philippe but men from the factory who live near by. Philippe says it was an incredible sight and well into the following morning before the fire brigade was able to bring it under control. What's left is still smouldering even now. I saw that for myself.'

'And there was no question of the Germans suspecting sabotage?'

'None at all. According to Philippe that hasn't even been mentioned. It all apparently appeared to happen accidentally.'

Christian was ecstatic. His mission had been successful and his parents had not been implicated. Precisely what he'd been aiming for. He turned towards the door.

'Where are you going?'

'I have to encode a message and send it to London. I must get it off as soon as possible.'

Aunt Sophie nodded her understanding. She'd been expecting Christian to help her with the horse and unload the supplies. No matter, she was well used to doing things on her own.

*   *   *

'Coffee?'

'Please.' Christian slumped into a chair, a great wave of tiredness having overtaken him. That, no doubt, was a reaction to the tension he'd been under.

'Get the message off all right?'

'Yes. They asked me to hang on for a reply, which I did. They then came through again saying they'd contact me tomorrow evening about eight.'

'So, when do you think you'll be leaving?'

'That depends on the RAF, Aunt, and how quickly they can arrange a pick-up. Tomorrow night at the earliest, possibly the night after. I'll just have to wait and find out.'

She gave him a steaming mug. 'You must be pleased with yourself?'

'Very. Not just for the job itself, but that Maman and Papa didn't fall under suspicion. If the Germans thought they were involved in any way it would be a firing squad for the pair of them. That or a concentration camp.'

'Well, there's no worry now on either score.' She smiled. 'Your father was quite hysterical at the blaze, I'm told, begging the Germans to save his precious factory. Delphine said it was a wonderful performance. If she hadn't known better even she would have been convinced.'

Christian smiled. 'Good old Papa.'

'You're a lot like him in many ways,' Sophie stated quietly.

'Am I?'

'Oh yes. There's far more of him in you than your mother. I've always thought that.' Sophie glanced out the window and sighed. 'I'd better get on with the chores. Farm work is never ending, you know. It just goes on and on.'

'You must enjoy it otherwise you wouldn't stay here?'

Sophie considered that. 'I suppose I do. But just occasionally

I'd like a break away from it all. Can't do that when I run the place by myself, I'm afraid. You get neither breaks nor holidays.'

Christian lit a cigarette. 'Well, you can have a little break right now. You sit down and I'll finish my coffee. Then I'll do what needs doing,' he volunteered, shrugging off his tiredness.

She stared at him. 'You'll make some woman a good husband one day, Christian. She'll be very fortunate.'

For a brief moment an anguished look creased his face. 'There's a war to be won first before I can start thinking about marriage,' he replied lightly.

Sophie eyed him speculatively. Now that *was* interesting.

Later that evening found Christian sprawled in front of a blazing fire thinking how warm and cosy the room was. He was sitting on a cushion with his back against the sofa, a glass of Aunt Sophie's homemade calvados by his side. It was a potent brew, if rather rough for his taste.

Sophie glanced up from her darning. 'How do you find the English then, Christian?' she asked, making conversation.

'Not bad. I rather like them actually. Once you get accustomed to their peculiar habits, that is.'

'Oh? What sort of peculiar habits?'

He mused on that. 'They eat differently for a start. The food's stodgy in my opinion, lacking flavour. And they're very . . . rigid, I suppose you could say, in their approach to life. They're not nearly as relaxed as we are. Why, what do *you* think of them?'

Sophie shrugged. 'I've only ever met a few. I can't say I was impressed.'

'They do unbend after a while, when you get to know them. I particularly like the Cornish people.'

'And why's that?'

'I've spent a lot of time there and become friendly with some of them. They're more relaxed in their attitude than those in London where I have a flat.'

'And did you meet her in Cornwall? Or was it London?'

Christian frowned. 'Meet who?'

'The woman you keep thinking about.'

He gaped at his aunt. 'How did you know that?'

She laughed at his expression. 'It wasn't too hard to work out. I am a woman myself, don't forget. And one who, despite now being a widow, does know men. You also gave it away when I mentioned marriage earlier. Oh yes, I'd bet my last *sou* there's a woman involved here. Do you love her?'

Christian had a swallow of his calvados while marvelling at his aunt's intuitiveness. It was true, he had been thinking a great deal about Maizie since arriving at the farm.

'Yes, there is someone,' he admitted reluctantly.

'Ah, so I was right then!'

'And I do love her. Very much.'

Sophie had a sip from her own glass of calvados. 'Will you marry after the war?'

'I'm afraid not.'

Sophie raised an eyebrow. 'Does that mean she doesn't love *you*?'

'No, it's because she's already married. Her husband's in the British Merchant Navy. A sailor.'

'But does she love you?'

He nodded, mind filled with pictures of Maizie. He could hear her talking, laughing, see her naked in bed. He felt absolutely wretched. 'She told me she does. A number of times. The trouble is she won't leave her husband because she takes her wedding vows seriously. Nor will she leave Coverack where they live and all her friends are.'

'Poor Christian,' Sophie sympathised.

'She hates Sam, that's the husband. When he was last home

he raped a young girl evacuee she has living with her. That's the sort of person he is. A pig.'

'Have you slept with her?'

Christian blushed slightly. Sophie was his aunt after all. 'Yes,' he mumbled.

'And it was good between you?'

'It couldn't have been better, Aunt. I'll never find anyone to replace her. I just know I won't.'

Sophie closed her eyes, those words causing her to wince inwardly. Hadn't it been the same for her? Even now, after all these years, the memory still caused her enormous pain.

'Poor Christian,' she repeated. 'This is something you're going to have to live with just as I have done.'

He glanced at her in surprise. 'You?'

'It was the same between me and your Uncle Antoine. The same, and not the same, for we did get married. Much against the family's wishes, I can tell you. They all warned me but I wouldn't listen. I was headstrong and thought I knew better.' She paused and smiled. 'The trouble is, I'd do exactly the same all over again. Our love was that strong.'

Christian was intrigued. 'My parents rarely mention Uncle Antoine, and certainly never discuss him, at least not in front of me. I've always wondered about that. When I was young I asked about him a number of times but never got an answer. They always somehow changed the subject.'

Sophie smiled wryly. 'They thought him a bad lot. And, in a way, they were proved right. But what we had was sheer magic. Perhaps if he hadn't been a gypsy things might have been different. It was his gypsy blood gave him itchy feet.' She suddenly laughed. 'And an itchy something else. One woman, no matter how much he loved her, was never enough for Antonie. That's why he left me in the end.'

'Left you!' Christian exclaimed. This was news to him.

Sophie nodded. 'For a younger woman from Hennebont. They ran off together.'

'I *am* sorry, Aunt,' Christian whispered.

Sophie had gone quiet, her voice introspective. 'I remember the day I met him. The circus had come to town and he was working with it as a roustabout. Do you know what a roustabout is?'

'I've no idea.' Gypsy. Circus. Whatever next!

'They're the men who put up the tents and generally do all the hard physical labour. Antonie was one of those. You should have seen him then, Christian, a Greek God if ever there was. Dark curly hair down to his shoulders, flashing black eyes, olive skin, a body as hard as iron. I was well and truly smitten the moment I saw him.'

'Hold on,' Christian said, getting up. He fetched the calvados bottle and refilled Sophie's glass, then his own. He was fascinated by all this.

'It was a whirlwind romance,' Sophie continued when he'd settled himself again. 'We were head over heels, besotted with one another. When it came time for the circus to move on he stayed behind and found a job in Hennebont. Two months later we were married.'

Christian simply couldn't imagine Sophie in this light. It seemed so against character. The story she was recounting was like something straight out of a cheap novel.

'Your parents weren't long married themselves and of course totally against our marriage, as were my mother and father. So much so they disowned me, your grandmother and grandfather that is, and never spoke to me again. I had some money that had been left me and used that to buy this place. We particularly chose somewhere remote to be away from others, to be more or less entirely on our own. Philippe said that Antoine had been after my money all along, but that just wasn't true. At least I can't believe it.'

'How long were you together?' Christian asked.

'Three years and eight months. The farm wasn't paying very well so Antonie took a part-time job in town to help make ends meet, and that was where he met the girl. I knew nothing about her, or their affair, until after they'd run off. It broke my heart the morning I found the letter saying he'd left me.'

Sophie shook her head.

'I still think it was the gypsy blood in him, those people are born wanderers and philanderers. I was foolish enough to believe I could change him and make him settle down. Well, I was wrong and paid the price.'

'So how did you discover he was dead?'

'A *gendarme* called here to tell me. I had to be notified as his next of kin. Apparently he was killed in a car crash. That was a long time after he'd gone. I doubt he stayed with the girl though she never returned to Hennebont. Most probably she too got discarded for someone else.'

'And you never remarried?'

Sophie swallowed some more calvados. 'I did have the opportunity when it became known I was widowed, even though I was getting on by then. But I had no interest. Antoine was the only man for me. There could never be anyone else. Not in this lifetime anyway.'

Christian reflected on all she'd said. No wonder his parents had never discussed Uncle Antoine. It was hardly surprising he'd been something of a taboo subject! He could understand why now.

'I don't know why I told you all this tonight,' Sophie said softly. 'Probably because of your own lost love. I can only hope you get over yours, for I certainly never got over mine.' Sophie came to her feet. 'I don't know about you but I want my bed. Will you put out the lamps and bar the door?'

'Of course, Aunt Sophie.'

She hesitated. 'We won't speak of this ever again. Understand?'

He nodded.

'Good.'

She crossed over and kissed him on the top of his head. 'Listen to me, Christian, for I'd hate to think of you suffering down through the years as I've done. If the woman is out of your reach then do your best to try to forget her. For your own sake. I don't want you ending up like me.'

And with that Sophie swept from the room leaving Christian deep in thought.

After a while he laughed. Aunt Sophie and a roustabout from the circus! A gypsy into the bargain. Who would ever have imagined!

But she was right about one thing. He must try to stop brooding over Maizie. She was in the past, gone for ever. He must come to terms with that and look to the future.

If he had one that was. There was still a war to get through.

'Maizie!' Alice exclaimed in alarm. 'What's the matter with ee?'

Maizie was standing stock still, her face drained to a muddy grey colour, a large vein in her neck visibly throbbing. She suddenly gagged and rushed over to the sink. Her entire body heaved and spasmed as she violently vomited.

Alice was instantly beside her, holding her, as Maizie vomited a second time. 'Christ Almighty,' Maizie muttered when it was finished.

She straightened and sucked in a deep breath, grimacing at the foul taste in her mouth. 'I don't know what brought that on,' she said at last.

'Shall I ring the doctor?'

Maizie ran a hand over her forehead which was beaded

with cold sweat. Her head was spinning. 'All I need is a lie down.'

'Are ee sure?'

Maizie nodded. 'Probably something I ate was a little off. Though I can't think what. No one else has been sick, have they?'

'Not that I knows of.'

'Well, whatever, a lie down will do. But first of all, get me a glass, will you.'

Alice hastily did as requested. When Maizie had the glass she filled it with water and rinsed out her mouth. Then she made to clean the mess in the sink.

'You leave that, I'll do it,' Alice protested. 'Now do you want some help upstairs?'

Maizie thought about that. 'I think so. My legs are none too steady.'

Alice slipped an arm round Maizie's waist. 'This is most unlike ee, maid. I's never known ee throw up before.'

'I was a child last time it happened.'

Rosemary came into the kitchen. 'What's wrong?'

'Maizie's had a funny turn. I'm taking her upstairs.'

'I'm all right now, don't you fret,' Maizie said when she saw Rosemary's concerned expression. 'I'll probably be as right as rain in a few minutes.'

It would take longer than that, Alice thought as they moved towards the doorway. 'We'll attend to things down here so you stay in bed till you're better,' she declared.

'Thanks, Alice.'

'I'll bring you up a nice cup of tea,' Rosemary volunteered.

'I'd like that.'

'It might be the flu coming on,' Alice conjectured as they mounted the stairs. 'It's the right time of year for it.'

That was entirely possible, Maizie thought, head still spinning.

'Are ee certain I shouldn't call the doctor?'

'Let's just wait and see how I do. I don't want to bother the man if it's nothing.'

Alice snorted. 'He's the doctor, 'tain't he! He's there to be bothered whether it's nothing or no.'

In the kitchen Rosemary was filling the kettle.

Sophie looked up from the dough she was kneading in preparation for the morning's bread bake. It was something she always enjoyed, finding it soothing and relaxing. 'Did you get through?' she inquired of Christian who'd just appeared having been with his wireless for the past hour.

He gave her the thumbs-up. 'Loud and clear.'

'So is the pick-up later tonight or tomorrow night?'

He came across and leant against the surface she was working on. 'Neither, I'm afraid.'

'Oh?'

'There's been a change of plan. I'm to stay on here for a while. If you'll continue to have me that is.'

'Of course, Christian. You don't even have to ask. What sort of change of plan?'

'A German General has moved into the area,' he said slowly. 'His name is Tanz and he's commandeered the Château d'Aubray as his headquarters. Do you know the place?'

'I've never actually been there but it's about fifteen kilometers away.'

'That's right, according to my map. The General is a renowned tank man and has brought four full divisions of Panzers with him. London's information is that there are others on their way. My instructions are to try to find out what's going on. Why the General is here and what his intentions are.'

'I see,' Sophie nodded.

Christian recalled the tanks he'd seen in Hennebont. Well, this explained their presence in the town. They must have been *en route* to Château d'Aubray.

'Are you disappointed?'

He frowned. 'About what?'

'Not returning to London right away.'

Christian shrugged. 'There's nothing there for me, Aunt Sophie. I'd much rather be here where I can do some good.'

'Four divisions,' she mused. 'That's a lot, isn't it?'

'A major force. And one that appears to be being enlarged. Something's up all right. Something big, I'd say. I've heard of Tanz. He made quite a name for himself in Poland where he butchered thousands of Jews. He's utterly ruthless apparently. A born killer.'

Sophie shuddered. 'And now he's hereabouts. Holy Mary Mother of God!'

Christian pulled out his cigarette packet and lit up, his mind going over the signal he'd decoded. London were worried about this, that was obvious. What was also obvious was that they hadn't the vaguest idea what the General was up to. Hence his latest assignment, the man on the spot so to speak.

'How will you go about this?' Sophie asked, attacking the dough again.

'As yet I don't know. It'll take some thinking on.'

Sophie was pleased Christian would be staying, she enjoyed his company and having him around. It was a break from the long spells of loneliness that she normally endured.

He crossed over to a chair and sat. It was a good hour before he spoke again. In the meantime Sophie got on with what she was doing and left him to it.

*   *   *

Maizie was serving alone behind the bar and busy when the couple came in. It was just after nine o'clock at night. They glanced around and then the man made his way over.

'Do you have a double room available?' he asked Maizie as she was pulling a pint for Charlie Treloar.

'We always have vacancies in March,' she smiled. 'It's hardly our busiest time.'

'Good. We were relying on that.'

'If you'll just hold on a moment.'

She took the pint to Charlie who paid her. 'Don't forget tomorrow evening,' she whispered, having first ensured she wouldn't be overheard.

He nodded. 'I'll be there, Maiz.' It was one of their regular meetings for the resistance in the tunnel.

Maizie spotted Rosemary picking up empty glasses and called her across. 'Can you book in that couple for me, please.'

'Why so busy tonight?'

Maizie shrugged. 'Search me. But I'm not complaining. Sometimes it just happens, that's all.' Recently the bar had been dead as a dodo in the evenings.

'What room will I put them in?'

'Number four. That's the biggest and nicest. When you take them up tell them if they want to eat there's only sandwiches.'

'Right,' Rosemary declared, and moved off.

Later the couple turned up in the bar for a drink, going up again to their room when last orders were called before Maizie had a chance to have a chat with them.

'A full English breakfast each for Mr and Mrs McEwen,' Rosemary announced, breezing into the kitchen.

'Right,' Maizie acknowledged. So that was the couple's name. She hadn't checked the register the previous night, being too tired, nor had she had time that morning to do so. 'What are they like?'

'Pleasant enough.'

'How long are they staying for?'

'They're not sure. Probably about a week.'

Good, Maizie thought. She could use the trade. 'Are they holidaymakers?' It seemed an odd month to go on holiday if they were.

'They didn't say.'

'And what about the other gentleman, Mr Hubert?'

'He's not down yet.'

'Well, he'd better hurry up or he'll have to go without.'

'Here, take that through,' instructed Alice, handing Rosemary a rack of fresh toast.

Rosemary disappeared back to the dining room.

Maizie glanced at the date on the calender later on that morning. There was no doubt, she'd missed her period. Still, that was nothing new. She'd often missed the occasional period. When it happened it was quite a relief actually.

'May I join you?'

Mr McEwen immediately came to his feet. 'Please do.'

'I'm Mrs Blackacre, the owner. I haven't had a chance to say hello yet. Is everything OK?'

'Absolutely fine, thank you,' Mr McEwen replied. 'Would you care for some coffee?'

'Not for me thanks.'

It was the afternoon and they were seated in the bar by a window, the McEwens indulging in coffee and tipsy cake.

'This your first time in Coverack?' Maizie inquired politely.

'No, we've been before.'

'But not for some years,' Mrs McEwen added.

'We've always had a soft spot for Coverack,' Mr McEwen said. 'We both love it here.'

'And now we've come to stay.'

'Really!' Maizie exclaimed, surprised to hear that.

'Yes, we've bought a cottage up at the back of the village. It's called Trewolsta.'

Of course, it all made sense now. Trewolsta had been lying empty ever since the German air raid. The Peaceys, an old couple, had been so upset by what had happened they'd decided to move to Porthleven where their only son was a vicar living in a large house all by himself.

'So you bought from the Peaceys,' Maizie said.

'That's right. We saw the property advertised in a London paper and decided to go for it sight unseen. And so here we are.'

'I wonder why a London paper?' Maizie mused.

'Probably thought they'd get a better price. Which undoubtedly they did.'

Rosemary had been right, Maizie thought. They did seem a pleasant enough couple. 'Anyway, welcome to Coverack. I hope you'll like it.'

'Oh we will, we're certain about that,' Mrs McEwen enthused.

'We've booked into the hotel because we're waiting for our furniture to come down,' Mr McEwen explained. 'It also gives us a little time to sort things out at the cottage before it arrives.'

Maizie nodded her understanding.

'We're very excited about it all,' Mr McEwen went on.

'I just hope you don't find it too remote. It's one thing spending a holiday here, another living all the year in the village.'

'We won't have any problem with that,' Mr McEwen replied. 'We keep ourselves to ourselves a lot anyway.'

'We've actually been in the Paris before,' Mrs McEwen declared. 'But it must have been before your time.'

'My God, look at that sky!' Mr McEwen suddenly exclaimed, having glanced out the window. 'Isn't it magnificent?' He was staring at it like a man transfixed.

Huge black clouds dominated the horizon, almost satanic in their appearance. As they watched jagged bolts of lightning flickered through them.

'I must get my pad,' Mr McEwen declared, jumping to his feet. And with that he rushed off.

'That's an artist for you,' Mrs McEwen apologised. 'Nothing else matters when the mood takes them.'

'An artist?'

'Professionally. That's how he makes his living.'

When Mr McEwen returned a few minutes later he was in a fever of excitement so Maizie decided to leave them to it.

It was almost half an hour later when the penny dropped. Could it be? Had to, surely. How many artists called McEwen were there? Especially ones who'd previously been to Coverack.

She bided her time till Mr McEwen had stopped sketching and laid his pad aside before going up to them again.

'Excuse me for asking, but would your first name be Ted?'

He smiled quizzically at her. 'That's right.'

'I thought so. Then you must know Christian Le Gall from Hennebont.'

Chapter 29

'The world truly is a small place right enough,' Ted McEwen mused when Maizie came to the end of her story about how she knew Christian.

'As I said, he often spoke about you. Told me that you helped him become fluent in English.'

'And Christian's been here. I just can't believe it,' Ted murmured, shaking his head.

'He's ever such a lovely man. A great favourite of ours. He was almost like a son to us,' Pet McEwen added.

'I have his phone number. Why don't you ring him later?' Maizie suggested.

'You do? We'd love to,' Ted replied quickly. 'Is he in for a shock!'

'He doesn't even know whether or not you escaped from France.'

Ted's face darkened. 'We nearly didn't. My fault for leaving it so long. But in the end we did get out if only by the skin of our teeth. We've been living with relatives of Pet's in Watford.' He saw Maizie frown. 'That's north of London.'

Ted suddenly barked out a laugh. 'What a turn up for the book! And an enormous relief to know Christian is OK. We've often wondered.'

'He was at Dunkirk and then posted to Plymouth. That

was when he first came down here. Lately he's been billeted in London.'

'With the French Army?'

Be careful here, Maizie warned herself. She mustn't mention SOE. 'Special duties of some sort,' she prevaricated.

'Interpreter most likely,' Pet said.

Heavy rain began hammering against the window. 'We're in for a real blow,' Maizie stated. 'If I was you I'd stay in for the rest of the day.'

Thunder crashed not far away, a great booming roll of it. Lightning flashed, followed by more thunder.

'I still can't get over this,' Ted commented in amazement. 'Do you think Christian will be able to get down here at some point?'

'I should imagine so,' Maizie replied. If he was in the country that is, she thought, but didn't articulate this thought. 'He's become almost part of our family. I have two evacuee children staying with me, one of them the girl who booked you in last night and served breakfast earlier. They think he's wonderful, particularly Bobby whom you'll meet later.'

Ted nodded. 'Christian has always been easy to get on with. Even as a teenager he was easy going.'

'I'd like to hear about those days,' Maizie smiled. 'When you were all in Hennebont together.'

'Where to start?' Ted smiled back.

'Why don't I make some fresh coffee while you think about it?'

'All right.'

Maizie was in a lighthearted mood as she returned to the kitchen. She was going to enjoy hearing all about the young Christian.

'Well, bugger I!' Alice exclaimed when she told her about the McEwens.

*　　*　　*

'Any luck?'

Ted shook his head. 'Still no answer.' It was the third time he'd tried to ring Christian.

Maizie glanced at a nearby clock. 'Oh well, you can try again later. And if he's still not in there's always tomorrow.'

'He's probably out on the town with some young piece no doubt,' Ted grinned. 'He always had an eye for the ladies did our Christian.'

Maizie turned swiftly away so Ted didn't see her expression.

Maizie woke with the alarm clanging. Another early start, another day, she thought grimly. Getting up in winter was so much worse than summer when it could be a real joy.

She switched off the alarm and lay back for her customary few additional minutes while she gathered herself. When her few minutes were up she swung her legs out of bed.

That was when it hit her, a violent wave of nausea that came seemingly from nowhere. She gagged as the hot bile rose in her throat.

Clamping a hand over her mouth she rushed to the sink and vomited, some of the vomit splashing back on to her nightdress. The inside of her head was hammering while her skin had gone clammy. Beads of cold sweat dotted her brow.

Just when she thought it was finished she vomited again, her stomach heaving as it ejected the rest of its contents.

Oh my God, she thought. Oh my God!

When it was finally all over she snatched up a towel and ran it across her mouth. What was going on? she wondered, recalling her vomiting in the kitchen when Alice was there. This was an exact repeat performance.

She must have caught something, that had to be it. There were all sorts of bugs doing the rounds in Coverack. She'd go and see Dr Renvoise later, she decided. He'd be able to help.

*   *   *

'You seem perfectly OK to me,' Dr Renvoise declared, after his examination of Maizie.

'I have to confess I feel right as rain now.'

'Your temperature's normal, so's your blood pressure.'

'Could it be food poisoning? That's what I thought the first time it happened.'

He shook his head. 'Most unlikely. The nausea would have continued if it had.'

Renvoise rocked back in his chair, studying Maizie speculatively. 'Have you missed a period or two by any chance?'

That surprised her. 'Why yes I . . .' Then the full implication of what he was suggesting struck home. Her face froze with shock.

'Just one?'

She nodded.

'I see.'

'It happens to me now and then. It's nothing to be concerned about.'

'Nonetheless, I think we should send a sample off to be tested, don't you?'

Pregnant? She couldn't be. Oh please God she wasn't. Her mind was whirling.

Renvoise knew full well that Sam had been away too long for it to be his. But that was none of his business, he didn't bother himself with others' morals.

Maizie was hastily checking dates. When was the last time she'd slept with Christian? Jesus, it could be. That would fit. She went chill all over.

Renvoise opened a drawer in his desk and produced a small, empty bottle. 'You know where the toilet is, Maizie. I'll see it gets sent off to Helston in the next post.'

She couldn't look Renvoise in the eye as she took the bottle. He had to be wrong. He just had to be.

But it did make sense. That was the trouble, the frightening thing. It did make sense.

It would take a week for the results to come through, a week that was sheer torture for Maizie. She was sick every morning. She prayed that was due to nerves.

Her hands started to shake almost uncontrollably during the walk to the surgery to hear the results of the test.

It had been confirmed. The test was positive. She was pregnant. Early days but she was pregnant nevertheless. There was no doubt about it.

She tried to fight down the panic that was threatening to engulf her. Sam would go berserk when he found out, beat her black and blue.

The ironic thing was she'd wanted a child for so long, prayed for one, and now a child was on the way it wasn't Sam's. Not only that, it was impossible for her to even try to pretend it was.

The gossip would be dreadful. She'd be called terrible names behind her back, be a figure of scorn and derision, a scarlet woman. She could already hear the whispers, the sniggers, the sly innuendoes. And of course there would be the avid speculation as to whom she'd slept with. Her reputation would be completely and utterly in tatters.

She'd be branded a slut, a tart, a whore. So-called friends would shun her.

Maizie worried a nail, shaking inside as all this went through her mind. Nor was she exaggerating, she knew the local people only too well. They'd be vicious towards her, the women in particular who'd see her as having let the side down.

It would affect business, of course. Bound to, even though the Paris was the only pub in the village.

As for Sam, it was entirely possible, being shamed, that he'd toss her out on her ear. Where would she go then? Not back to Porthoustock where she came from for it would be exactly the same there.

She lit a cigarette. What a mess to get herself into! What a bloody awful mess. She and Christian had been careful right from the word go. At least they'd thought they had. But not careful enough it seemed.

She couldn't even get in touch with him, ask him to help. The McEwens had finally got an answer when ringing. A man, possibly Dutch, Ted had thought by the sound of him, had told Ted that Christian had moved away and no, he had neither a forwarding address nor telephone number.

That meant Christian was in France. At least she presumed it did. And gone for some while if they'd put someone else into the flat. Whatever, she couldn't contact him.

The answer would be to have an abortion, but even thinking about that made her cringe. She knew in her heart of hearts she could never consent to have that. Her whole being revolted against the idea. Not that she would know where to locate an abortionist. She wouldn't even begin to guess where to look or who to ask. That sort of thing was completely outside her experience.

An alternative was to have a self-induced miscarriage. A bottle of gin and a piping hot bath she'd heard, or throw herself down the stairs in the hope that was the result. She couldn't do that either. As far as she was concerned a self-induced miscarriage was exactly the same as an abortion. Cold-blooded murder.

The thought of telling Sam made her shudder. Though she might not have to do so. Chances were that when he next returned she'd either have a belly on her the size of a barrage balloon or else the actual baby itself. She could just imagine his face contorted with rage and humiliation and the physical assault that would follow. There again, if she was that far gone he just might not hit her. But she wouldn't have bet on it.

What to do? That was the question. What to do? It seemed the only recourse open to her was to run away. But that would mean leaving her adored Coverack and Lizard, something she'd refused to do for Christian whom she truly loved.

That had been different though, there she'd had a choice. In this matter it wouldn't appear she did. It would be impossible to continue living in the village. It would be a daily nightmare that would begin when she started to show, for that's when tongues would begin wagging.

Maizie shook her head, brain now befuddled by all of this. What to do? she asked herself yet again. What to do?

'Maizie, whose is this?'

Maizie, wiping down shelves, turned to Ted McEwen who was sitting at the bar. As had become his custom he dropped in every afternoon around one o'clock for a pint of cider. He worked early, had a break during which he'd stroll round the village or surrounding area, then come to the Paris for about twenty minutes before returning home for lunch followed by another stint of painting.

Maizie glanced at the pad he was holding up. 'Rosemary's.'

'It was lying on the bar here and I took the liberty of looking inside. Her portraits are excellent.'

'That's what I think.'

'Truly they are. Does she paint?'

'Not that I know of. Sketching is as far as it goes.'

Ted flipped the pad open and stared at the portrait revealed. It was of Denzil Eustis and captured the very essence of the man. 'A remarkable talent for someone her age,' he commented.

Maizie laid down her duster and went over. 'They aren't bad, are they?'

'They're a lot better than that, Maizie. I'm most impressed.'

'You should tell her that. She'll be thrilled.'

'I shall tell her, Maizie. Believe you me I will.'

If any possible doubt had remained, that the result of her test might have been wrong, then it was gone. She'd now missed two periods in a row which, even given her history of missed months, had never happened before. She was well and truly in the pudding club as the locals might say.

And still she didn't know what she was going to do. Whenever she tried to think about that her mind remained a blank. At least the vomiting had stopped, that was something to be thankful for. But her skirts were becoming tight on her. Soon she'd have to start letting them out.

She must make a plan, Maizie told herself. She must. That's all there was to it.

'Aunt Maiz, do you mind if I go to the McEwens tomorrow afternoon? It is my day off.'

'Of course I don't mind, Rosemary. Do as you wish.'

Rosemary's eyes were sparkling. 'Ted has promised to give me a few lessons. Isn't that wonderful?'

'Ted! Mr McEwen to you, my girl.'

'But he insisted I call him Ted. He said it made him feel like a geriatric when I called him Mr McEwen.'

Maizie laughed. Geriatric indeed! Ted was old but not that old. He still cut a handsome figure even if he was grey. 'I suppose that's the Bohemian in him,' Maizie commented.

Rosemary frowned. 'Bohemian?'

'The artist. Most of them are very eccentric, unconventional, from what I understand. All right, you can call him

Ted outside of the hotel, but inside you refer to him as Mr McEwen. Understand?'

Rosemary nodded.

'What sort of lessons is he intending giving you anyway?'

'I don't know. On drawing I suppose.'

'Whatever, it's very kind of him. Make sure you thank him afterwards.'

'I will, Aunt Maiz, don't worry.'

'Now get on with your work. There's a lot to do.'

'Yes, Aunt Maiz.' And with that Rosemary scampered away.

It would seem Rosemary had made a friend, Maizie reflected. Well that was good. She certainly hadn't made any particular ones at school, which had always surprised her. So this was a good thing.

This was the third occasion Rosemary had visited the McEwens, each previous visit a real treat. She felt so relaxed in their house, so at home. As for the studio where Ted worked, it was as if she belonged there. The smells, the clutter, the entire atmosphere was heady in the extreme.

'Ah, there you are,' Ted smiled, wiping his hands on a rag, as she entered the studio. 'I've prepared a canvas for you. You're going to paint.'

Rosemary, completely taken by surprise, gaped at him. 'Paint?'

'That's what I said. A portrait of your Aunt Maiz, I think. You've already done the preparatory sketching so now you can transfer that to oils.'

'But I don't know how to paint,' she stammered.

'Of course you don't. Not yet anyway. But I'm here to help and guide. Now take your coat off and let's get started.'

Rosemary was a real find, Ted thought. Well, she had to be, he didn't waste his time on just anyone. He had high hopes for her. All she needed was reassurance and the guidance he'd already mentioned for her gift to grow and develop.

He'd already decided she would eventually be suitable material for the Slade school in London. If she wanted to be an artist that is. Which she believed she did.

She simply hadn't realised it yet.

'I'm starving,' Bobby declared, sliding on to his seat at the table.

Maizie laughed. 'When are you not?'

'What is it?'

'Stew,' Rosemary informed him.

'Well, I'll have lots please.'

'And what about you, Emily?'

Emily, sitting next to Bobby, smiled back. 'I love stew.'

'Is there a sweet for afters?' Bobby asked anxiously.

'Lemon tart.'

His eyes gleamed. 'Goody goody.'

Rosemary placed mashed potatoes and winter vegetables on the table. 'And there's clotted cream to go with the tart,' she added.

Bobby glanced at Emily. He always enjoyed it when she came over for a meal. Just as he enjoyed going to her house. Later on her father would call and collect her in the van. But it was hours till then. Hours during which they'd be together.

Maizie was the last to sit down. 'Help yourself, Emily. Don't let it go cold.'

'Thank you, Mrs Blackacre.'

Rosemary's face suddenly froze, her eyes widening with shock.

'Is there enough there for another?' Sam asked from where he was standing in the doorway.

Maizie would later swear her heart stopped. Stunned, she turned round. 'Sam!'

He grinned at her. 'Home is the hunter home from the hill, and the sailor home from the sea. Or some such twaddle. I see I've timed my arrival spot on.'

He strode forward to kiss Maizie on the cheek. 'Hello, my lover. How are you?'

'Fine,' she managed to smile.

Rosemary looked down at her plate feeling sick inside. Any appetite she'd had had disappeared.

'Bobby, get Sam a chair,' Maizie instructed.

Bobby hastily rose to do as he was bid.

'How long are you back for?'

'Only three days, then I'm away again, sailing out of Plymouth.'

Maizie's mind was whirling. This was a miracle, truly a miracle. Her problem was solved and she was filled with jubilation. She could now pass the baby off as Sam's. Of course that meant sleeping with him, which she'd somehow force herself to do, even though it would fill her with revulsion and make her flesh creep. There would be no confrontation for the present, no accusing Sam of raping Rosemary. No righteous condemnation and banishment from the marital bed. Due to present circumstances all that had been turned topsy turvy.

'You're a welcome sight,' she managed to say to Sam, both meaning it and despising herself at the same time. How she loathed and detested the man.

Sam glanced over at Emily. 'And who are you, young maid?'

Emily's presence was explained as Sam sat down to join in the meal.

'Now ain't this just dandy!' he exclaimed, beaming at all present.

'Christ, Sam, not yet!' Maizie complained as Sam's meaty

hands grabbed hold of her breasts. 'Rosemary's only gone out for a moment.'

He leered at her, eyes bright with lust. 'I'm hard as bloody iron from just looking at ee across that table. I want ee so much, Maizie my darling. I hurt from it.'

'Well, you'll just have to wait, that's all there is to it,' she riposted, wriggling away.

'Upstairs for a quick one, eh?'

'Sam, I can't. I have to open up the bar.'

'Let the maid do that.'

'She's under age, Sam, and certainly not experienced enough to be behind the bar on her own. No, it has to be me.'

'Ring Trudy Curnow.'

'Trudy's laid up with bronchitis. You'll just have to wait.'

He reluctantly accepted that; he had three full days ahead of him after all. And maybe this was for the best, he wanted to take his time with her, indulge himself. A quickie would only be frustrating.

'OK then,' he nodded. 'I'll go and have meself a drink in the meantime. I'll even open up for you if you like.'

'Thank you, Sam. That would be helpful.'

'But I wants a proper kiss first. I must have that.'

They were still kissing when Rosemary came back into the kitchen. 'Excuse me,' she mumbled, going bright red.

Sam broke away with a laugh, smacking Maizie on the rear as he did. 'I'll be in the bar,' he declared, and strode off.

Maizie tidied her hair, unable to look Rosemary in the eye.

It was a wild night, Maizie thought, closing a set of curtains in the bar. The wind was howling and the Channel running high. She could hear the boom of breakers exploding on the shore.

It had been a bad winter, one of the worst she could remember, storms and gales aplenty. The fishermen had been moaning non-stop about it as they'd been severely restricted on getting out. Their incomes had plummeted.

Sam was at a table with several of his cronies, all of them having a right old time by the sound of things and judging by the amount of alcohol they'd consumed. Sam was drunk and intent on getting drunker. Not that that would interfere with his performance when he got to bed, it never did. All that happened was it took him longer.

Her mind was still in a turmoil at Sam's unexpected return. On the one hand her relief was profound, for there was still enough time left for her to claim the baby was his. If any questions were asked she'd simply say it had been premature. So her life and reputation in Coverack were saved.

On the other hand she had to sleep with Sam knowing what she did about him. That was going to take some doing, but do it she would. For the baby if nothing else, because now it wouldn't be born illegitimate but could bear the name Blackacre. She was truly thankful for that. God had answered her prayers for which she'd be eternally grateful.

Maizie shot home the bolt. That was the last customer gone. The time she'd been dreading had come.

Sam was standing propping up the bar, his face flushed, a silly smile on his face. ''Twas a grand evening,' he pronounced. ''Tis always good to see some of me old mates.'

Maizie went behind the bar and poured herself a large gin. She was going to need it.

'Shall we go on up, Maiz?'

'Let me finish this first.'

'Why not just bring it with ee?'

She sighed. Dog tired, what she really wanted was sleep. Well, there would be precious little of that tonight if she knew Sam. She saw off the gin and poured herself another even larger.

'I'll do the lights and follow,' he said.

In the bedroom she had another swallow of gin. Rain was lashing the window when she pulled the curtains and the wind was howling even louder than before. When she turned round Sam was standing staring at her.

'Christ, but you're gorgeous,' he declared throatily.

She had to laugh, for gorgeous she wasn't and never had been. 'Aren't you exaggerating, Sam? It must be the drink talking.'

'Drink, my arse. Come here, girl. I want to get my hands on ee.'

He'd meant that quite literally, his hands were suddenly everywhere. Groping, feeling, kneading. His beard had never bothered her before, but now it was scratching. She decided she didn't really like being kissed by a man with a beard.

He undid her blouse then pulled up her bra causing her to suck in a breath.

'That hurt,' she complained.

He didn't reply, his mouth already fastening on to a nipple which he greedily, and loudly, sucked. Maizie winced; that too hurt.

'Get your clothes off,' he ordered her, taking a step backwards.

'Right here?'

'Right there.'

'Can't I go to the toilet first?'

He frowned in annoyance. 'If you have to, but be quick about it. I want ee naked, Maiz, naked as the day you was born.'

He was standing in exactly the same spot when she returned. Closing the door she came to the foot of the bed. Despite herself, she was aroused.

'Now take them off,' he commanded.

She stripped slowly, all the while his eyes never leaving her. He seemed not even to blink. She had to sit on the end of the bed to remove her stockings. 'There,' she said softly.

'Stand up again.'

She did, feeling extremely vulnerable standing in the nude. He came closer and she noted that his nostrils were dilated, his breath coming in short, sharp pants.

Reaching out he gently touched first one breast, then the other. He trailed a calloused finger down her middle, stopping at the beginnings of her pubic hair. She trembled.

'Cold, Maiz?'

She shook her head.

'Ahh!' he exhaled. 'That's good. That's very good.'

He began removing his own clothes, tossing each article casually aside. When his underpants came off she saw he was massively excited.

'It's all for ee, Maiz. What do you think of that?'

She didn't reply.

'Now I want ee to get on the bed, lie on your back and spread your legs wide.'

She did as instructed, while he moved to the end of the bed to stare down at her. 'Put your arms out to the side.'

Again she did as told.

He was gazing at her crotch, anticipation written all over his flushed face. 'You don't know how much I've been looking forward to this, girl. How many times I've dreamt of it these past months.'

'Come on then,' she urged.

He climbed on to the bed to straddle her. Maizie was hypnotised by the tumescent penis bobbing in front of him.

He moved to between her legs which he spread even wider. A finger found her, causing her to gasp. She was so wet she was almost running with it.

'I'm going to give ee a seeing to like ee's never had before. And that's saying something,' he croaked.

Maizie could well believe it. She closed her eyes, waiting for the onslaught.

He was on the very point of entering her when there was a sudden loud bang. He immediately jerked backwards. 'Christ Almighty, it's the fucking maroon!' he exclaimed.

Instantly Sam was off the bed and hurrying to the window where he threw back the curtains just in time to see the last flare of a distress rocket expire in the sky.

'A ship's in trouble, gone aground most likely,' he shouted to Maizie over his shoulder.

He was galvanised into action, hastily throwing his clothes on again.

Maizie was now sitting up in bed. 'You're not part of the lifeboat crew any more, Sam.'

'I bloody well am!' he roared. 'Means nothing that I been away. I've been part of the Coverack crew man and boy. If the boat is going out then I go with her.'

The next minute he was gone, the sound of his boots echoing along the corridor as he clattered down the stairs.

Chapter 30

The weather was as foul as she could recall. Maizie lowered her head against the driving rain as she hurried down to the quay where a group of people had already gathered. She was thankful for the wet-weather gear she'd put on.

When she arrived at the quay she stood beside Miss Hitchon, the schoolteacher, whose brother Fred was also a member of the crew. Both unmarried, they lived together.

Maizie could just make out the lifeboat being severely buffeted by waves, so it had been launched safely. As she watched, another distress flare was fired.

Maizie noted Charlie Treloar was amongst the group, as was Adam Daw who owned a truck. Each had a relative out there on the lifeboat. Charlie came over.

'I saw Sam went with them,' he said, having to raise his voice to be heard above the wind.

Maizie nodded. 'Insisted on it.'

'Good man.'

He glanced up at the sky. 'Christ, what a night. They don't come no worse.'

'Do we know anything about the ship in trouble?'

Charlie shook his head.

Maizie would have liked to have had a cigarette but that was impossible in these conditions. If the boat was out for long she'd return to the hotel and make up flasks of tea for those waiting. If asked, Molly Hitchon would no doubt come and help her.

When she looked again there was no sign of the lifeboat which had been completely swallowed up by the inky blackness.

'There she is!' Denzil Eustis cried. 'She's still got a light or two burning.'

'That's the Little Wrea Rock,' Sam said, wishing he had a clearer head. 'Run aground probably.'

Denzil wiped his face to try to get a better view. 'Small freighter by the looks of her,' he declared.

Sam thought so too. He had to quickly grab a hold as the boat pitched violently over on the port side.

''Tis a Portugee out of Lisbon,' Denzil shouted a few minutes later as they came up on the ship astern.

Sam could see faces peering over the side now. He counted half a dozen, all white with fear.

'Stupid Portugees,' Fred Hitchon commented to his neighbour, Jack Trevalyan. Jack didn't reply, thinking about what salvage there might be to be had. If they were lucky it could be a profitable night's work. Strictly on the QT of course. Saving lives was the priority.

'Ahoy!' a voice shouted from the ship.

'Ahoy there!' Denzil, as coxswain, yelled back.

'We're badly holed and sinking fast!' the Portuguese shouted in heavily accented English.

Denzil could now see she was doing exactly that. There wasn't much time left. 'We're coming alongside and will throw you a line. Make it fast!'

'I hear you, Englis.'

Sam scooped up the line. He was the strongest of the crew and able to throw the furthest. This was his job.

'Try and steady her, lads,' Denzil instructed as they came into position.

Sam readied himself for the throw.

'They're coming back,' John Corin said, stabbing a finger into the night.

Maizie peered in the direction he was pointing, and sure enough, there was the faint outline of the lifeboat. She'd been about to suggest to Molly Hitchon that they make some tea, but that would have to wait now.

God, she was cold, her feet, despite the heavy socks she was wearing, positively icy. She wished she'd had the foresight to bring along some spirits with her. Anything would have done.

Denzil was the first ashore as it touched the harbour wall. Yabbering and thoroughly frightened Portuguese sailors quickly followed him. Denzil's eyes swept the crowd. When he spotted Maizie he went straight to her.

'Did you get them all off?'

He nodded.

She glanced back at the boat and frowned. 'Where's Sam?'

Denzil took a deep breath. 'There ain't no easy way to say this, Maiz. Sam's dead.'

She thought she hadn't heard him correctly, that the wind had somehow distorted his words. 'What was that, Denzil?'

'Sam's dead, Maiz. I'm sorry.'

She stared at Denzil in horror. 'How?' she eventually managed to ask.

'He was about to throw the line when the boat did a sudden yawing, corkscrew motion. I don't know if he slipped or lost his balance, but he pitched overboard and never came up again. He sank like a stone.'

He'd been drunk, was all Maizie could think. That would never have happened if he'd been sober. Never in a million years. He'd been drunk, that had to be the reason.

'Thank you, Denzil,' she heard herself reply.

'I'll take ee back to the hotel, Maiz,' he said, placing a comforting hand on her arm.

She pulled herself free. 'That's all right, Denzil. I can manage.'

''Tis no trouble, Maiz.'

'I said I can manage,' she insisted, almost crossly.

He nodded. 'I really am sorry, Maiz. There aren't any words.'

She was dimly aware of everyone else staring at her. Even the Portuguese had gone quiet, getting the drift that she was the woman of the man who'd drowned.

Maizie turned and walked slowly up the incline to the Paris. She was numb with shock. Sam dead! It was unbelievable. Why, only a short while ago they'd been in the bedroom together, he about to . . . And now he was gone. Not killed in the war as she'd often half expected, but here in Coverack, their own village, fallen from the lifeboat. One moment alive, the next drowned.

When she got into the Paris she bolted the door again, then went directly to the bar where she poured herself a huge gin. She drank that in one swallow, and shuddered. Gasping as it burnt her insides, she poured another.

She suddenly smiled, and then began to laugh. Laughter that reached such a pitch it was almost hysterical. Sometime during the outburst tears starting running down her face.

'Push!' the doctor instructed.

The pain was almost ripping her apart. She could easily have believed that a team of farm horses had been harnessed to either leg and both teams were pulling in opposite directions. 'I am fucking pushing!' she shrieked in reply.

The doctor wasn't fazed in the least. He'd heard it all before. Even the most genteel of women became extremely unladylike during childbirth.

The pain subsided a little, Maizie gulping in deep breath after breath. How much longer could this go on for?

A nurse's face swam into view, as she dabbed at her sopping forehead with a cloth. 'Baby's head's been born. You're almost there, Mrs Blackacre.'

Maizie tried to smile her gratitude, but it was beyond her.

'He's a fine baby boy, Mrs Blackacre,' the doctor informed her.

She was awash with sweat, completely drained, more tired than she'd ever have thought possible. 'Is everything . . . as it should be?' she croaked anxiously.

That was the first thing they all asked, the doctor reflected. His own wife included, when she'd had their two. 'Ten fingers, ten toes, a perfect specimen,' he was delighted to reply.

Maizie breathed a great sigh of relief. 'Can I hold him?'

Catching her by surprise, her body spasmed, then again as the afterbirth slipped free. The nurse who'd been mopping her forehead bent to deal with that.

'Here he is,' crooned Mrs Fitzhugh, the Irish midwife in attendance. 'And isn't he the darling little man to be sure.'

Maizie accepted the tiny bundle and cradled it in her arms. Not it, but *he*, she reminded herself. She gazed down into a red face topped by a shock of black hair. It might have been her imagination, but she was sure he was the mirror of Christian.

'Hello, my angel,' she whispered. At long last she had the child she'd always wanted, craved. Her emotions at that moment were almost spiritual.

And then, wonder of wonders, the baby's eyelids fluttered open to reveal pale blue eyes staring directly at her.

The doctor nodded his approval. He'd long since lost count of the number of babies he'd brought into the world. But even now, after all that while, the miracle of it never ceased to amaze him and bring a lump to his throat.

Alice dashed out of the Paris the moment Maizie's hired car drew up in front. The old, wrinkled face was alight with excitement. Rosemary and Bobby, one after the other, appeared in her wake.

Alice yanked open the car door and beamed at mother and son. 'Welcome home, Maiz, me dear.'

'Why thank you, Alice.'

Alice's beam broadened even further when she gazed full on the baby's face. 'And there he is! Wrapped up snug as a bug in a rug. Can I take him?'

Maizie frowned. 'You will be careful?'

'Of course I will, silly,' Alice cackled. 'Don't forget I've got a family of me own. 'Tain't much about babas I don't know about.'

'He's absolutely gorgeous,' Rosemary breathed, peering over Alice's shoulder. 'And ever so small.'

'Newborn babies are small,' Alice scolded. 'What do you expect?'

'Well, I don't know.'

Maizie laughed. It was good to be home, especially to her own bed. She'd found the one in the hospital excruciatingly hard.

The driver had unloaded her case from the boot and now stood waiting to be paid. A family man himself he smiled at the happy group. Though his three were now all grown up, this little scene being enacted before him brought back happy memories.

'Bobby, can you take the case up to my room, please?' Maizie requested.

'Yes, Aunt Maiz. Can I see Christopher?'

'Come and have a look,' Alice said expansively, gently rocking the sleeping baby in her arms.

While they were doing this Maizie got stiffly out of the car. There had been several stitches after the birth which weren't at all pleasant. Still, they and the stiffness were just something she'd have to put up with for the time being. A small price to pay, after all.

Maizie gave the driver a handsome tip and thanked him for driving so carefully. She'd dreaded being jolted but there had been none of that.

'I think Christopher is lovely,' Bobby declared proudly.

'Why, thank you, Bobby.'

Christopher, Maizie smiled inwardly to herself. Christine if a girl, Christopher if a boy, she'd decided before the birth. When he was older she'd call him Chris, just like his father. His real father.

What an amazing night it had been, a thoroughly exhausted Maizie reflected, slumped in the wicker chair in her bedroom enjoying a last cigarette before turning in. At long last it was over. The Germans had surrendered three months previously, and now the Japanese too after several of their major cities had been utterly destroyed by some sort of new super bomb. The Second World War was finally over.

It had been pandemonium in the bar ever since the announcement on the wireless. So much alcohol had been consumed she doubted she'd have any left when she opened again next day. The hotel had been drunk dry.

Blackout curtains had been thrown open and all over the village lights blazed for the first time since the restriction had been imposed all those long weary years ago.

She glanced over to where Christopher lay fast asleep in his cot. At almost two he was growing quickly, toddling everywhere and forever into mischief. He was quite a handful, which is exactly what she'd have expected of a little lad that age.

Thankfully he was taking after her in looks. No sign yet of his father's distinct Gallic nose. That might have caused a few frowns and speculations. No, as far as everyone was concerned he was Sam's child, conceived that fateful night of his father's death.

She'd had to take on a new girl to help out because of the time she had to devote to Christopher. Alice was, and continued to be, a tower of strength, as was Rosemary. The new girl, Biddy Wynyack, was a Coverack maid just turned eighteen. She worked full time and helped out mainly in the bar as well as assisting Rosemary in other general duties. A sweet maid, she was popular with everyone.

Maizie kicked off her shoes and arched her feet which were killing her. It really had been a long day and an even longer night. At one point she'd spotted Rosemary being kissed by a young chap her own age. Now that had pleased her, particularly as Rosemary had been so obviously enjoying the experience.

She'd worried that Rosemary would be put off men for life after what she'd gone through with Sam. And for a while it had seemed that might be the case. Now the indications were she'd recovered from the trauma, for which Maizie thanked God. It would have been awful for the youngster to go through the rest of her life permanently scarred by her ordeal at Sam's hands.

As for Sam, he was a hero. Or at least that's how folk remembered him. Just as well they didn't know him the way she did. Or Rosemary. They had their own separate memories of the man. There was a plaque to his memory on the lifeboat station recording the date and how he'd died. His body had never been recovered. The sea had been his life and had claimed him for its own in death.

Dear Rosemary, Maizie thought. Ted McEwen was pleased with her progress at painting, still convinced she was extremely talented. The plan was for her to try for the Slade school in London in a few years' time. Now that she thought about it, she was sure Ted had been responsible for Rosemary's rehabilitation where men were concerned. He'd become something of a father figure to her as well as tutor. Yes, Rosemary had a lot to thank Ted for.

Maizie yawned, thinking if she wasn't careful she'd fall asleep there in the chair, which would never do.

It was hard to believe the war was really over. Maybe now they could return to normal, If that was possible. For how could anything ever be normal again?

She'd often wondered what had become of Christian. Was he alive or dead? She had no way of finding out. Occasionally she'd thought, hoped, he'd get in touch again. But in her heart of hearts she'd known he wouldn't. She'd turned him down for Sam, and her beloved Coverack, which had been the end of their relationship. He'd gone out of her life, and stayed out.

She closed her eyes, recalling him as she'd last seen him, a great surge of emotion and love welling through her. Dear Christian, please let him be alive and God grant him happiness if he was.

Maizie lit another cigarette, her mind filled with memories. Not only of Chris but all manner of things. She smiled, recalling the afternoon at the cove beyond the tunnel. That had been the most perfect of days, one to remember for ever. How passionately they'd made love, and how sublimely. No matter what happened to her in the future, she'd never make love, or be made love to, like that again.

At least she had Christopher. At least she had him.

Epilogue

How Hennebont had changed, Ted McEwen marvelled. Changed, and yet not changed at the same time. He felt no affinity with it any more, the town had become a stranger to him. Even now, two years after the war ended, there were still signs of the occupation everywhere, little things that hadn't yet been torn down and cleared away. He wouldn't have been at all surprised if a column of Germans had suddenly appeared, goosestepping and singing the Horst Wessel song. The echo of their tainted presence hung in the air.

He needed a coffee, he decided. And a cassis. He'd go to the Café Emile Zola which was an old haunt of his — if it still existed that was.

To his delight it did. Settling himself at an outside table he waited for his order to be taken. Overhead the July sun shone strongly down, making him grateful for the umbrella shade casting its shadow over him. For some reason he'd forgotten how hot it was in Hennebont during summer.

He'd been seated a good five minutes and started on his drinks before noticing the man occupying another table further along the pavement. The man's nose was buried deep in the local newspaper, *Le Télégramme*. Ted smiled in recognition and immediately came to his feet.

'Hello, Christian, remember me?'

Christian glanced up, his eyes opening wide. 'Ted!'

Next moment the two men were hugging one another.

'Where did you come from?' Christian demanded.

'That table over there actually,' Ted replied, tongue in cheek, pointing.

'That's not what I mean.'

'I know what you mean, Christian. But let's sit down and let me have a look at you. It's been years.'

'I knew you and Pet had got away. I made inquiries. I could only hope the pair of you were well.'

Ted nodded. 'We are. Never better. Living in England now.'

'Really!'

'Quite settled actually. But you, I want to hear about you. Last I heard you'd joined the army.'

Christian's face darkened. 'That's right. I too was in England for a while then ended up here again in forty-three. I belonged to a unit called the SOE, Special Operations Executive. Ring any bells?'

Ted shook his head.

'Well, I was sent back here as a spy and saboteur. Which is what I did until the Germans left.'

'Well well,' Ted mused. 'And your parents?'

'Both fine. Though Papa's factory was destroyed.'

'The Germans?'

'No, me.'

'You!'

Christian explained all about that. 'Papa still talks of rebuilding but I think that's all it is, talk. He's too old now for that sort of thing, being more or less settled into retirement. Luckily, he and Maman don't have any money worries thanks to various foreign accounts he'd opened up before the war. Accounts to do with the business.'

'I see. And what about your studies?'

Christian laughed softly. 'I can't see myself going back to those after what I've been through. Besides, being a surveyor just doesn't appeal any more.' He shrugged. 'I'll do something in time, but what I haven't yet decided. Now, why are you here?'

'I have legal affairs to deal with. Don't forget I still own a house in Hennebont for a start. As chance would have it the house is exactly as we left it. I had thought the Germans might have commandeered it, but apparently not. It's quite intact. Even some paintings I left behind are still there. They're quite valuable and will be going back to England with me.'

'England,' Christian murmured, his eyes taking on a far-away look. 'I had some happy times there.'

'Yes I know, I heard.'

Christian frowned. 'From whom?'

'Maizie Blackacre.'

A completely dumbfounded Christian stared at his friend. 'Maizie?' he repeated eventually.

Ted laughed at Christian's expression. 'Pet and I bought a cottage in Coverack when we decided to resettle over there. We stayed at the Paris to begin with which is how we made Maizie's acquaintance. We're now the best of chums.'

'How . . . how is she?' His mind had gone quite numb.

'Same as always. Rosemary comes to me several times a week for painting lessons, the girl has a remarkable talent and I predict a big future for her. Bobby has left school and taken up an apprenticeship with the electricity people. Maizie is a bit pushed nowadays mind you, having the hotel and baby to look after.'

That rocked Christian. 'Baby?'

'Yes, a little boy called Christopher. Lovely little chap. It was a pity the father, whom I didn't know, never got to see him.'

Christian quickly lowered his gaze. 'What does that mean, Ted?'

'Sam Blackacre was killed, drowned, while out on the lifeboat attempting a rescue. Fell overboard apparently. He'd only arrived back in Coverack that day too.'

Sam dead, Maizie a widow, a baby Christian's mind was reeling.

'Maizie often speaks about you,' Ted went on. 'As do Bobby, Rosemary and Alice. It seems you were a big hit with all of them.'

Christian lifted a hand to attract the waiter's attention. He badly needed a drink. Something strong.

'What's wrong?' Delphine Le Gall queried 'You're quite the picture of misery.'

Christian roused himself from his reverie. 'Am I?'

'Ever since you came back from bumping into Ted McEwen earlier. Black as black. Was it something Ted said?'

'Yes,' Christian reluctantly admitted.

'I see.' She waited for him to elaborate, but he gave no sign of doing so. 'Do you want to talk about it?'

Christian glanced over at his mother busy at the stove. Unlike with Aunt Sophie, he'd never mentioned a word about Maizie to either of his parents.

'I met a woman while I was in England,' he said slowly. 'Ted knows her too, as it happens, and was bringing me up to date.'

Delphine eyed Christian speculatively. 'A special woman?'

He nodded.

'How special?'

'I loved her, Maman. There was only one problem, she was married.'

'Aaahh!' Delphine exhaled. Now she was beginning to understand.

'I learnt from Ted she's now a widow.'

Delphine thought about that. 'You said loved, past tense. Does that mean you don't love her any more?'

He had to be honest. 'No, Maman, I still do.'

'And did she love you?'

The pain he'd thought long since gone, or at least buried, had now returned, as intense and sickening as ever. 'Yes, Maman. I asked her to leave her husband and come away with me, but she wouldn't. She's an honourable woman who refused to renege on her marriage vows. Albeit she certainly had cause to do so, for the husband was a bastard. Scum.'

'Now he's dead,' Delphine said softly.

'According to Ted.'

There was a pause between them. 'So what are you going to do about it?' she queried eventually.

He shook his head. 'I don't know.'

'Do you want my advice, Christian?'

'Please.'

She stopped what she was doing and turned to face him. 'You must see her again to find out how things now stand between you. If you don't you'll regret it for the rest of your life.'

He knew she was right. That it was sound advice. 'Thanks, Maman.'

'I'll tell you this. Love is hard enough to find. Just because you've found it once doesn't mean you'll do so a second time. Don't let it go unless it's completely out of reach.'

Delphine busied herself again with her cooking.

'I'll pack you a valise when you're ready to leave.'

It was late afternoon when he walked into the Paris, the sunlight dappling in through the windows creating an almost magical effect. As luck would have it, as though it was meant to be, the only person present was Maizie standing behind the bar with her back to him. She was busy with some paperwork.

He stood for a few moments staring at her, drinking her in. His heart felt so full it must surely explode. He continued towards the bar.

'We're not open for another hour yet,' Maizie declared without turning round, having heard his approach.

'I thought guests could be served at any time.'

She went suddenly very still, the breath catching in her throat. The voice was exactly as she remembered it. Slowly she did now turn round.

'Hello, Maizie,' he smiled.

'You've come back,' was all she could think of to say.

'I ran into Ted in Hennebont. He told me everything.'

Tears welled in her eyes. Not everything, only she knew that. 'I didn't know if you were alive or dead.'

'Alive, Maiz, as you can see. Very much so.'

He'd aged. When they'd first met he'd been a young man, the bloom of youth still about him, now he was fully mature. The lines on his face bore testament to that. Why, there was even the odd fleck of grey in his hair.

'I have a decent bottle of cognac. Would you like a glass?'

'Please.'

She dashed away the tears, wishing she'd had some warning he was coming. She'd have worn something more suitable. And she was sure her hair was a mess.

'Will you join me, Maiz?'

'I'd like that.' Her hand was trembling as she poured out two measures.

Christian was praying no one else would appear to spoil this. 'There's something I have to say,' he declared as she pushed a glass across the bar to him.

She didn't reply.

'I've rehearsed this a dozen times, but now I'm actually here I'm simply going to be blunt. The way you English prefer.'

Maizie smiled to hear that.

'Do you still love me, Maizie?'

She swallowed hard. He'd meant it when he'd said he was going to be blunt. There was no beating about the bush, or subtlety, here. 'Do you still love *me*, Christian?' she queried, turning the question back on him.

'I do, Maizie. I've never stopped loving you.'

It was as if a huge load had been lifted from her shoulders. Her eyes were fastened on to his, Christian's boring into hers. Each was holding their breath.

'And I've never stopped loving you.'

There they were, the words he'd so desperately wanted to hear. 'Will you marry me?'

'Of course. But not right away, for appearances' sake. The fact you've been here before. There's a reason for that.'

'Oh?'

'There's someone I want you to meet. He's the reason.'

'Who's that, Maiz?'

'Your son.'

'My—!'

'His name's Christopher, Chris, the same as you. That was the closest I could come without giving the game away.'

Christian's expression reflected his profound shock at this bombshell. It had never crossed his mind. 'A son!' he breathed. 'Where is he?'

'Upstairs.'

She raised her glass. 'To us, Christian. The three of us.'

'To us,' he toasted in a daze. Then he couldn't contain himself any longer. He was round the bar and wrapping Maizie in his arms. 'We'll run the hotel together as man and wife. That suit you?'

'What do you think?'

He kissed her long and hard. And again and again. When they finally went upstairs it was hand in hand, the years apart as if they'd never been.